HORSE TROUBLE

Kristin Varner

:01

First Second
New York

First Second

Published by First Second
First Second is an imprint of Roaring Brook Press,
a division of Holtzbrinck Publishing Holdings Limited Partnership
120 Broadway, New York, NY 10271
firstsecondbooks.com
mackids.com

Library of Congress Control Number: 2021906631

Our books may be purchased in bulk for promotional, educational, or business use.
Please contact your local bookseller or the Macmillan Corporate and Premium Sales Department
at (800) 221-7945 ext. 5442 or by email at MacmillanSpecialMarkets@macmillan.com.

First edition, 2021
Edited by Robyn Chapman and Rachel Stark
Cover design by Kirk Benshoff
Interior book design by Kristin Varner and Molly Johanson
Equestrian consultant: Allison Wicks

The artwork for this book was sketched by hand using Staedtler non-photo blue pencils.
Final art was digitally inked and colored in Adobe Photoshop.

Printed in China by RR Donnelley Asia Printing Solutions Ltd., Dongguan City, Guangdong Province

ISBN 978-1-250-22588-7 (paperback)
10 9 8 7 6 5 4 3 2 1

ISBN 978-1-250-22587-0 (hardcover)
10 9 8 7 6 5 4 3 2 1

Don't miss your next favorite book from First Second! For the latest updates go to
firstsecondnewsletter.com and sign up for our enewsletter.

For Mom and Dad,
who lovingly supported all the horse years

Chapter 1
Saddle Slip

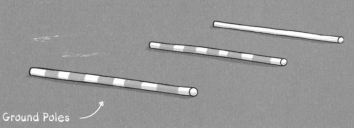

Ground Poles

A basic training tool to help build balance, focus, and coordination in both the horse and rider before jumping fences.

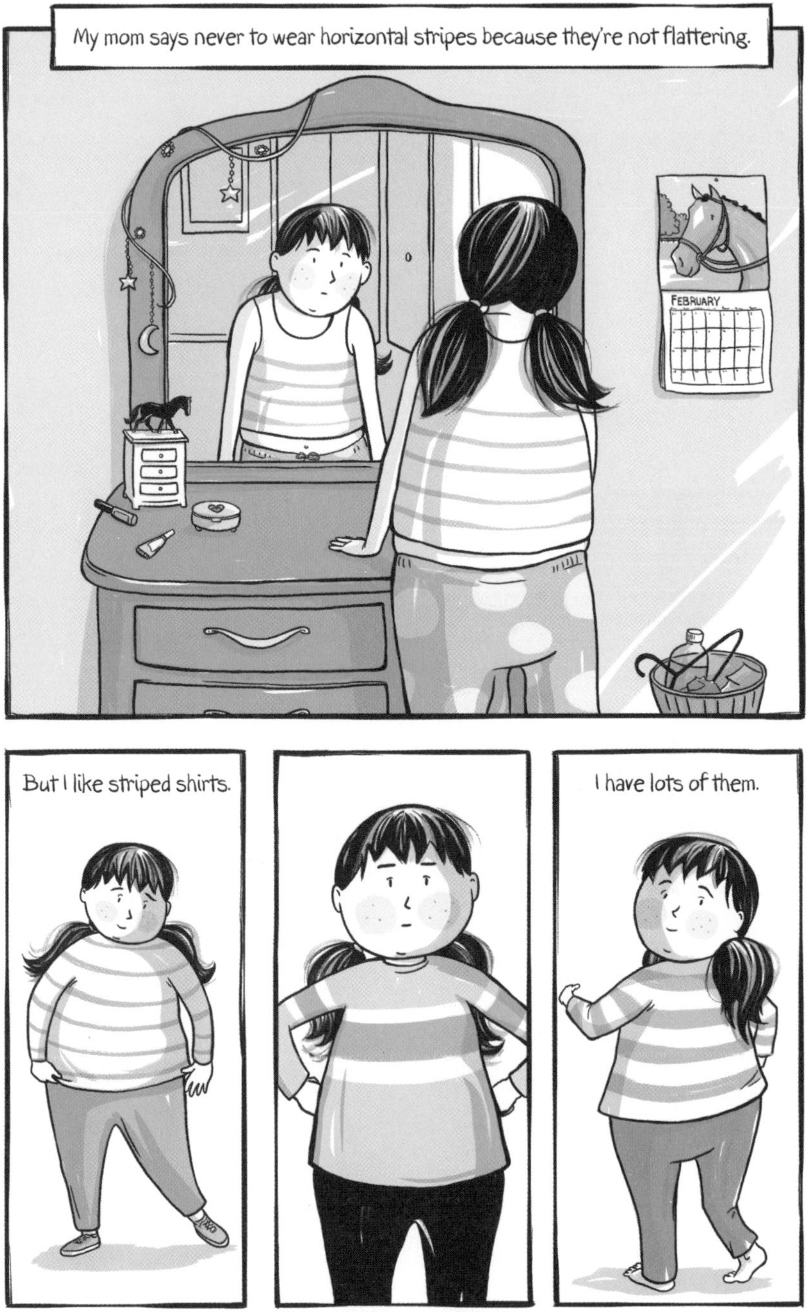
My mom says never to wear horizontal stripes because they're not flattering.
FEBRUARY
But I like striped shirts.
I have lots of them.

My mom means well, she just doesn't get it.
She wasn't chubby as a kid or at any point in her life.

I don't know when I started getting pudgy.

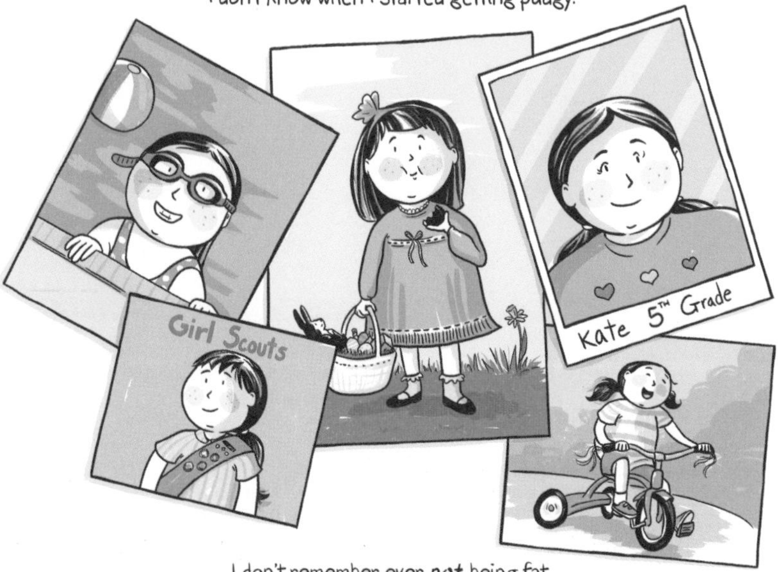
Girl Scouts
Kate 5TH Grade

I don't remember ever ***not*** being fat.

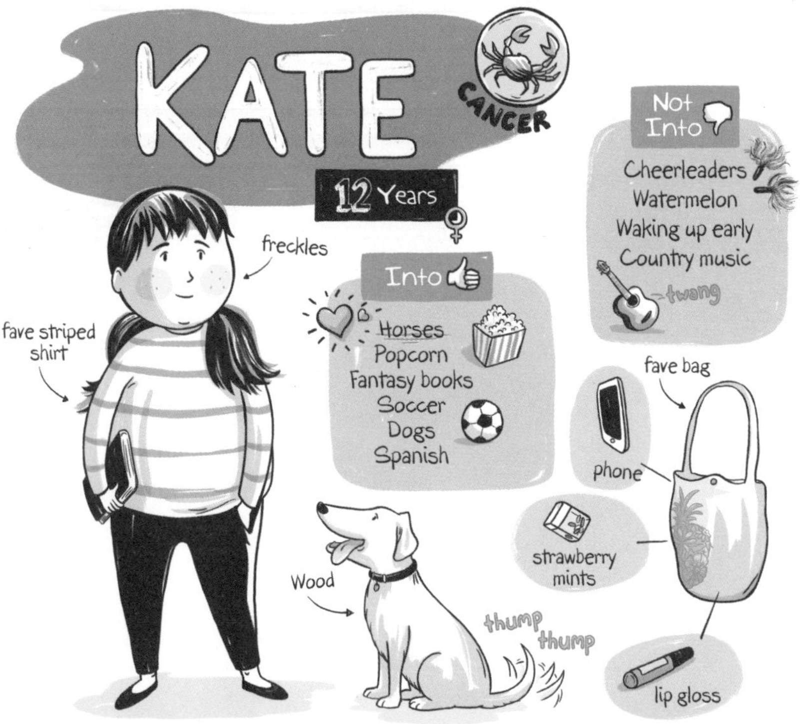
KATE
CANCER
12 Years
freckles
fave striped shirt
Into
Horses
Popcorn
Fantasy books
Soccer
Dogs
Spanish
Not Into
Cheerleaders
Watermelon
Waking up early
Country music
twang
fave bag
phone
strawberry mints
lip gloss
Wood
thump
thump

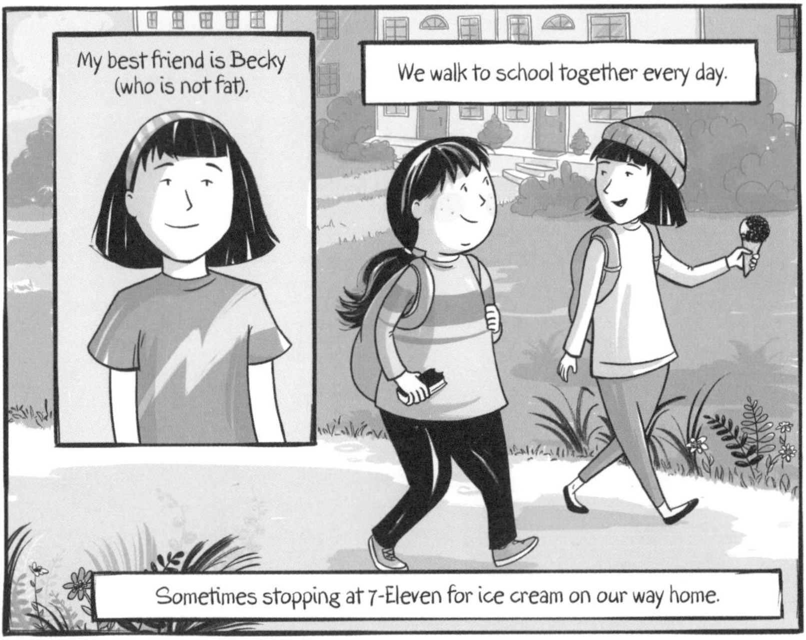
My best friend is Becky (who is not fat).
We walk to school together every day.
Sometimes stopping at 7-Eleven for ice cream on our way home.

Becky and I have been friends since preschool when the Lee family moved in up the street. Our families started hanging out, a lot.

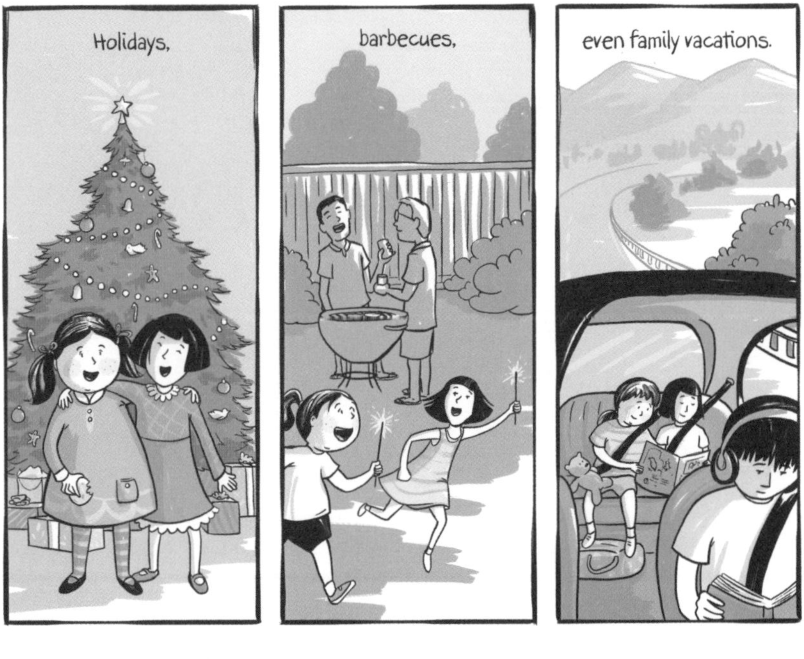
Holidays,
barbecues,
even family vacations.

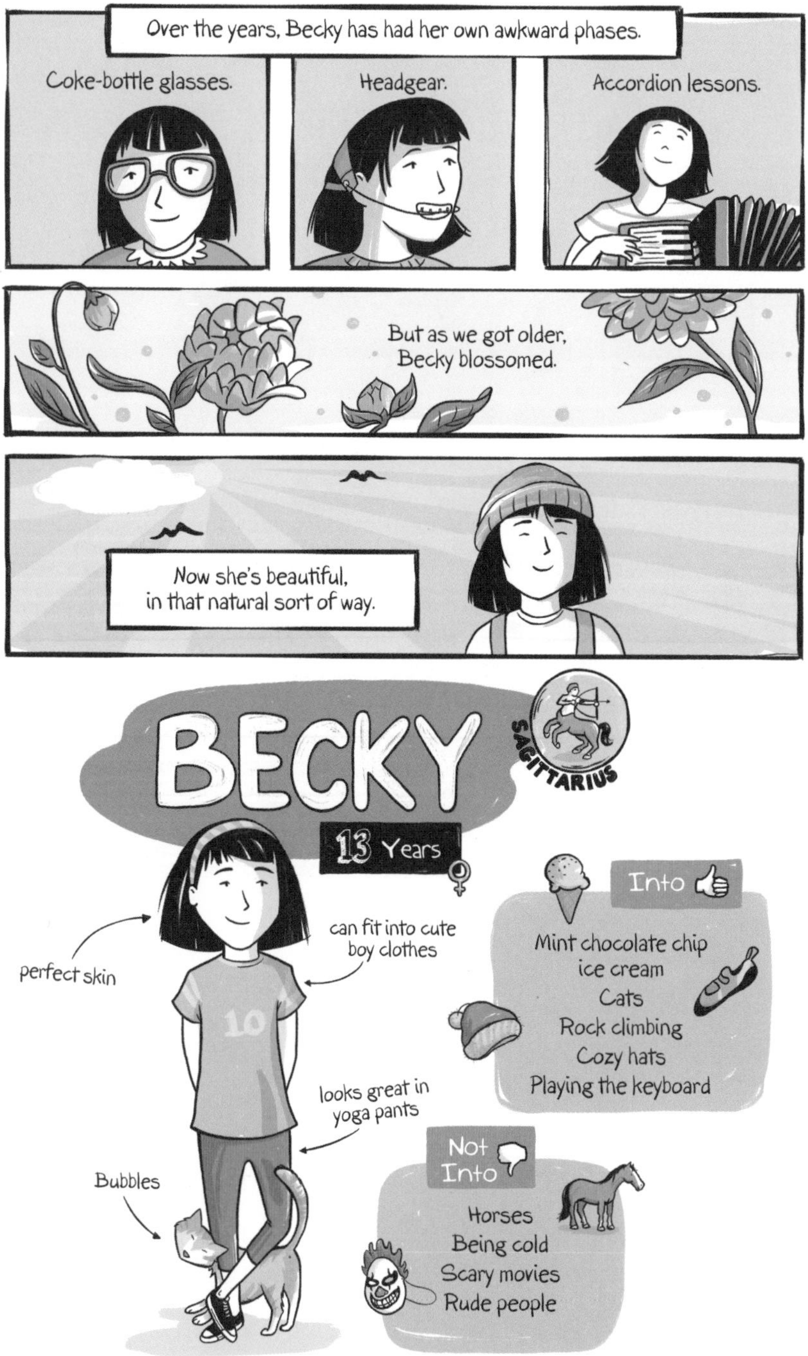
Over the years, Becky has had her own awkward phases.
Coke-bottle glasses.
Headgear.
Accordion lessons.
But as we got older, Becky blossomed.
Now she's beautiful, in that natural sort of way.
BECKY
SAGITTARIUS
13 Years
perfect skin
can fit into cute boy clothes
10
looks great in yoga pants
Bubbles
Into
Mint chocolate chip ice cream
Cats
Rock climbing
Cozy hats
Playing the keyboard
Not Into
Horses
Being cold
Scary movies
Rude people

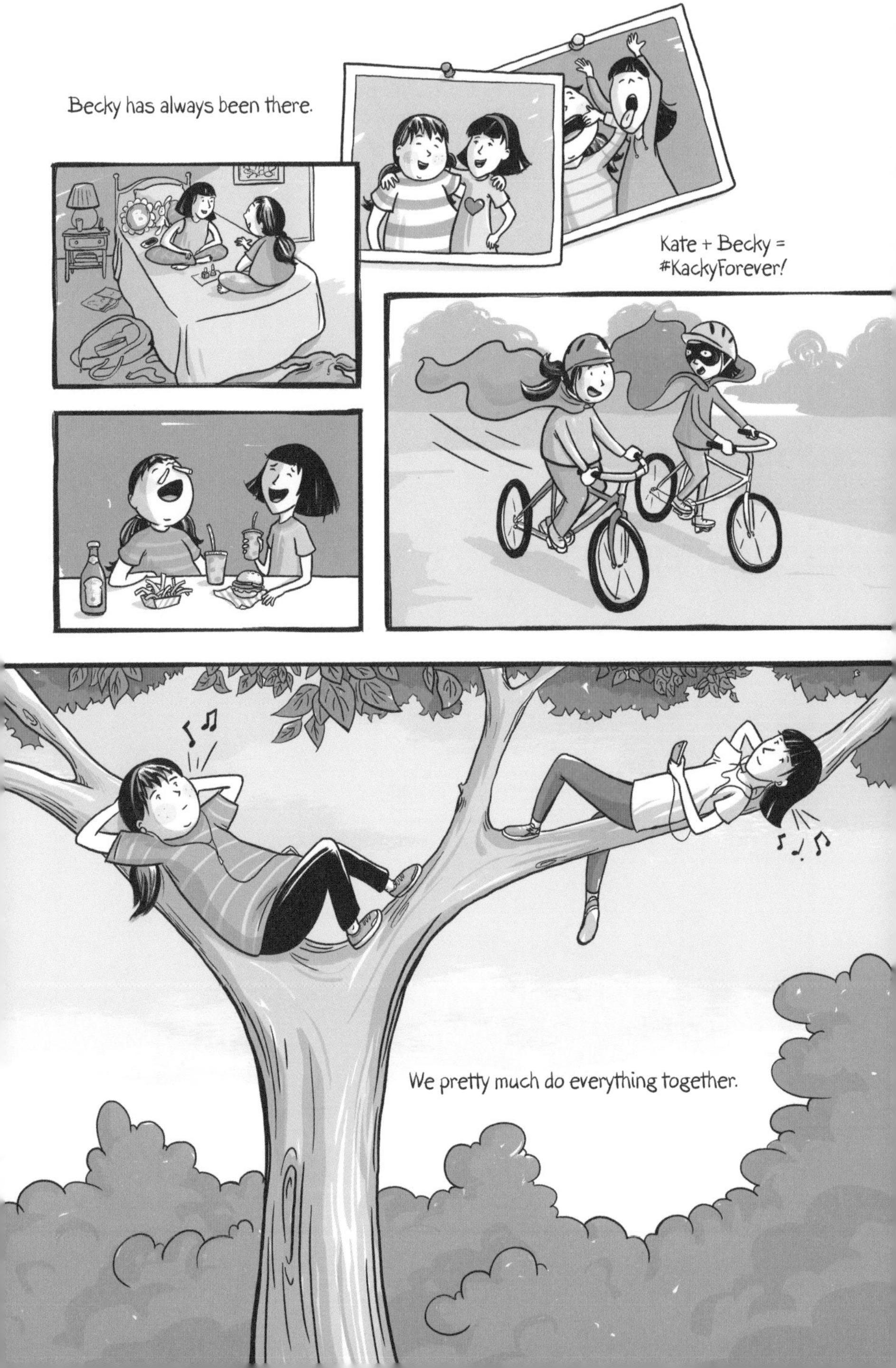

Becky has always been there.
Kate + Becky =
#KackyForever!
We pretty much do everything together.

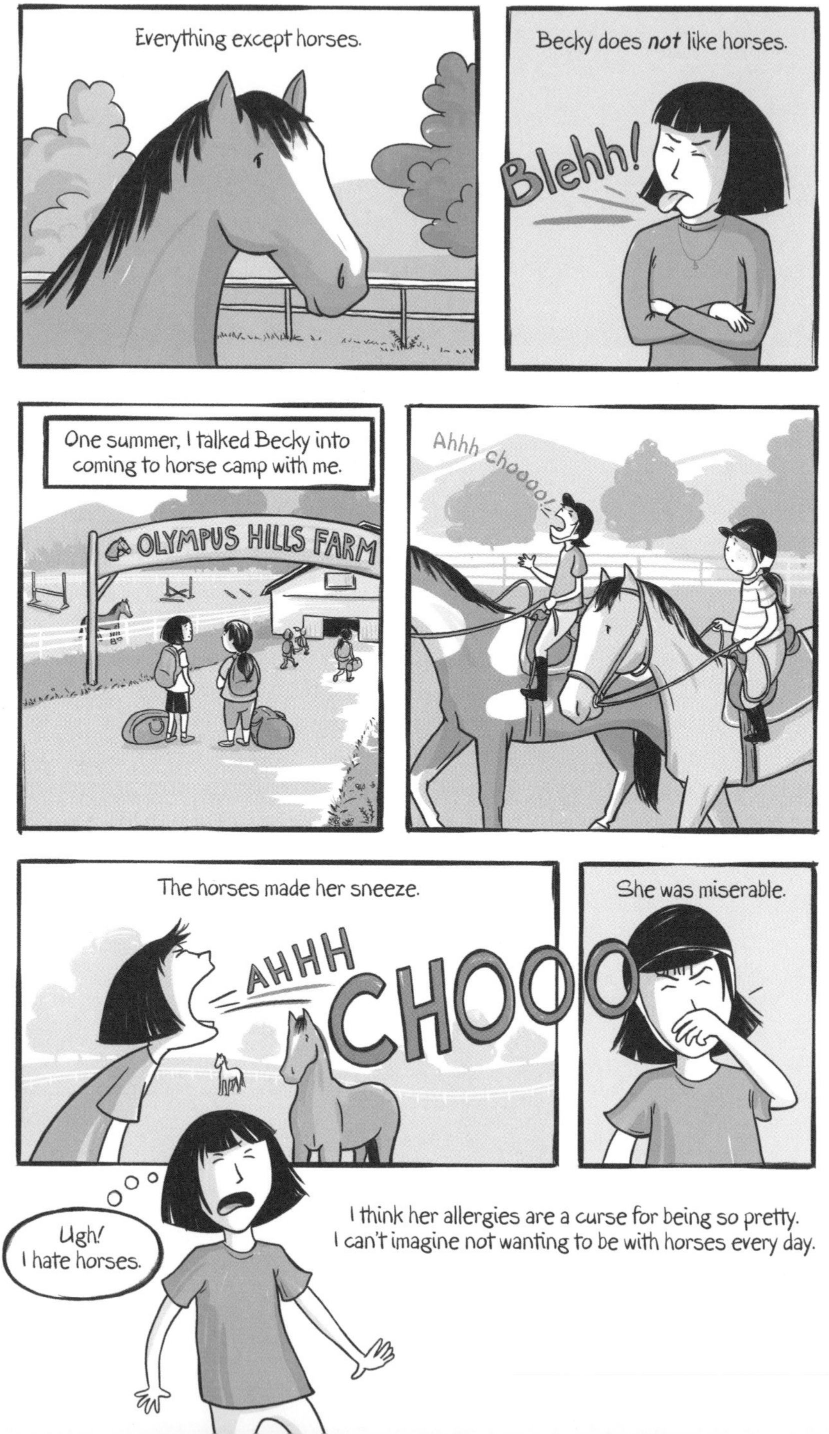
Everything except horses.
Becky does *not* like horses.
Blehh!
One summer, I talked Becky into coming to horse camp with me.
OLYMPUS HILLS FARM
Ahhh chooooo!
The horses made her sneeze.
AHHH CHOOO
She was miserable.
Ugh! I hate horses.
I think her allergies are a curse for being so pretty.
I can't imagine not wanting to be with horses every day.

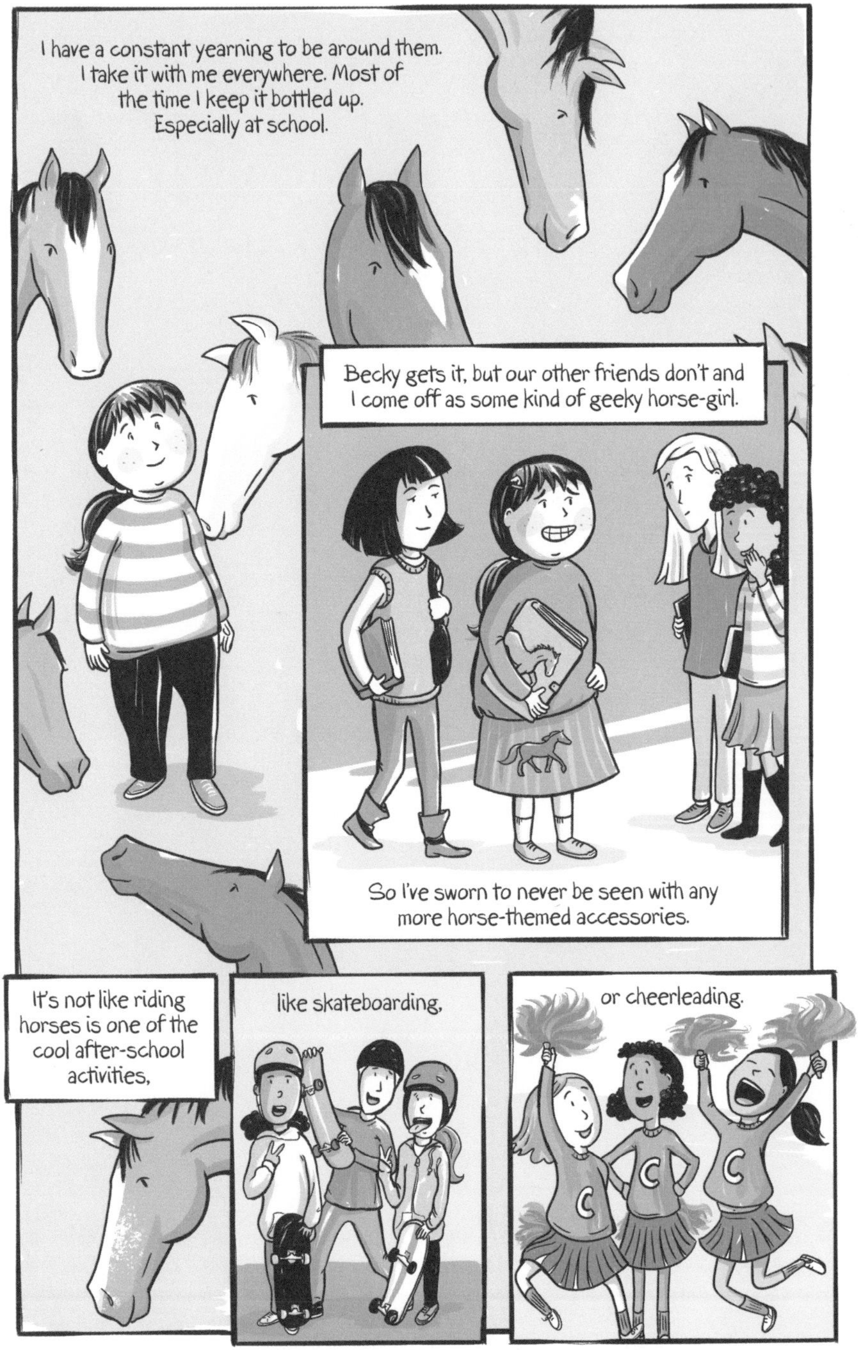
I have a constant yearning to be around them. I take it with me everywhere. Most of the time I keep it bottled up. Especially at school.
Becky gets it, but our other friends don't and I come off as some kind of geeky horse-girl.
So I've sworn to never be seen with any more horse-themed accessories.
It's not like riding horses is one of the cool after-school activities,
like skateboarding,
or cheerleading.

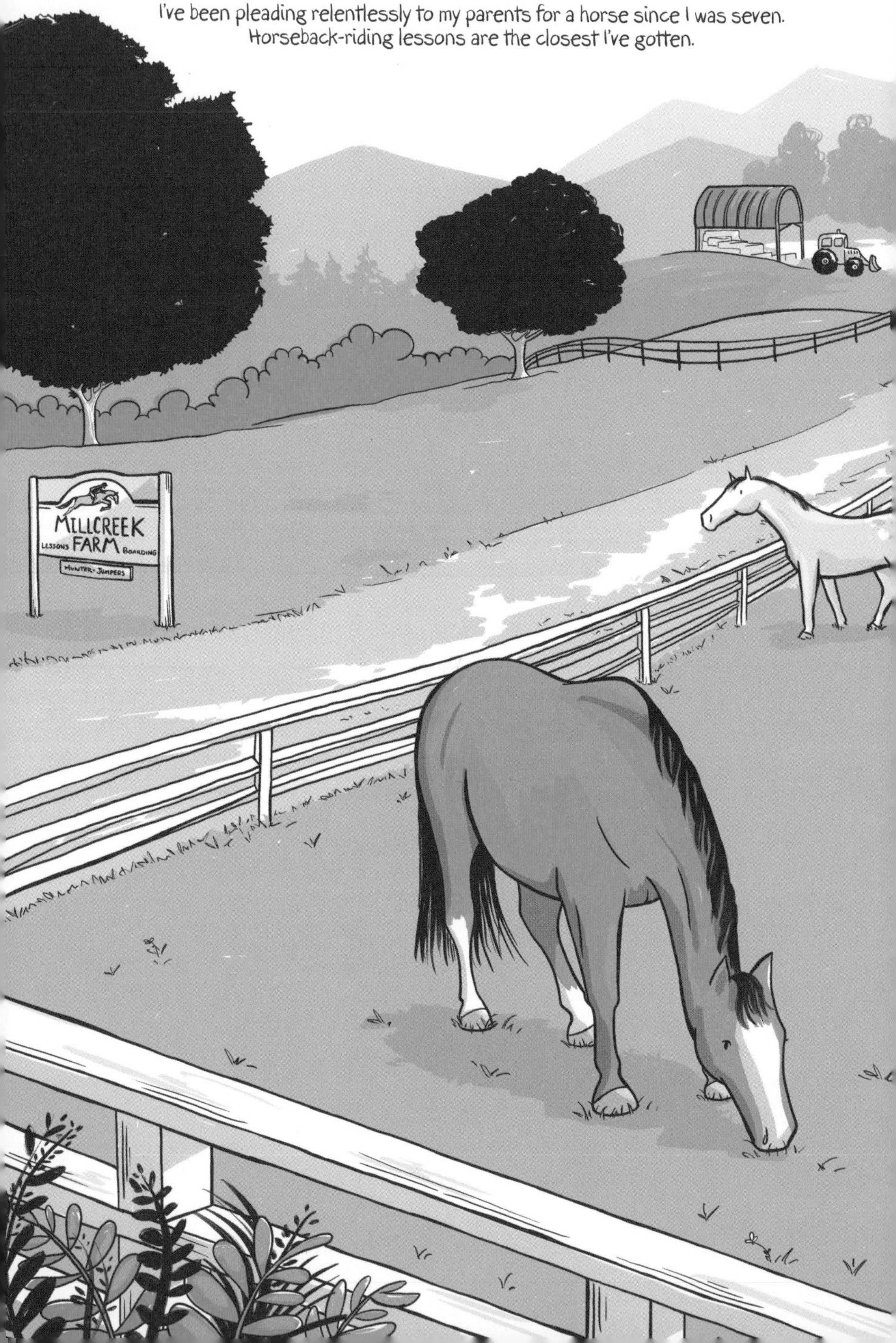
I've been pleading relentlessly to my parents for a horse since I was seven.
Horseback-riding lessons are the closest I've gotten.
MILLCREEK
LESSONS FARM BOARDING
HUNTER-JUMPERS

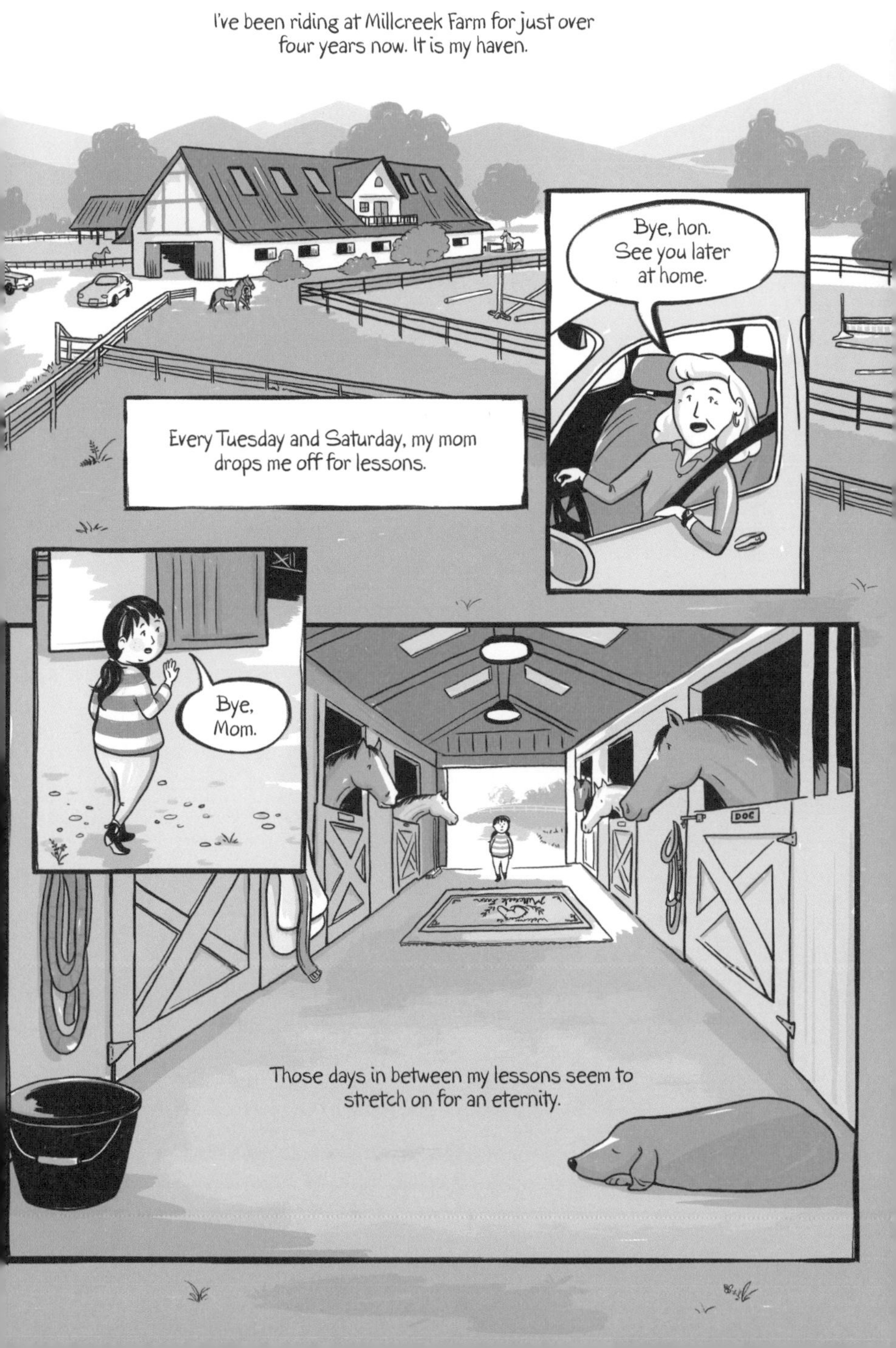
I've been riding at Millcreek Farm for just over four years now. It is my haven.
Every Tuesday and Saturday, my mom drops me off for lessons.
Bye, hon. See you later at home.
Bye, Mom.
DOC
Those days in between my lessons seem to stretch on for an eternity.

I clean stalls and do whatever job is needed around the barn.
It allows me more time with the horses and helps pay off my lessons.

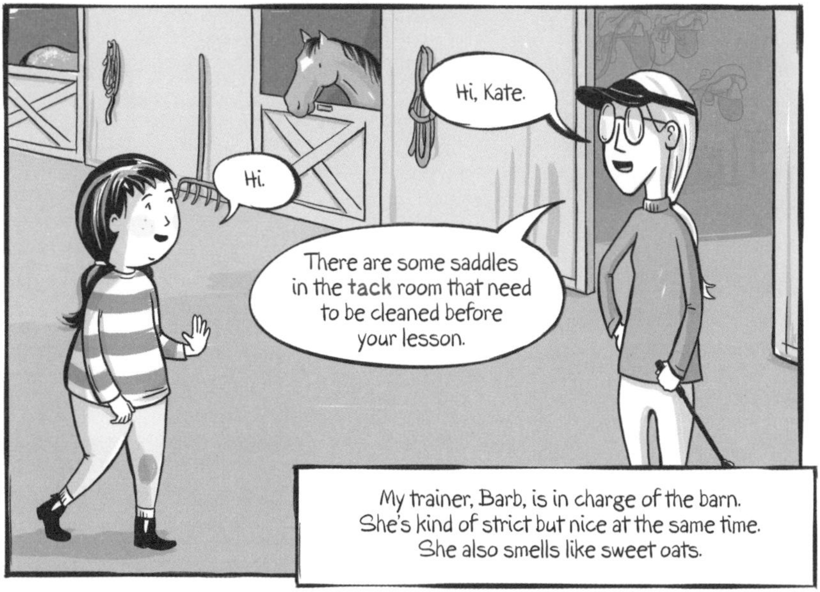
Hi, Kate.
Hi.
There are some saddles in the **tack** room that need to be cleaned before your lesson.
My trainer, Barb, is in charge of the barn. She's kind of strict but nice at the same time. She also smells like sweet oats.

I love being around Barb and the horses.

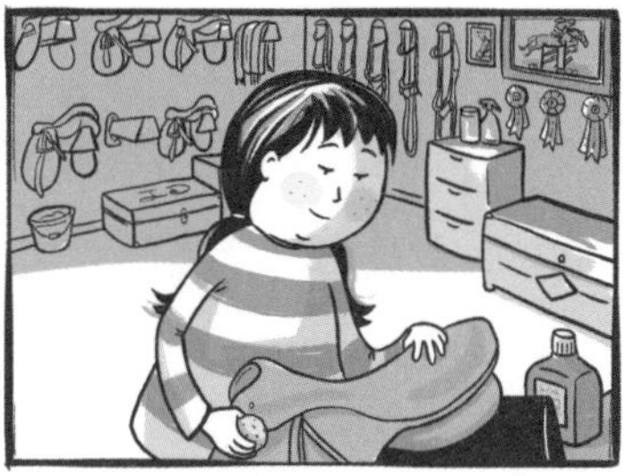

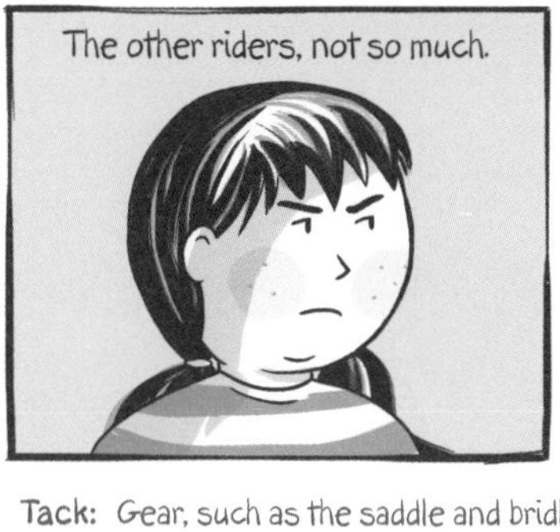
The other riders, not so much.

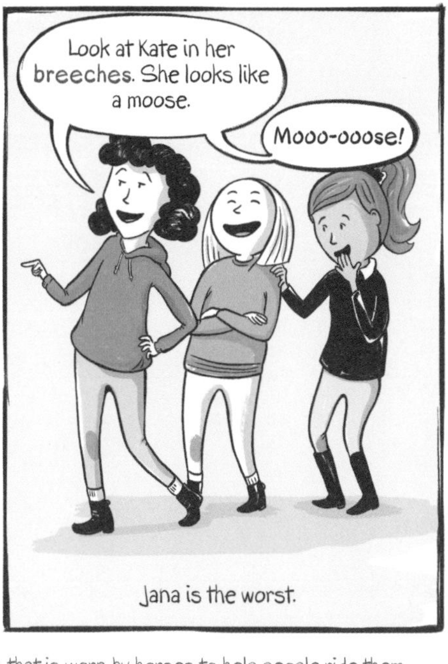
Look at Kate in her **breeches**. She looks like a moose.
Mooo-ooose!
Jana is the worst.

Tack: Gear, such as the saddle and bridle, that is worn by horses to help people ride them.

Breeches: Riding pants

Jana is a snobby rich girl.

She is also skinny and can eat doughnuts to her heart's content.

designer bag

ARIES

JANA

14 Years

Into 👍
- Nice cars
- Junk food
- Tennis club
- Prep school
- Makeup

fresh manicure

Not Into 👎
- Camping
- Gaming
- Dark chocolate
- Babies

$$$$

cool boots

Being around Jana makes me feel like I'm back in my fourth grade dance class.

Staring into the mirror, flanked by leggy girls in leotards.

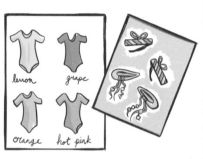

lemon   grape

orange   hot pink

Everyone got to choose their own color leotard with matching hair accessories.

I picked green.

Not the best choice.

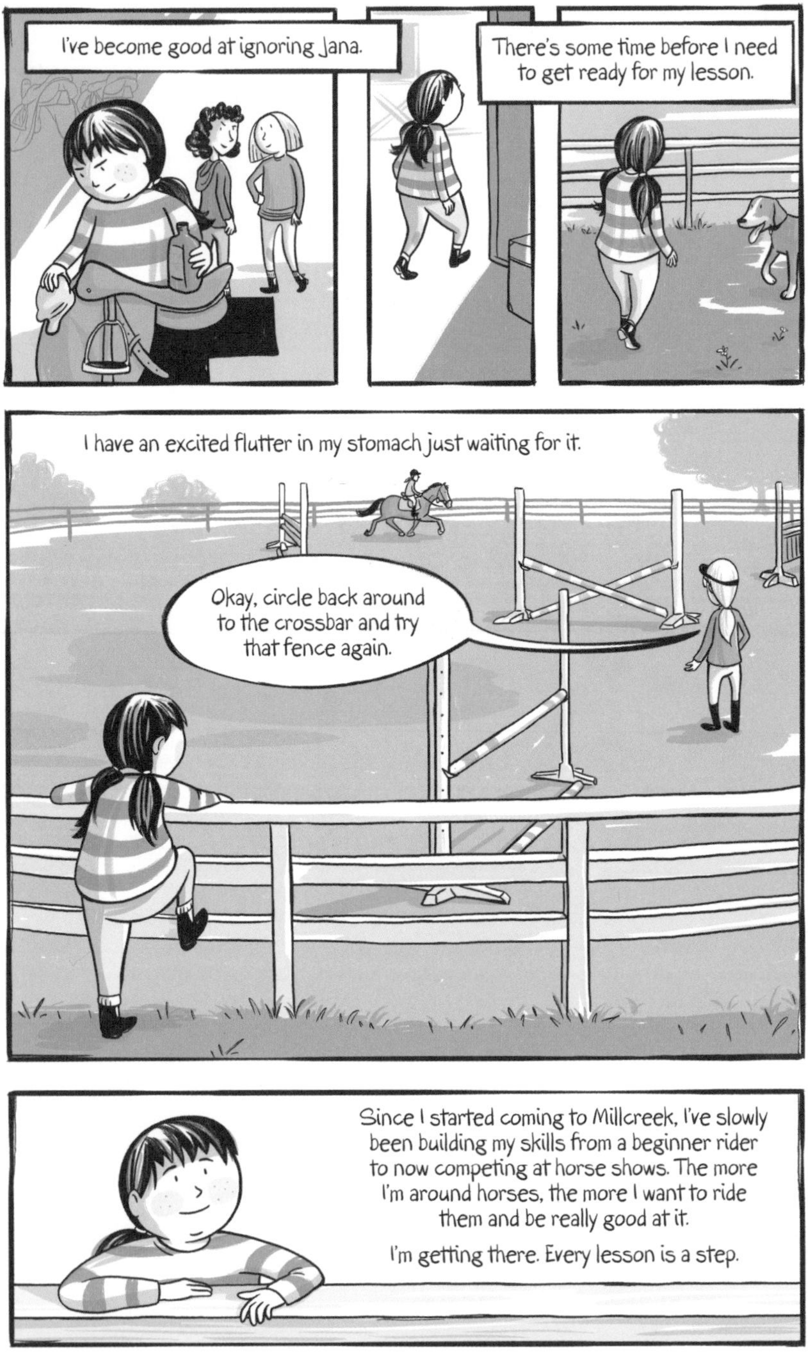

I've become good at ignoring Jana.
There's some time before I need to get ready for my lesson.
I have an excited flutter in my stomach just waiting for it.
Okay, circle back around to the crossbar and try that fence again.
Since I started coming to Millcreek, I've slowly been building my skills from a beginner rider to now competing at horse shows. The more I'm around horses, the more I want to ride them and be really good at it.
I'm getting there. Every lesson is a step.

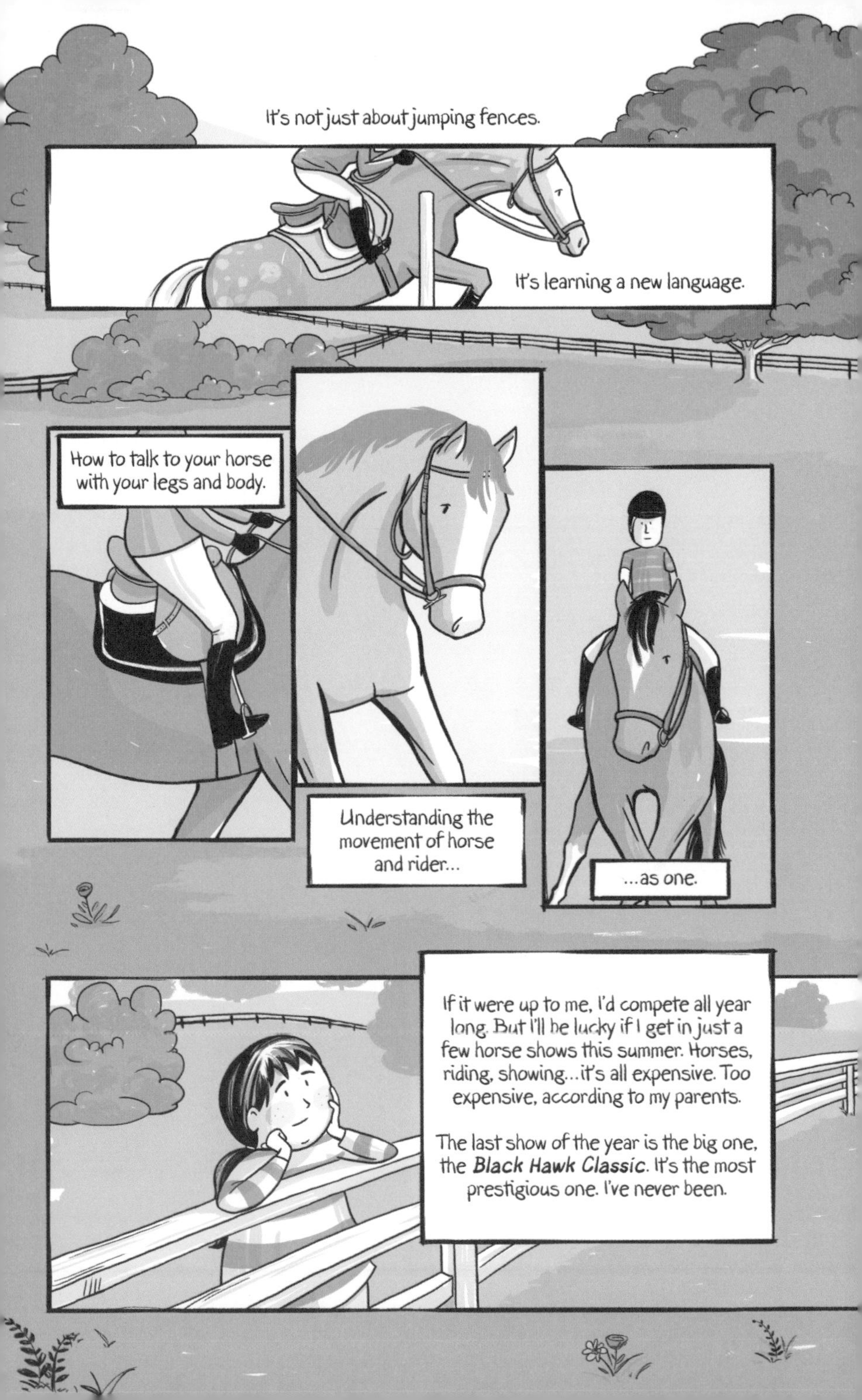
It's not just about jumping fences.
It's learning a new language.
How to talk to your horse with your legs and body.
Understanding the movement of horse and rider...
...as one.
If it were up to me, I'd compete all year long. But I'll be lucky if I get in just a few horse shows this summer. Horses, riding, showing...it's all expensive. Too expensive, according to my parents.
The last show of the year is the big one, the *Black Hawk Classic*. It's the most prestigious one. I've never been.

When it's almost time for my lesson, I get Felix ready.
He's one of my favorite horses at the barn.

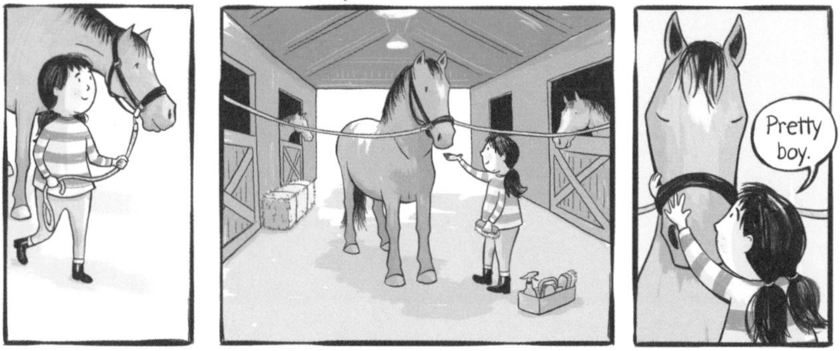
Pretty boy.

Halfway through my ride, my saddle comes loose. It slips all the way over
to Felix's side when we take a sharp turn after a jump.

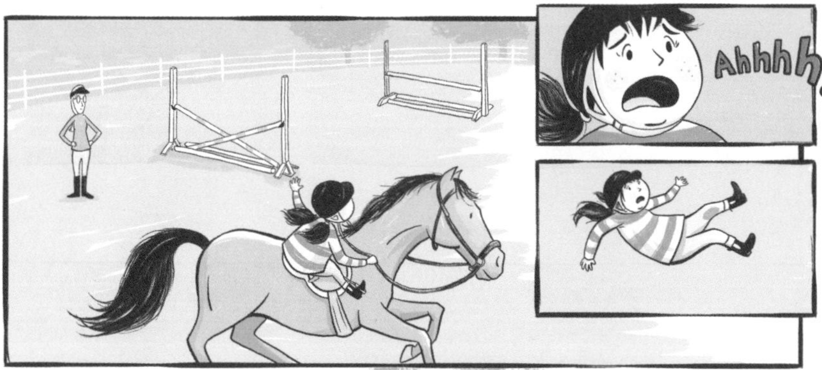
Ahhhh!

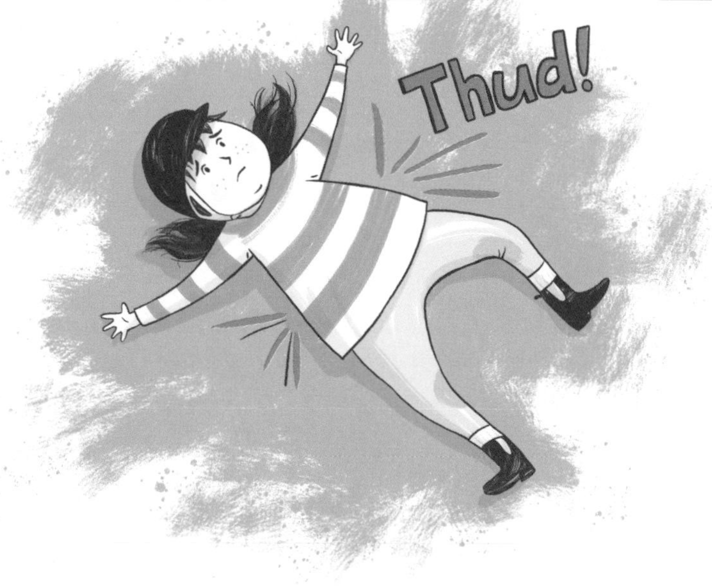
Thud!

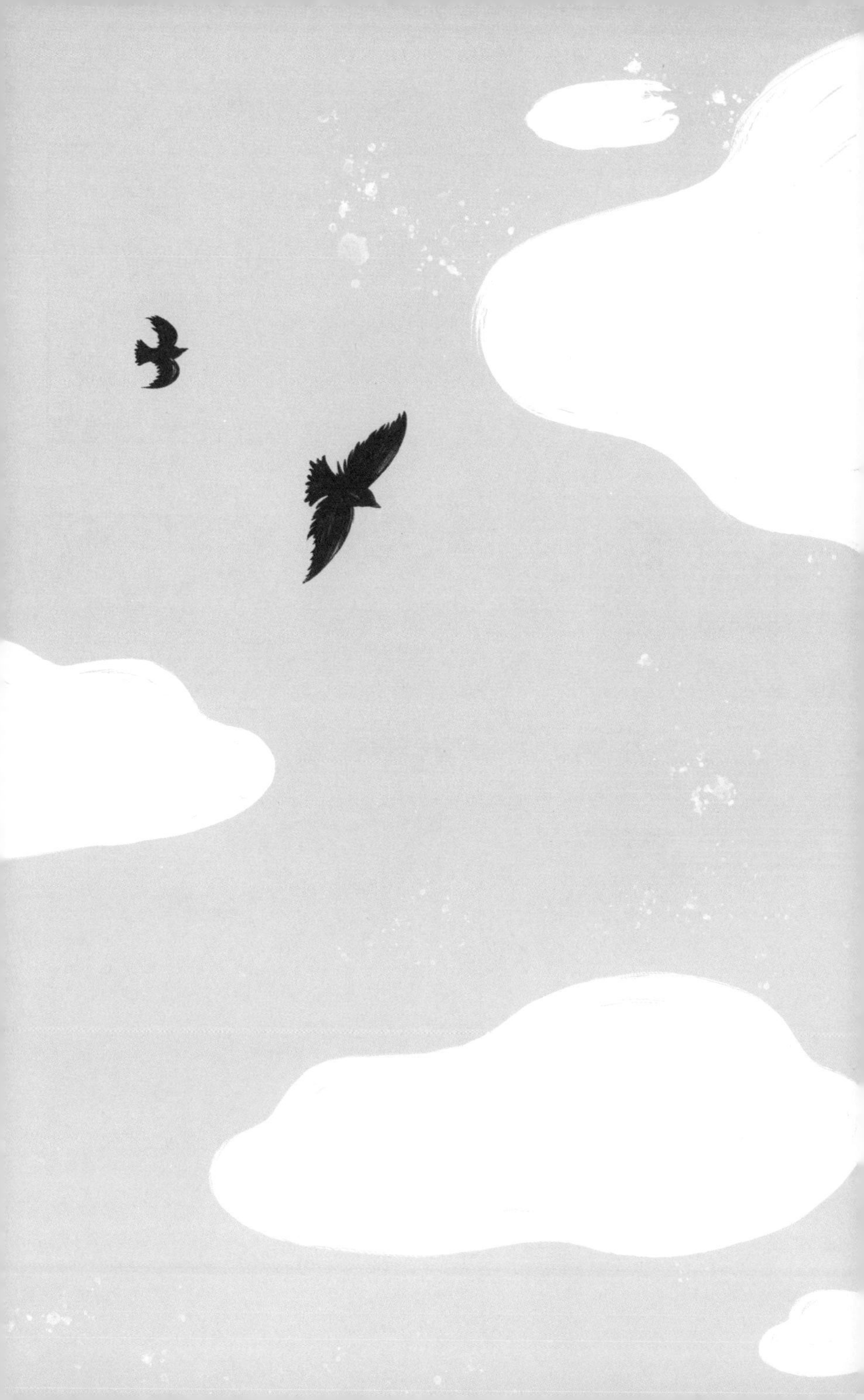

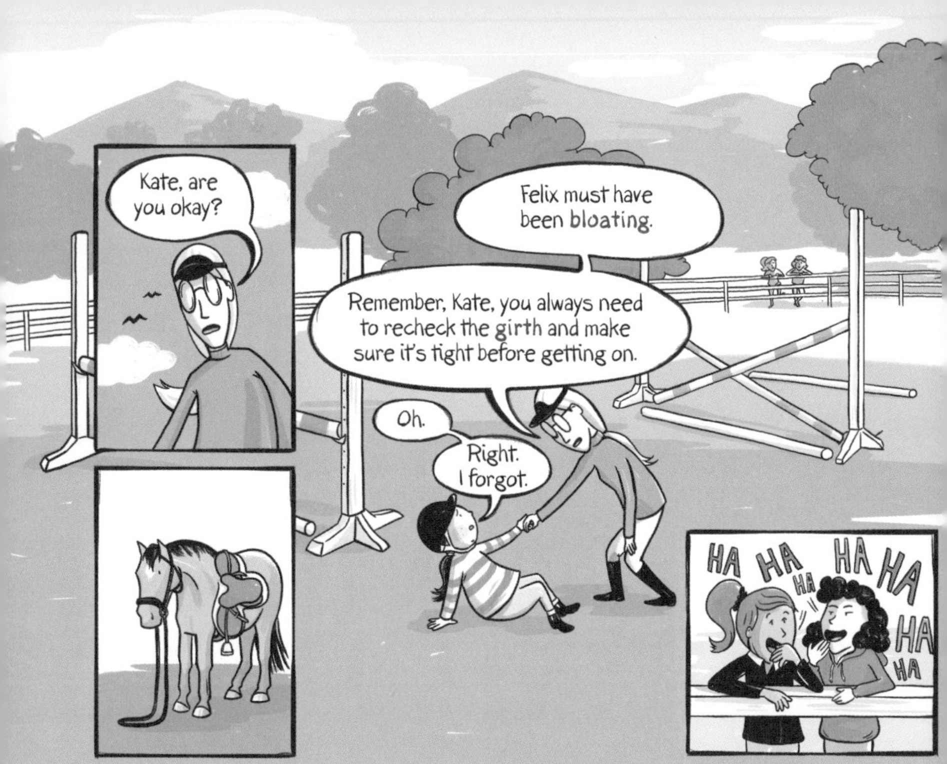
Kate, are you okay?
Felix must have been bloating.
Remember, Kate, you always need to recheck the girth and make sure it's tight before getting on.
Oh.
Right. I forgot.
HA HA HA HA HA HA HA HA

How could I be so ***stupid?!***
Rechecking the girth was one of the first things I learned about putting a saddle on.

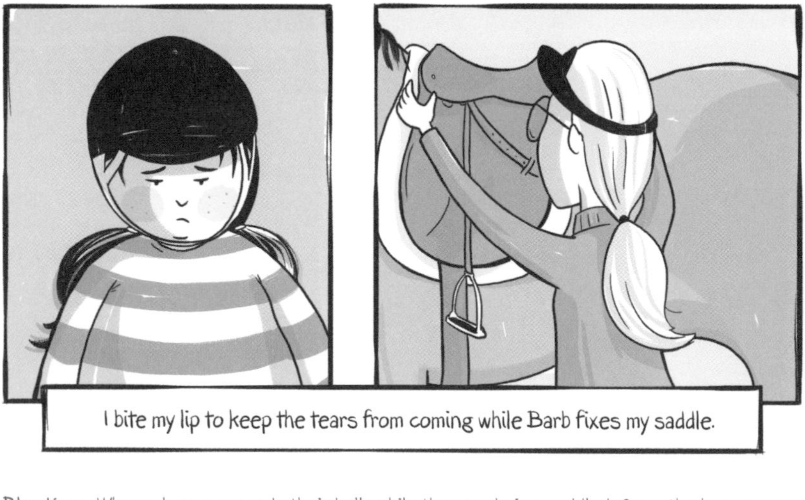
I bite my lip to keep the tears from coming while Barb fixes my saddle.

Bloating: When a horse expands their belly while they are being saddled. Once the horse relaxes their abdominal muscles, the girth loosens, allowing the saddle to slip.

Girth: The band that's attached to the saddle, used to secure it on the horse by fastening around its belly.

It's not like I haven't fallen off before. If you ride horses long enough, you'll eventually have a fall.

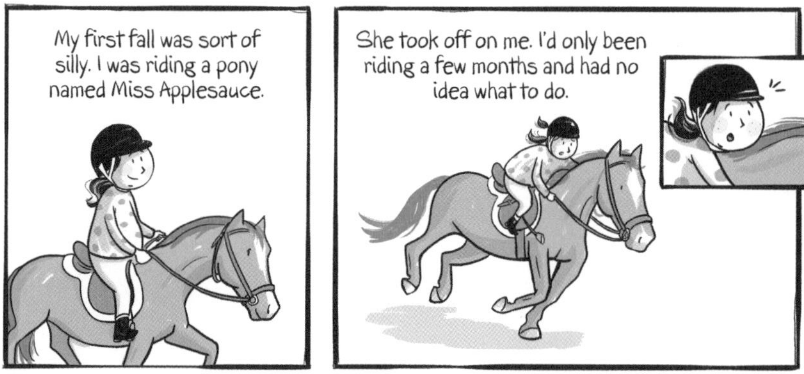

My first fall was sort of silly. I was riding a pony named Miss Applesauce.
She took off on me. I'd only been riding a few months and had no idea what to do.

She was so short that I just slid off her back onto the ground.

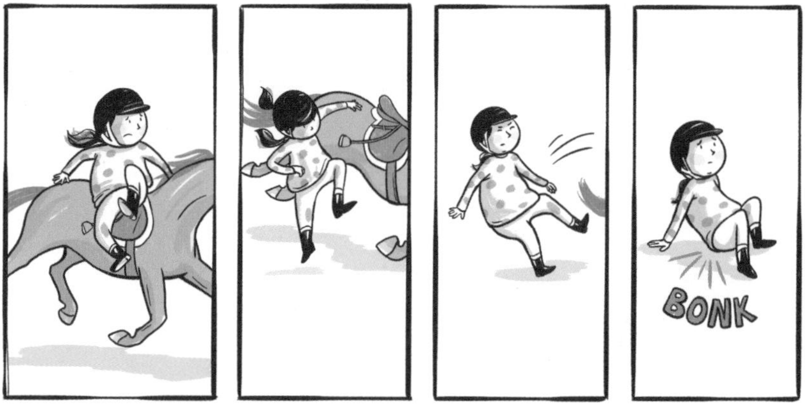

BONK

But sometimes falling is scary. Really scary.

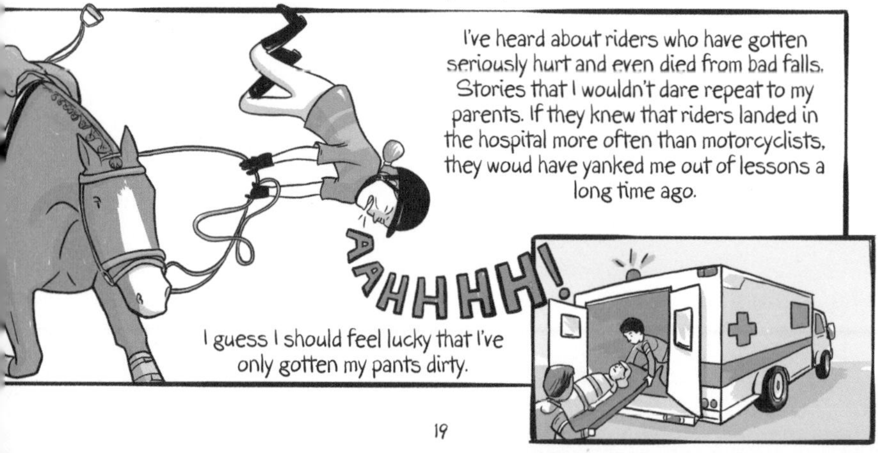

I've heard about riders who have gotten seriously hurt and even died from bad falls. Stories that I wouldn't dare repeat to my parents. If they knew that riders landed in the hospital more often than motorcyclists, they woud have yanked me out of lessons a long time ago.
AAHHHHH!
I guess I should feel lucky that I've only gotten my pants dirty.

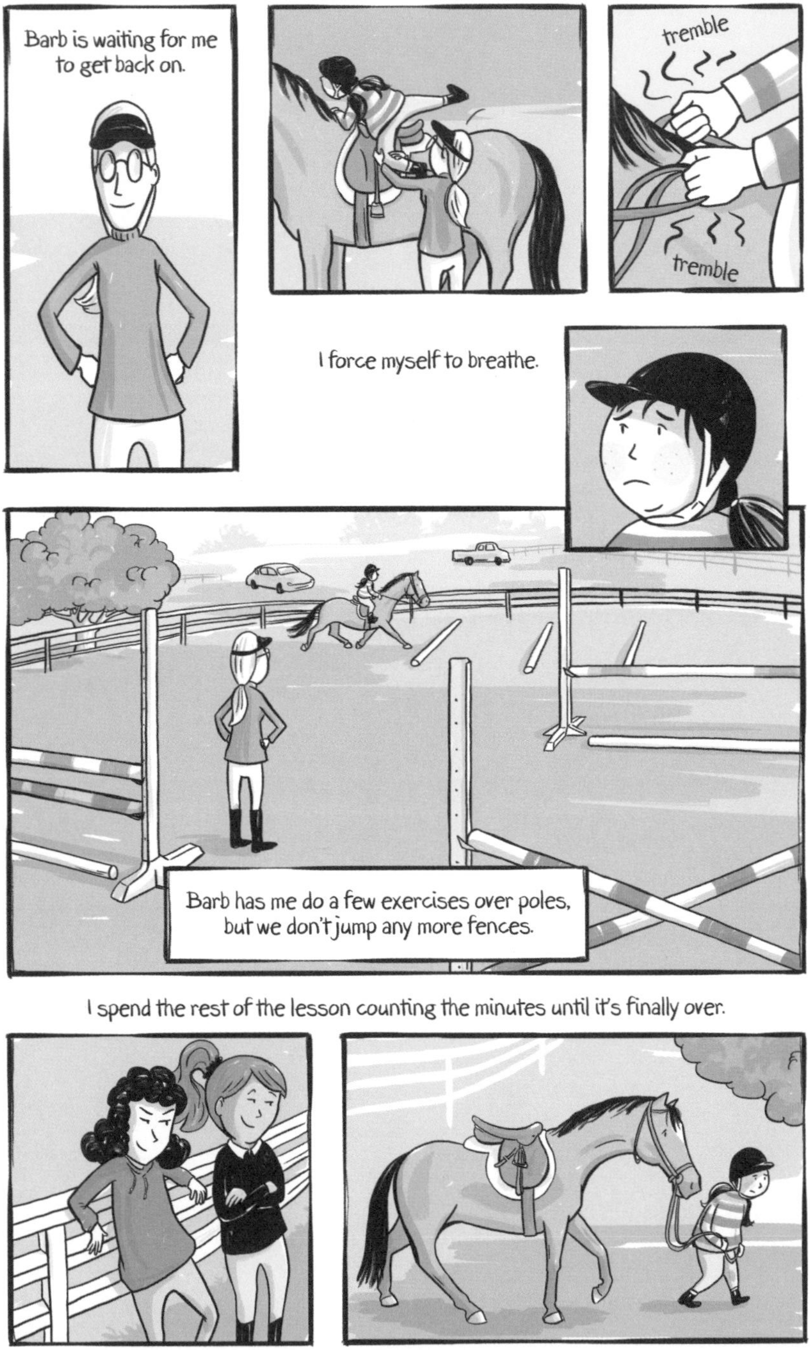

Barb is waiting for me to get back on.
tremble
tremble
I force myself to breathe.
Barb has me do a few exercises over poles, but we don't jump any more fences.
I spend the rest of the lesson counting the minutes until it's finally over.

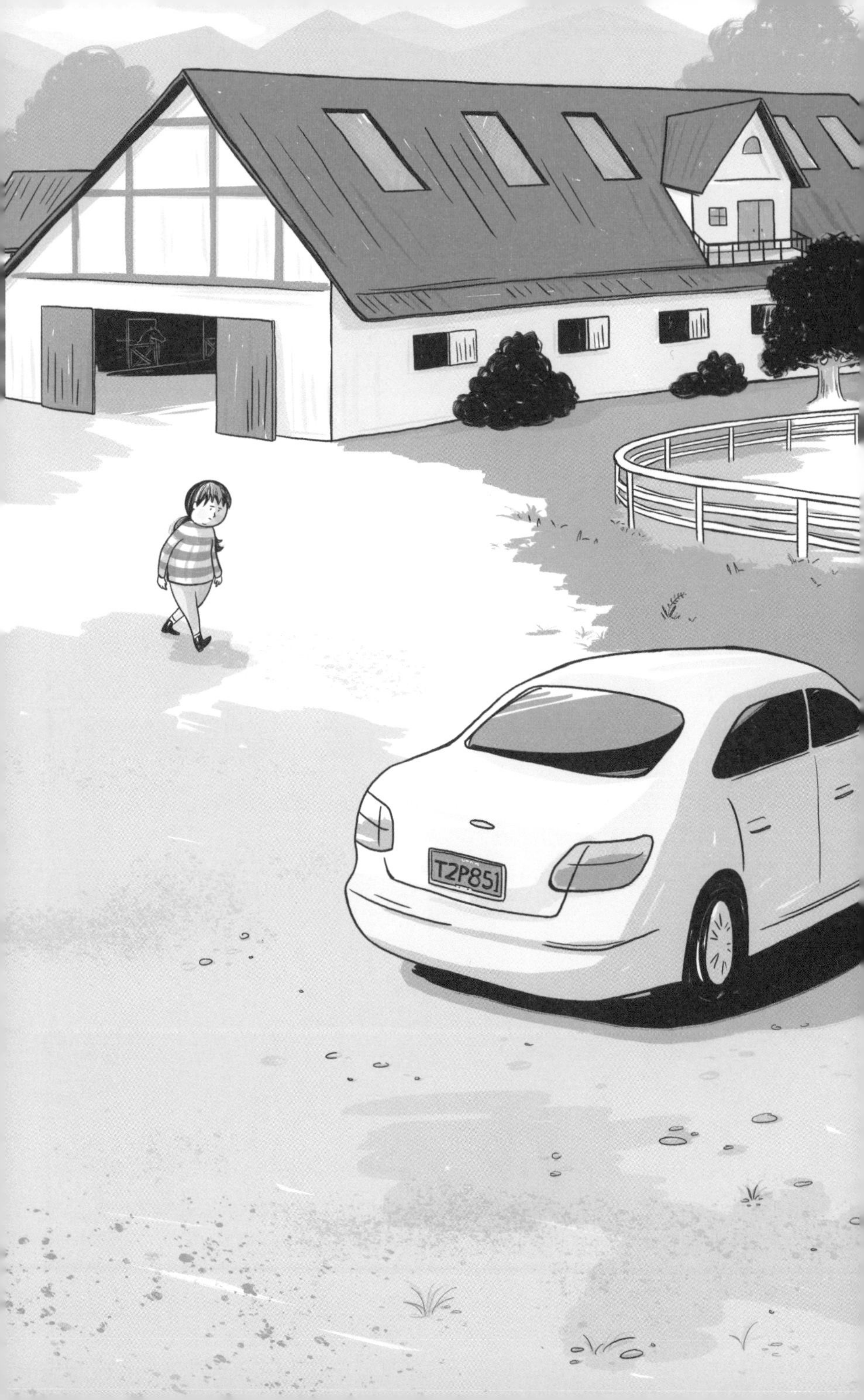
T2P851

To make matters worse, my brother, Ross, has shown up early.

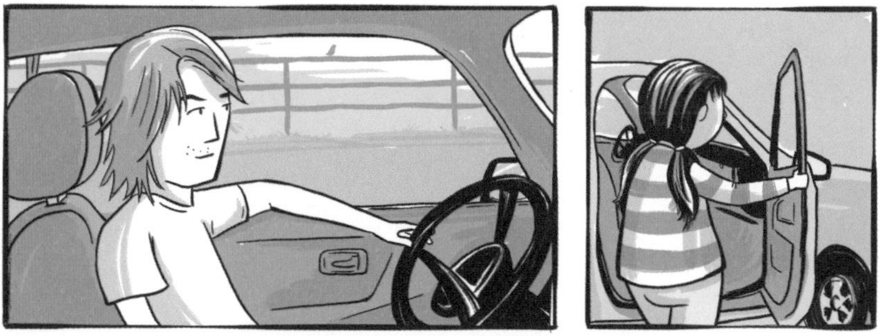

Ross is not a fan of the barn. My mom makes him pick me up every Tuesday on his way home from band practice.

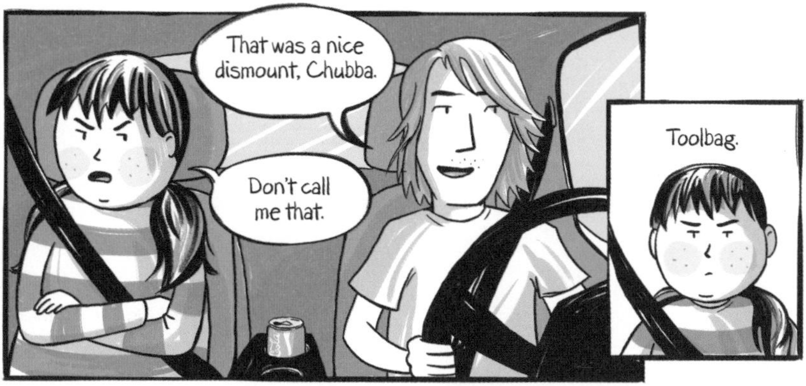

That was a nice dismount, Chubba.
Don't call me that.
Toolbag.

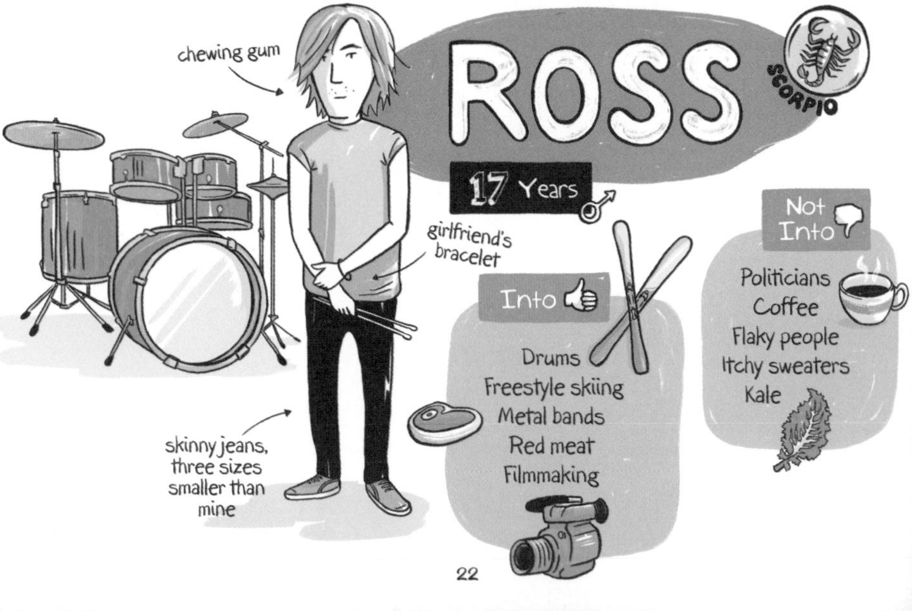

ROSS
SCORPIO
chewing gum
17 Years
girlfriend's bracelet
Into
Drums
Freestyle skiing
Metal bands
Red meat
Filmmaking
Not Into
Politicians
Coffee
Flaky people
Itchy sweaters
Kale
skinny jeans, three sizes smaller than mine

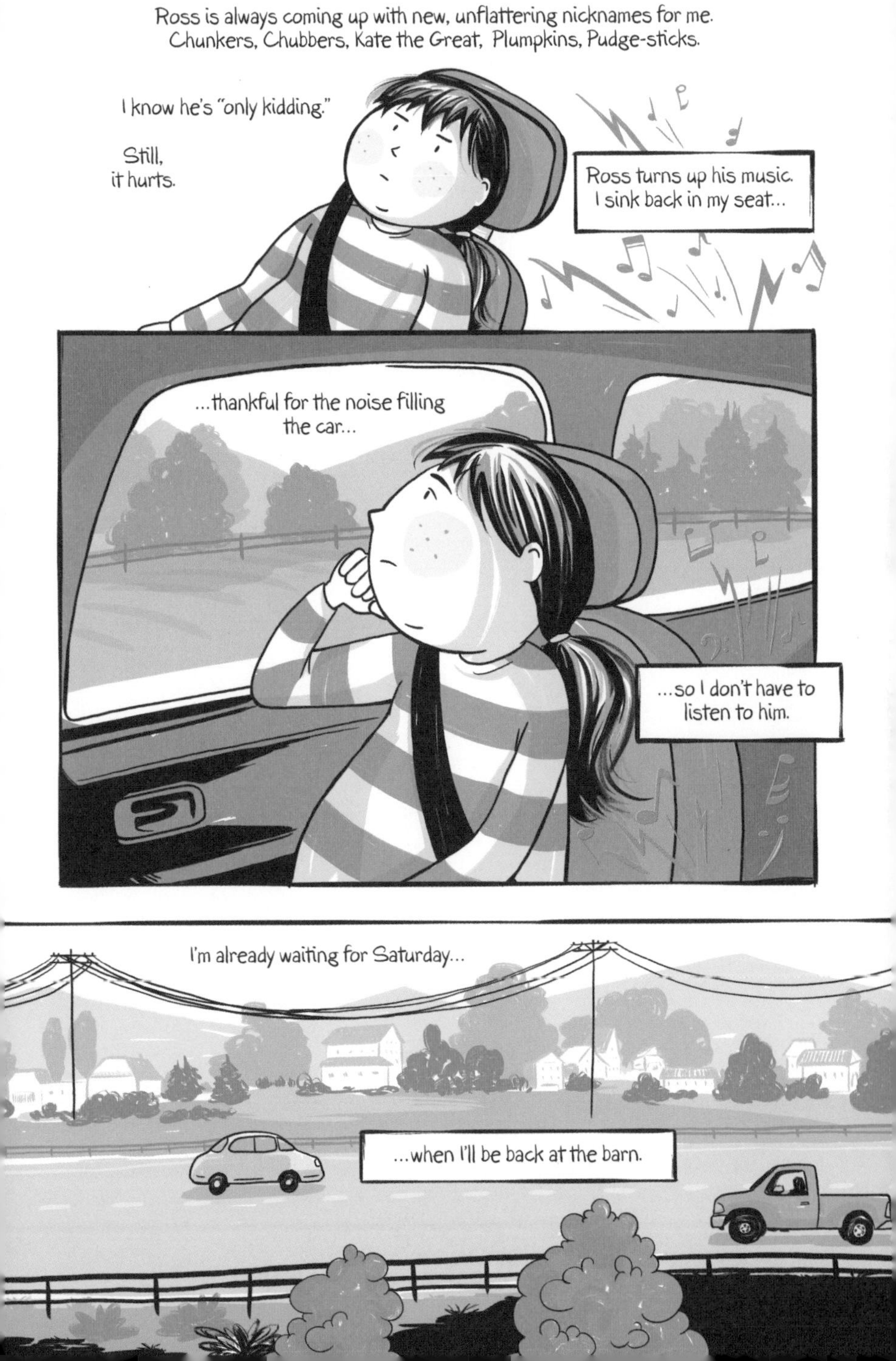
Ross is always coming up with new, unflattering nicknames for me. Chunkers, Chubbers, Kate the Great, Plumpkins, Pudge-sticks.
I know he's "only kidding."
Still, it hurts.
Ross turns up his music. I sink back in my seat...
...thankful for the noise filling the car...
...so I don't have to listen to him.
I'm already waiting for Saturday...
...when I'll be back at the barn.

Chapter 2
Gravel Toss

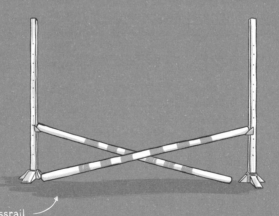

Crossrail

Normally the first kind of fence used for horses and riders just learning how to jump. The center is lower than the sides and encourages the horse to jump the middle of the fence.

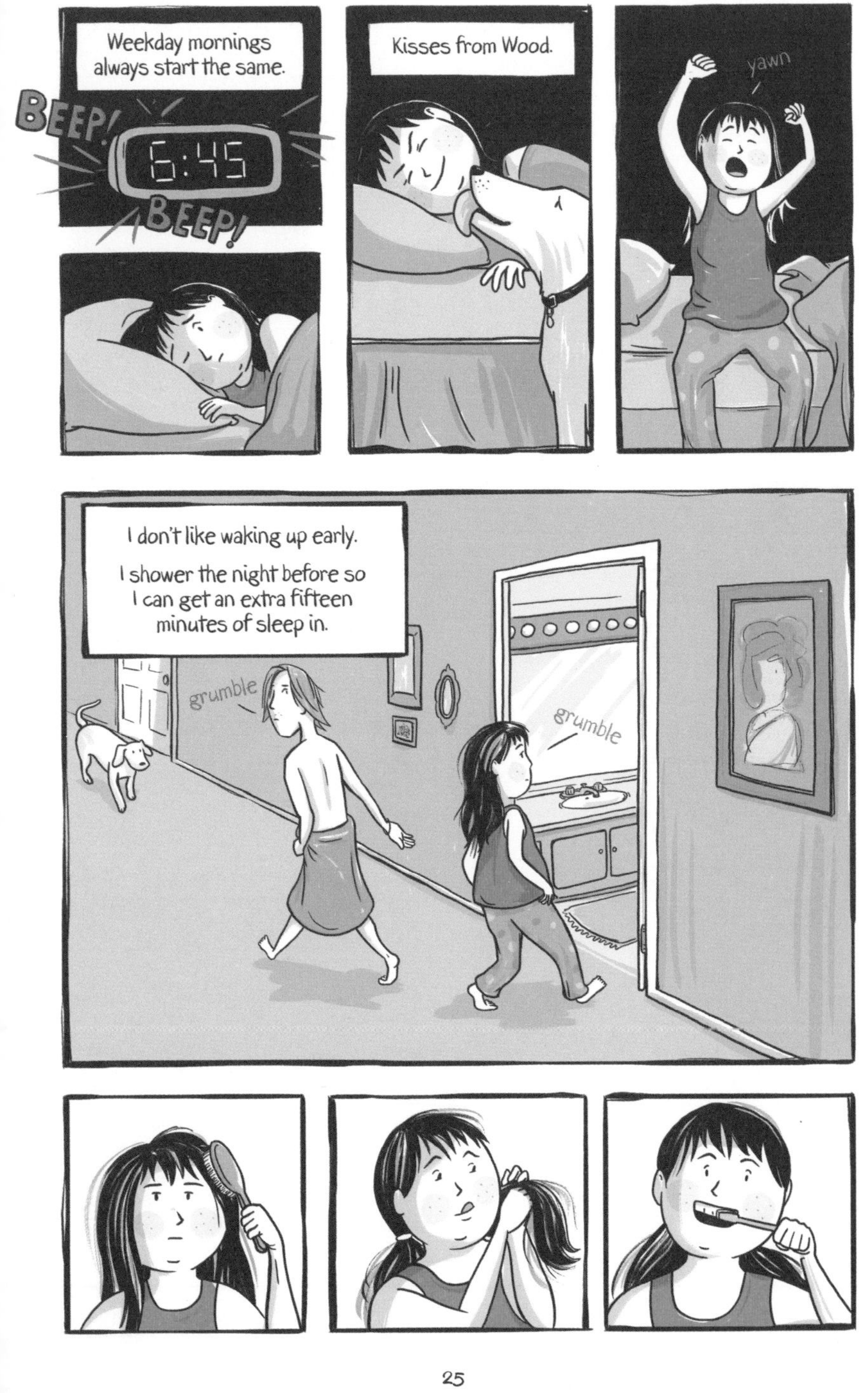

Weekday mornings always start the same.
BEEP!
6:45
BEEP!
Kisses from Wood.
yawn
I don't like waking up early.
I shower the night before so I can get an extra fifteen minutes of sleep in.
grumble
grumble

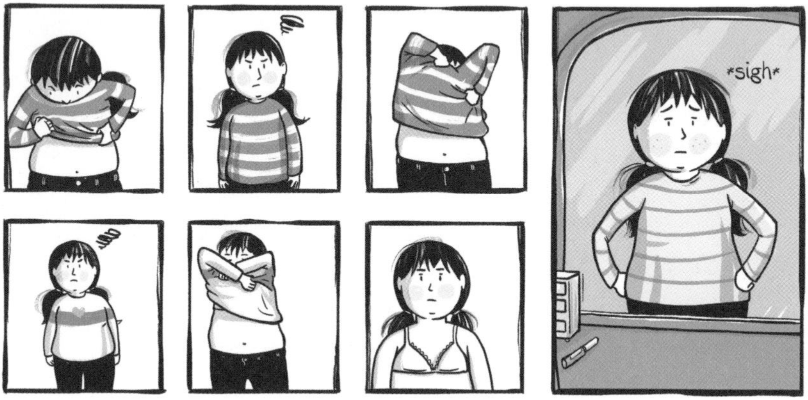
sigh

I get a whiff of my dad's aftershave in the hallway.
He's always annoyingly chipper in the morning.

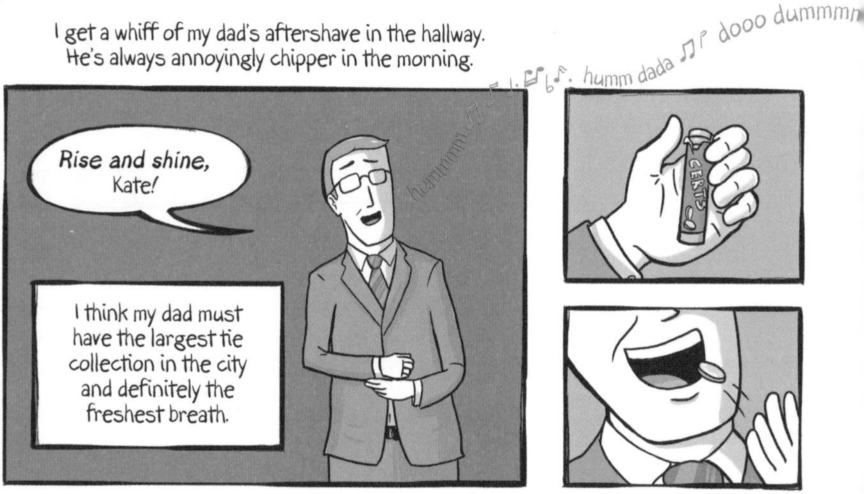
hummmm
humm dada
dooo dummmm
Rise and shine, Kate!
I think my dad must have the largest tie collection in the city and definitely the freshest breath.
CERTS

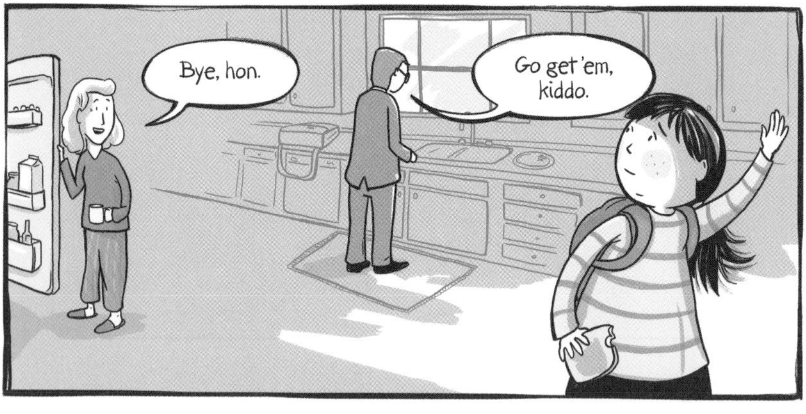
Bye, hon.
Go get 'em, kiddo.

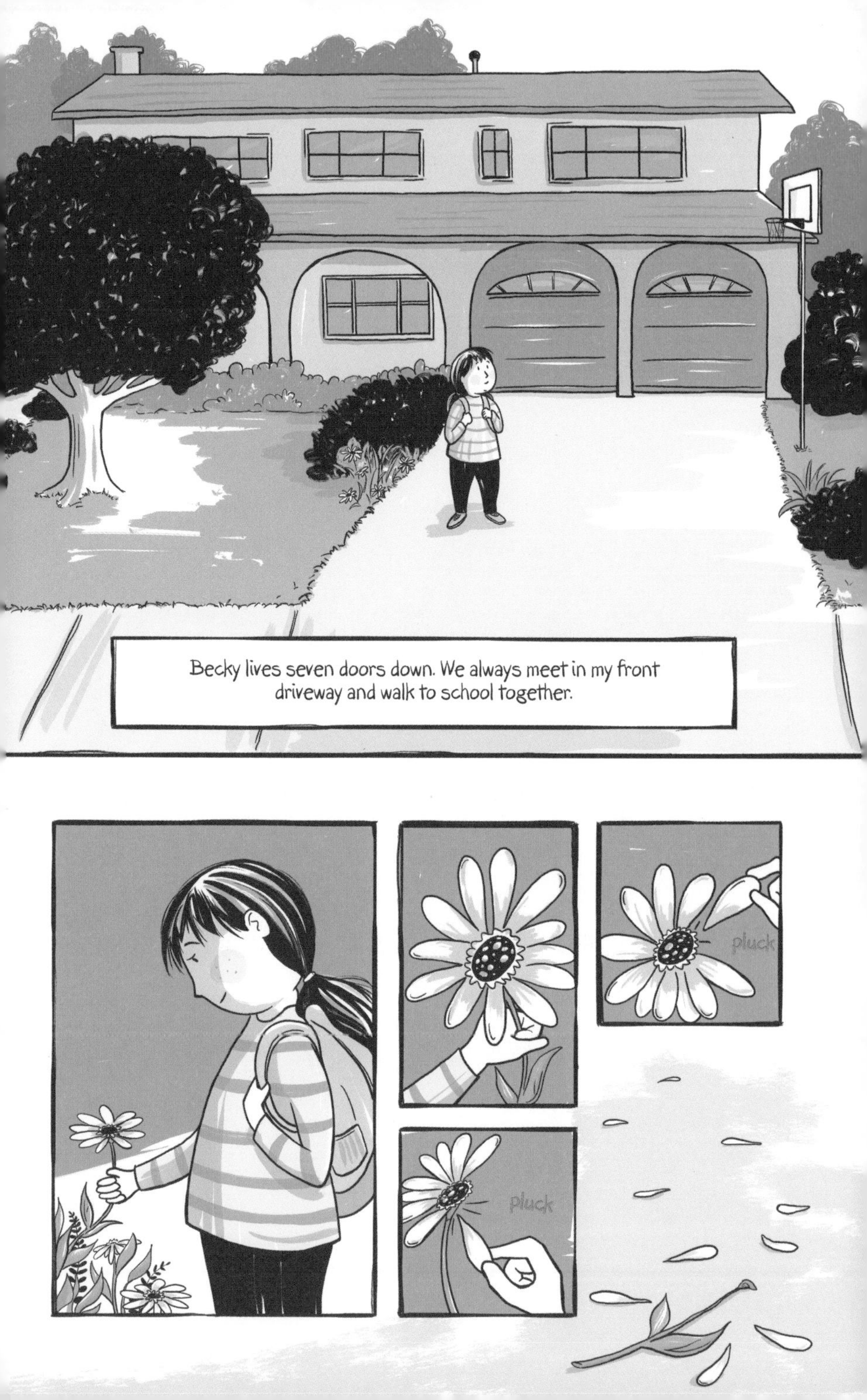
Becky lives seven doors down. We always meet in my front driveway and walk to school together.
pluck
pluck

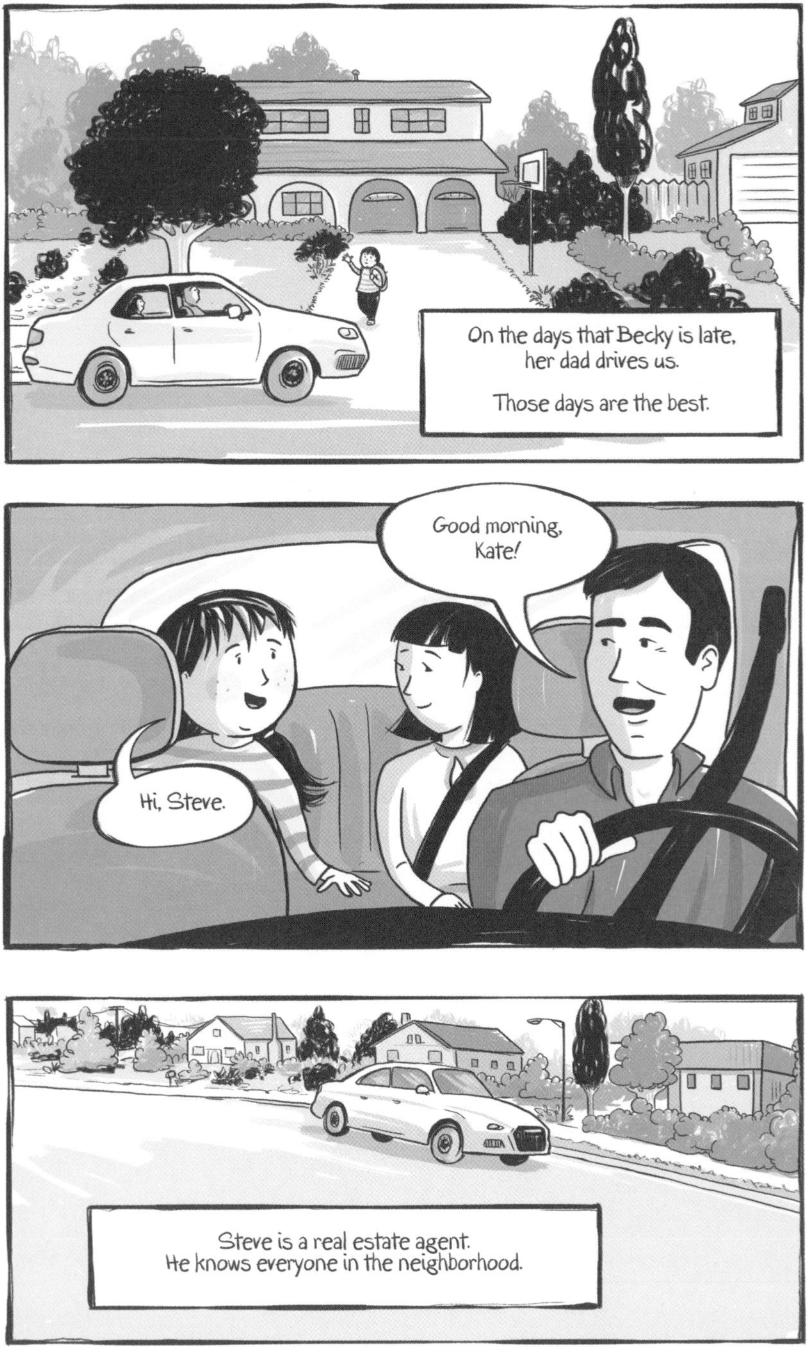
On the days that Becky is late, her dad drives us.
Those days are the best.
Good morning, Kate!
Hi, Steve.
Steve is a real estate agent. He knows everyone in the neighborhood.

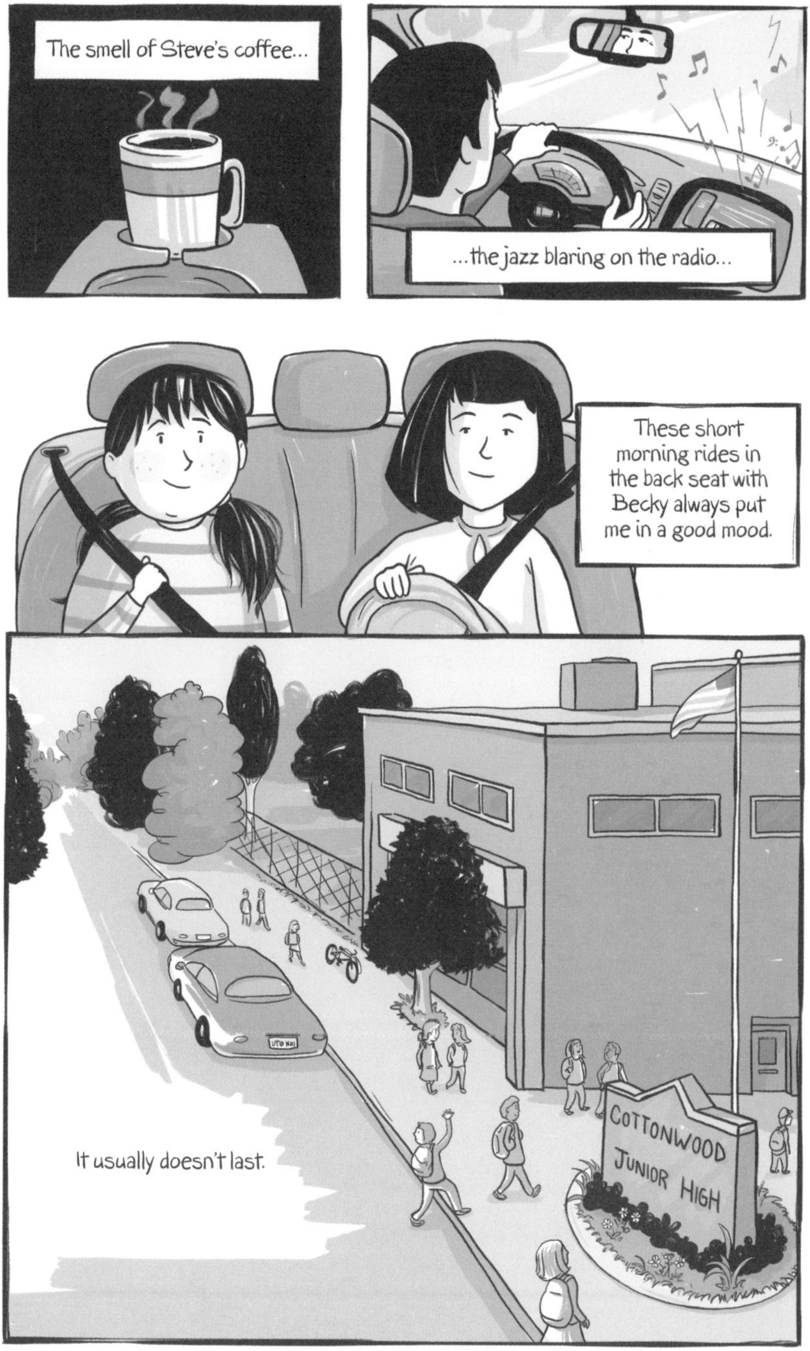
The smell of Steve's coffee...
...the jazz blaring on the radio...
These short morning rides in the back seat with Becky always put me in a good mood.
COTTONWOOD JUNIOR HIGH
It usually doesn't last.

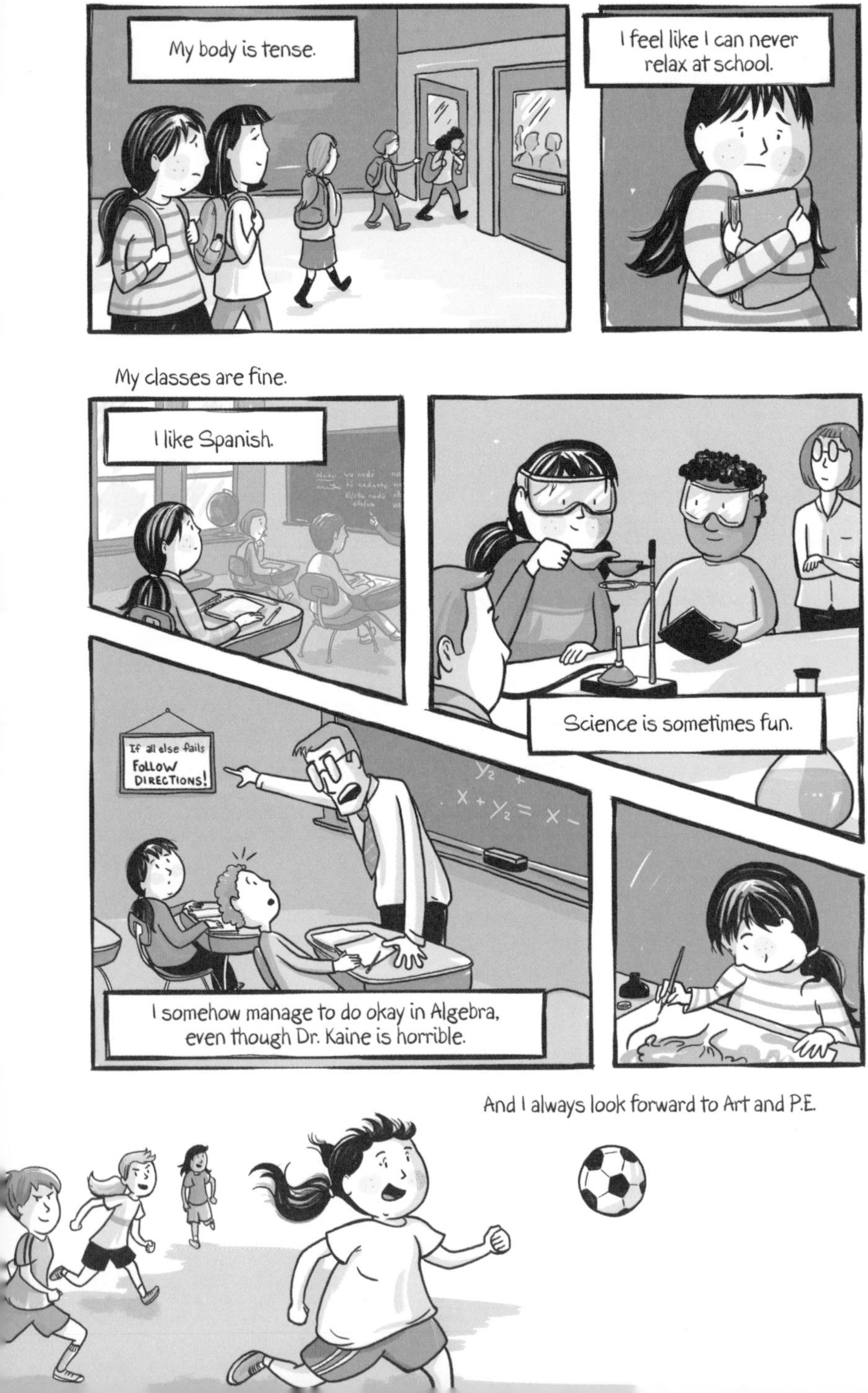

My body is tense.
I feel like I can never relax at school.
My classes are fine.
I like Spanish.
Science is sometimes fun.
If all else fails FOLLOW DIRECTIONS!
I somehow manage to do okay in Algebra, even though Dr. Kaine is horrible.
And I always look forward to Art and P.E.

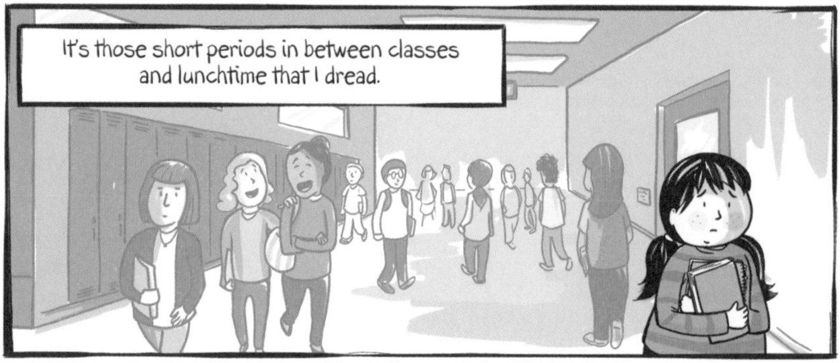
It's those short periods in between classes and lunchtime that I dread.

I'm in with the popular girls at school...

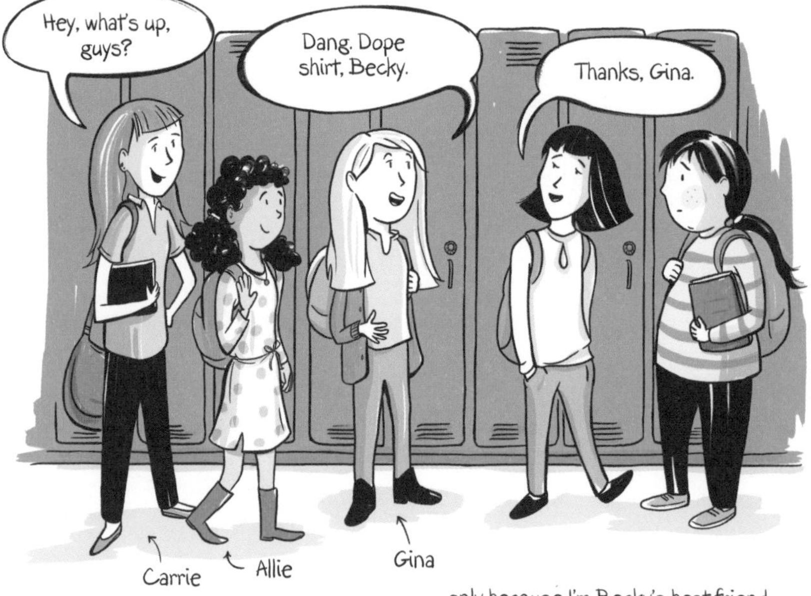
Hey, what's up, guys?
Dang. Dope shirt, Becky.
Thanks, Gina.
Carrie
Allie
Gina

...only because I'm Becky's best friend.

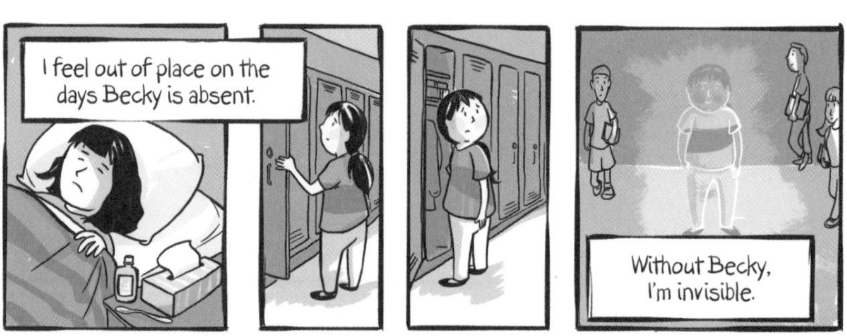
I feel out of place on the days Becky is absent.
Without Becky, I'm invisible.

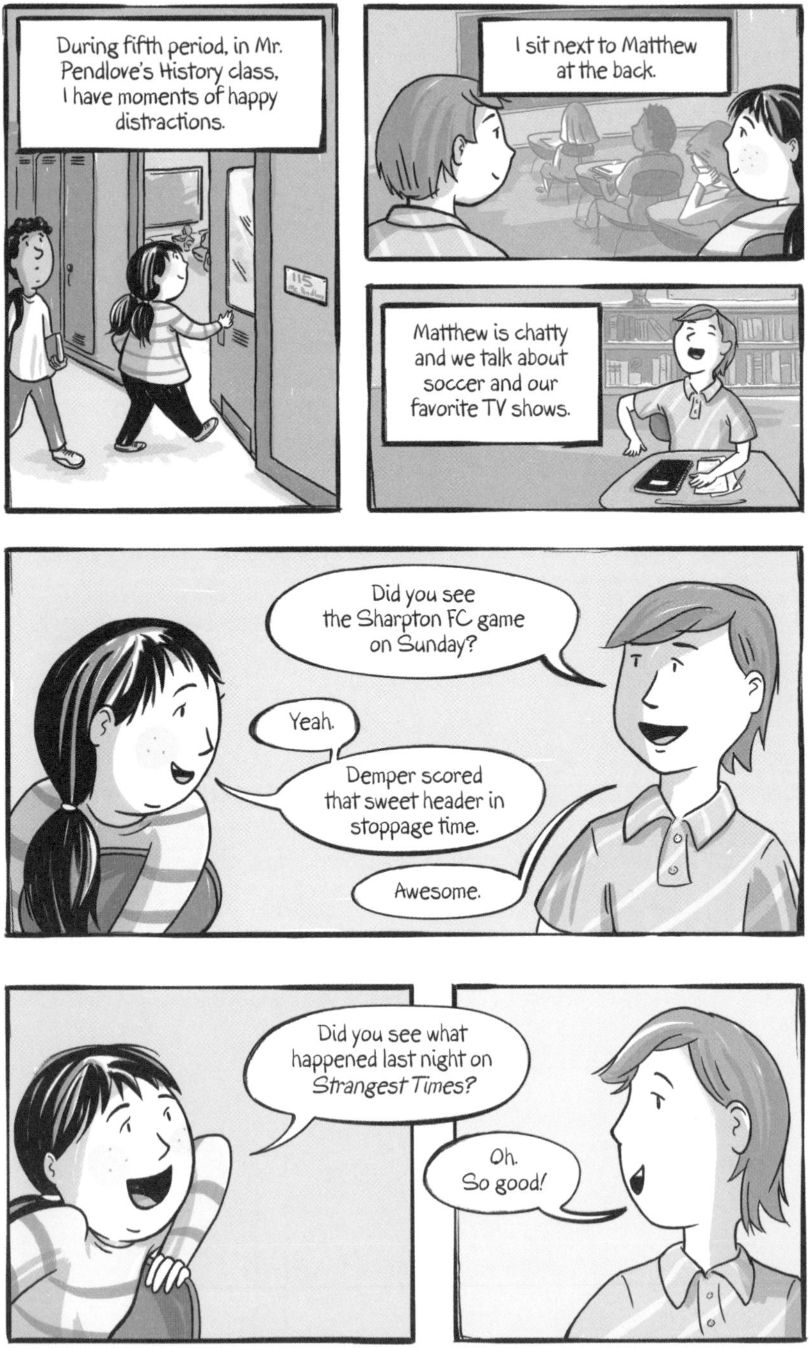
During fifth period, in Mr. Pendlove's History class, I have moments of happy distractions.
115
I sit next to Matthew at the back.
Matthew is chatty and we talk about soccer and our favorite TV shows.
Did you see the Sharpton FC game on Sunday?
Yeah.
Demper scored that sweet header in stoppage time.
Awesome.
Did you see what happened last night on *Strangest Times*?
Oh.
So good!

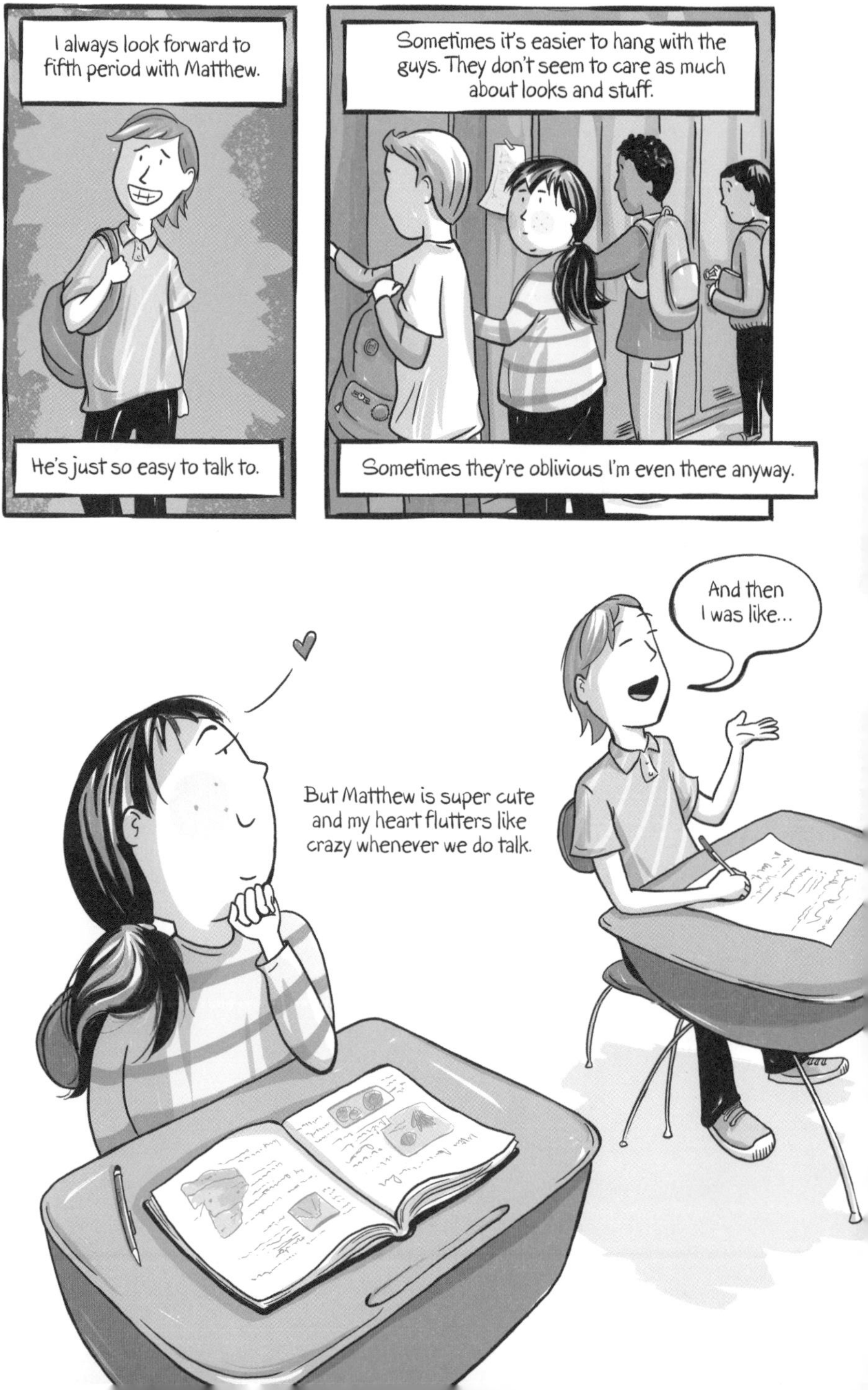
I always look forward to fifth period with Matthew.
He's just so easy to talk to.
Sometimes it's easier to hang with the guys. They don't seem to care as much about looks and stuff.
Sometimes they're oblivious I'm even there anyway.
And then I was like...
But Matthew is super cute and my heart flutters like crazy whenever we do talk.

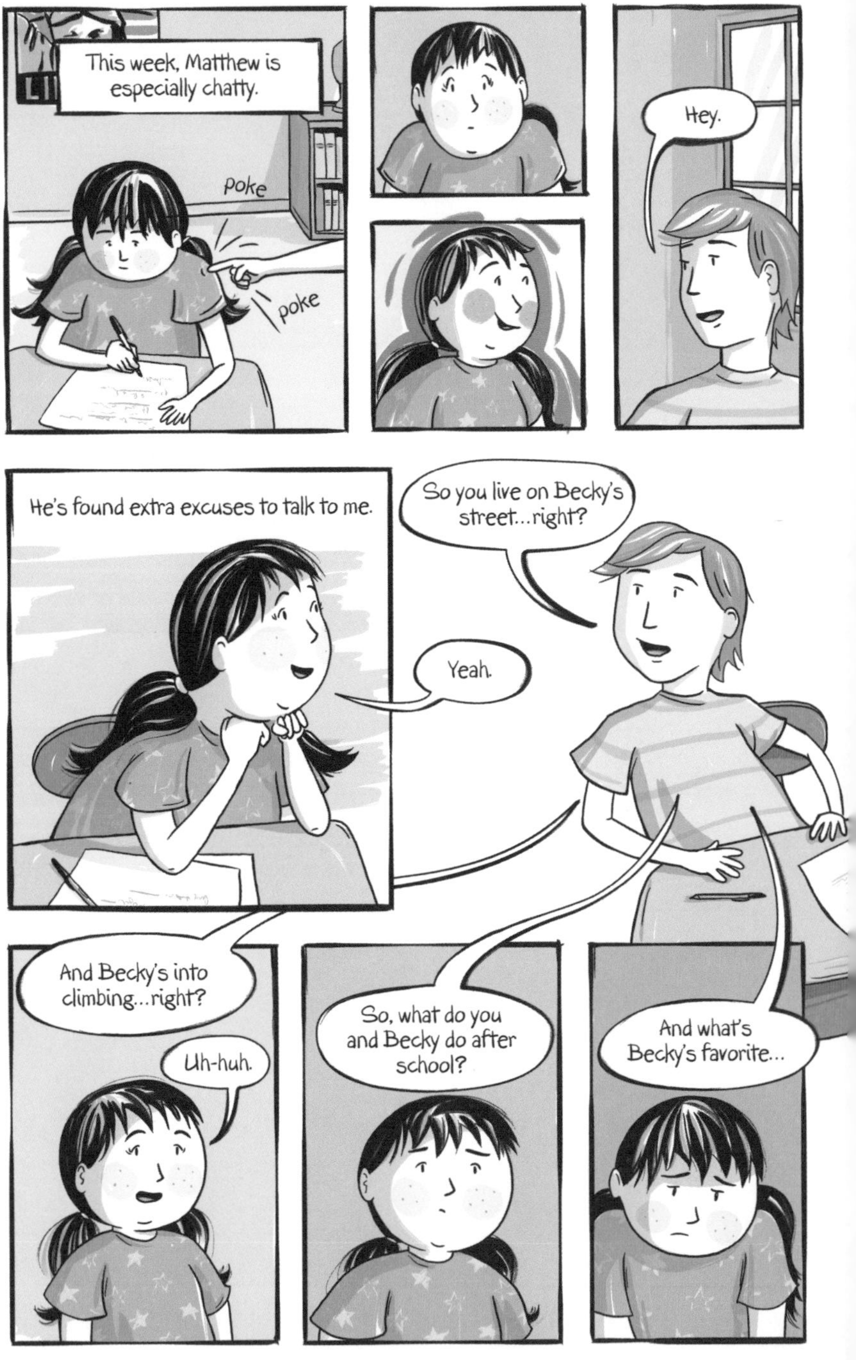
This week, Matthew is especially chatty.
poke
poke
Hey.
He's found extra excuses to talk to me.
So you live on Becky's street...right?
Yeah.
And Becky's into climbing...right?
Uh-huh.
So, what do you and Becky do after school?
And what's Becky's favorite...

He *only* wants to talk about Becky.

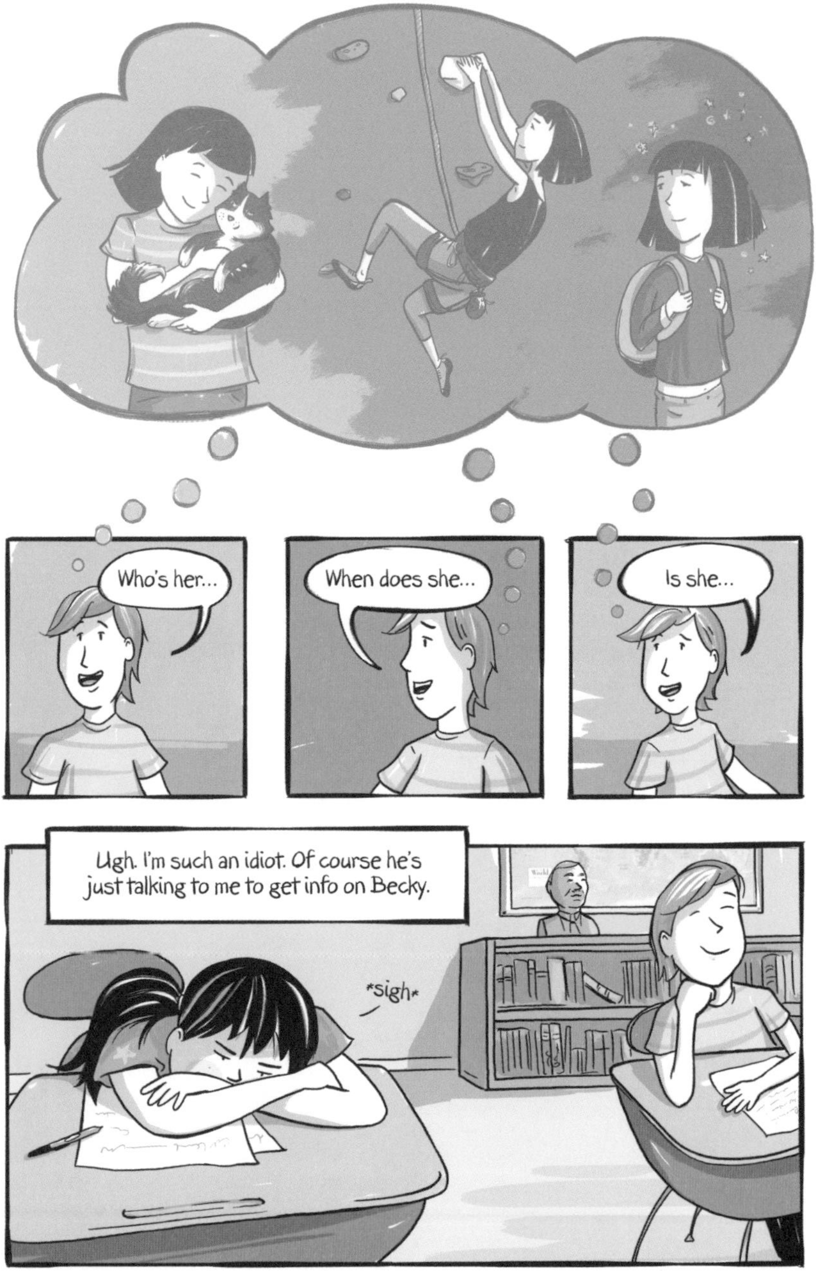
Who's her...
When does she...
Is she...
Ugh. I'm such an idiot. Of course he's just talking to me to get info on Becky.
sigh

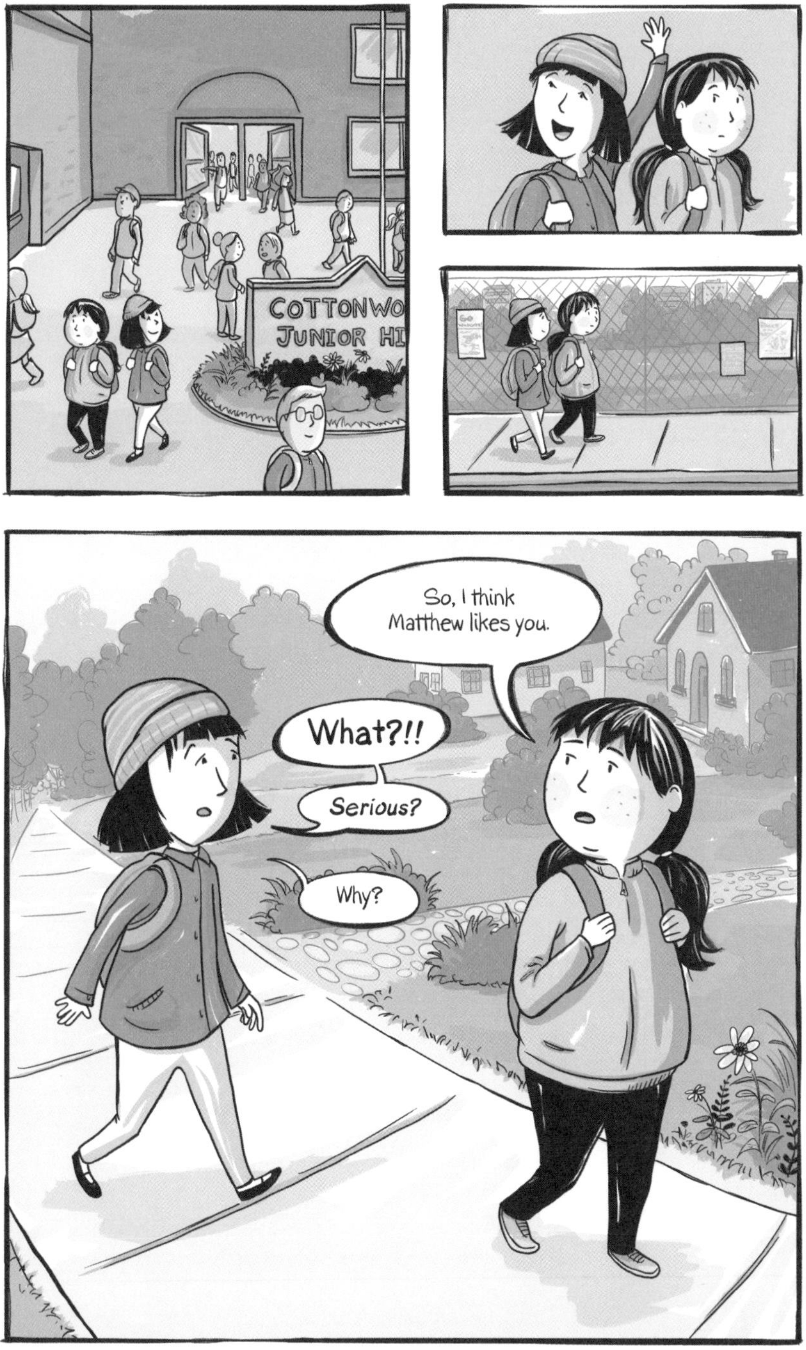
COTTONWO
JUNIOR HI
So, I think Matthew likes you.
What?!!
Serious?
Why?

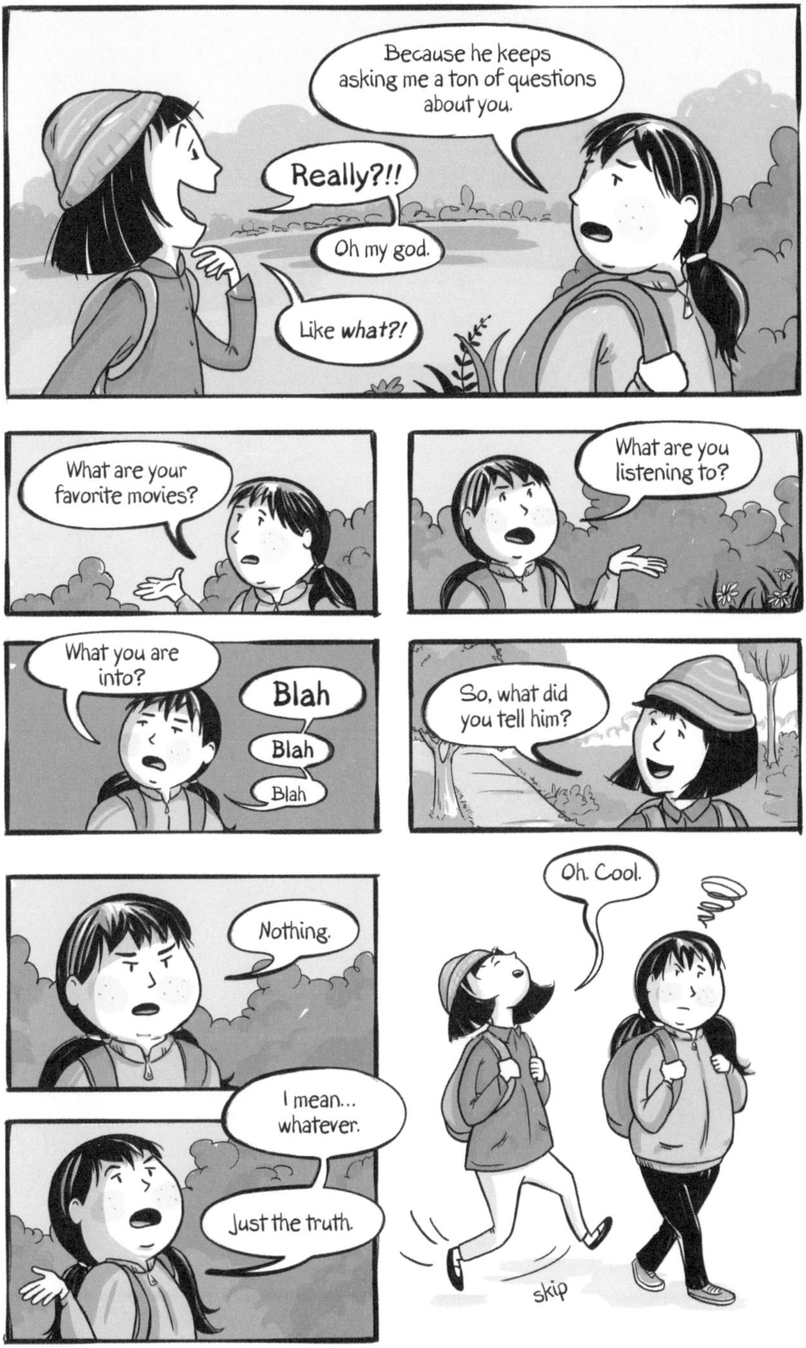
Because he keeps asking me a ton of questions about you.
Really?!!
Oh my god.
Like *what?!*
What are your favorite movies?
What are you listening to?
What you are into?
Blah
Blah
Blah
So, what did you tell him?
Nothing.
I mean... whatever.
Just the truth.
Oh. Cool.
skip

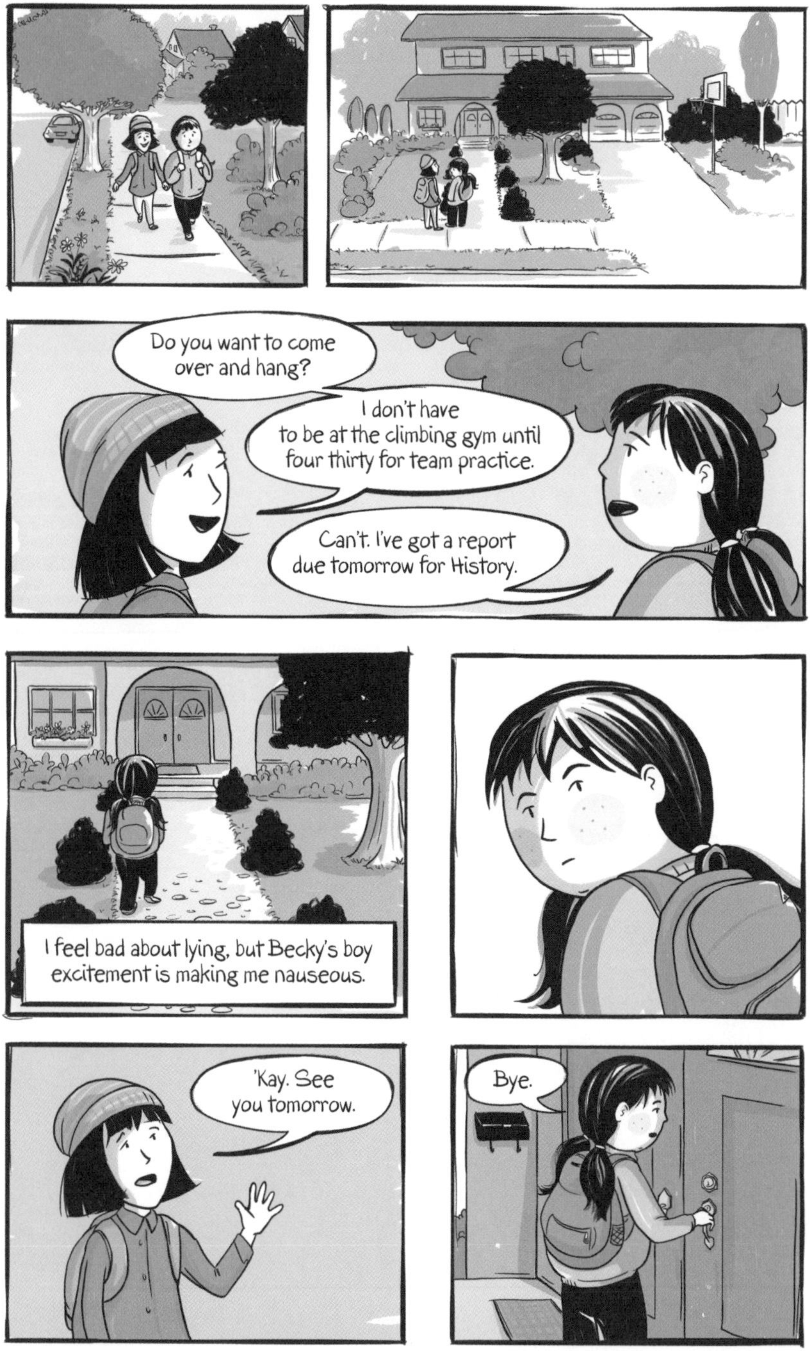

Do you want to come over and hang?
I don't have to be at the climbing gym until four thirty for team practice.
Can't. I've got a report due tomorrow for History.
I feel bad about lying, but Becky's boy excitement is making me nauseous.
'Kay. See you tomorrow.
Bye.

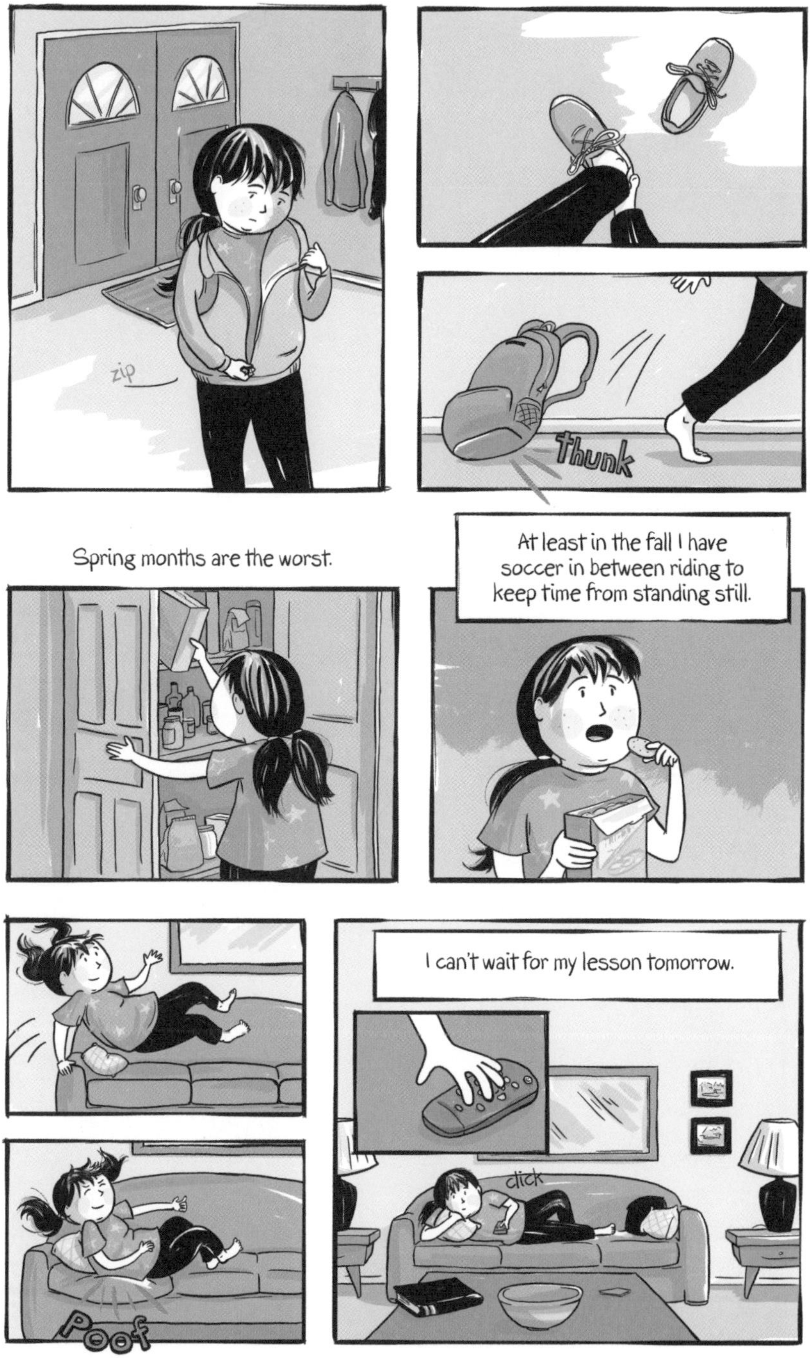
zip
thunk
Spring months are the worst.
At least in the fall I have soccer in between riding to keep time from standing still.
Poof
I can't wait for my lesson tomorrow.
click

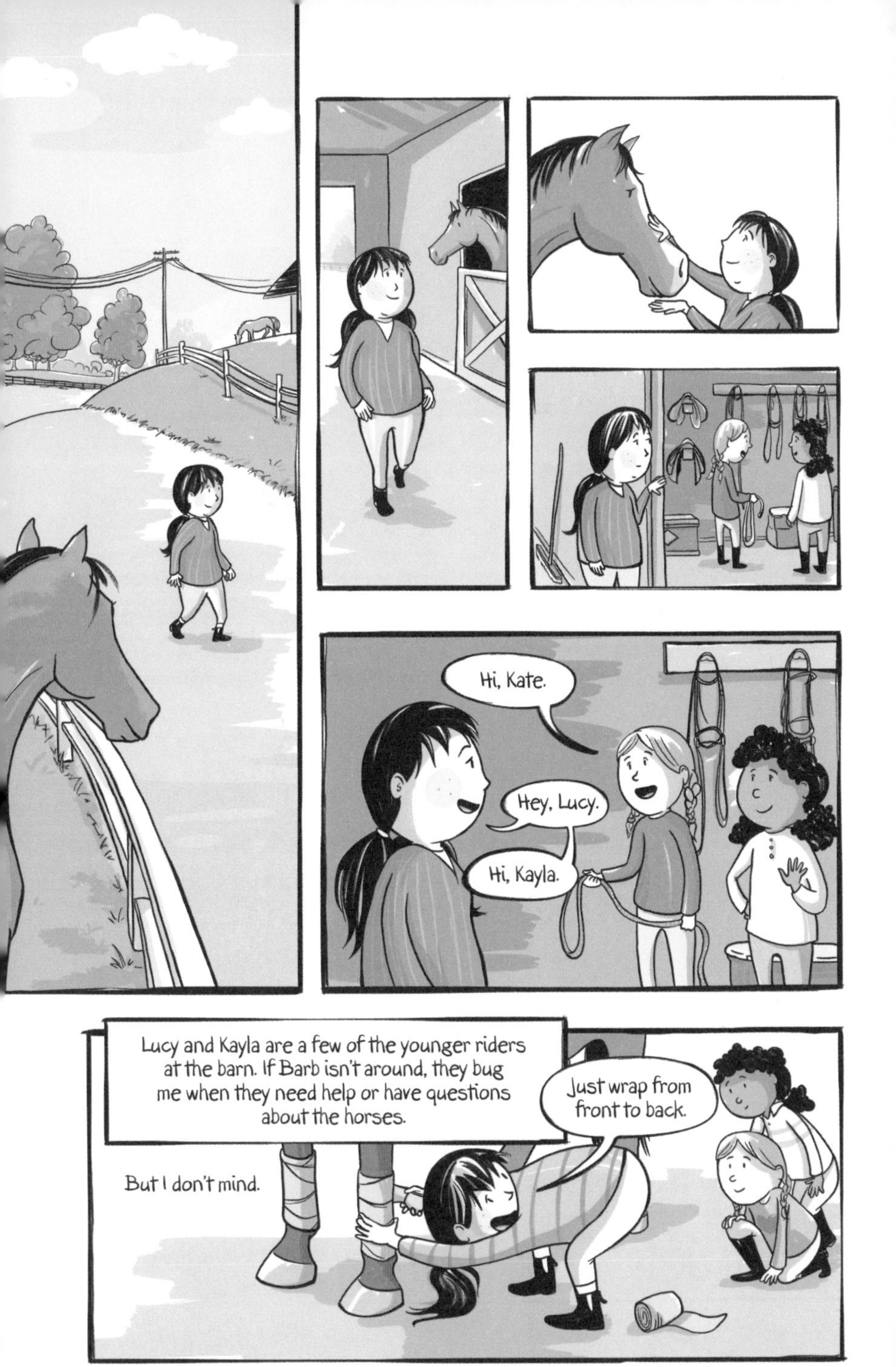
Hi, Kate.
Hey, Lucy.
Hi, Kayla.
Lucy and Kayla are a few of the younger riders at the barn. If Barb isn't around, they bug me when they need help or have questions about the horses.
Just wrap from front to back.
But I don't mind.

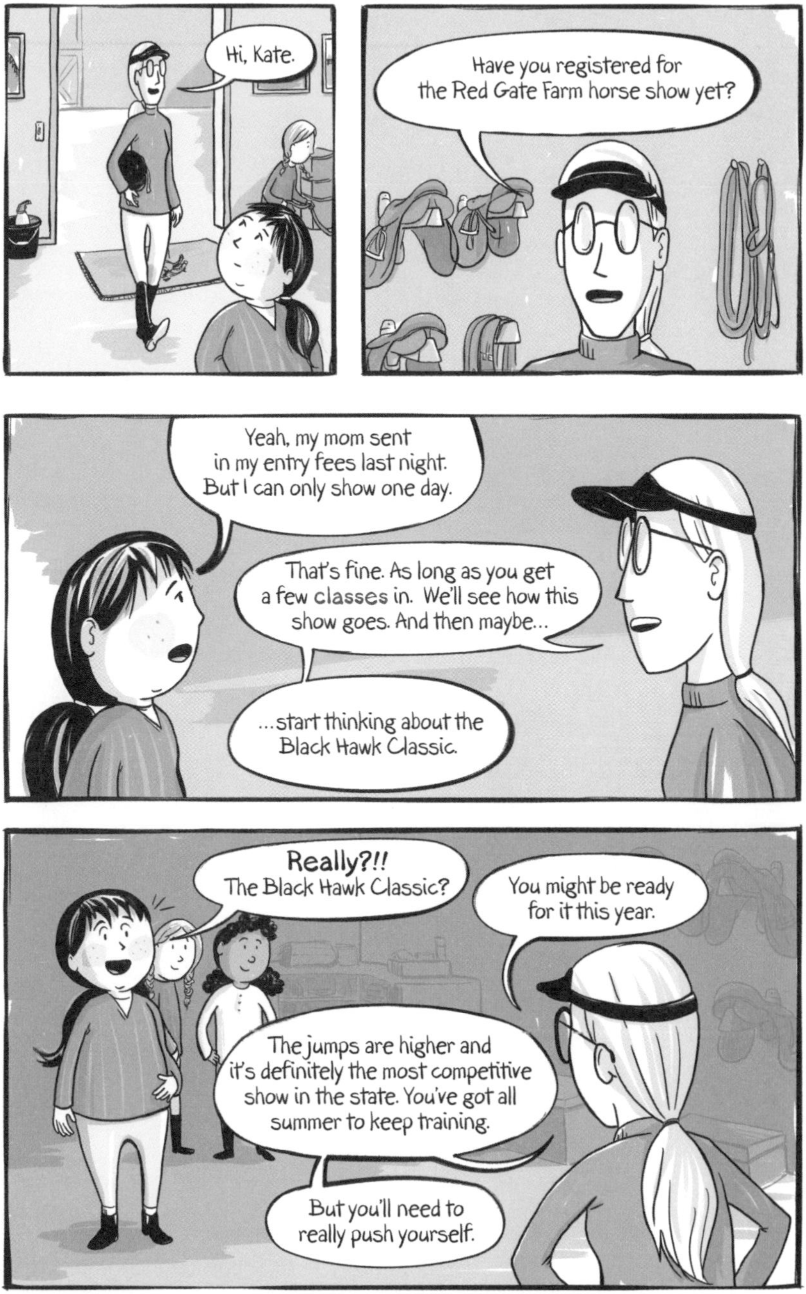
Hi, Kate.
Have you registered for the Red Gate Farm horse show yet?
Yeah, my mom sent in my entry fees last night. But I can only show one day.
That's fine. As long as you get a few classes in. We'll see how this show goes. And then maybe...
...start thinking about the Black Hawk Classic.
Really?!! The Black Hawk Classic?
You might be ready for it this year.
The jumps are higher and it's definitely the most competitive show in the state. You've got all summer to keep training.
But you'll need to really push yourself.

Class: The specific event at the horse show in which the horse and rider are competing. Classes are often divided by ability levels, the rider's age, fence height, etc.

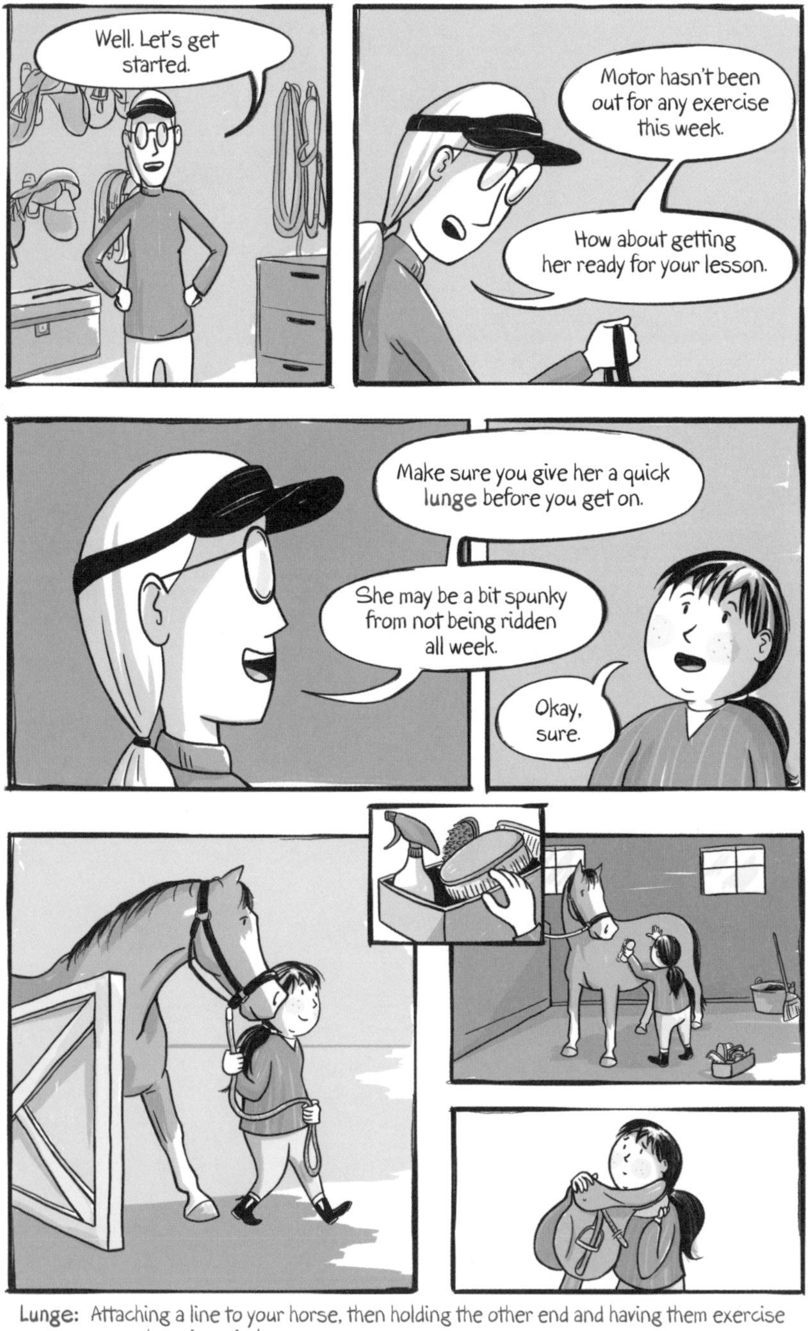
Well. Let's get started.
Motor hasn't been out for any exercise this week.
How about getting her ready for your lesson.
Make sure you give her a quick lunge before you get on.
She may be a bit spunky from not being ridden all week.
Okay, sure.

Lunge: Attaching a line to your horse, then holding the other end and having them exercise around you in a circle.

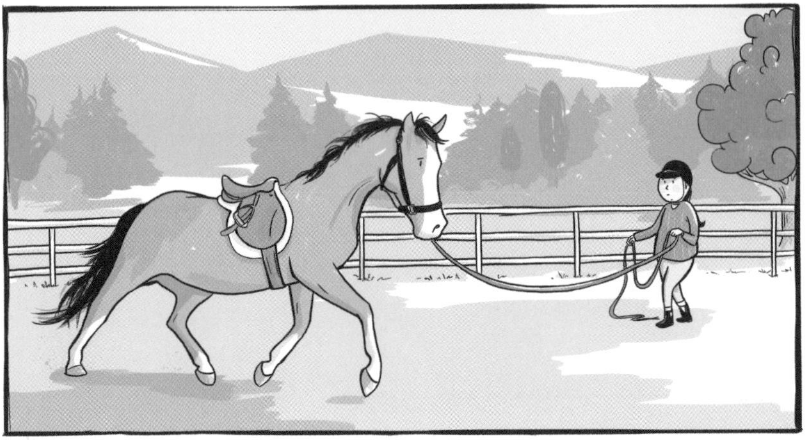

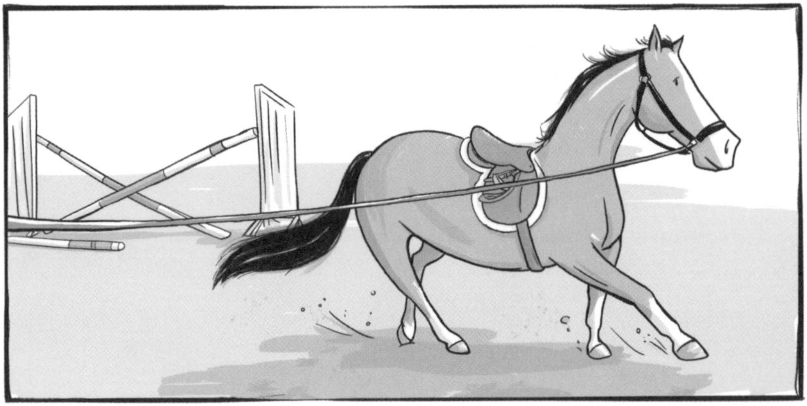

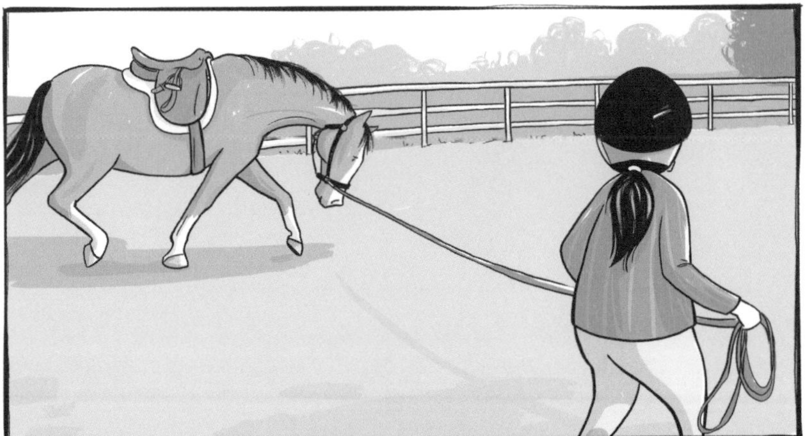

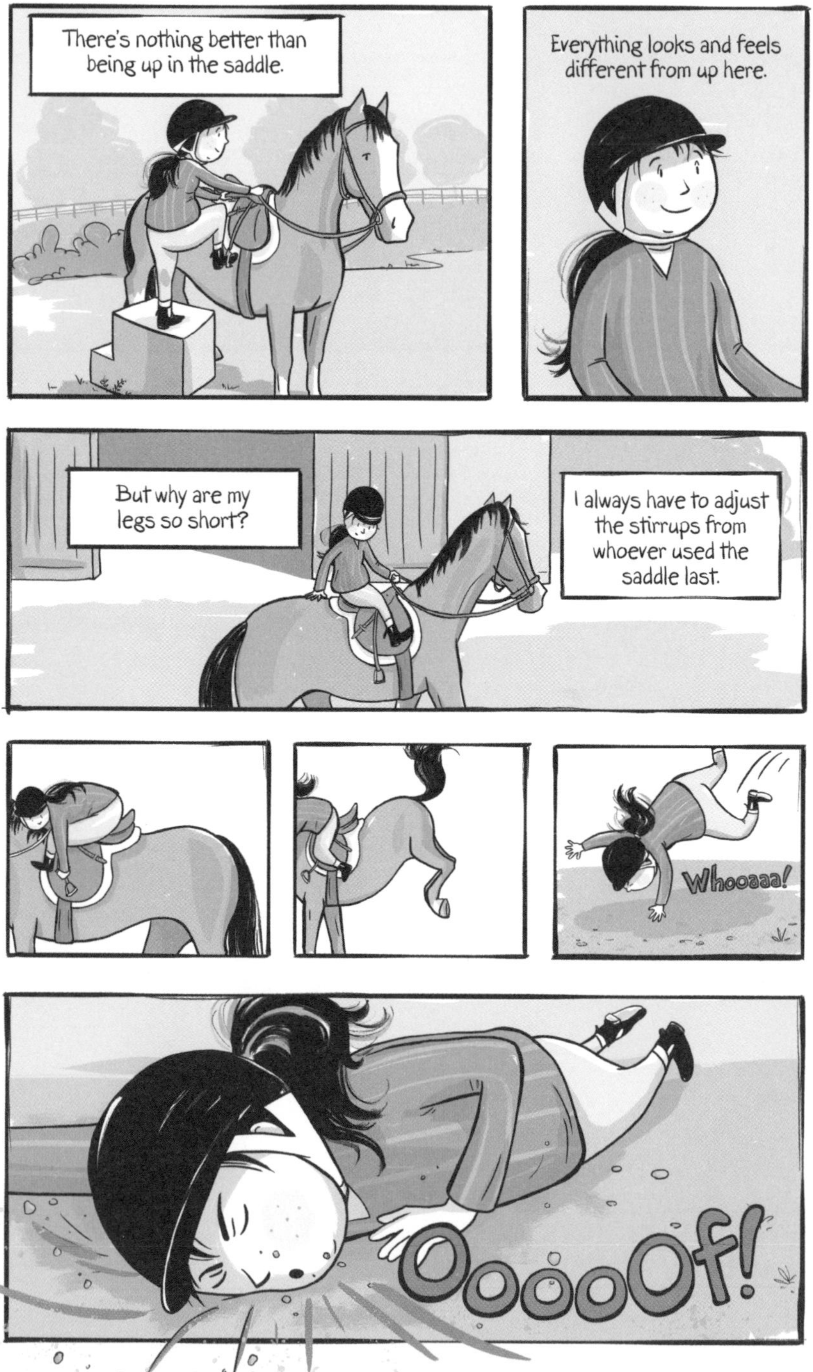
There's nothing better than being up in the saddle.
Everything looks and feels different from up here.
But why are my legs so short?
I always have to adjust the stirrups from whoever used the saddle last.
Whooaaa!
OooooF!

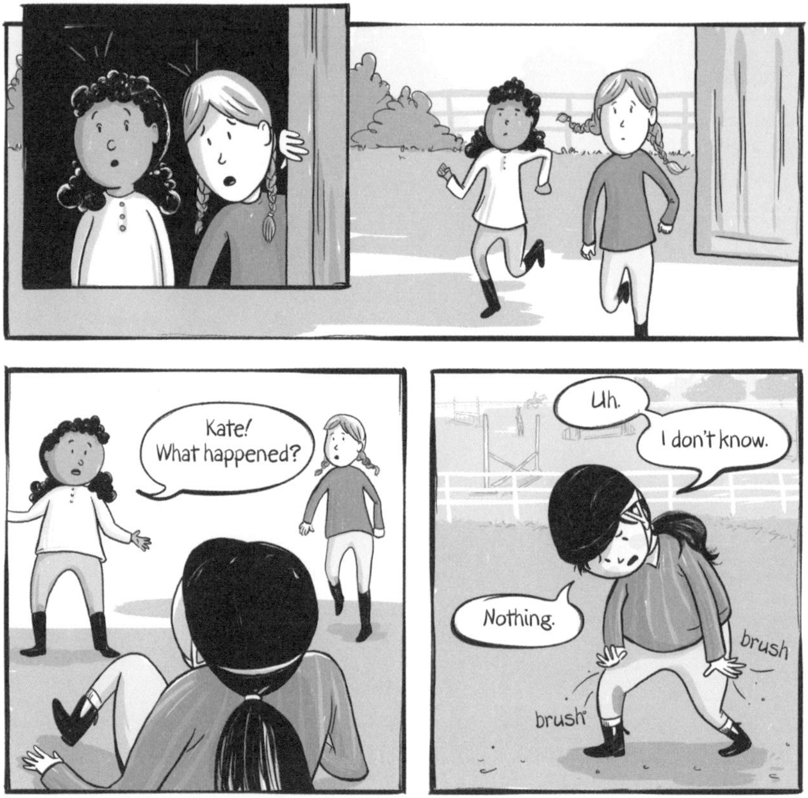
Kate!
What happened?
Uh.
I don't know.
Nothing.
brush
brush

Oh, great! I don't want Barb to think that I didn't lunge Motor first like she asked. If she thinks I can't follow directions—or worse, that I can't stay on my horse—how will she ever think I'm ready for the Black Hawk Classic?!

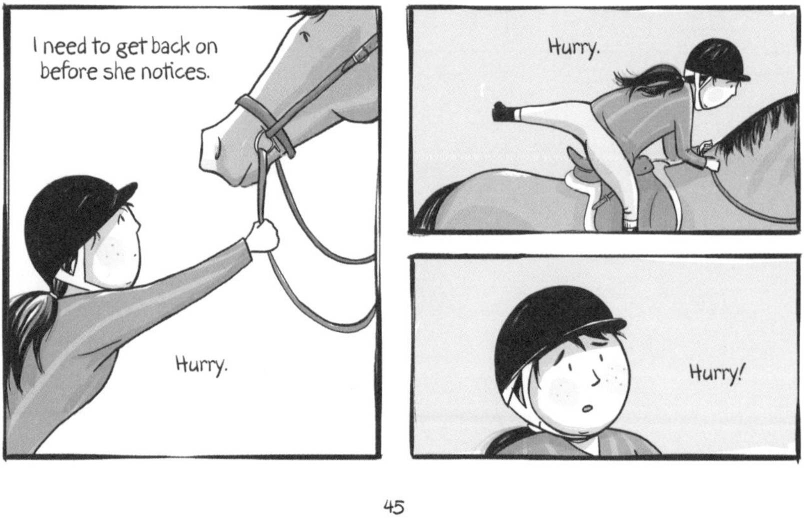
I need to get back on before she notices.
Hurry.
Hurry.
Hurry!

I don't think Barb saw me.

Phew!

My eyes are wet and my cheek is stinging.

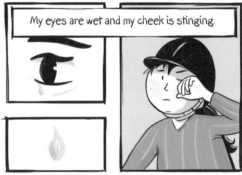

I didn't even have a chance to get all the pea gravel out that is still stuck up my nose.

BLOW!

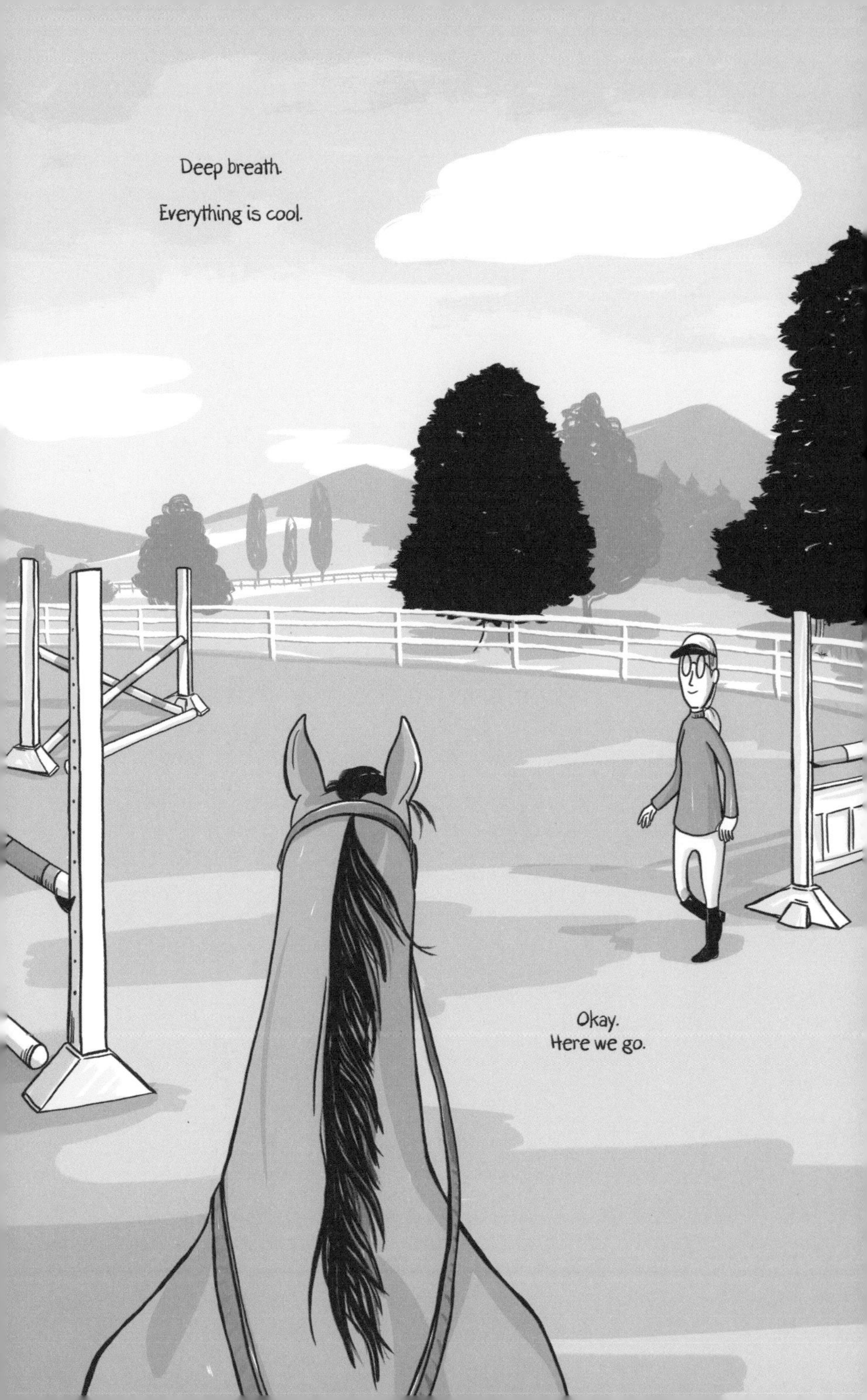
Deep breath.
Everything is cool.
Okay.
Here we go.

Chapter 3
Butt Clench

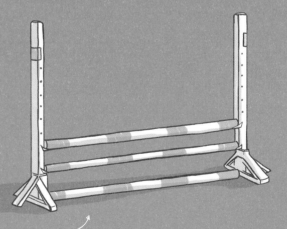

Vertical

A singular fence with poles or planks placed one directly above another.

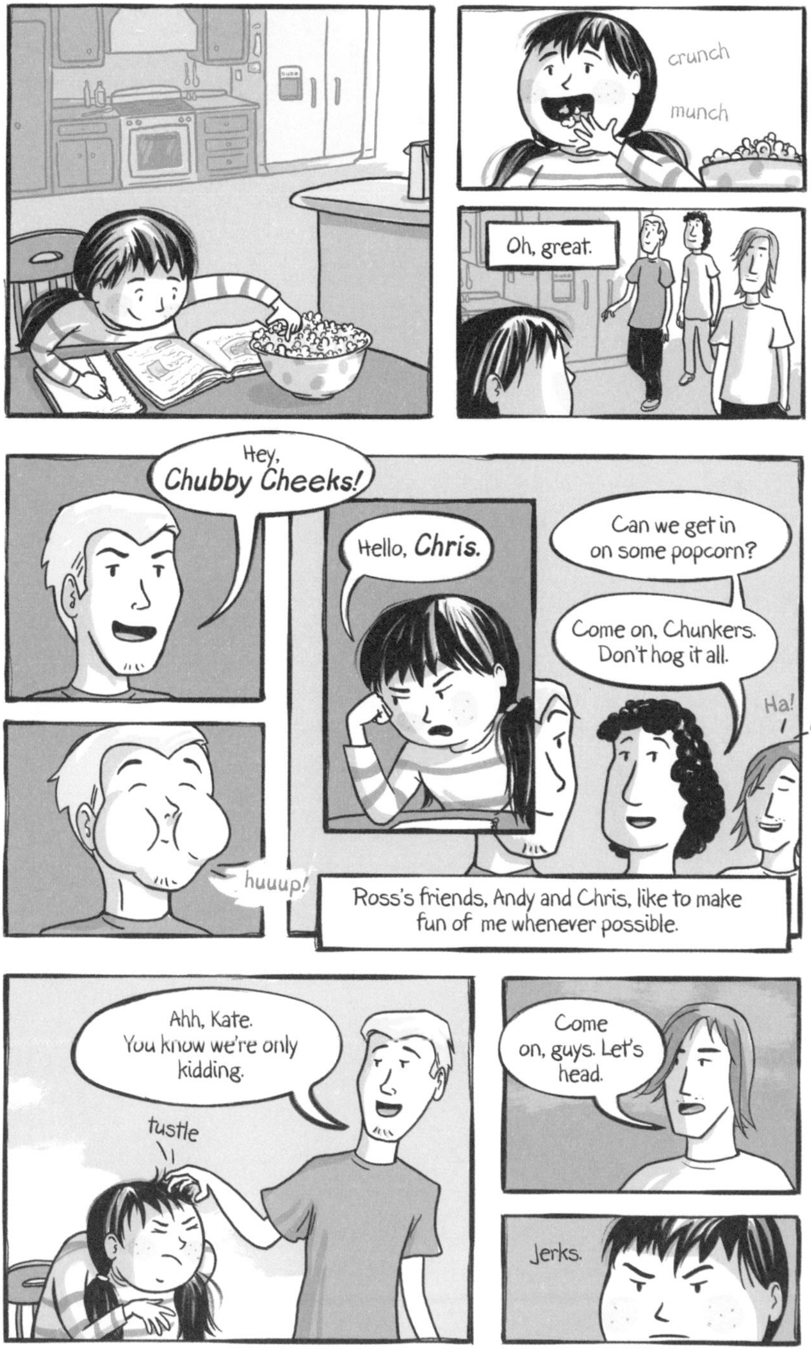
crunch
munch
Oh, great.
Hey, Chubby Cheeks!
huuup!
Hello, Chris.
Can we get in on some popcorn?
Come on, Chunkers. Don't hog it all.
Ha! Ha!
Ross's friends, Andy and Chris, like to make fun of me whenever possible.
Ahh, Kate. You know we're only kidding.
tustle
Come on, guys. Let's head.
Jerks.

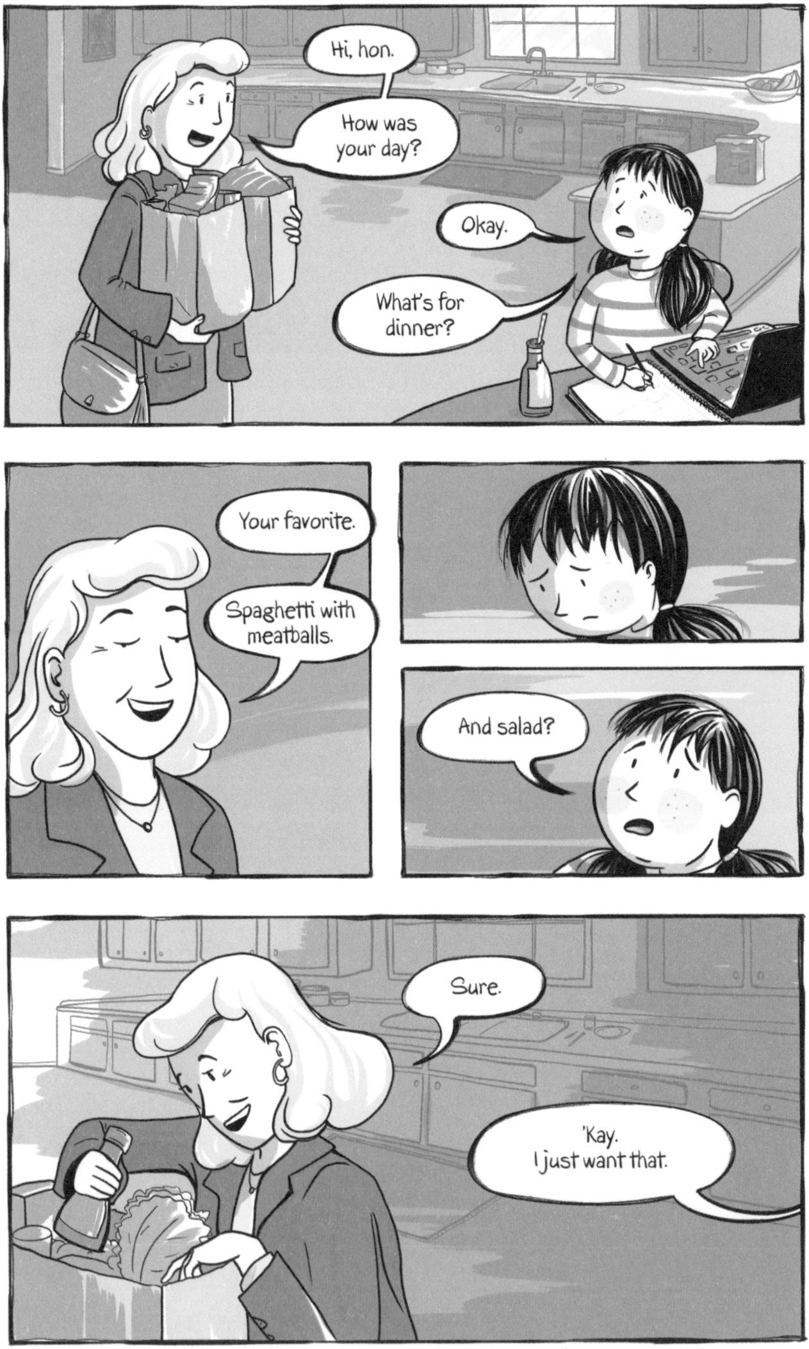
Hi, hon.
How was your day?
Okay.
What's for dinner?
Your favorite.
Spaghetti with meatballs.
And salad?
Sure.
'Kay. I just want that.

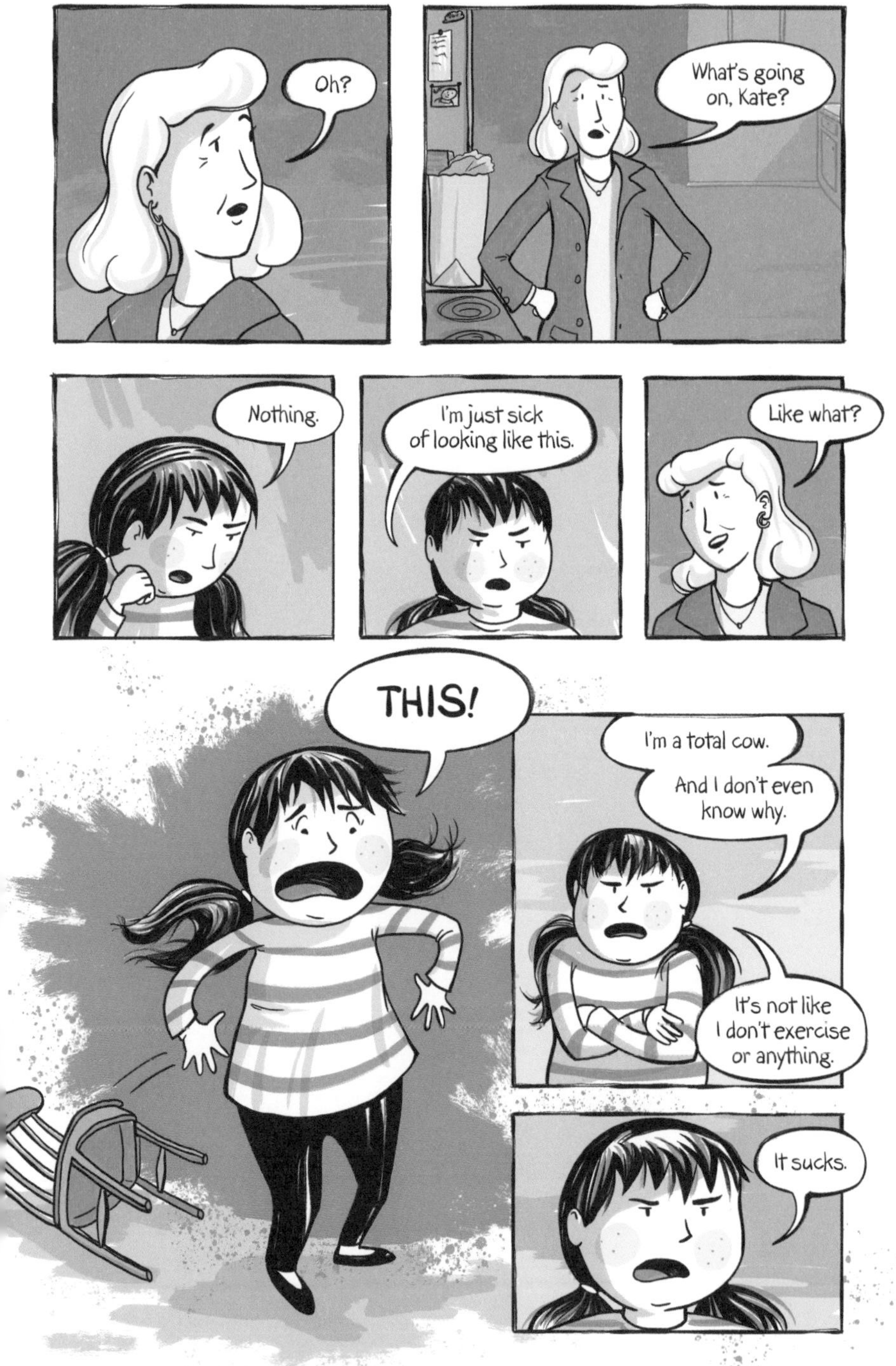
Oh?
What's going on, Kate?
Nothing.
I'm just sick of looking like this.
Like what?
THIS!
I'm a total cow.
And I don't even know why.
It's not like I don't exercise or anything.
It sucks.

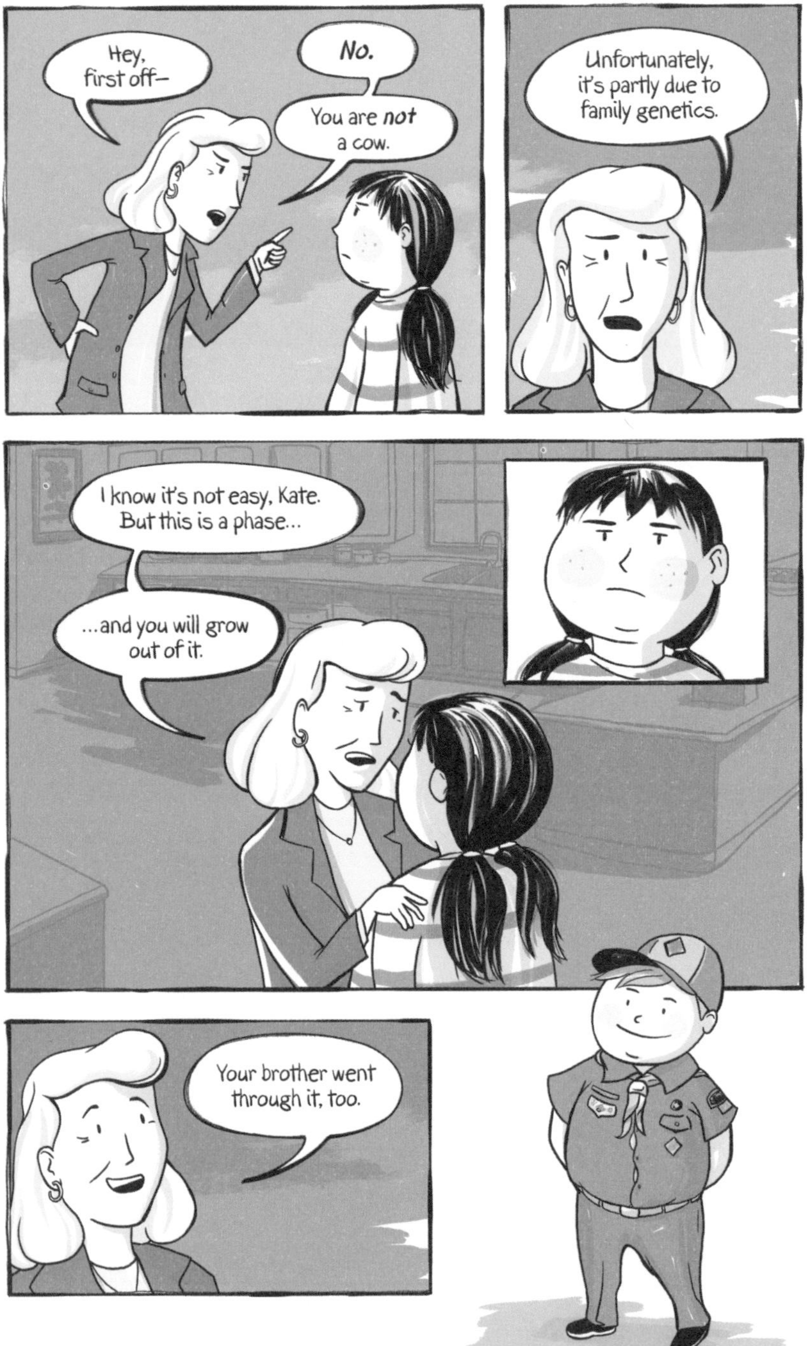

Hey, first off—
No.
You are *not* a cow.
Unfortunately, it's partly due to family genetics.
I know it's not easy, Kate. But this is a phase...
...and you will grow out of it.
Your brother went through it, too.

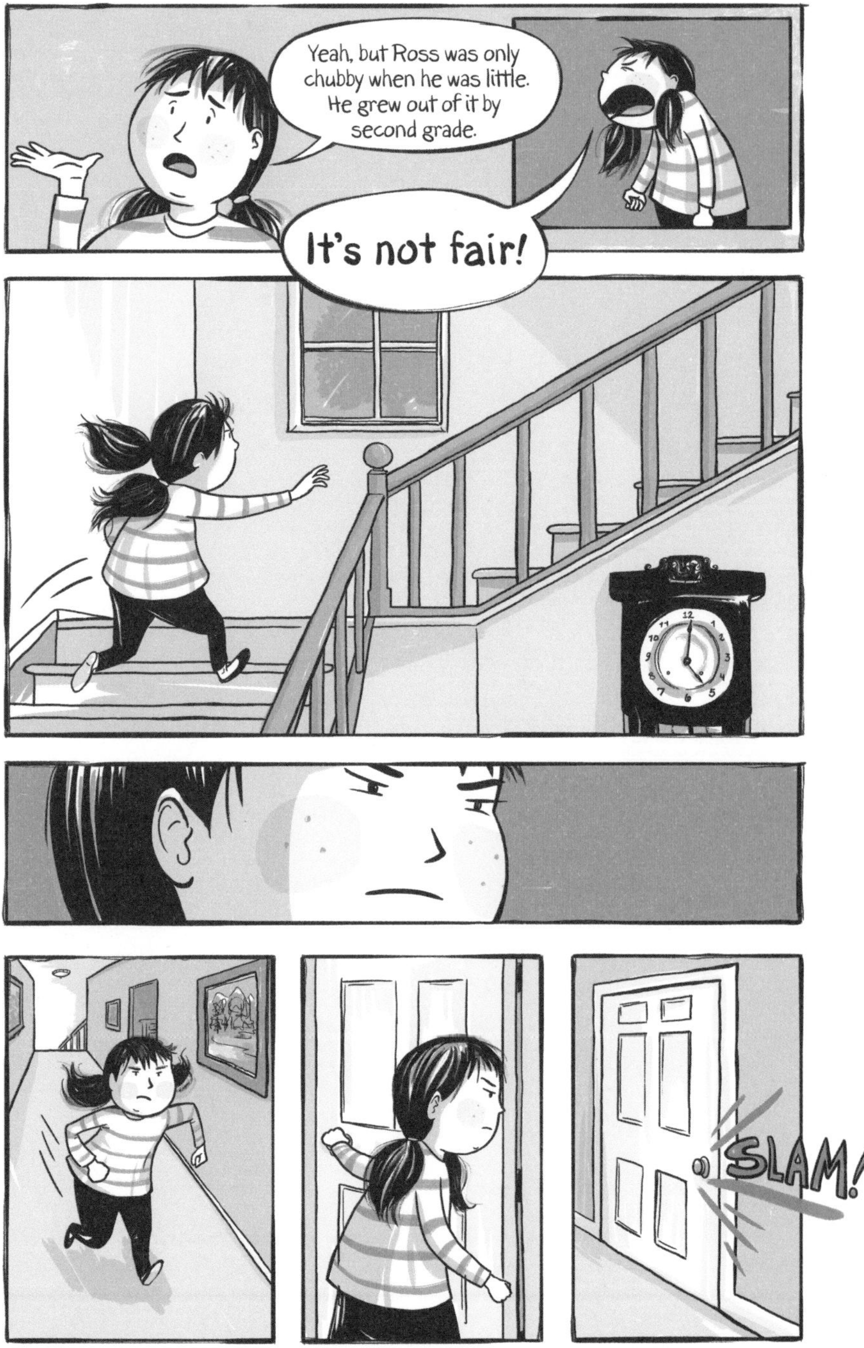
Yeah, but Ross was only chubby when he was little. He grew out of it by second grade.
It's not fair!
SLAM!

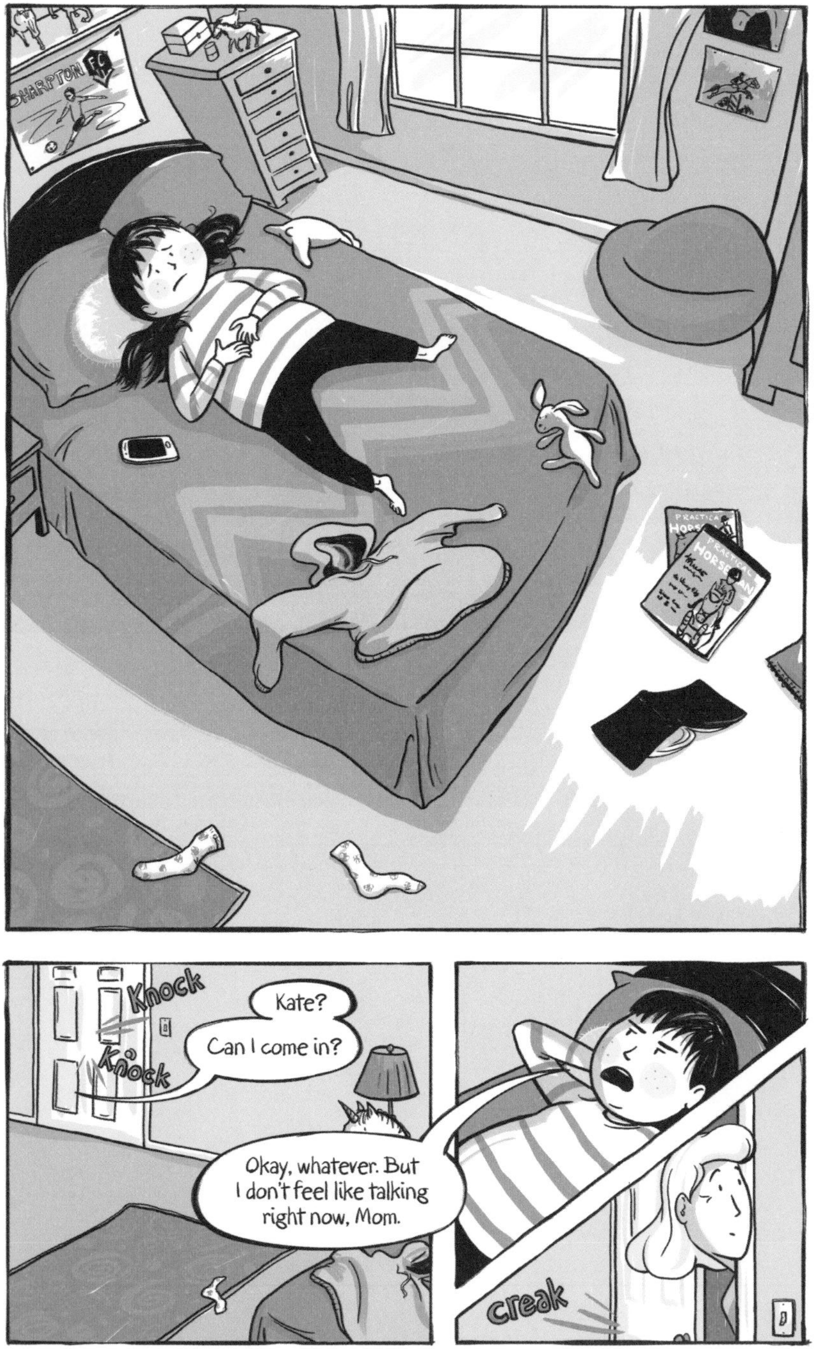
SHARPTON FC
Knock
Knock
Kate?
Can I come in?
Okay, whatever. But I don't feel like talking right now, Mom.
creak

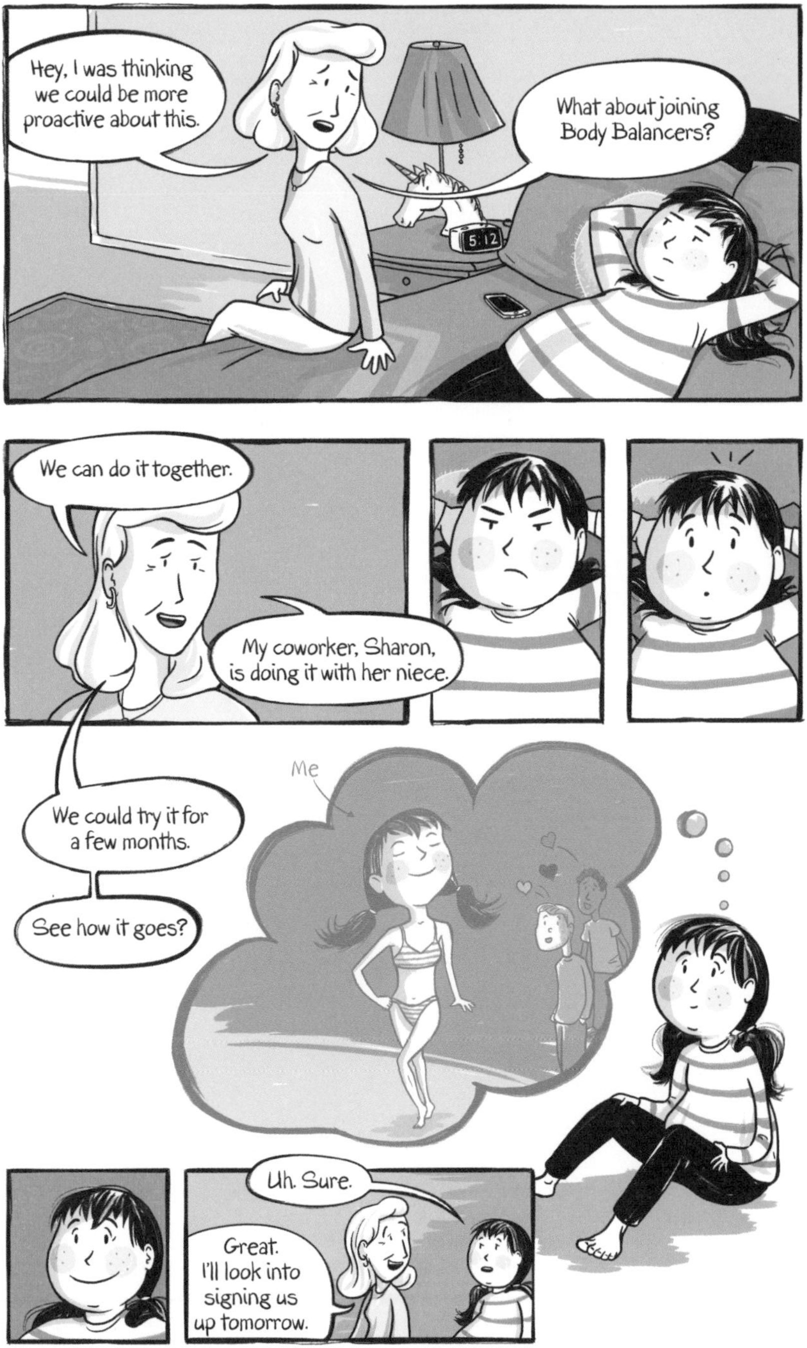
Hey, I was thinking we could be more proactive about this.
What about joining Body Balancers?
5:12
We can do it together.
My coworker, Sharon, is doing it with her niece.
We could try it for a few months.
See how it goes?
Me
Uh. Sure.
Great. I'll look into signing us up tomorrow.

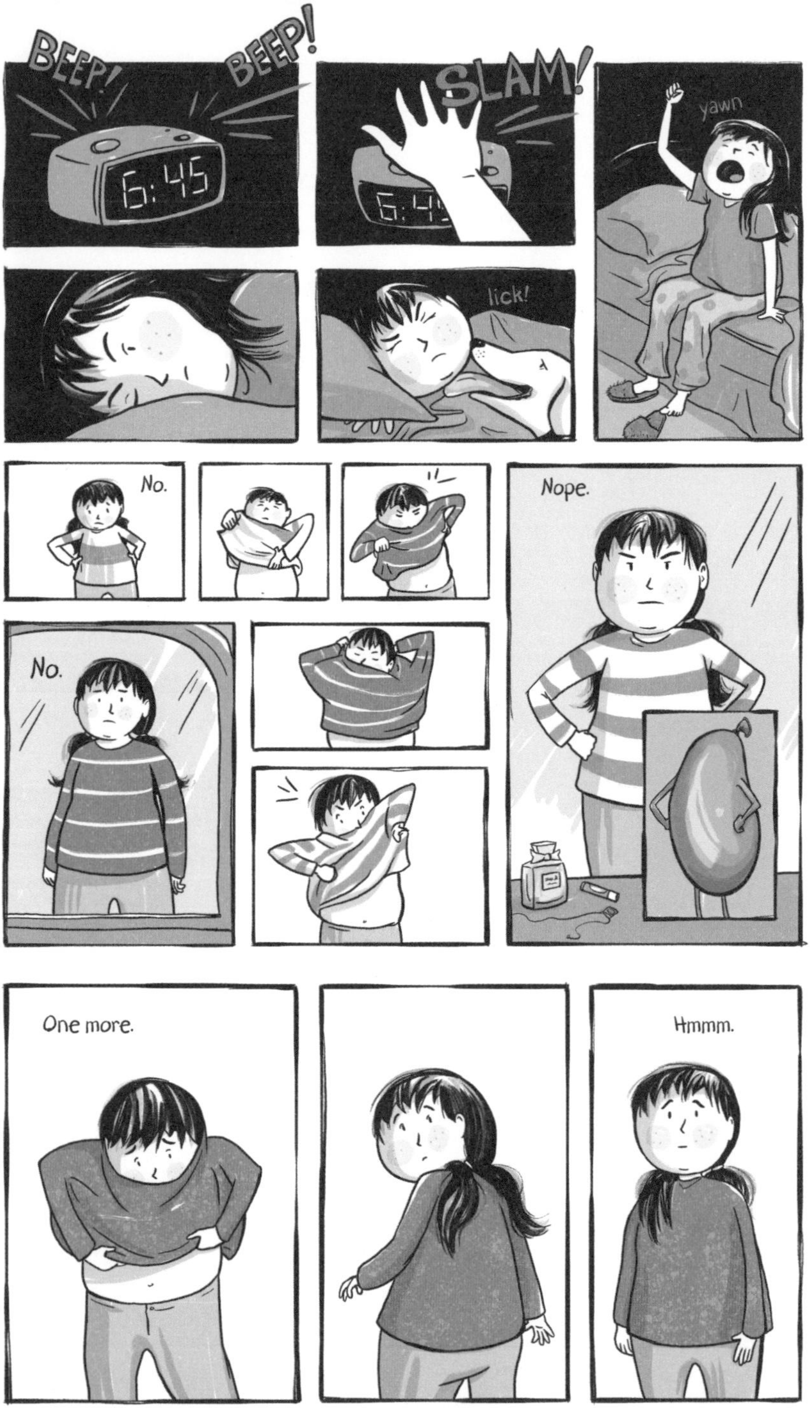
BEEP!
BEEP!
6:45
SLAM!
yawn
lick!
No.
Nope.
No.
One more.
Hmmm.

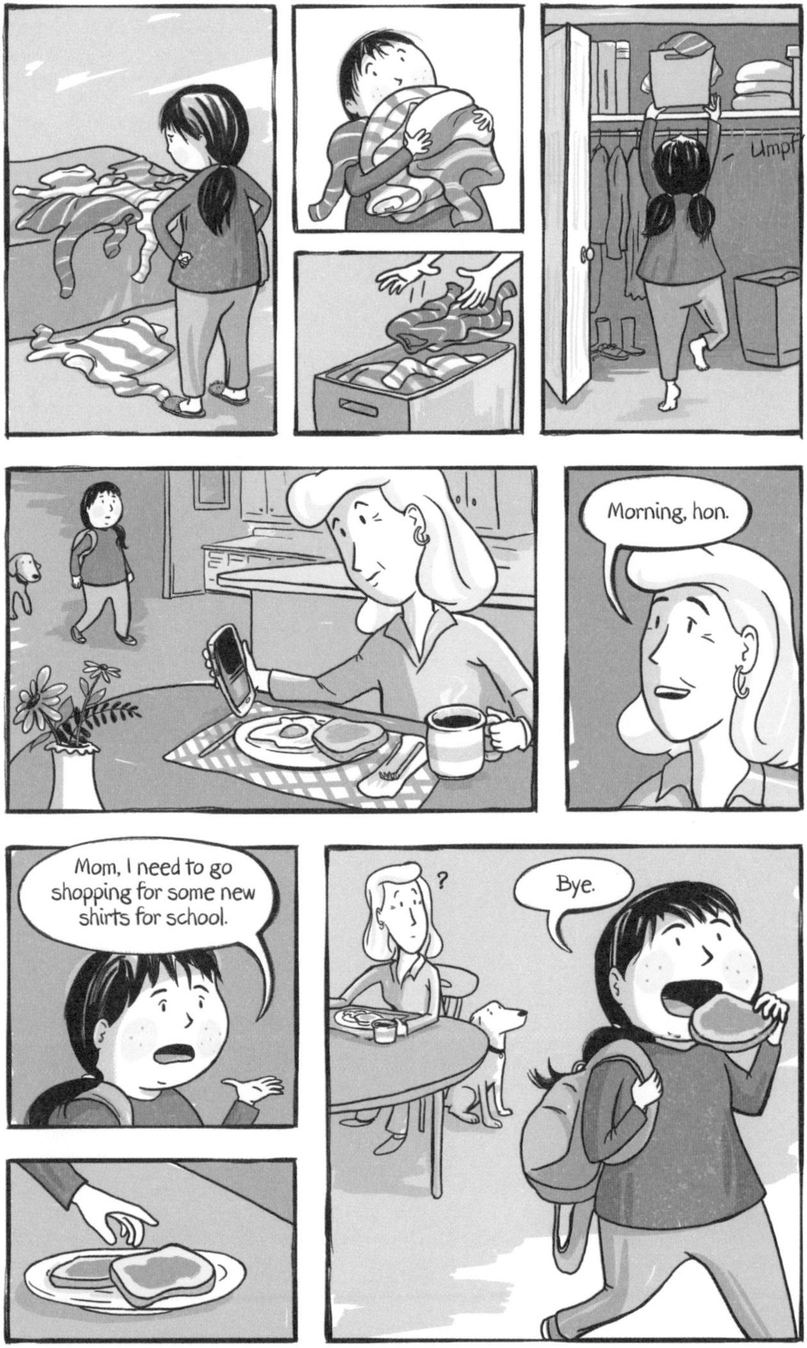
Umpf
Morning, hon.
Mom, I need to go shopping for some new shirts for school.
?
Bye.

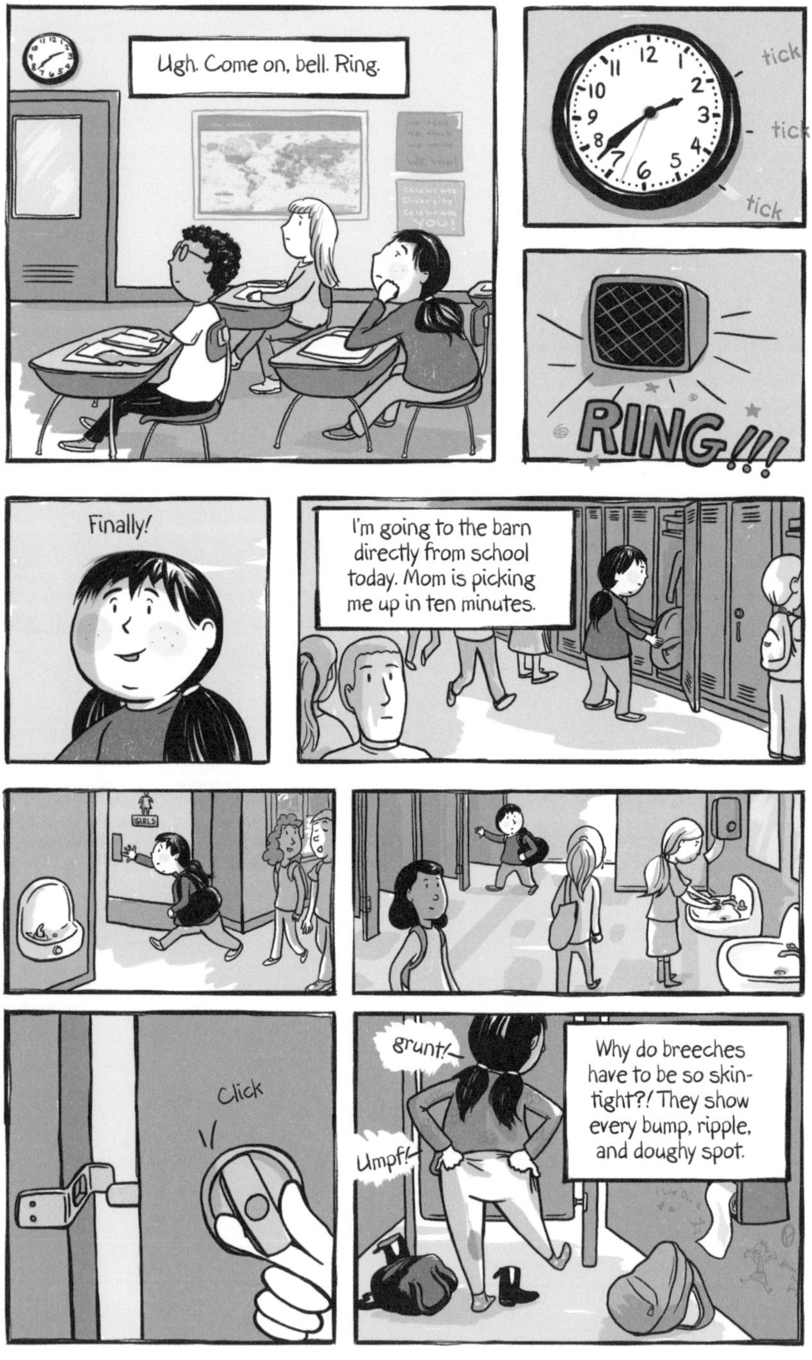
Ugh. Come on, bell. Ring.
tick
tick
tick
RING!!!
Finally!
I'm going to the barn directly from school today. Mom is picking me up in ten minutes.
GIRLS
Click
grunt!
Umpf!
Why do breeches have to be so skin-tight?! They show every bump, ripple, and doughy spot.

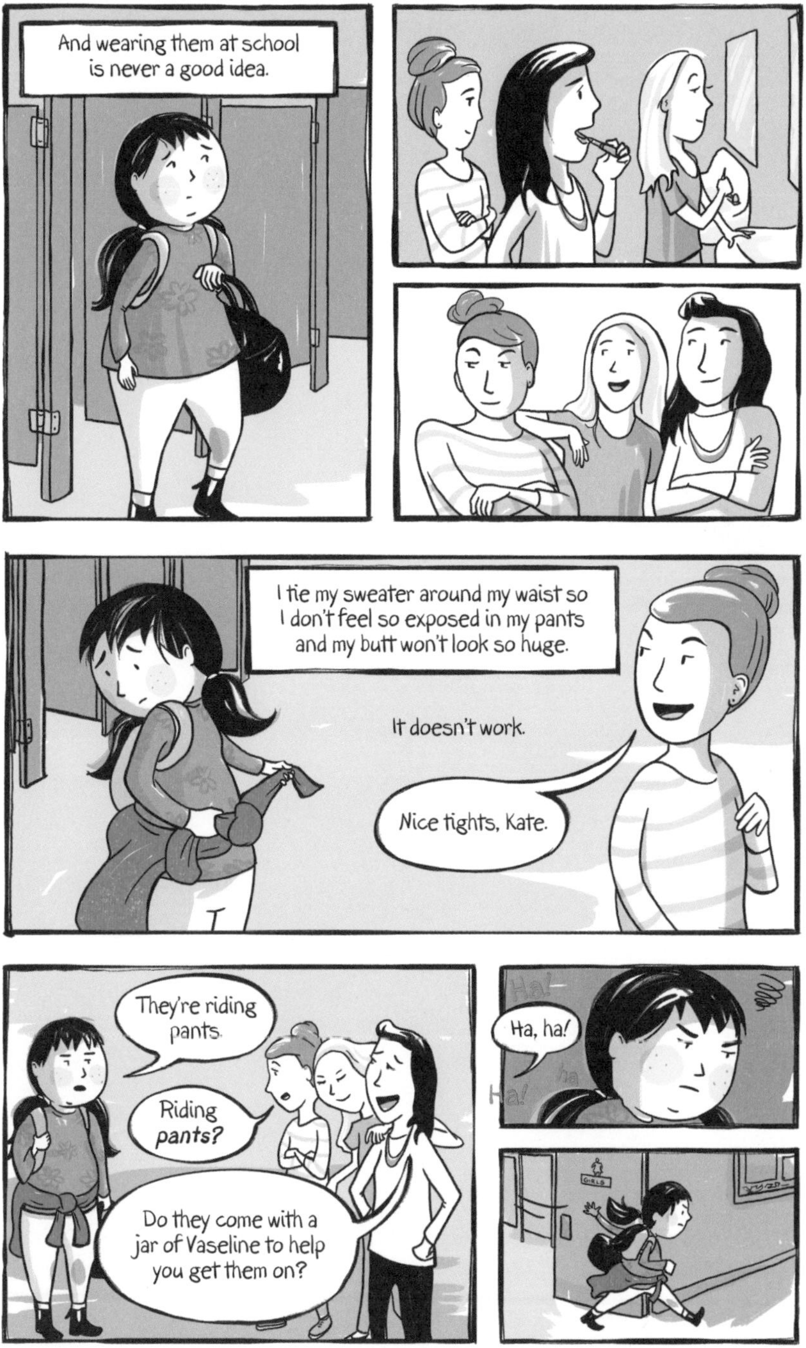
And wearing them at school is never a good idea.
I tie my sweater around my waist so I don't feel so exposed in my pants and my butt won't look so huge.
It doesn't work.
Nice tights, Kate.
They're riding pants.
Riding *pants?*
Do they come with a jar of Vaseline to help you get them on?
Ha!
Ha, ha!
ha
Ha!
GIRLS

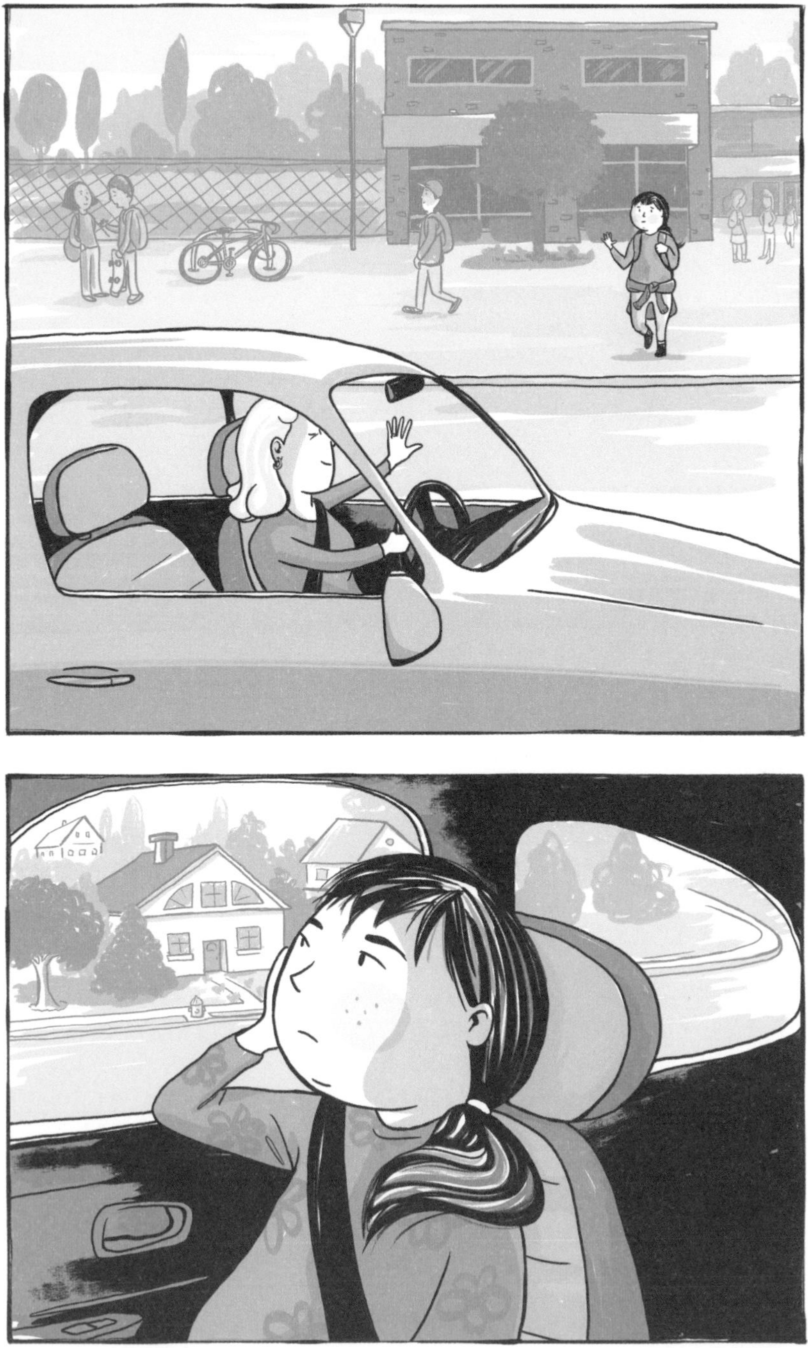

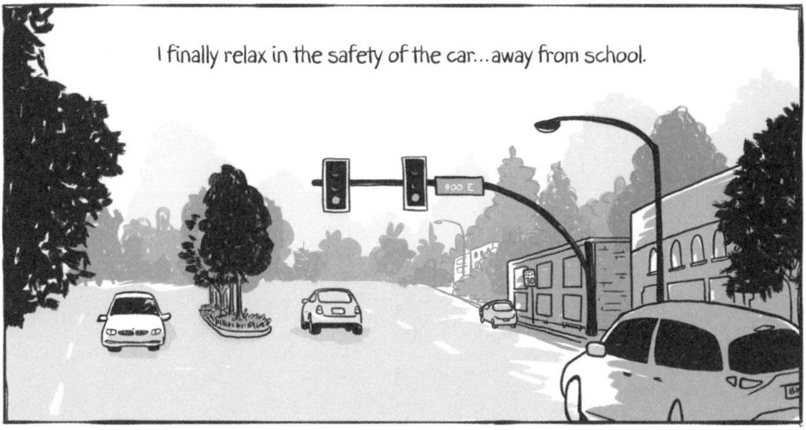
I finally relax in the safety of the car... away from school.
900 E
30

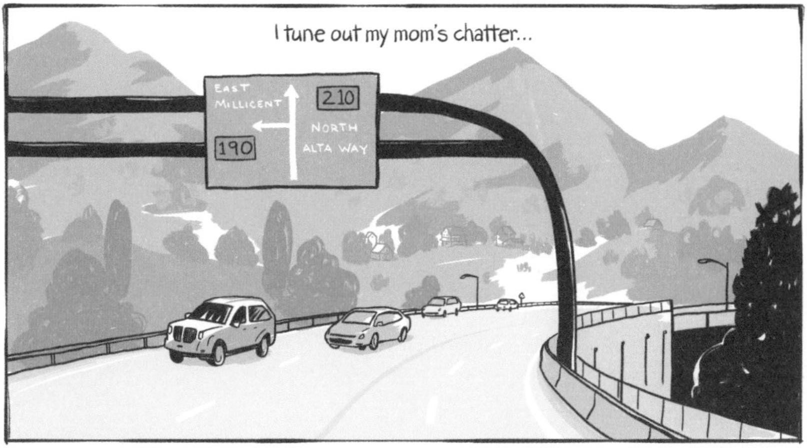
I tune out my mom's chatter...
EAST MILLICENT
210
NORTH ALTA WAY
190

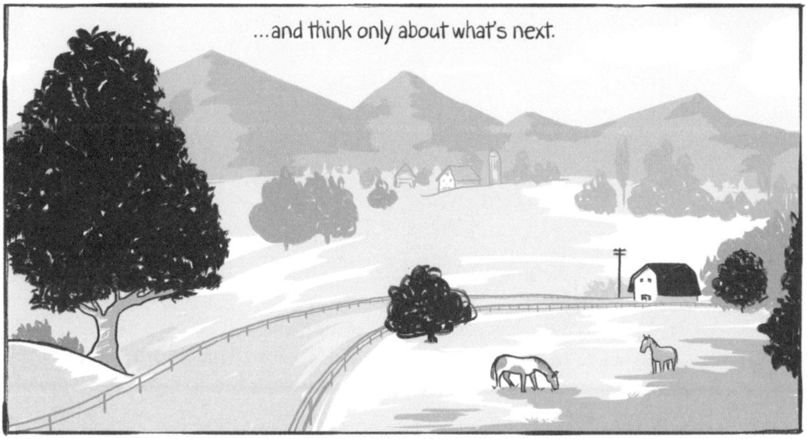
...and think only about what's next.

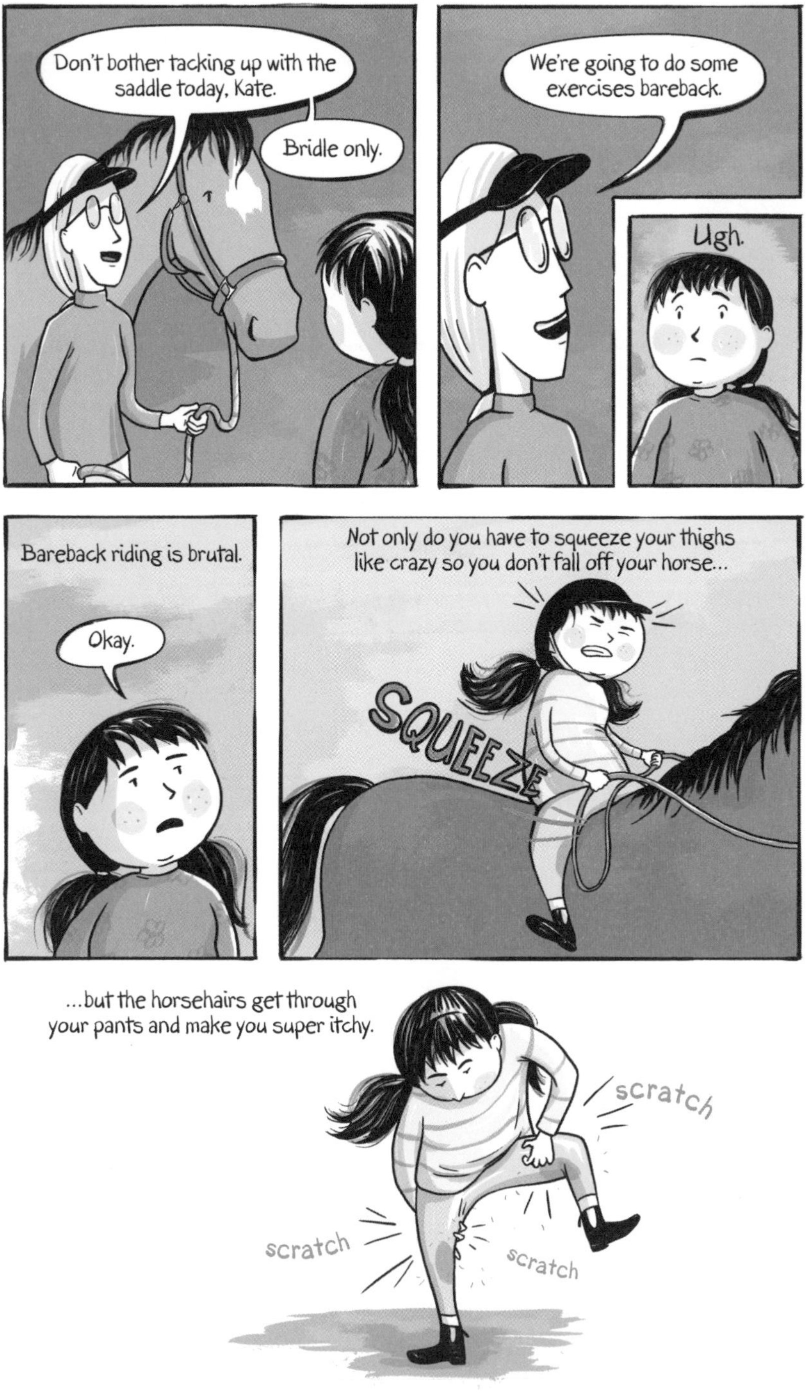

Don't bother tacking up with the saddle today, Kate.
Bridle only.
We're going to do some exercises bareback.
Ugh.
Bareback riding is brutal.
Okay.
Not only do you have to squeeze your thighs like crazy so you don't fall off your horse...
SQUEEZE
...but the horsehairs get through your pants and make you super itchy.
scratch
scratch
scratch

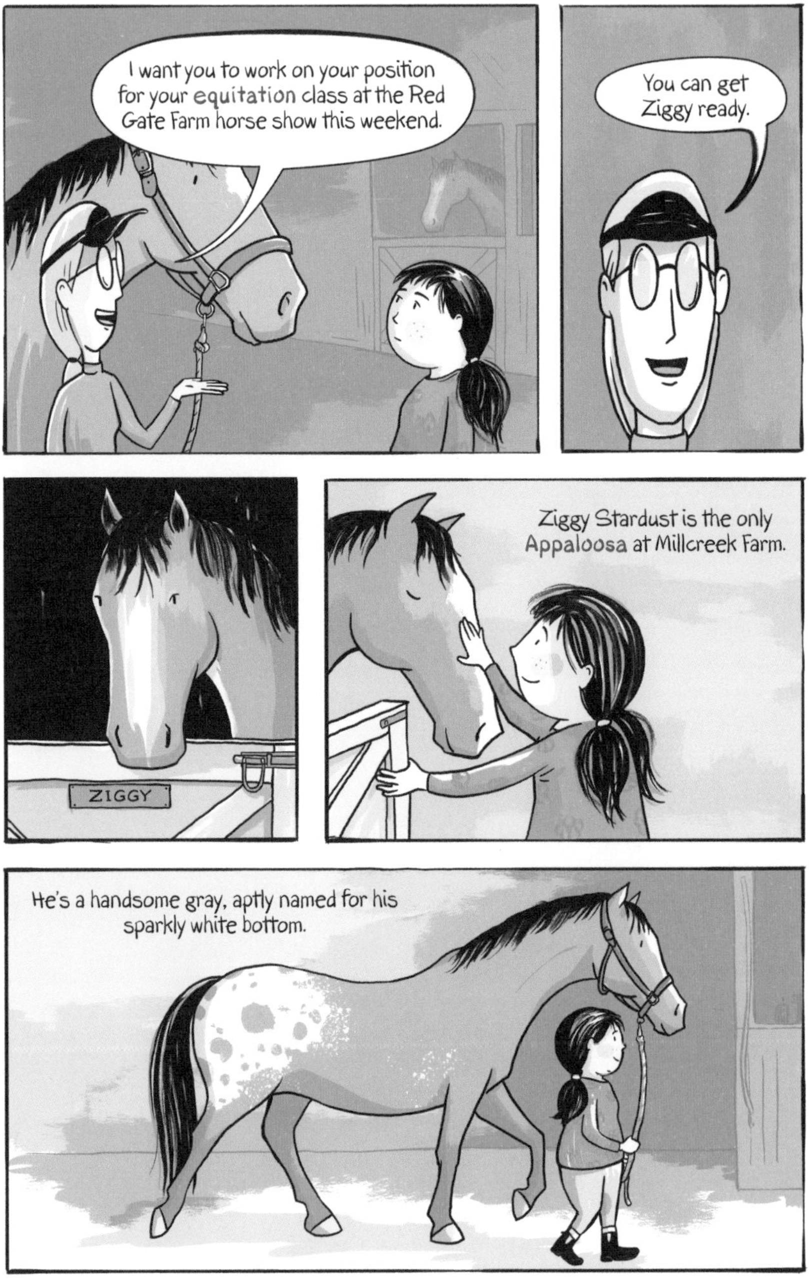
I want you to work on your position for your equitation class at the Red Gate Farm horse show this weekend.
You can get Ziggy ready.
ZIGGY
Ziggy Stardust is the only Appaloosa at Millcreek Farm.
He's a handsome gray, aptly named for his sparkly white bottom.

Equitation: One of the three main divisions at a horse show (hunter, jumper, and equitation). Equitation is judged solely on the rider's ability and their positioning on the horse.

Appaloosa: A breed of horse best known for their colorful, spotted coat patterns.

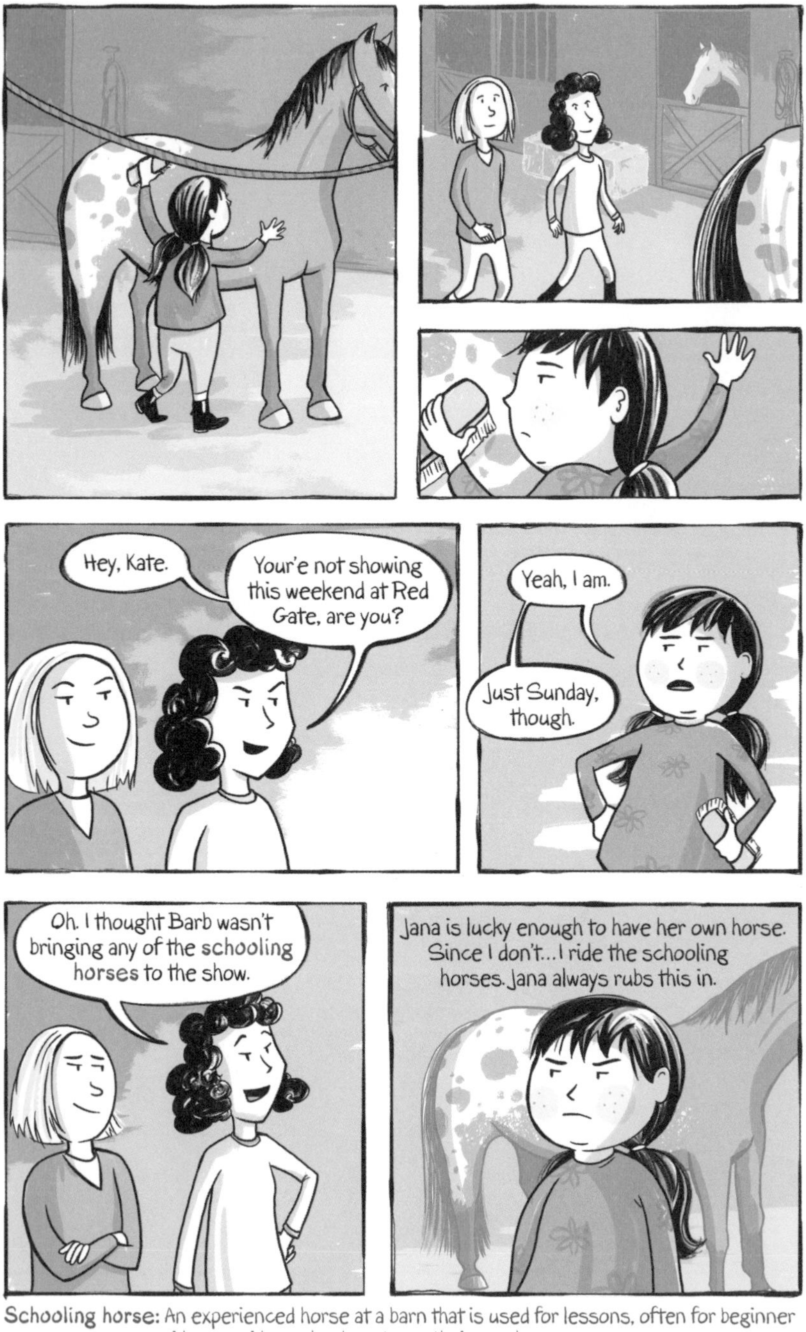
Hey, Kate.
Your'e not showing this weekend at Red Gate, are you?
Yeah, I am.
Just Sunday, though.
Oh. I thought Barb wasn't bringing any of the schooling horses to the show.
Jana is lucky enough to have her own horse. Since I don't...I ride the schooling horses. Jana always rubs this in.

Schooling horse: An experienced horse at a barn that is used for lessons, often for beginner riders or riders who do not own their own horse.

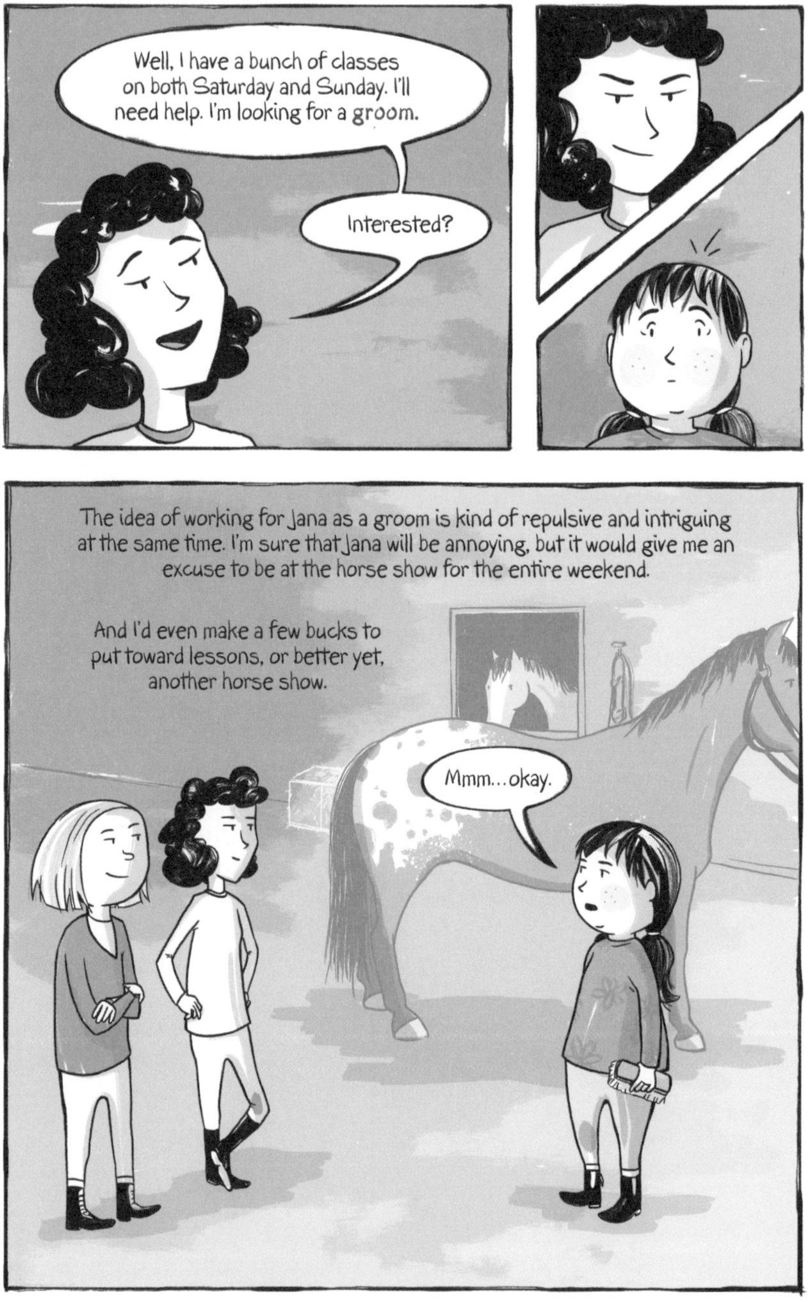
Well, I have a bunch of classes on both Saturday and Sunday. I'll need help. I'm looking for a groom.
Interested?
The idea of working for Jana as a groom is kind of repulsive and intriguing at the same time. I'm sure that Jana will be annoying, but it would give me an excuse to be at the horse show for the entire weekend.
And I'd even make a few bucks to put toward lessons, or better yet, another horse show.
Mmm...okay.

Groom: Someone hired to help clean, braid, and ready a horse for a horse show as well as perform any other jobs that the rider requires.

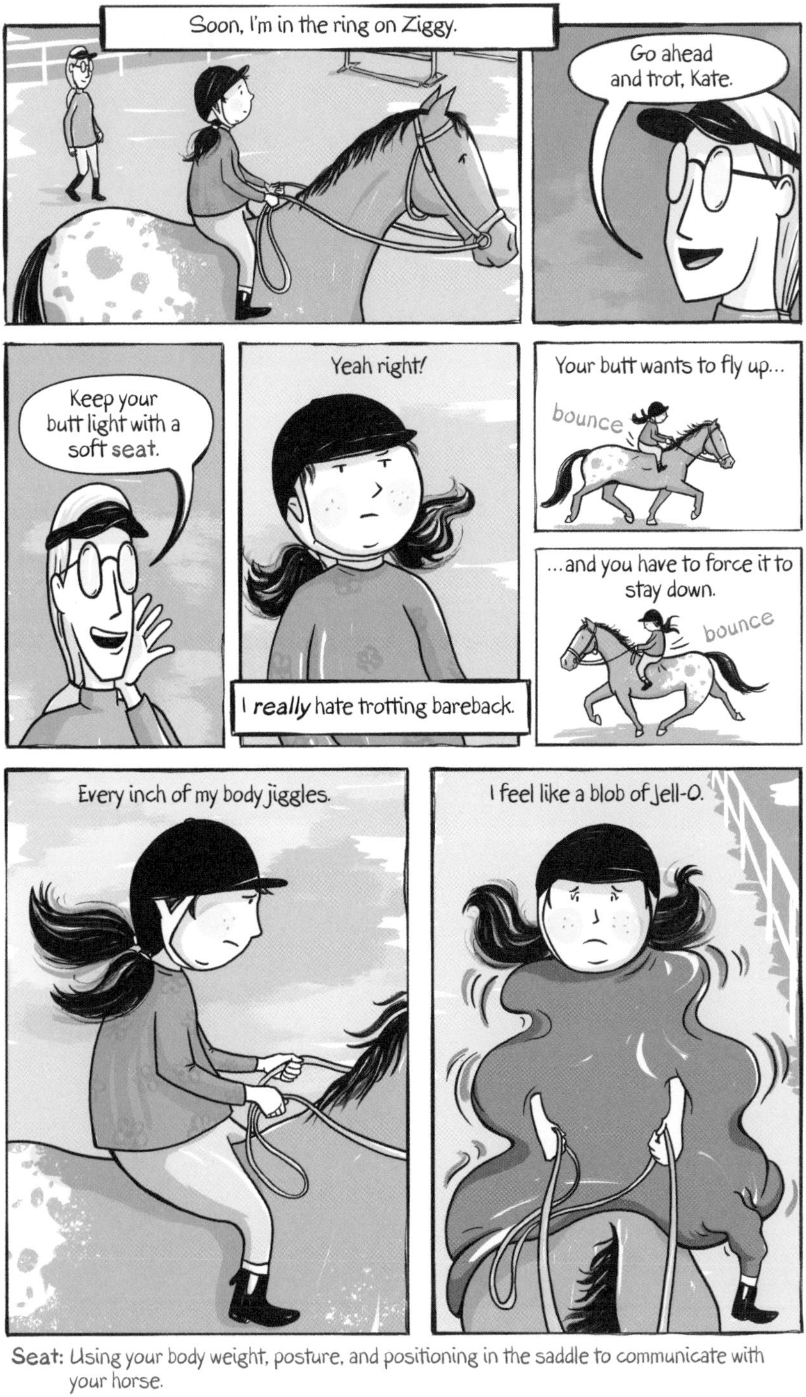
Soon, I'm in the ring on Ziggy.
Go ahead and trot, Kate.
Keep your butt light with a soft seat.
Yeah right!
I *really* hate trotting bareback.
Your butt wants to fly up...
bounce
...and you have to force it to stay down.
bounce
Every inch of my body jiggles.
I feel like a blob of Jell-O.

Seat: Using your body weight, posture, and positioning in the saddle to communicate with your horse.

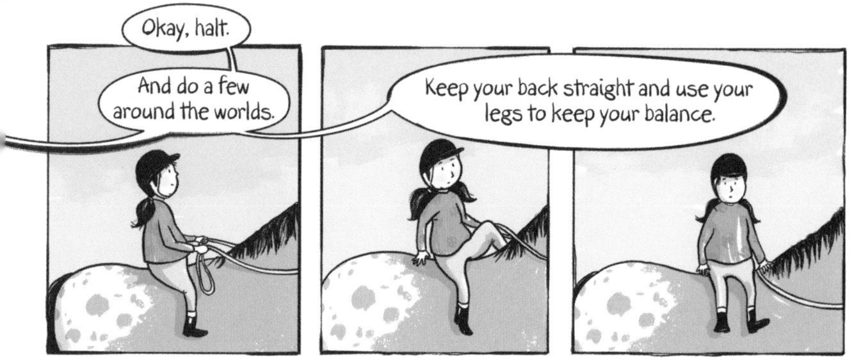
Okay, halt.
And do a few around the worlds.
Keep your back straight and use your legs to keep your balance.

Ziggy patiently stands in the middle of the arena while I do 360-degree rotations on his back.

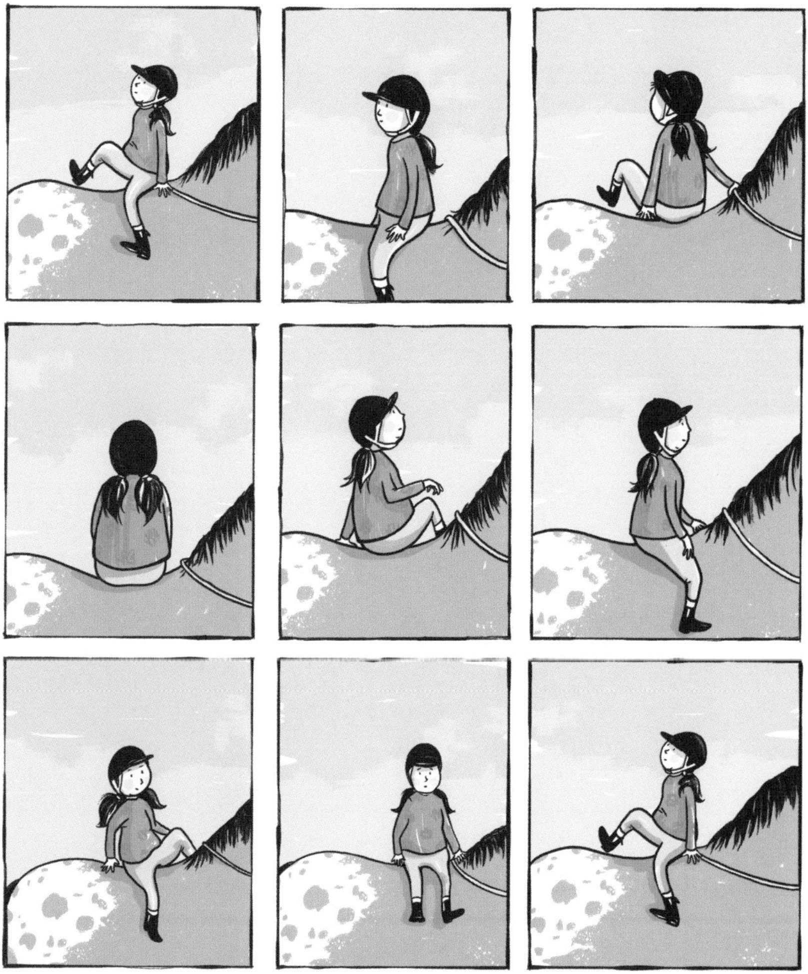

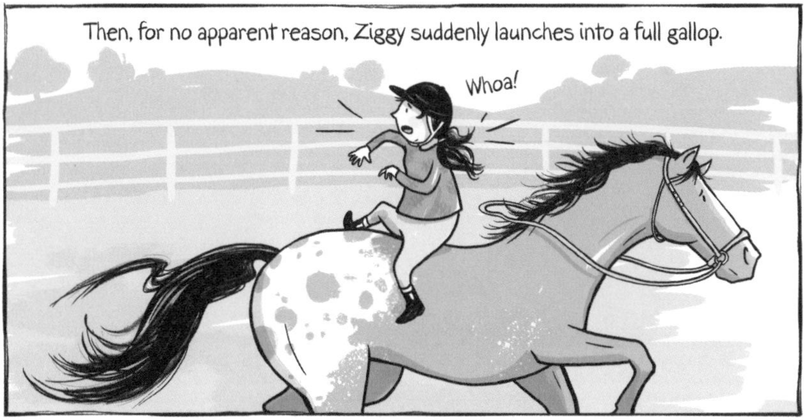
Then, for no apparent reason, Ziggy suddenly launches into a full gallop.
Whoa!

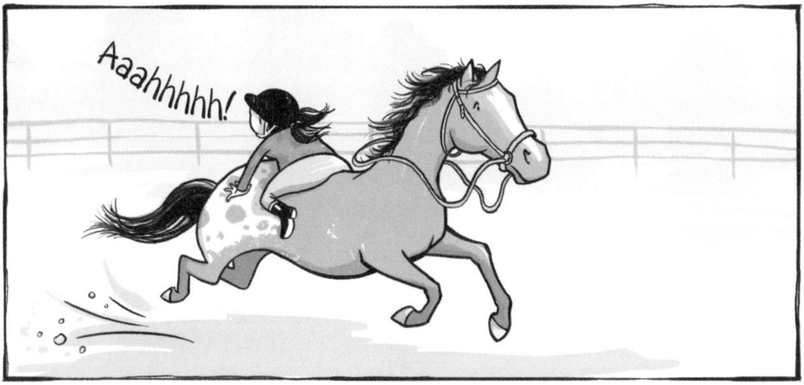
Aaahhhhh!

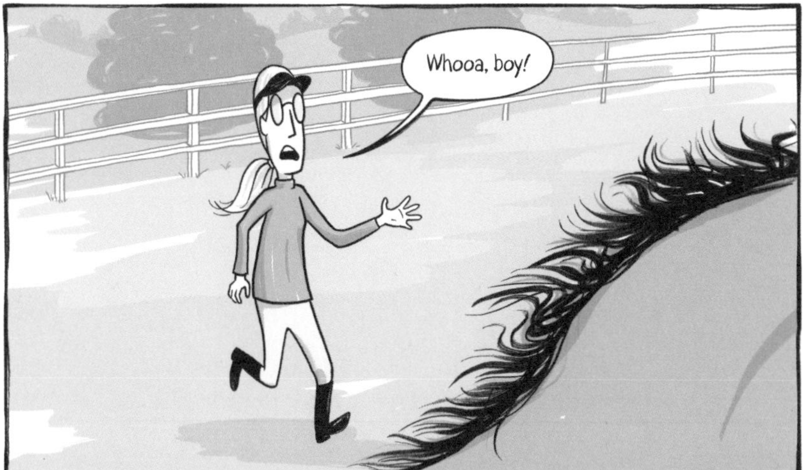
Whooa, boy!

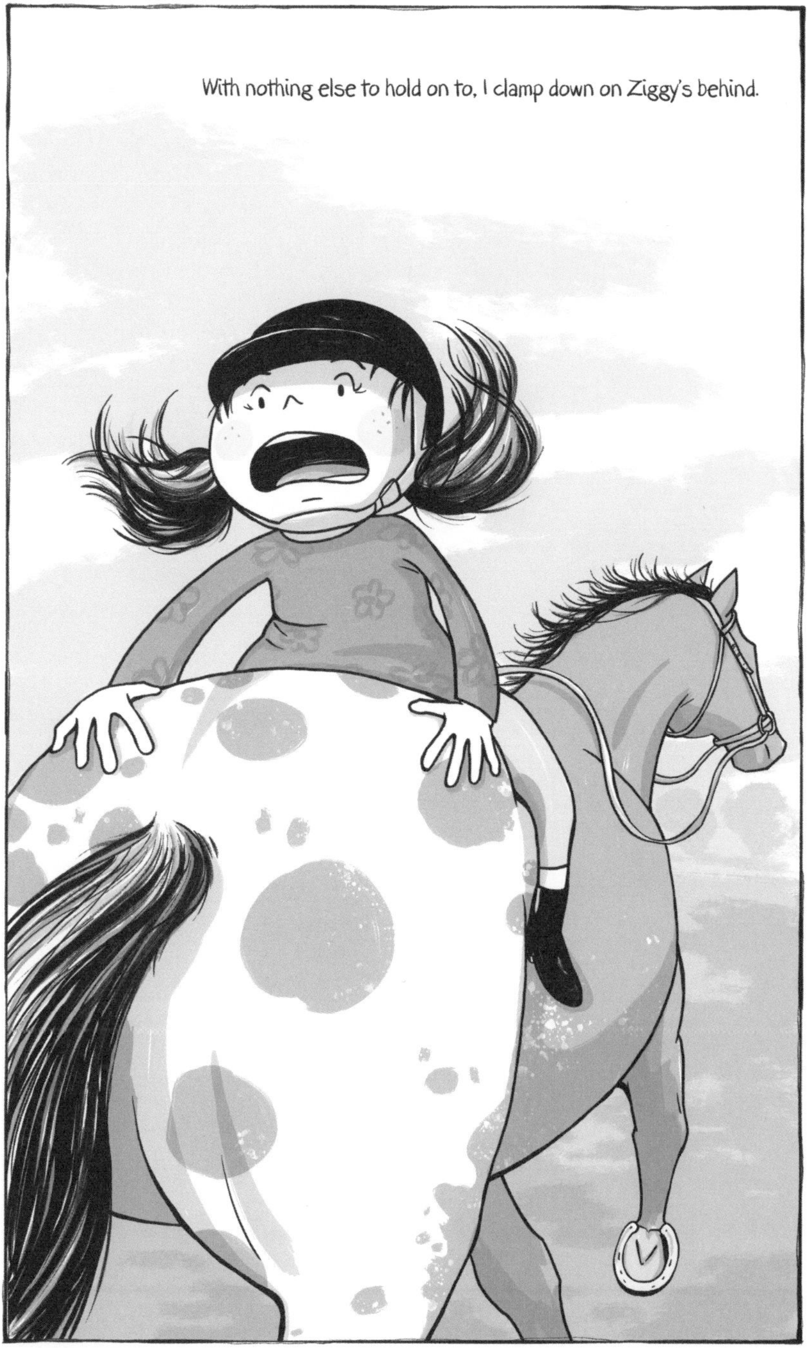
With nothing else to hold on to, I clamp down on Ziggy's behind.

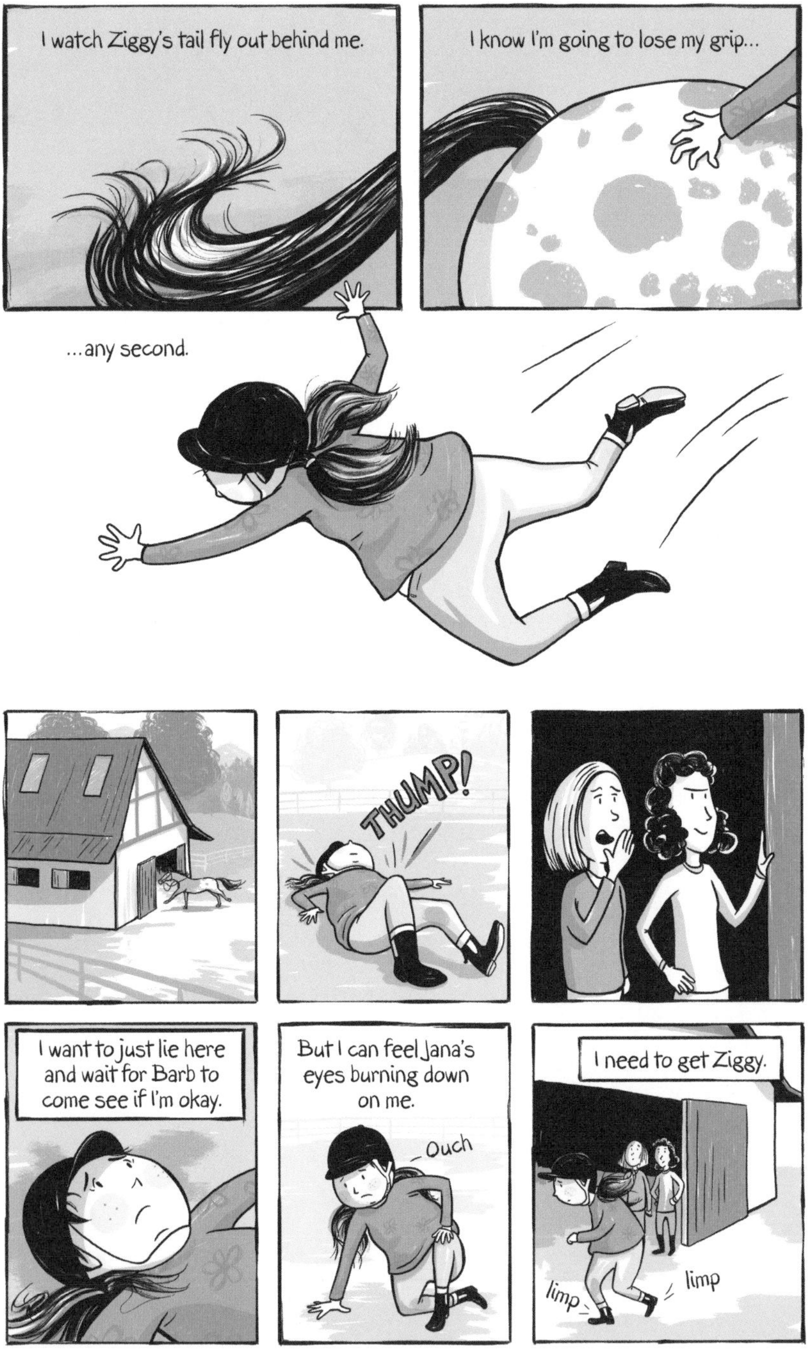
I watch Ziggy's tail fly out behind me.
I know I'm going to lose my grip...
...any second.
THUMP!
I want to just lie here and wait for Barb to come see if I'm okay.
But I can feel Jana's eyes burning down on me.
Ouch
I need to get Ziggy.
limp
limp

Well, I don't know what got into Ziggy.

But, we'll go easy on you today, Kate, and put your saddle back on.

She seriously wants me to get back on?

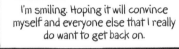
I'm smiling. Hoping it will convince myself and everyone else that I really do want to get back on.

I clench my teeth, trying to ignore the pain in my left butt cheek.

All good, Kate?

Yep.

No.

71

Chapter 4
Shadow Spook

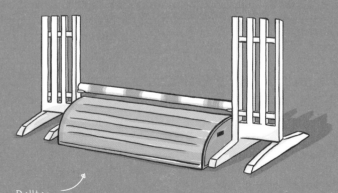

Rolltop

A jump with a rounded, half-barrel appearance.

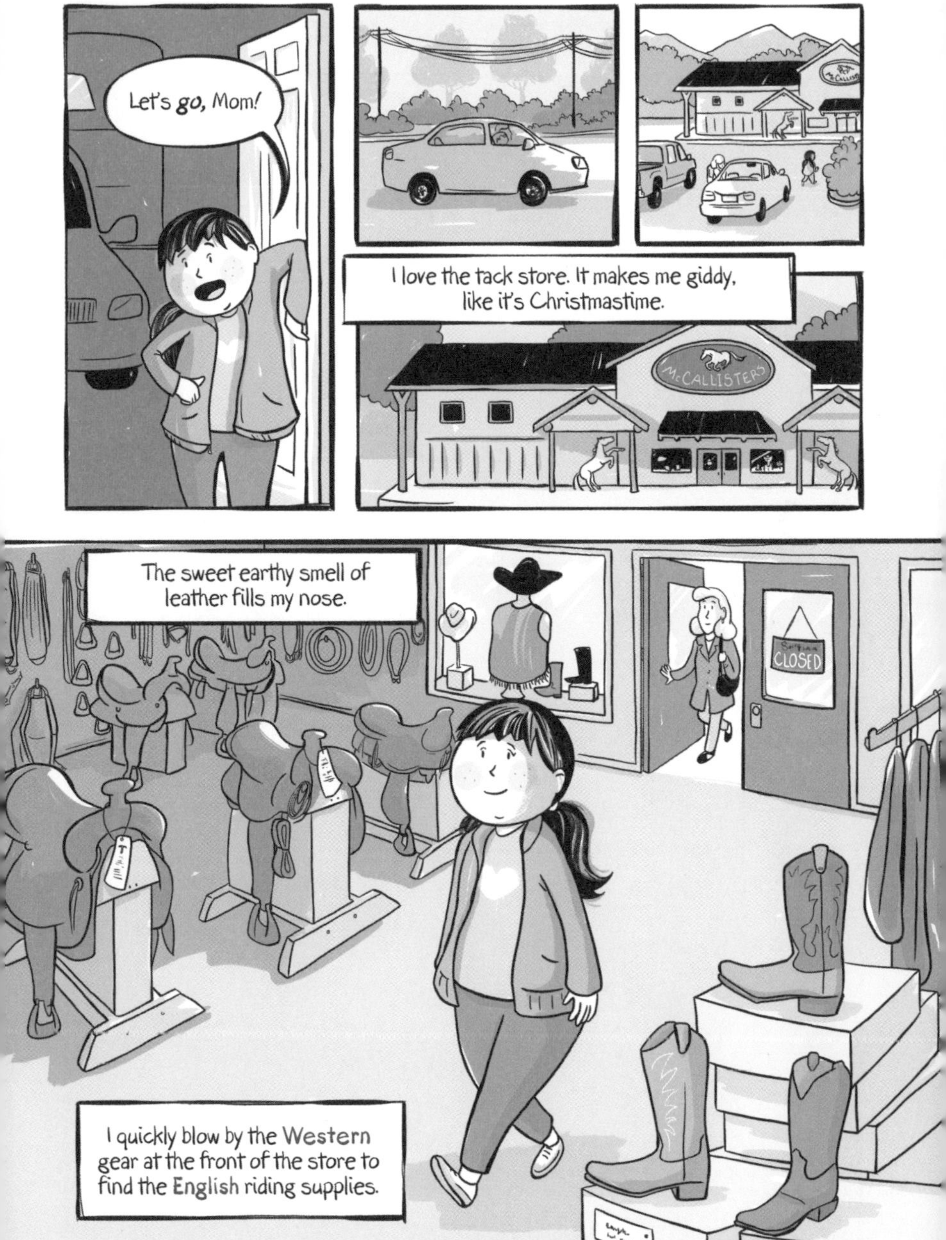
Let's go, Mom!
I love the tack store. It makes me giddy, like it's Christmastime.
McCALLISTERS
The sweet earthy smell of leather fills my nose.
CLOSED
I quickly blow by the Western gear at the front of the store to find the English riding supplies.

Western vs. English: Two different types of riding styles, with differing equipment and attire. Western developed from the needs of cowboys who worked cattle from horseback. English riding takes many of its traditions and equipment from European mounted military styles.

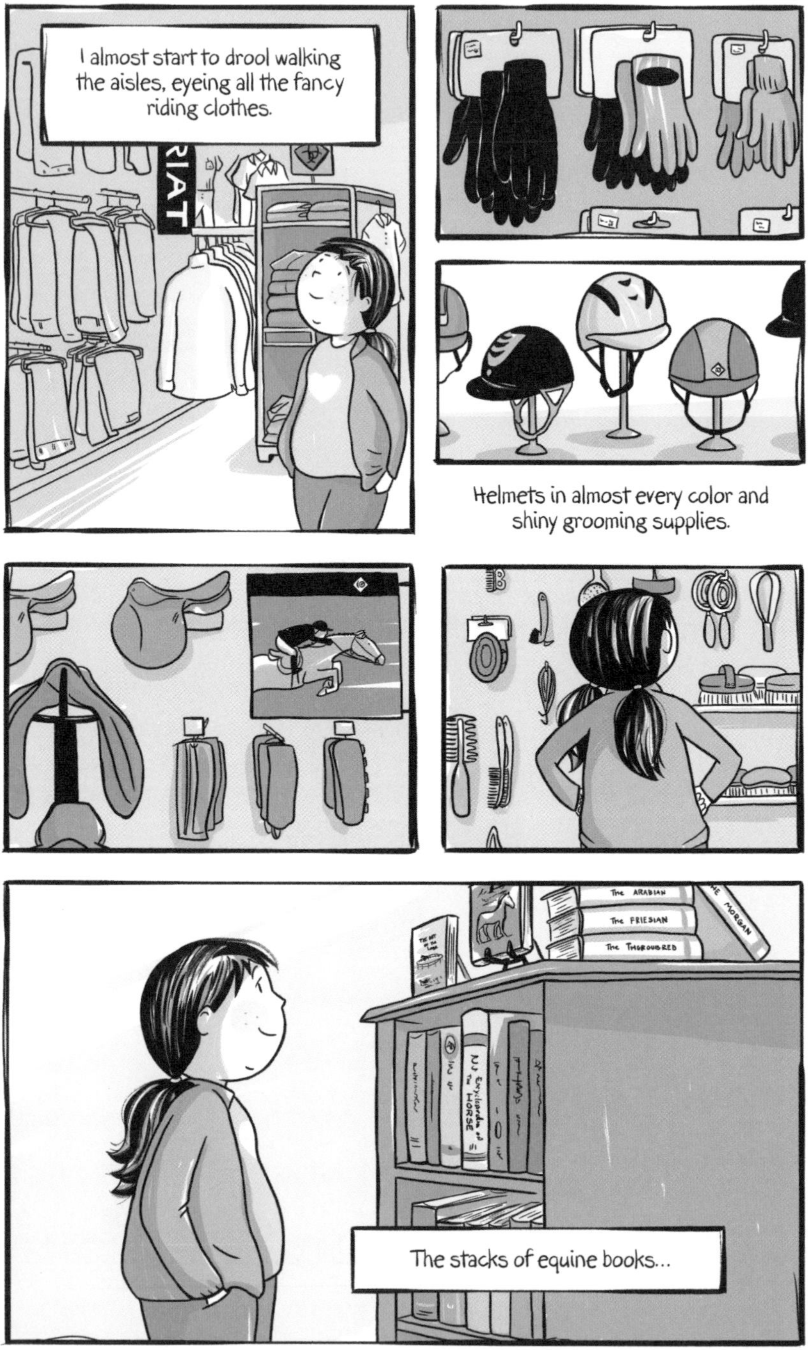
I almost start to drool walking the aisles, eyeing all the fancy riding clothes.
Helmets in almost every color and shiny grooming supplies.
The ARABIAN
The FRIESIAN
The stacks of equine books...

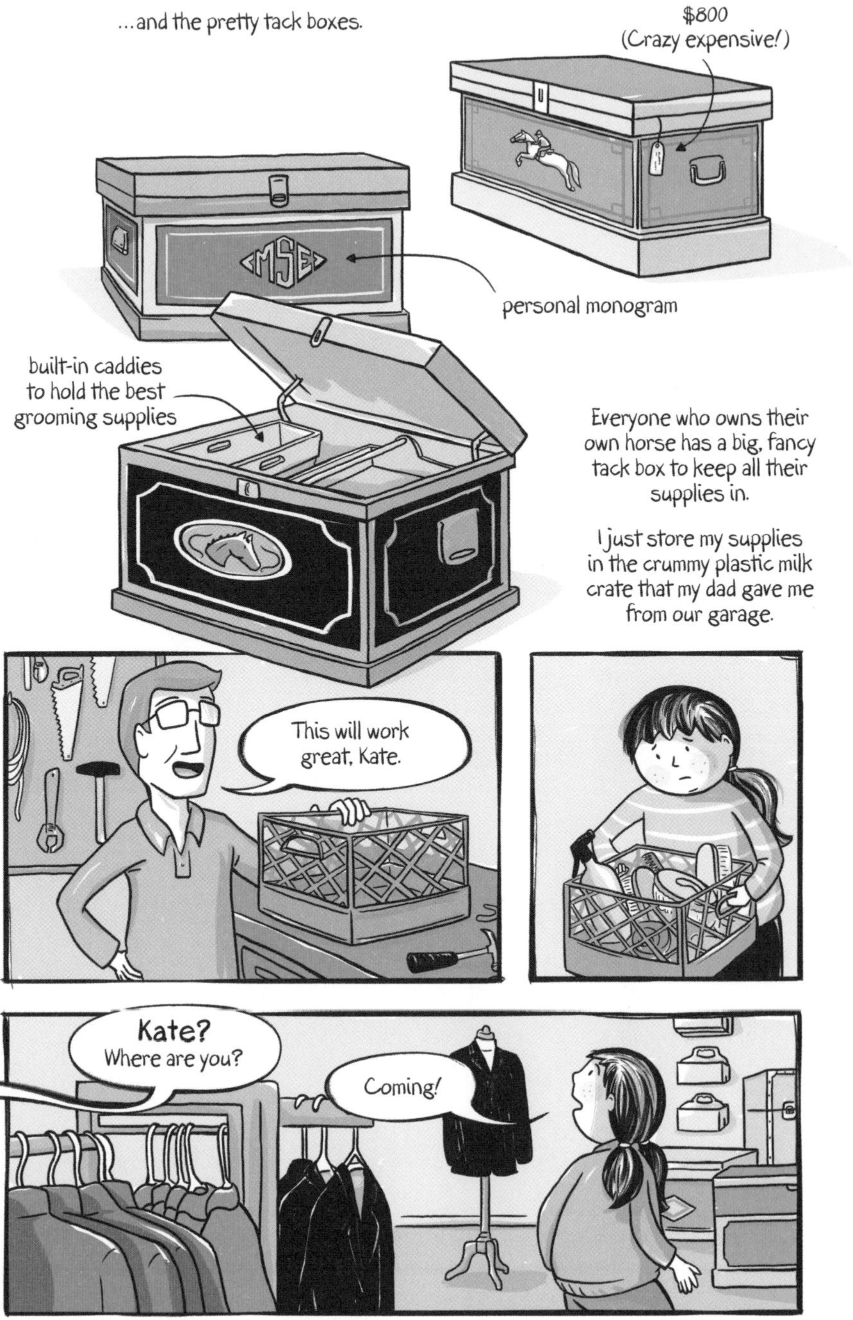
...and the pretty tack boxes.
$800
(Crazy expensive!)
MSE
personal monogram
built-in caddies to hold the best grooming supplies
Everyone who owns their own horse has a big, fancy tack box to keep all their supplies in.
I just store my supplies in the crummy plastic milk crate that my dad gave me from our garage.
This will work great, Kate.
Kate?
Where are you?
Coming!

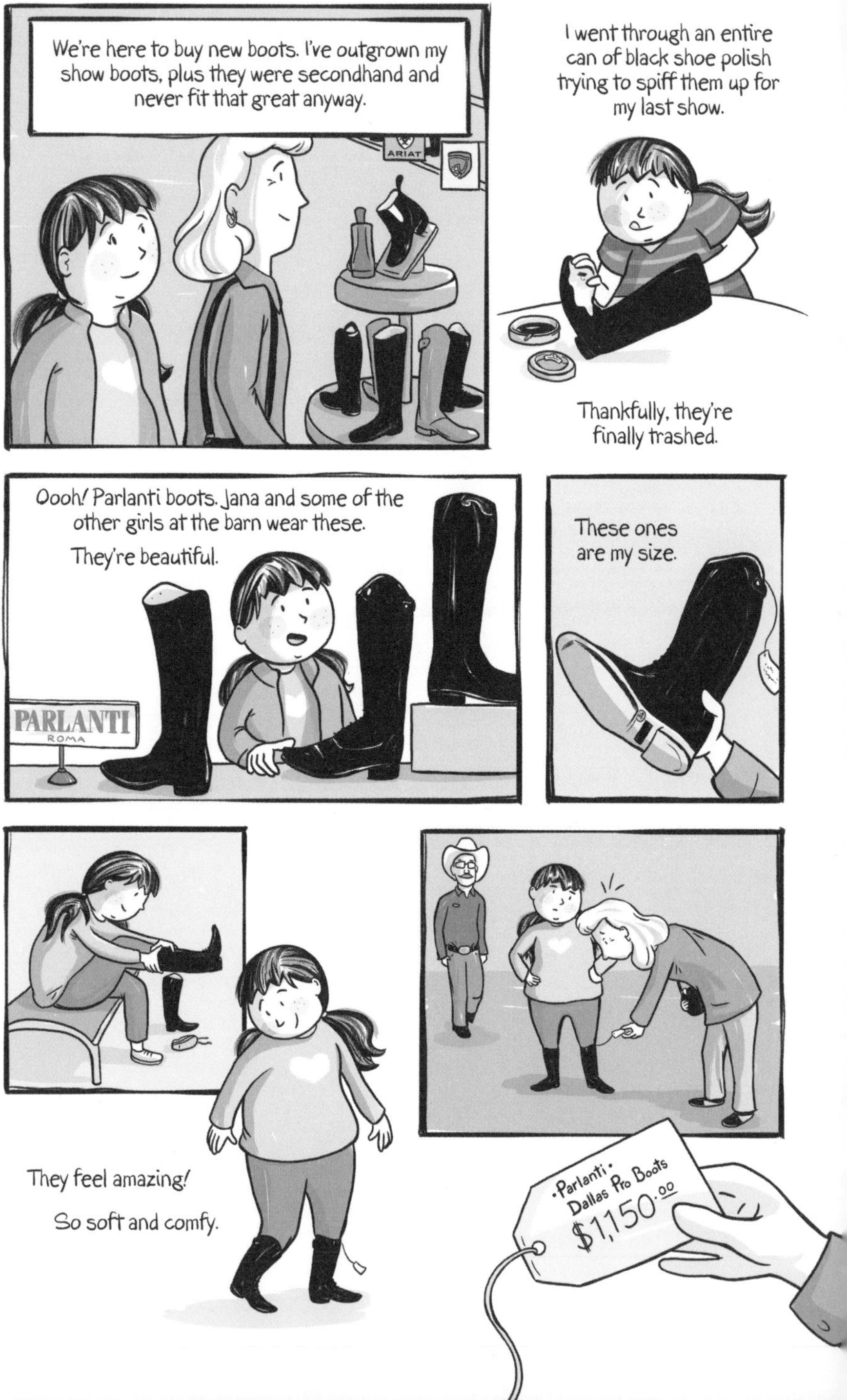
We're here to buy new boots. I've outgrown my show boots, plus they were secondhand and never fit that great anyway.
ARIAT
I went through an entire can of black shoe polish trying to spiff them up for my last show.
Thankfully, they're finally trashed.
Oooh! Parlanti boots. Jana and some of the other girls at the barn wear these.
They're beautiful.
PARLANTI
ROMA
These ones are my size.
They feel amazing!
So soft and comfy.
•Parlanti•
Dallas Pro Boots
$1,150.00

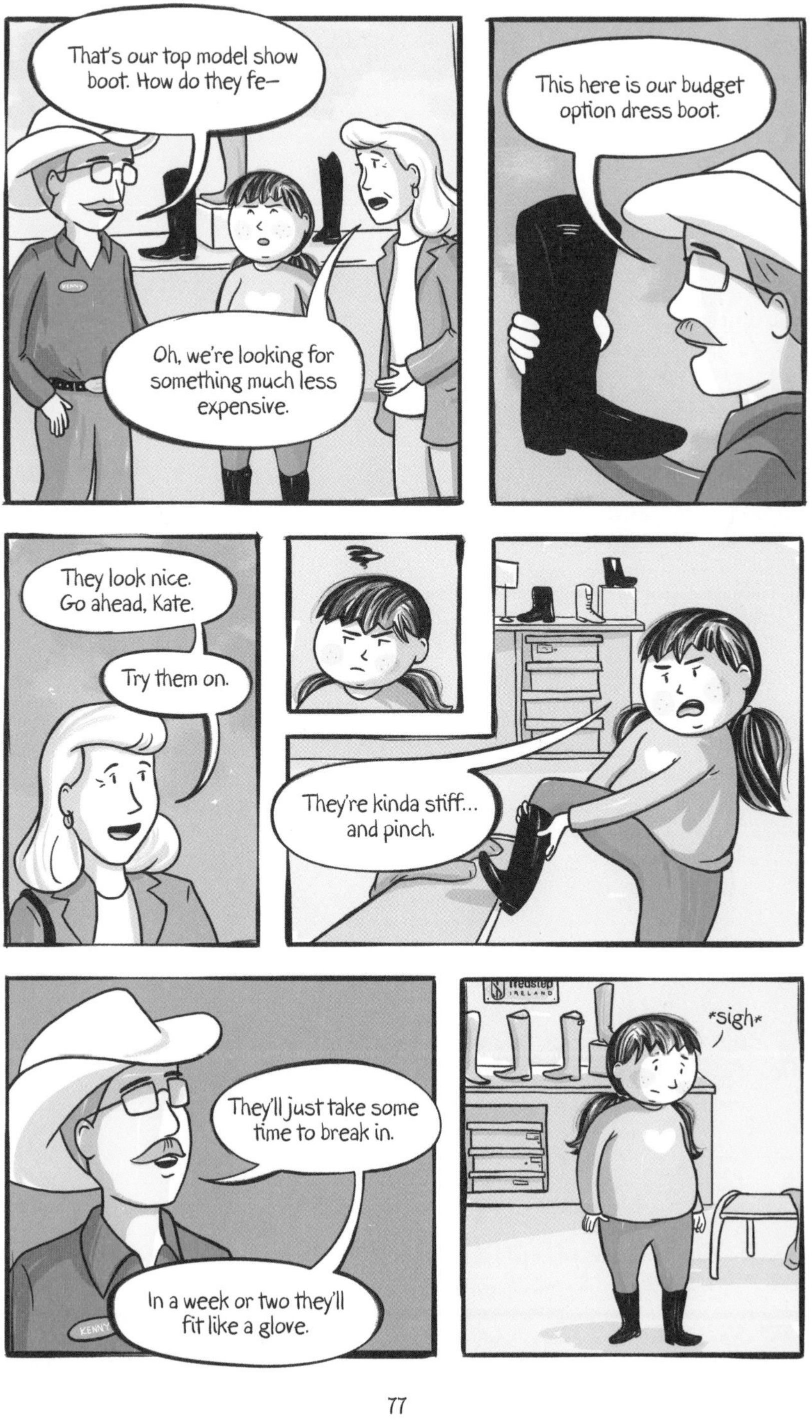

That's our top model show boot. How do they fe–
Oh, we're looking for something much less expensive.
This here is our budget option dress boot.
They look nice. Go ahead, Kate.
Try them on.
They're kinda stiff... and pinch.
They'll just take some time to break in.
In a week or two they'll fit like a glove.
KENNY
sigh

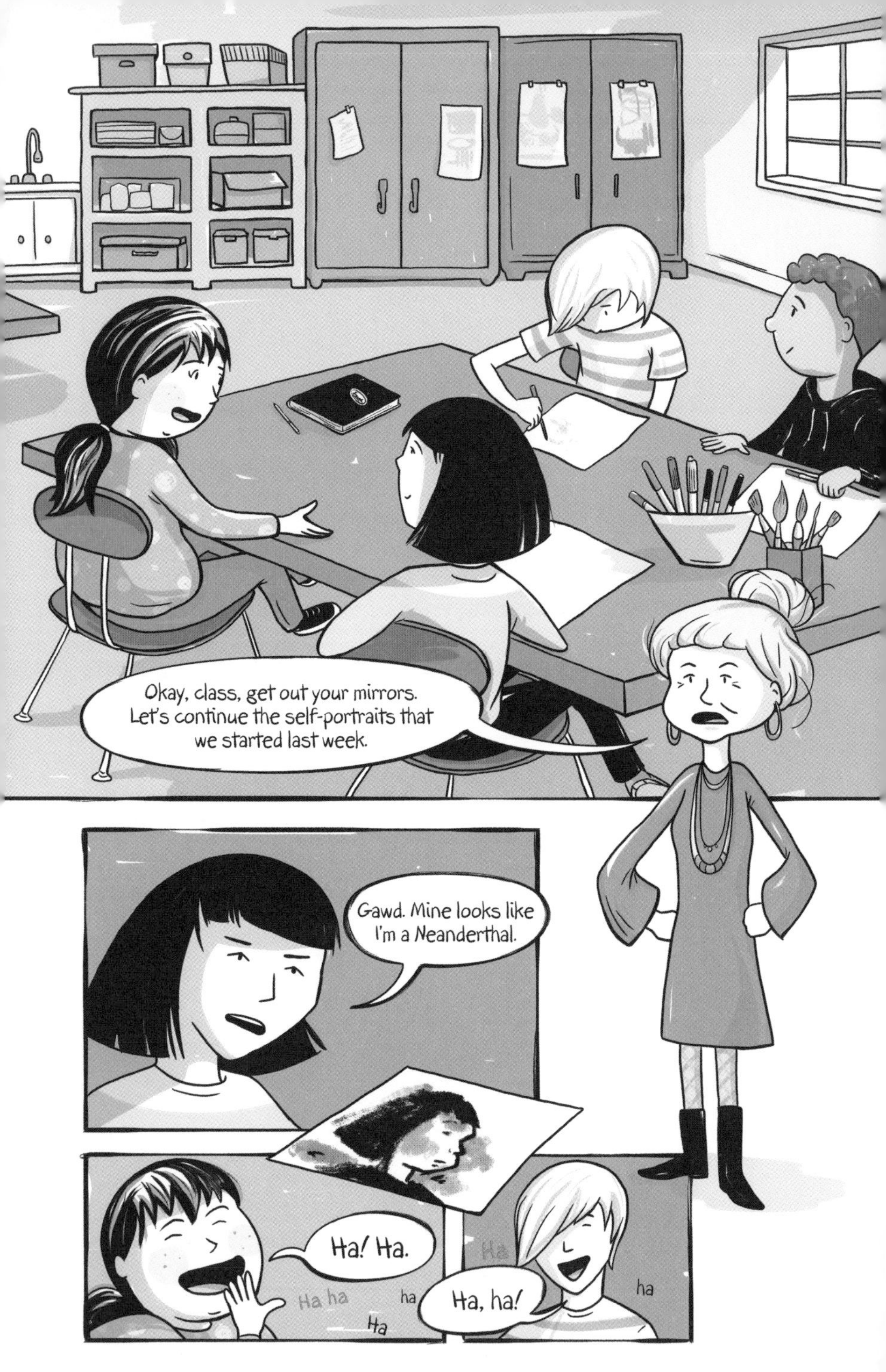
Okay, class, get out your mirrors. Let's continue the self-portraits that we started last week.
Gawd. Mine looks like I'm a Neanderthal.
Ha! Ha.
Ha ha
ha
Ha
Ha
Ha, ha!
ha

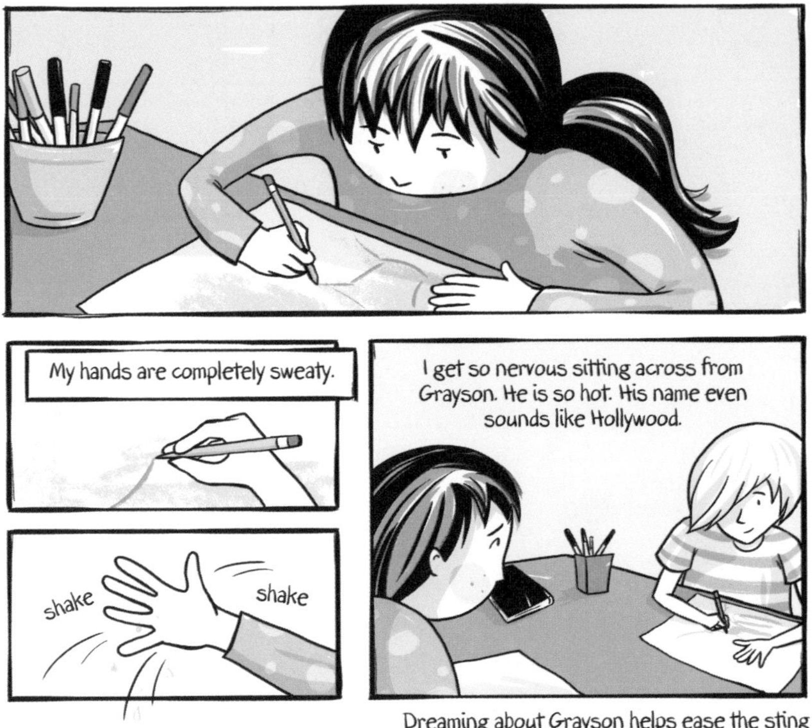
My hands are completely sweaty.
shake
shake
I get so nervous sitting across from Grayson. He is so hot. His name even sounds like Hollywood.

Dreaming about Grayson helps ease the sting of Matthew's Becky obsession.

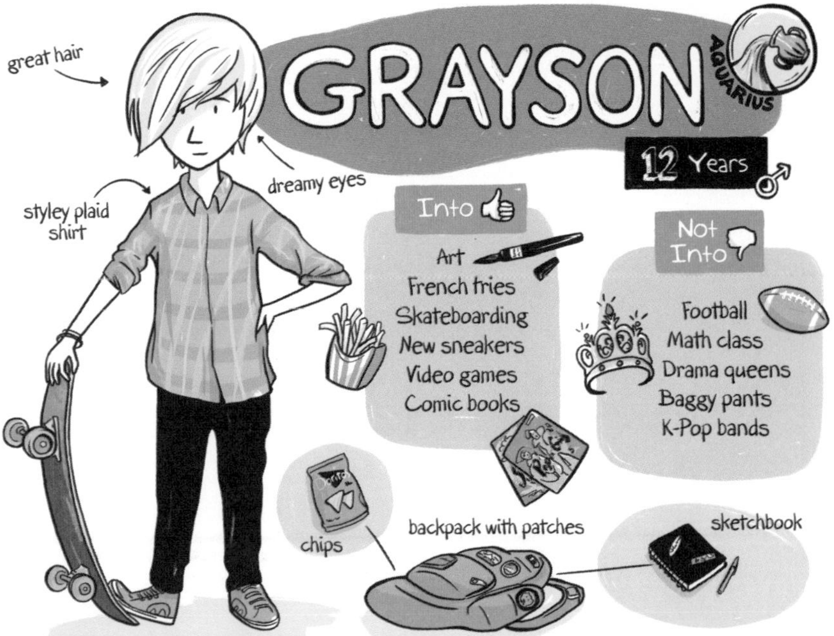
GRAYSON
AQUARIUS
12 Years
great hair
dreamy eyes
styley plaid shirt
Into
Art
French fries
Skateboarding
New sneakers
Video games
Comic books
Not Into
Football
Math class
Drama queens
Baggy pants
K-Pop bands
chips
backpack with patches
sketchbook

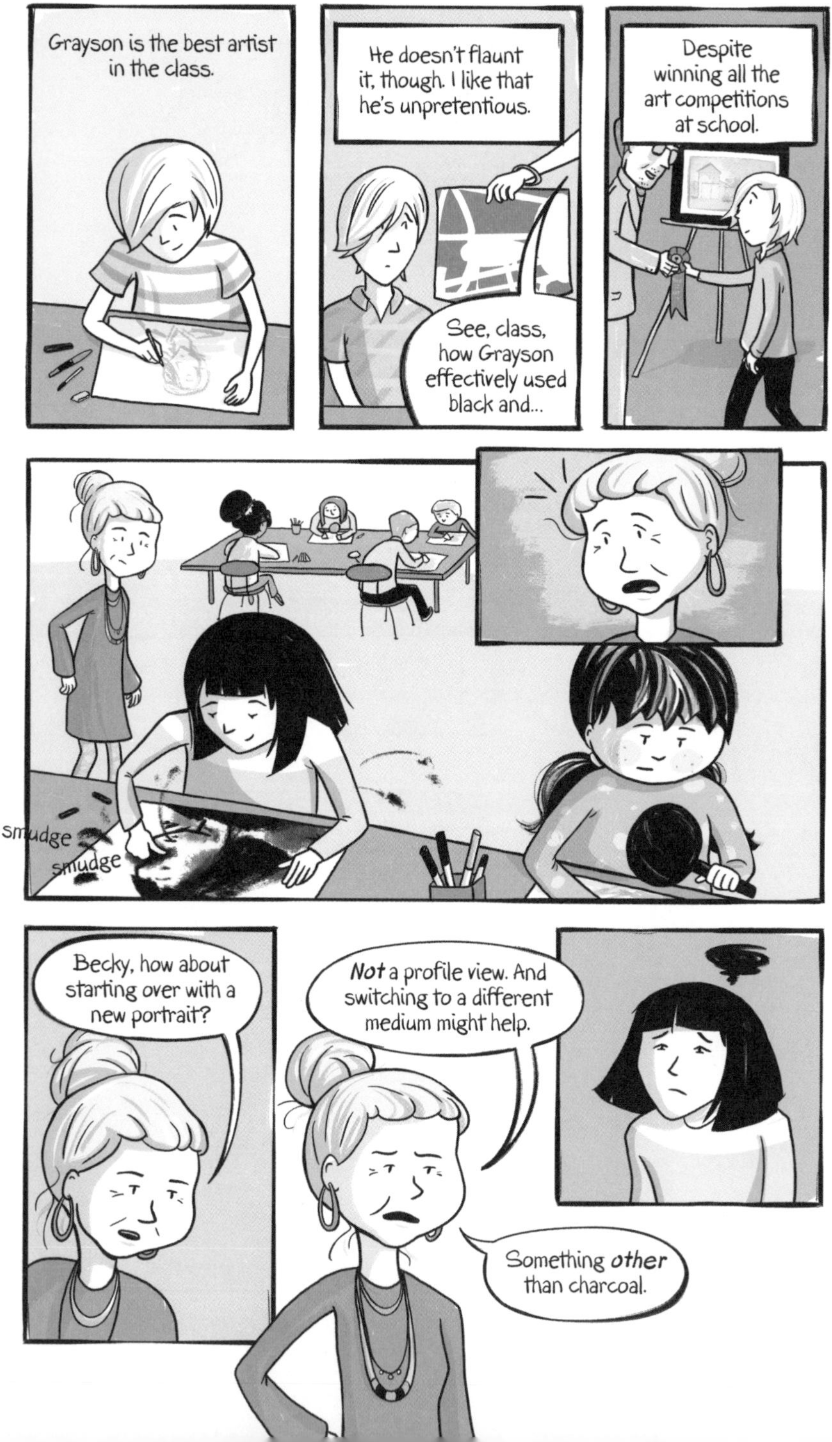
Grayson is the best artist in the class.
He doesn't flaunt it, though. I like that he's unpretentious.
See, class, how Grayson effectively used black and...
Despite winning all the art competitions at school.
smudge
smudge
Becky, how about starting over with a new portrait?
Not a profile view. And switching to a different medium might help.
Something *other* than charcoal.

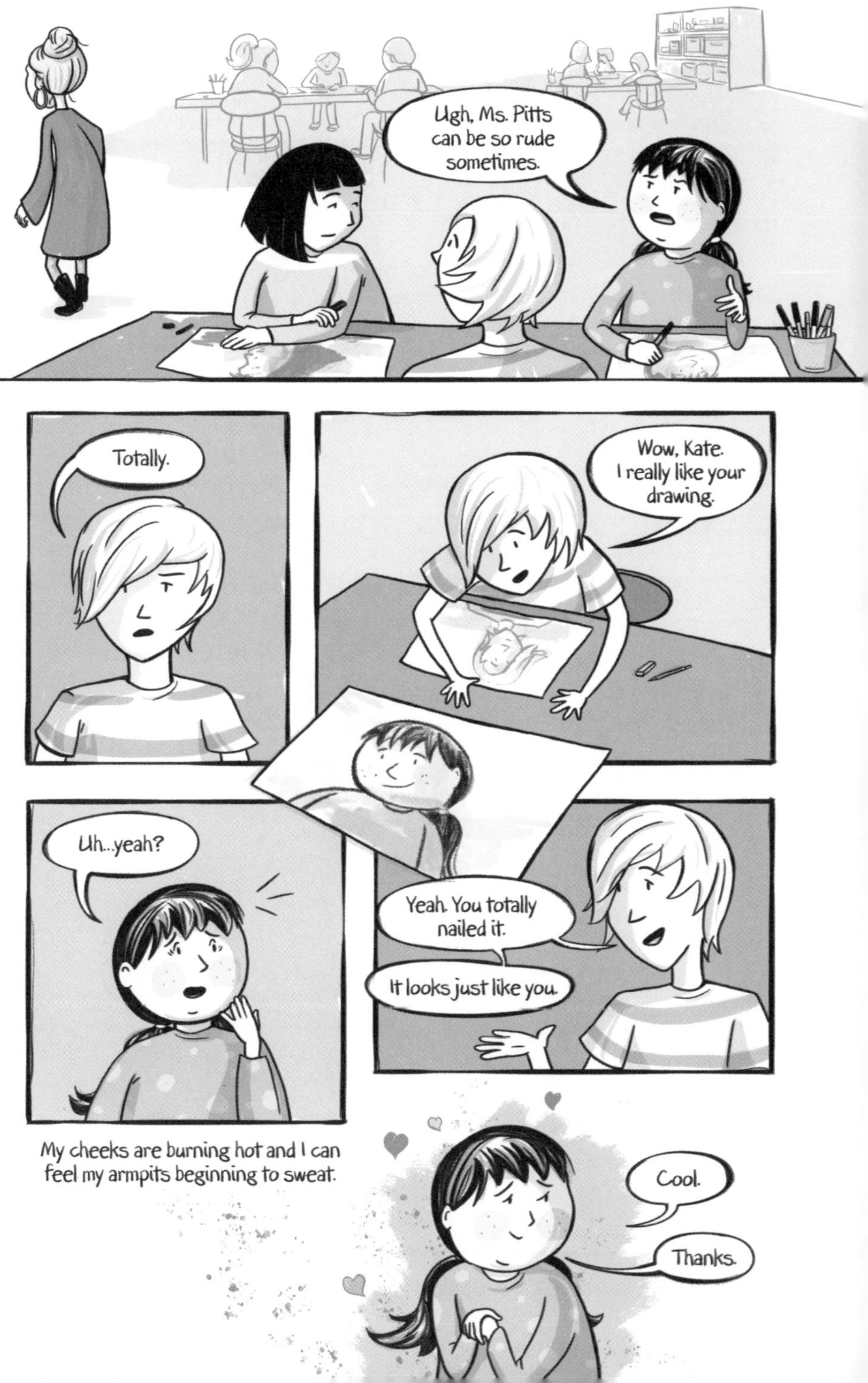
Ugh, Ms. Pitts can be so rude sometimes.
Totally.
Wow, Kate. I really like your drawing.
Uh...yeah?
Yeah. You totally nailed it.
It looks just like you.
My cheeks are burning hot and I can feel my armpits beginning to sweat.
Cool.
Thanks.

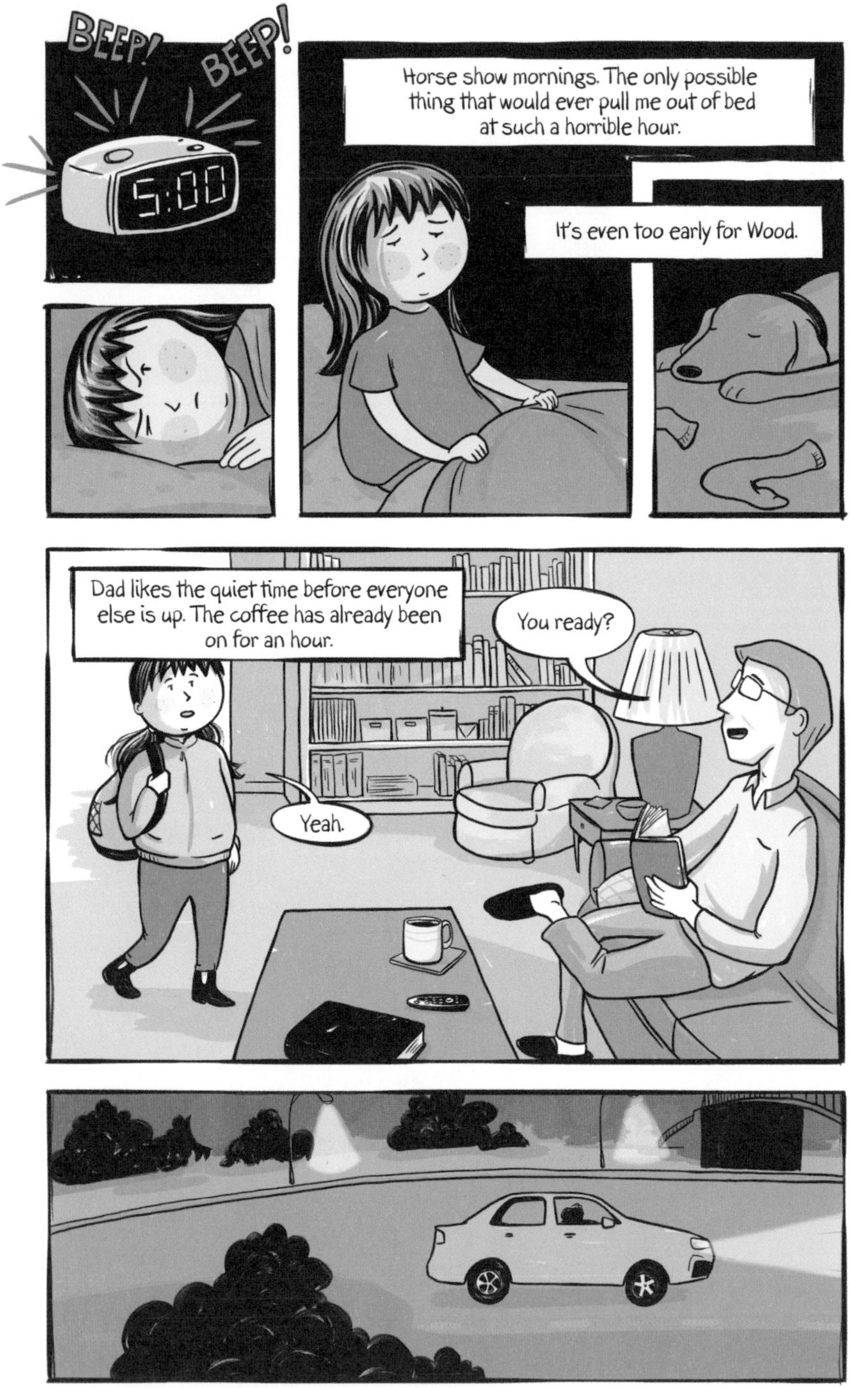
BEEP! BEEP!
5:00
Horse show mornings. The only possible thing that would ever pull me out of bed at such a horrible hour.
It's even too early for Wood.
Dad likes the quiet time before everyone else is up. The coffee has already been on for an hour.
You ready?
Yeah.

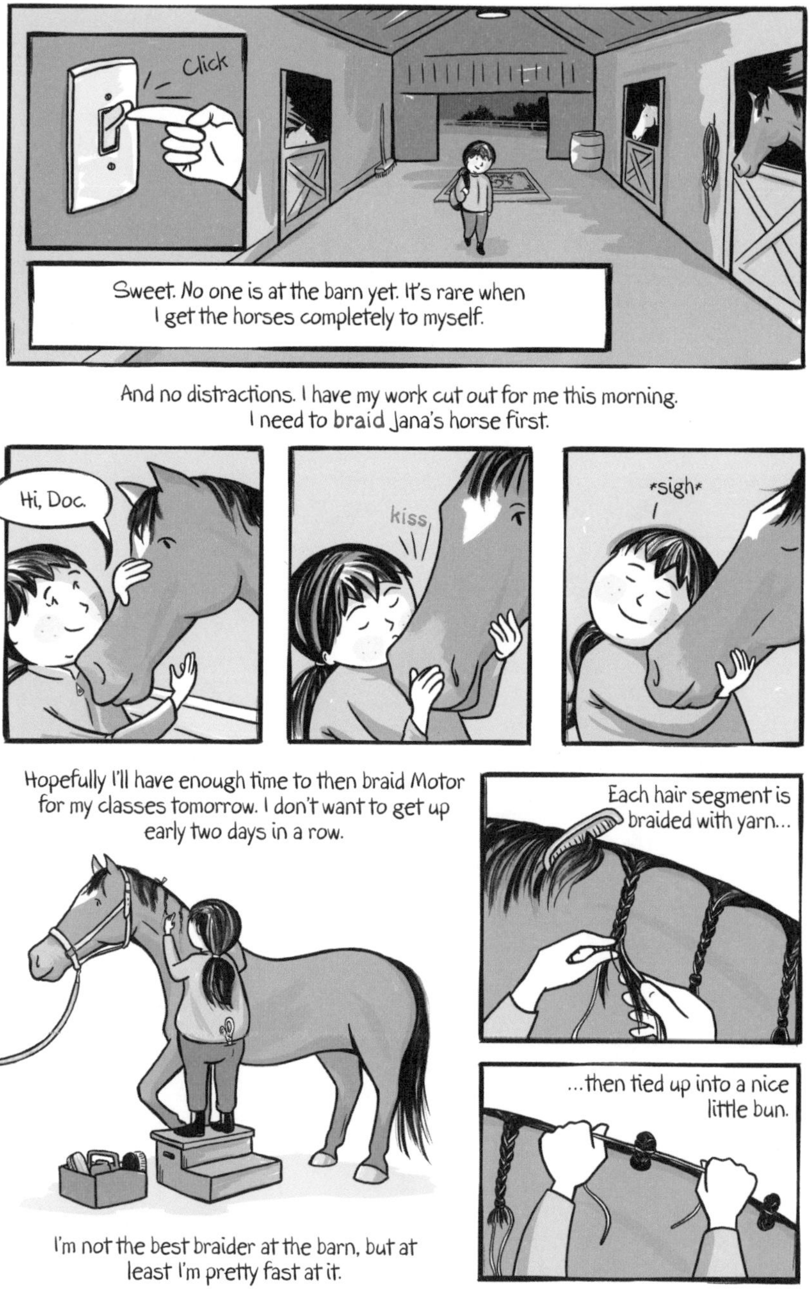
Click
Sweet. No one is at the barn yet. It's rare when I get the horses completely to myself.
And no distractions. I have my work cut out for me this morning. I need to braid Jana's horse first.
Hi, Doc.
kiss
sigh
Hopefully I'll have enough time to then braid Motor for my classes tomorrow. I don't want to get up early two days in a row.
Each hair segment is braided with yarn...
I'm not the best braider at the barn, but at least I'm pretty fast at it.
...then tied up into a nice little bun.

Braids: Braided manes are required for most classes at horse shows. They give the horse's neck a clean line and a more polished look.

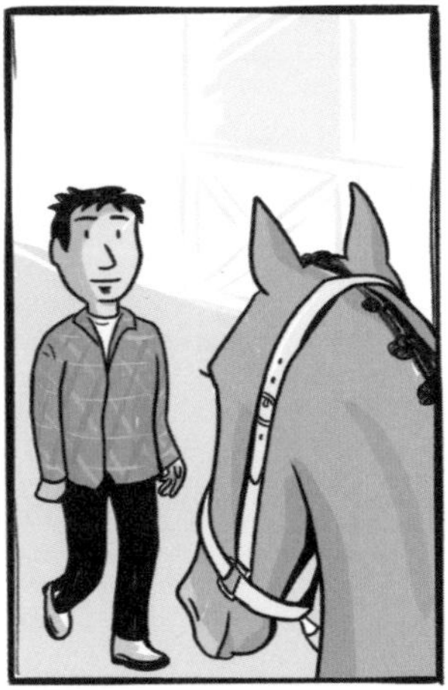

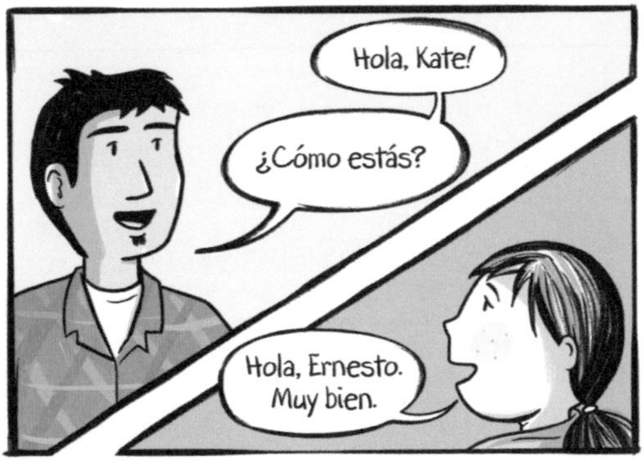
Hola, Kate!
¿Cómo estás?
Hola, Ernesto. Muy bien.

Ernesto works as a barn hand at Millcreek Farm. Barb hired him last year. He lives in a trailer at the far end of the property, all alone.

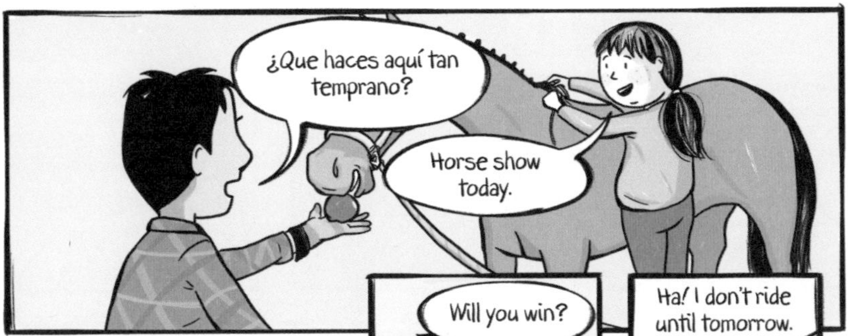
¿Que haces aquí tan temprano?
Horse show today.

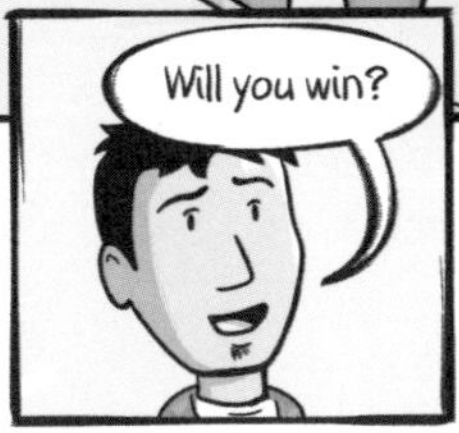
Will you win?

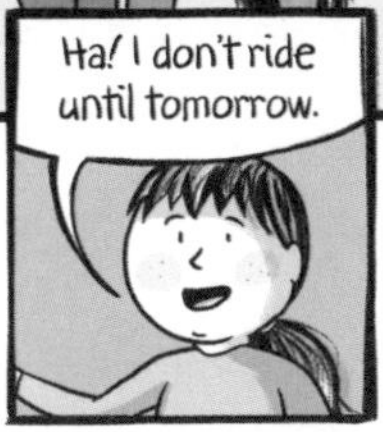
Ha! I don't ride until tomorrow.

Ernesto is great. He loves the horses, too. Something about his smile puts me at ease. I also get to practice my Spanish with him. He thinks it's really cool that I'm learning.

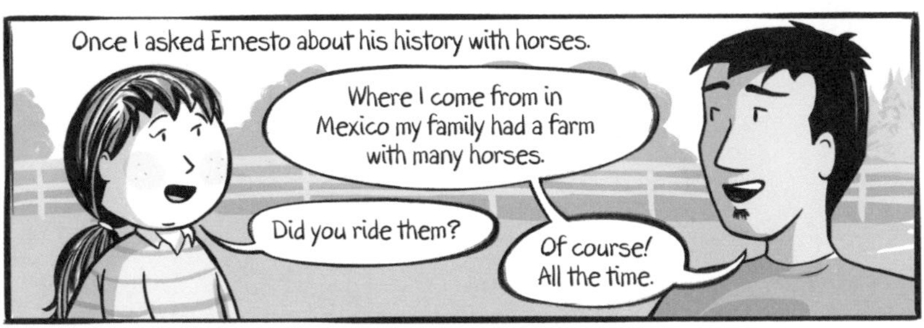
Once I asked Ernesto about his history with horses.
Where I come from in Mexico my family had a farm with many horses.
Did you ride them?
Of course! All the time.

I've never seen him riding any of the horses at Millcreek. That makes me sad.

We do many of the same barn jobs, so there was an instant respect between us. But sometimes I wonder how Ernesto really feels about working here.

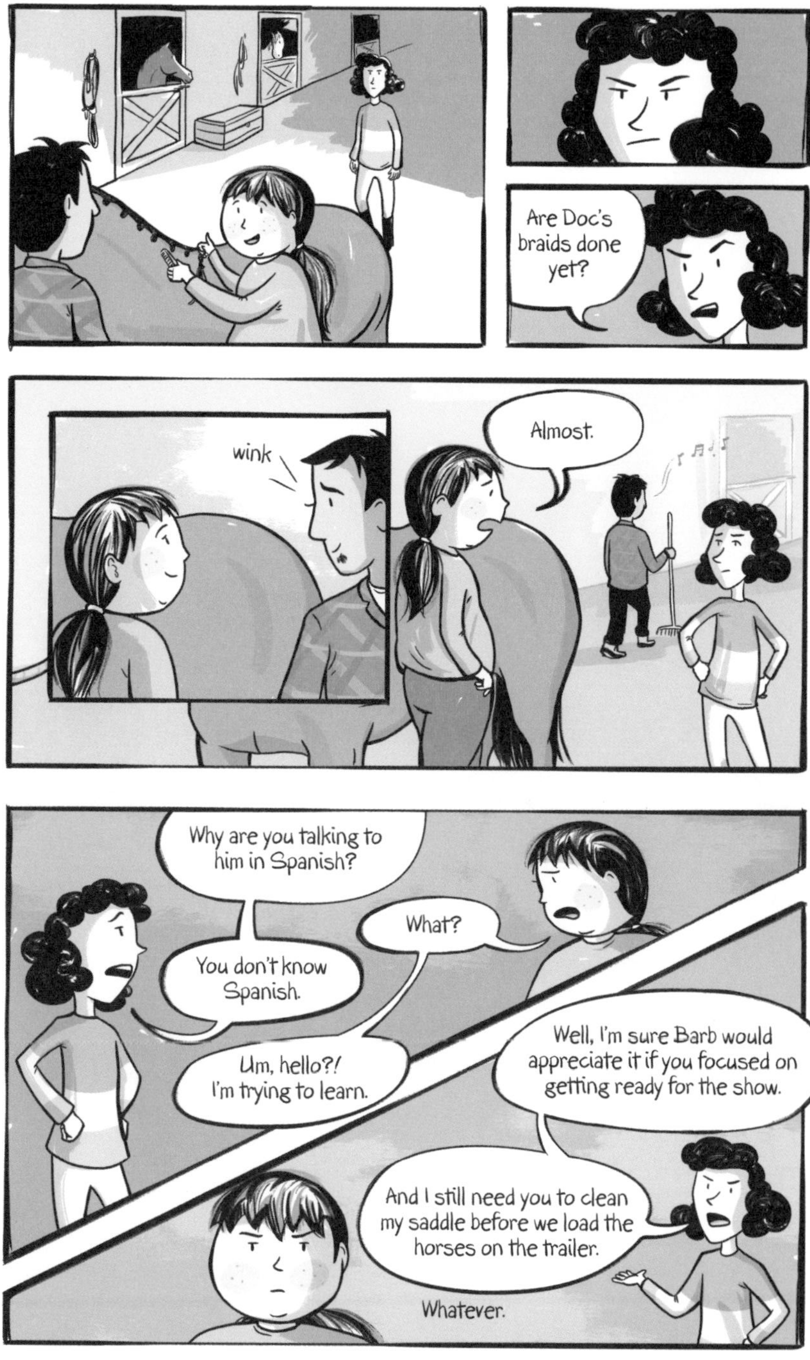

Are Doc's braids done yet?
wink
Almost.
Why are you talking to him in Spanish?
You don't know Spanish.
What?
Um, hello?! I'm trying to learn.
Well, I'm sure Barb would appreciate it if you focused on getting ready for the show.
And I still need you to clean my saddle before we load the horses on the trailer.
Whatever.

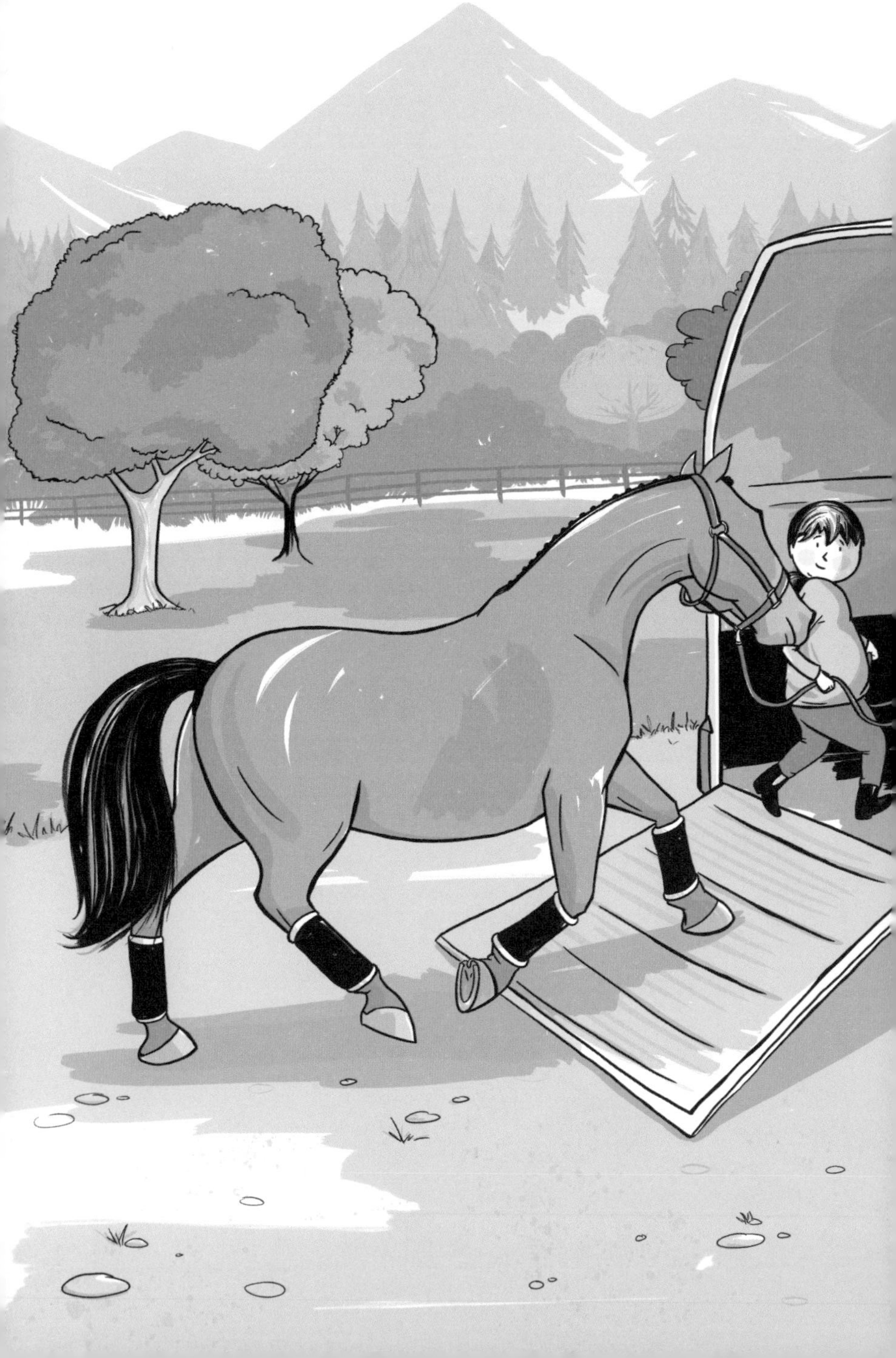

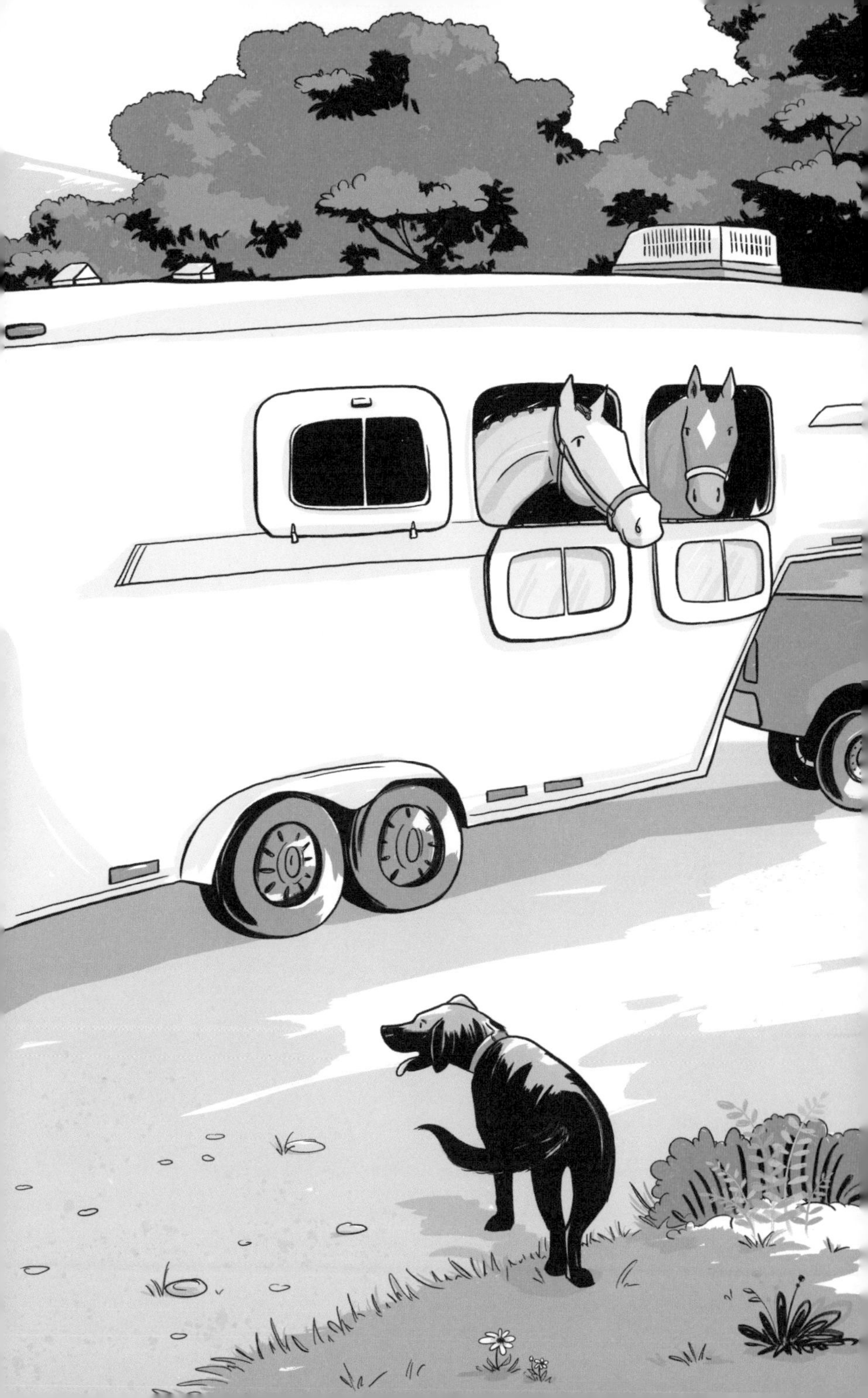

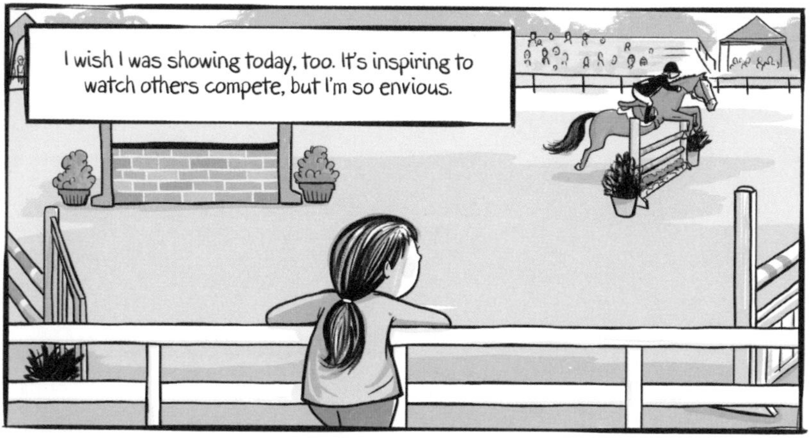
I wish I was showing today, too. It's inspiring to watch others compete, but I'm so envious.

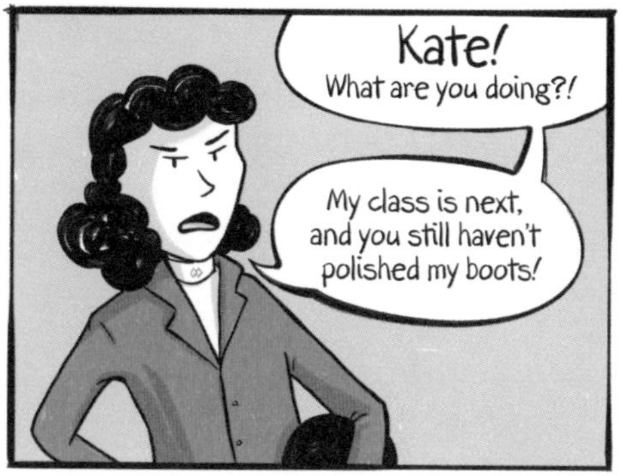
Kate!
What are you doing?!
My class is next, and you still haven't polished my boots!

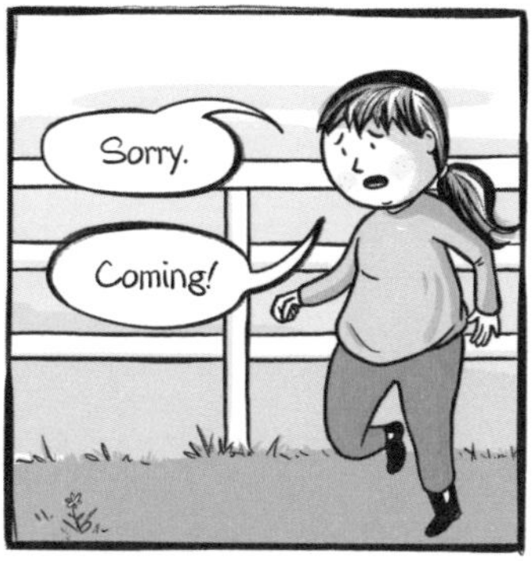
Sorry.
Coming!

Jana keeps me busy the rest of the day.

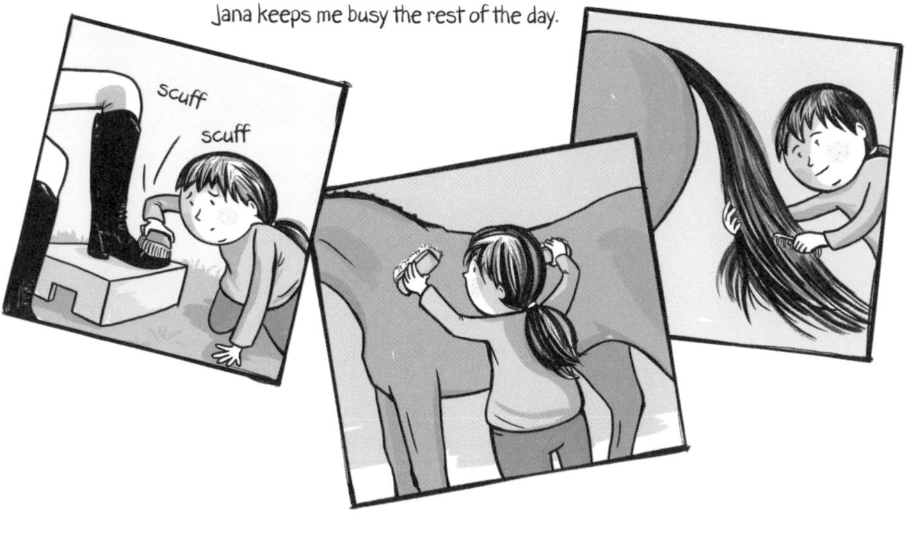
scuff
scuff

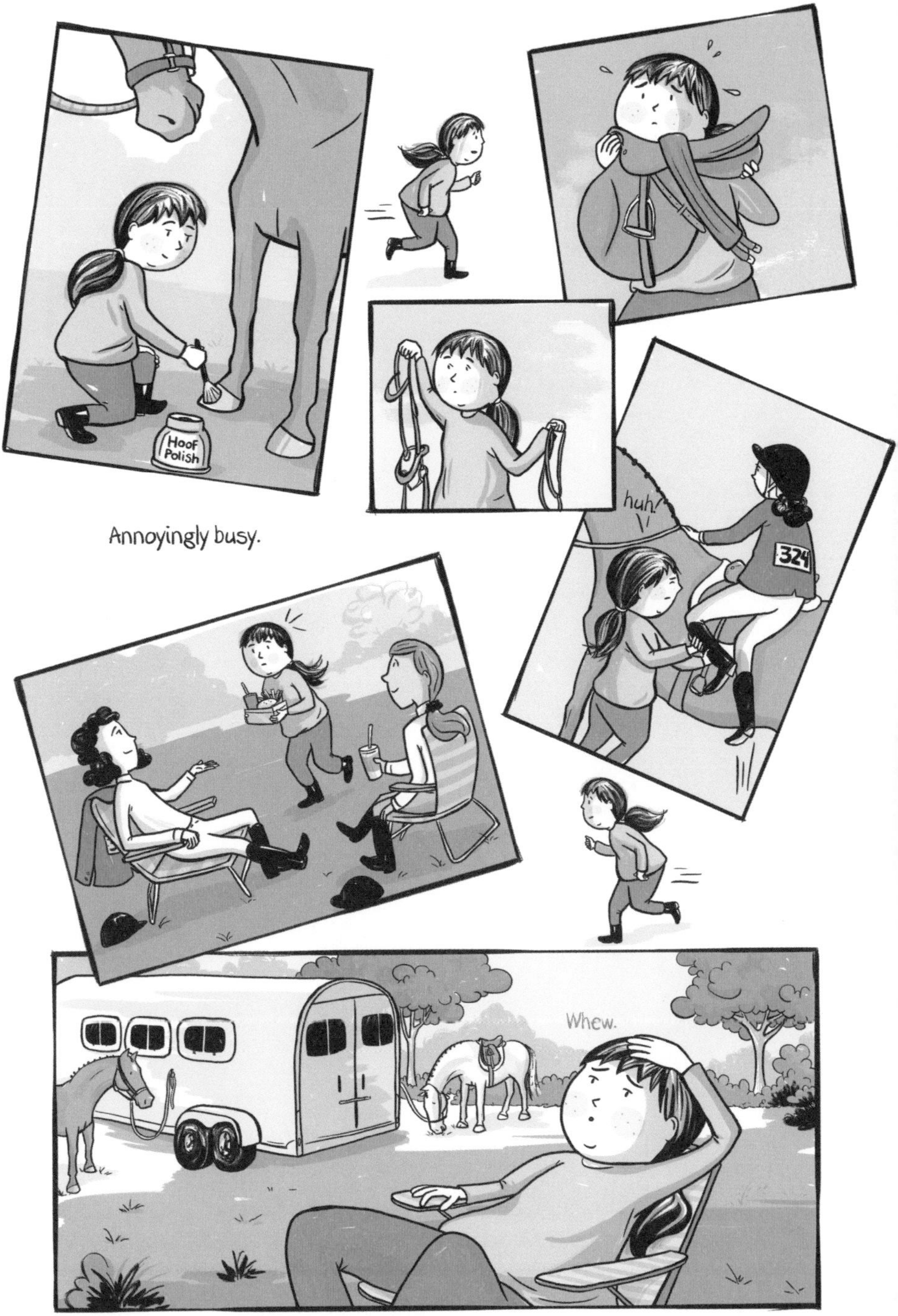
Hoof Polish
Annoyingly busy.
huh!
324
Whew.

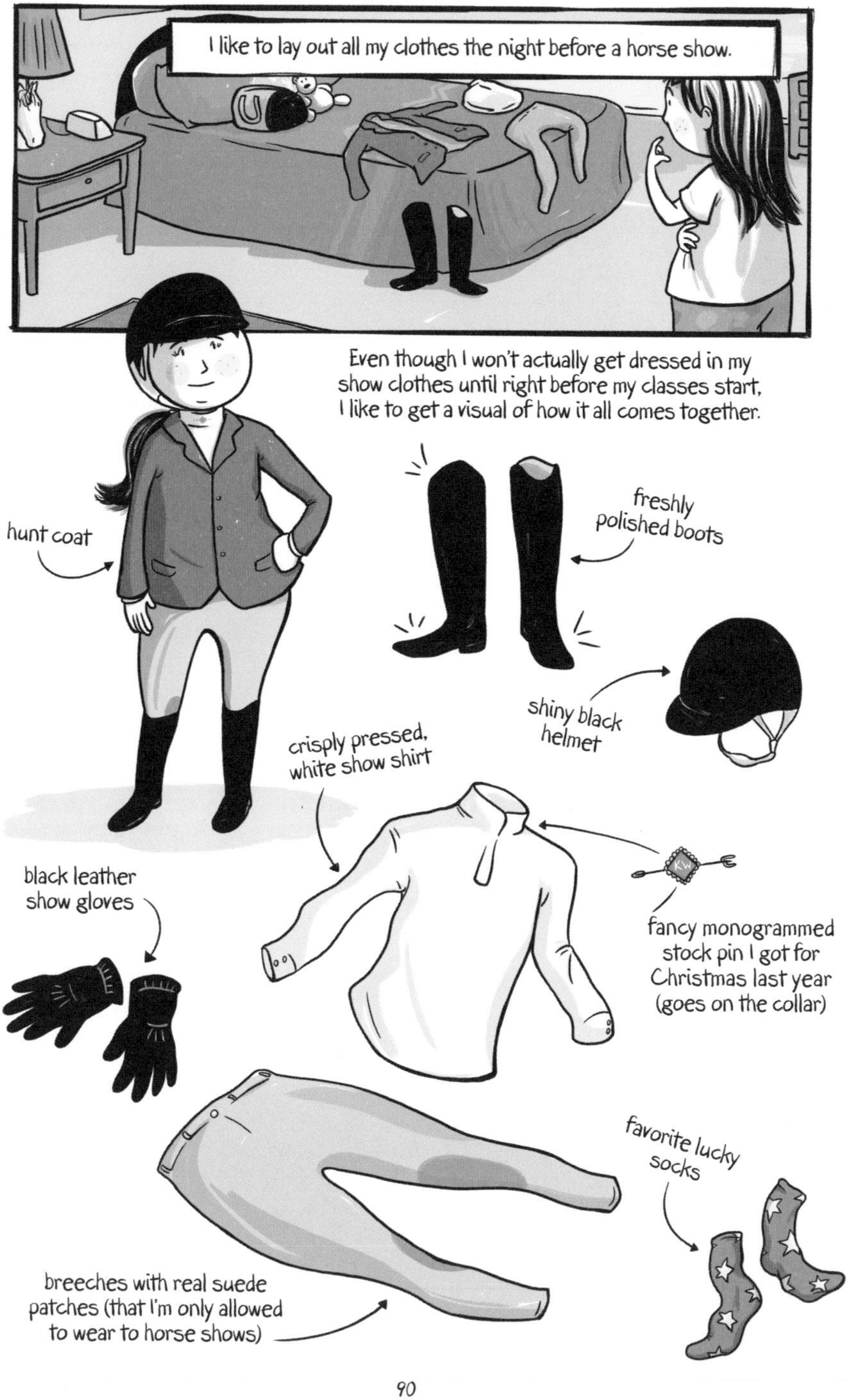
I like to lay out all my clothes the night before a horse show.
Even though I won't actually get dressed in my show clothes until right before my classes start, I like to get a visual of how it all comes together.
hunt coat
freshly polished boots
shiny black helmet
crisply pressed, white show shirt
black leather show gloves
fancy monogrammed stock pin I got for Christmas last year (goes on the collar)
KW
favorite lucky socks
breeches with real suede patches (that I'm only allowed to wear to horse shows)

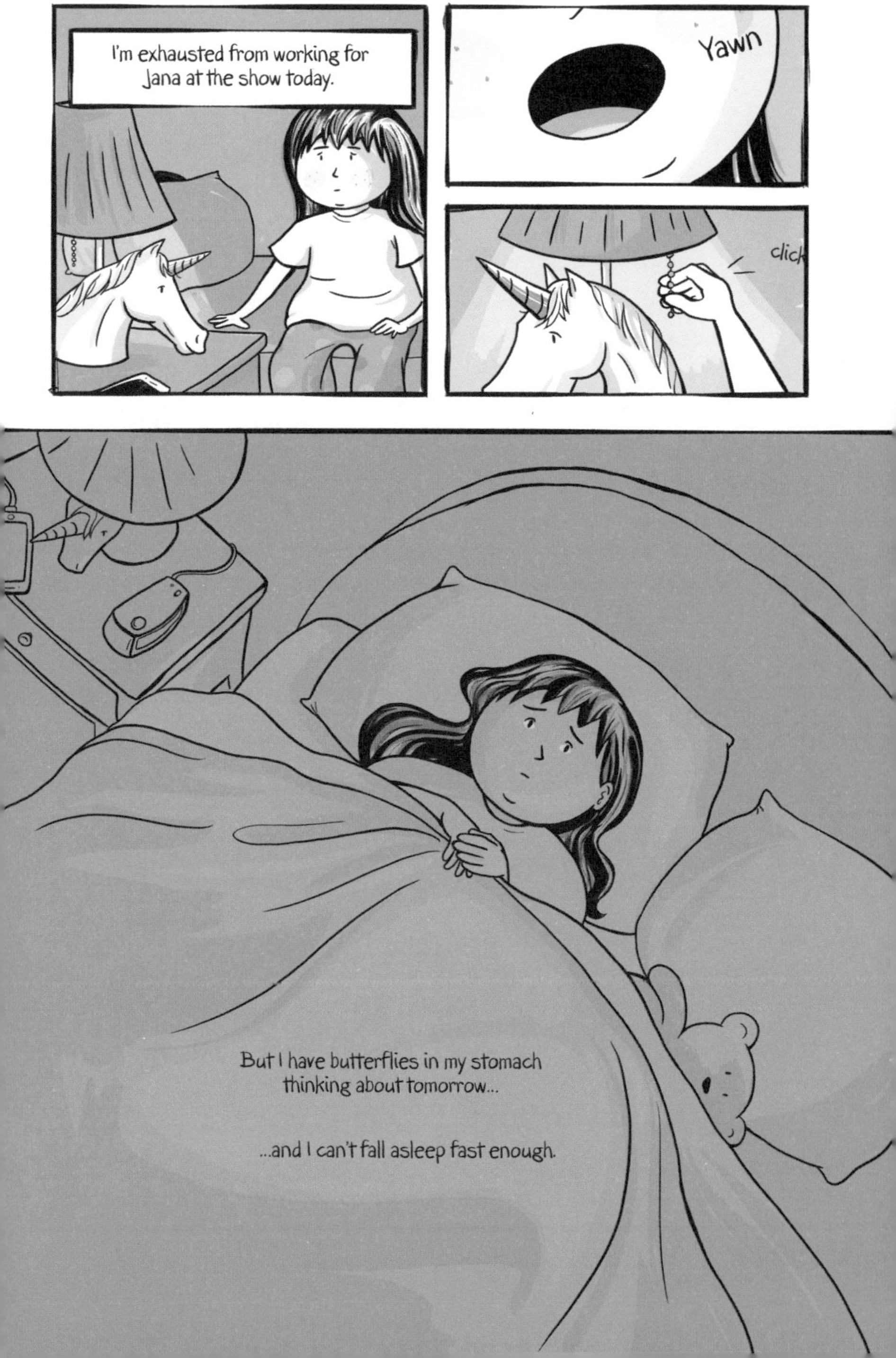
I'm exhausted from working for Jana at the show today.
Yawn
click
But I have butterflies in my stomach thinking about tomorrow...
...and I can't fall asleep fast enough.

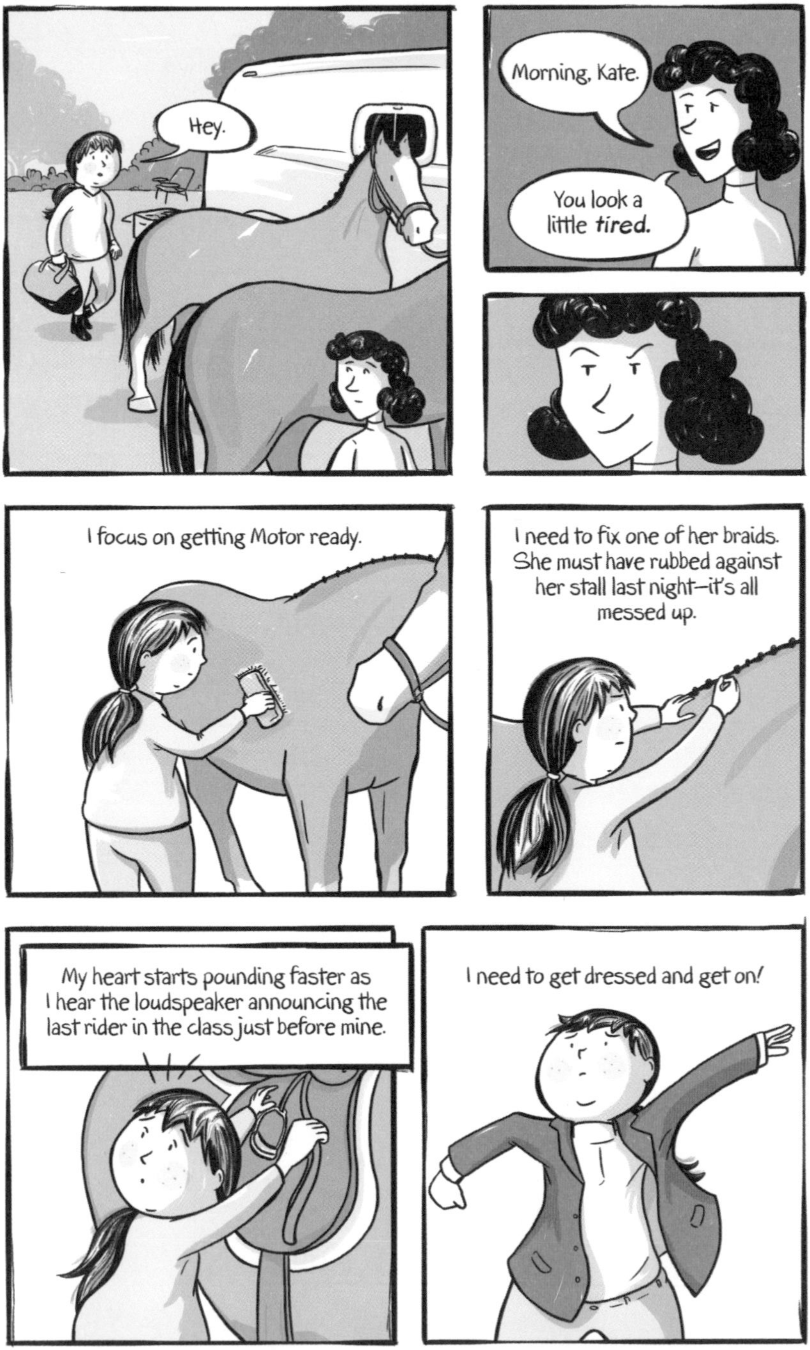
Hey.
Morning, Kate.
You look a little *tired.*
I focus on getting Motor ready.
I need to fix one of her braids. She must have rubbed against her stall last night—it's all messed up.
My heart starts pounding faster as I hear the loudspeaker announcing the last rider in the class just before mine.
I need to get dressed and get on!

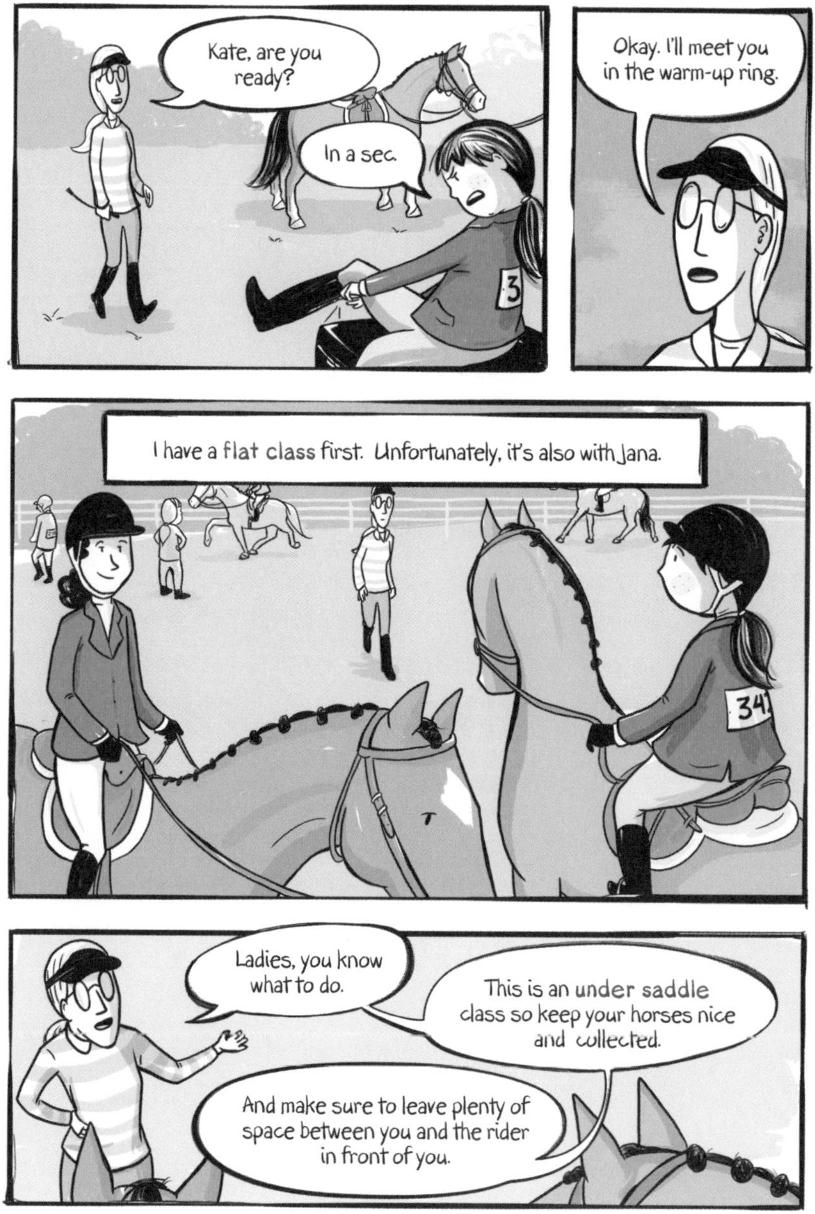
Kate, are you ready?
In a sec.
3
Okay. I'll meet you in the warm-up ring.
I have a flat class first. Unfortunately, it's also with Jana.
34
Ladies, you know what to do.
This is an under saddle class so keep your horses nice and collected.
And make sure to leave plenty of space between you and the rider in front of you.

Flat class: All riders are directed by a judge and ride along the outside of the ring at a walk, trot, and canter. There is no jumping and winners are chosen out of a lineup at the class's end.

Under saddle: The class is judged on how well the horse (not the rider) moves and performs.

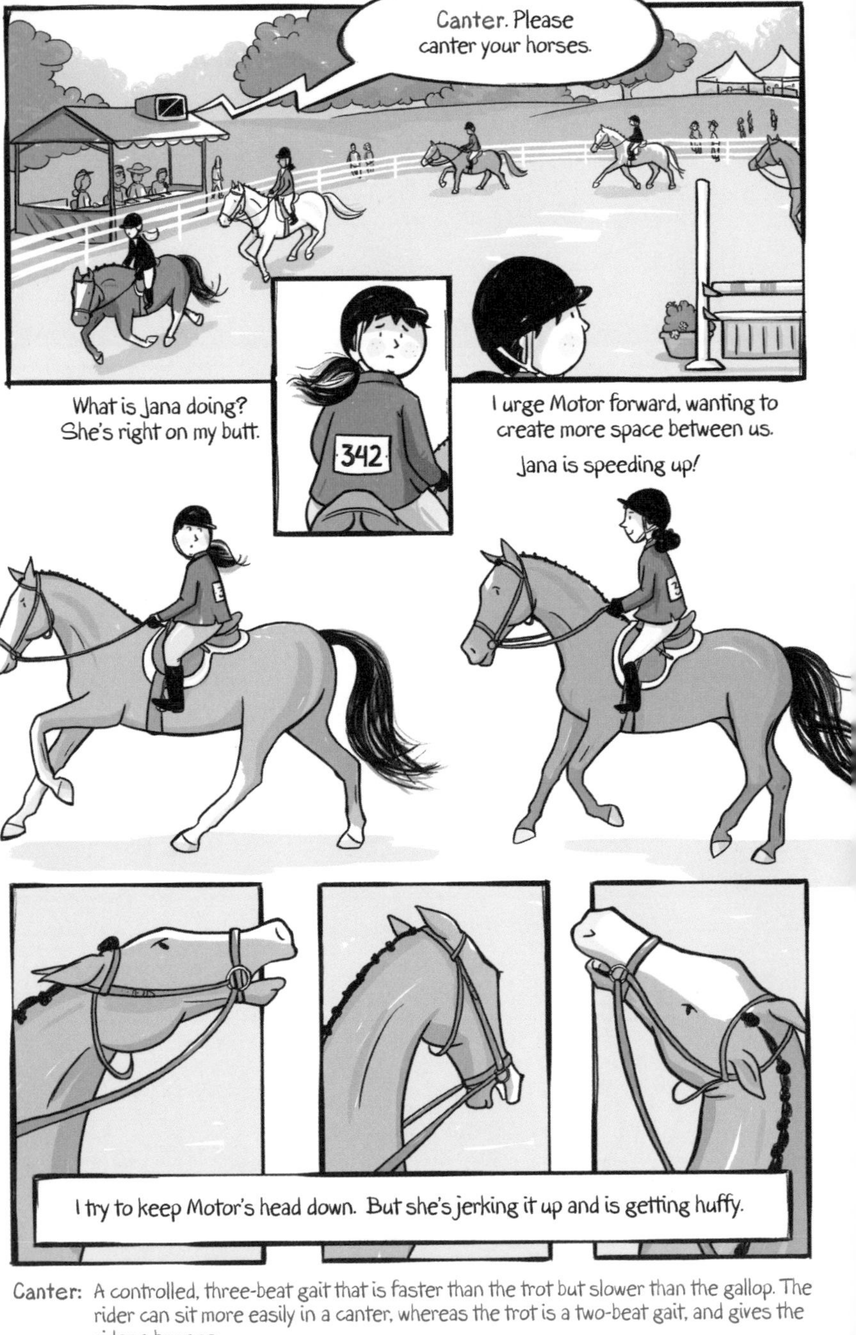
Canter. Please canter your horses.
What is Jana doing? She's right on my butt.
342
I urge Motor forward, wanting to create more space between us.
Jana is speeding up!
I try to keep Motor's head down. But she's jerking it up and is getting huffy.

Canter: A controlled, three-beat gait that is faster than the trot but slower than the gallop. The rider can sit more easily in a canter, whereas the trot is a two-beat gait, and gives the rider a bounce.

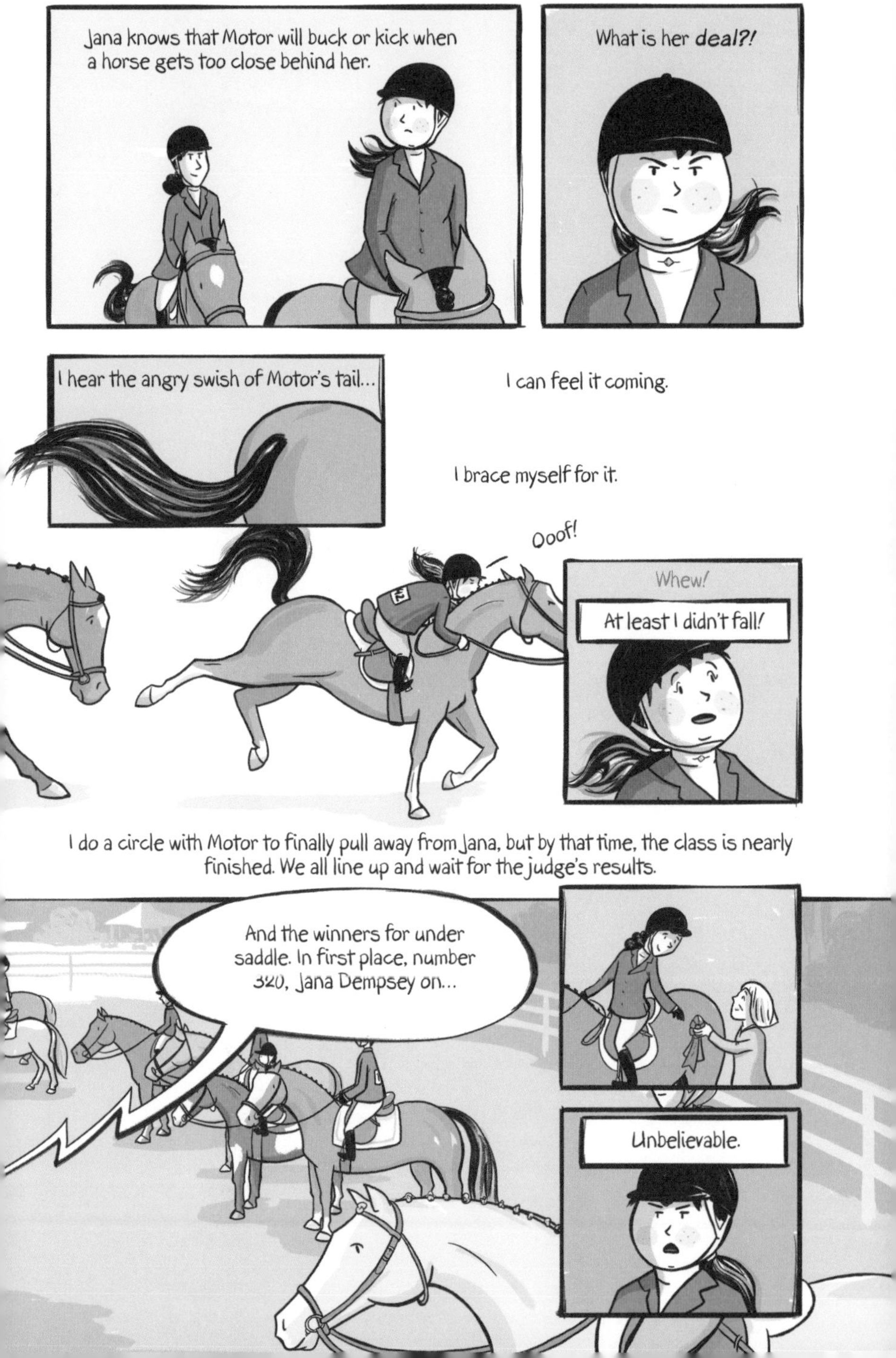
Jana knows that Motor will buck or kick when a horse gets too close behind her.
What is her *deal?!*
I hear the angry swish of Motor's tail...
I can feel it coming.
I brace myself for it.
Ooof!
Whew!
At least I didn't fall!
I do a circle with Motor to finally pull away from Jana, but by that time, the class is nearly finished. We all line up and wait for the judge's results.
And the winners for under saddle. In first place, number 320, Jana Dempsey on...
Unbelievable.

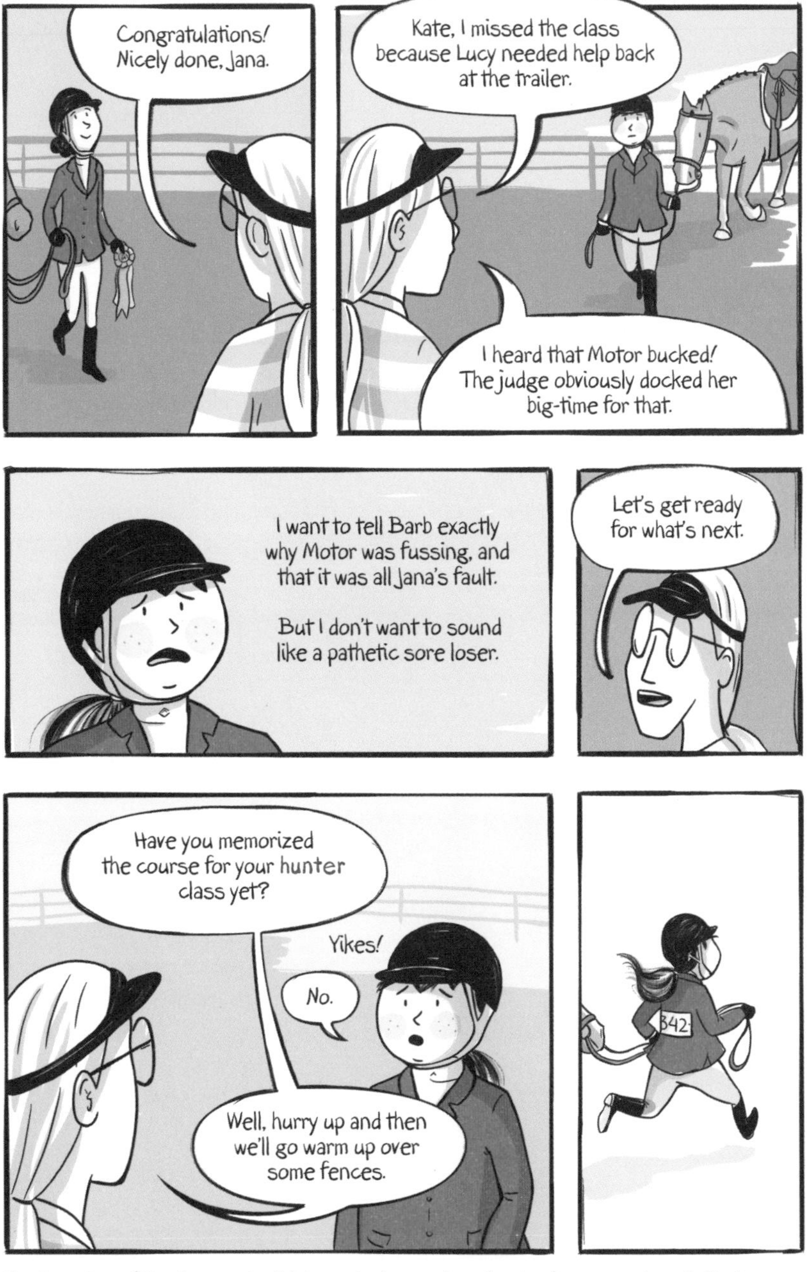

Congratulations! Nicely done, Jana.
Kate, I missed the class because Lucy needed help back at the trailer.
I heard that Motor bucked! The judge obviously docked her big-time for that.
I want to tell Barb exactly why Motor was fussing, and that it was all Jana's fault.
But I don't want to sound like a pathetic sore loser.
Let's get ready for what's next.
Have you memorized the course for your hunter class yet?
Yikes!
No.
Well, hurry up and then we'll go warm up over some fences.
342

Hunter: One of the three main divisions at a horse show (hunter, jumper, and equitation). Hunter is judged on the horse's form, style, and manners going around a course of jumps that are designed to emulate a classic fox hunt.

I quickly forget about Jana and the flat class in a panic to study the jump sequence.

I run it through my head:

- smooth transition in and out of the ring
- always end with a circle
- keep a steady pace, don't rush it!

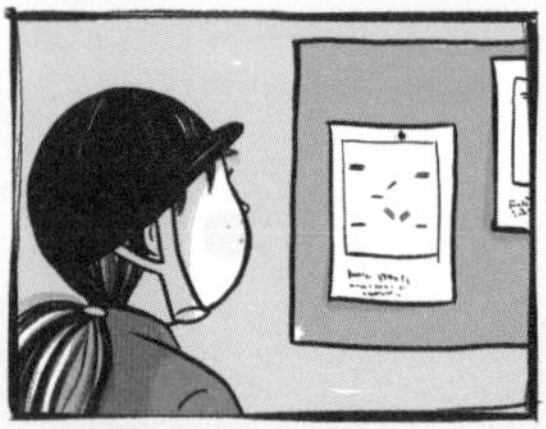

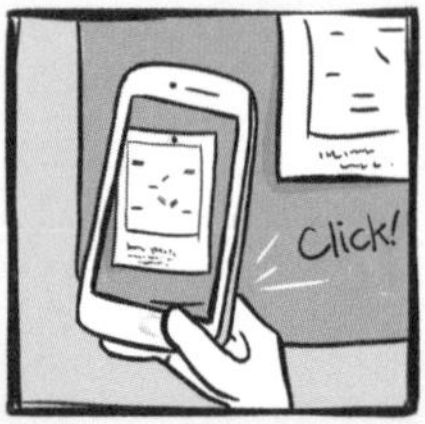
Click!

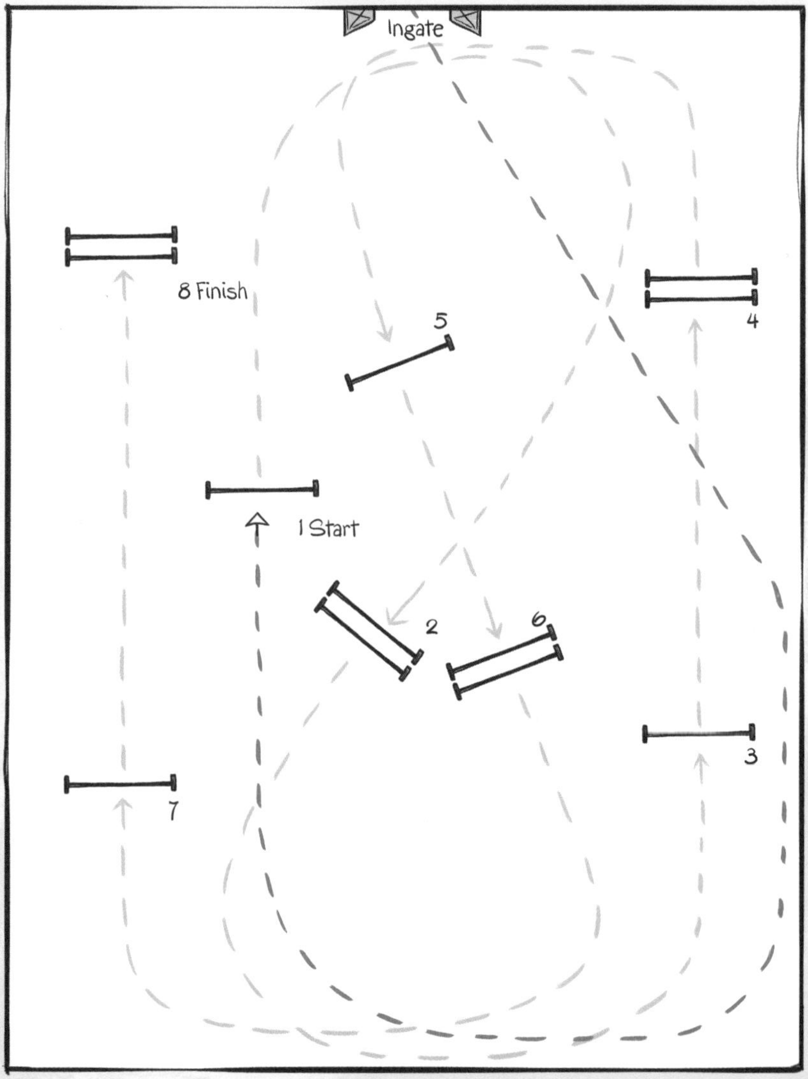
Ingate
8 Finish
5
4
1 Start
2
6
3
7

Entering the ring is always scary. Just you and your horse. Everyone watching.

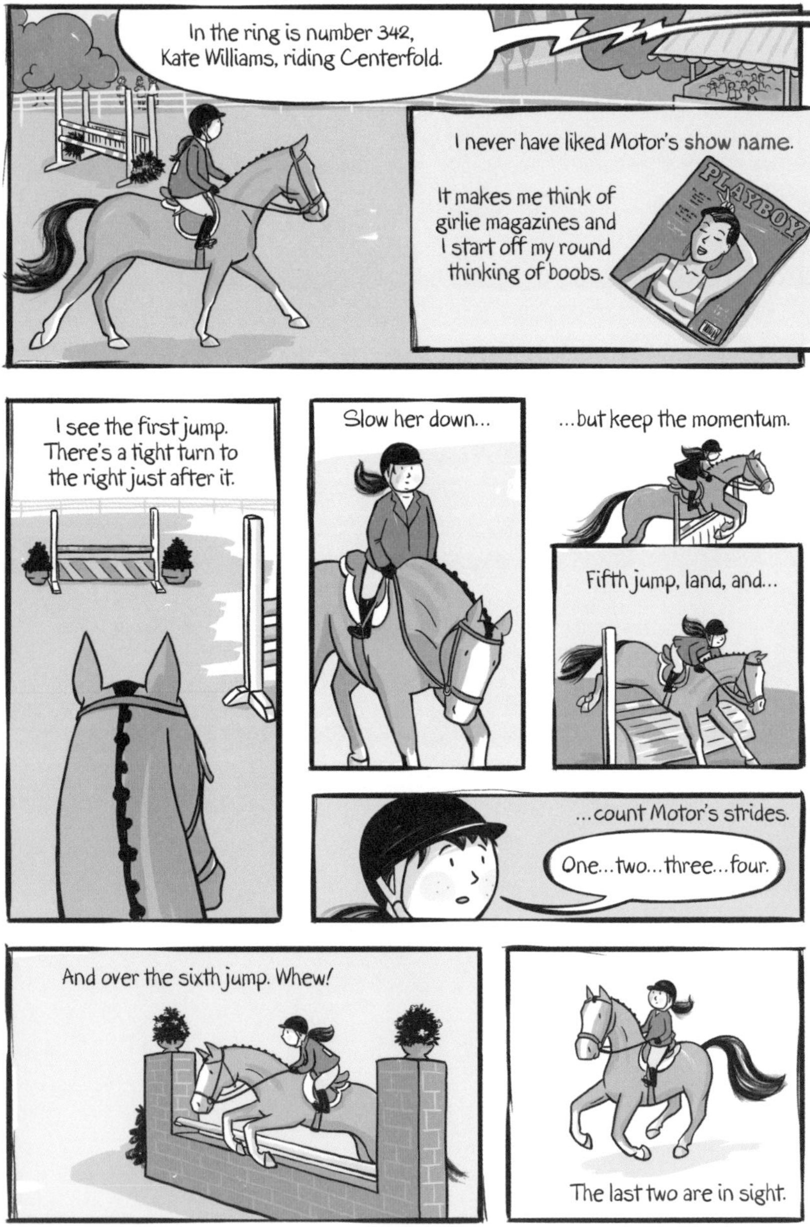
In the ring is number 342,
Kate Williams, riding Centerfold.
I never have liked Motor's show name.
It makes me think of girlie magazines and I start off my round thinking of boobs.
PLAYBOY
I see the first jump. There's a tight turn to the right just after it.
Slow her down...
...but keep the momentum.
Fifth jump, land, and...
...count Motor's strides.
One...two...three...four.
And over the sixth jump. Whew!
The last two are in sight.

Show name: Often horses use a different name (usually flashier, longer, or descriptive of their personality or physical traits) when they are competing at a horse show.

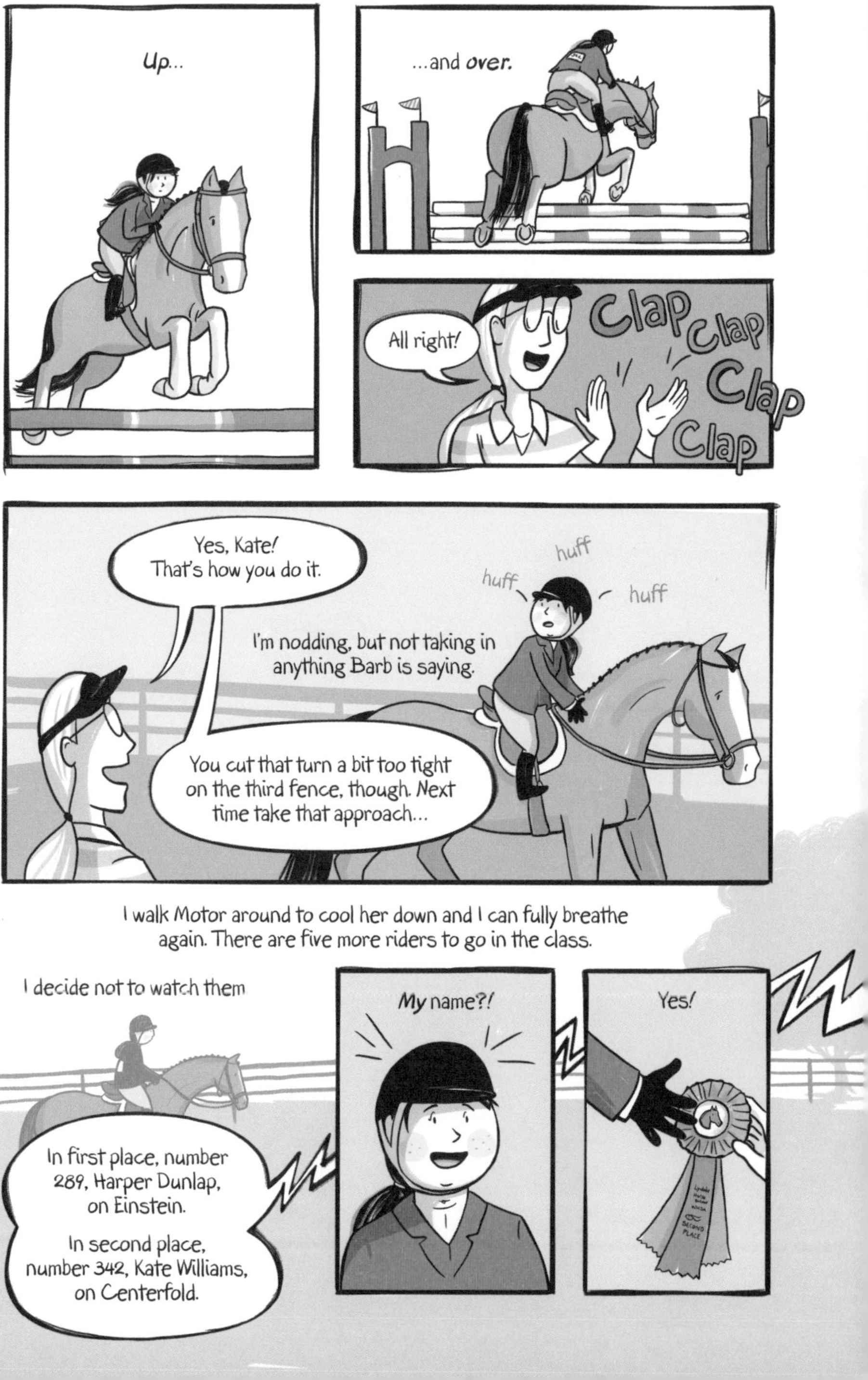
Up...
...and over.
All right!
Clap Clap Clap Clap
Yes, Kate! That's how you do it.
huff huff huff
I'm nodding, but not taking in anything Barb is saying.
You cut that turn a bit too tight on the third fence, though. Next time take that approach...
I walk Motor around to cool her down and I can fully breathe again. There are five more riders to go in the class.
I decide not to watch them.
In first place, number 289, Harper Dunlap, on Einstein.
In second place, number 342, Kate Williams, on Centerfold.
My name?!
Yes!

I walk Motor back to the trailer the long way.

pat

pat

I want to soak in every last second of my time sitting upon Motor's back...

...and replay the near win again in my mind.

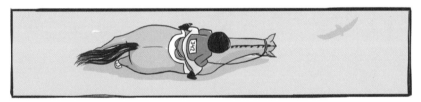

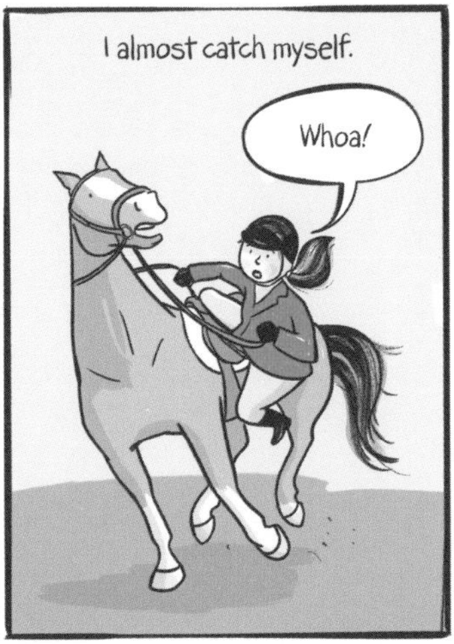
I almost catch myself.
Whoa!

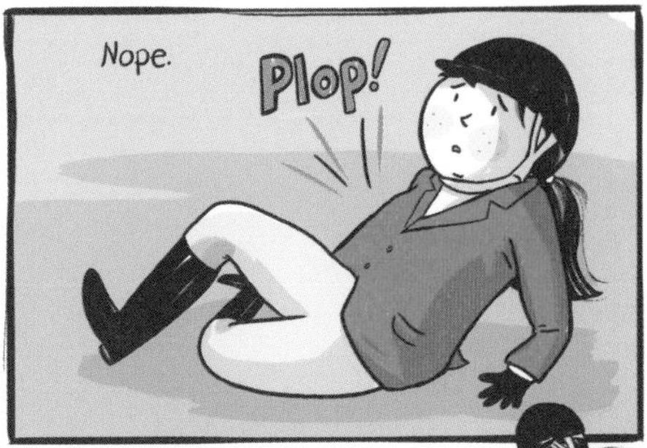
Nope.
Plop!

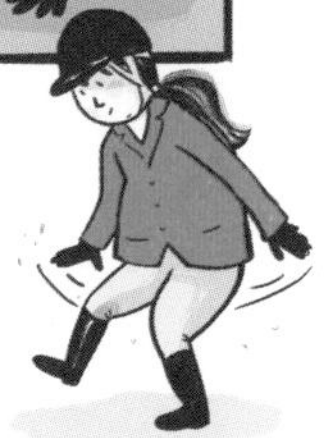

I laugh at myself while brushing off the dirt.

I don't think anyone saw me, but I don't want to leave any evidence of my spill.

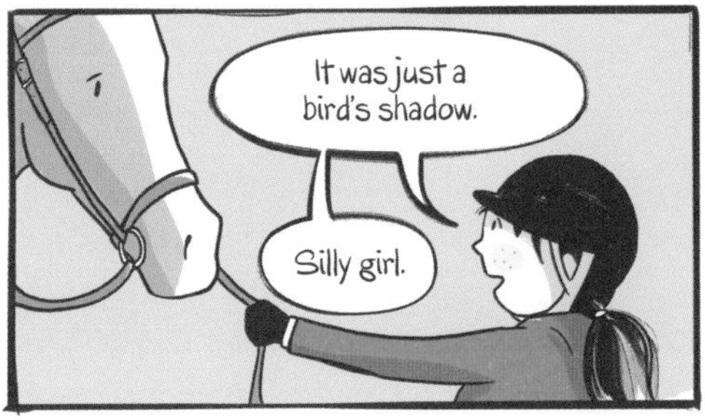
It was just a bird's shadow.
Silly girl.

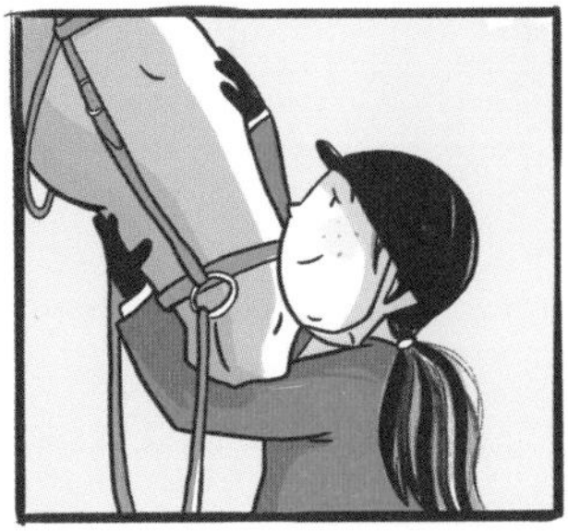

I walk Motor back to the trailer. Jana is there.

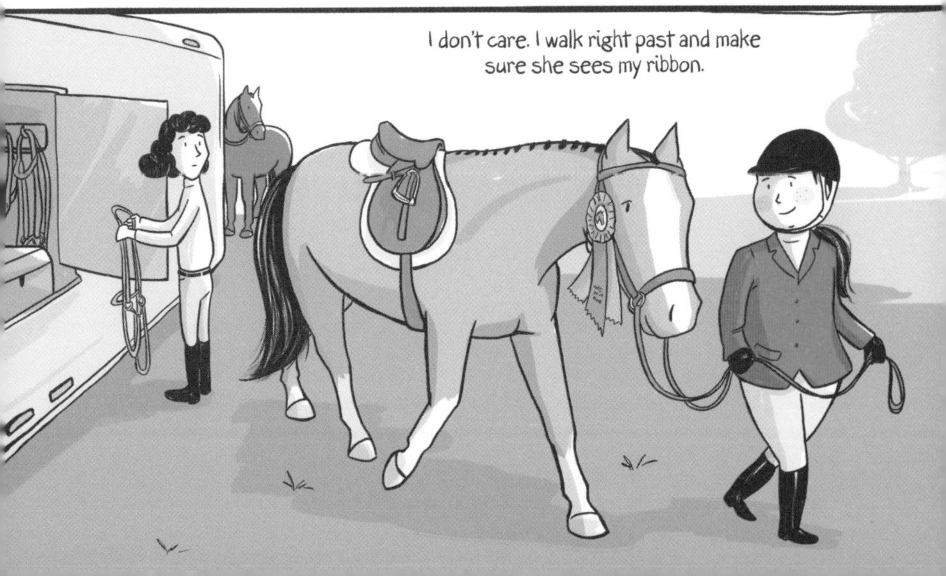
I don't care. I walk right past and make sure she sees my ribbon.

Chapter 5
Stream Dunk

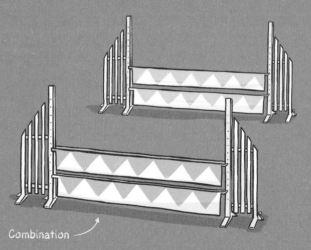

Combination

Two (or three) jumps in succession with no more than two strides between each.

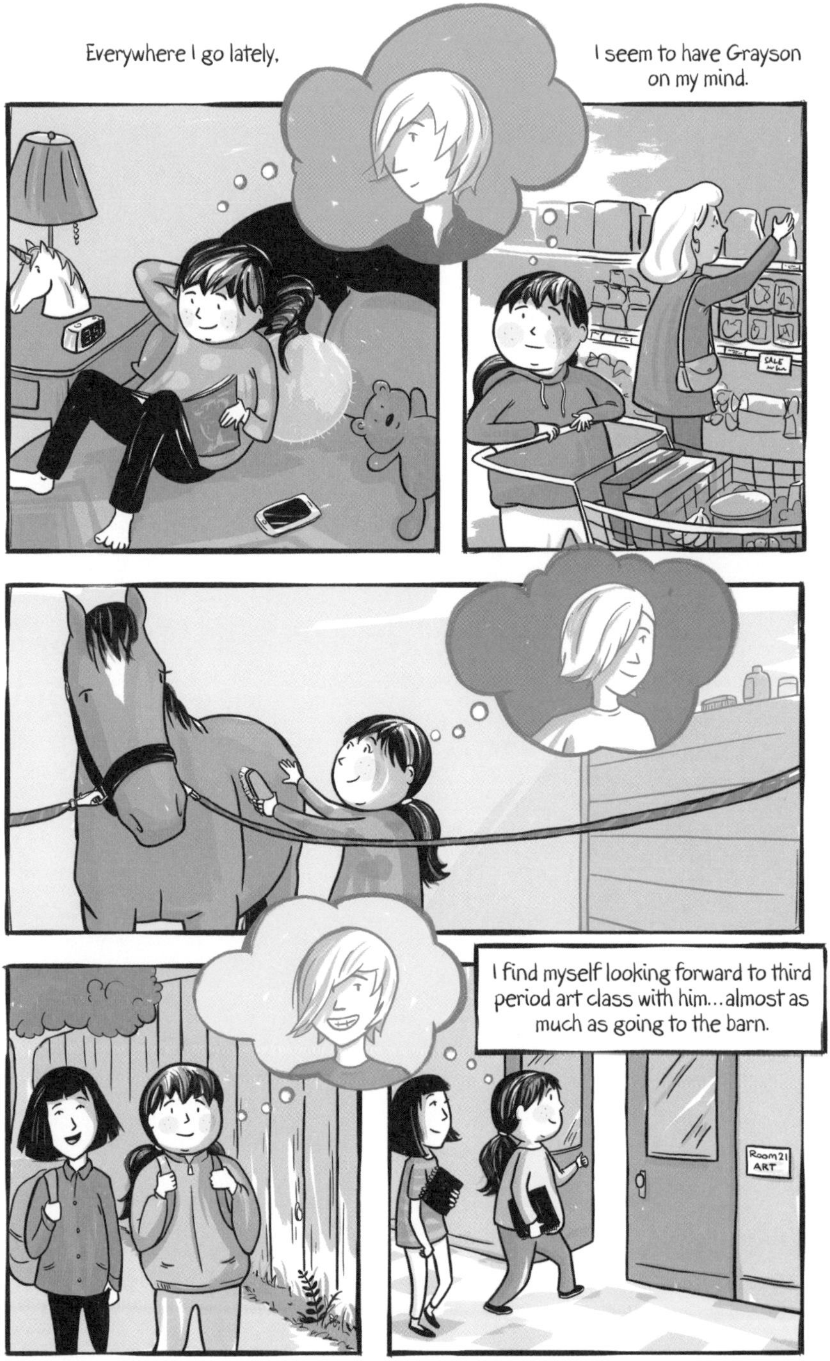
Everywhere I go lately,
I seem to have Grayson on my mind.
SALE
I find myself looking forward to third period art class with him...almost as much as going to the barn.
Room 21 ART

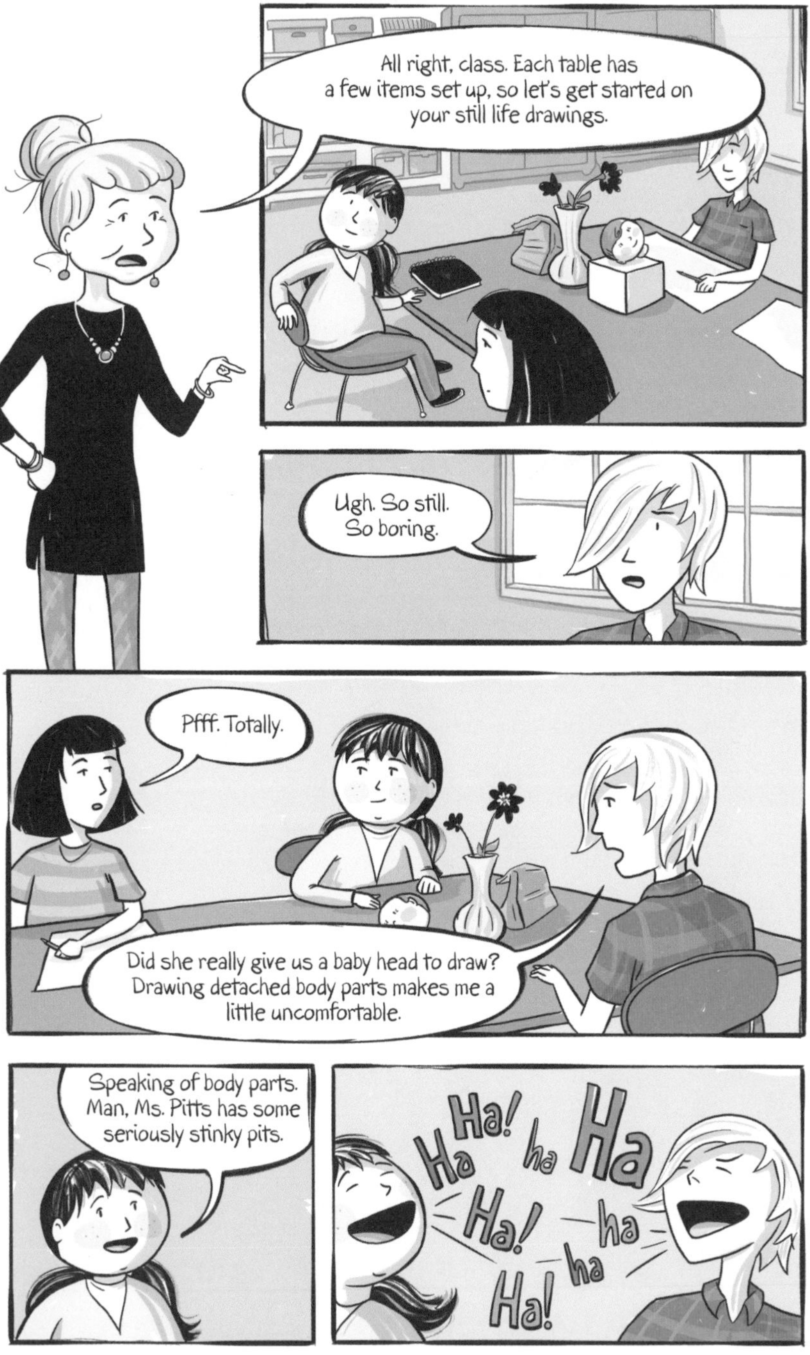
All right, class. Each table has a few items set up, so let's get started on your still life drawings.
Ugh. So still. So boring.
Pfff. Totally.
Did she really give us a baby head to draw? Drawing detached body parts makes me a little uncomfortable.
Speaking of body parts. Man, Ms. Pitts has some seriously stinky pits.
Ha Ha! ha Ha Ha! ha ha Ha!

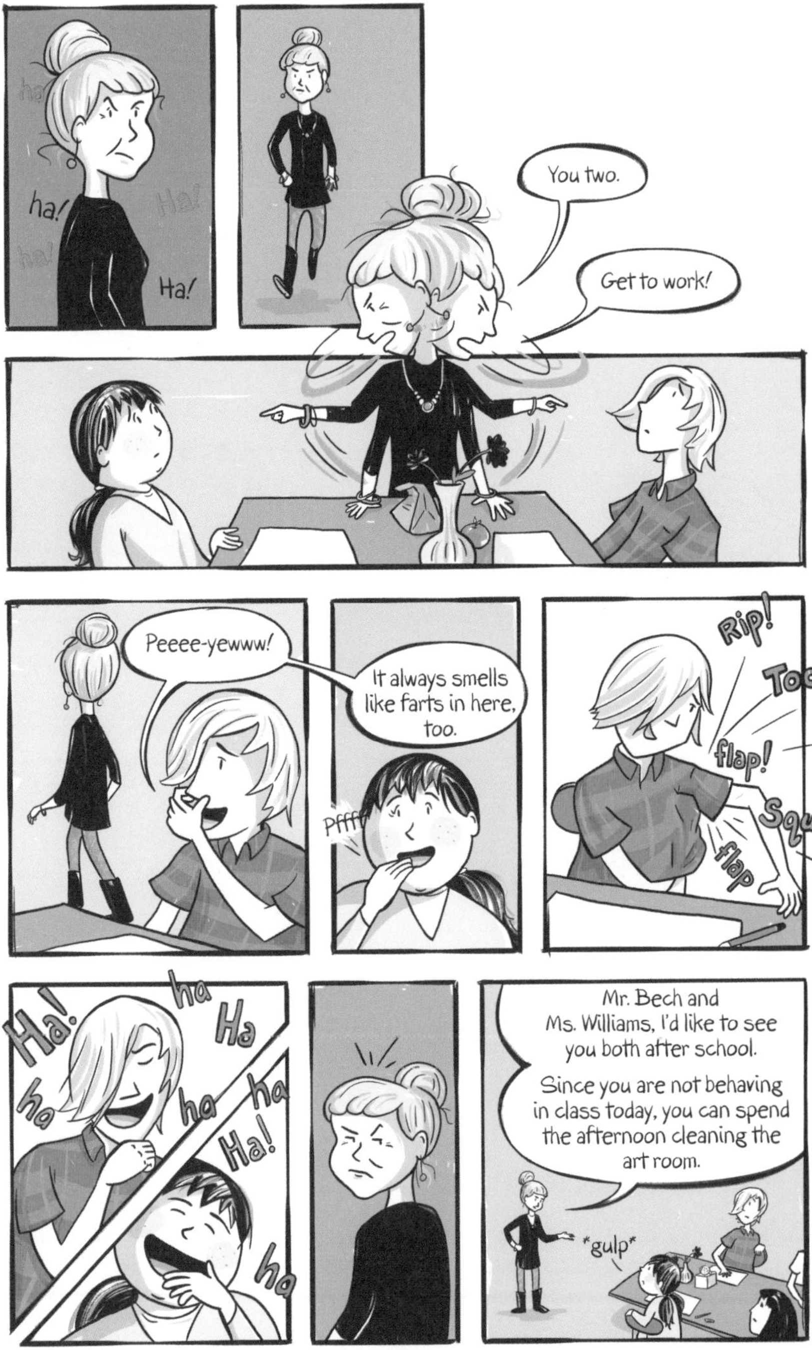
ha!
Ha!
Ha!
You two.
Get to work!
Peeee-yewww!
It always smells like farts in here, too.
Pfff
Rip!
Toot!
flap!
Squirt!
flap
Ha!
ha
Ha
ha
ha
ha
Ha!
ha
Mr. Bech and Ms. Williams, I'd like to see you both after school.
Since you are not behaving in class today, you can spend the afternoon cleaning the art room.
gulp

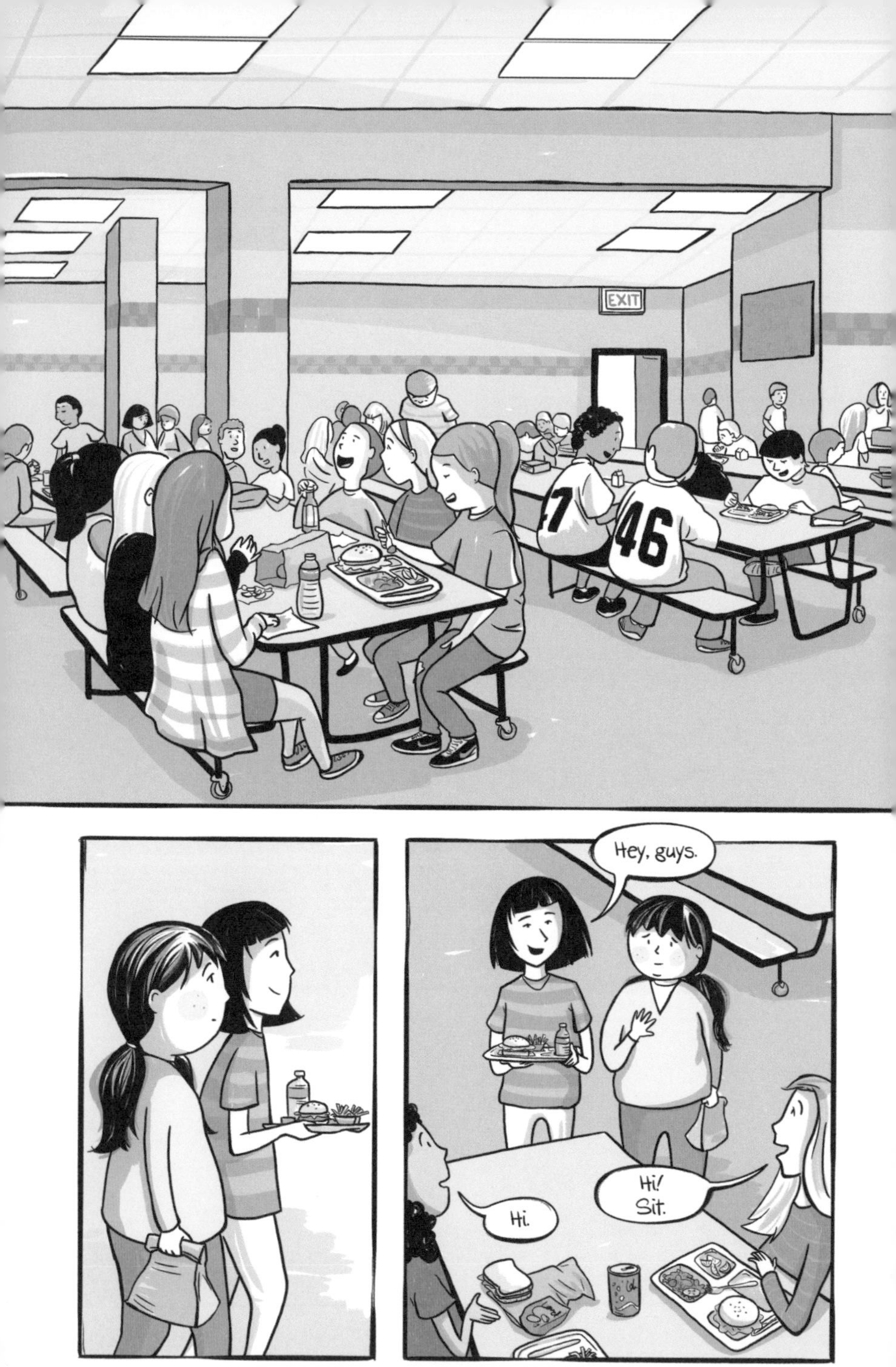
EXIT
Hey, guys.
Hi.
Hi!
Sit.

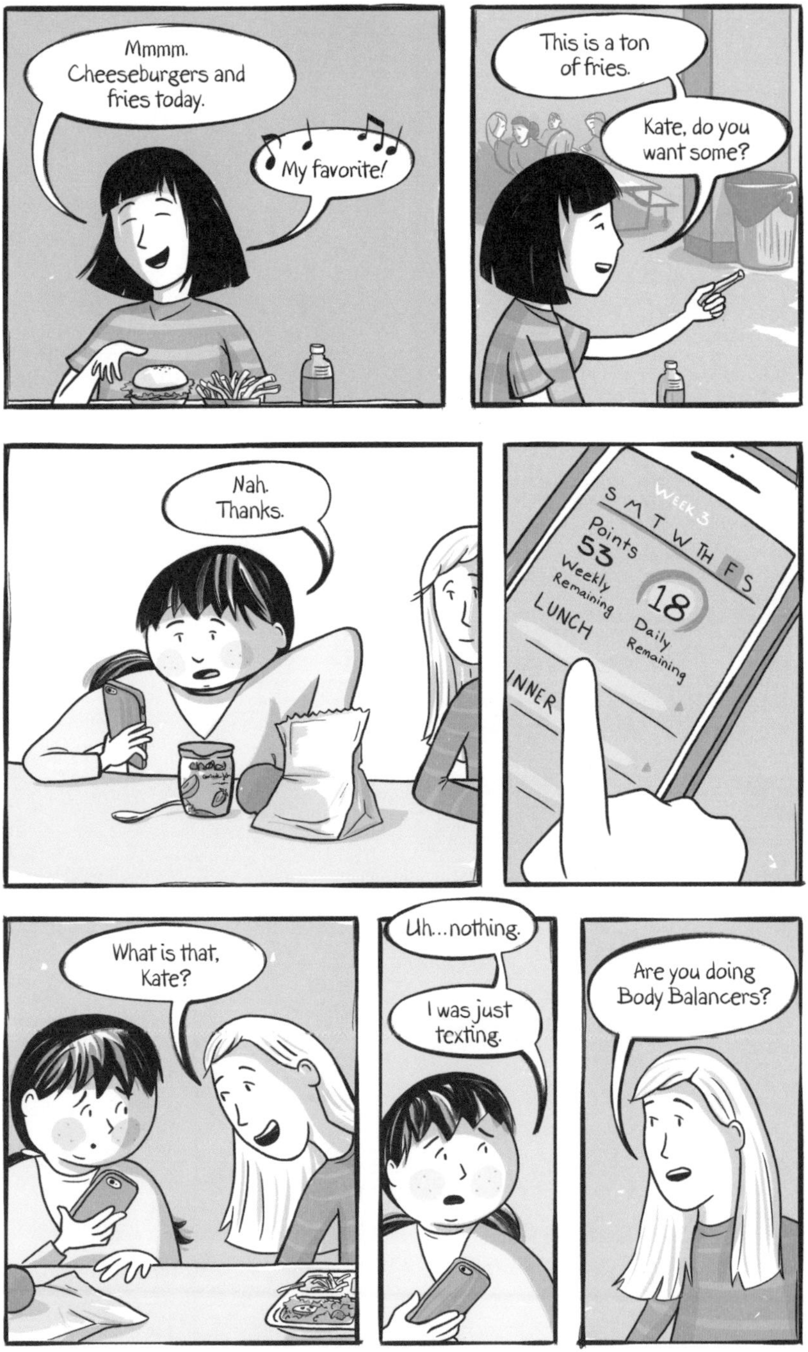
Mmmm. Cheeseburgers and fries today.
My favorite!
This is a ton of fries.
Kate, do you want some?
Nah. Thanks.
WEEK 3
S M T W TH F S
Points
53
Weekly Remaining
18
Daily Remaining
LUNCH
INNER
What is that, Kate?
Uh...nothing.
I was just texting.
Are you doing Body Balancers?

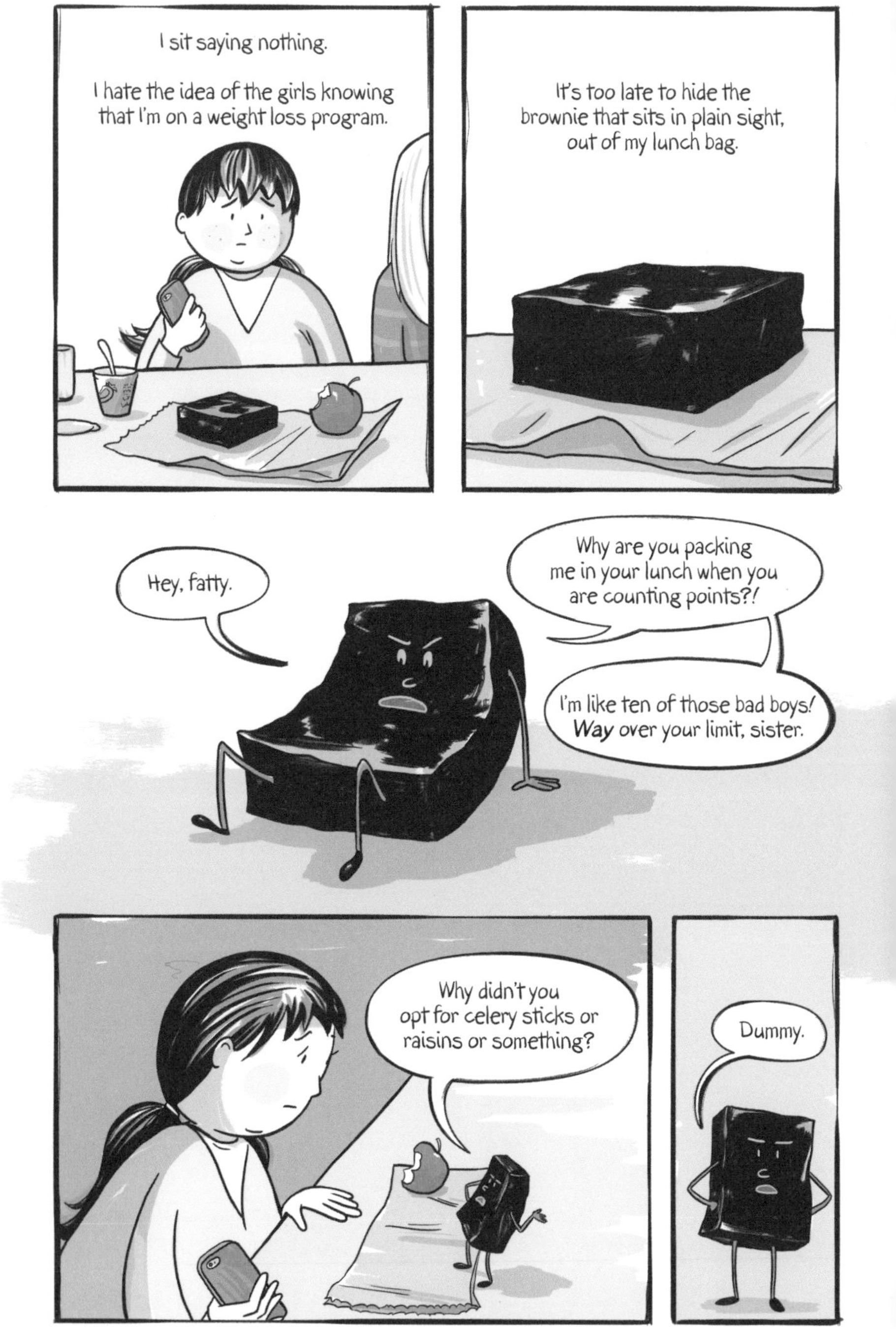
I sit saying nothing.
I hate the idea of the girls knowing that I'm on a weight loss program.
It's too late to hide the brownie that sits in plain sight, out of my lunch bag.
Hey, fatty.
Why are you packing me in your lunch when you are counting points?!
I'm like ten of those bad boys! *Way* over your limit, sister.
Why didn't you opt for celery sticks or raisins or something?
Dummy.

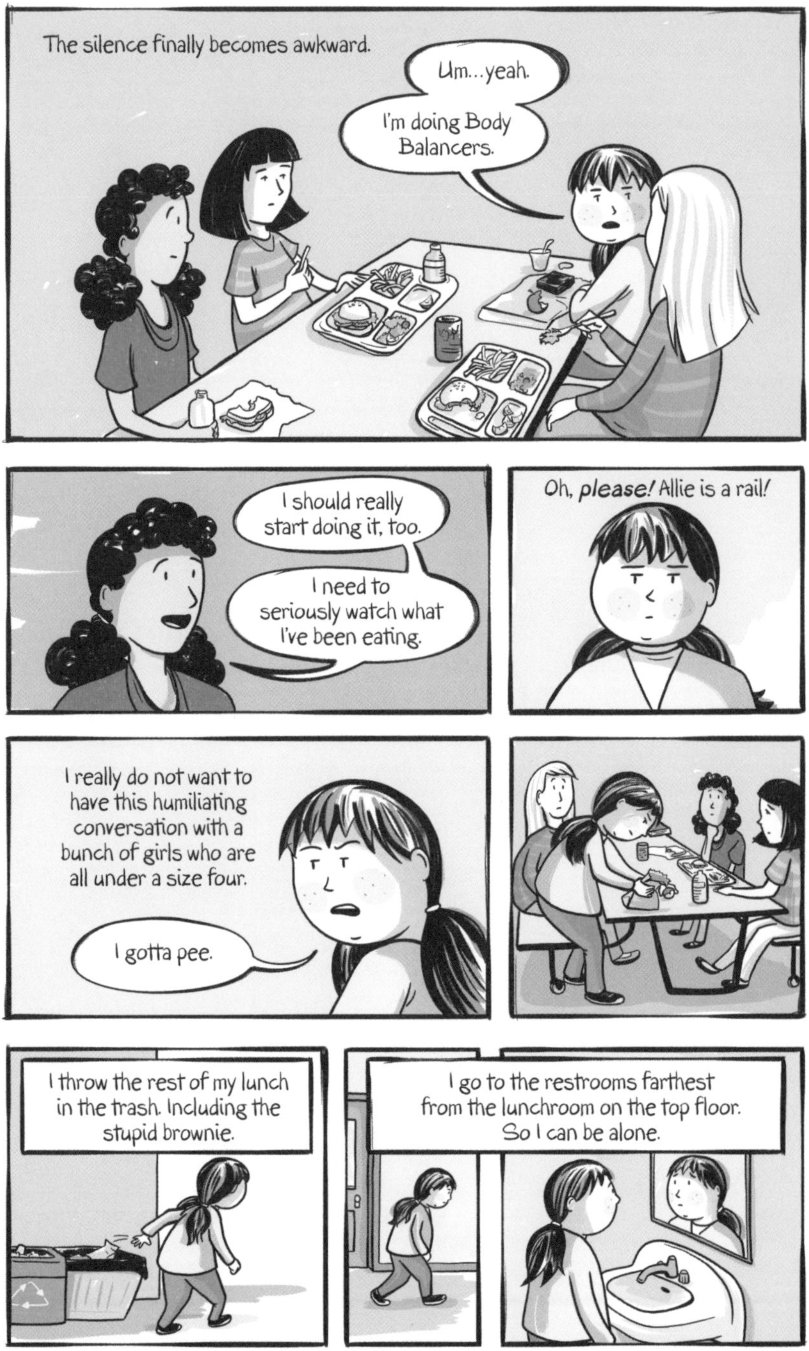

The silence finally becomes awkward.
Um...yeah.
I'm doing Body Balancers.
I should really start doing it, too.
I need to seriously watch what I've been eating.
Oh, *please!* Allie is a rail!
I really do not want to have this humiliating conversation with a bunch of girls who are all under a size four.
I gotta pee.
I throw the rest of my lunch in the trash. Including the stupid brownie.
I go to the restrooms farthest from the lunchroom on the top floor. So I can be alone.

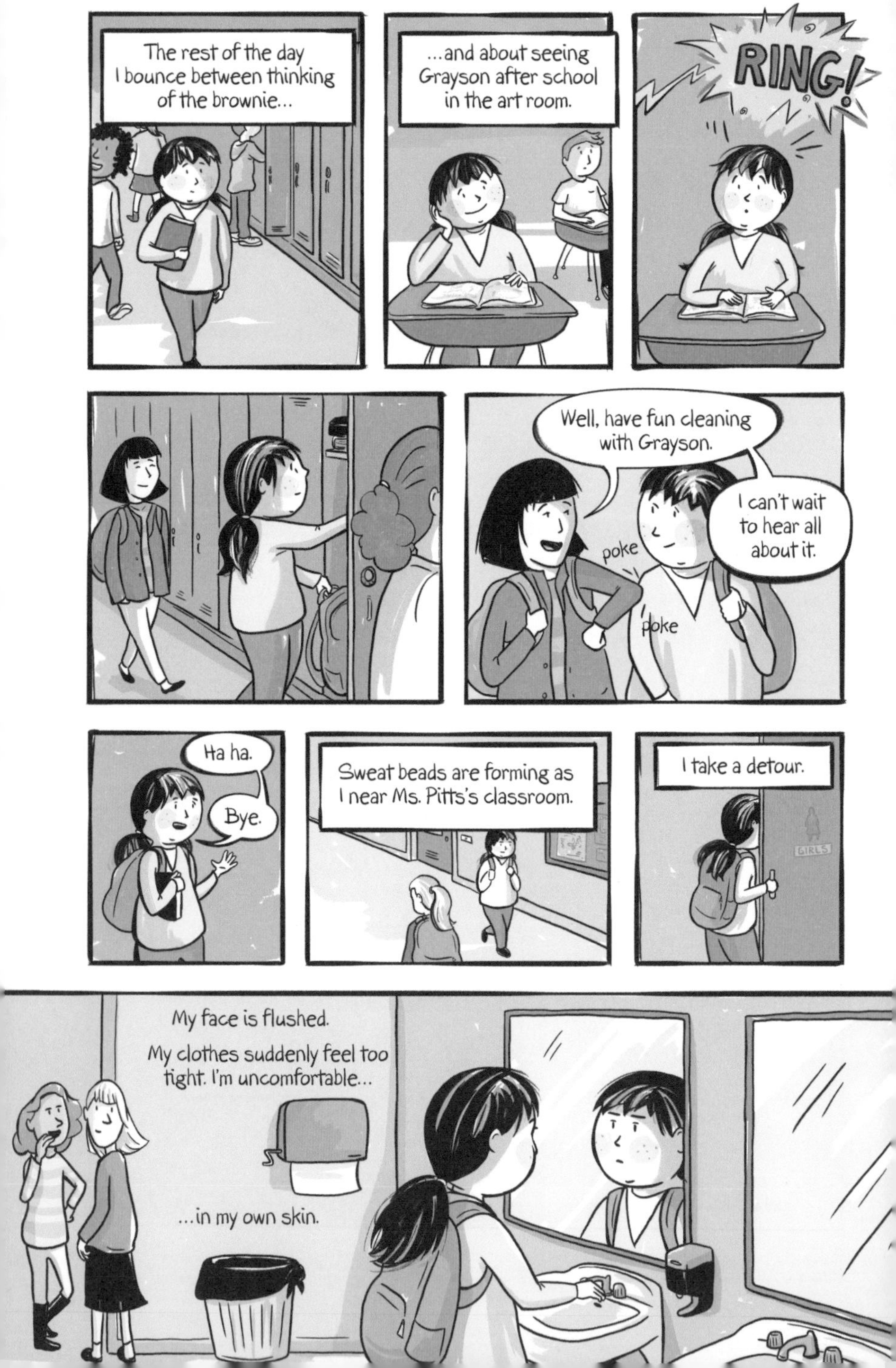

The rest of the day I bounce between thinking of the brownie...
...and about seeing Grayson after school in the art room.
RING!
Well, have fun cleaning with Grayson.
I can't wait to hear all about it.
poke
poke
Ha ha.
Bye.
Sweat beads are forming as I near Ms. Pitts's classroom.
I take a detour.
GIRLS
My face is flushed.
My clothes suddenly feel too tight. I'm uncomfortable...
...in my own skin.

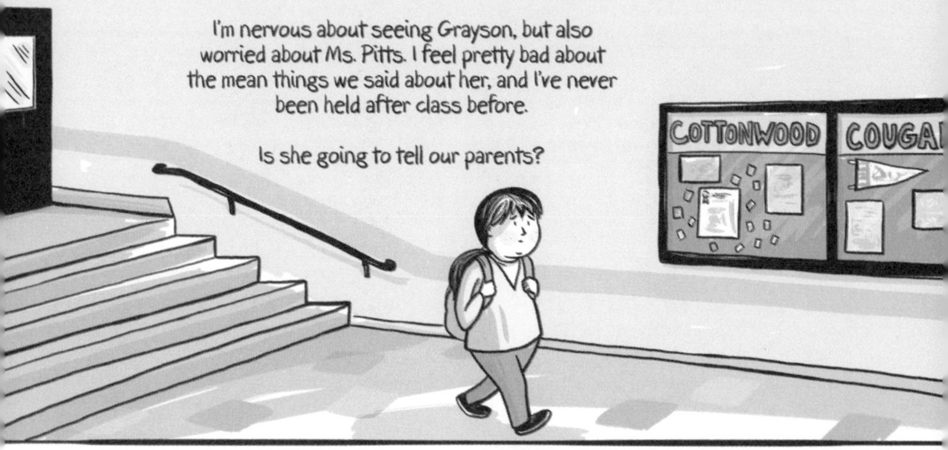
I'm nervous about seeing Grayson, but also worried about Ms. Pitts. I feel pretty bad about the mean things we said about her, and I've never been held after class before.
Is she going to tell our parents?
COTTONWOOD
COUGA

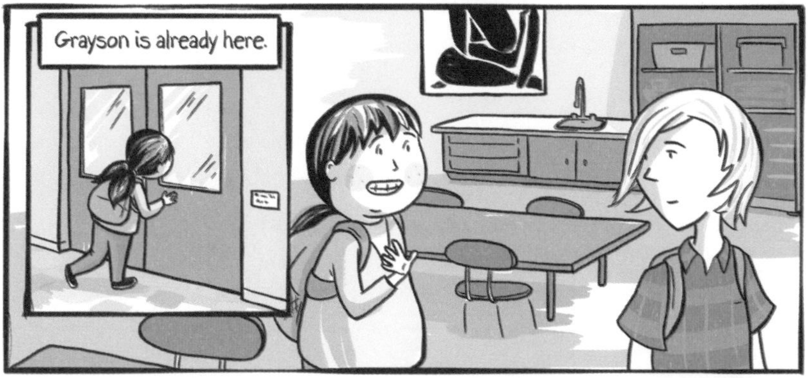
Grayson is already here.

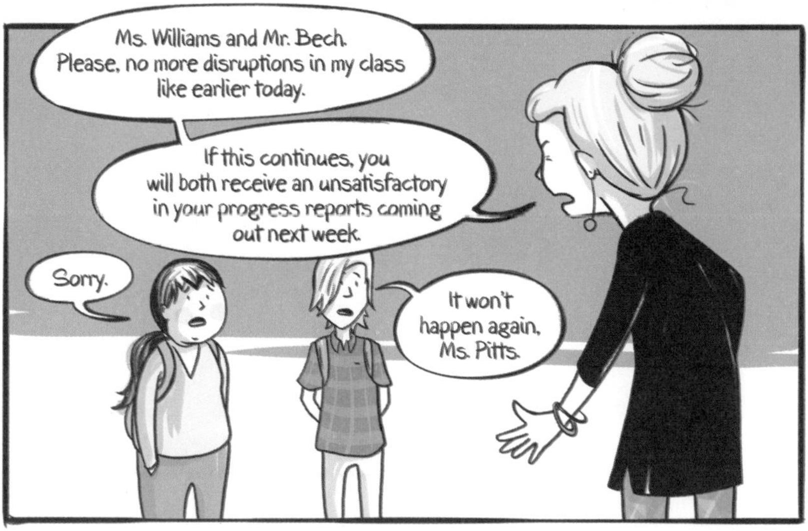
Ms. Williams and Mr. Bech. Please, no more disruptions in my class like earlier today.
If this continues, you will both receive an unsatisfactory in your progress reports coming out next week.
Sorry.
It won't happen again, Ms. Pitts.

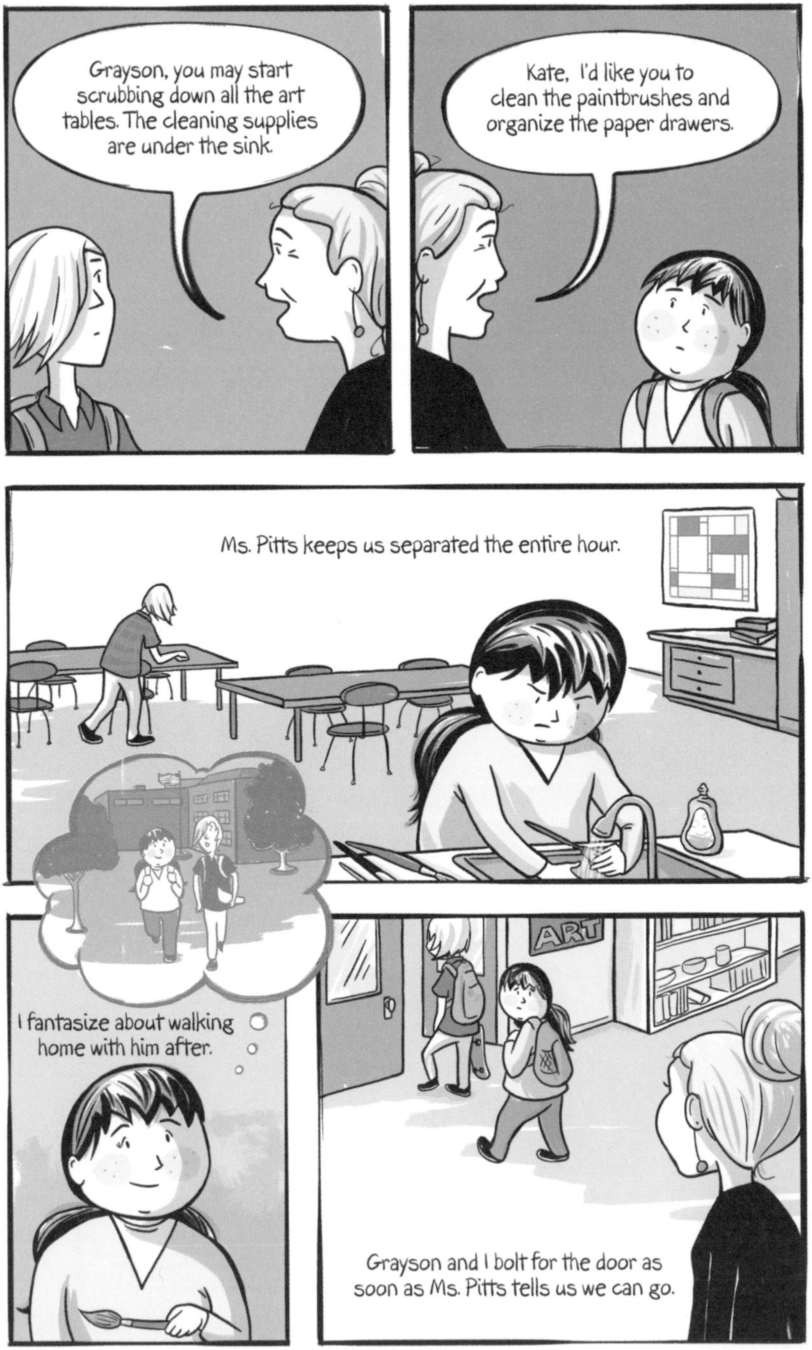

Grayson, you may start scrubbing down all the art tables. The cleaning supplies are under the sink.
Kate, I'd like you to clean the paintbrushes and organize the paper drawers.
Ms. Pitts keeps us separated the entire hour.
I fantasize about walking home with him after.
ART
Grayson and I bolt for the door as soon as Ms. Pitts tells us we can go.

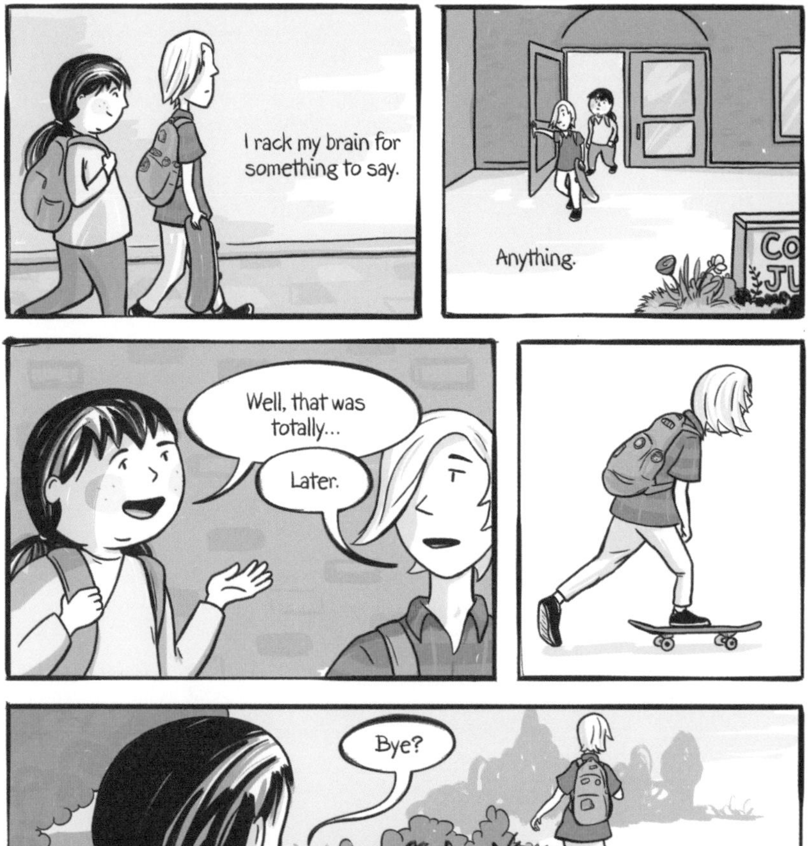
I rack my brain for something to say.
Anything.
Well, that was totally...
Later.
Bye?

I'm starving since I trashed most of my lunch, but I've got some money in my backpack.

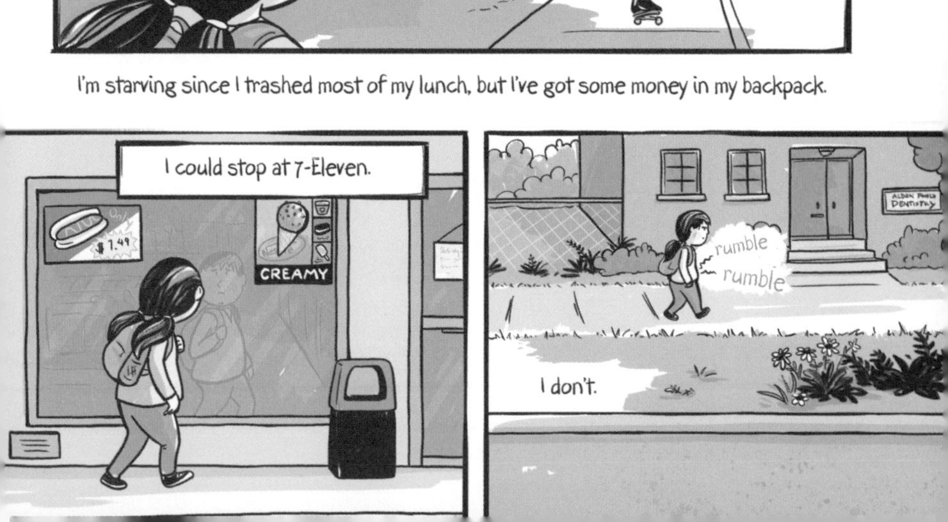
I could stop at 7-Eleven.
$7.49
CREAMY
rumble
rumble
I don't.

Knock

Knock

Hey, hon.
I've got your laundry.

'Kay.

Thanks.

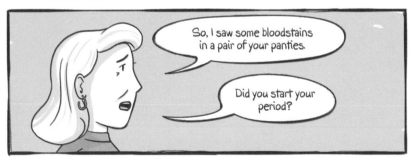

So, I saw some bloodstains
in a pair of your panties.

Did you start your
period?

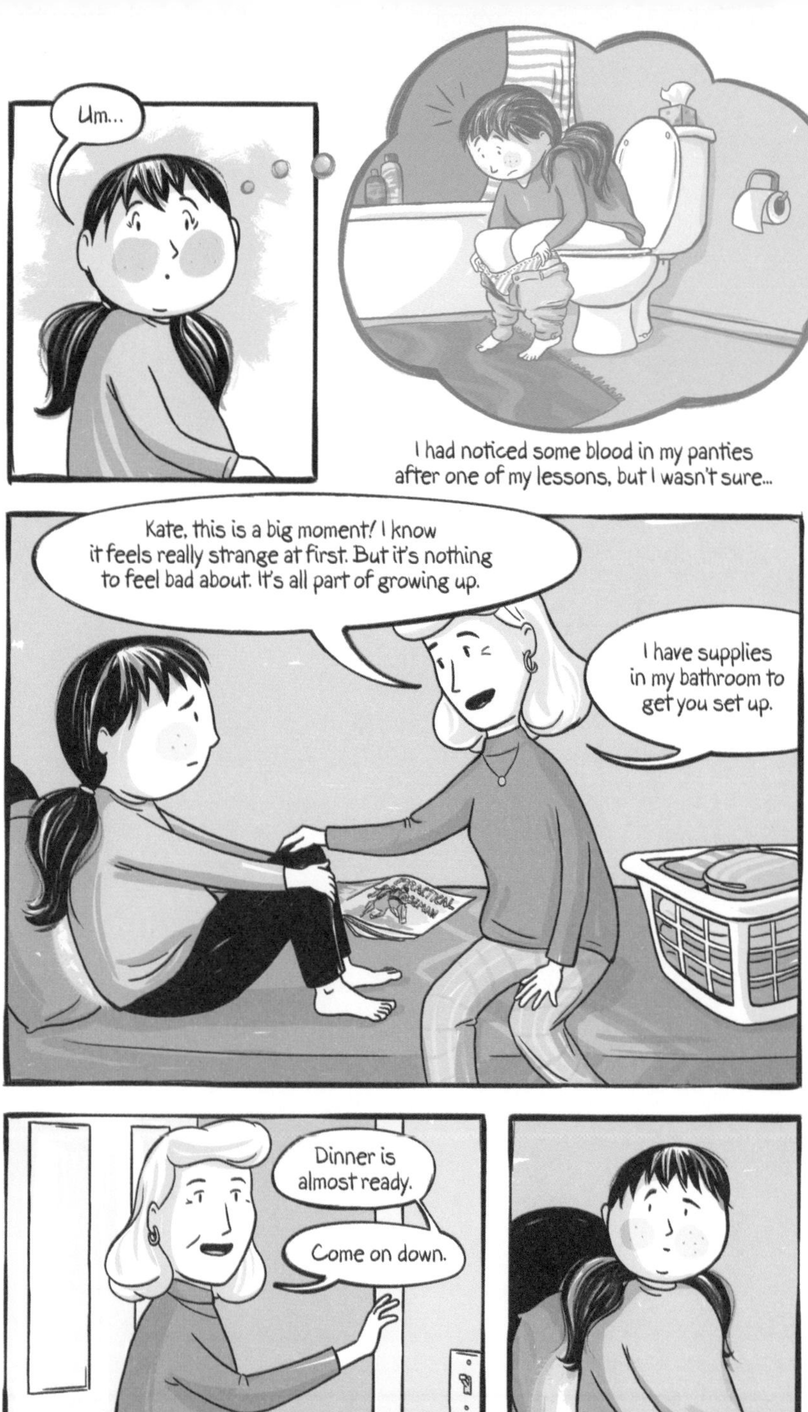
Um...
I had noticed some blood in my panties after one of my lessons, but I wasn't sure...
Kate, this is a big moment! I know it feels really strange at first. But it's nothing to feel bad about. It's all part of growing up.
I have supplies in my bathroom to get you set up.
Dinner is almost ready.
Come on down.

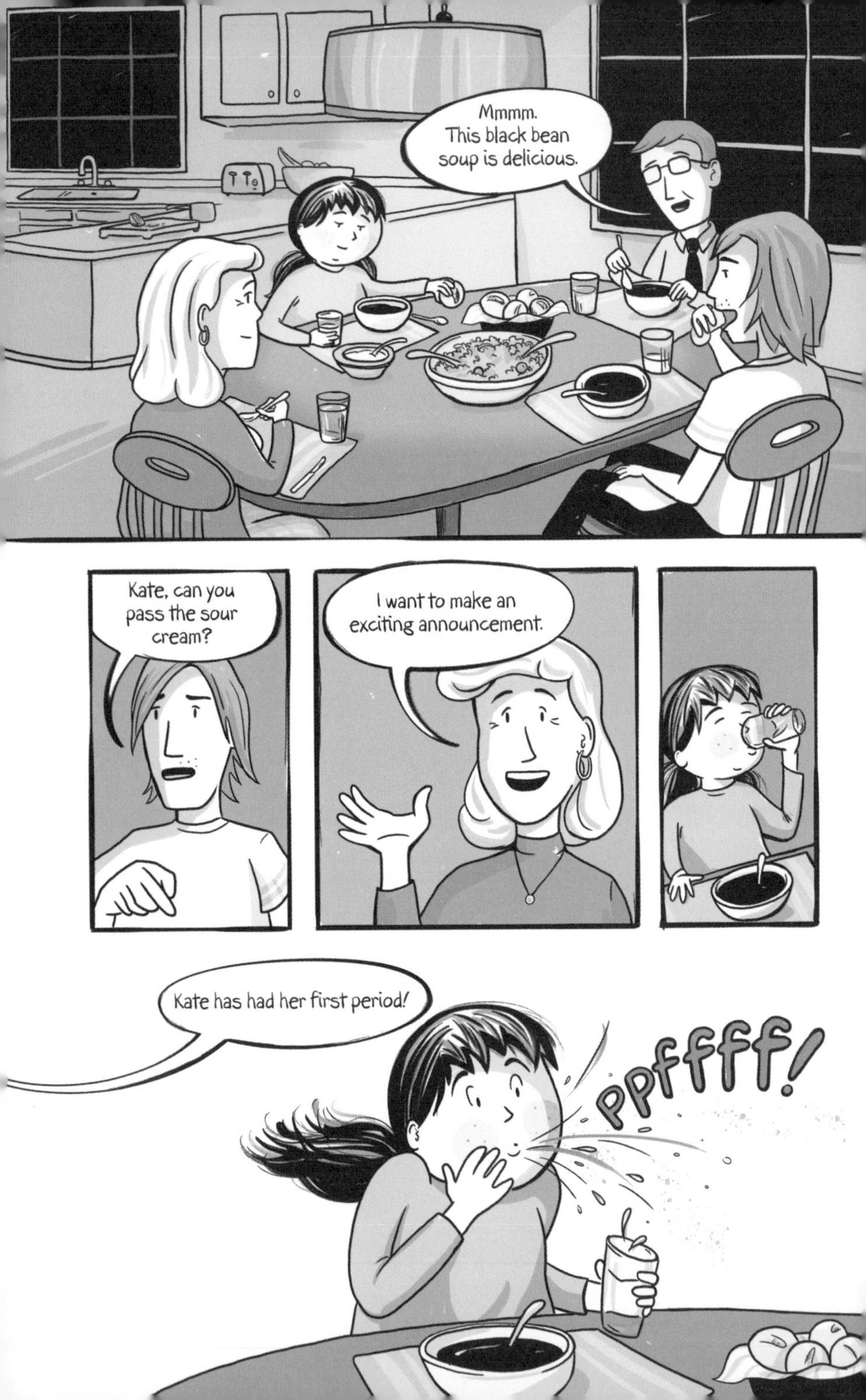
Mmmm.
This black bean soup is delicious.
Kate, can you pass the sour cream?
I want to make an exciting announcement.
Kate has had her first period!
PPFFFF!

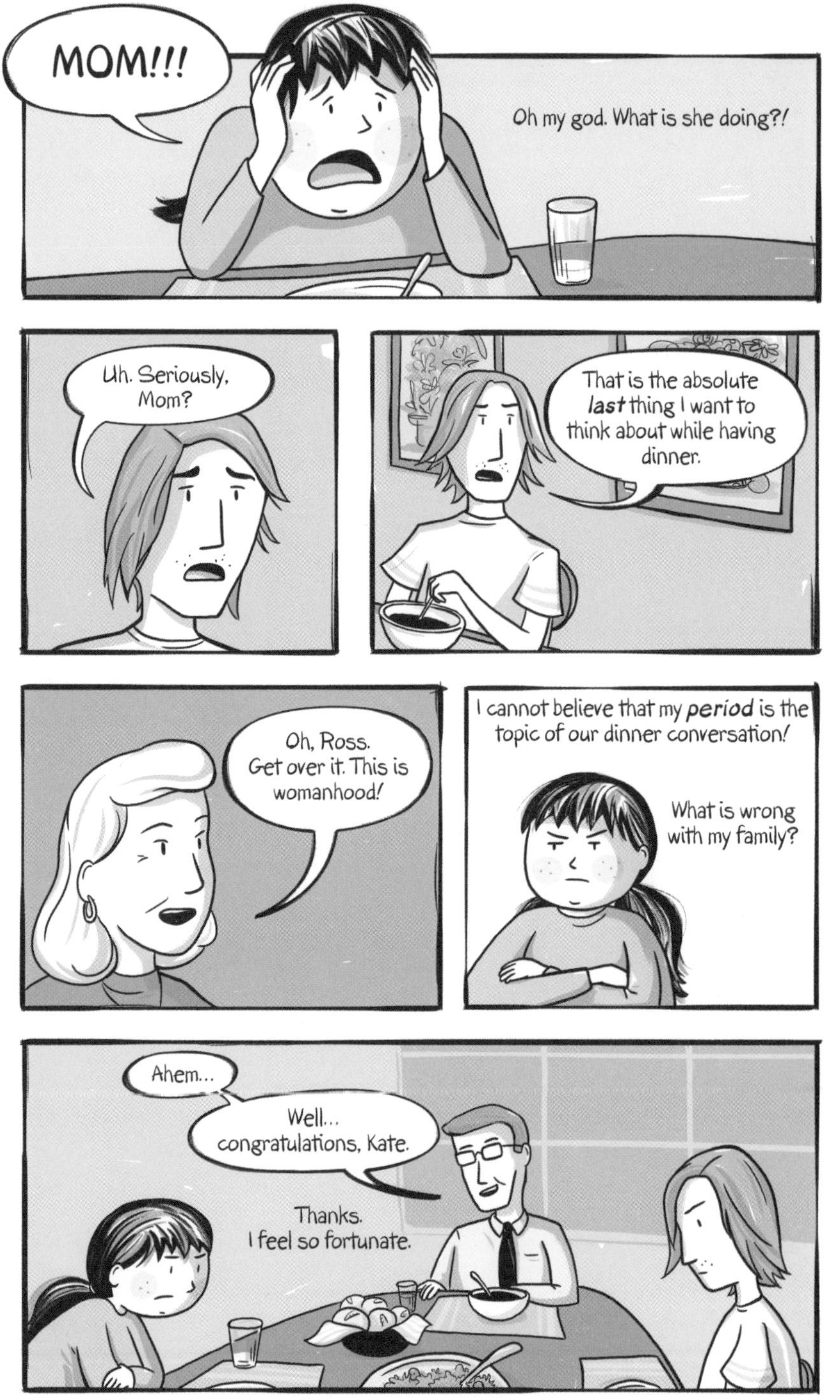
MOM!!!
Oh my god. What is she doing?!
Uh. Seriously, Mom?
That is the absolute *last* thing I want to think about while having dinner.
Oh, Ross. Get over it. This is womanhood!
I cannot believe that my *period* is the topic of our dinner conversation!
What is wrong with my family?
Ahem...
Well... congratulations, Kate.
Thanks. I feel so fortunate.

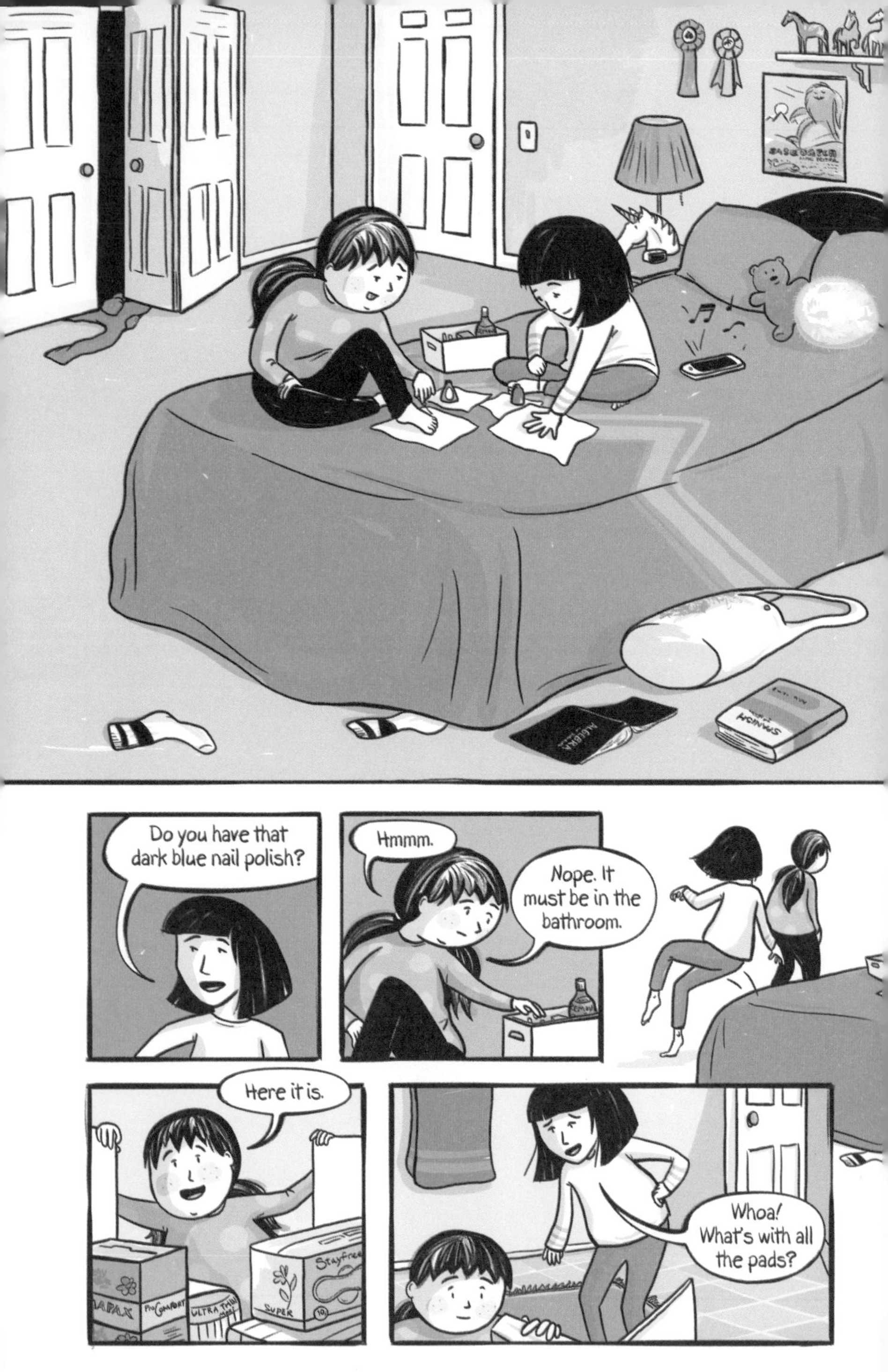
Do you have that dark blue nail polish?
Hmmm.
Nope. It must be in the bathroom.
Here it is.
Whoa! What's with all the pads?

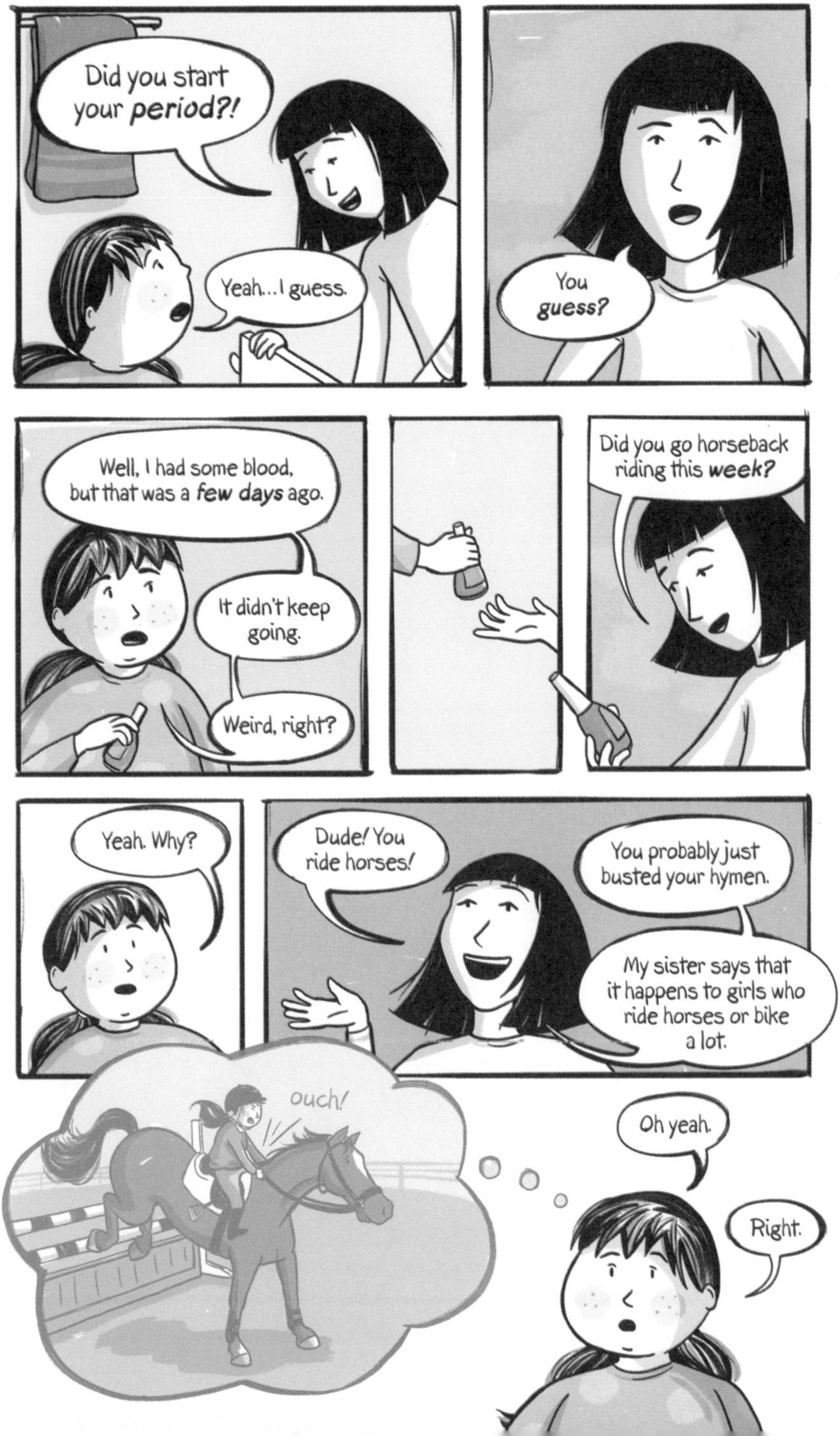
Did you start your *period?!*
Yeah...I guess.
You *guess?*
Well, I had some blood, but that was a *few days* ago.
It didn't keep going.
Weird, right?
Did you go horseback riding this *week?*
Yeah. Why?
Dude! You ride horses!
You probably just busted your hymen.
My sister says that it happens to girls who ride horses or bike a lot.
ouch!
Oh yeah.
Right.

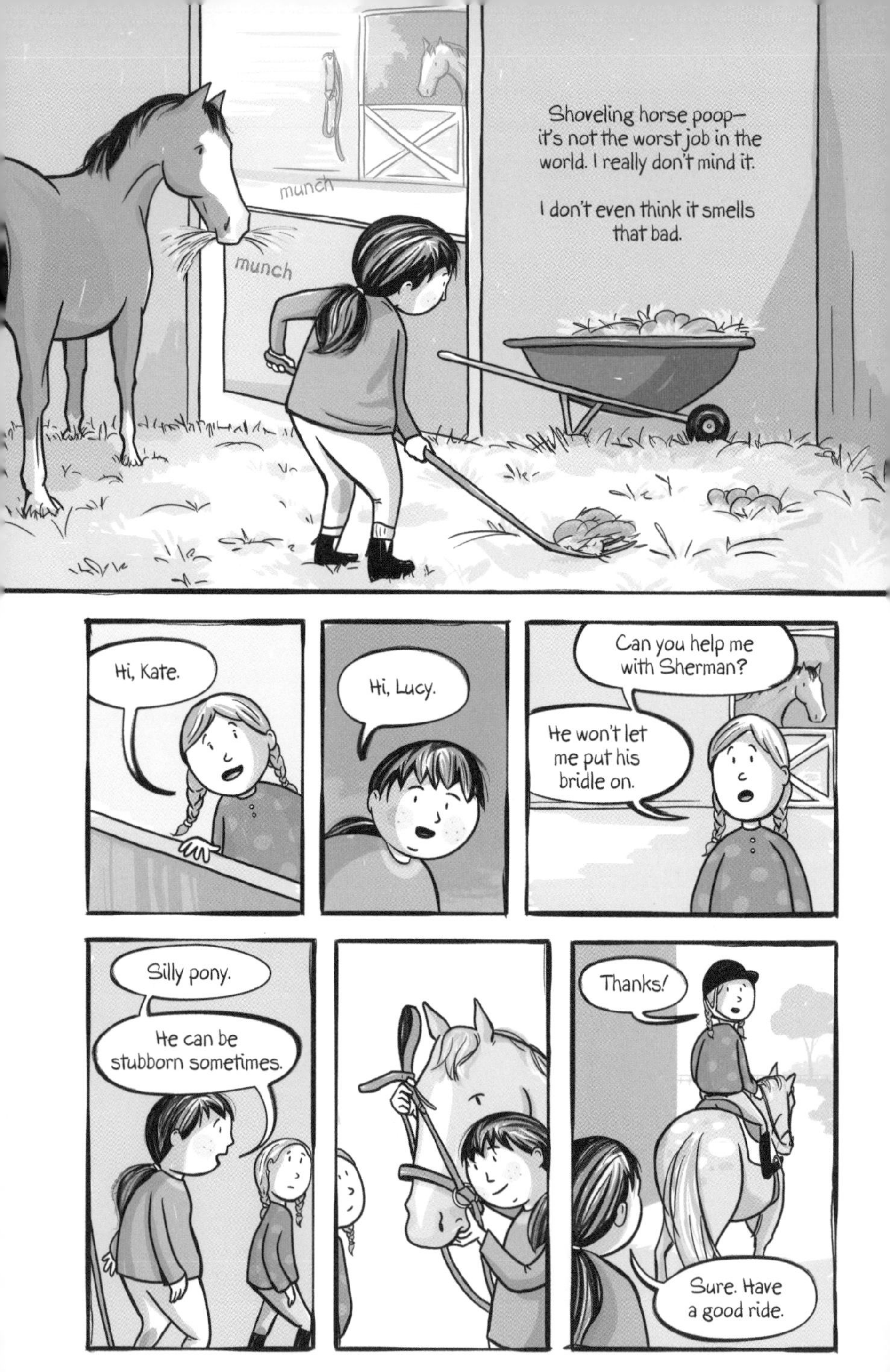

Shoveling horse poop—it's not the worst job in the world. I really don't mind it.
I don't even think it smells that bad.
munch
munch
Hi, Kate.
Hi, Lucy.
Can you help me with Sherman?
He won't let me put his bridle on.
Silly pony.
He can be stubborn sometimes.
Thanks!
Sure. Have a good ride.

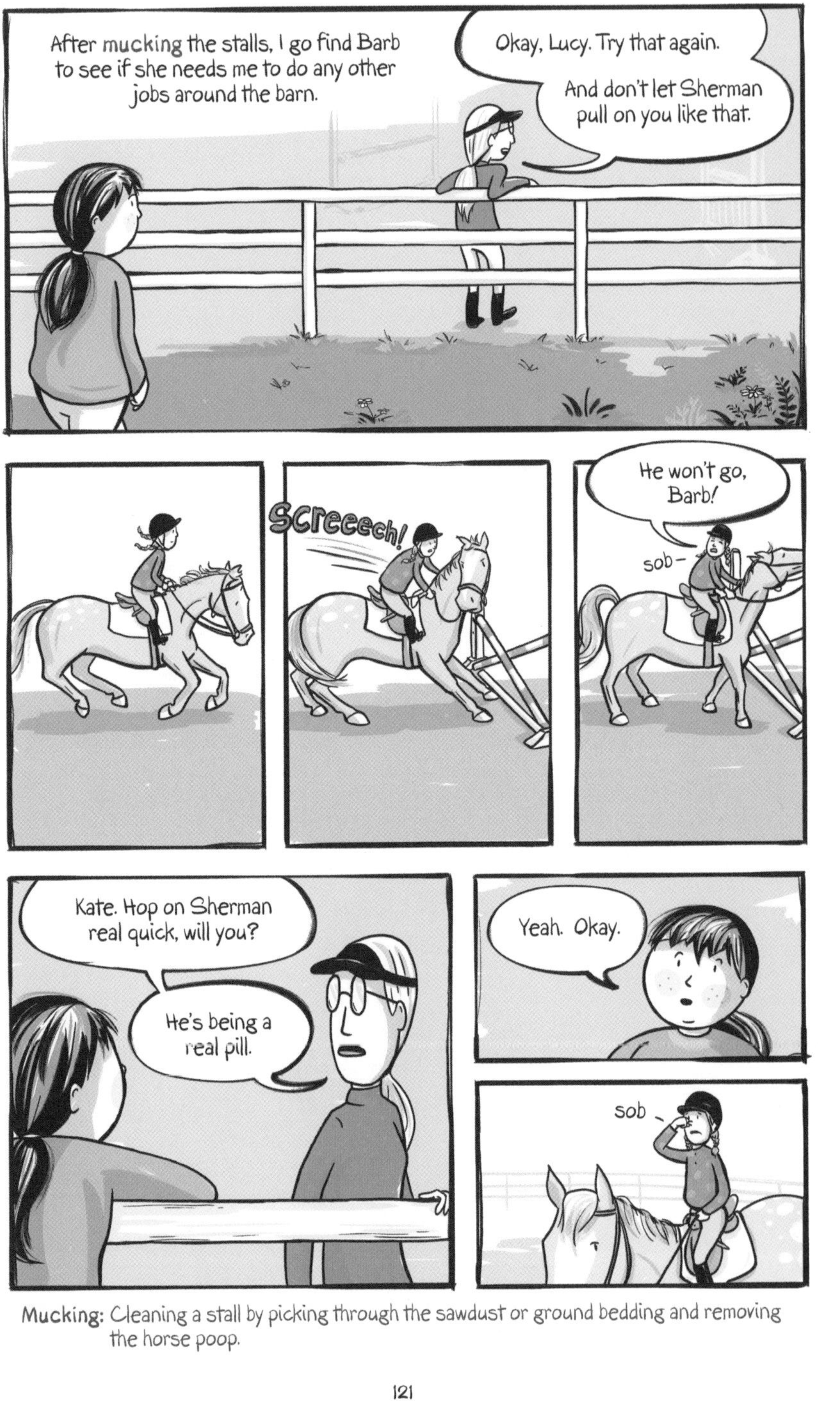
After mucking the stalls, I go find Barb to see if she needs me to do any other jobs around the barn.
Okay, Lucy. Try that again.
And don't let Sherman pull on you like that.
SCREEECH!
He won't go, Barb!
sob–
Kate. Hop on Sherman real quick, will you?
He's being a real pill.
Yeah. Okay.
sob

Mucking: Cleaning a stall by picking through the sawdust or ground bedding and removing the horse poop.

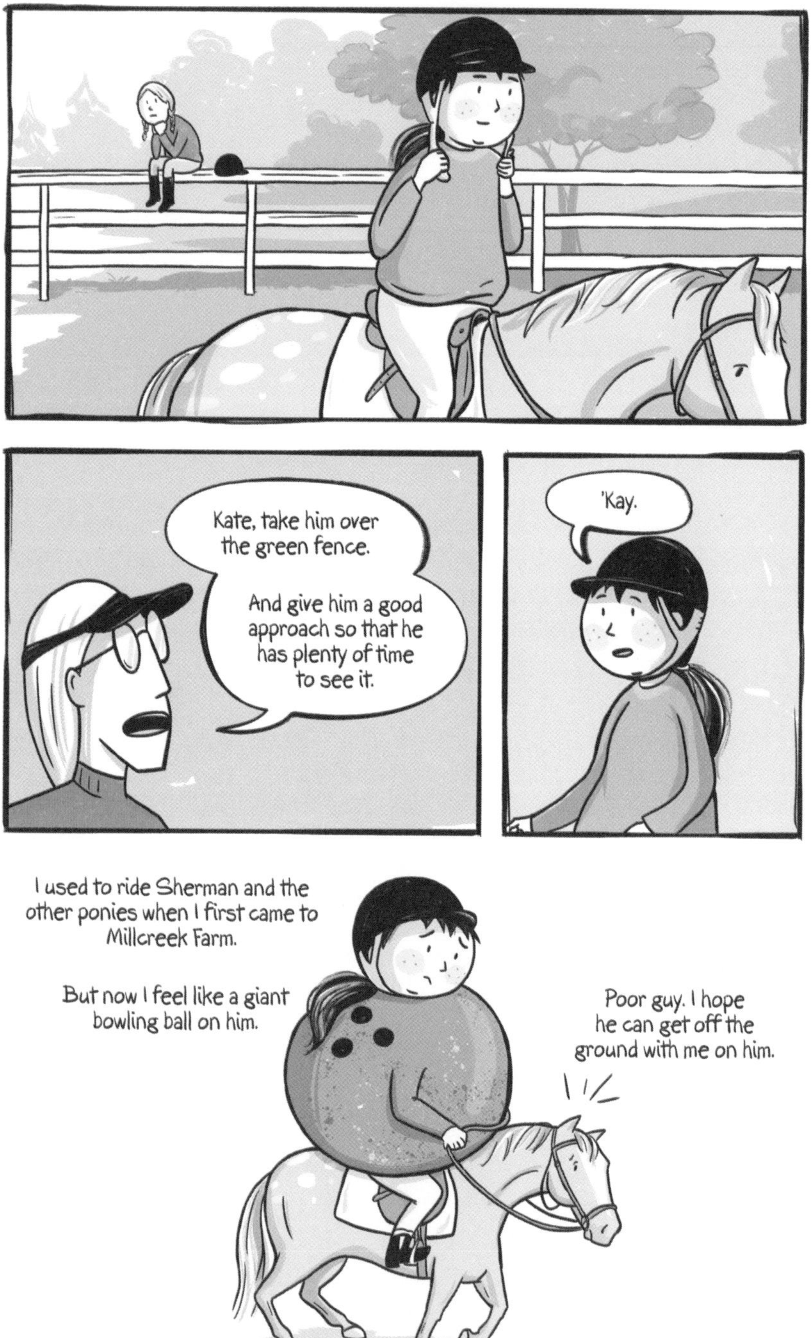
Kate, take him over the green fence.
And give him a good approach so that he has plenty of time to see it.
'Kay.
I used to ride Sherman and the other ponies when I first came to Millcreek Farm.
But now I feel like a giant bowling ball on him.
Poor guy. I hope he can get off the ground with me on him.

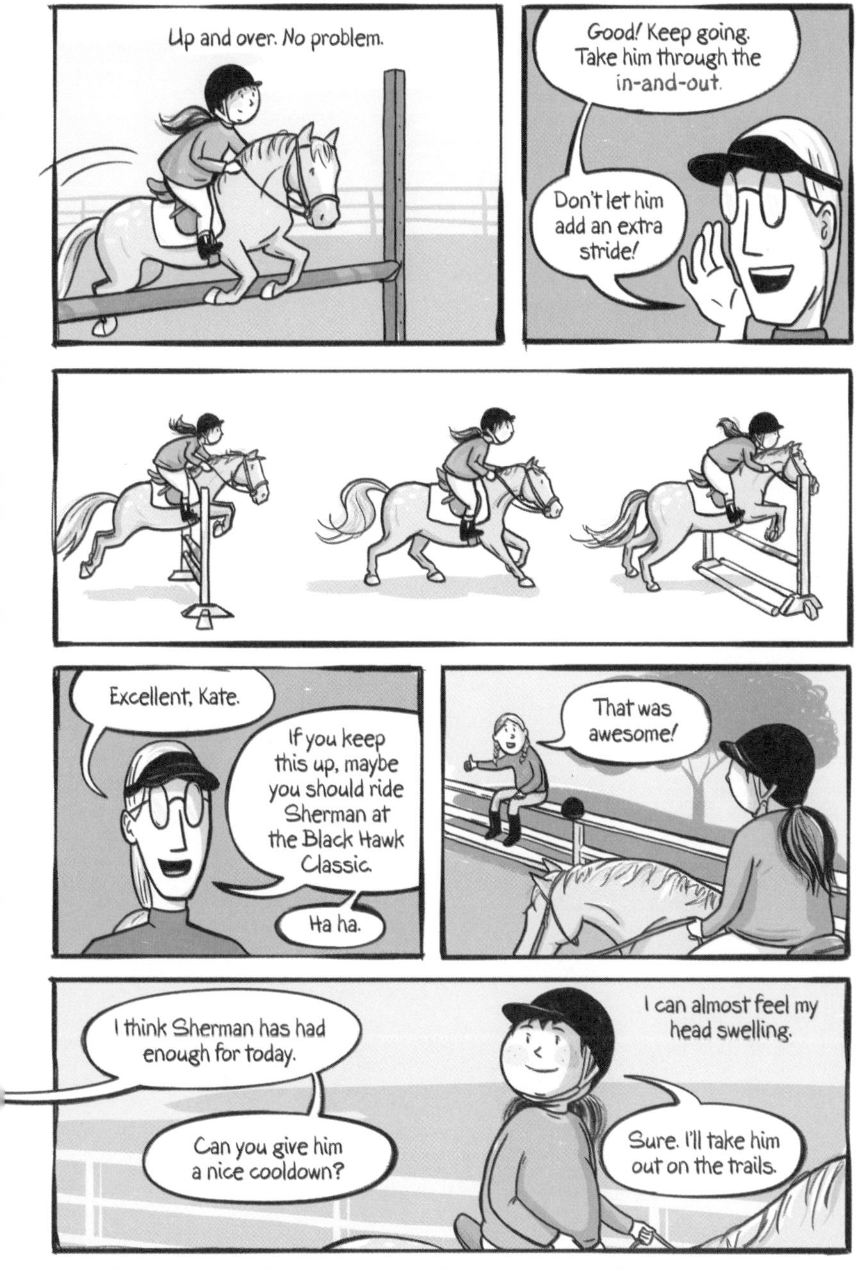
Up and over. No problem.
Good! Keep going. Take him through the in-and-out.
Don't let him add an extra stride!
Excellent, Kate.
If you keep this up, maybe you should ride Sherman at the Black Hawk Classic.
Ha ha.
That was awesome!
I think Sherman has had enough for today.
Can you give him a nice cooldown?
I can almost feel my head swelling.
Sure. I'll take him out on the trails.

In-and-Out: Two jumps that are separated with just enough space for the horse to land from the first jump and take one or two strides before jumping the second fence (also called a combination).

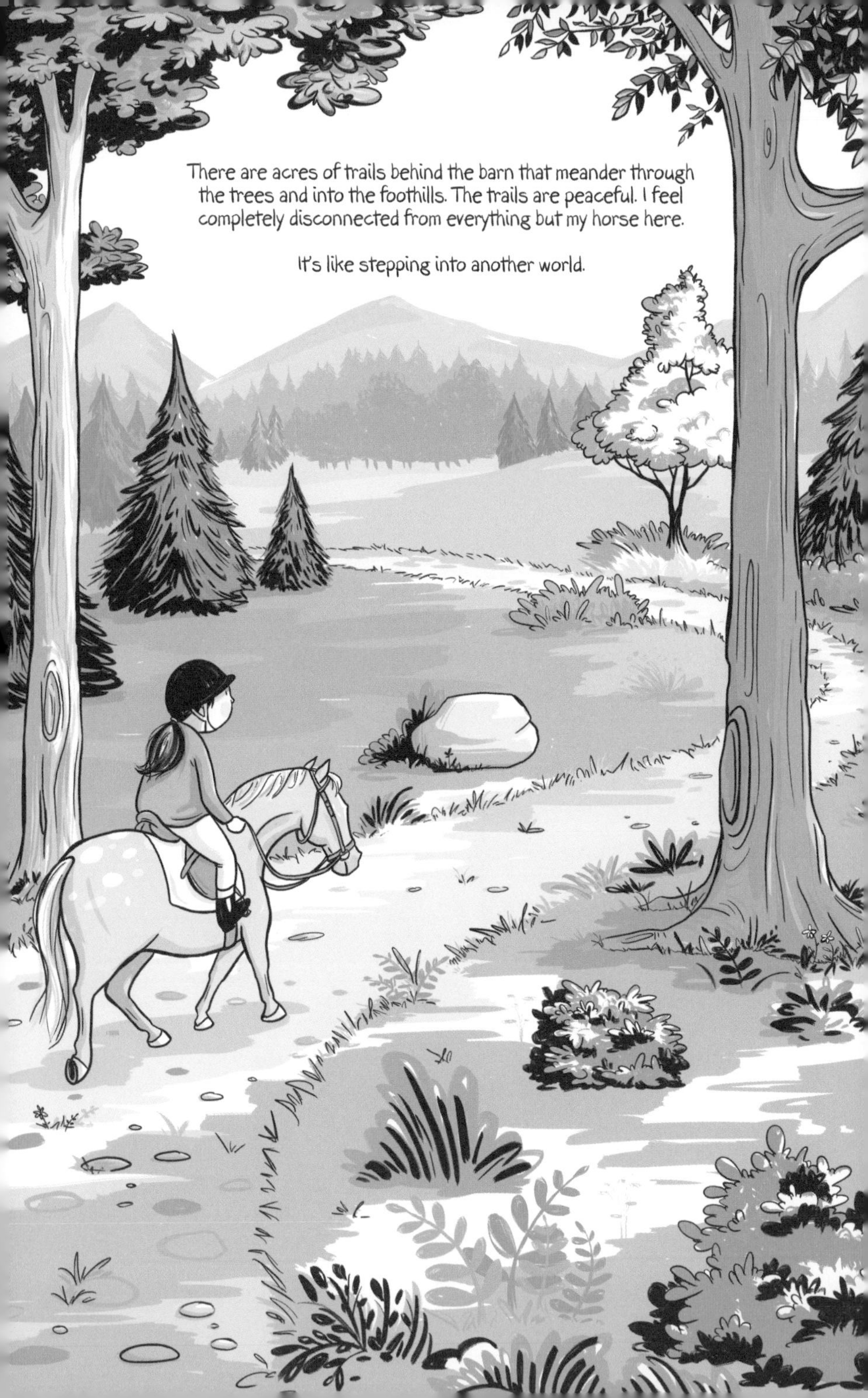
There are acres of trails behind the barn that meander through the trees and into the foothills. The trails are peaceful. I feel completely disconnected from everything but my horse here.
It's like stepping into another world.

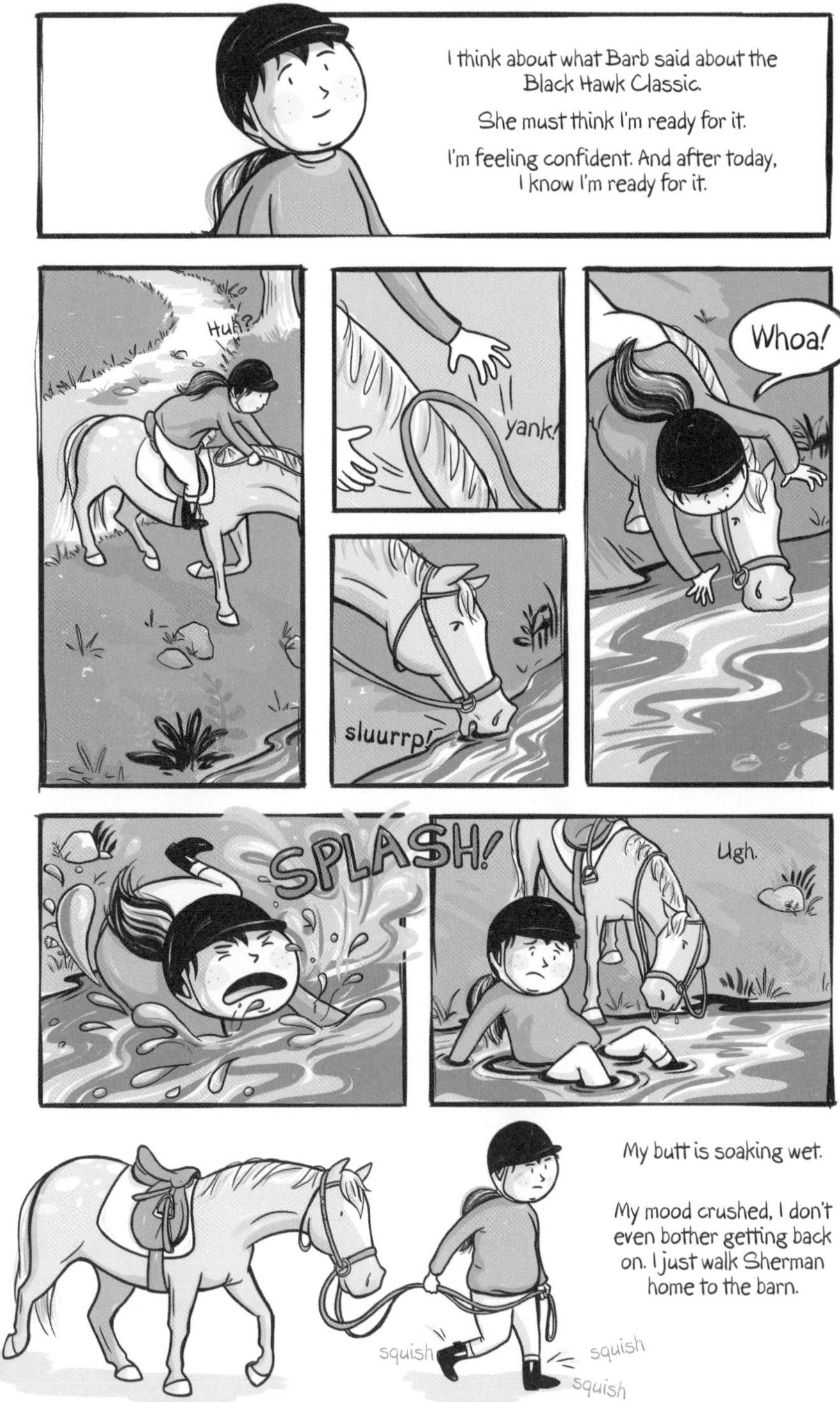

I think about what Barb said about the Black Hawk Classic.
She must think I'm ready for it.
I'm feeling confident. And after today, I know I'm ready for it.
Huh?
yank!
sluurrp!
Whoa!
SPLASH!
Ugh.
My butt is soaking wet.
My mood crushed, I don't even bother getting back on. I just walk Sherman home to the barn.
squish
squish
squish

Chapter 6
Piggy Buck

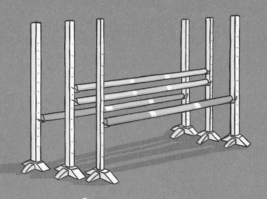

Hogsback

A type of spread (distance) fence with three rails where the tallest pole is in the center.

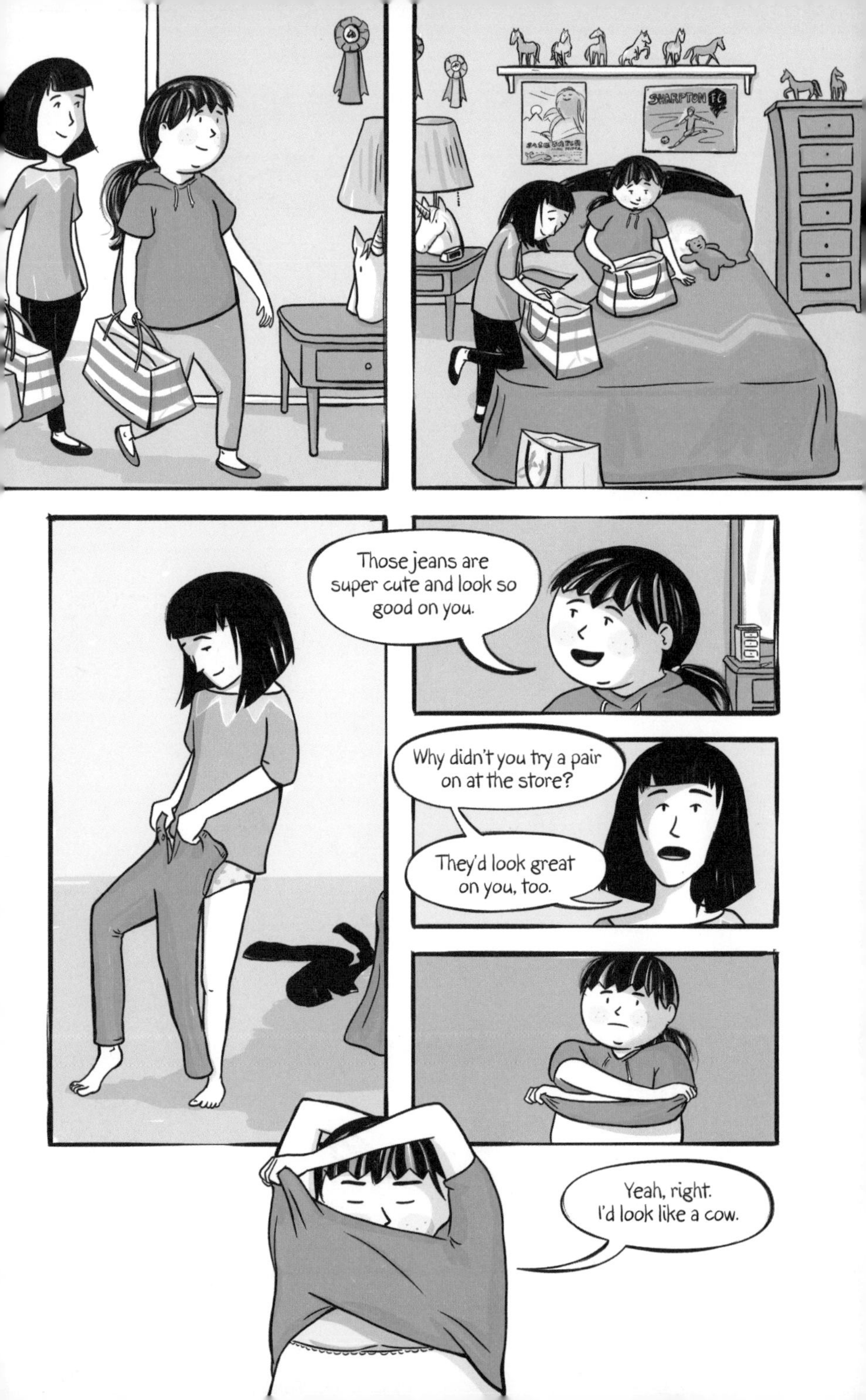
Those jeans are super cute and look so good on you.
Why didn't you try a pair on at the store?
They'd look great on you, too.
Yeah, right. I'd look like a cow.

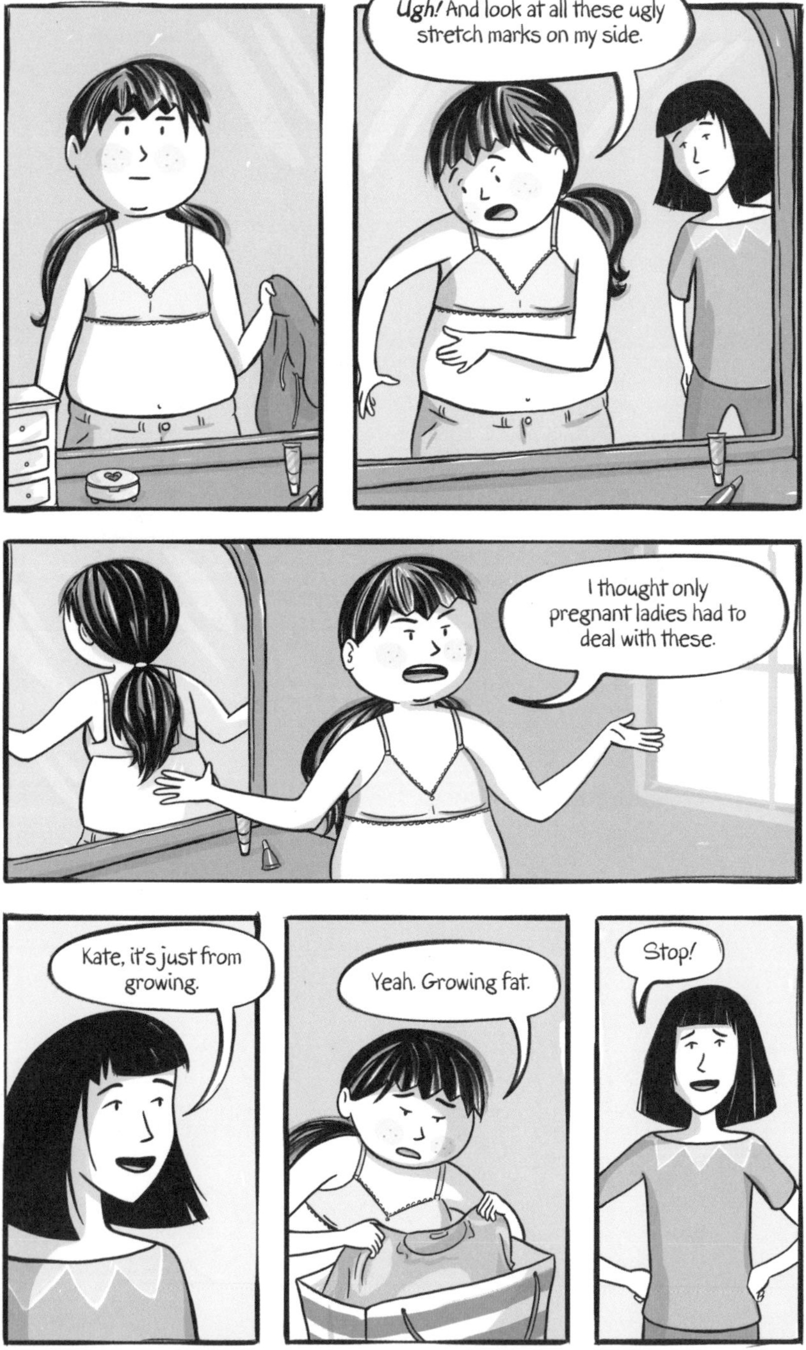
Ugh! And look at all these ugly stretch marks on my side.
I thought only pregnant ladies had to deal with these.
Kate, it's just from growing.
Yeah. Growing fat.
Stop!

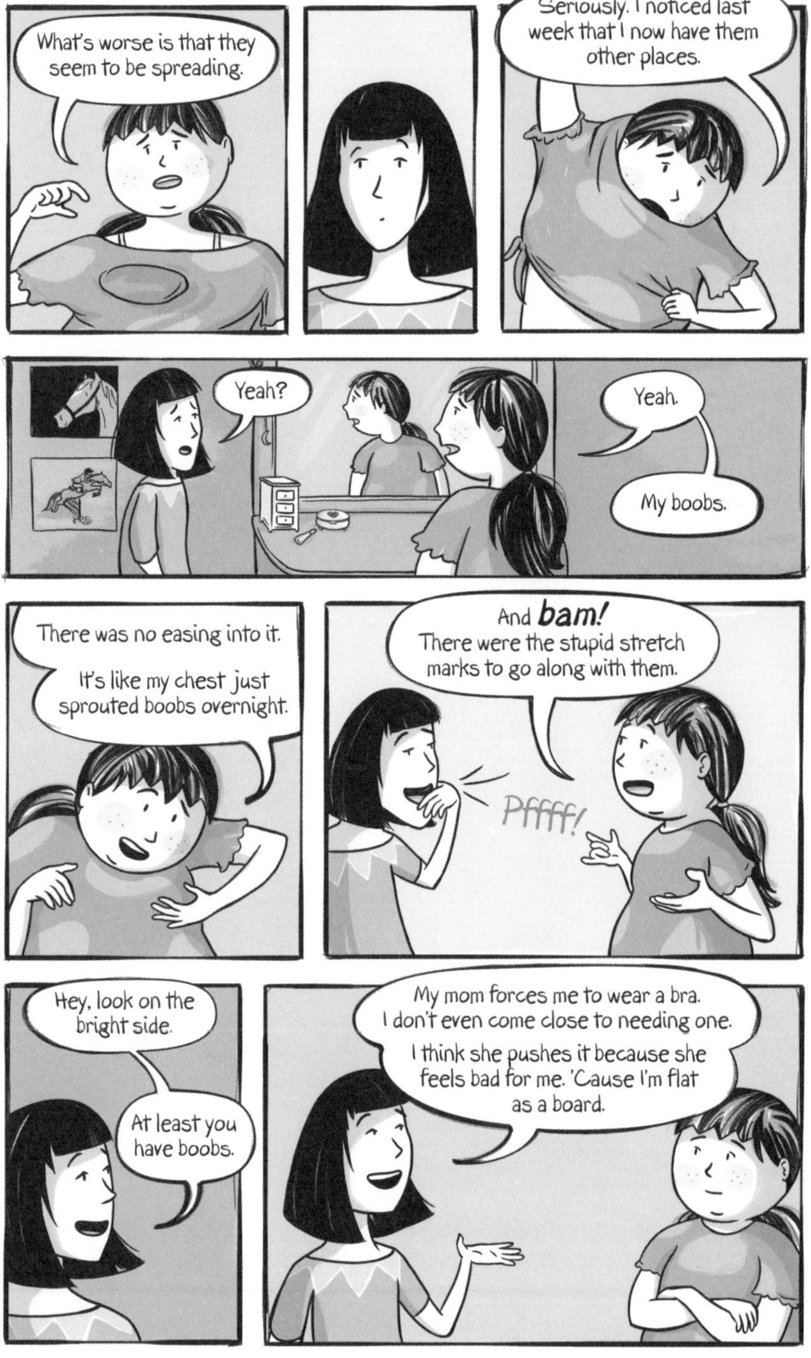
What's worse is that they seem to be spreading.
Seriously. I noticed last week that I now have them other places.
Yeah?
Yeah.
My boobs.
There was no easing into it.
It's like my chest just sprouted boobs overnight.
And **bam!** There were the stupid stretch marks to go along with them.
Pffff!
Hey, look on the bright side.
At least you have boobs.
My mom forces me to wear a bra. I don't even come close to needing one.
I think she pushes it because she feels bad for me. 'Cause I'm flat as a board.

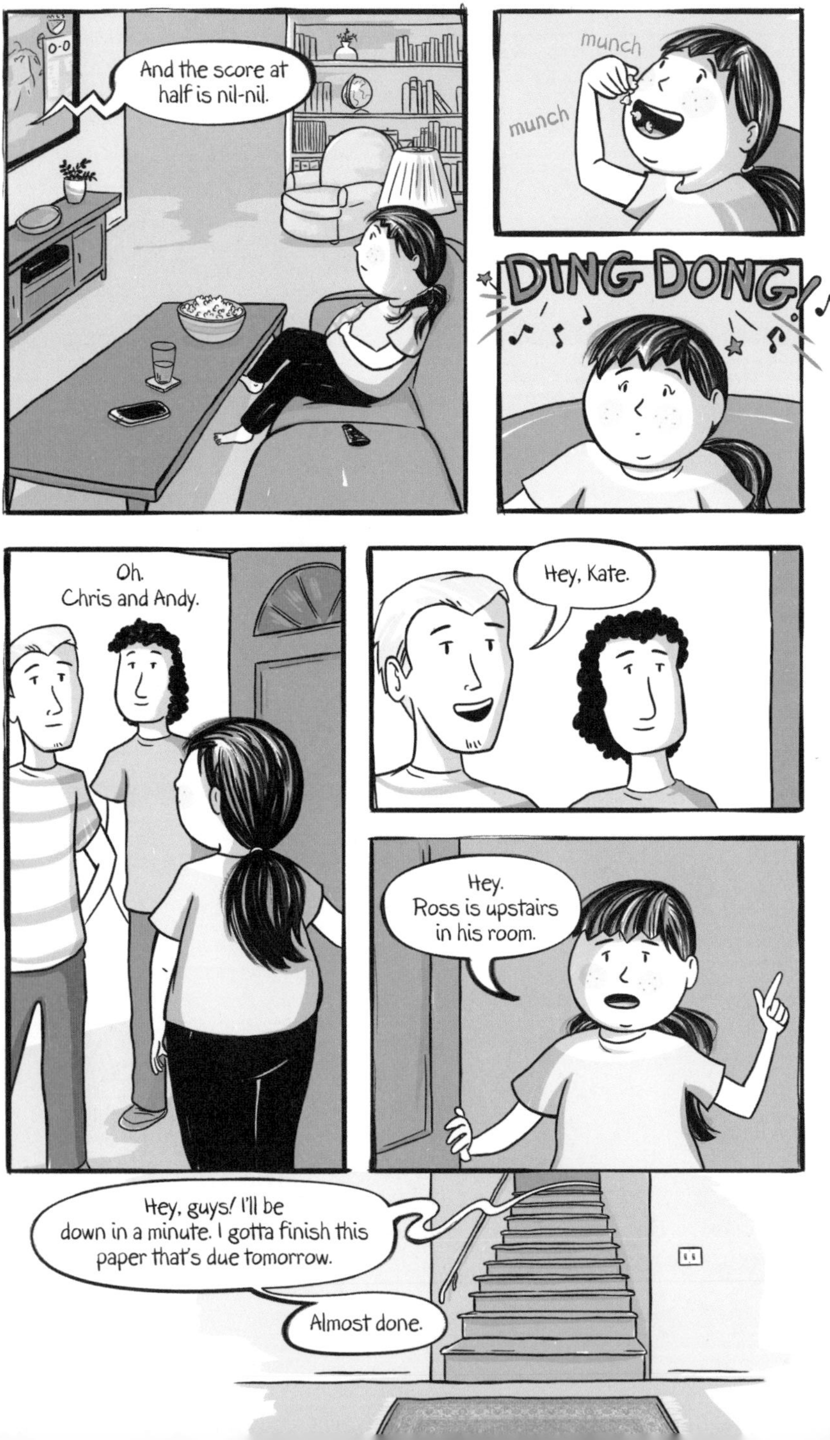
0-0
And the score at half is nil-nil.
munch
munch
DING DONG!
Oh.
Chris and Andy.
Hey, Kate.
Hey.
Ross is upstairs in his room.
Hey, guys! I'll be down in a minute. I gotta finish this paper that's due tomorrow.
Almost done.

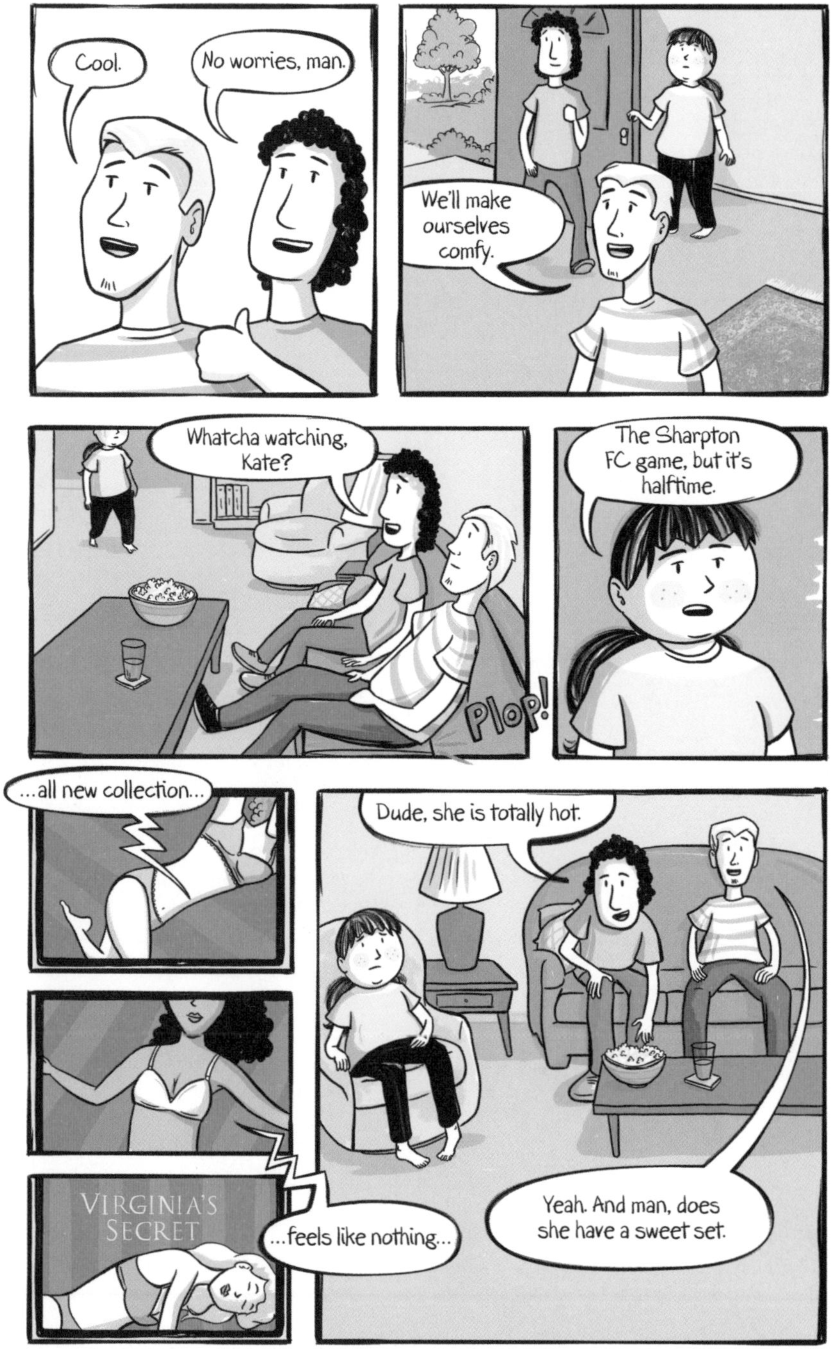
Cool.
No worries, man.
We'll make ourselves comfy.
Whatcha watching, Kate?
PLOP!
The Sharpton FC game, but it's halftime.
...all new collection...
VIRGINIA'S SECRET
...feels like nothing...
Dude, she is totally hot.
Yeah. And man, does she have a sweet set.

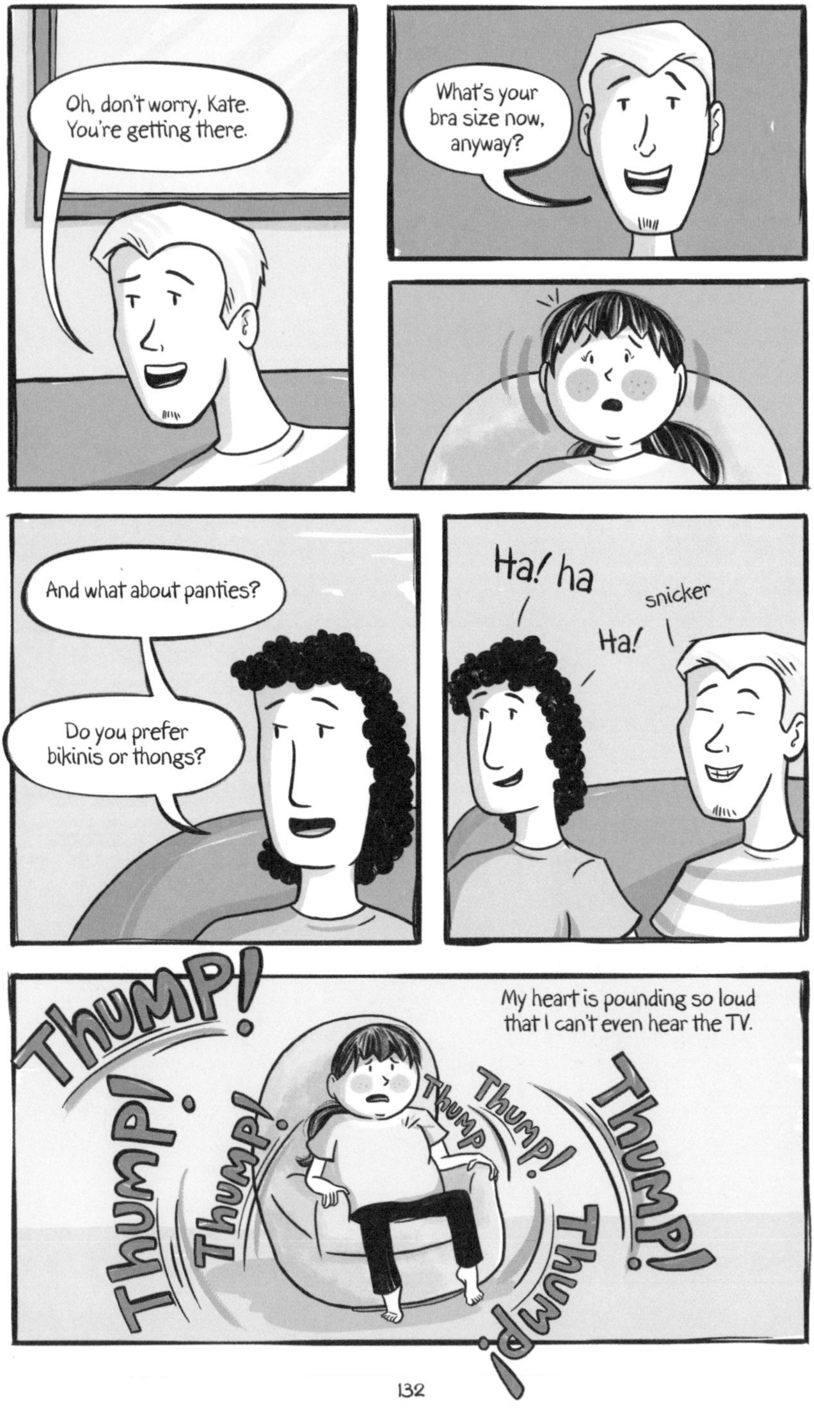
Oh, don't worry, Kate. You're getting there.
What's your bra size now, anyway?
And what about panties?
Do you prefer bikinis or thongs?
Ha! ha
Ha!
snicker
My heart is pounding so loud that I can't even hear the TV.
THUMP!
THUMP!
Thump!
Thump
Thump!
THUMP!
Thump!

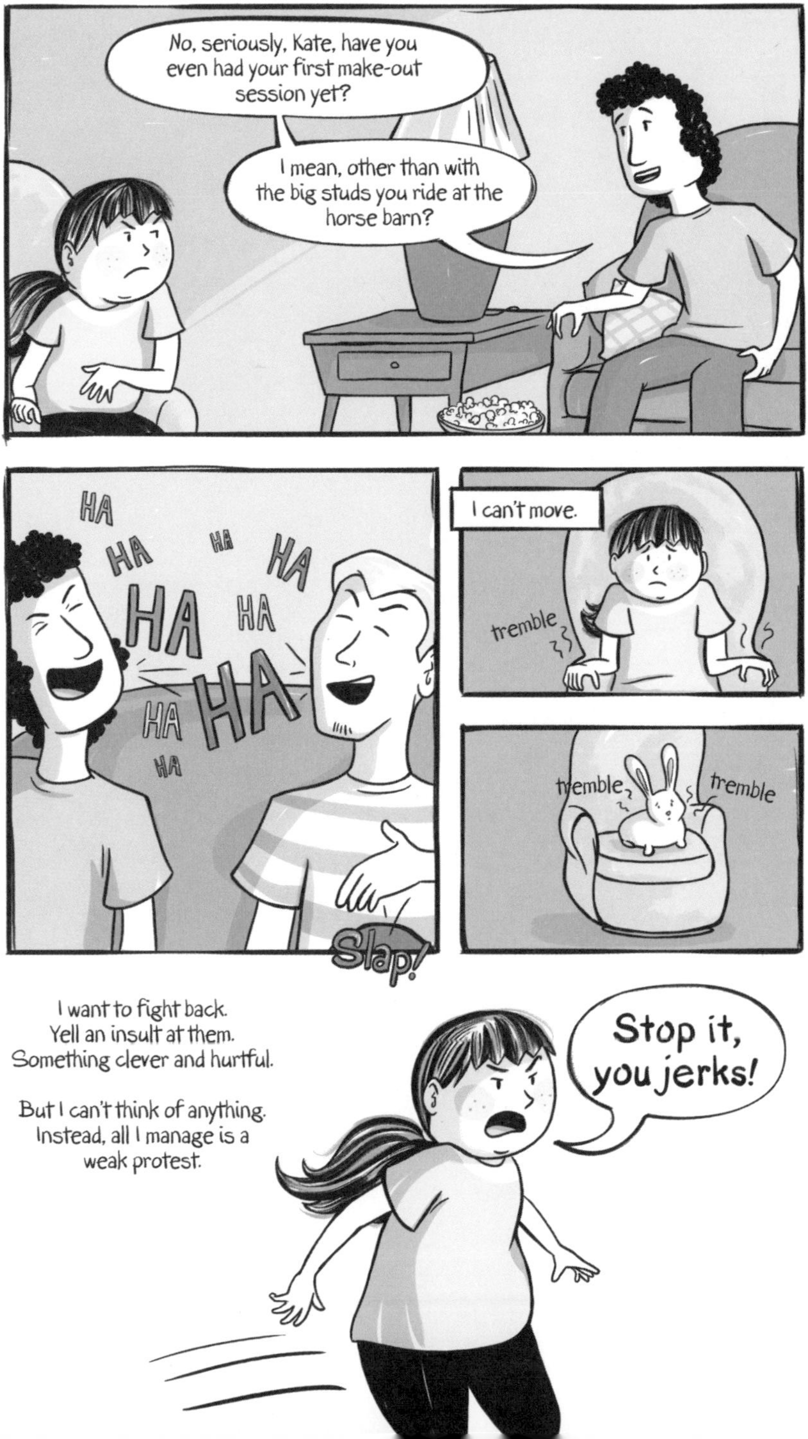
No, seriously, Kate, have you even had your first make-out session yet?
I mean, other than with the big studs you ride at the horse barn?
HA HA HA HA HA HA HA HA HA HA
Slap!
I can't move.
tremble
tremble
tremble
I want to fight back. Yell an insult at them. Something clever and hurtful.
But I can't think of anything. Instead, all I manage is a weak protest.
Stop it, you jerks!

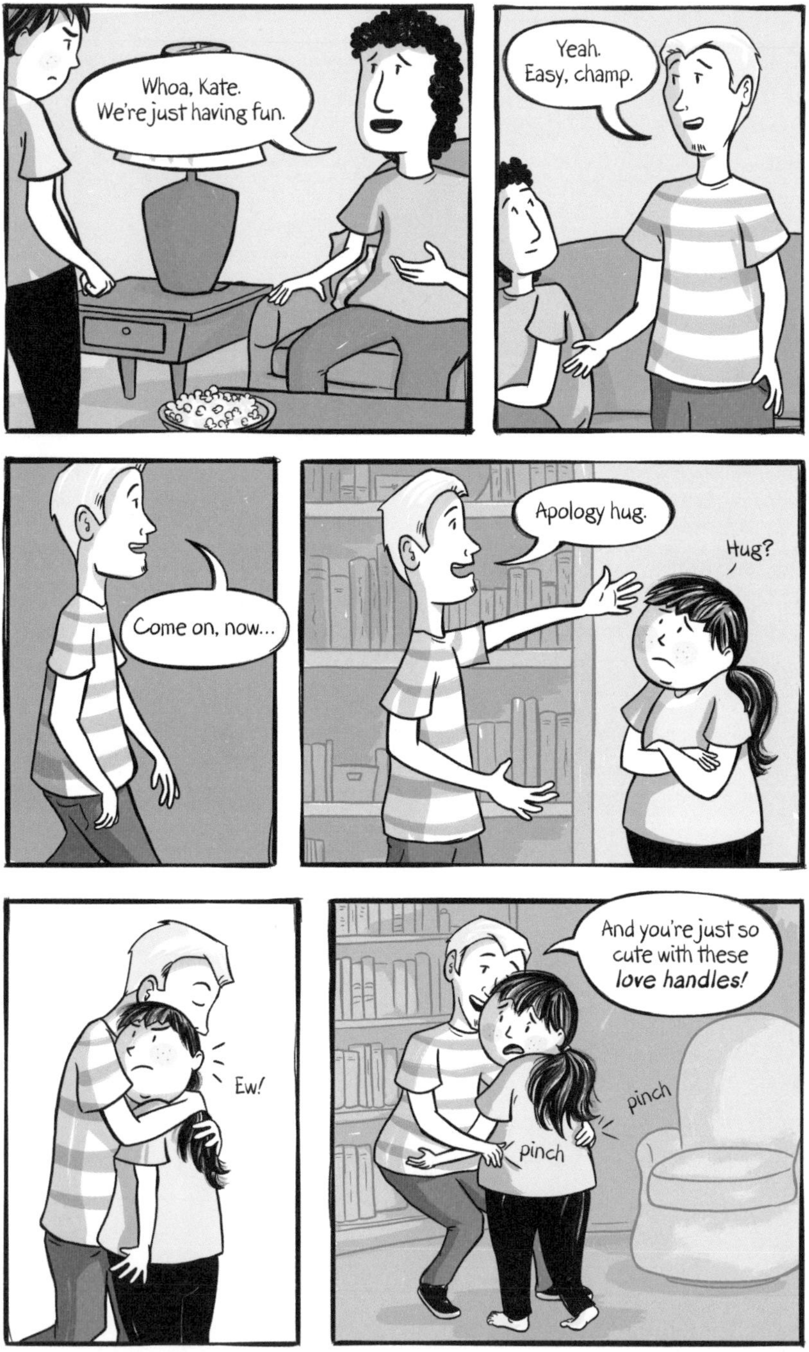
Whoa, Kate.
We're just having fun.
Yeah.
Easy, champ.
Come on, now...
Apology hug.
Hug?
Ew!
And you're just so cute with these **love handles!**
pinch
pinch

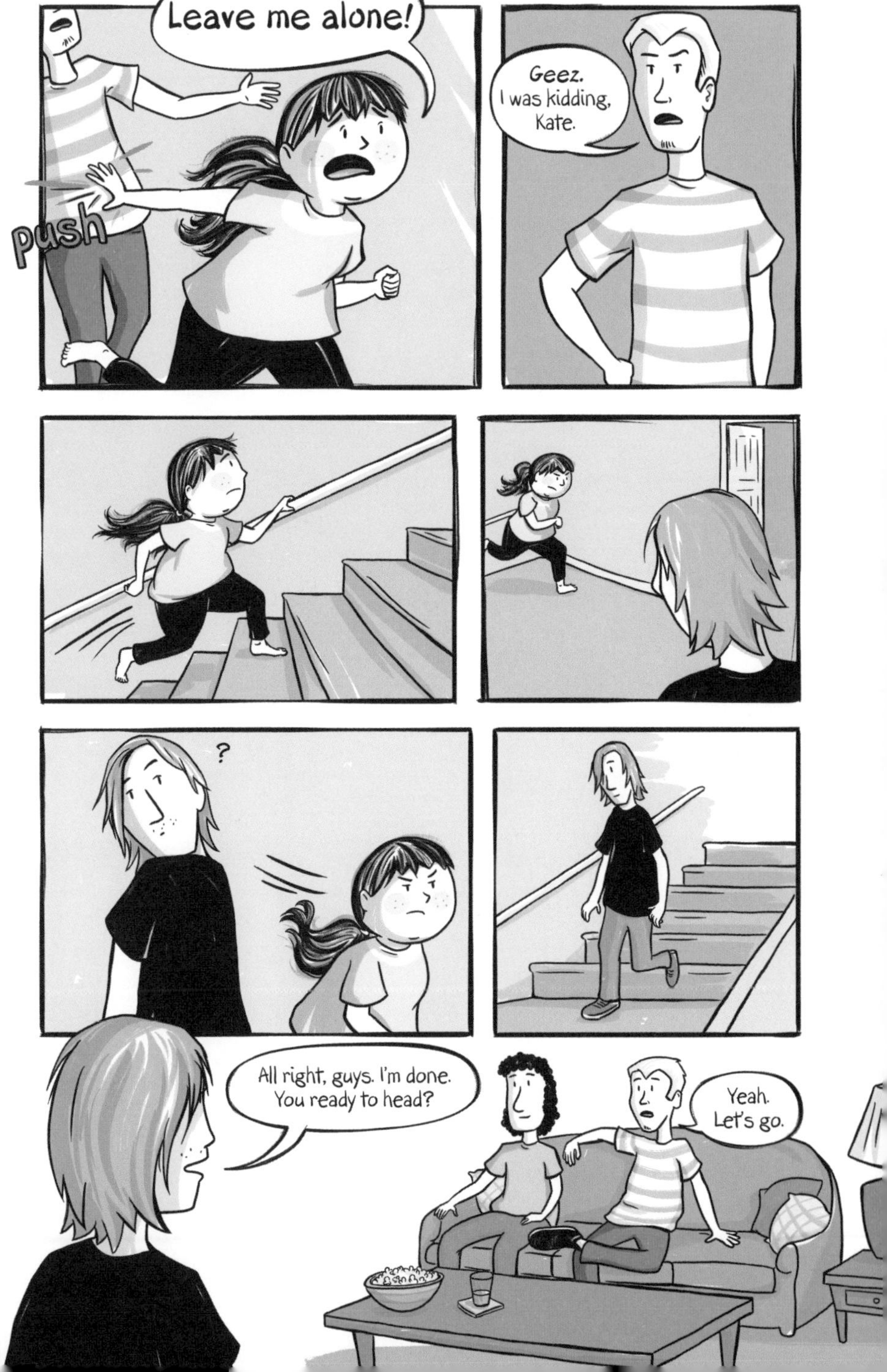
Leave me alone!
push
Geez. I was kidding, Kate.
?
All right, guys. I'm done. You ready to head?
Yeah. Let's go.

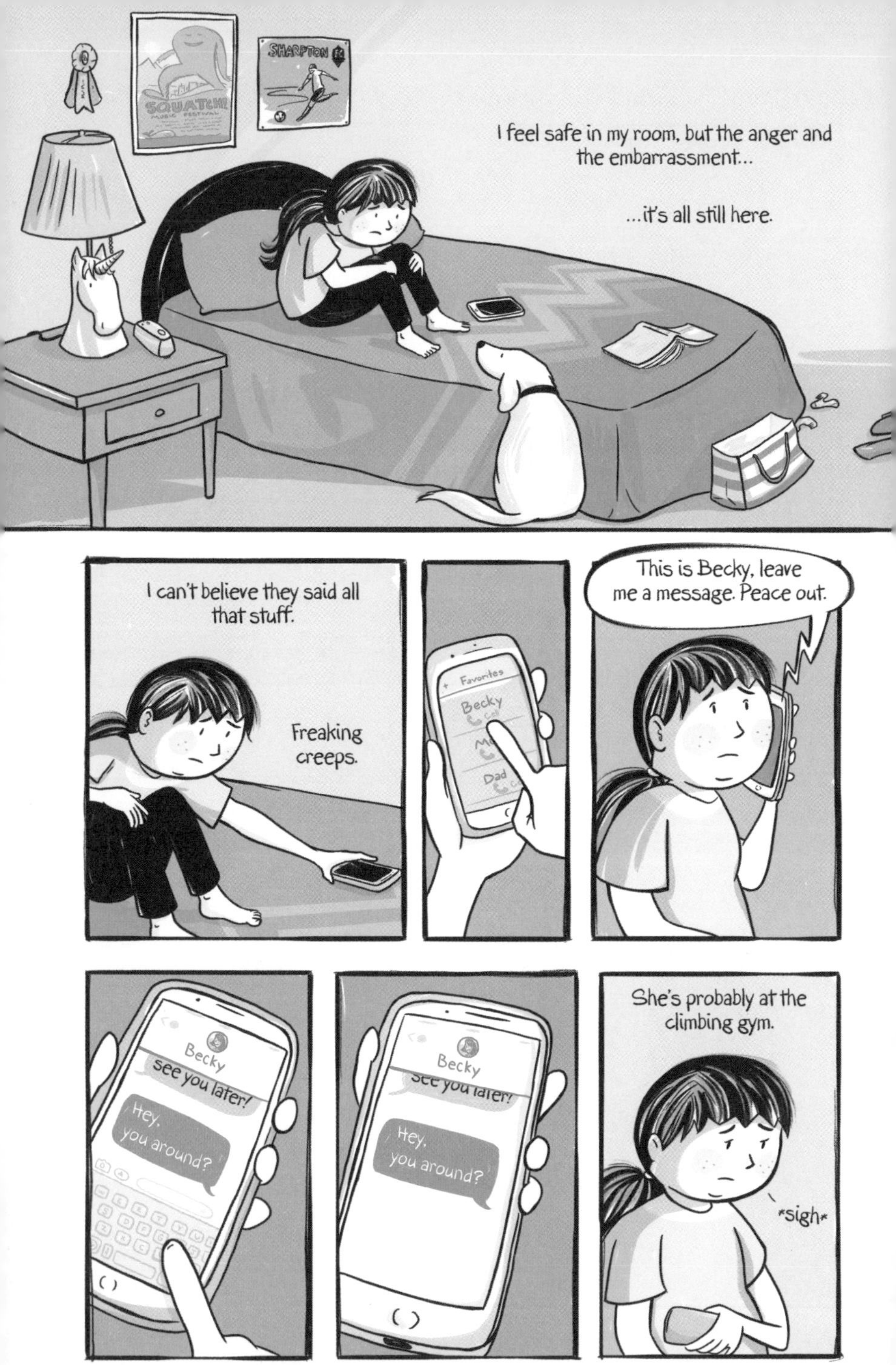
SHARPTON FC
SQUATCH! MUSIC FESTIVAL
I feel safe in my room, but the anger and the embarrassment...
...it's all still here.
I can't believe they said all that stuff.
Freaking creeps.
Favorites
Becky
Dad
This is Becky, leave me a message. Peace out.
Becky
see you later!
Hey, you around?
Becky
see you later!
Hey, you around?
She's probably at the climbing gym.
sigh

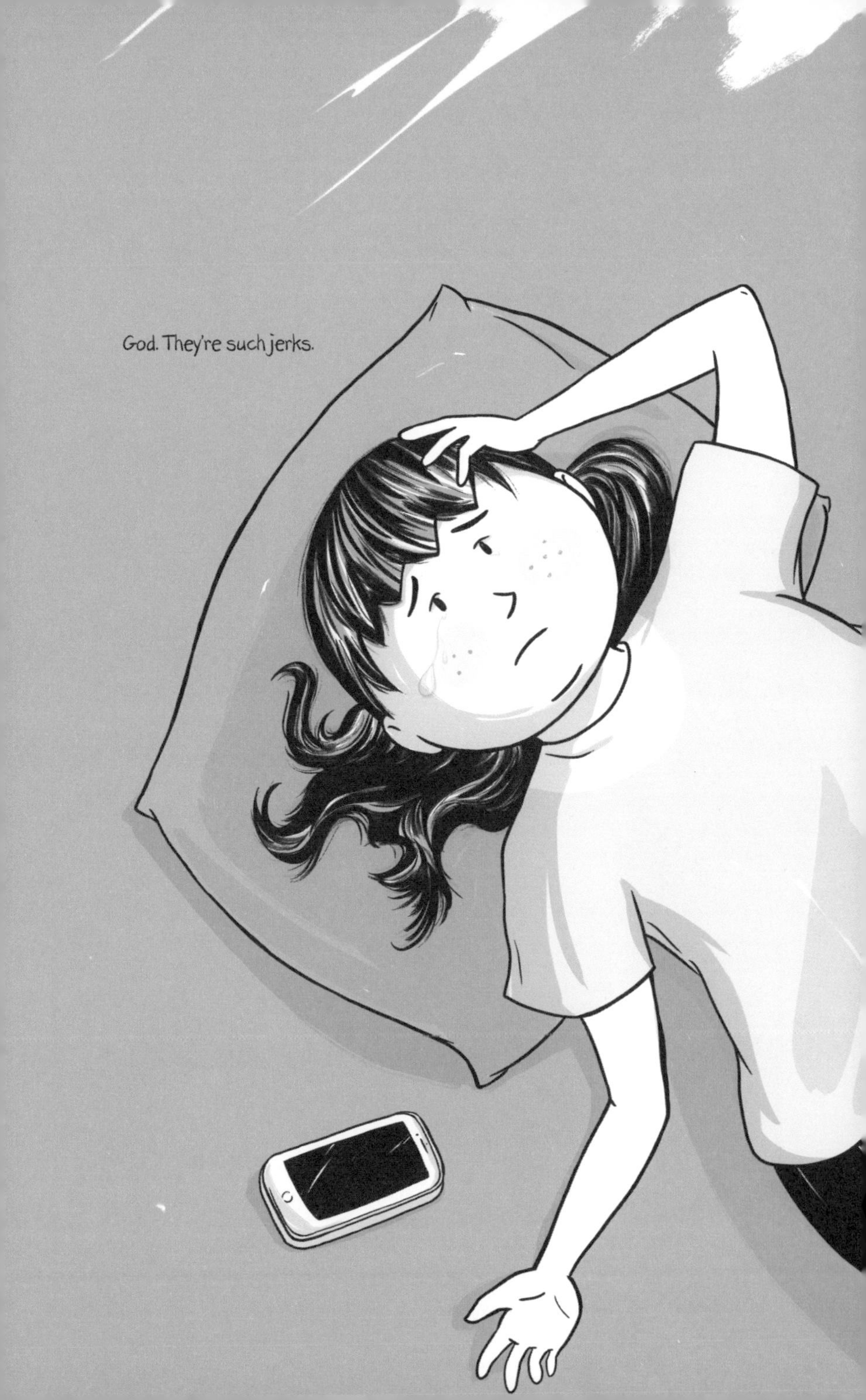
God. They're such jerks.

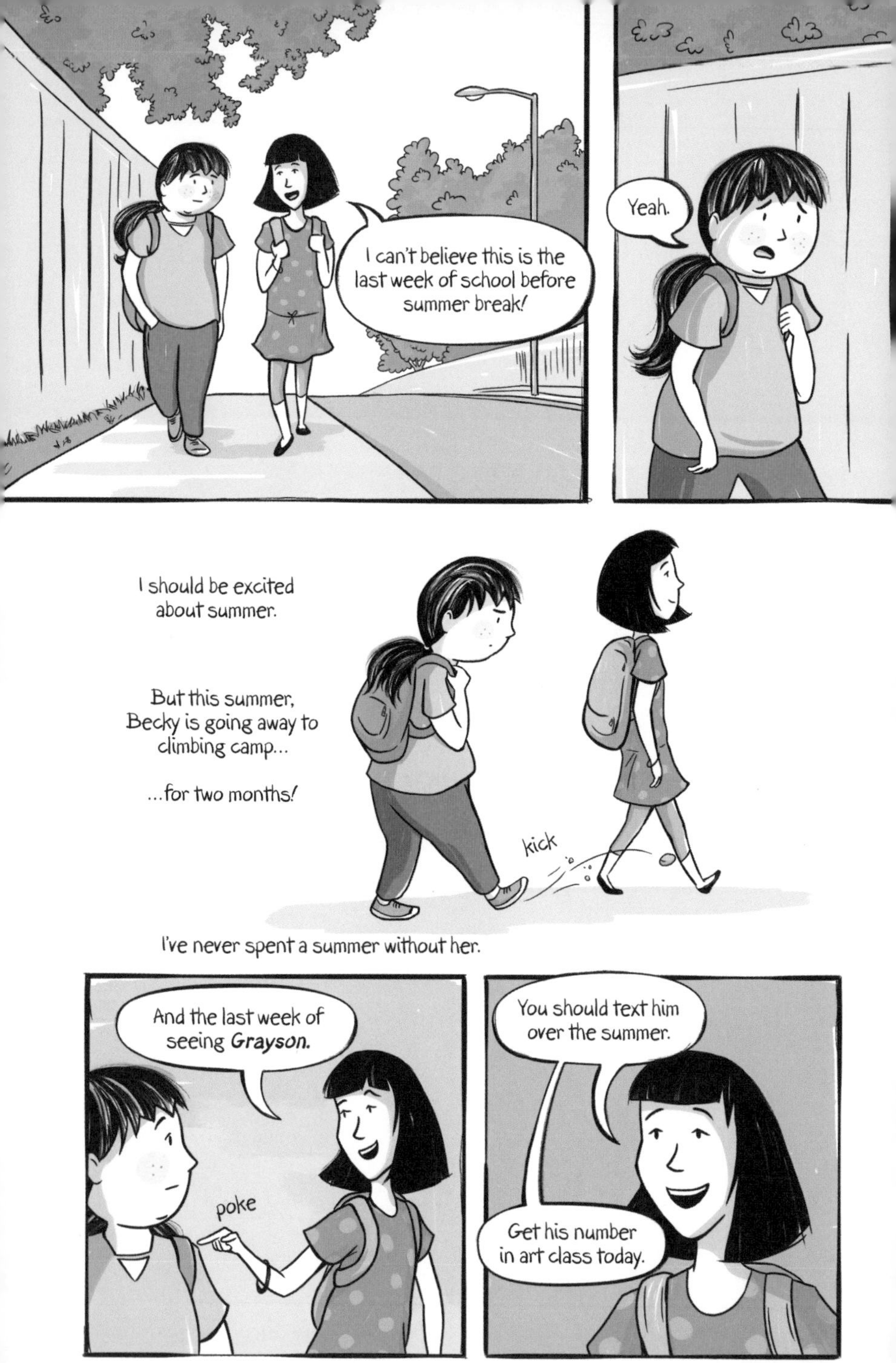
I can't believe this is the last week of school before summer break!
Yeah.
I should be excited about summer.
But this summer, Becky is going away to climbing camp...
...for two months!
kick
I've never spent a summer without her.
And the last week of seeing **Grayson.**
poke
You should text him over the summer.
Get his number in art class today.

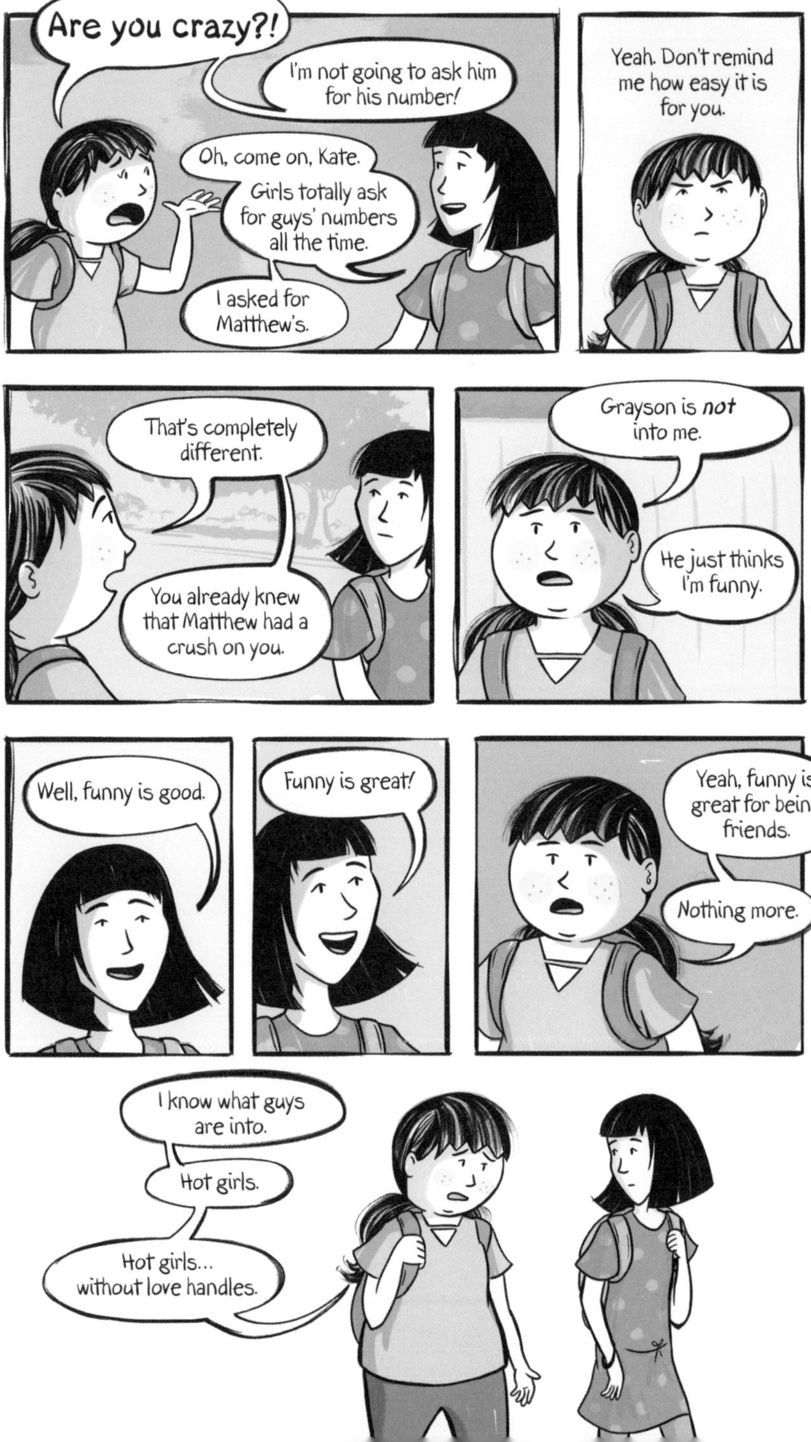
Are you crazy?!
I'm not going to ask him for his number!
Oh, come on, Kate.
Girls totally ask for guys' numbers all the time.
I asked for Matthew's.
Yeah. Don't remind me how easy it is for you.
That's completely different.
You already knew that Matthew had a crush on you.
Grayson is *not* into me.
He just thinks I'm funny.
Well, funny is good.
Funny is great!
Yeah, funny is great for being friends.
Nothing more.
I know what guys are into.
Hot girls.
Hot girls... without love handles.

FREQUENT FLYER CLUB

Rider	Falls
Kate	4
Finley	2
Emilia	1

Vet
Dr. Allen
(801) 943-1754

Farrier on Tues 6/15

happy summer!

FLYER CLUB

Falls
4
2
1

Vet
Dr. Allen
‑1754

6/15

Did Jana write this?

She must have. Piper's handwriting is far worse.

Speak of the devil.

Hey, Kate.

Hey, guys.

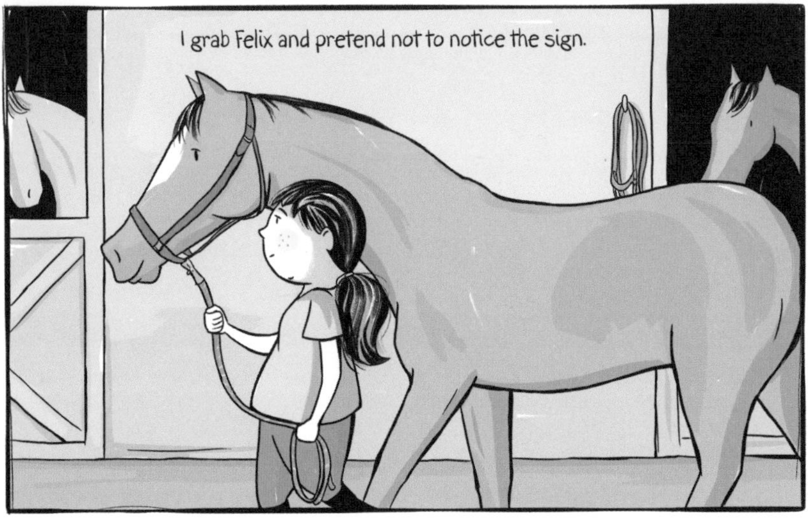
I grab Felix and pretend not to notice the sign.

I quickly get him ready to ride, trying hard to ignore the chatter coming from inside the tack room.

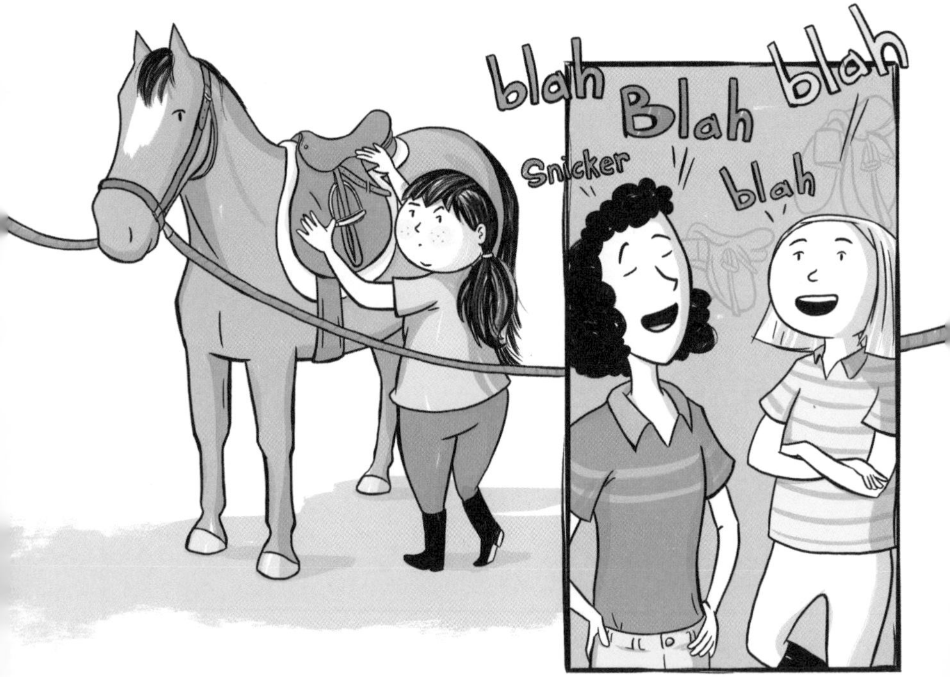
blah
Blah
blah
Snicker
blah

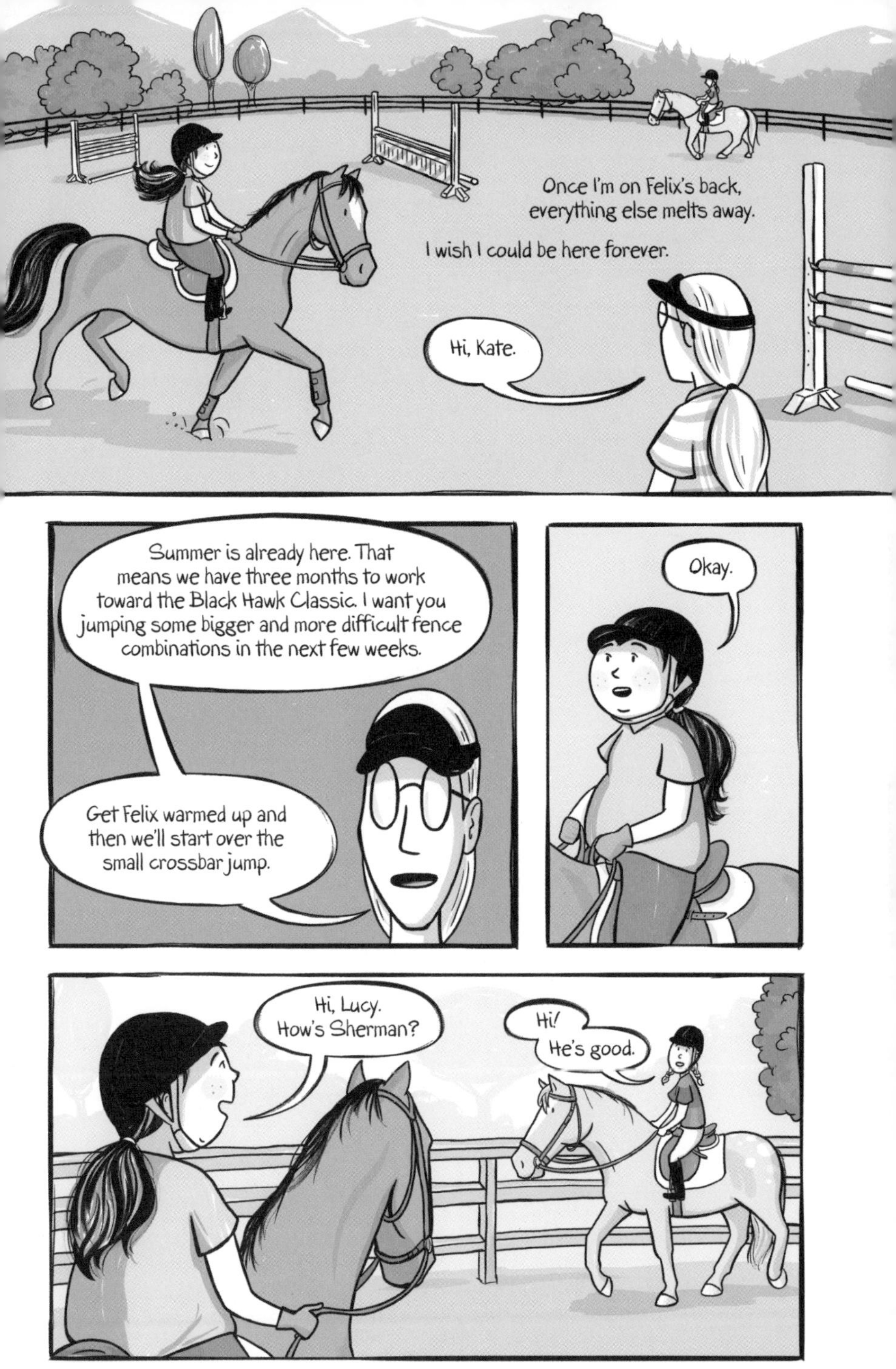
Once I'm on Felix's back, everything else melts away.
I wish I could be here forever.
Hi, Kate.
Summer is already here. That means we have three months to work toward the Black Hawk Classic. I want you jumping some bigger and more difficult fence combinations in the next few weeks.
Get Felix warmed up and then we'll start over the small crossbar jump.
Okay.
Hi, Lucy. How's Sherman?
Hi! He's good.

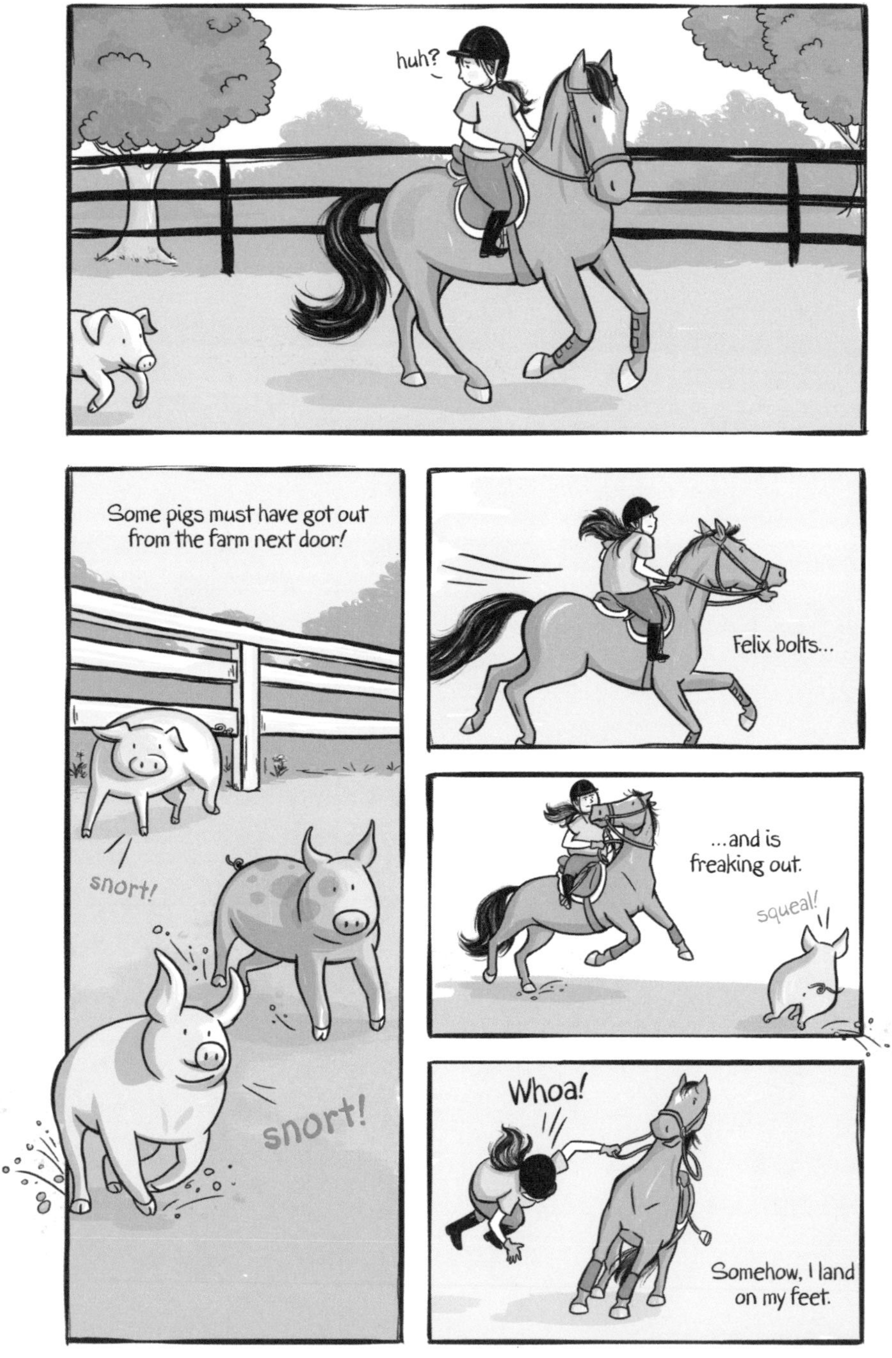
huh?
Some pigs must have got out from the farm next door!
snort!
snort!
Felix bolts...
...and is freaking out.
squeal!
Whoa!
Somehow, I land on my feet.

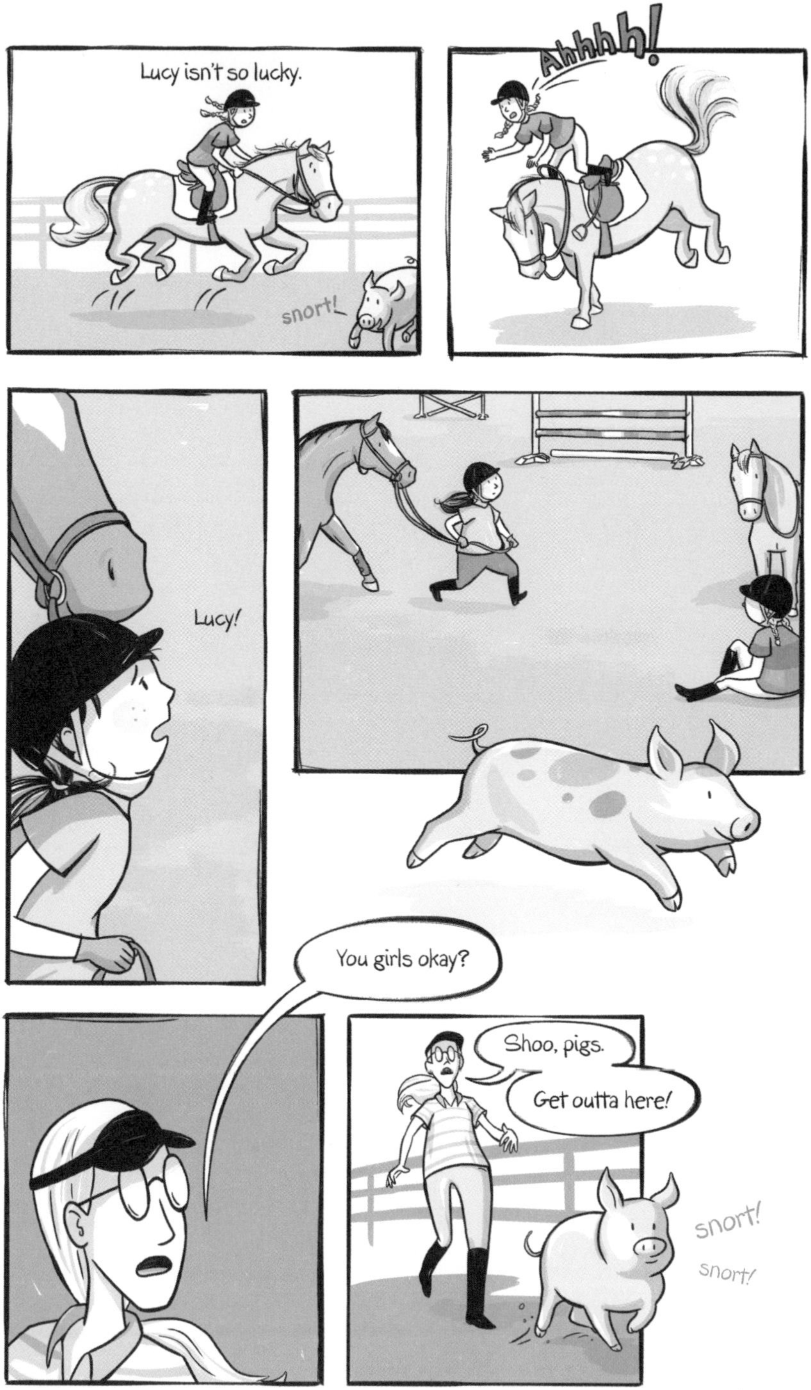
Lucy isn't so lucky.
snort!
Ahhhh!
Lucy!
You girls okay?
Shoo, pigs.
Get outta here!
snort!
snort!

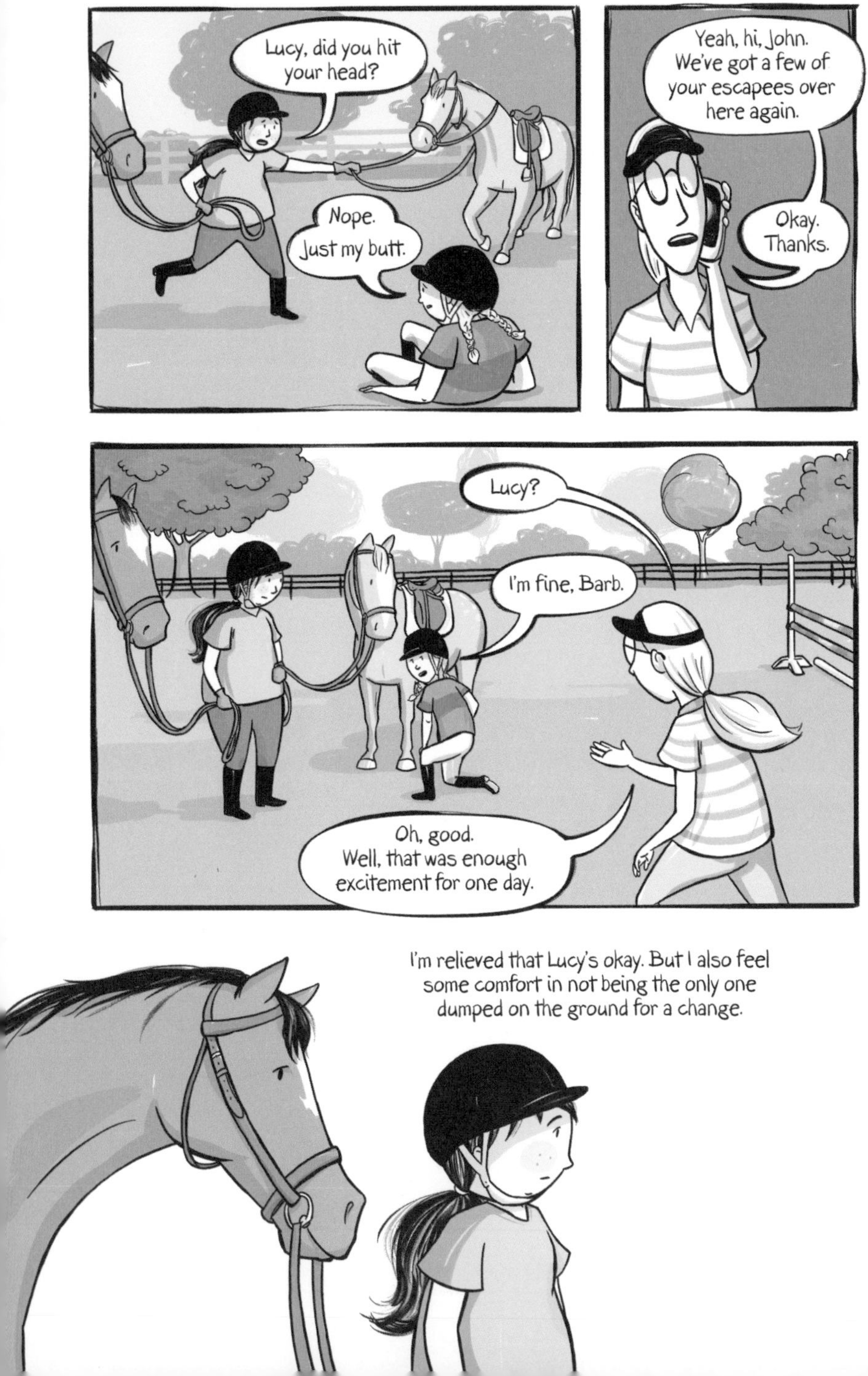
Lucy, did you hit your head?
Nope. Just my butt.
Yeah, hi, John. We've got a few of your escapees over here again.
Okay. Thanks.
Lucy?
I'm fine, Barb.
Oh, good. Well, that was enough excitement for one day.
I'm relieved that Lucy's okay. But I also feel some comfort in not being the only one dumped on the ground for a change.

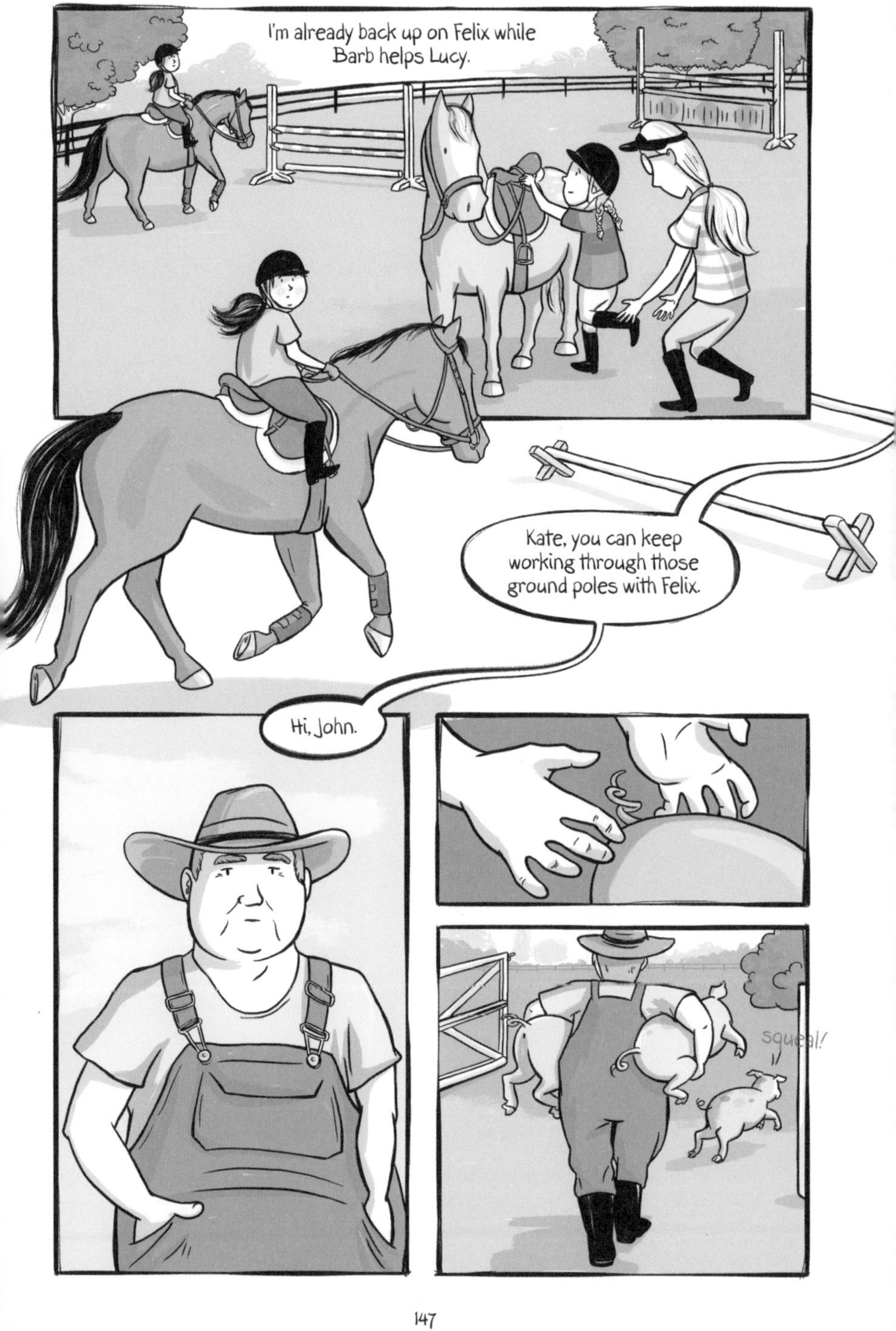
I'm already back up on Felix while Barb helps Lucy.
Kate, you can keep working through those ground poles with Felix.
Hi, John.
squeal!

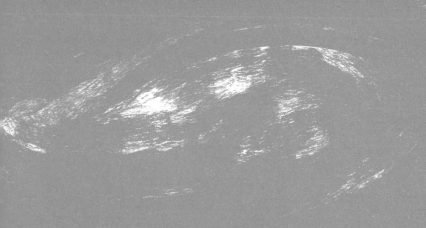

Chapter 7
Bridle Swipe

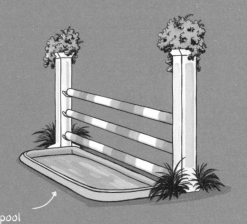

Liverpool

A ditch or large tray of water placed beneath a vertical fence.

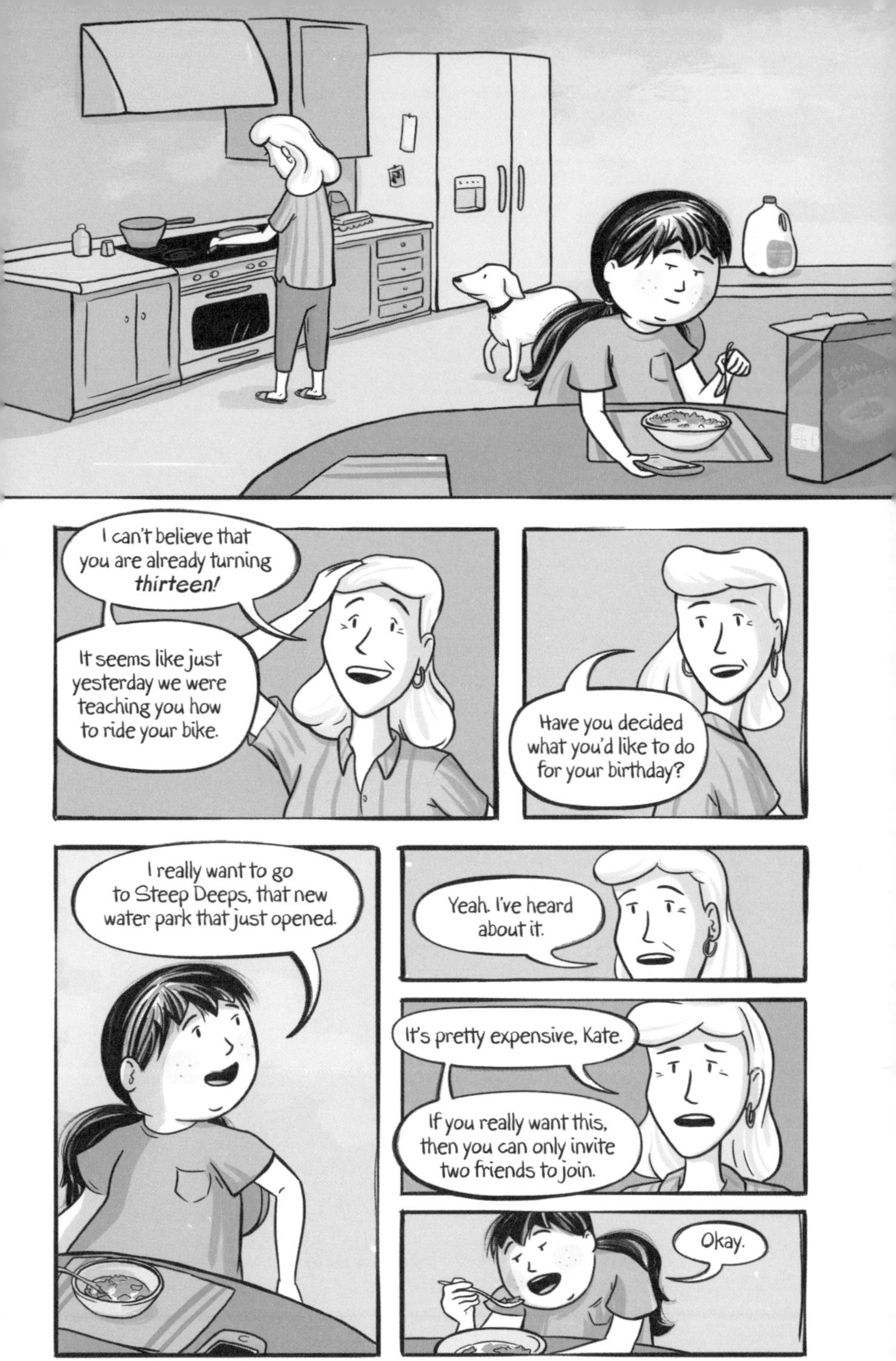
I can't believe that you are already turning *thirteen!*
It seems like just yesterday we were teaching you how to ride your bike.
Have you decided what you'd like to do for your birthday?
I really want to go to Steep Deeps, that new water park that just opened.
Yeah. I've heard about it.
It's pretty expensive, Kate.
If you really want this, then you can only invite two friends to join.
Okay.

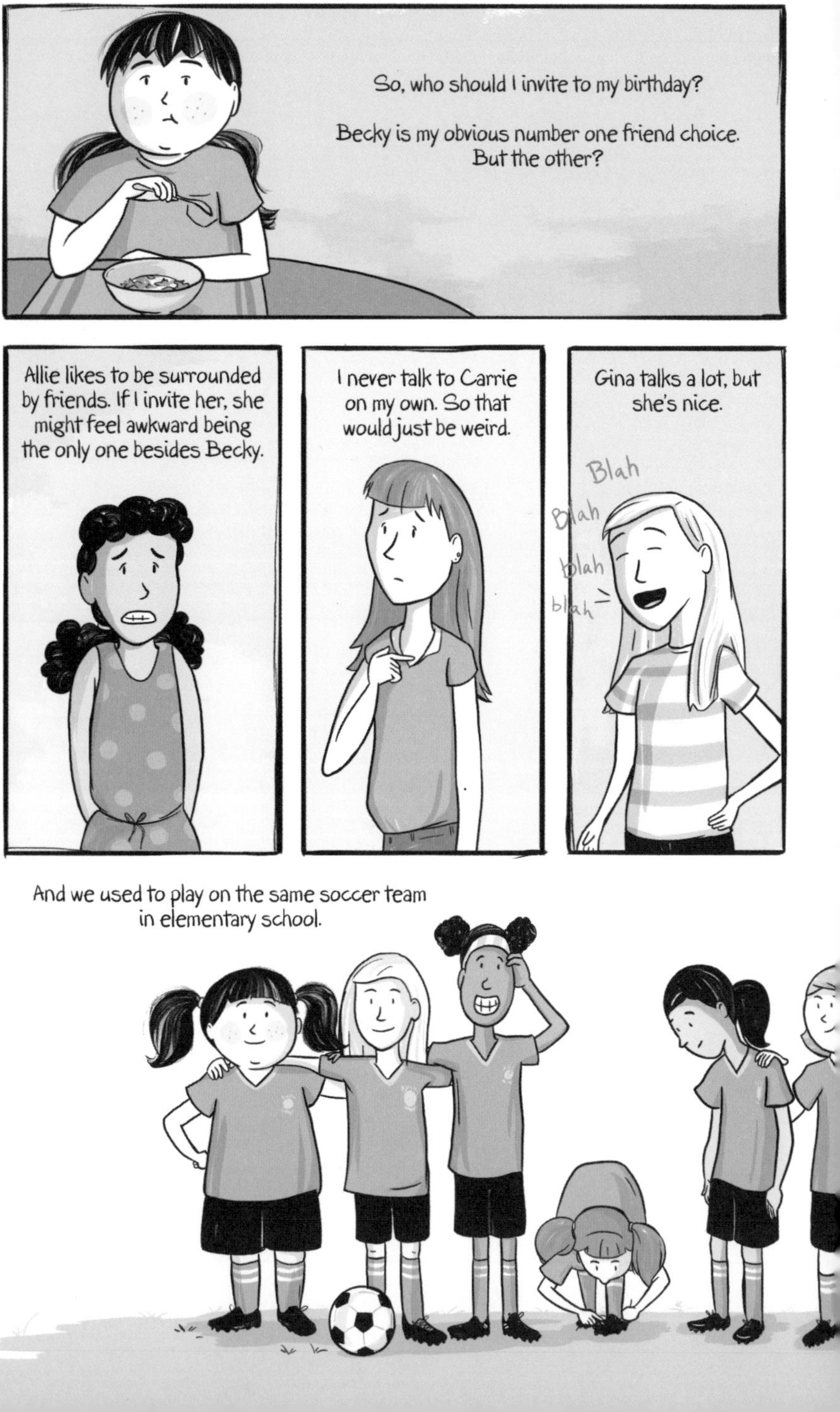
So, who should I invite to my birthday?
Becky is my obvious number one friend choice. But the other?
Allie likes to be surrounded by friends. If I invite her, she might feel awkward being the only one besides Becky.
I never talk to Carrie on my own. So that would just be weird.
Gina talks a lot, but she's nice.
Blah
Blah
blah
blah
And we used to play on the same soccer team in elementary school.

I also ran into her at the grocery store last week and she actually seemed like she wanted to hang out this summer.

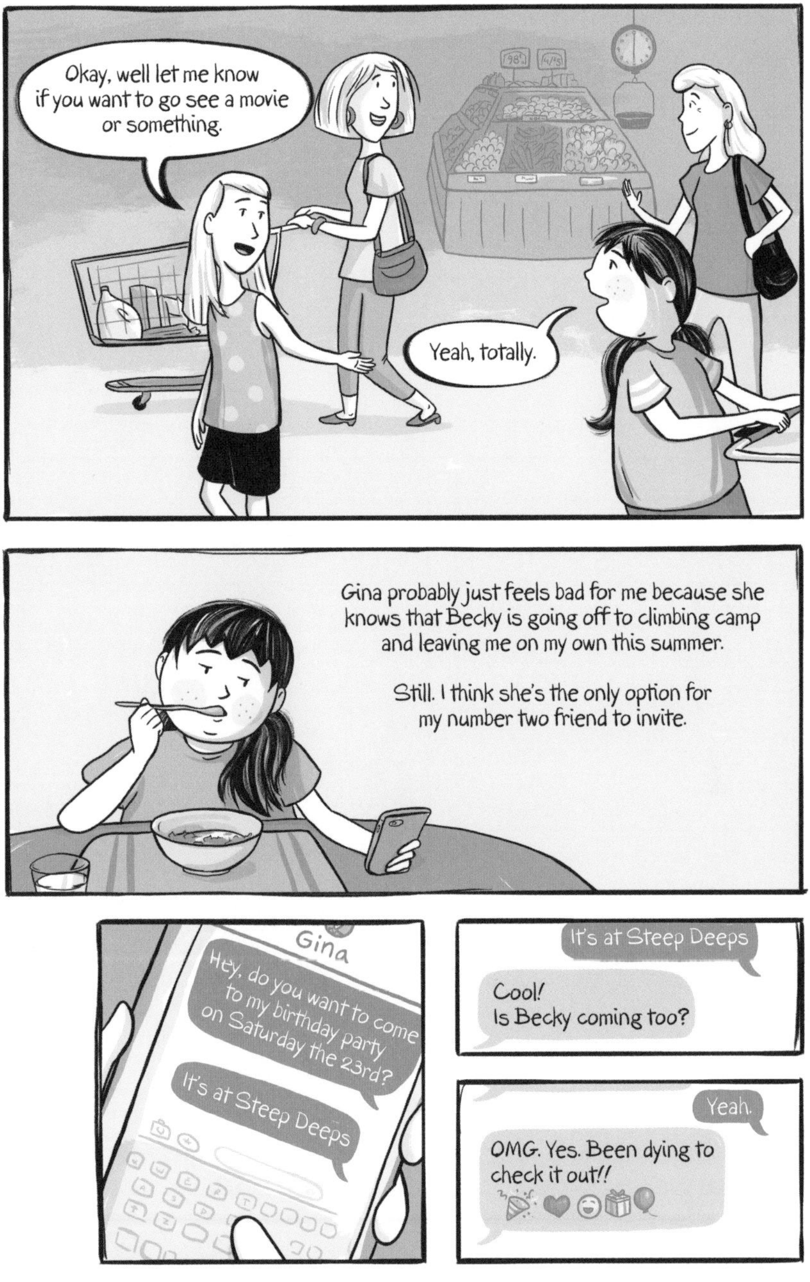
Okay, well let me know if you want to go see a movie or something.
Yeah, totally.
Gina probably just feels bad for me because she knows that Becky is going off to climbing camp and leaving me on my own this summer.
Still. I think she's the only option for my number two friend to invite.
Gina
Hey, do you want to come to my birthday party on Saturday the 23rd?
It's at Steep Deeps
It's at Steep Deeps
Cool! Is Becky coming too?
Yeah.
OMG. Yes. Been dying to check it out!!

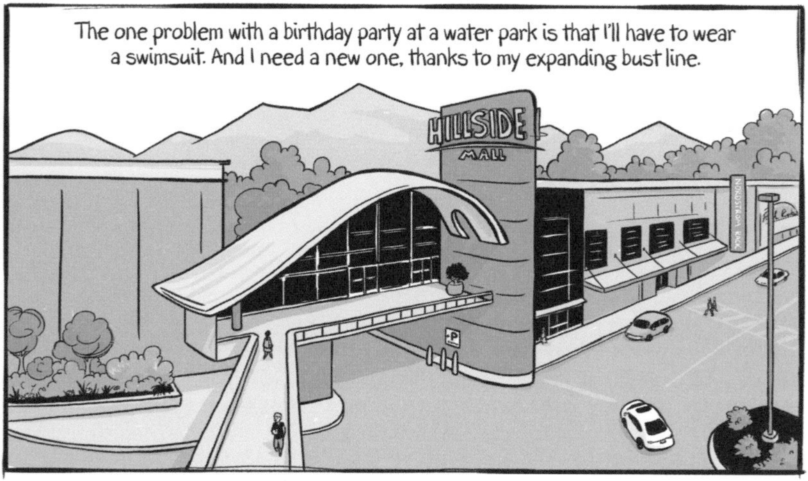
The one problem with a birthday party at a water park is that I'll have to wear a swimsuit. And I need a new one, thanks to my expanding bust line.
HILLSIDE
MALL

There is something really depressing about an indoor shopping mall during summertime.

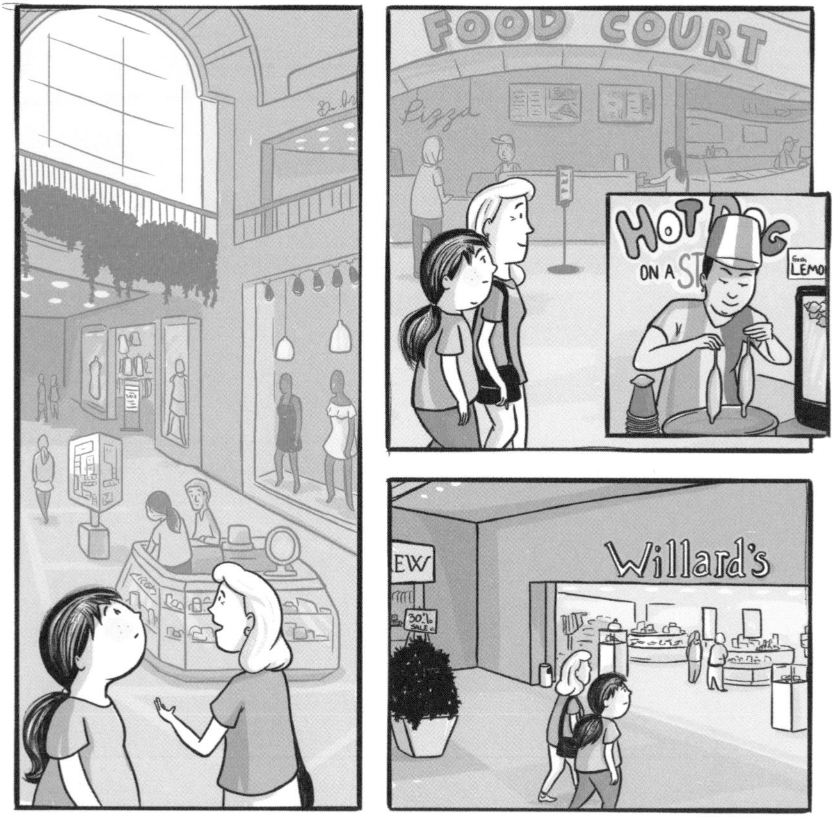
FOOD COURT
Pizza
Willard's

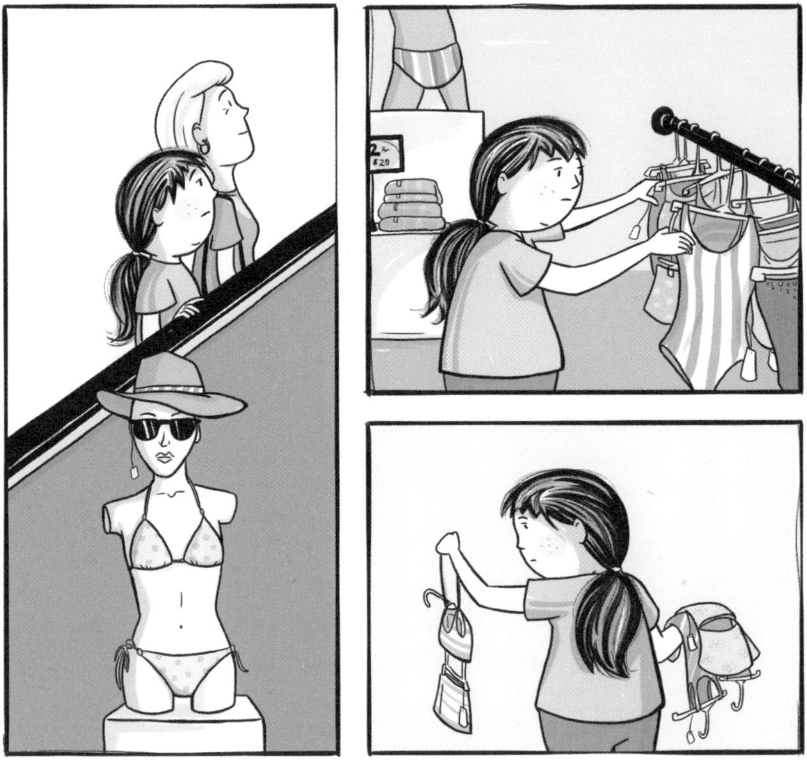

And there's probably nothing more horrible than trying on swimsuits.

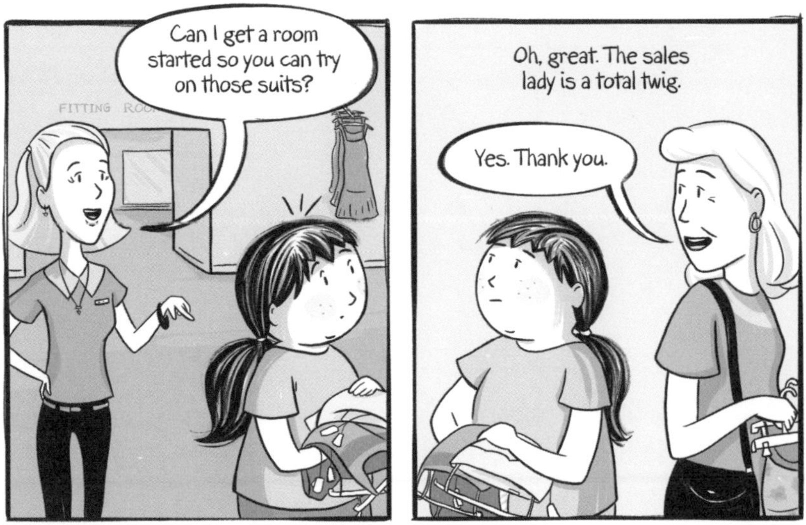
Can I get a room started so you can try on those suits?
Oh, great. The sales lady is a total twig.
Yes. Thank you.

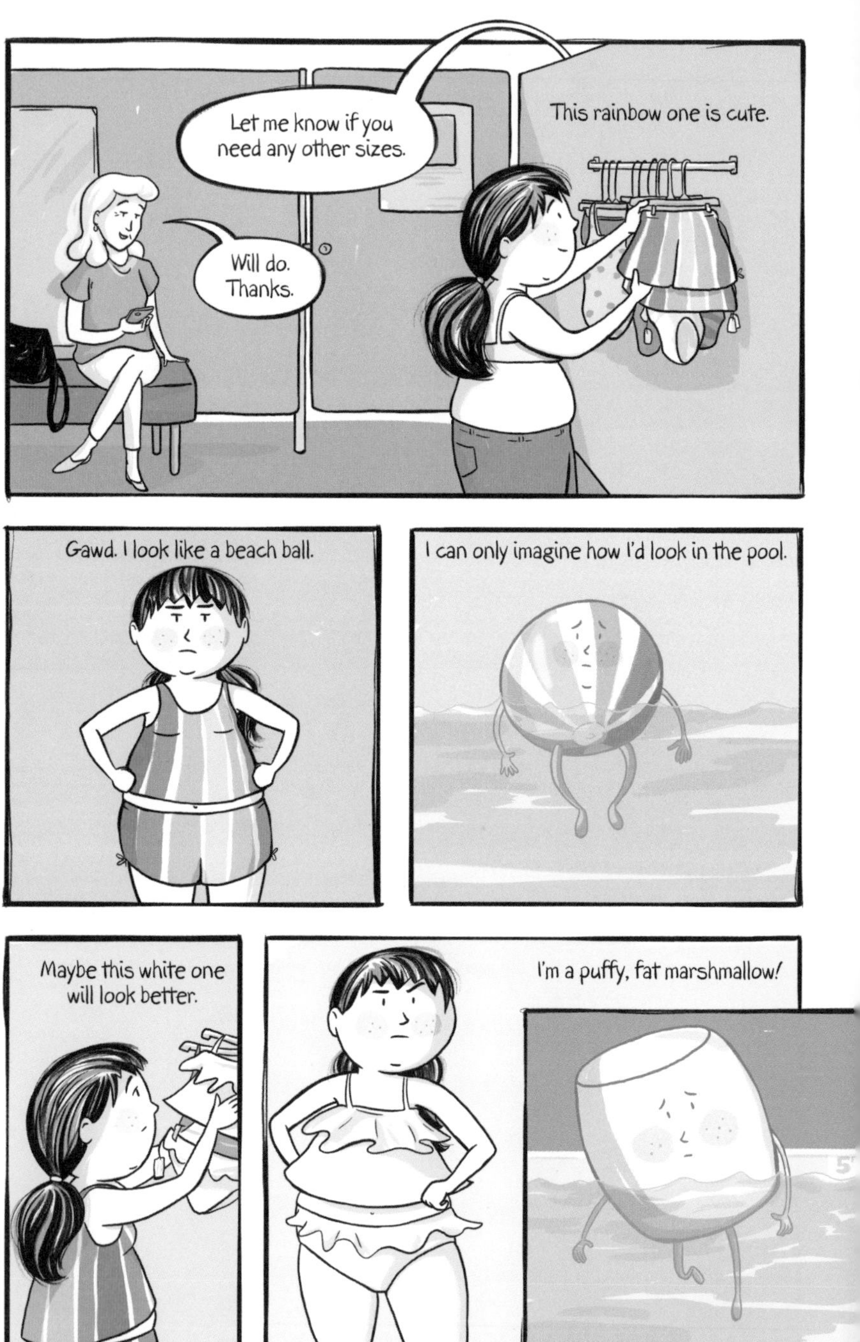
Let me know if you need any other sizes.
Will do. Thanks.
This rainbow one is cute.
Gawd. I look like a beach ball.
I can only imagine how I'd look in the pool.
Maybe this white one will look better.
I'm a puffy, fat marshmallow!
5'

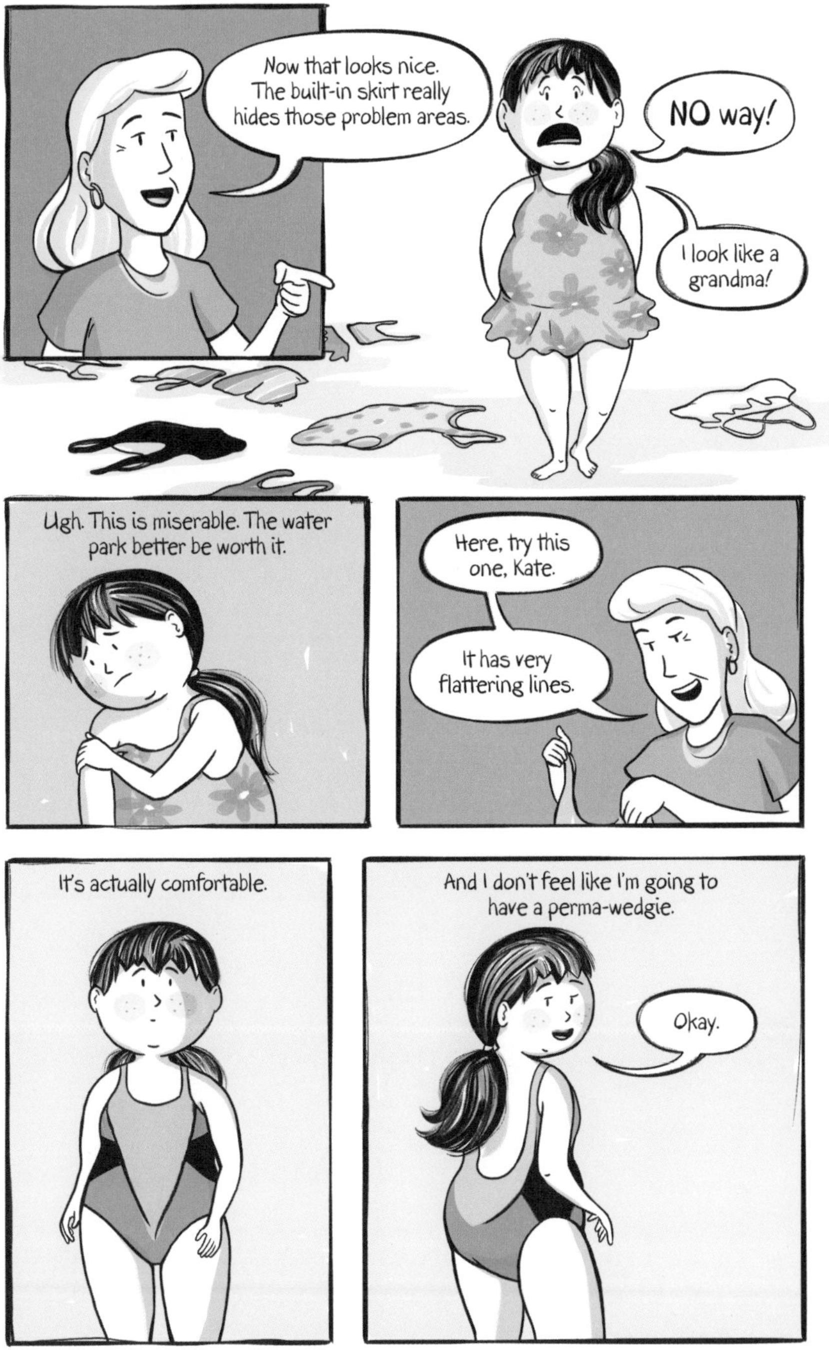
Now that looks nice. The built-in skirt really hides those problem areas.
NO way!
I look like a grandma!
Ugh. This is miserable. The water park better be worth it.
Here, try this one, Kate.
It has very flattering lines.
It's actually comfortable.
And I don't feel like I'm going to have a perma-wedgie.
Okay.

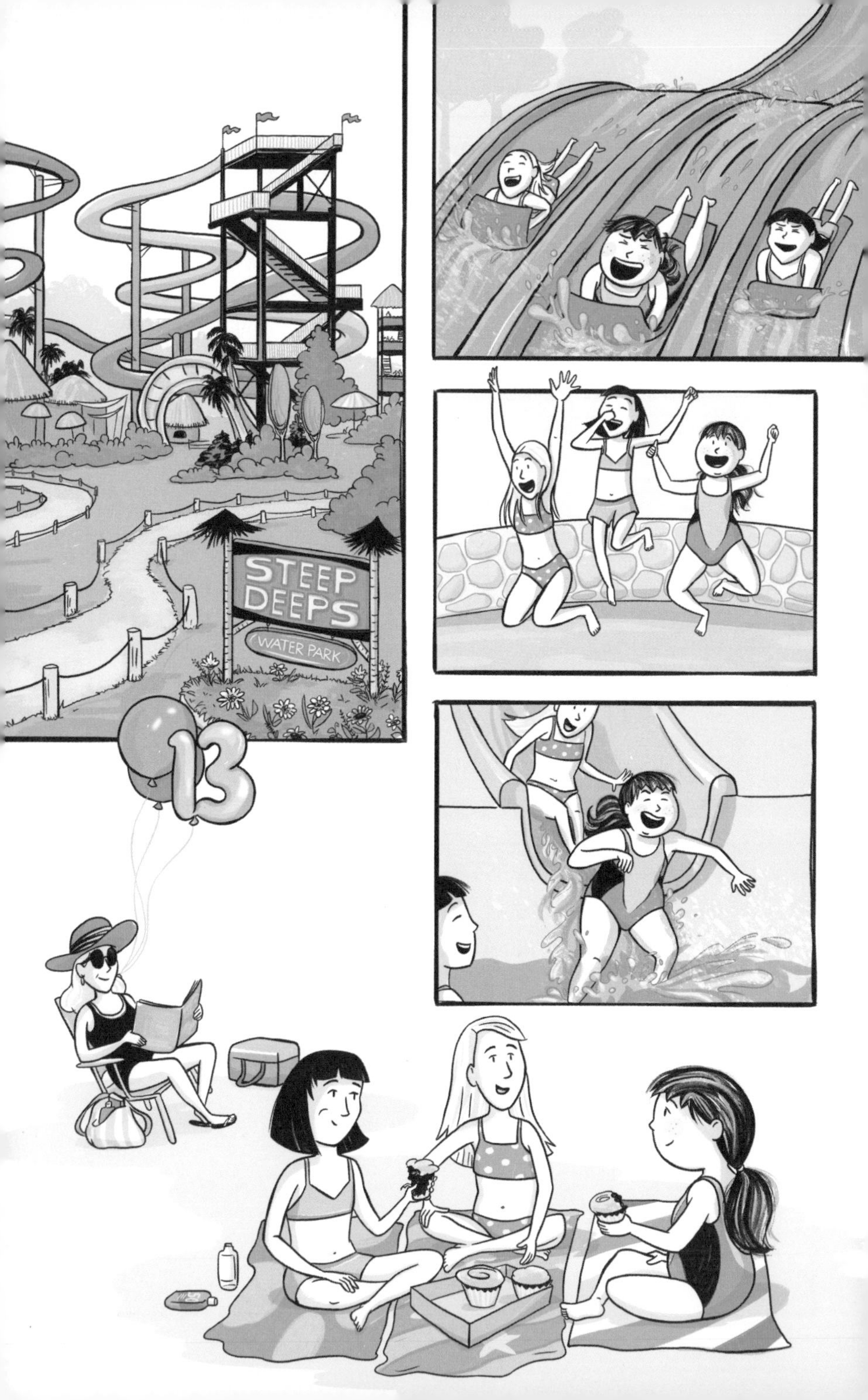
STEEP DEEPS
WATER PARK
13

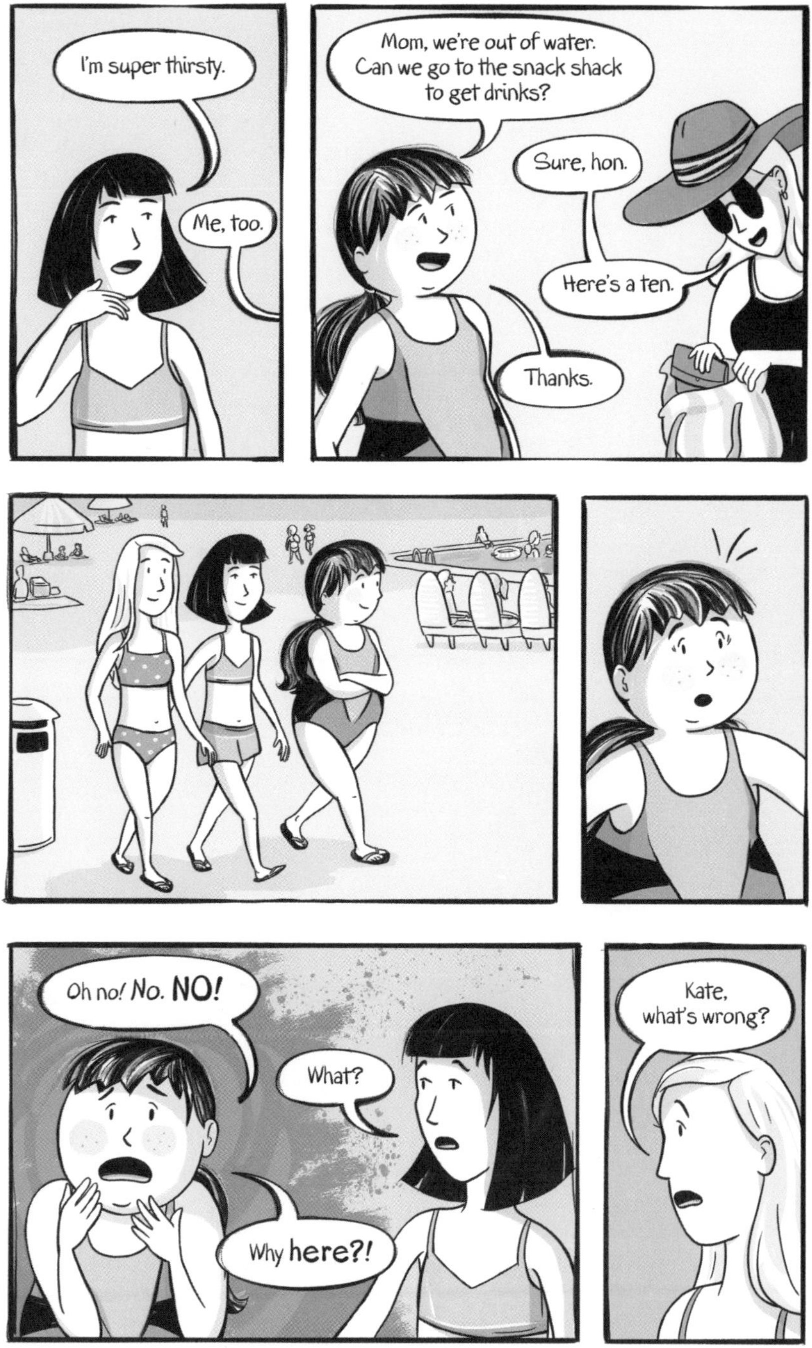
I'm super thirsty.
Me, too.
Mom, we're out of water. Can we go to the snack shack to get drinks?
Sure, hon.
Here's a ten.
Thanks.
Oh no! No. NO!
What?
Why here?!
Kate, what's wrong?

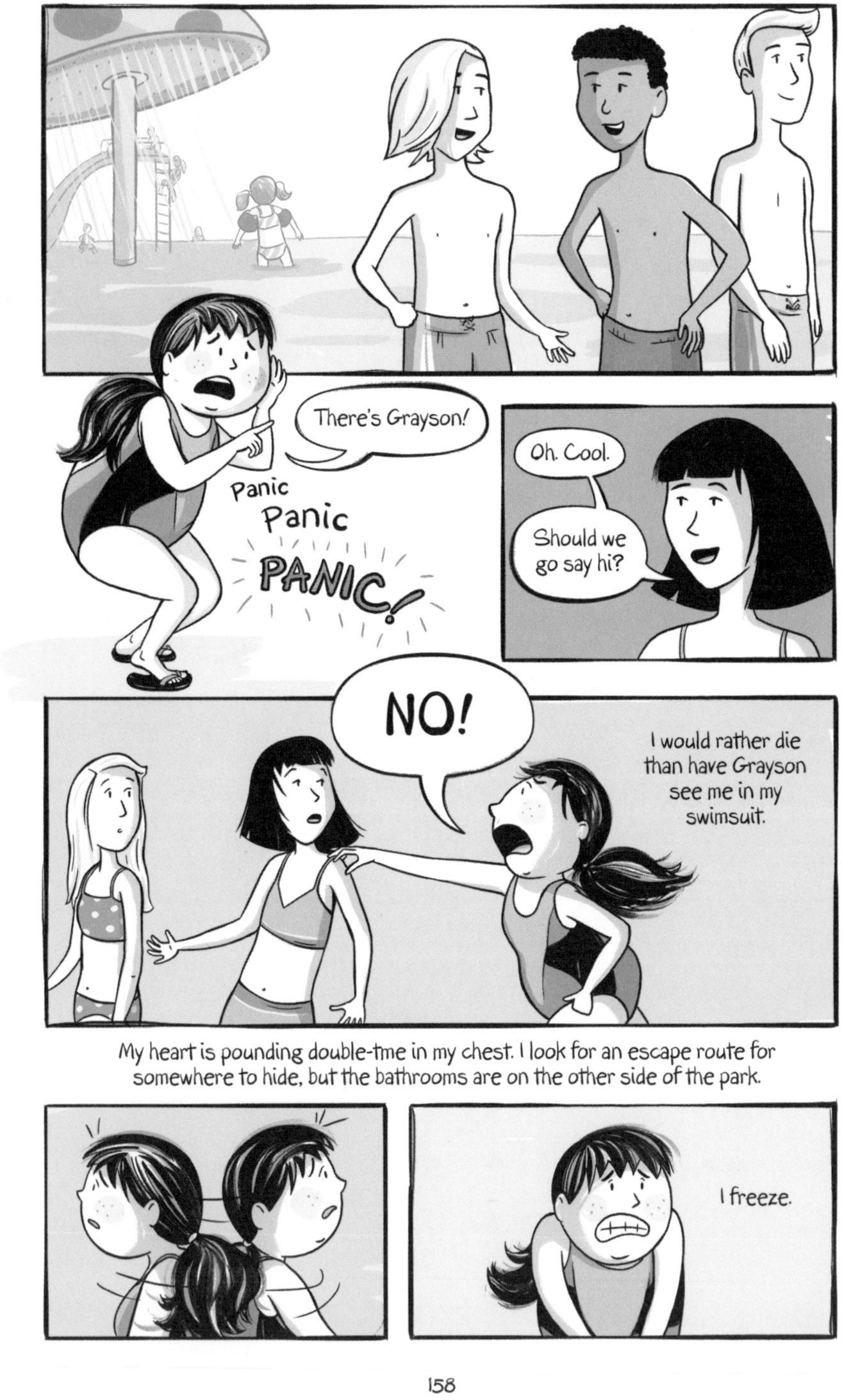
There's Grayson!
Panic
Panic
PANIC!
Oh. Cool.
Should we go say hi?
NO!
I would rather die than have Grayson see me in my swimsuit.
My heart is pounding double-tme in my chest. I look for an escape route for somewhere to hide, but the bathrooms are on the other side of the park.
I freeze.

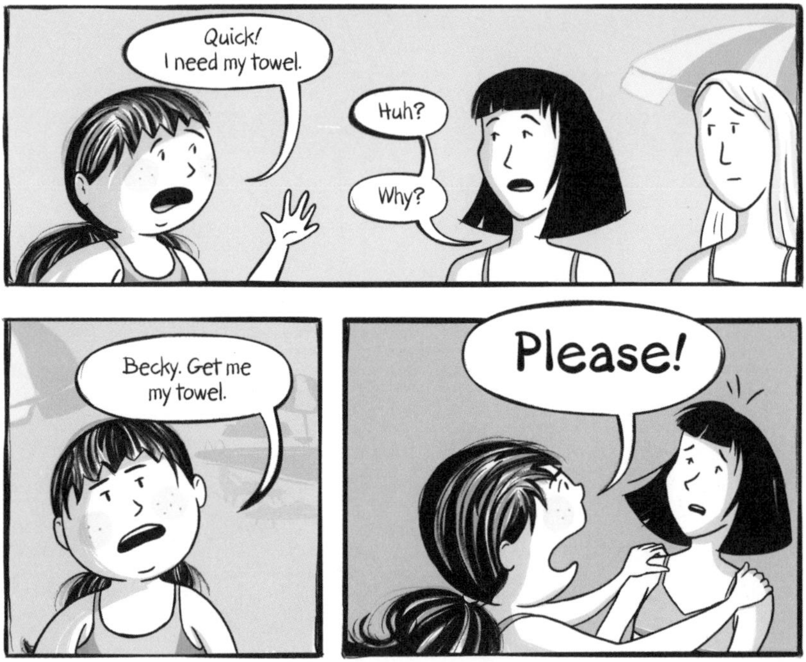
Quick!
I need my towel.
Huh?
Why?
Becky. Get me
my towel.
Please!

I feel completely exposed, like I'm stuck in one of those horrible dreams where you're caught in public (worst of all, a crowded school hallway) without your clothes on.

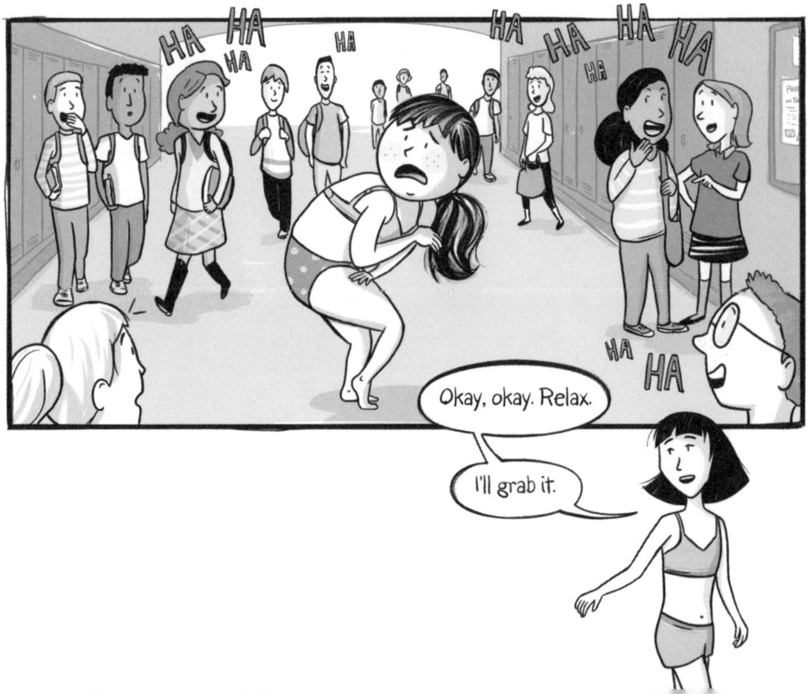
HA HA HA
HA
HA HA HA HA
HA
HA HA
Okay, okay. Relax.
I'll grab it.

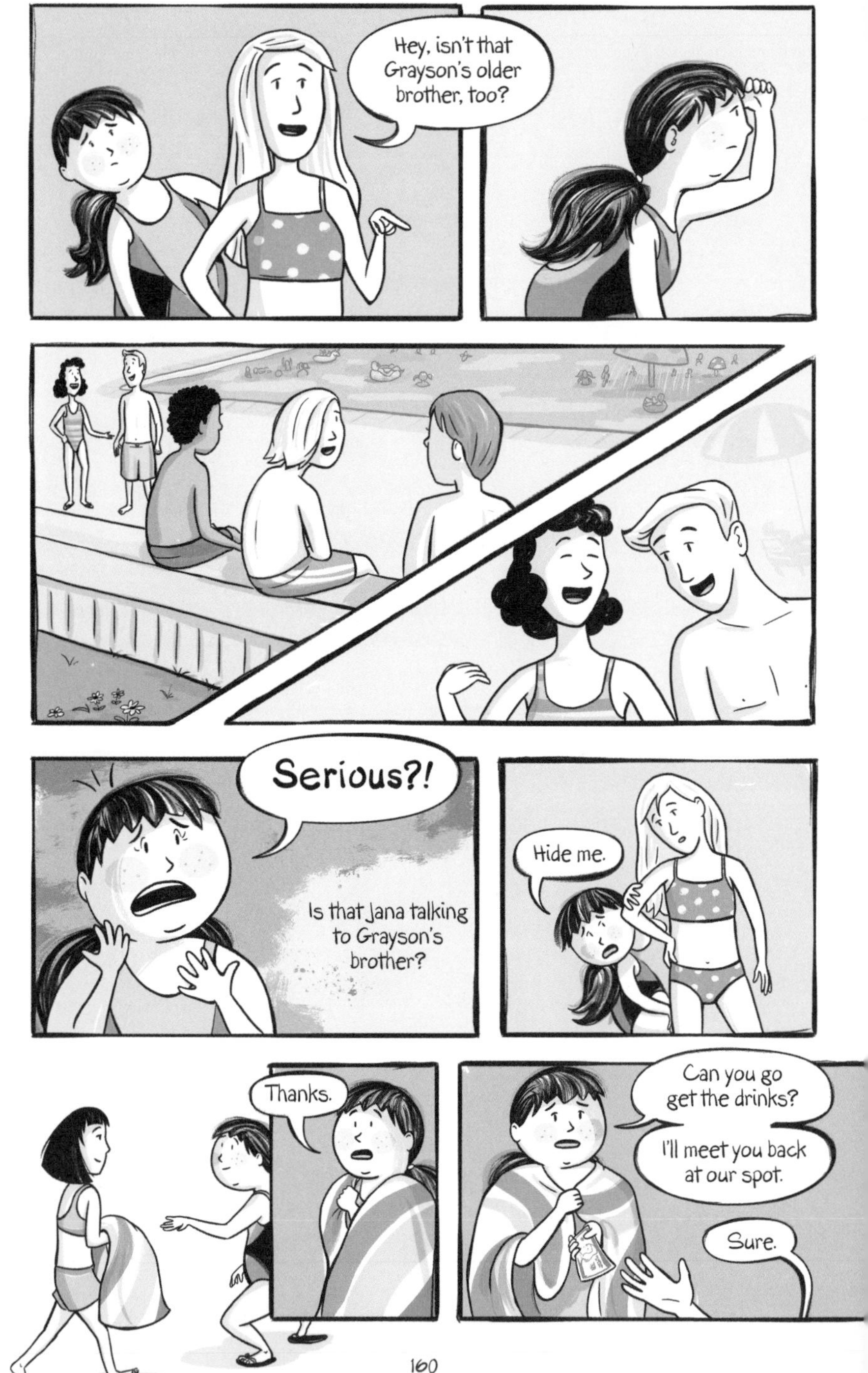
Hey, isn't that Grayson's older brother, too?
Serious?!
Is that Jana talking to Grayson's brother?
Hide me.
Thanks.
Can you go get the drinks?
I'll meet you back at our spot.
Sure.

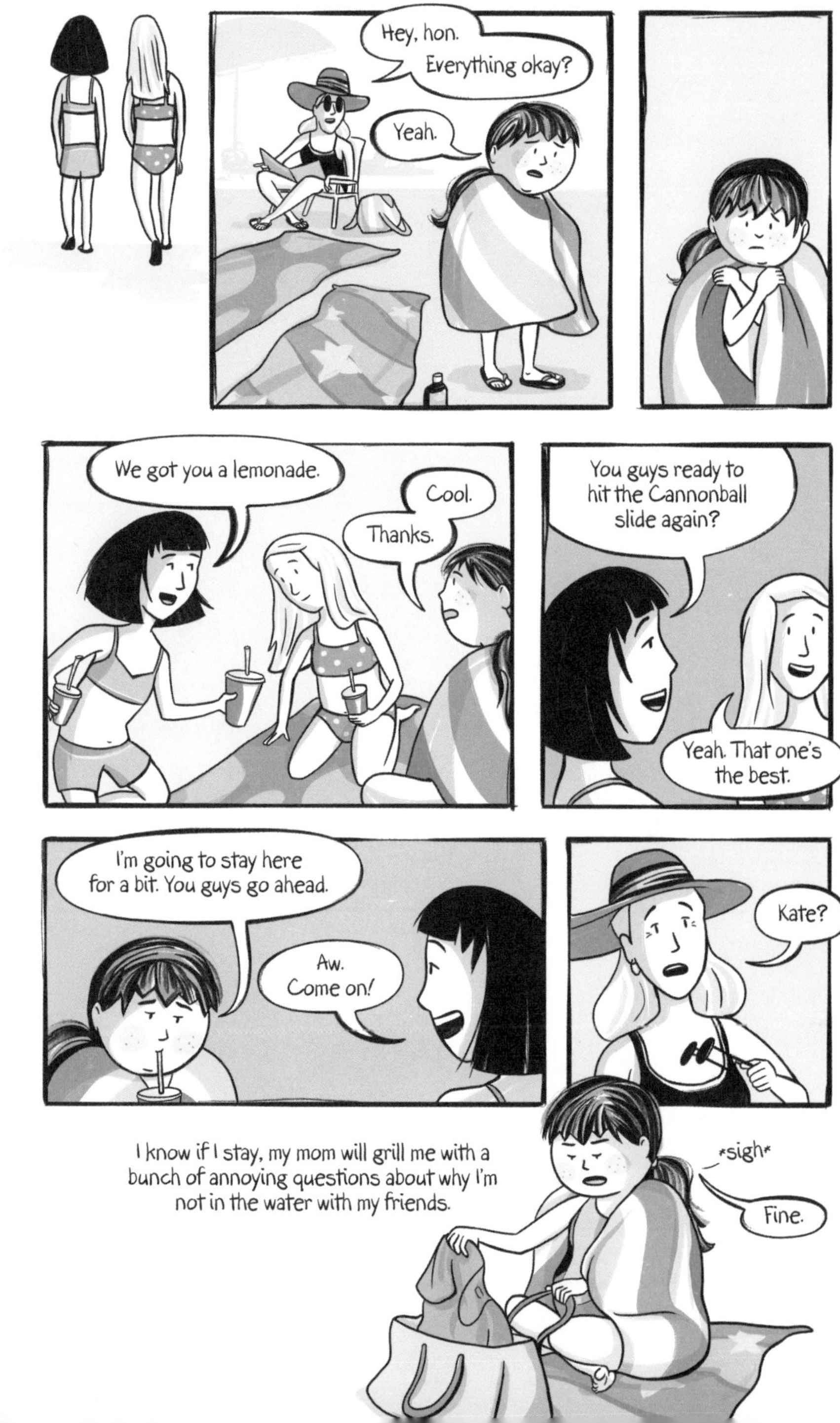
Hey, hon.
Everything okay?
Yeah.
We got you a lemonade.
Cool.
Thanks.
You guys ready to hit the Cannonball slide again?
Yeah. That one's the best.
I'm going to stay here for a bit. You guys go ahead.
Aw. Come on!
Kate?
I know if I stay, my mom will grill me with a bunch of annoying questions about why I'm not in the water with my friends.
sigh
Fine.

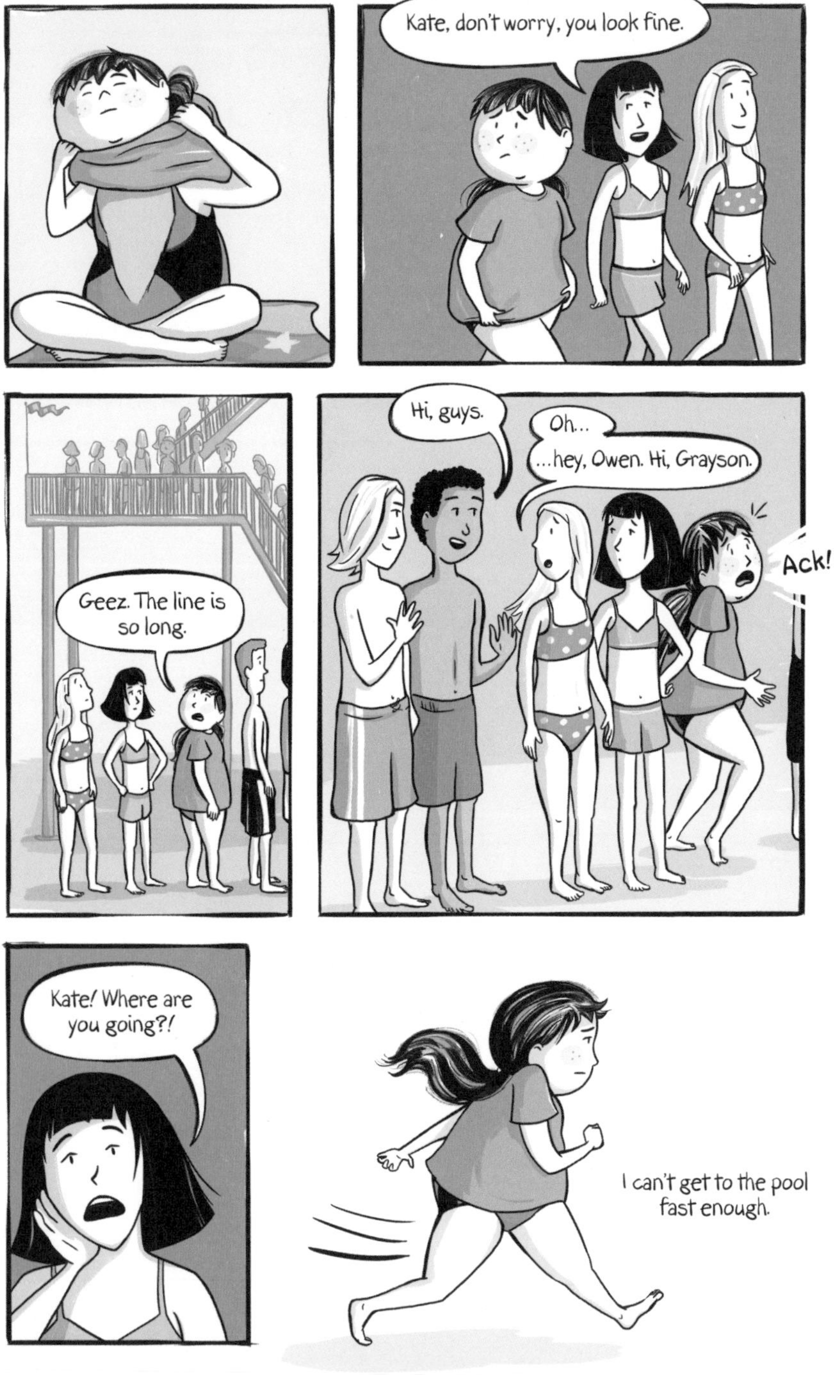
Kate, don't worry, you look fine.
Geez. The line is so long.
Hi, guys.
Oh...
...hey, Owen. Hi, Grayson.
Ack!
Kate! Where are you going?!
I can't get to the pool fast enough.

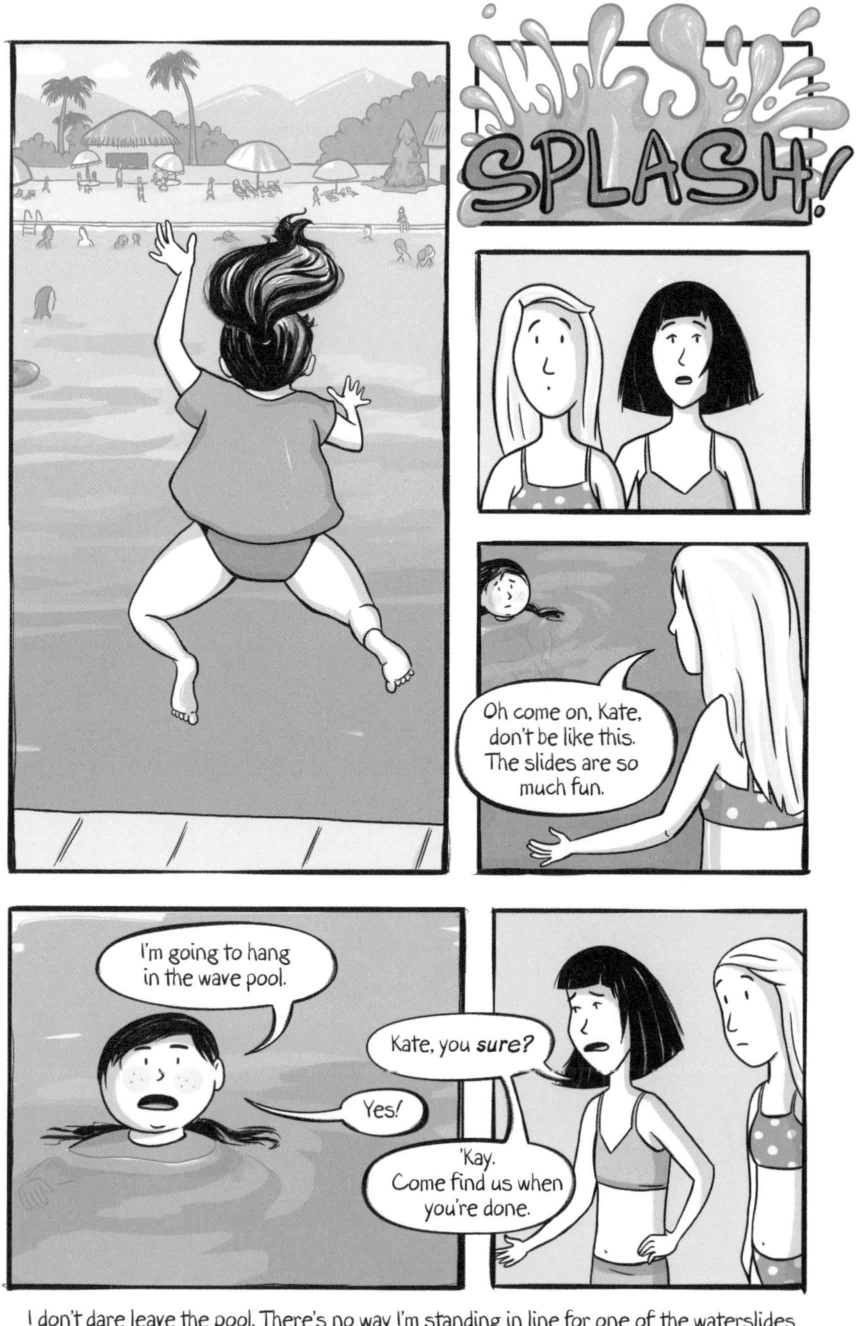
SPLASH!
Oh come on, Kate, don't be like this. The slides are so much fun.
I'm going to hang in the wave pool.
Kate, you *sure?*
Yes!
'Kay. Come find us when you're done.

I don't dare leave the pool. There's no way I'm standing in line for one of the waterslides with my thunder thighs in plain view for Grayson to see.

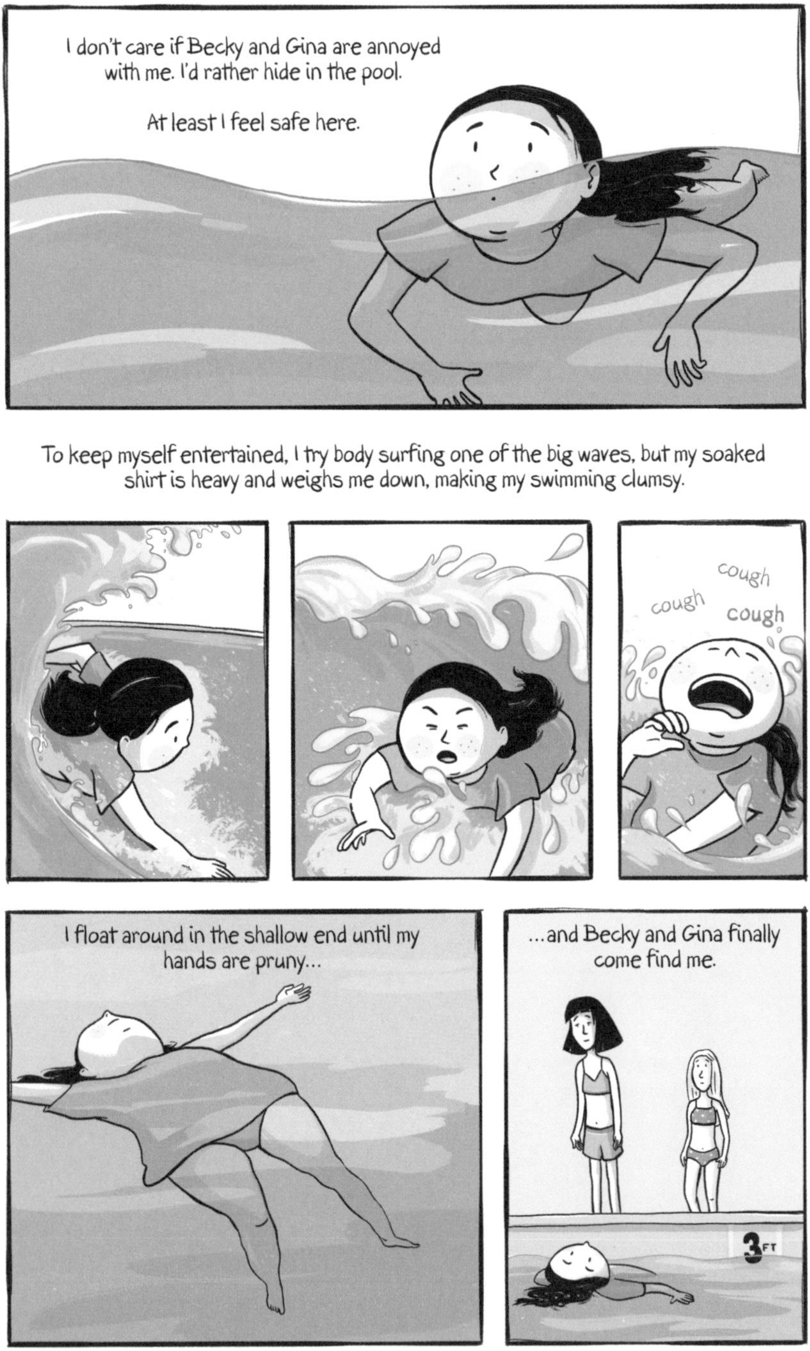
I don't care if Becky and Gina are annoyed with me. I'd rather hide in the pool.
At least I feel safe here.
To keep myself entertained, I try body surfing one of the big waves, but my soaked shirt is heavy and weighs me down, making my swimming clumsy.
cough
cough
cough
I float around in the shallow end until my hands are pruny...
...and Becky and Gina finally come find me.
3 FT

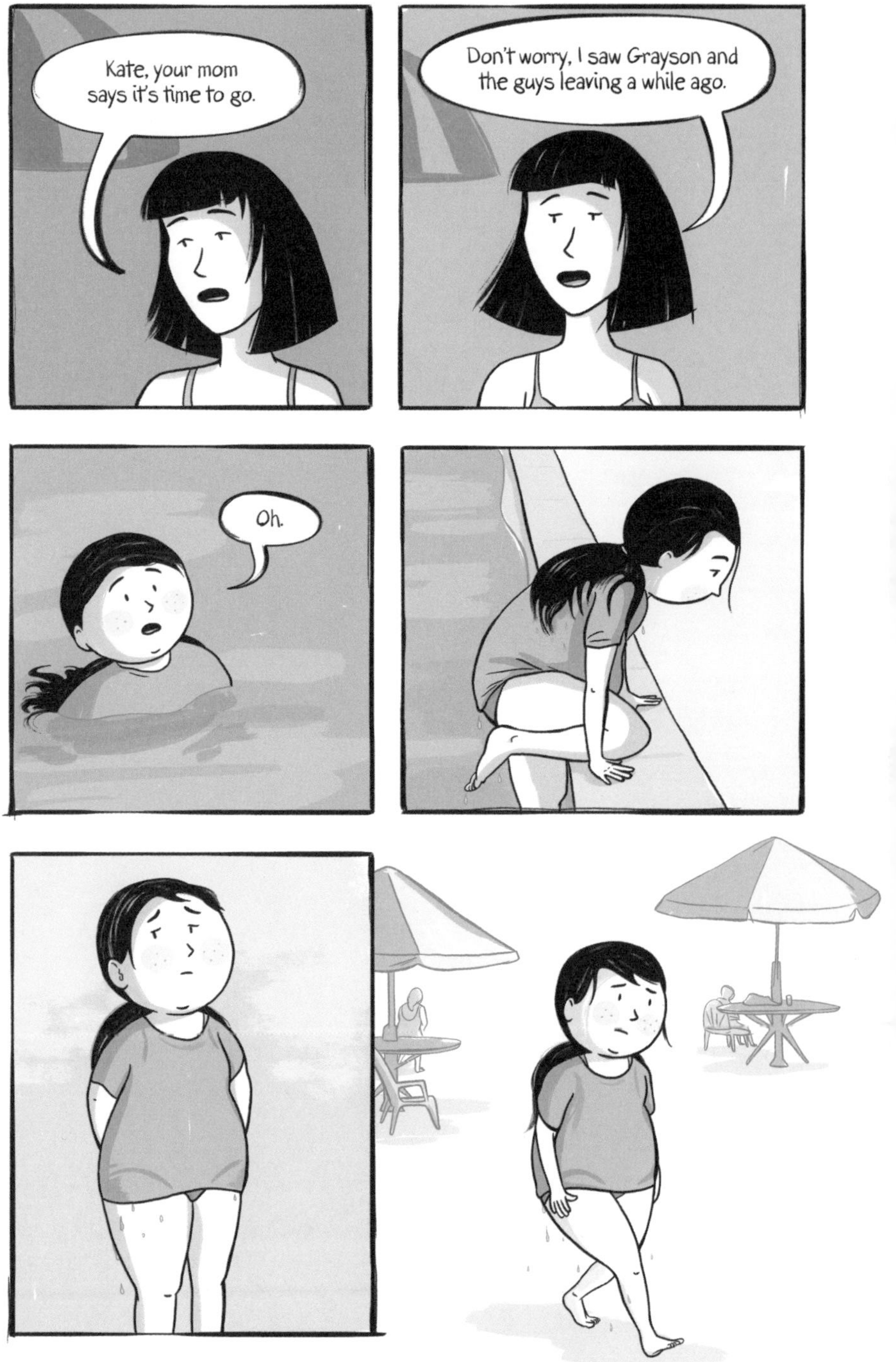
Kate, your mom says it's time to go.
Don't worry, I saw Grayson and the guys leaving a while ago.
Oh.

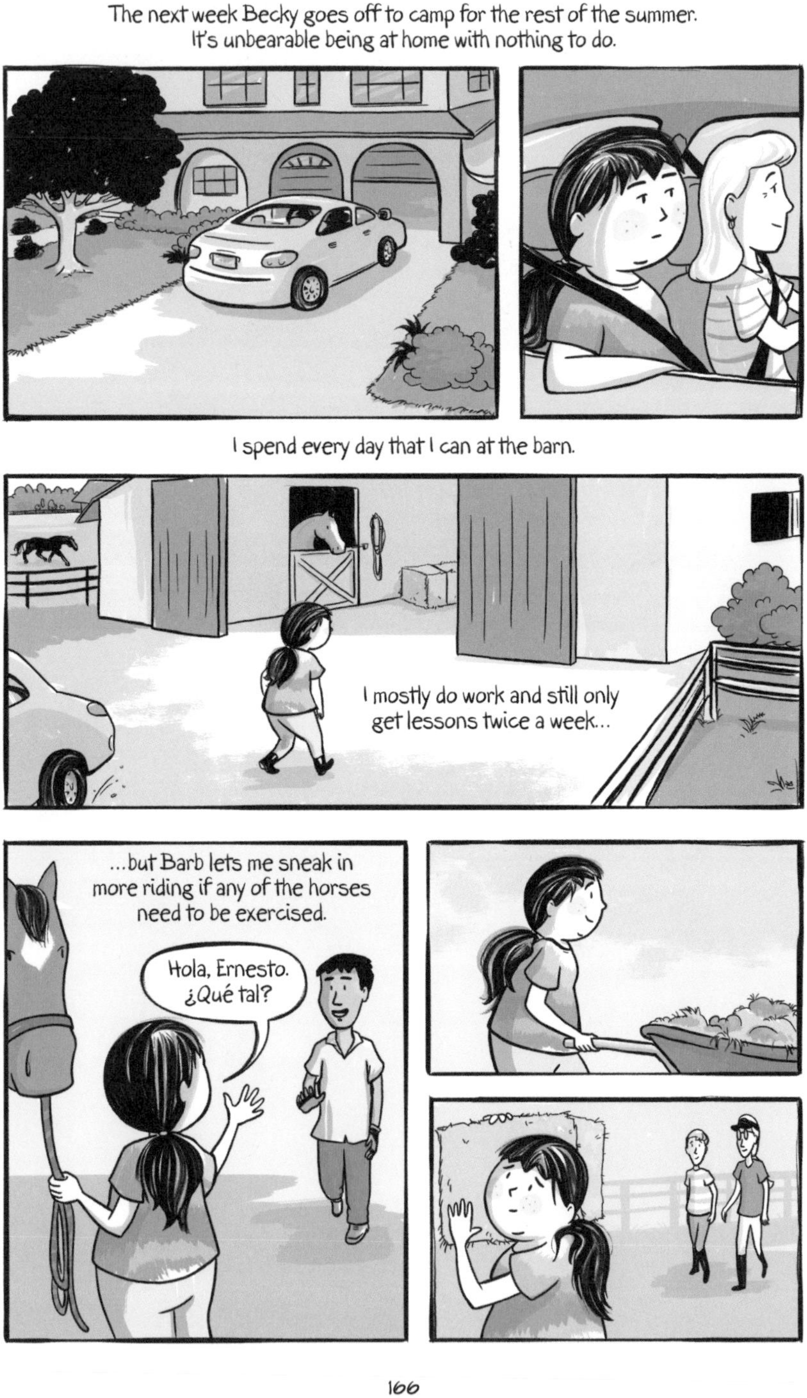
The next week Becky goes off to camp for the rest of the summer.
It's unbearable being at home with nothing to do.
I spend every day that I can at the barn.
I mostly do work and still only get lessons twice a week...
...but Barb lets me sneak in more riding if any of the horses need to be exercised.
Hola, Ernesto. ¿Qué tal?

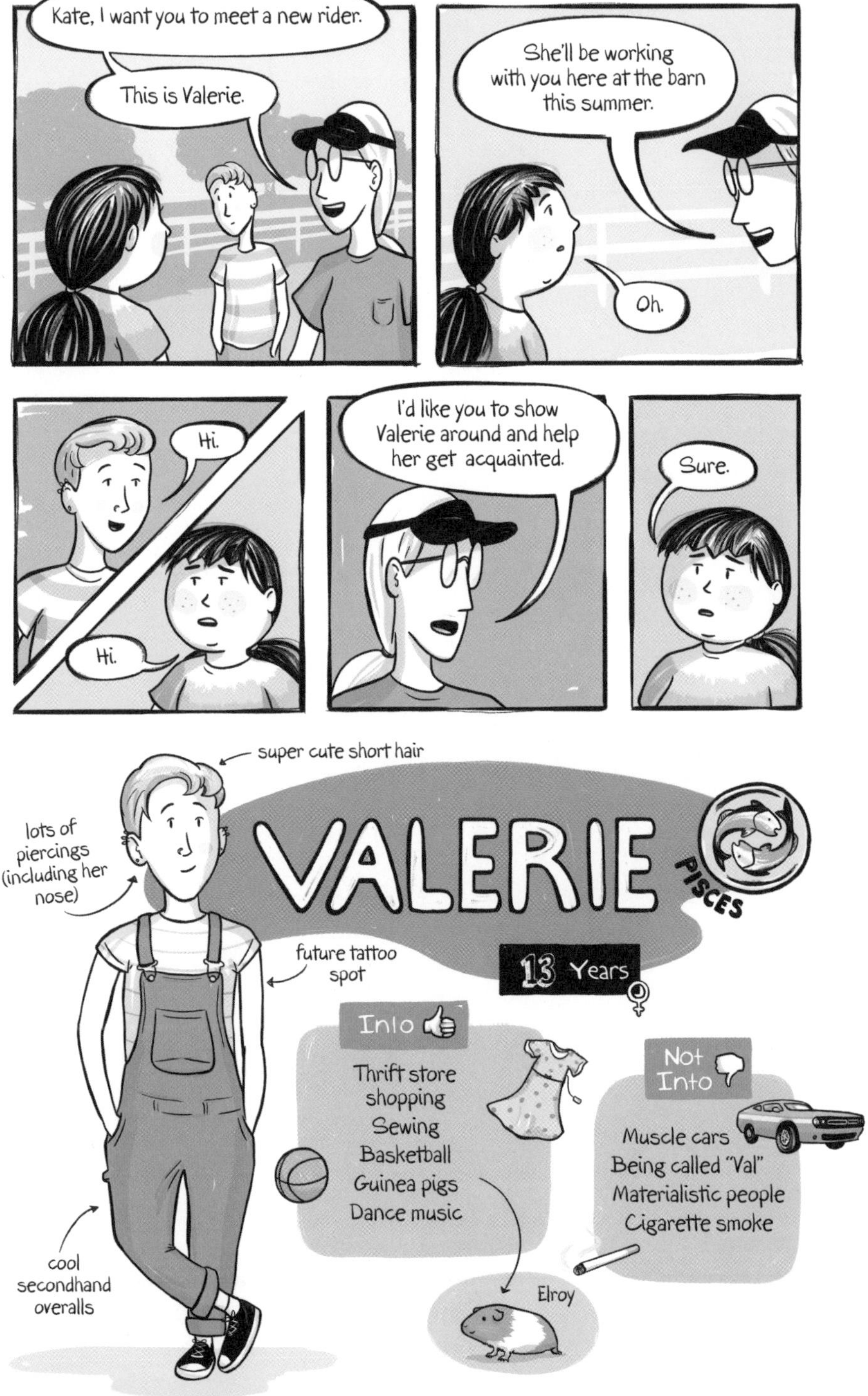
Kate, I want you to meet a new rider.
This is Valerie.
She'll be working with you here at the barn this summer.
Oh.
Hi.
Hi.
I'd like you to show Valerie around and help her get acquainted.
Sure.
super cute short hair
lots of piercings (including her nose)
VALERIE
PISCES
future tattoo spot
13 Years
Into
Thrift store shopping
Sewing
Basketball
Guinea pigs
Dance music
Not Into
Muscle cars
Being called "Val"
Materialistic people
Cigarette smoke
cool secondhand overalls
Elroy

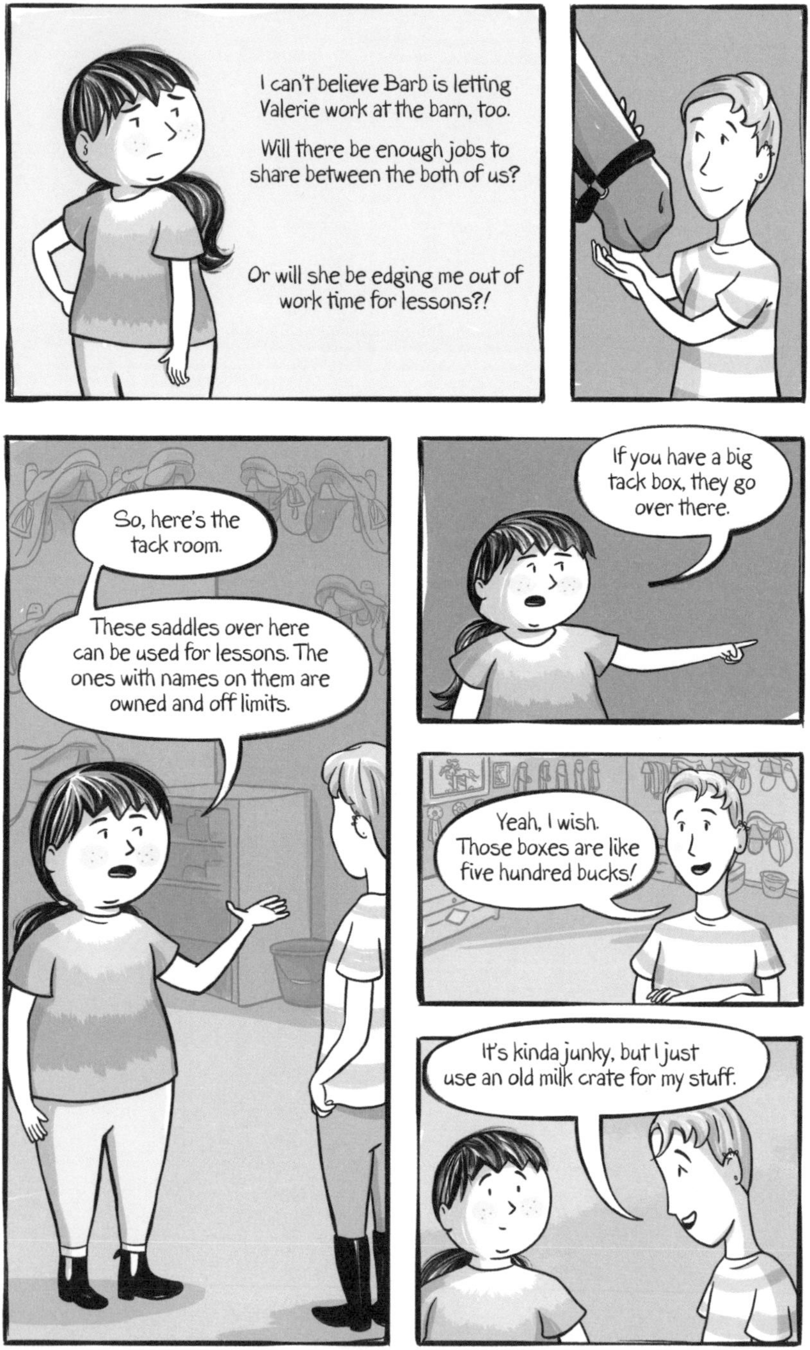
I can't believe Barb is letting Valerie work at the barn, too.
Will there be enough jobs to share between the both of us?
Or will she be edging me out of work time for lessons?!
So, here's the tack room.
These saddles over here can be used for lessons. The ones with names on them are owned and off limits.
If you have a big tack box, they go over there.
Yeah, I wish. Those boxes are like five hundred bucks!
It's kinda junky, but I just use an old milk crate for my stuff.

Here's the spray-down and washing area.

Hey, Lucy and Jana, this is Valerie.

Hi, Valerie.

Hi.

So...you're a new barn-cleaning buddy of Kate's?

Actually, Valerie is a new *rider* here.

Oh.

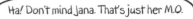

Geez. What's stuck up her butt?

Ha! Don't mind Jana. That's just her M.O.

Come on, let me introduce you to some of my favorite horses.

Despite some of my initial feelings about Valerie, I'm starting to become a big fan.

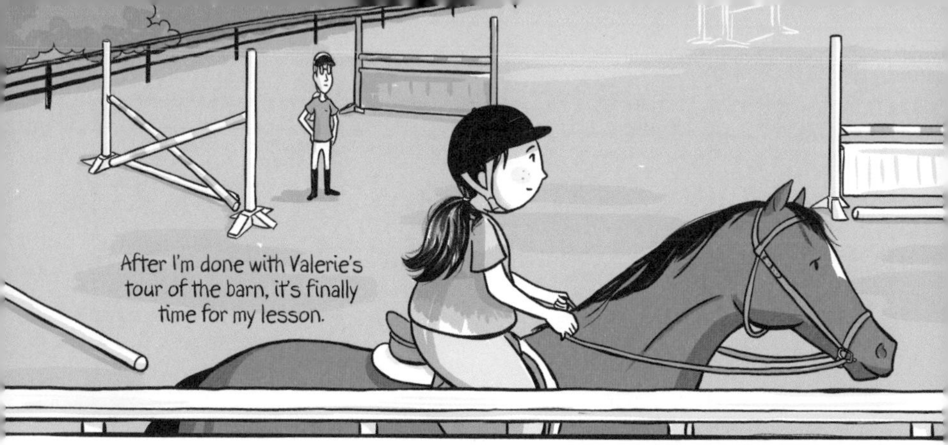
After I'm done with Valerie's tour of the barn, it's finally time for my lesson.

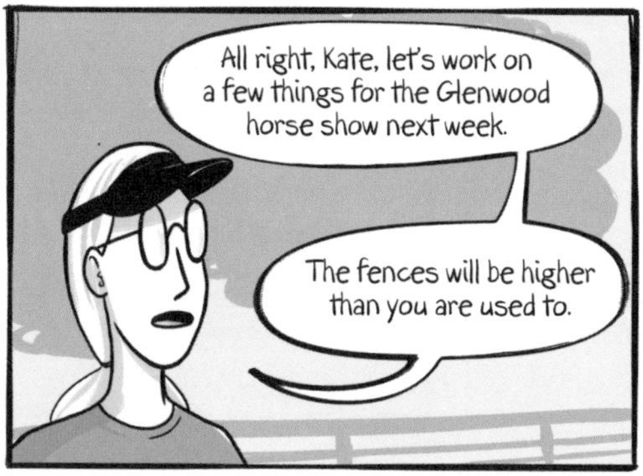
All right, Kate, let's work on a few things for the Glenwood horse show next week.
The fences will be higher than you are used to.

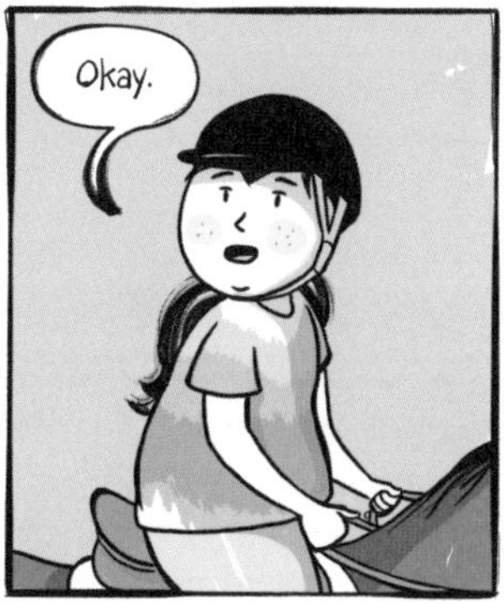
Okay.

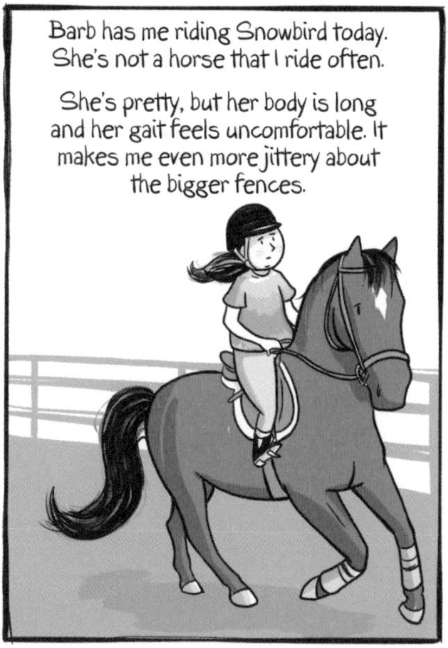
Barb has me riding Snowbird today. She's not a horse that I ride often.
She's pretty, but her body is long and her gait feels uncomfortable. It makes me even more jittery about the bigger fences.

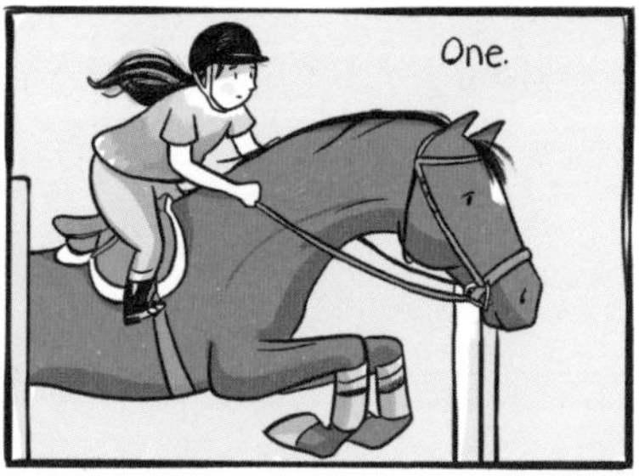
One.

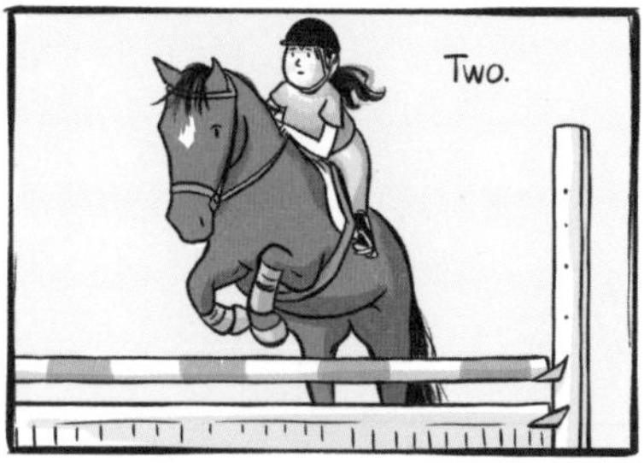
Two.

My nerves settle a bit.

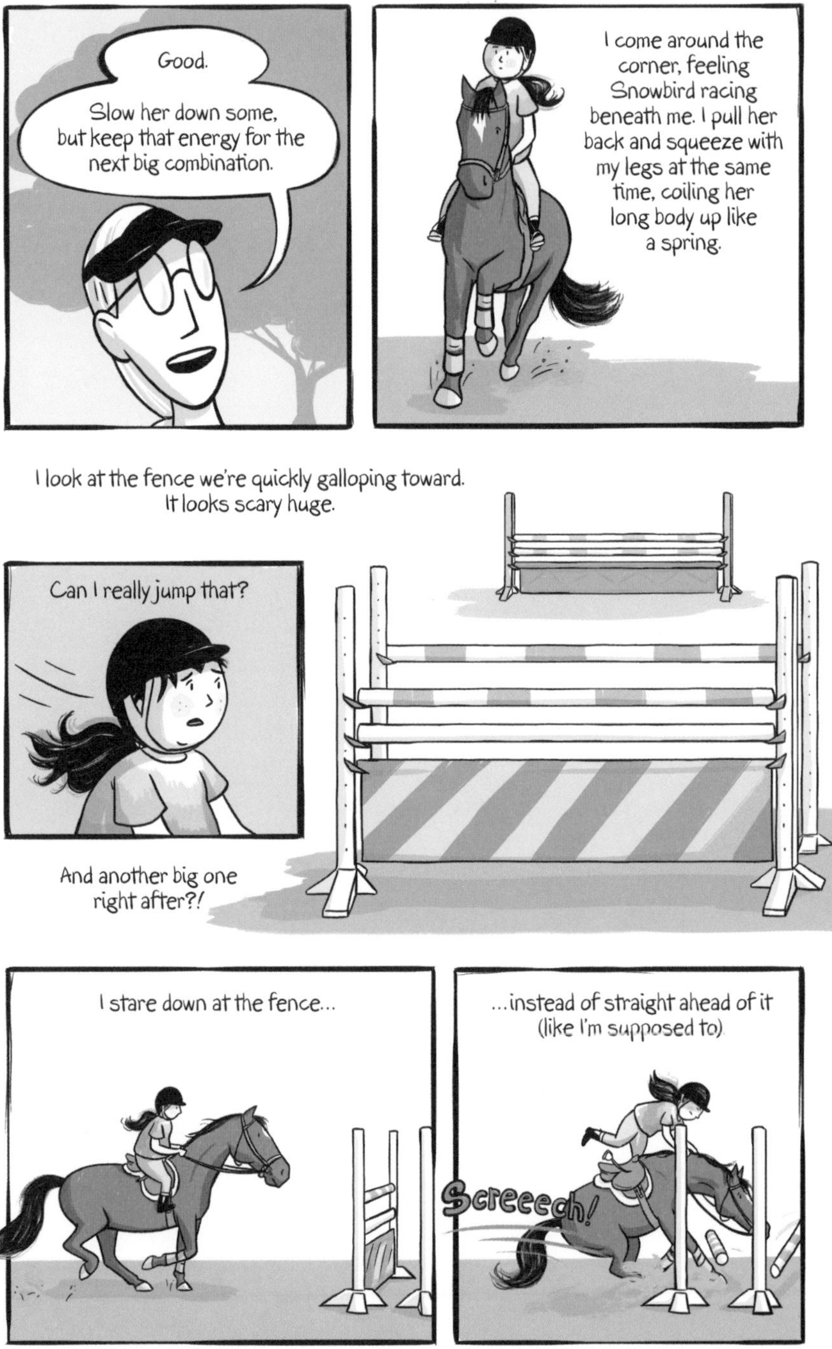
Good.
Slow her down some, but keep that energy for the next big combination.
I come around the corner, feeling Snowbird racing beneath me. I pull her back and squeeze with my legs at the same time, coiling her long body up like a spring.
I look at the fence we're quickly galloping toward. It looks scary huge.
Can I really jump that?
And another big one right after?!
I stare down at the fence...
...instead of straight ahead of it (like I'm supposed to).
Screeech!

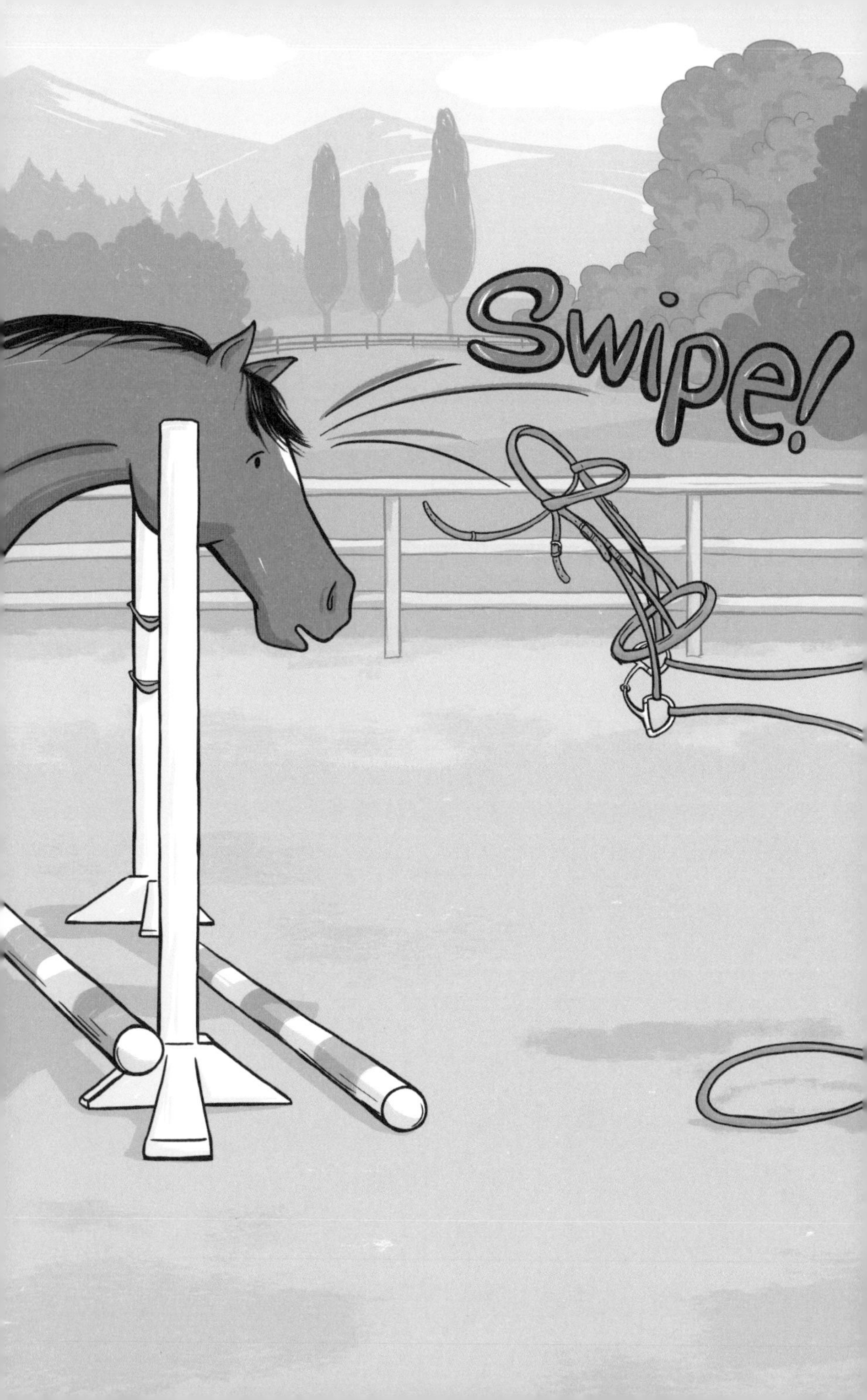
Swipe!

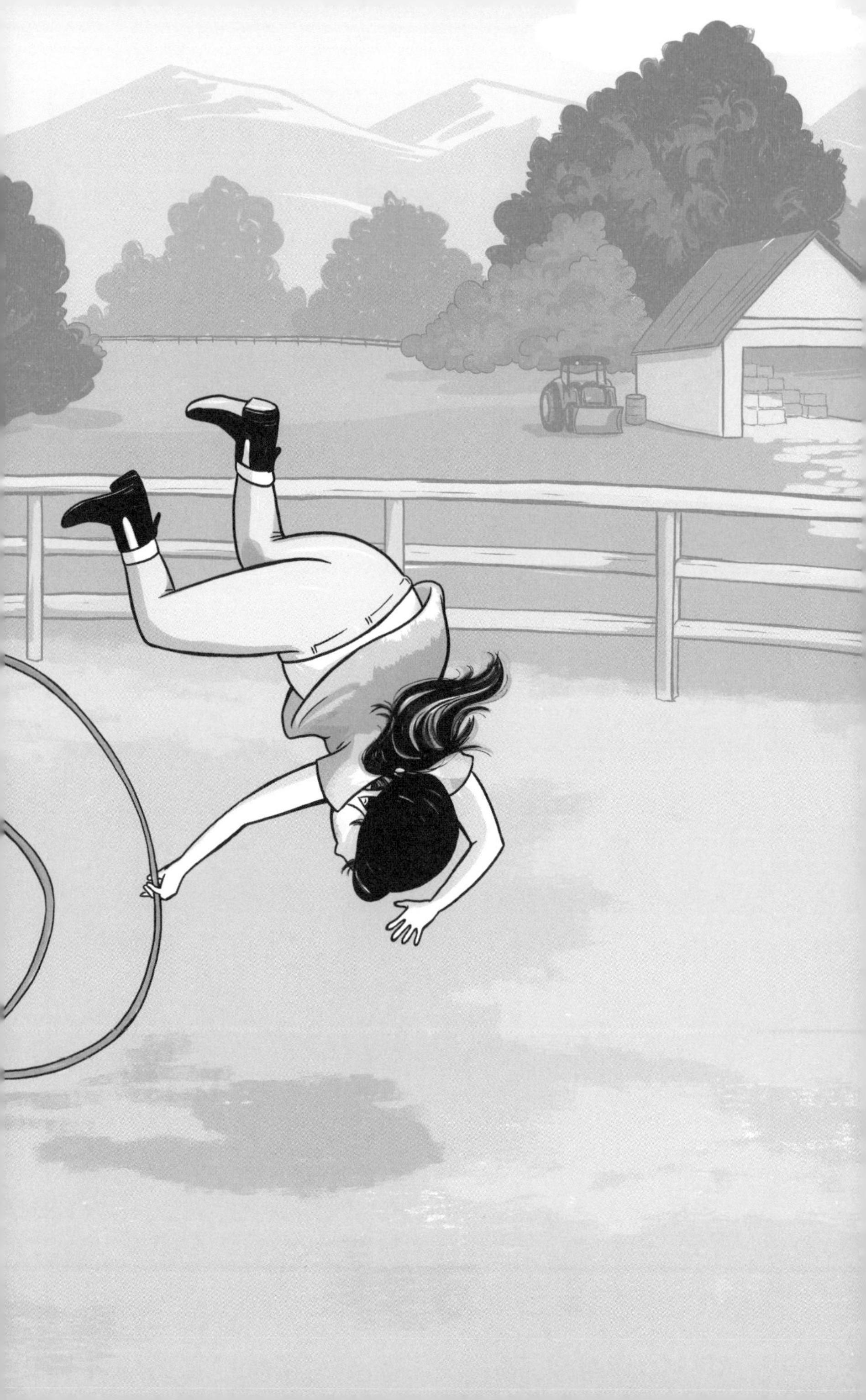

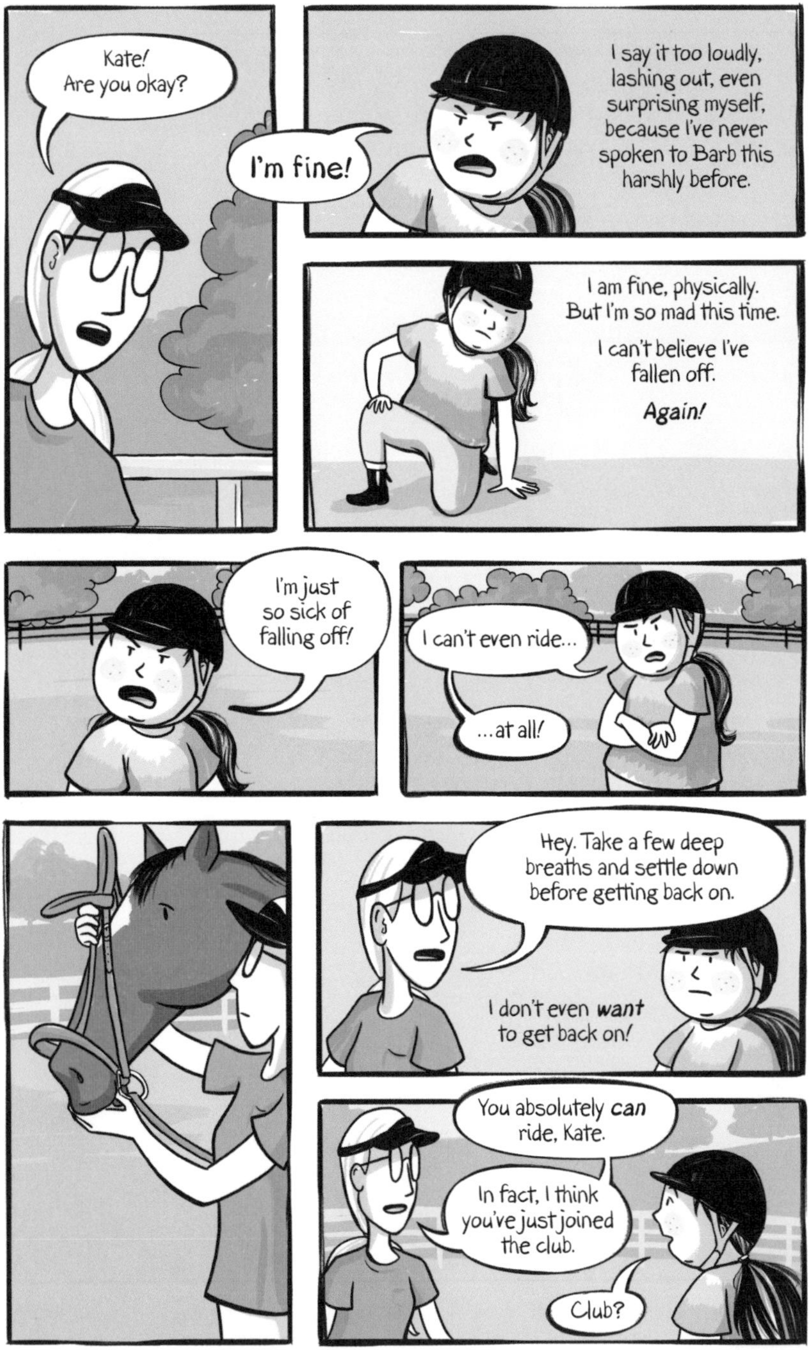
Kate!
Are you okay?
I'm fine!
I say it too loudly, lashing out, even surprising myself, because I've never spoken to Barb this harshly before.
I am fine, physically. But I'm so mad this time.
I can't believe I've fallen off.
Again!
I'm just so sick of falling off!
I can't even ride...
...at all!
Hey. Take a few deep breaths and settle down before getting back on.
I don't even want to get back on!
You absolutely can ride, Kate.
In fact, I think you've just joined the club.
Club?

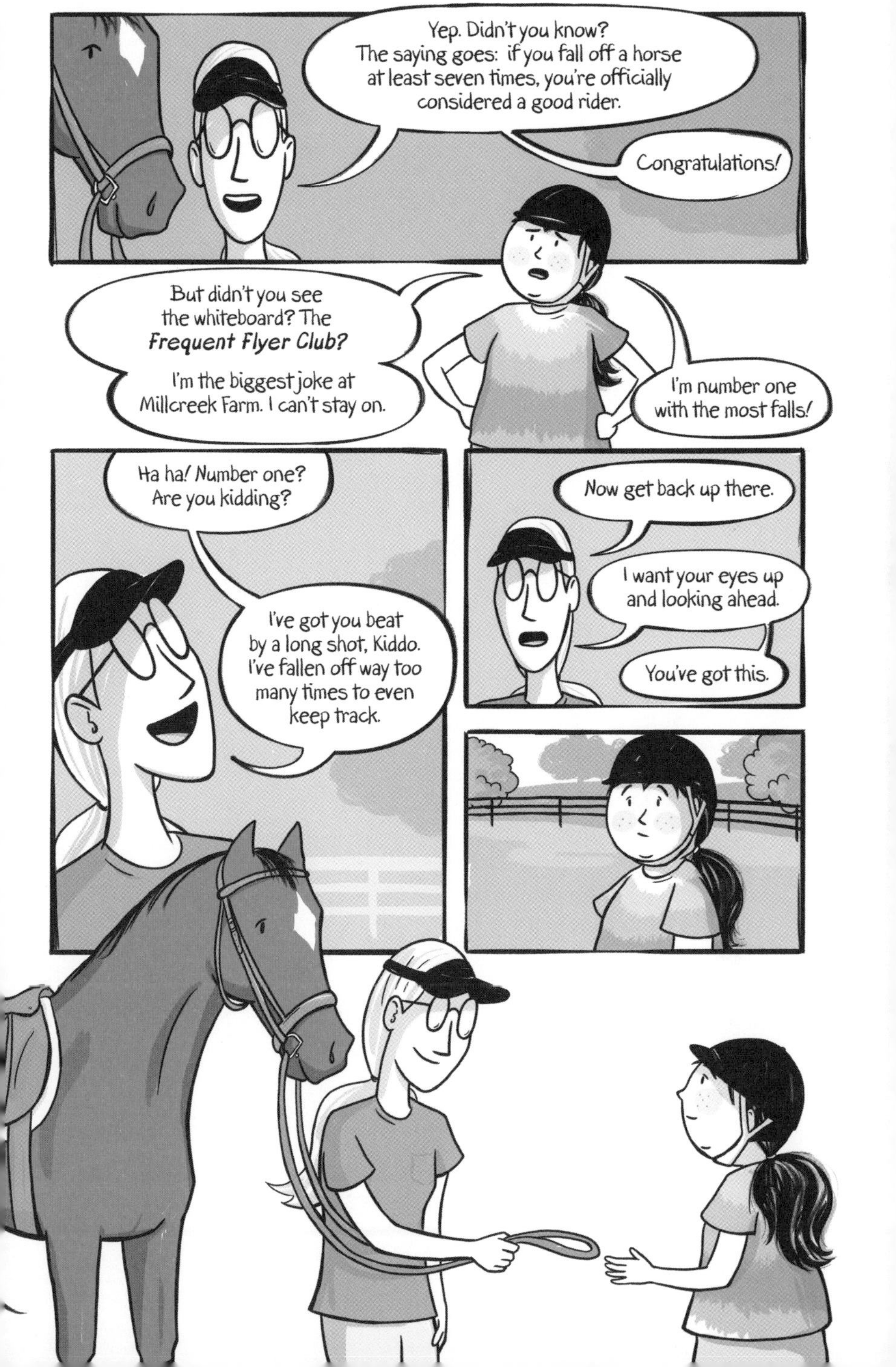
Yep. Didn't you know? The saying goes: if you fall off a horse at least seven times, you're officially considered a good rider.
Congratulations!
But didn't you see the whiteboard? The *Frequent Flyer Club?*
I'm the biggest joke at Millcreek Farm. I can't stay on.
I'm number one with the most falls!
Ha ha! Number one? Are you kidding?
I've got you beat by a long shot, Kiddo. I've fallen off way too many times to even keep track.
Now get back up there.
I want your eyes up and looking ahead.
You've got this.

Chapter 8
Dump and Jump

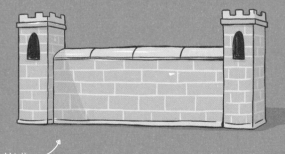

Wall

A jump that is painted to look like a brick or stone wall, but the "bricks" are made of a lightweight material and fall easily when knocked.

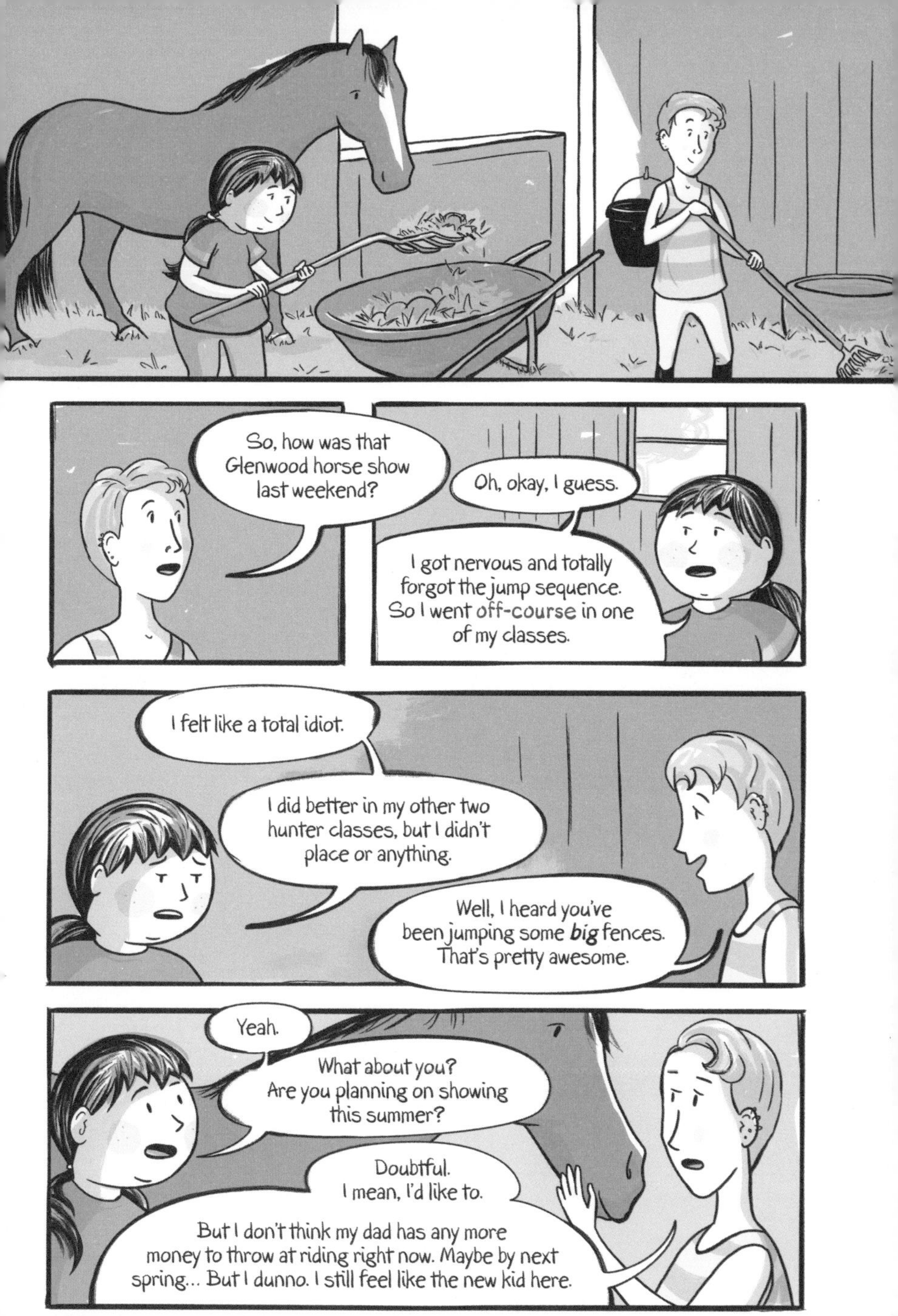
So, how was that Glenwood horse show last weekend?
Oh, okay, I guess.
I got nervous and totally forgot the jump sequence. So I went off-course in one of my classes.
I felt like a total idiot.
I did better in my other two hunter classes, but I didn't place or anything.
Well, I heard you've been jumping some *big* fences. That's pretty awesome.
Yeah.
What about you? Are you planning on showing this summer?
Doubtful. I mean, I'd like to.
But I don't think my dad has any more money to throw at riding right now. Maybe by next spring... But I dunno. I still feel like the new kid here.

Off-course: When a rider jumps fences during a competition in the incorrect order, which results in an immediate disqualification from the class.

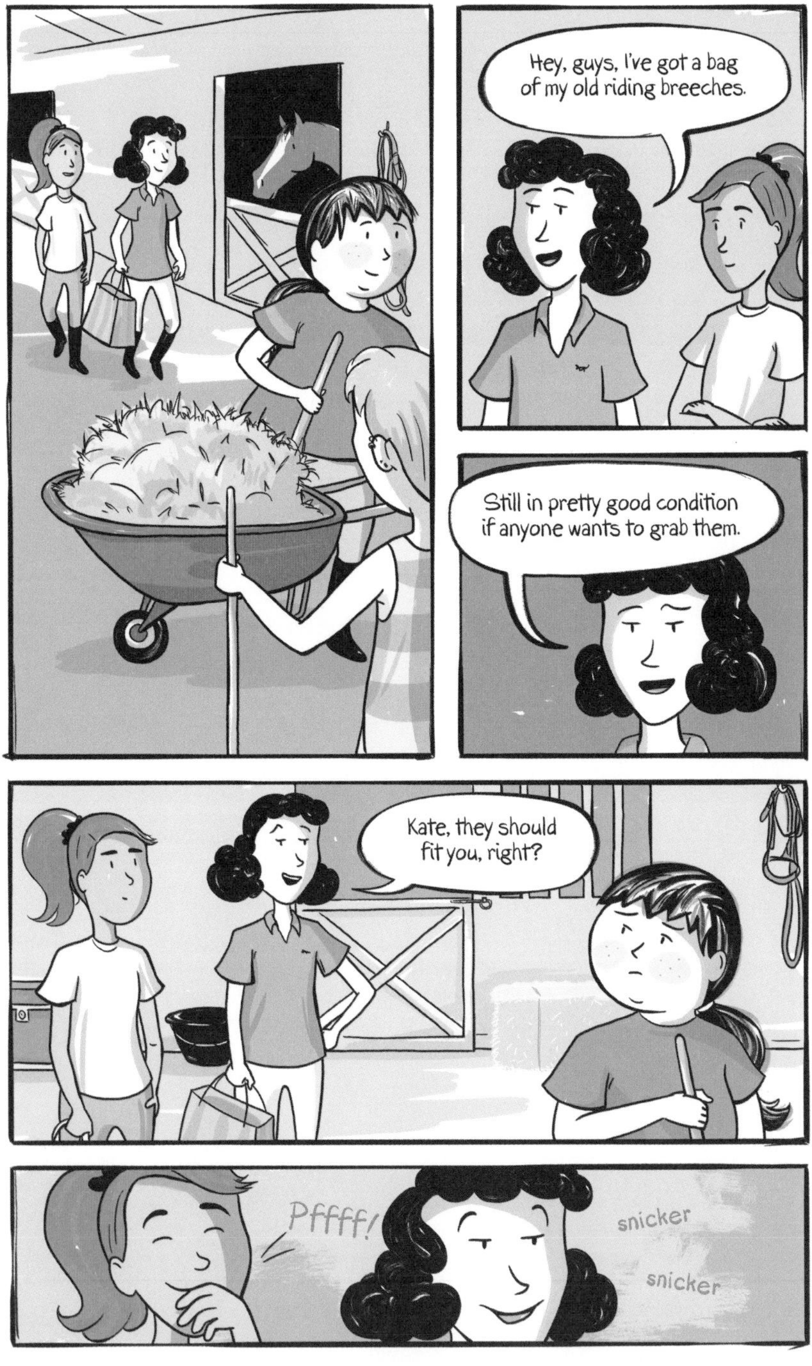
Hey, guys, I've got a bag of my old riding breeches.
Still in pretty good condition if anyone wants to grab them.
Kate, they should fit you, right?
Pffff!
snicker
snicker

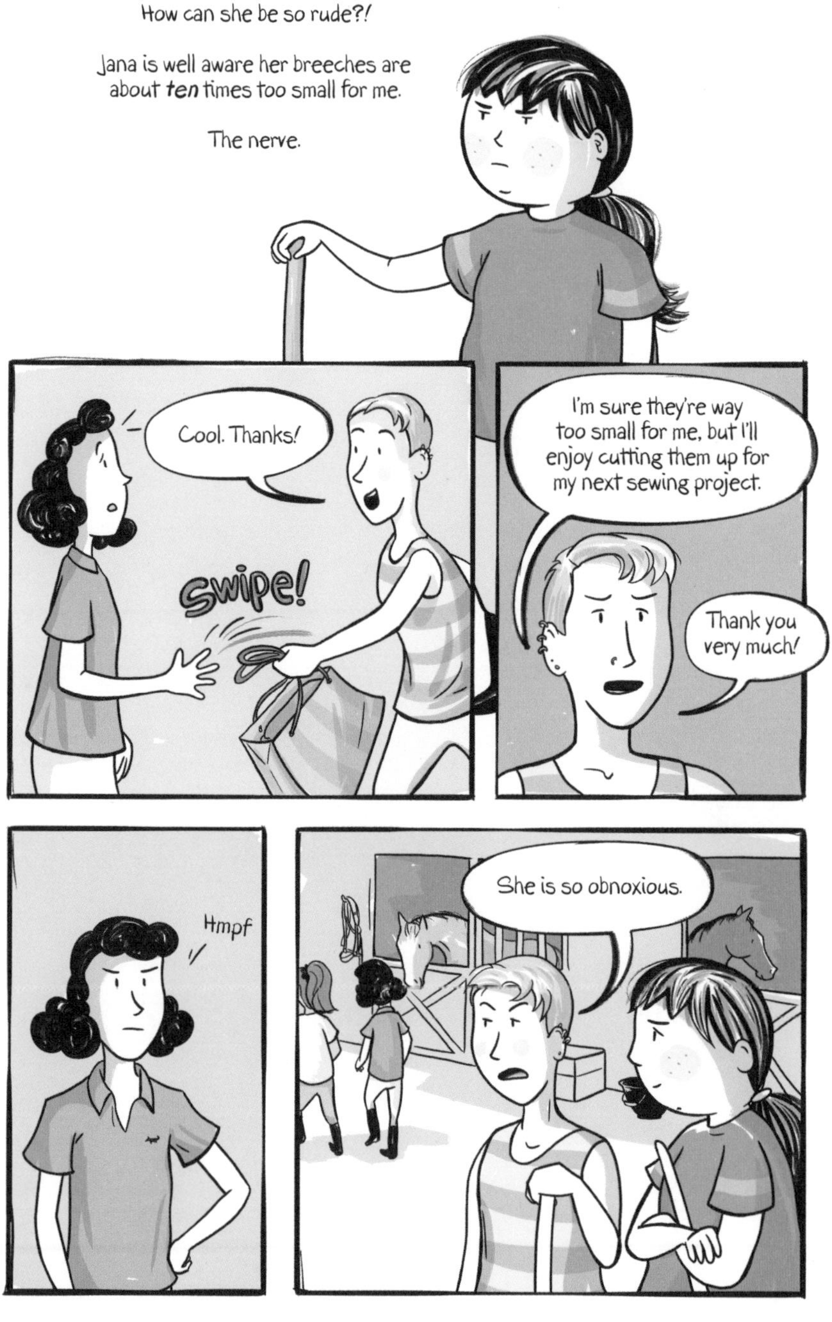
How can she be so rude?!
Jana is well aware her breeches are about *ten* times too small for me.
The nerve.
Cool. Thanks!
Swipe!
I'm sure they're way too small for me, but I'll enjoy cutting them up for my next sewing project.
Thank you very much!
Hmpf
She is so obnoxious.

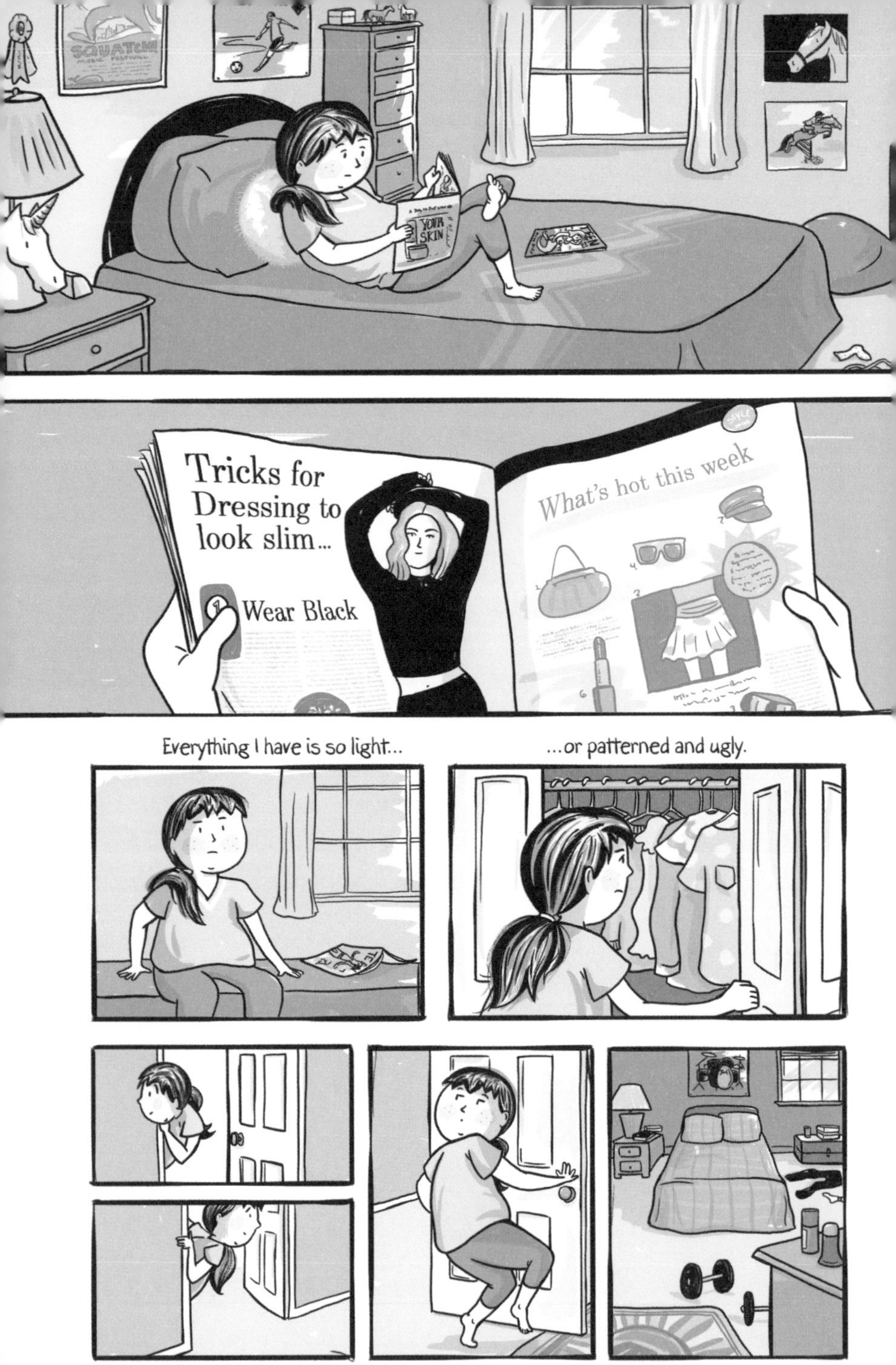
SQUATCH!
MUSIC FESTIVAL
YOUR SKIN
Tricks for Dressing to look slim...
1 Wear Black
What's hot this week
Everything I have is so light...
...or patterned and ugly.

drumming

Beat! Thump! Thump! Beat!

CHEEEEEs Crisps!

squeak

Ross!

CHEEEEEs Crisps!

If I sneak out through the garage, maybe he won't see me wearing his shirt.

click

Hmmm.

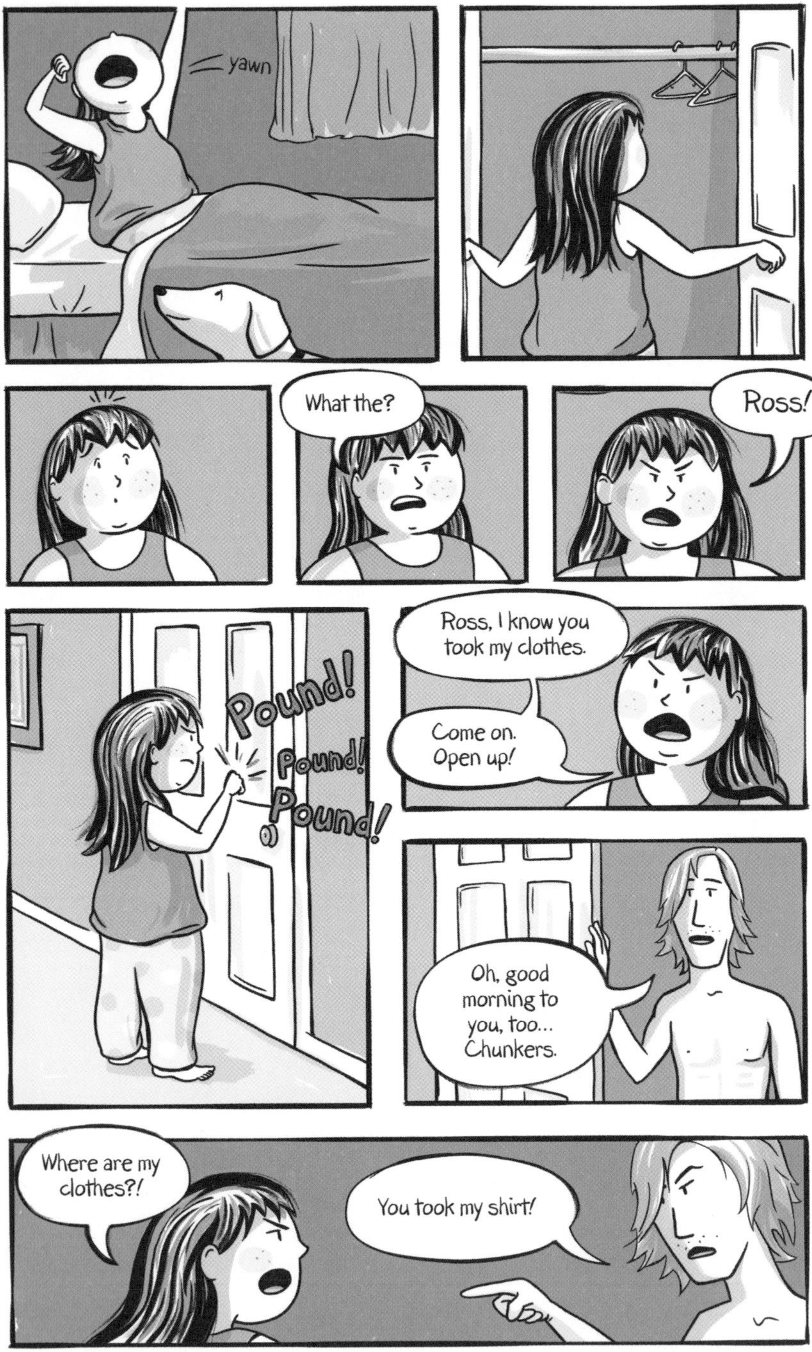
yawn
What the?
Ross!
Pound!
Pound!
Pound!
Ross, I know you took my clothes.
Come on. Open up!
Oh, good morning to you, too... Chunkers.
Where are my clothes?!
You took my shirt!

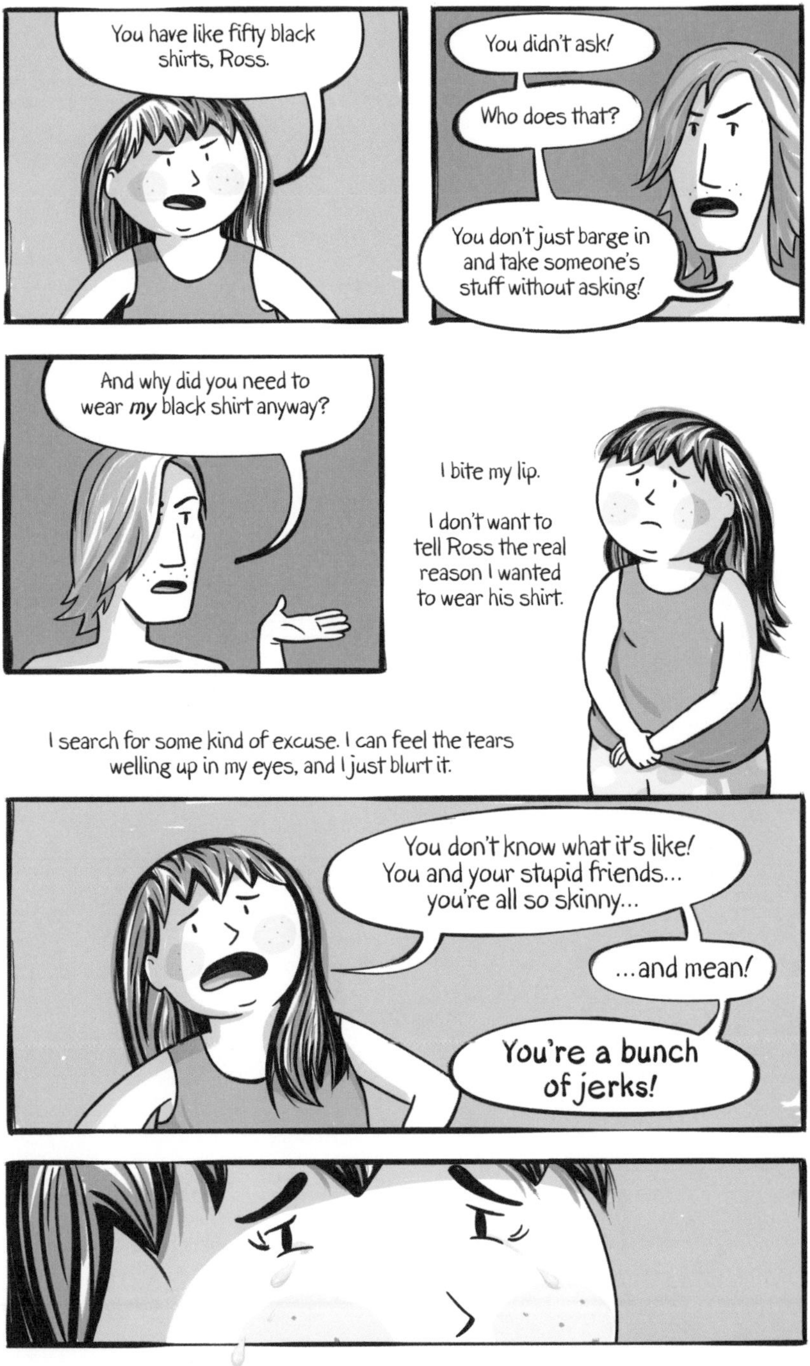
You have like fifty black shirts, Ross.
You didn't ask!
Who does that?
You don't just barge in and take someone's stuff without asking!
And why did you need to wear *my* black shirt anyway?
I bite my lip.
I don't want to tell Ross the real reason I wanted to wear his shirt.
I search for some kind of excuse. I can feel the tears welling up in my eyes, and I just blurt it.
You don't know what it's like! You and your stupid friends... you're all so skinny...
...and mean!
You're a bunch of jerks!

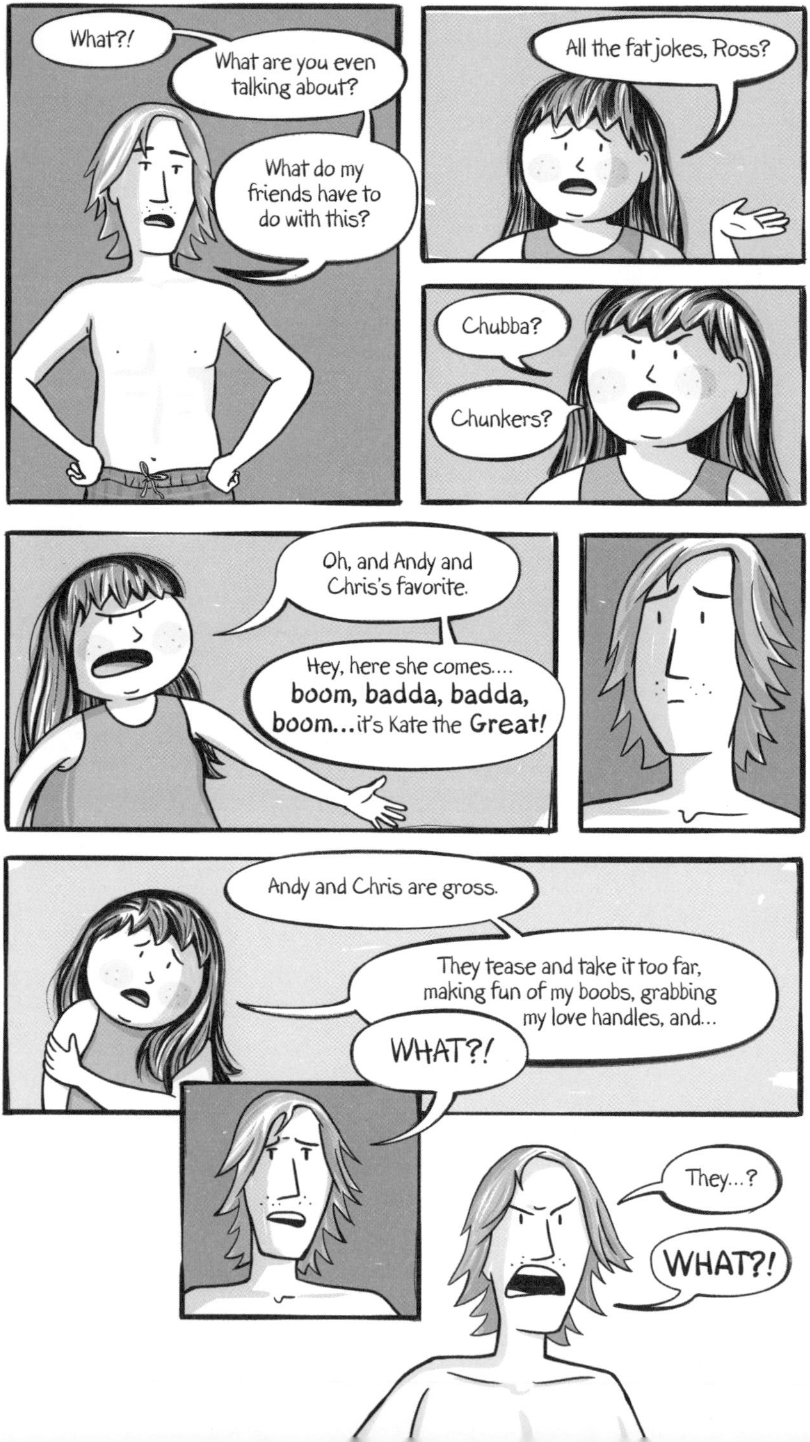
What?!
What are you even talking about?
What do my friends have to do with this?
All the fat jokes, Ross?
Chubba?
Chunkers?
Oh, and Andy and Chris's favorite.
Hey, here she comes.... **boom, badda, badda, boom...** it's Kate the **Great!**
Andy and Chris are gross.
They tease and take it too far, making fun of my boobs, grabbing my love handles, and...
WHAT?!
They...?
WHAT?!

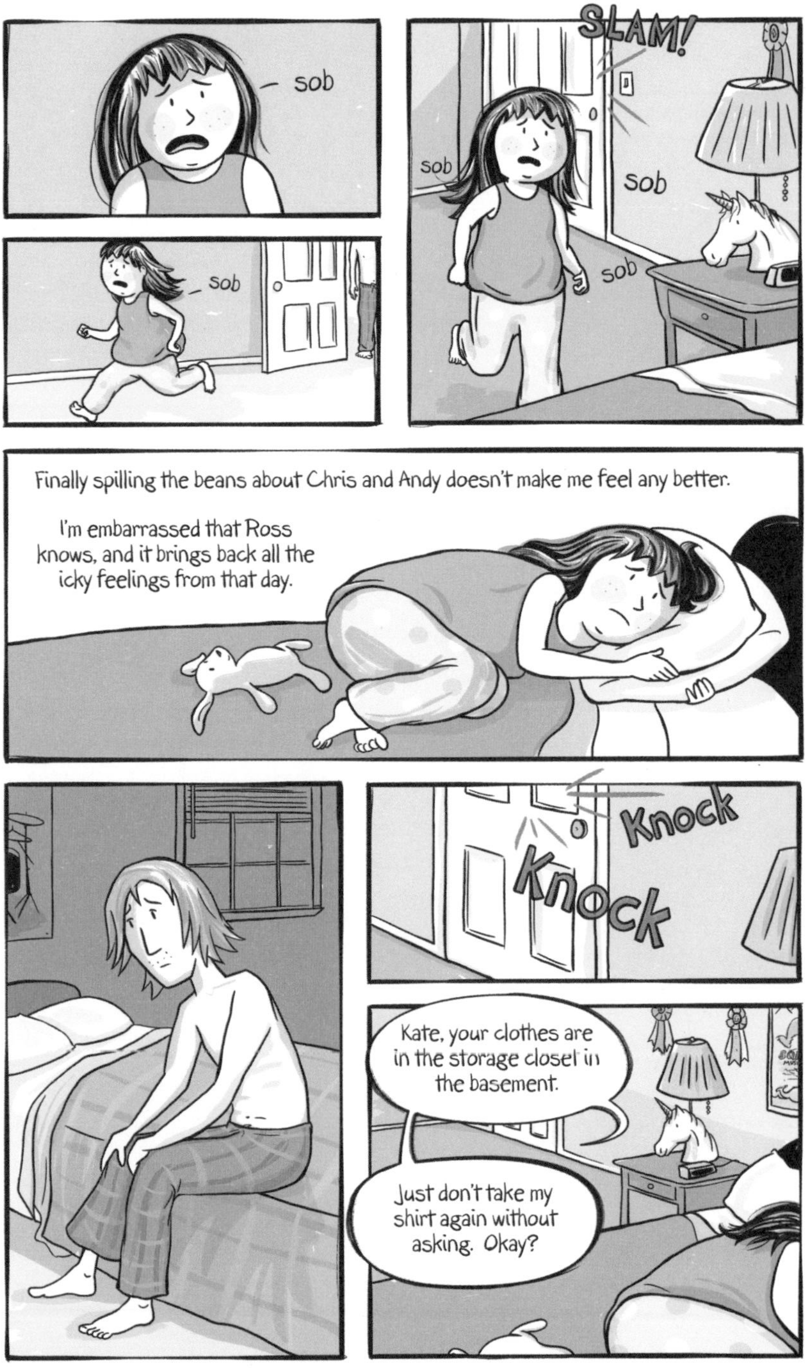
sob
sob
SLAM!
sob
sob
sob
sob
Finally spilling the beans about Chris and Andy doesn't make me feel any better.
I'm embarrassed that Ross knows, and it brings back all the icky feelings from that day.
Knock
Knock
Kate, your clothes are in the storage closet in the basement.
Just don't take my shirt again without asking. Okay?

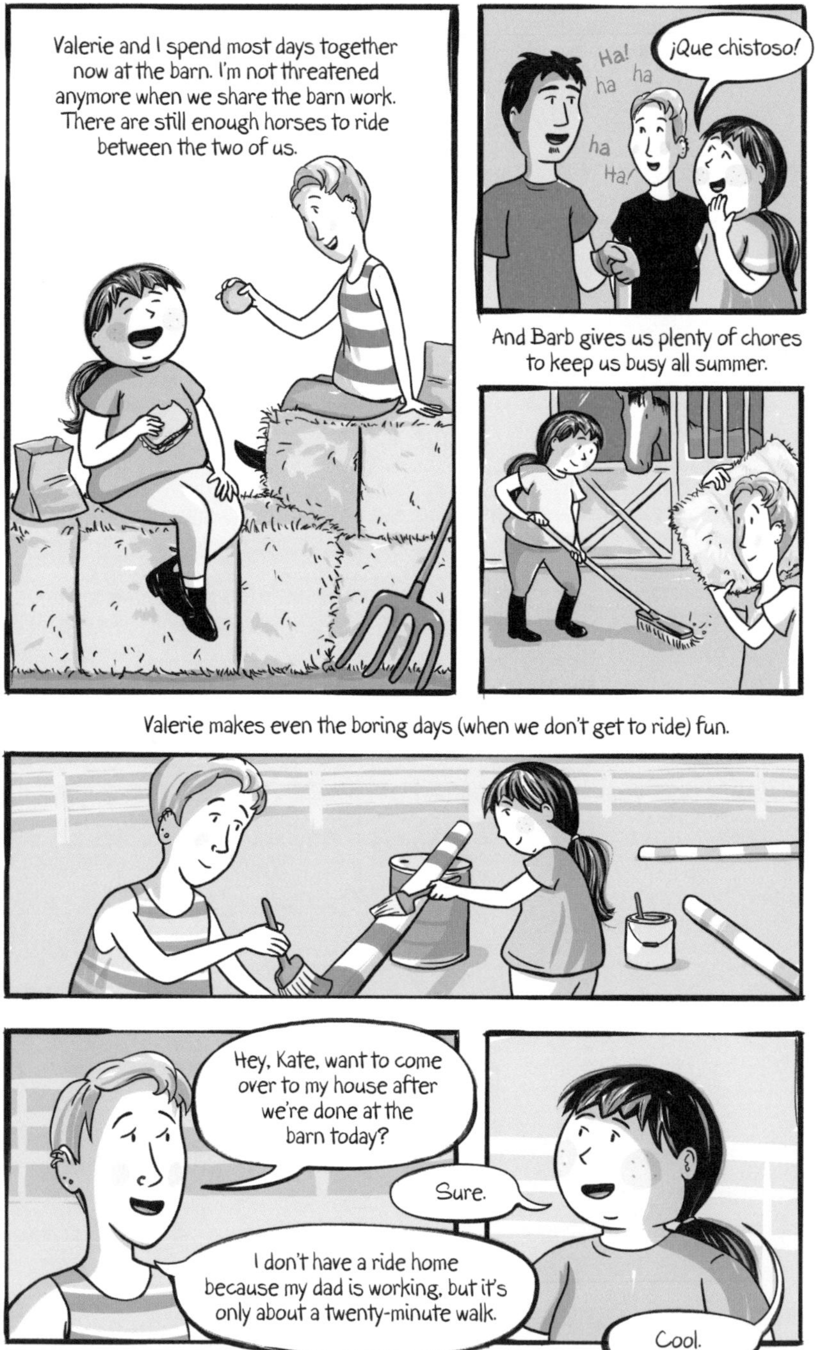
Valerie and I spend most days together now at the barn. I'm not threatened anymore when we share the barn work. There are still enough horses to ride between the two of us.
Ha! ha ha ha Ha!
¡Que chistoso!
And Barb gives us plenty of chores to keep us busy all summer.
Valerie makes even the boring days (when we don't get to ride) fun.
Hey, Kate, want to come over to my house after we're done at the barn today?
Sure.
I don't have a ride home because my dad is working, but it's only about a twenty-minute walk.
Cool.

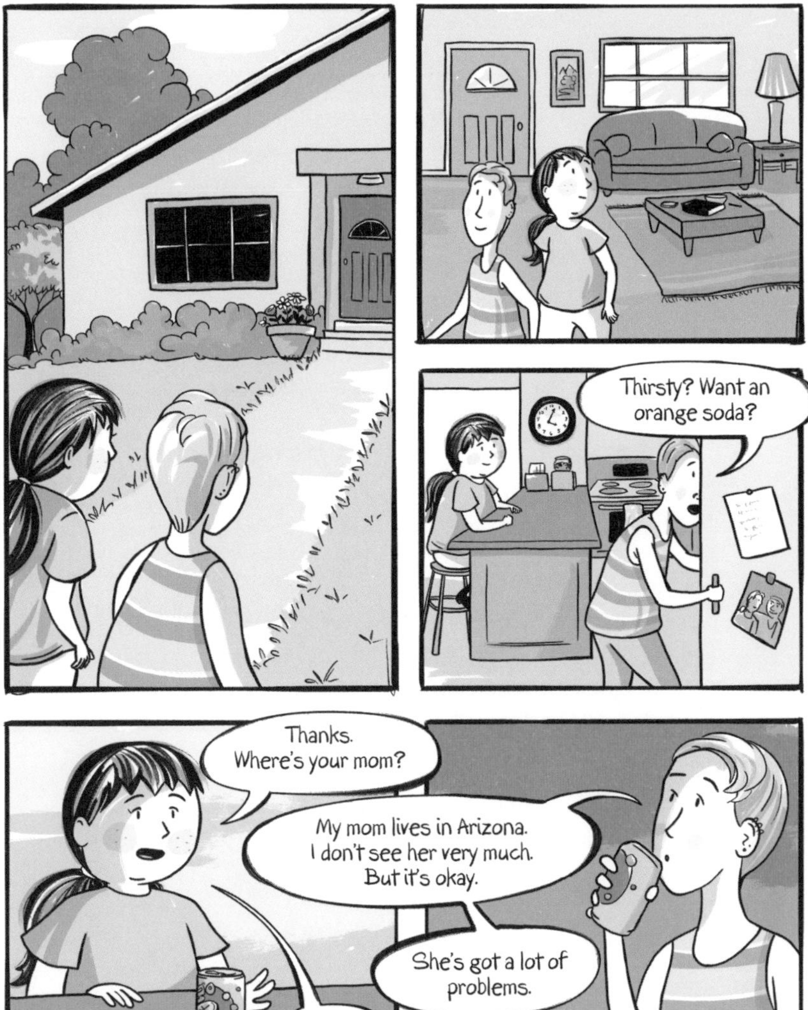
Thirsty? Want an orange soda?
Thanks. Where's your mom?
My mom lives in Arizona. I don't see her very much. But it's okay.
She's got a lot of problems.
Oh.

I don't ask any more questions about Valerie's mom, even though I'm curious.

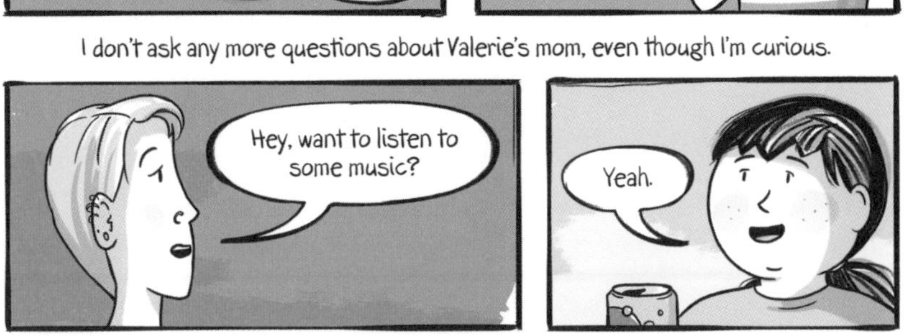
Hey, want to listen to some music?
Yeah.

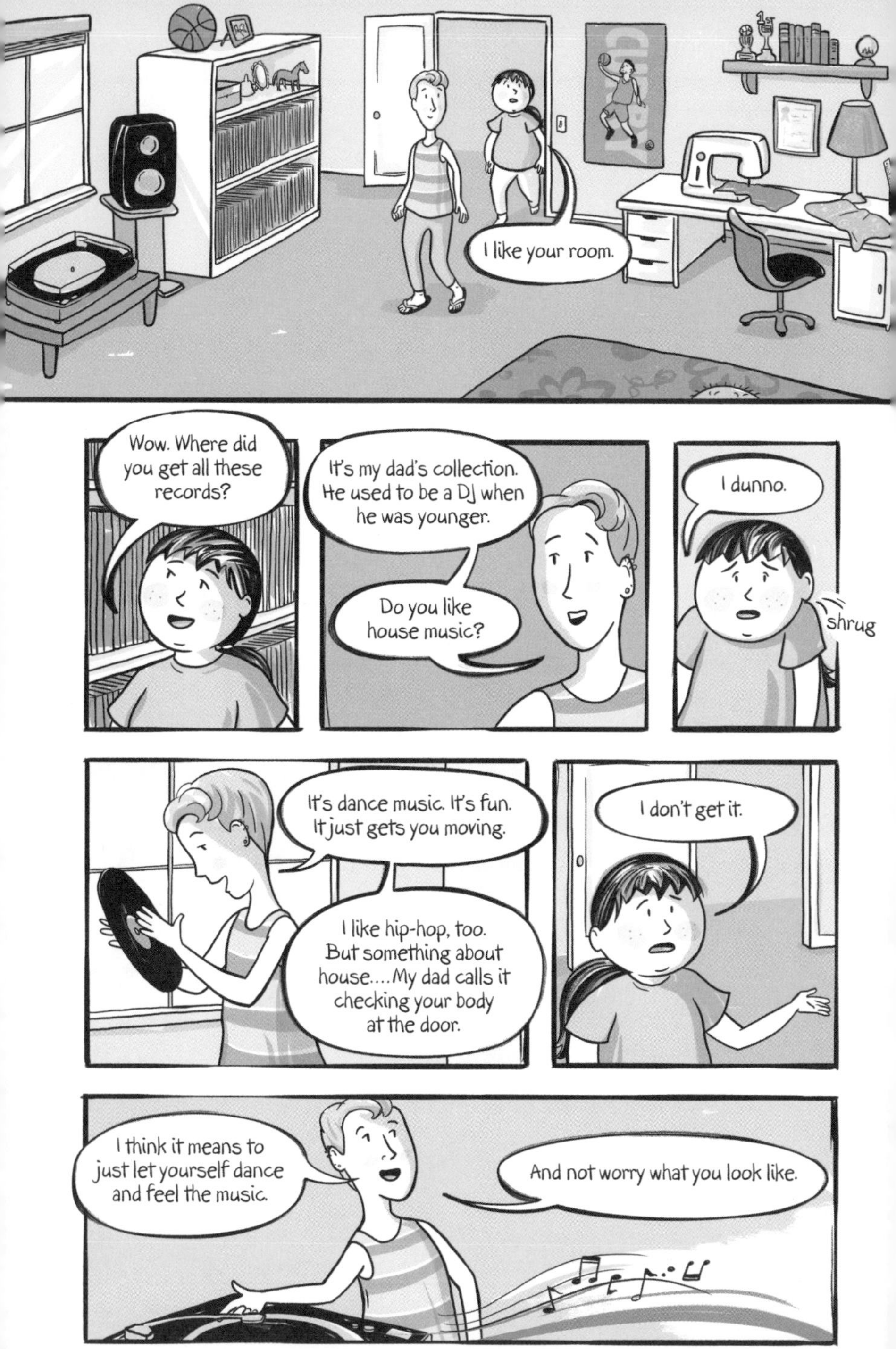
I like your room.
Wow. Where did you get all these records?
It's my dad's collection. He used to be a DJ when he was younger.
Do you like house music?
I dunno.
shrug
It's dance music. It's fun. It just gets you moving.
I like hip-hop, too. But something about house....My dad calls it checking your body at the door.
I don't get it.
I think it means to just let yourself dance and feel the music.
And not worry what you look like.

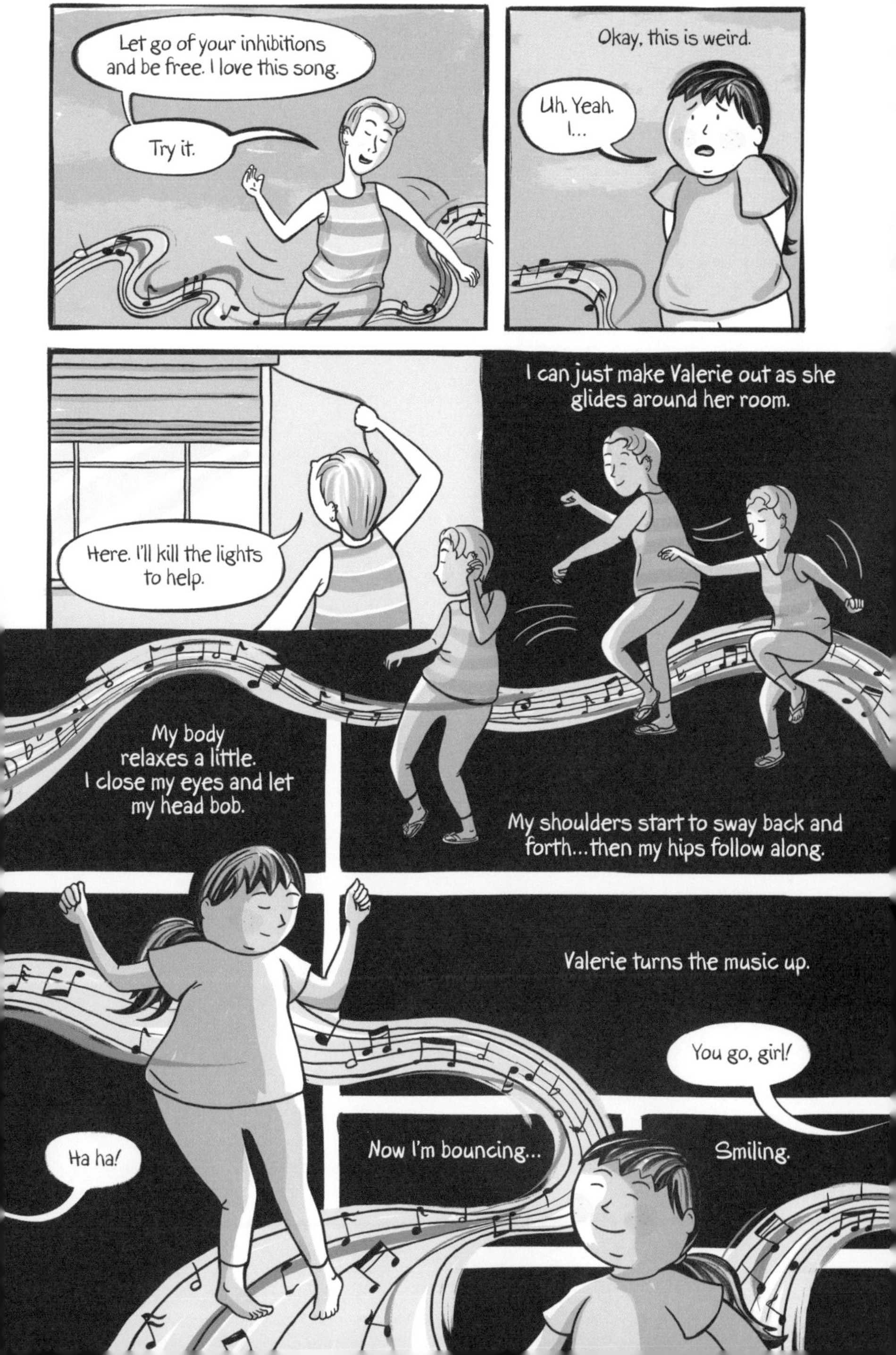
Let go of your inhibitions and be free. I love this song.
Try it.
Okay, this is weird.
Uh. Yeah. I...
Here. I'll kill the lights to help.
I can just make Valerie out as she glides around her room.
My body relaxes a little. I close my eyes and let my head bob.
My shoulders start to sway back and forth...then my hips follow along.
Valerie turns the music up.
You go, girl!
Ha ha!
Now I'm bouncing...
Smiling.

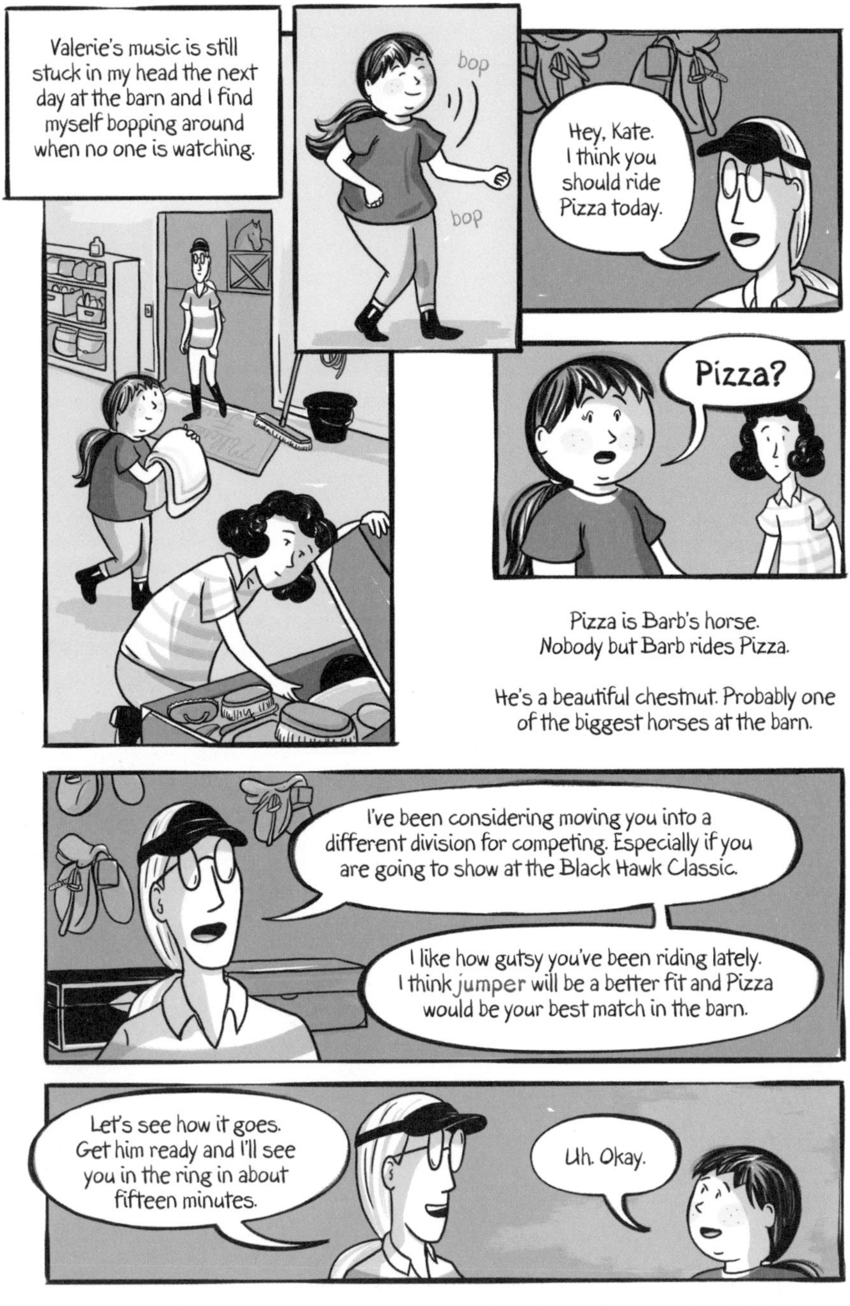
Valerie's music is still stuck in my head the next day at the barn and I find myself bopping around when no one is watching.
bop
bop
Hey, Kate. I think you should ride Pizza today.
Pizza?
Pizza is Barb's horse. Nobody but Barb rides Pizza.
He's a beautiful chestnut. Probably one of the biggest horses at the barn.
I've been considering moving you into a different division for competing. Especially if you are going to show at the Black Hawk Classic.
I like how gutsy you've been riding lately. I think jumper will be a better fit and Pizza would be your best match in the barn.
Let's see how it goes. Get him ready and I'll see you in the ring in about fifteen minutes.
Uh. Okay.

Jumper: One of the three main divisions at a horse show (hunter, jumper, and equitation). Jumper classes are not scored on style, but the speed at which the rider completes the course.

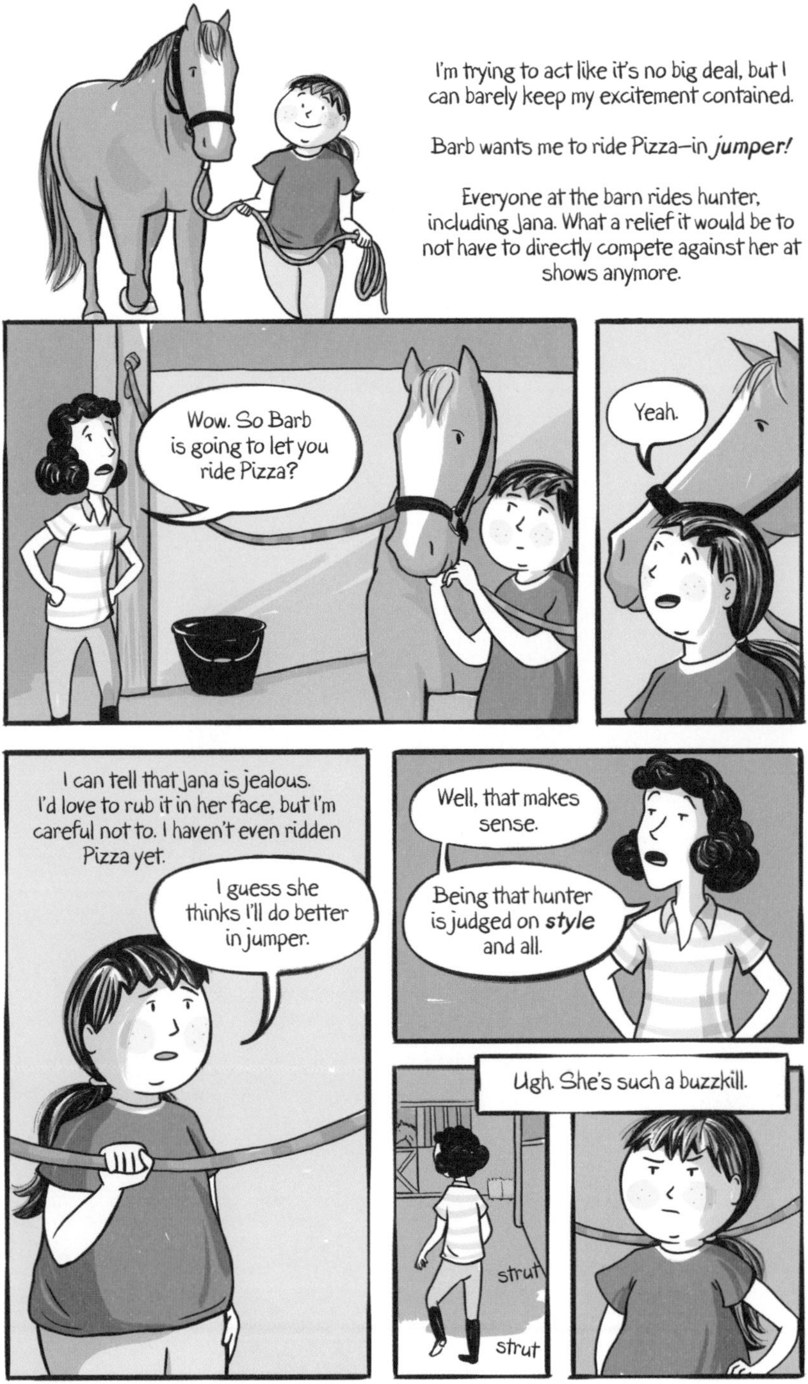

I'm trying to act like it's no big deal, but I can barely keep my excitement contained.
Barb wants me to ride Pizza—in *jumper!*
Everyone at the barn rides hunter, including Jana. What a relief it would be to not have to directly compete against her at shows anymore.
Wow. So Barb is going to let you ride Pizza?
Yeah.
I can tell that Jana is jealous. I'd love to rub it in her face, but I'm careful not to. I haven't even ridden Pizza yet.
I guess she thinks I'll do better in jumper.
Well, that makes sense.
Being that hunter is judged on *style* and all.
Ugh. She's such a buzzkill.
strut
strut

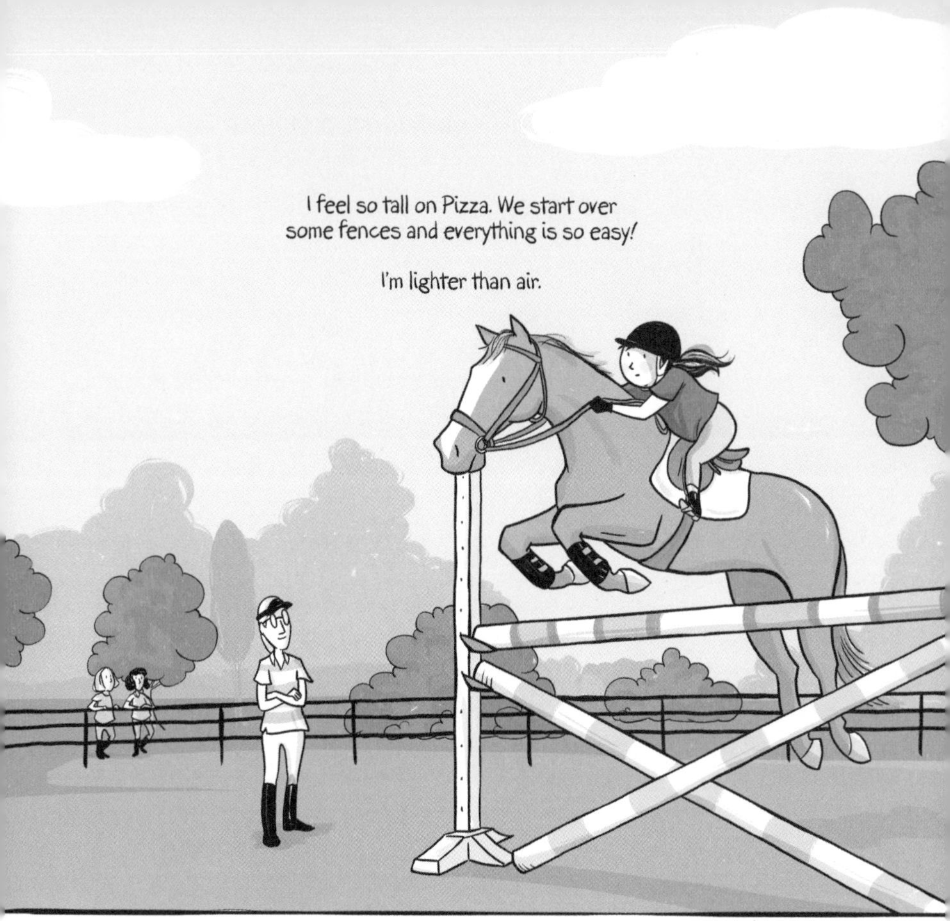
I feel so tall on Pizza. We start over some fences and everything is so easy!
I'm lighter than air.

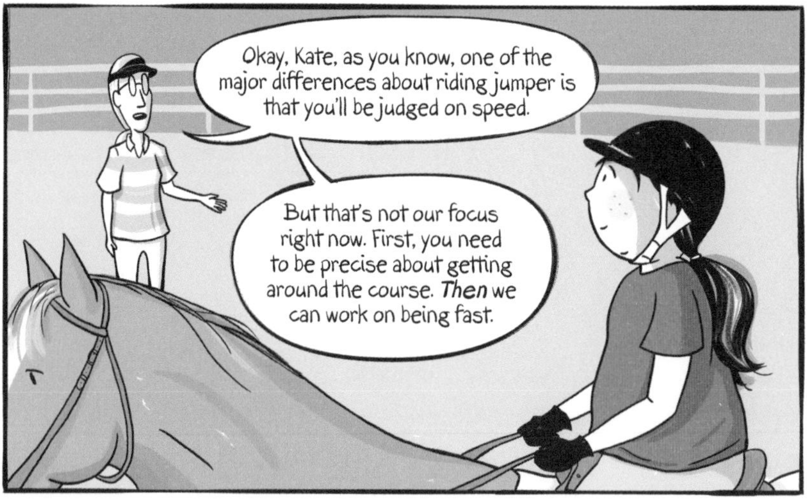
Okay, Kate, as you know, one of the major differences about riding jumper is that you'll be judged on speed.
But that's not our focus right now. First, you need to be precise about getting around the course. *Then* we can work on being fast.

I'm amped up, full of adrenaline, and my head is swirling with emotions.

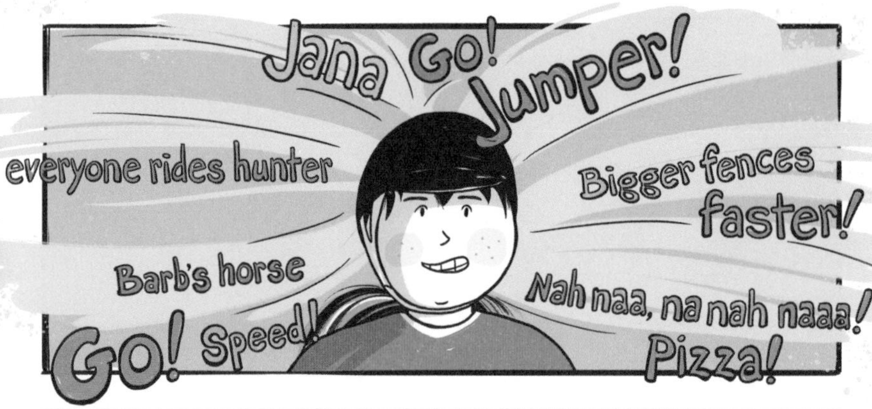
Jana
Go!
Jumper!
everyone rides hunter
Bigger fences
faster!
Barb's horse
Nah naa, na nah naaa!
Go!
Speed!
Pizza!

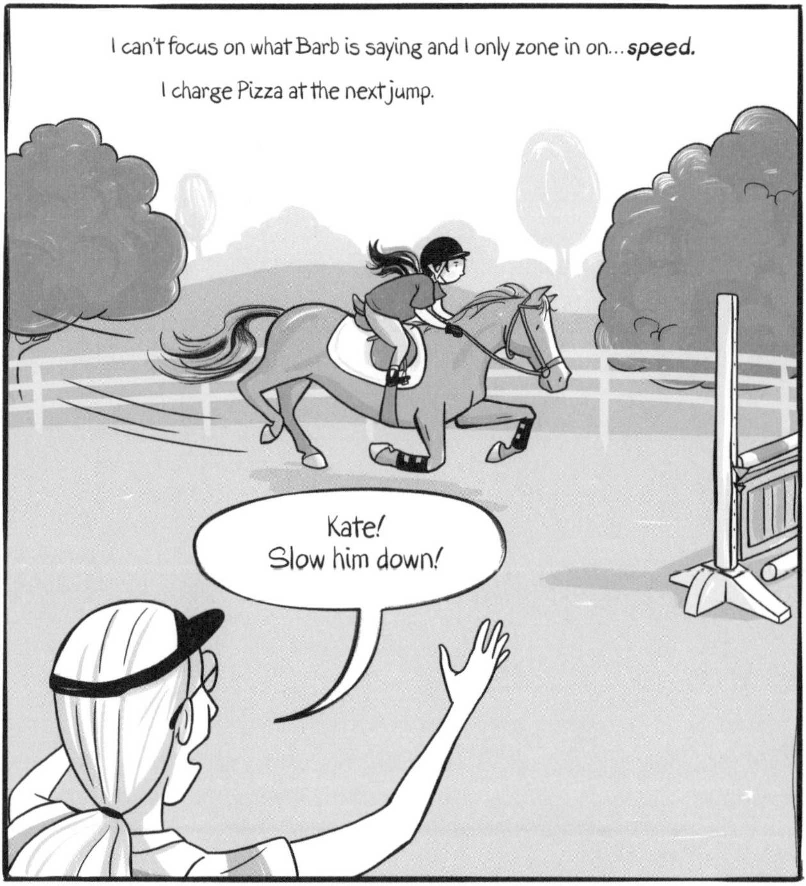
I can't focus on what Barb is saying and I only zone in on... *speed.*
I charge Pizza at the next jump.
Kate!
Slow him down!

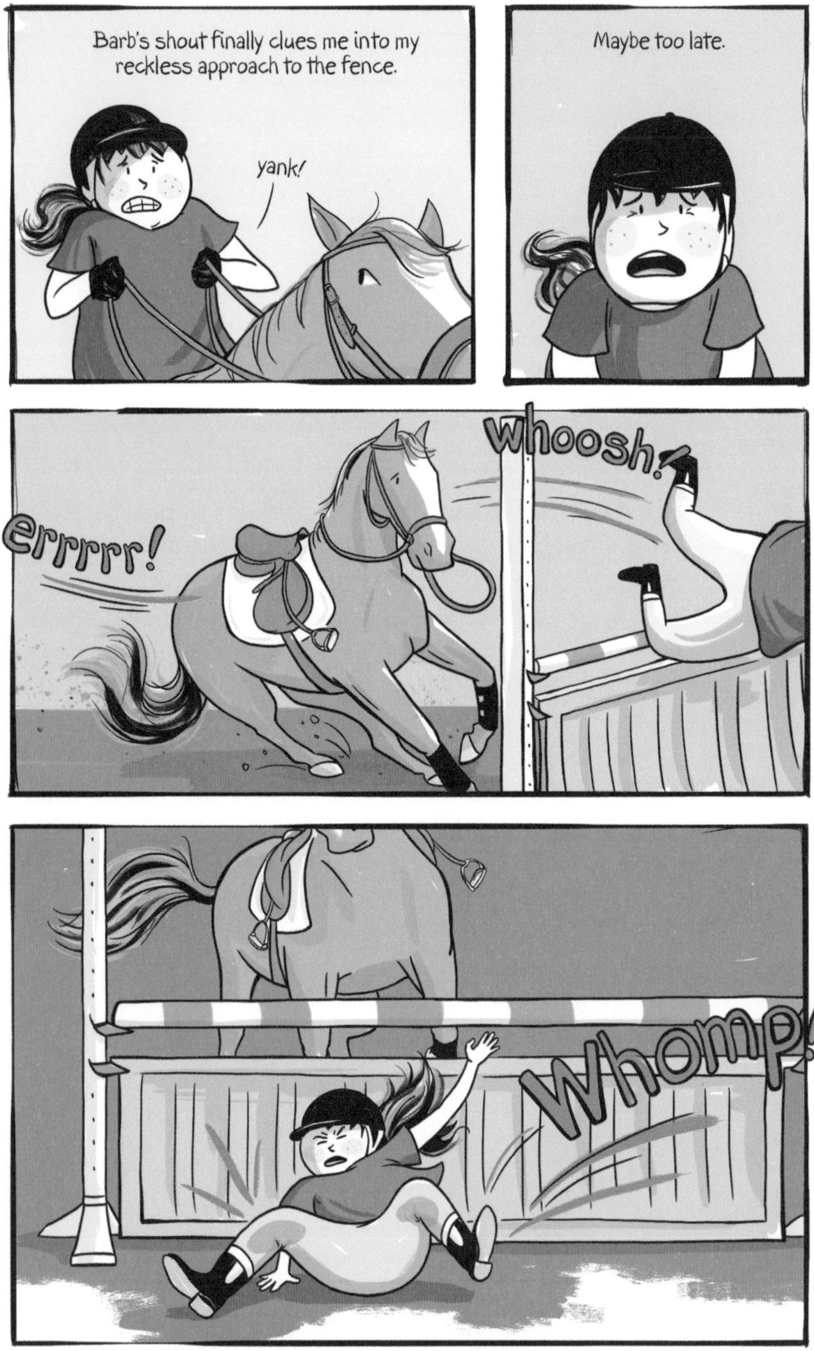

Barb's shout finally clues me into my reckless approach to the fence.
yank!
Maybe too late.
errrrr!
whoosh!
Whomp!

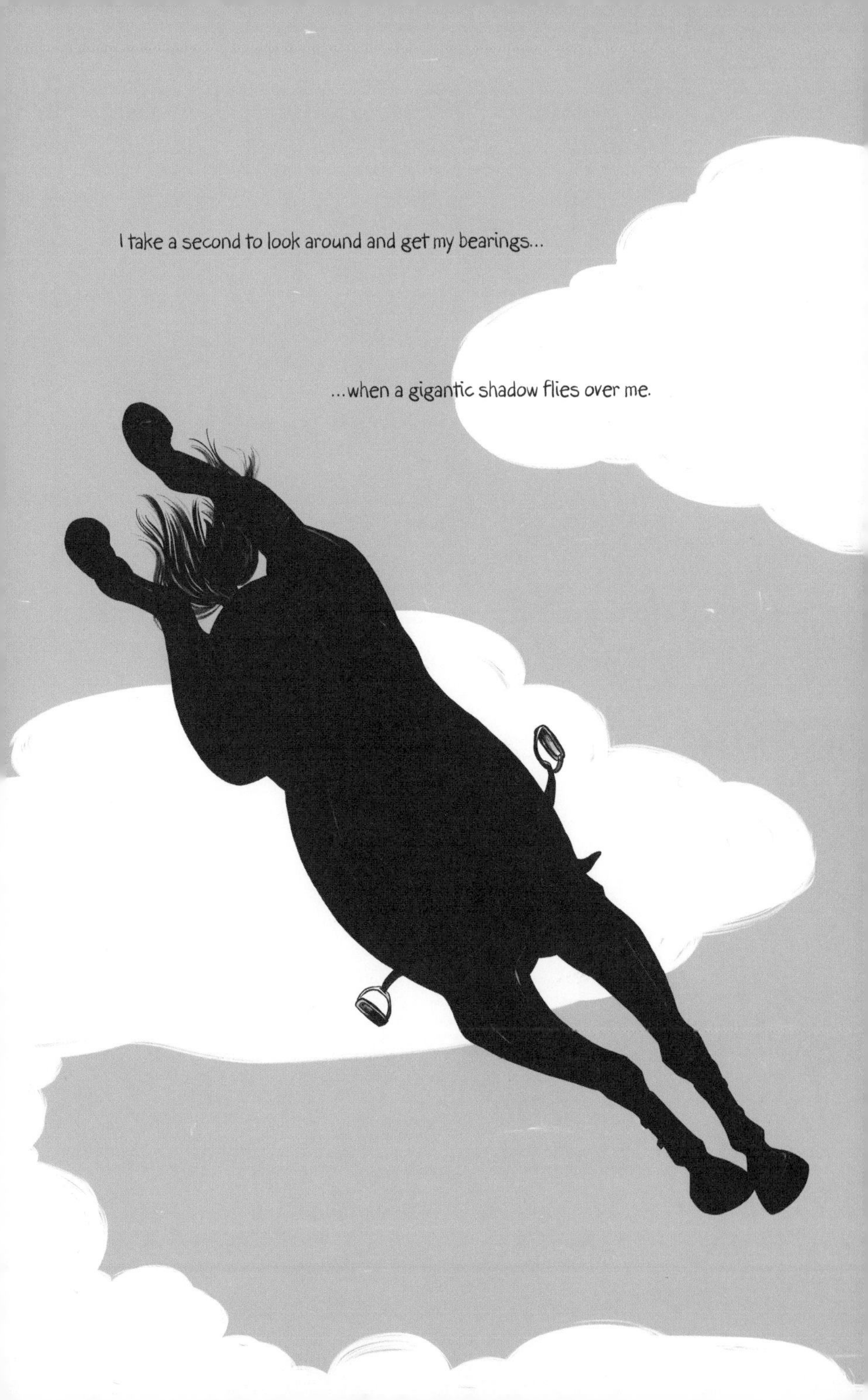
I take a second to look around and get my bearings...
...when a gigantic shadow flies over me.

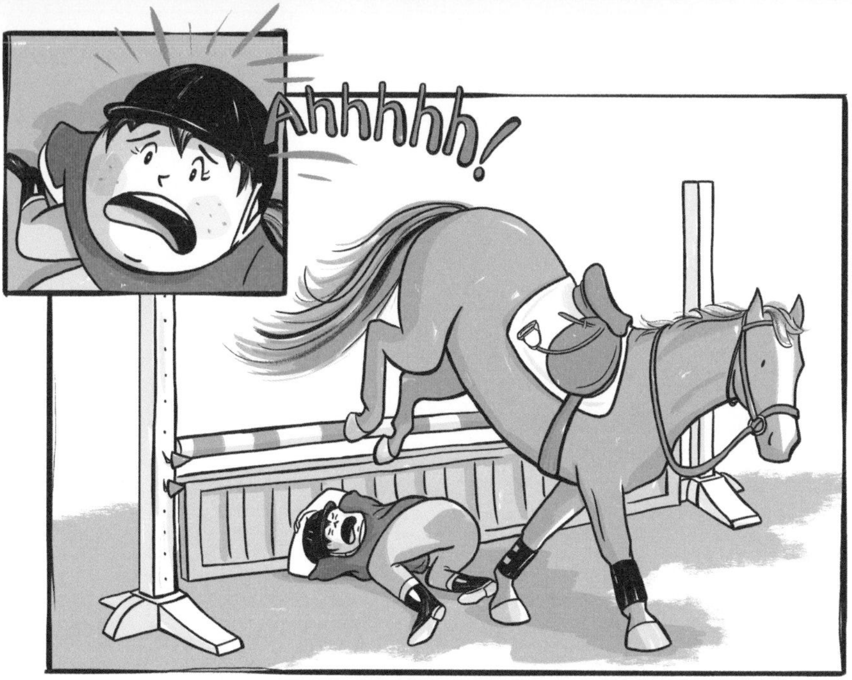
Ahhhhh!

I don't know how Pizza missed landing on me.
Or why he even jumped the fence by himself?!

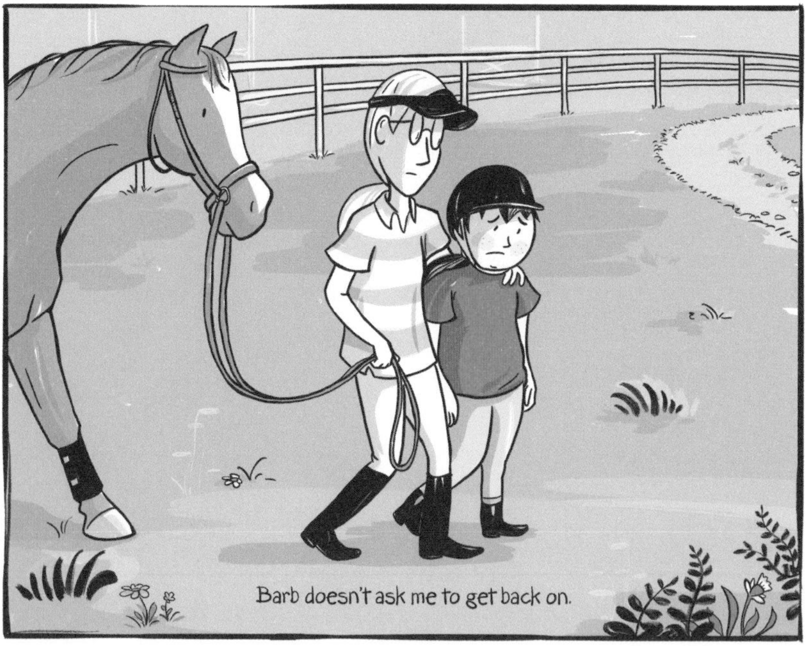
Barb doesn't ask me to get back on.

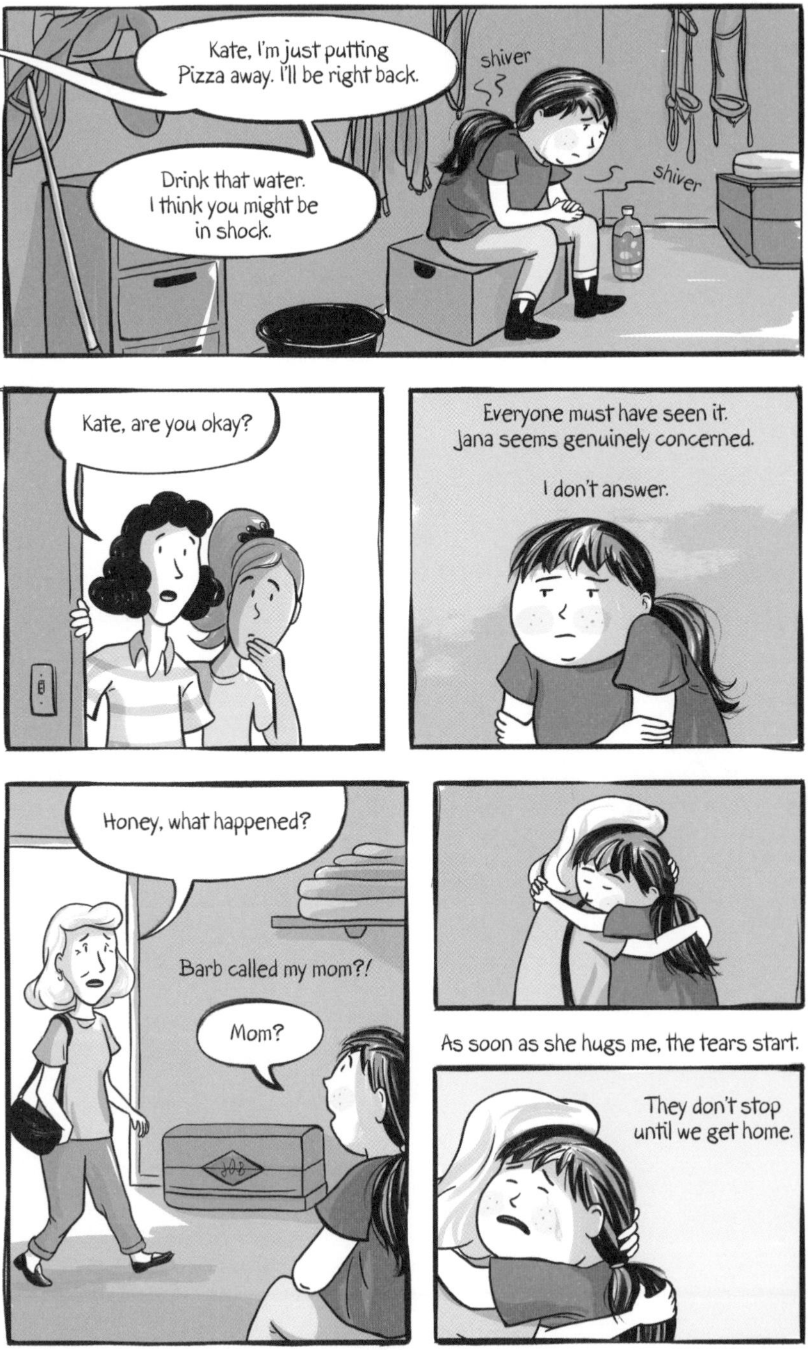
Kate, I'm just putting Pizza away. I'll be right back.
Drink that water. I think you might be in shock.
shiver
shiver
Kate, are you okay?
Everyone must have seen it. Jana seems genuinely concerned.
I don't answer.
Honey, what happened?
Barb called my mom?!
Mom?
As soon as she hugs me, the tears start.
They don't stop until we get home.

Chapter 9
BMX Bounce

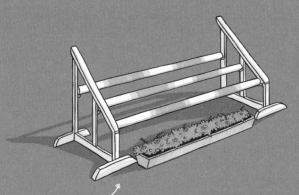

Triple Bar

A spread (distance) fence consisting of three elements at different heights, usually in ascending order.

It's been more than a week since I had my fall off Pizza.

Everything at the barn has gone on as normal. Everything except
I haven't dared to get back on a horse.

I replay the fall over and over in my head.

I've even had a few nightmares where Pizza jumps and this time lands right on top of me.

Farrier 8/1

Kate + Valerie
• Stalls
• Exercise: Motor-Speedy

Kate, Motor is on the exercise list today.

You want to hop on her?

Uh, no. That's okay.

You can take her out.

Pfffff_

Valerie didn't see the Pizza disaster, but she heard about it.

Kate, you are such a solid rider.

Most people here just ride their one horse, but you can ride any horse in the barn. Which ain't easy. And you do it well!

I know that Valerie is trying to make me feel better. But it doesn't help.

I want to ride... I just can't.

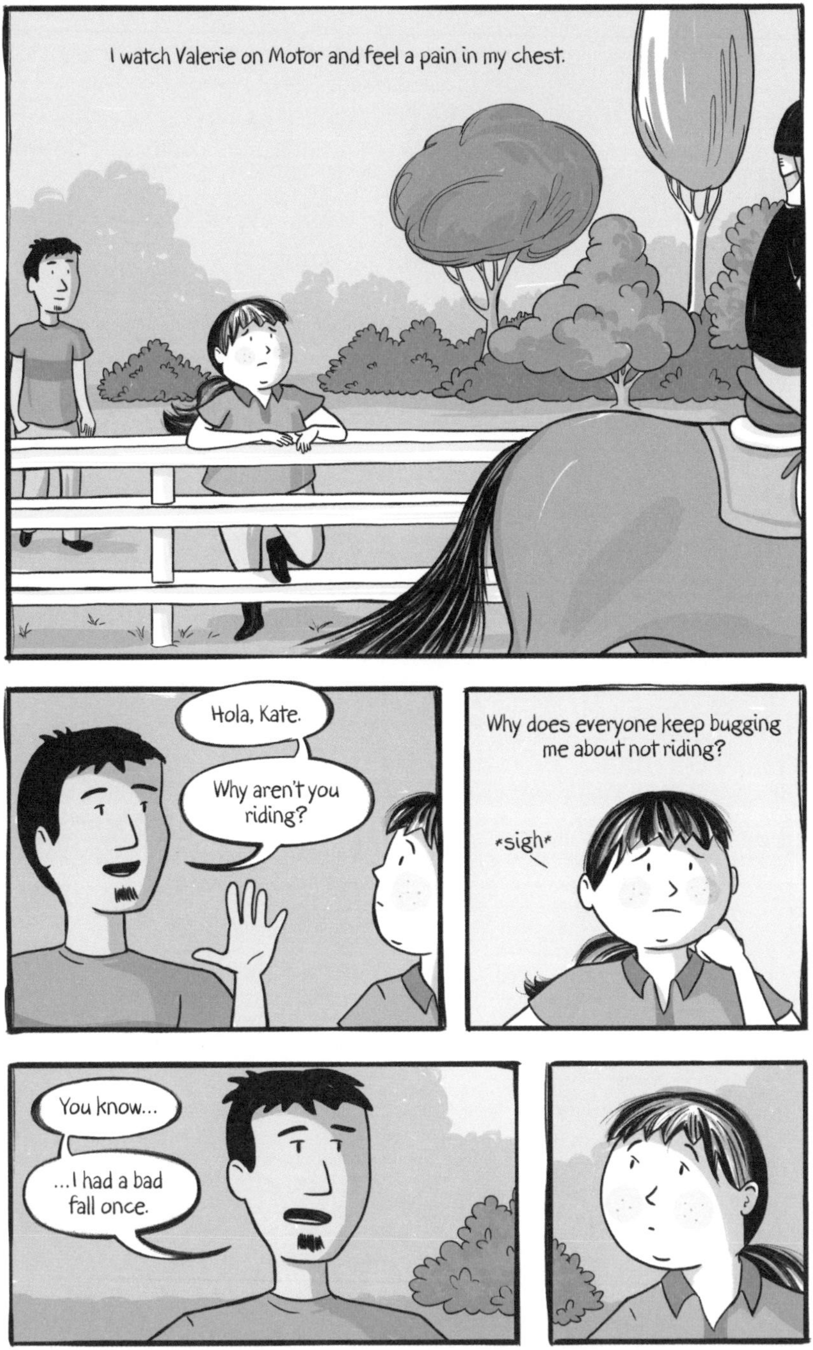
I watch Valerie on Motor and feel a pain in my chest.
Hola, Kate.
Why aren't you riding?
Why does everyone keep bugging me about not riding?
sigh
You know...
...I had a bad fall once.

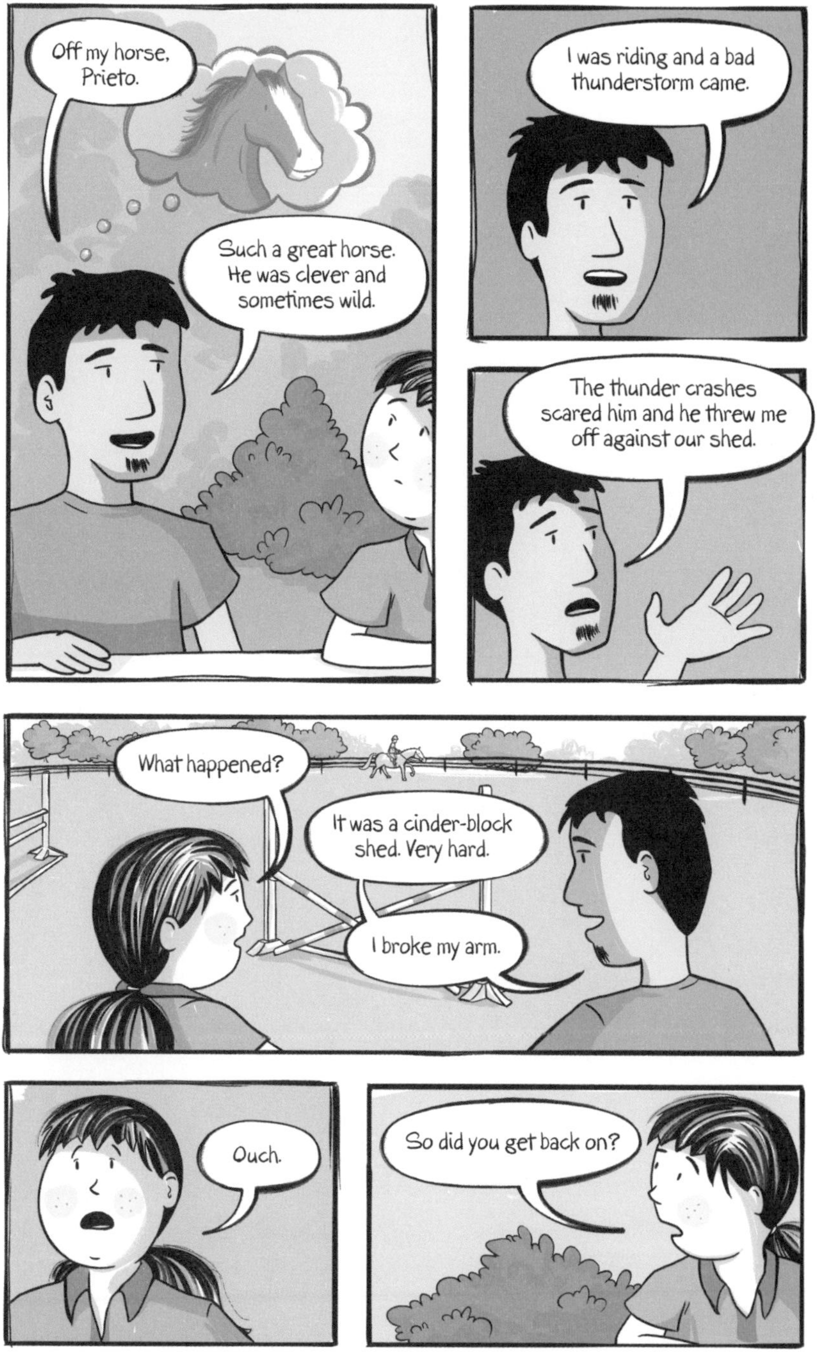
Off my horse, Prieto.
Such a great horse. He was clever and sometimes wild.
I was riding and a bad thunderstorm came.
The thunder crashes scared him and he threw me off against our shed.
What happened?
It was a cinder-block shed. Very hard.
I broke my arm.
Ouch.
So did you get back on?

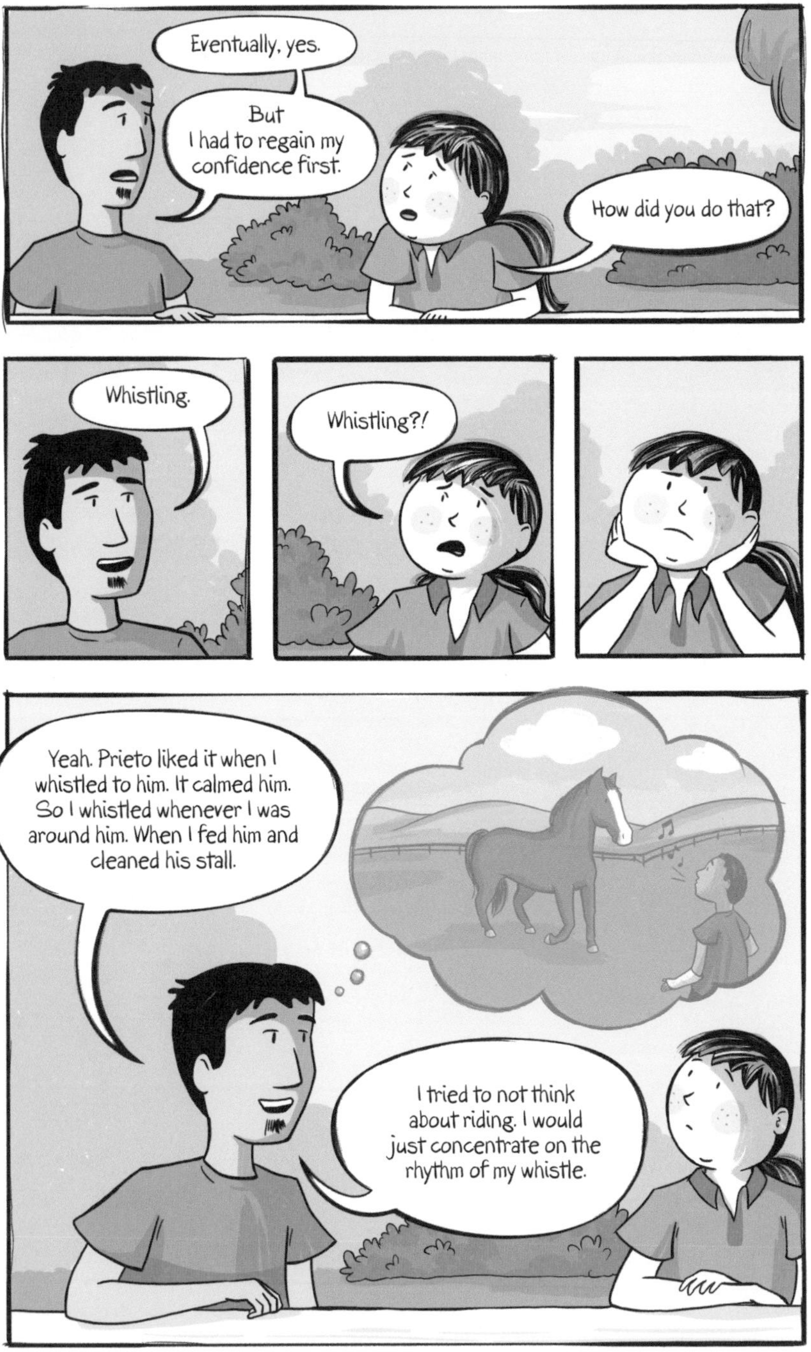
Eventually, yes.
But I had to regain my confidence first.
How did you do that?
Whistling.
Whistling?!
Yeah. Prieto liked it when I whistled to him. It calmed him. So I whistled whenever I was around him. When I fed him and cleaned his stall.
I tried to not think about riding. I would just concentrate on the rhythm of my whistle.

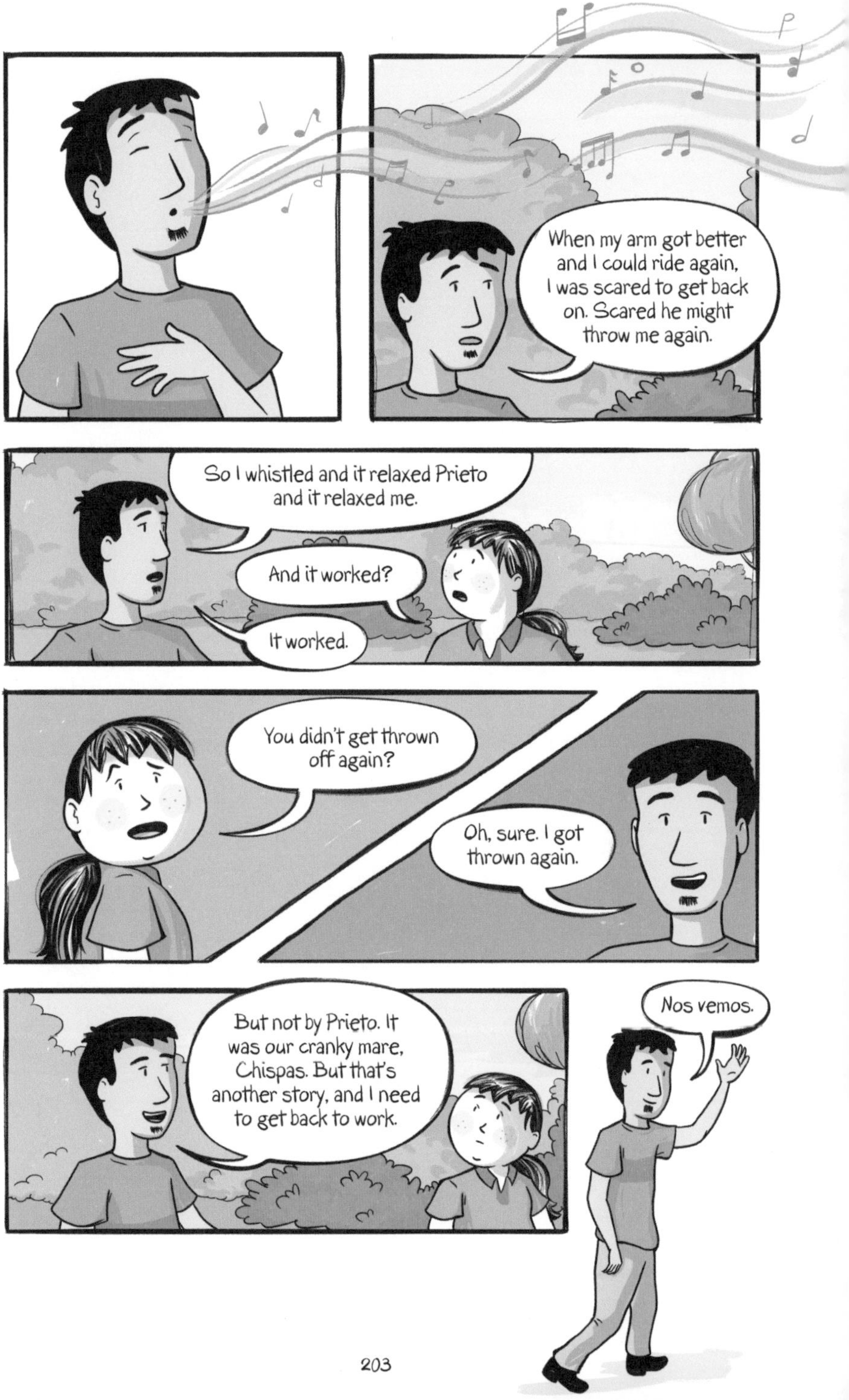
When my arm got better and I could ride again, I was scared to get back on. Scared he might throw me again.
So I whistled and it relaxed Prieto and it relaxed me.
And it worked?
It worked.
You didn't get thrown off again?
Oh, sure. I got thrown again.
But not by Prieto. It was our cranky mare, Chispas. But that's another story, and I need to get back to work.
Nos vemos.

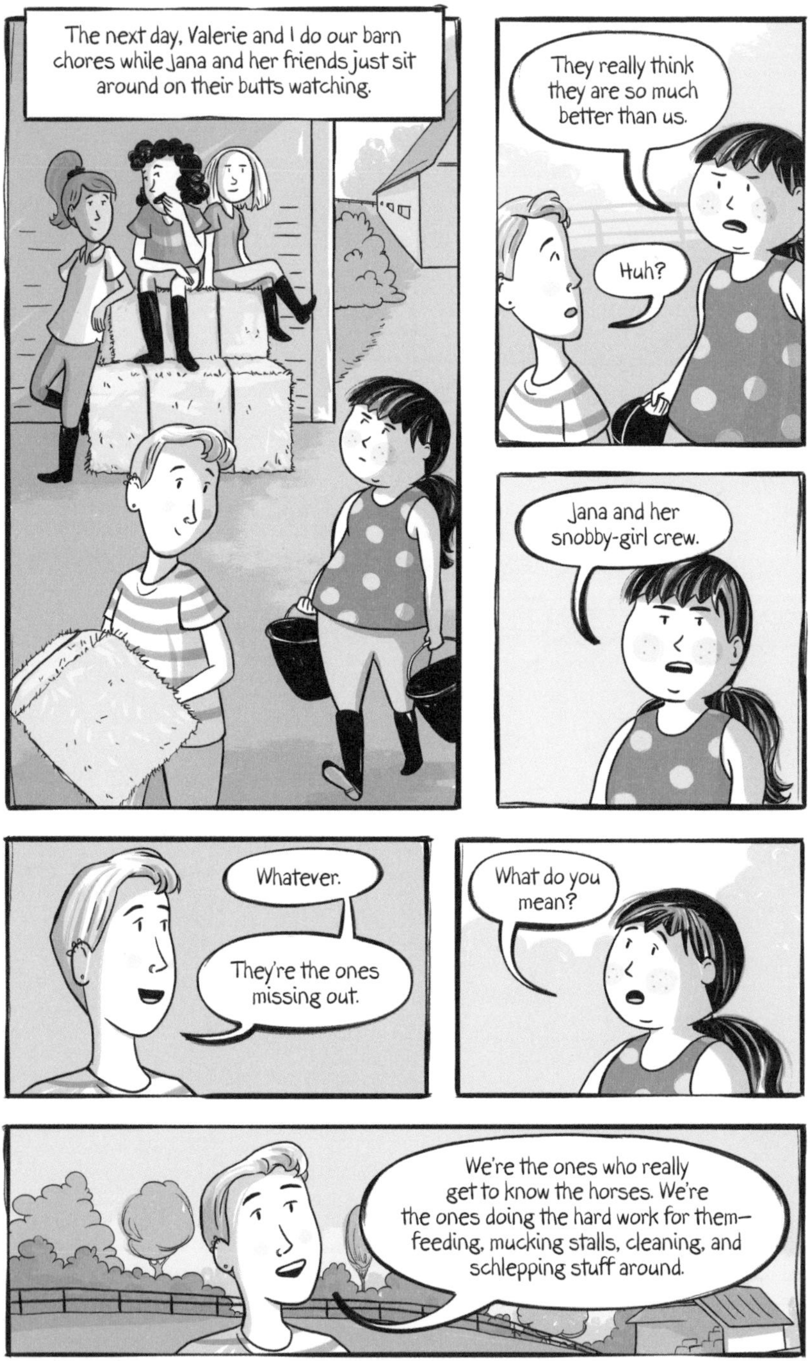
The next day, Valerie and I do our barn chores while Jana and her friends just sit around on their butts watching.
They really think they are so much better than us.
Huh?
Jana and her snobby-girl crew.
Whatever.
They're the ones missing out.
What do you mean?
We're the ones who really get to know the horses. We're the ones doing the hard work for them—feeding, mucking stalls, cleaning, and schlepping stuff around.

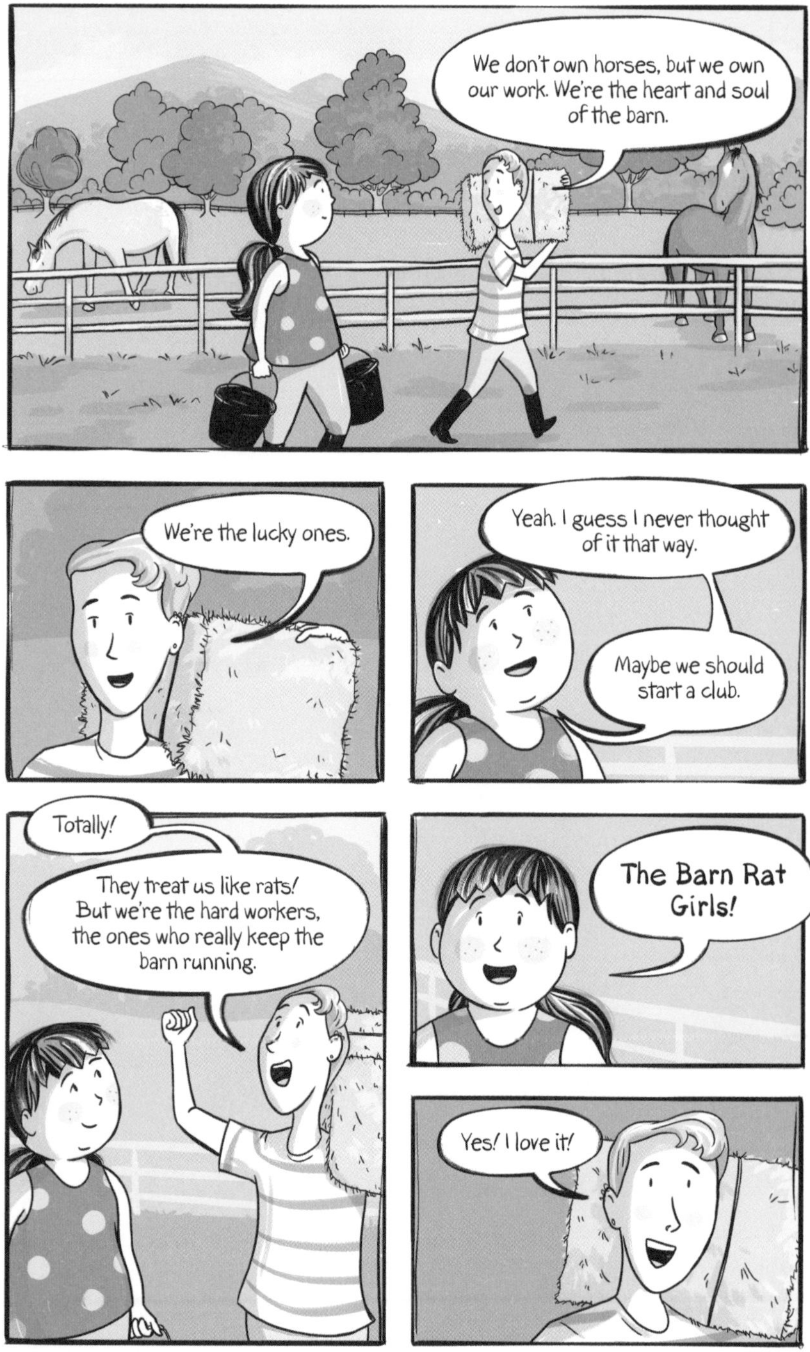
We don't own horses, but we own our work. We're the heart and soul of the barn.
We're the lucky ones.
Yeah. I guess I never thought of it that way.
Maybe we should start a club.
Totally!
They treat us like rats! But we're the hard workers, the ones who really keep the barn running.
The Barn Rat Girls!
Yes! I love it!

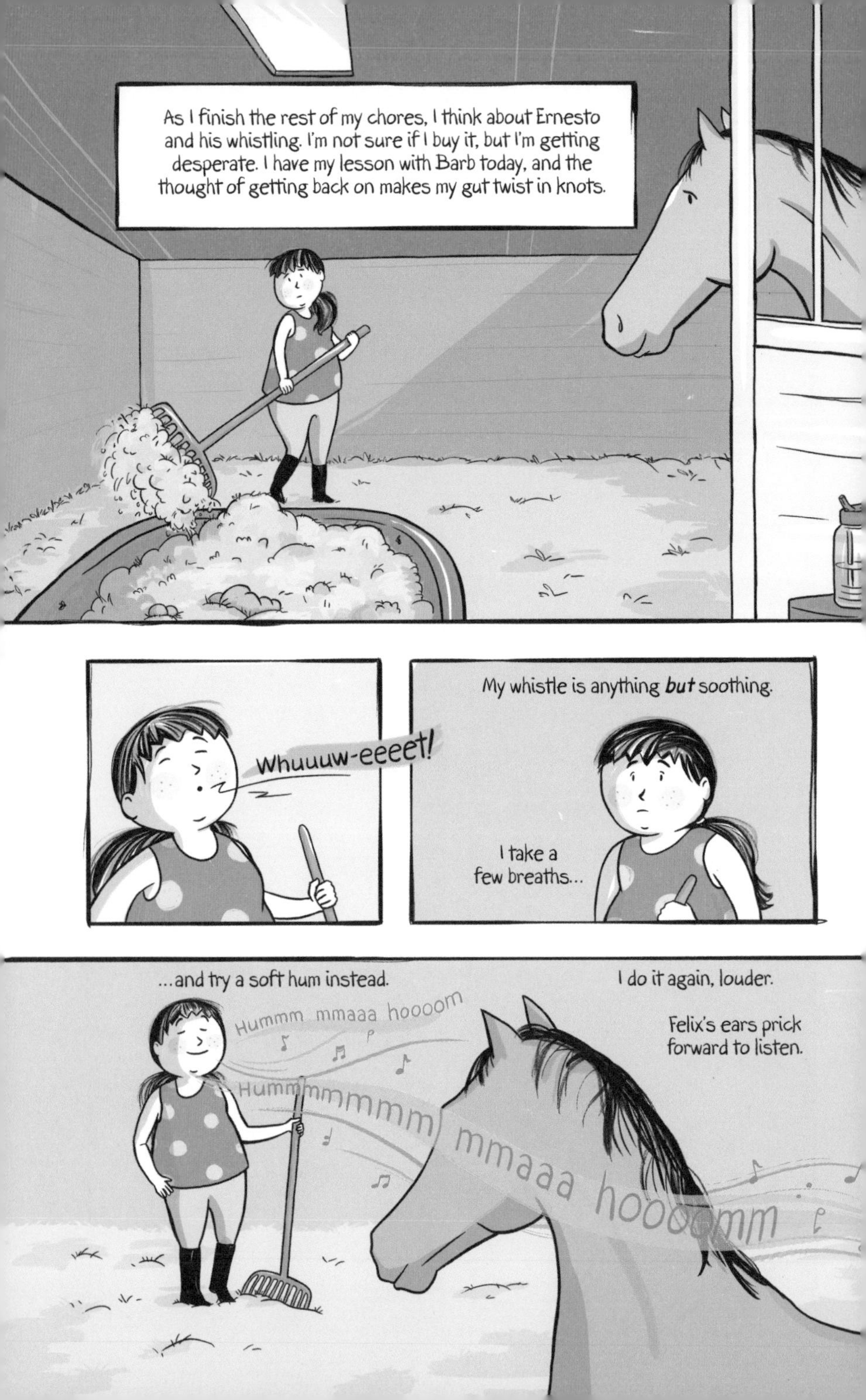

As I finish the rest of my chores, I think about Ernesto and his whistling. I'm not sure if I buy it, but I'm getting desperate. I have my lesson with Barb today, and the thought of getting back on makes my gut twist in knots.
Whuuuw-eeeet!
My whistle is anything **but** soothing.
I take a few breaths...
...and try a soft hum instead.
Hummm mmaaa hoooom
Hummmmmmmm mmaaa hoooomm
I do it again, louder.
Felix's ears prick forward to listen.

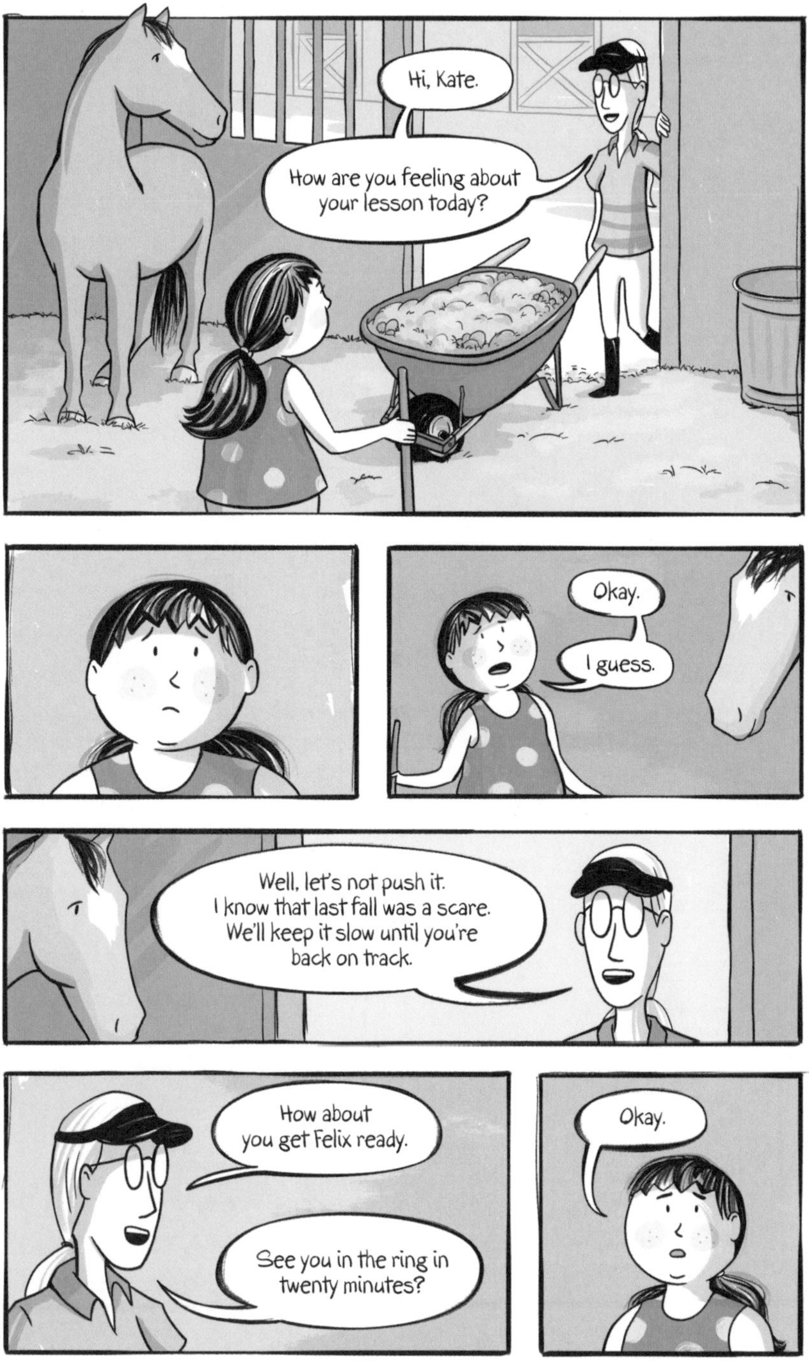

Hi, Kate.
How are you feeling about your lesson today?
Okay.
I guess.
Well, let's not push it. I know that last fall was a scare. We'll keep it slow until you're back on track.
How about you get Felix ready.
See you in the ring in twenty minutes?
Okay.

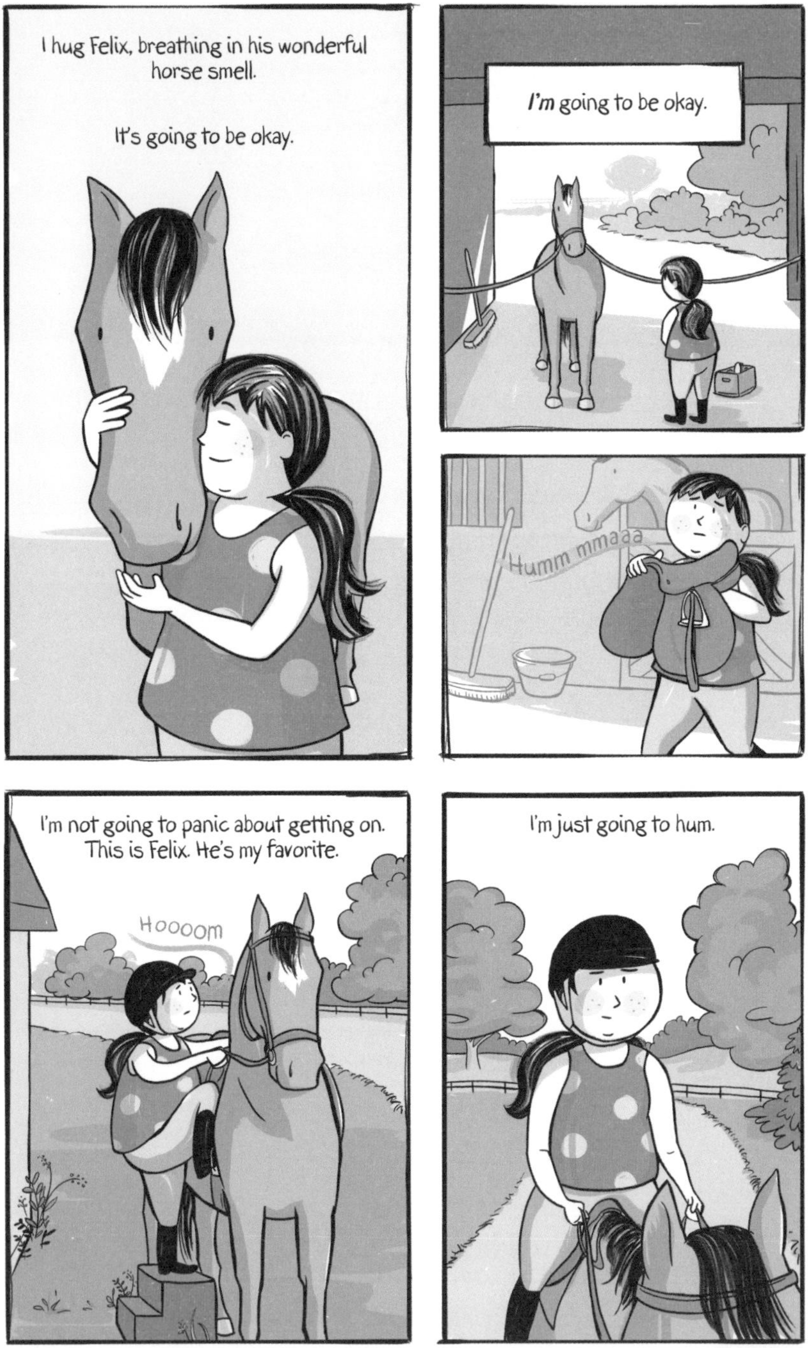
I hug Felix, breathing in his wonderful horse smell.
It's going to be okay.
I'm going to be okay.
Humm mmaaa
I'm not going to panic about getting on. This is Felix. He's my favorite.
Hoooom
I'm just going to hum.

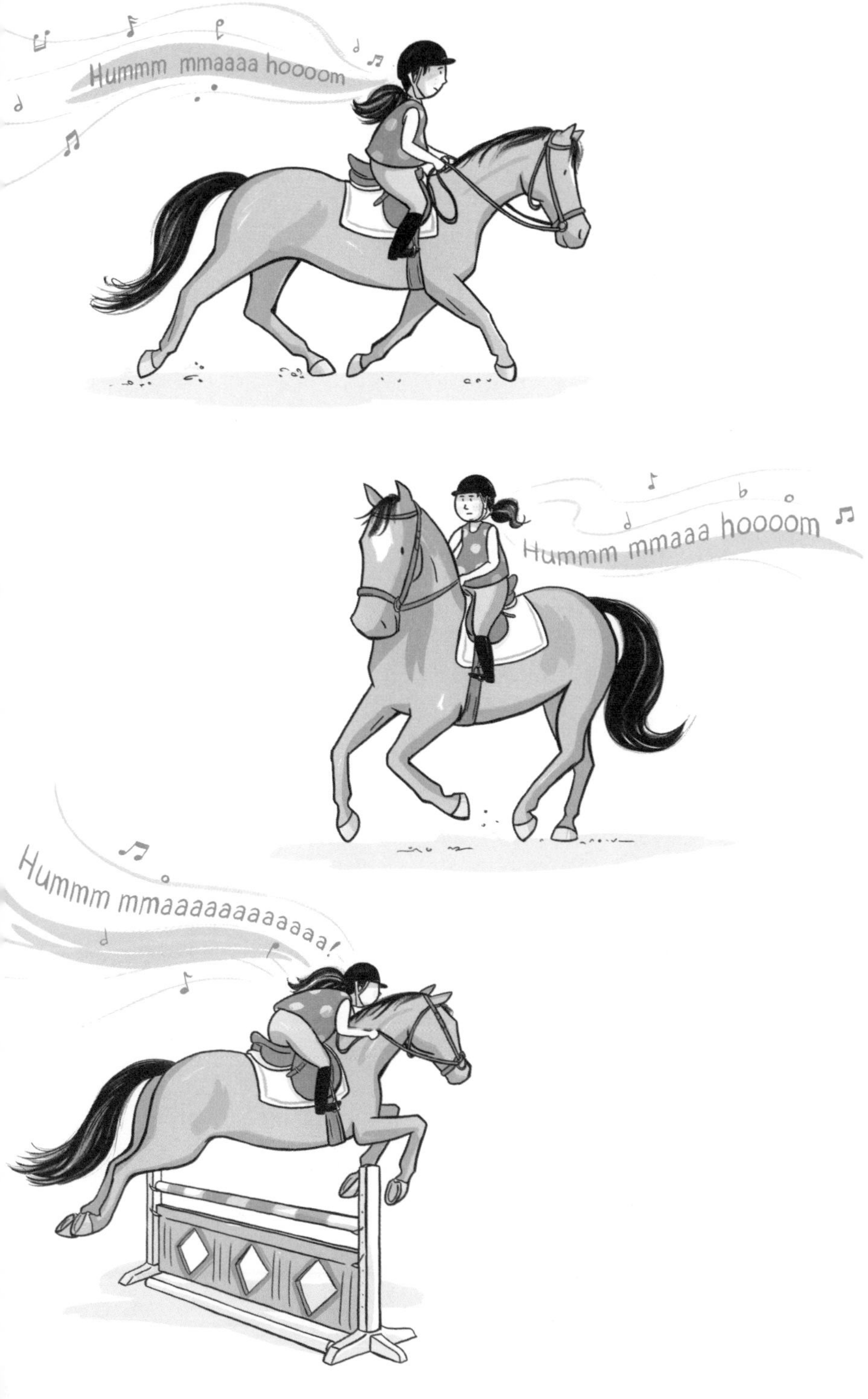
Hummm mmaaaa hoooom
Hummm mmaaa hoooom
Hummm mmaaaaaaaaaaaa!

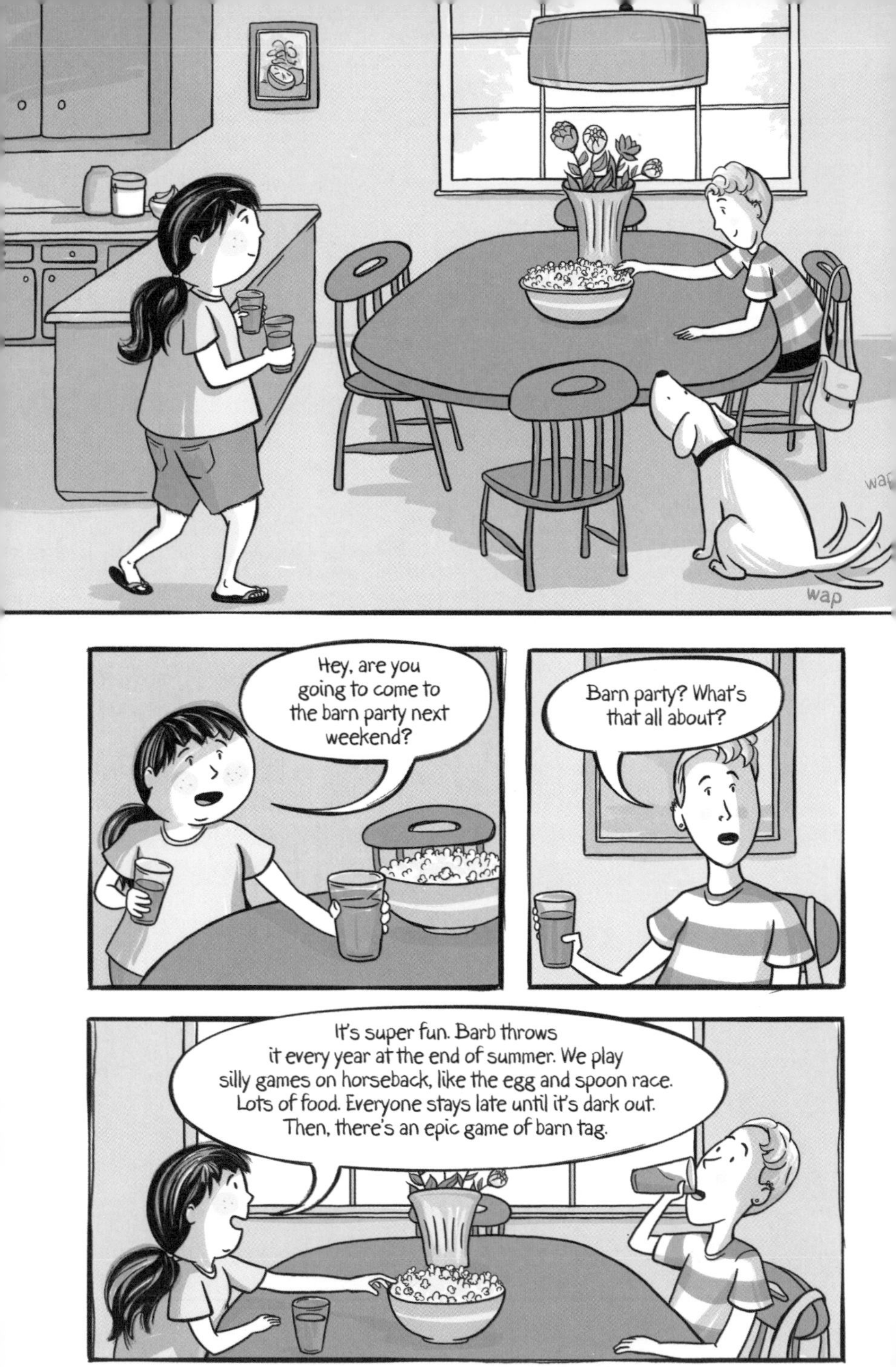
wap
wap
Hey, are you going to come to the barn party next weekend?
Barn party? What's that all about?
It's super fun. Barb throws it every year at the end of summer. We play silly games on horseback, like the egg and spoon race. Lots of food. Everyone stays late until it's dark out. Then, there's an epic game of barn tag.

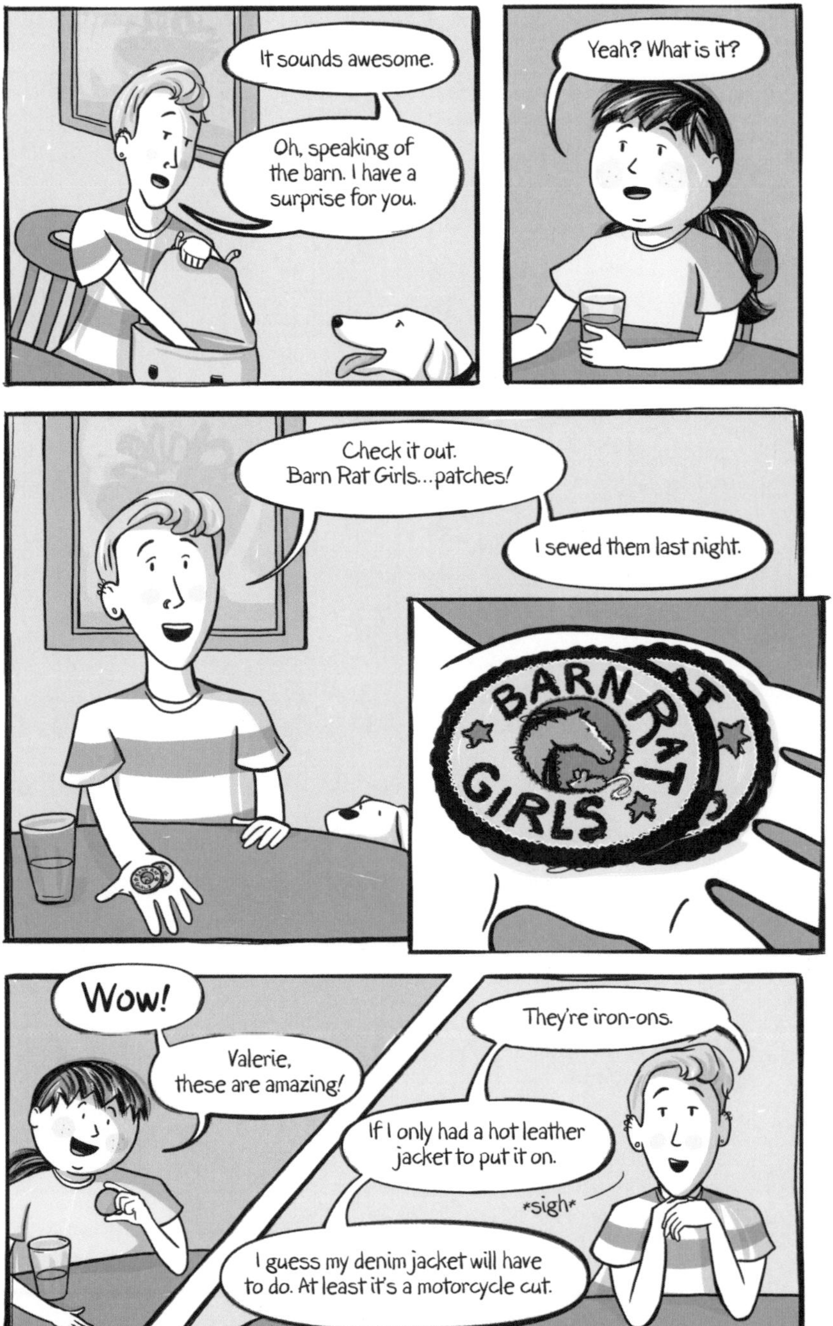
It sounds awesome.
Oh, speaking of the barn. I have a surprise for you.
Yeah? What is it?
Check it out. Barn Rat Girls...patches!
I sewed them last night.
BARN RAT GIRLS
Wow!
Valerie, these are amazing!
They're iron-ons.
If I only had a hot leather jacket to put it on.
sigh
I guess my denim jacket will have to do. At least it's a motorcycle cut.

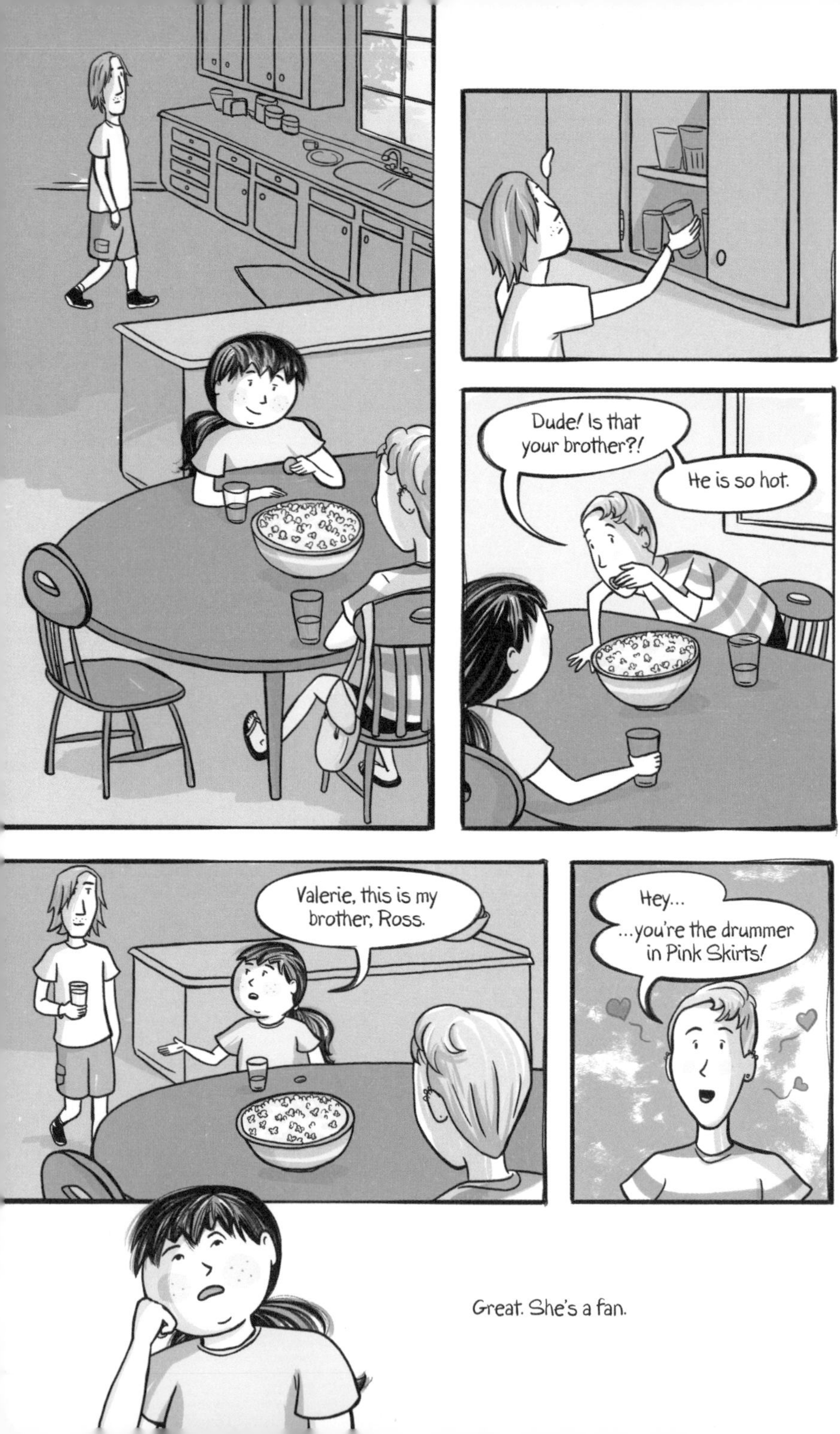

Dude! Is that your brother?!
He is so hot.
Valerie, this is my brother, Ross.
Hey...
...you're the drummer in Pink Skirts!
Great. She's a fan.

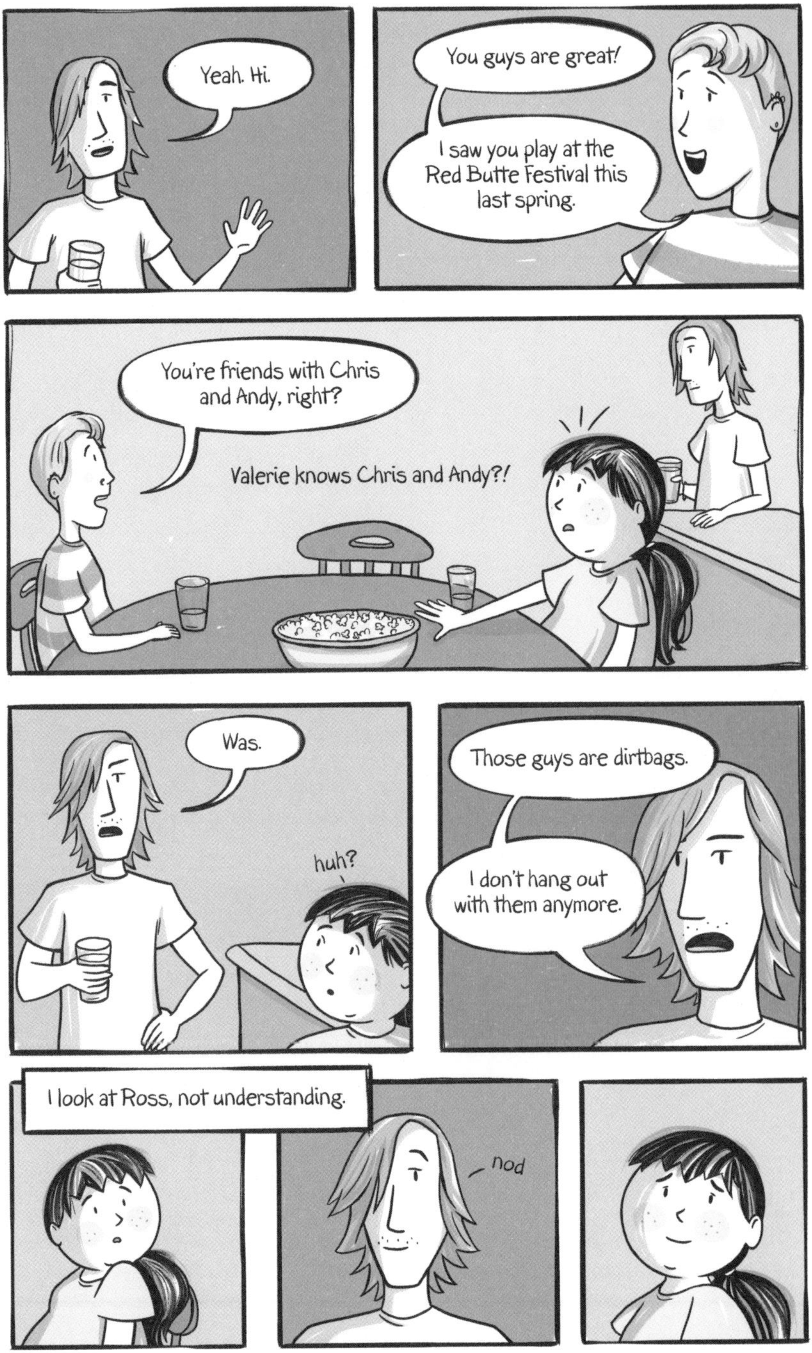
Yeah. Hi.
You guys are great!
I saw you play at the Red Butte Festival this last spring.
You're friends with Chris and Andy, right?
Valerie knows Chris and Andy?!
Was.
huh?
Those guys are dirtbags.
I don't hang out with them anymore.
I look at Ross, not understanding.
nod

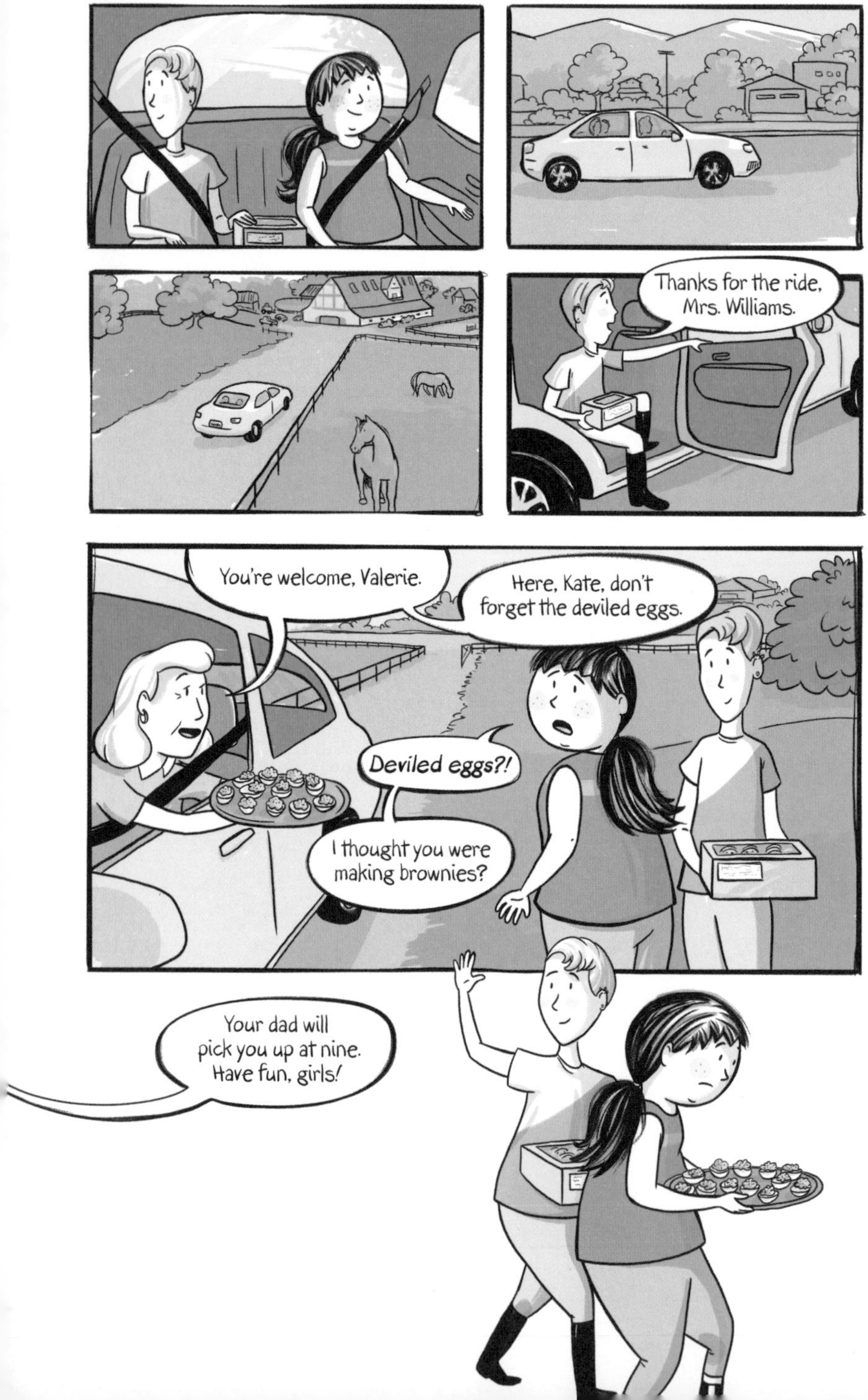
Thanks for the ride, Mrs. Williams.
You're welcome, Valerie.
Here, Kate, don't forget the deviled eggs.
Deviled eggs?!
I thought you were making brownies?
Your dad will pick you up at nine. Have fun, girls!

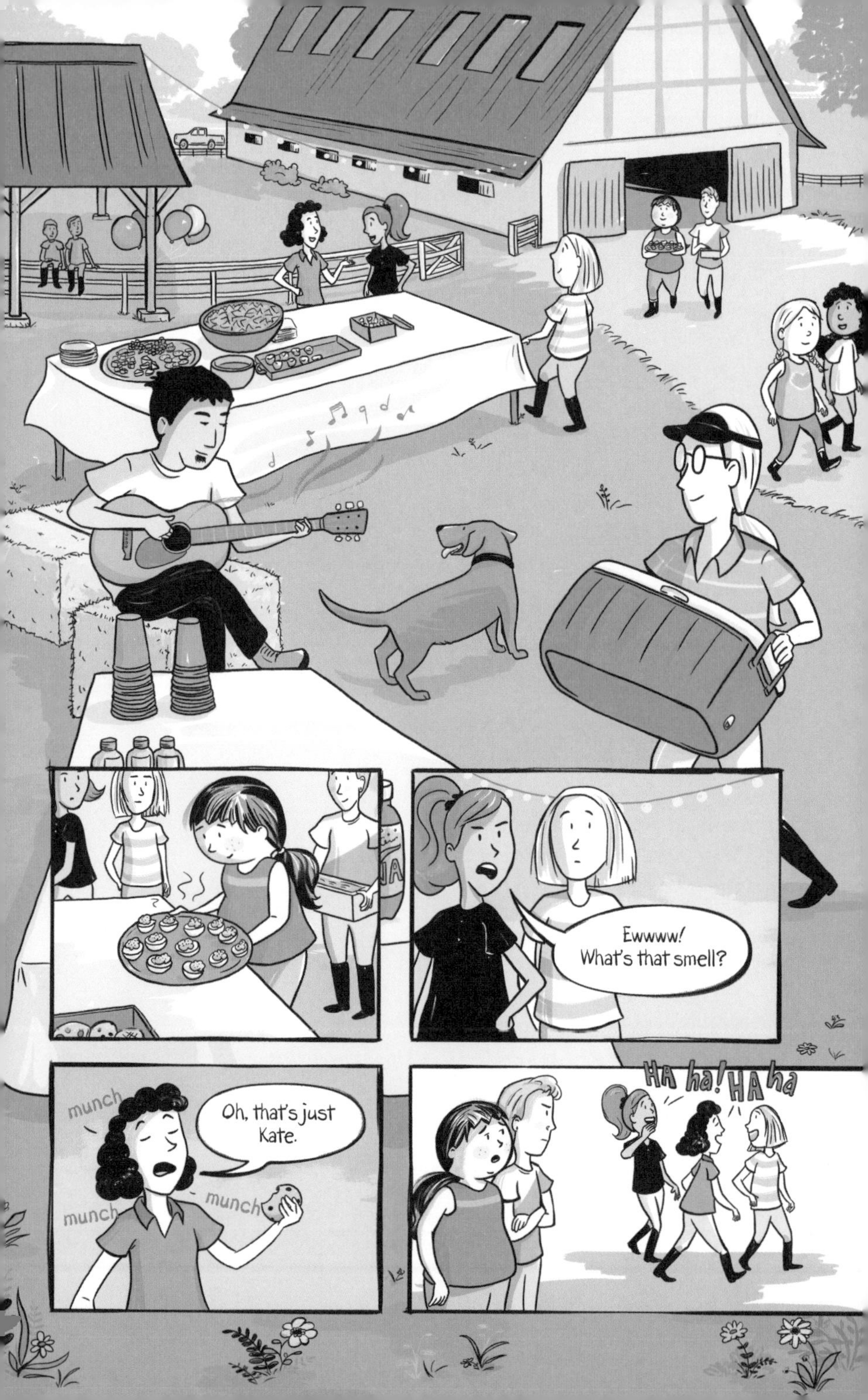
Ewwww! What's that smell?
munch
Oh, that's just Kate.
munch
munch
HA ha! HA ha

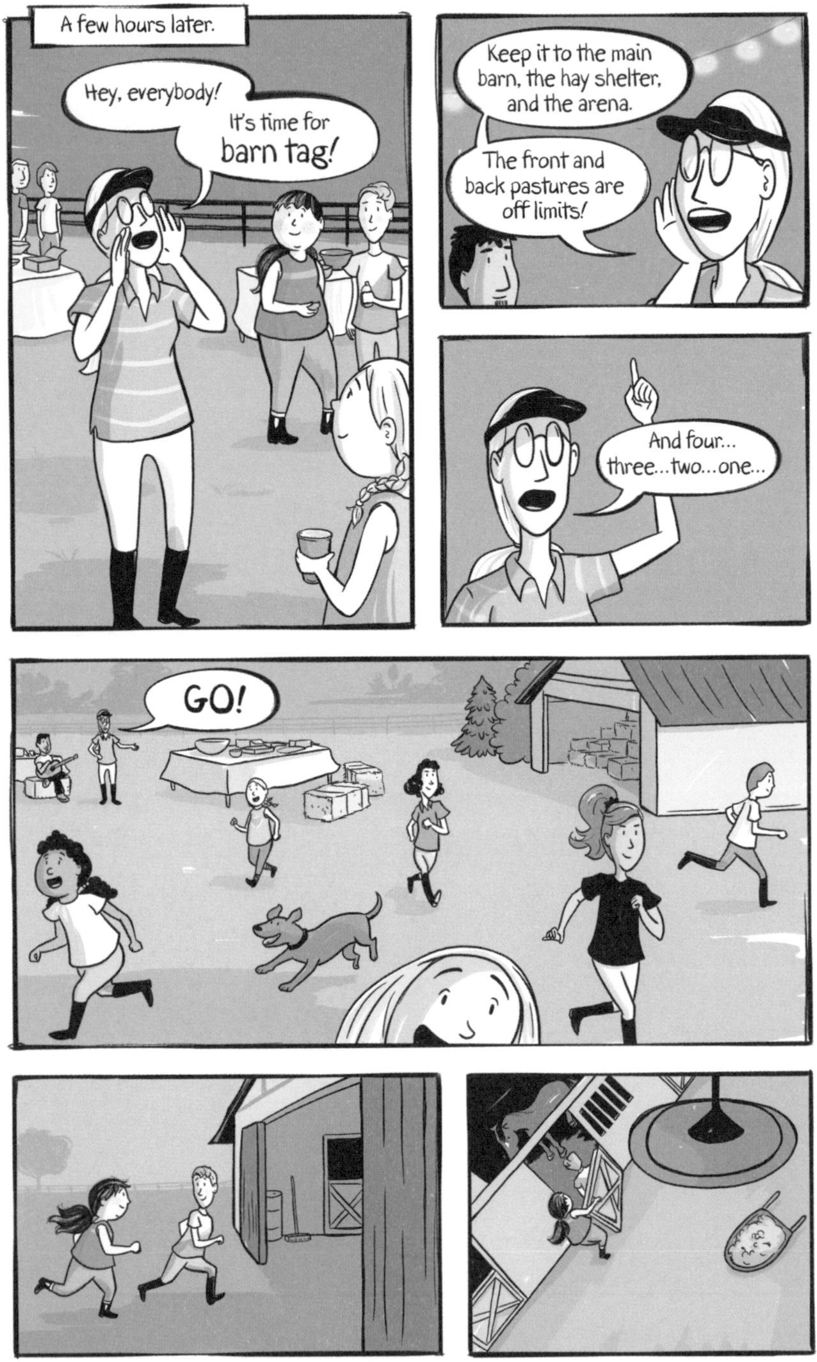
A few hours later.
Hey, everybody!
It's time for barn tag!
Keep it to the main barn, the hay shelter, and the arena.
The front and back pastures are off limits!
And four... three...two...one...
GO!

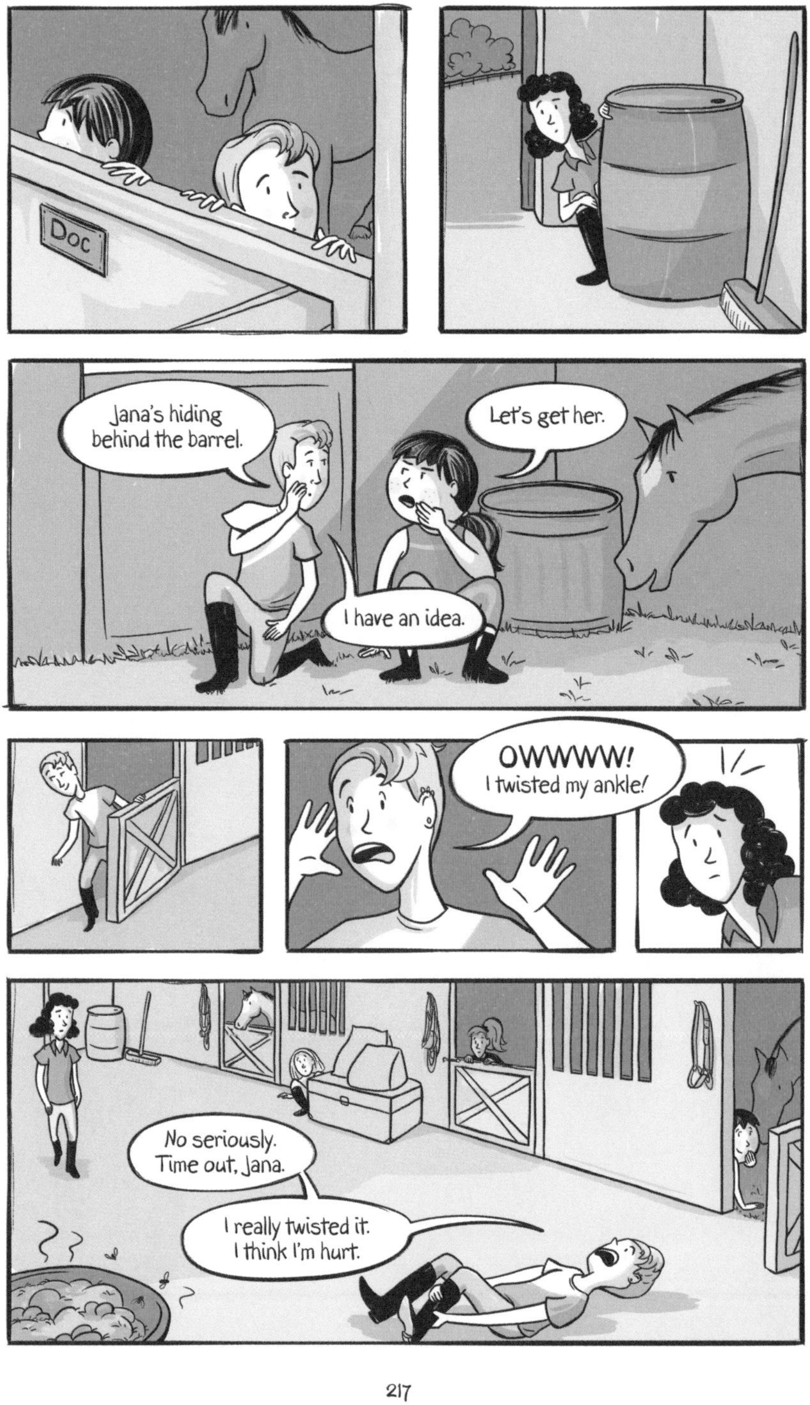
Doc
Jana's hiding behind the barrel.
Let's get her.
I have an idea.
OWWWW!
I twisted my ankle!
No seriously. Time out, Jana.
I really twisted it. I think I'm hurt.

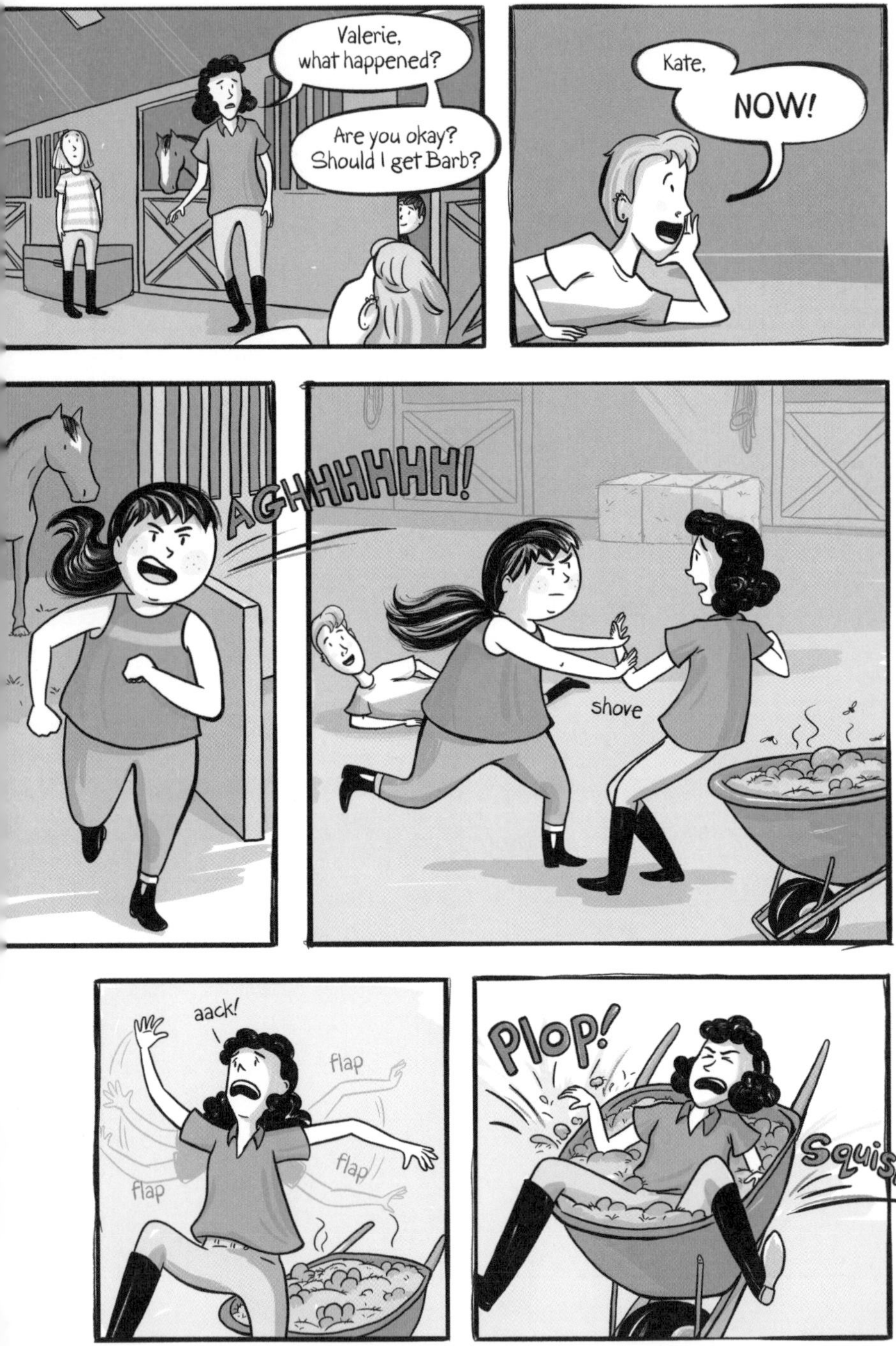
Valerie, what happened?
Are you okay? Should I get Barb?
Kate,
NOW!
AGHHHHHH!
shove
aack!
flap
flap
flap
PLOP!
Squish

Uuughhh!

I brace myself for Jana to get me back.

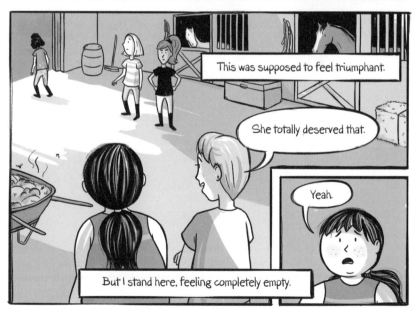

This was supposed to feel triumphant.

She totally deserved that.

Yeah.

But I stand here, feeling completely empty.

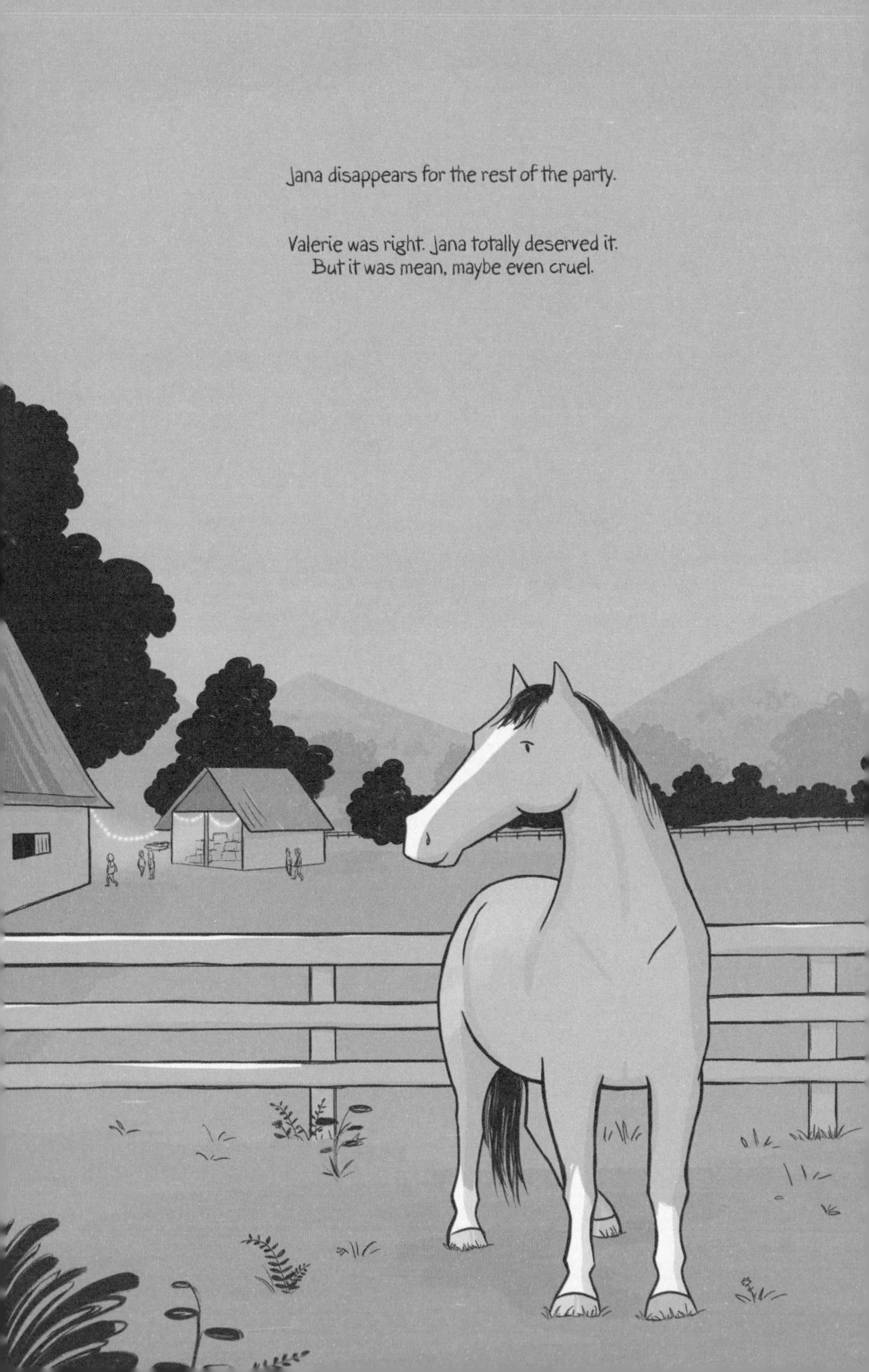
Jana disappears for the rest of the party.
Valerie was right. Jana totally deserved it. But it was mean, maybe even cruel.

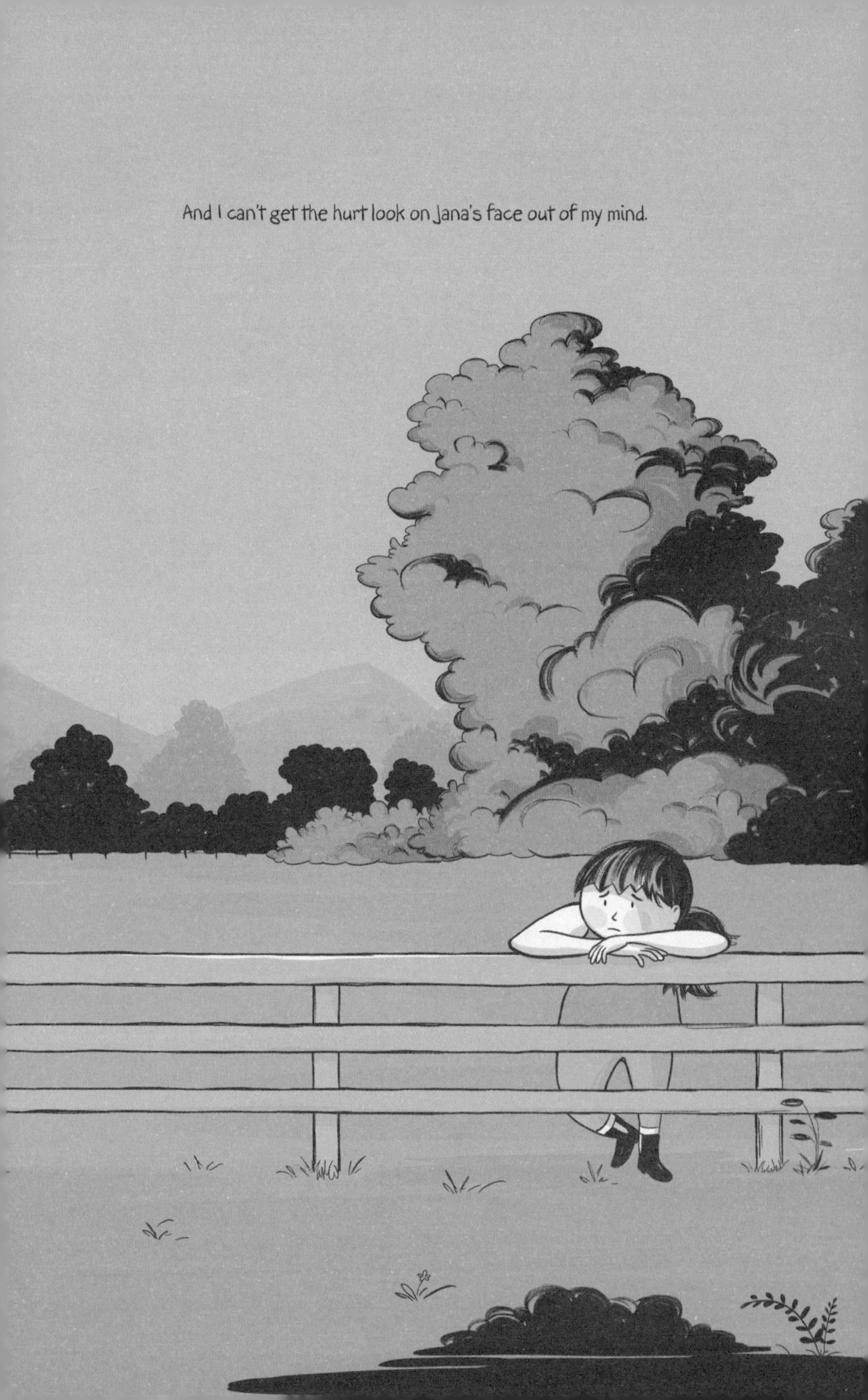
And I can't get the hurt look on Jana's face out of my mind.

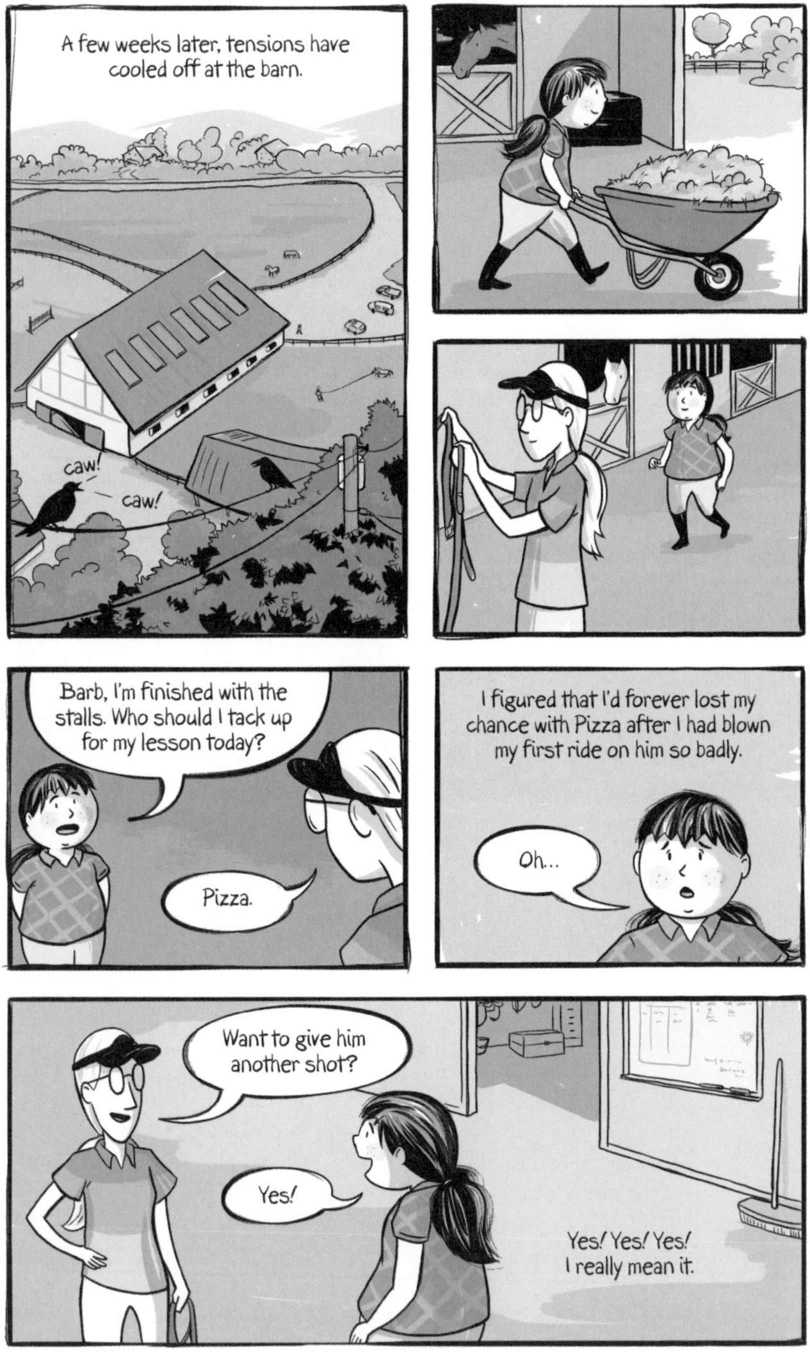
A few weeks later, tensions have cooled off at the barn.
caw!
caw!
Barb, I'm finished with the stalls. Who should I tack up for my lesson today?
Pizza.
I figured that I'd forever lost my chance with Pizza after I had blown my first ride on him so badly.
Oh...
Want to give him another shot?
Yes!
Yes! Yes! Yes! I really mean it.

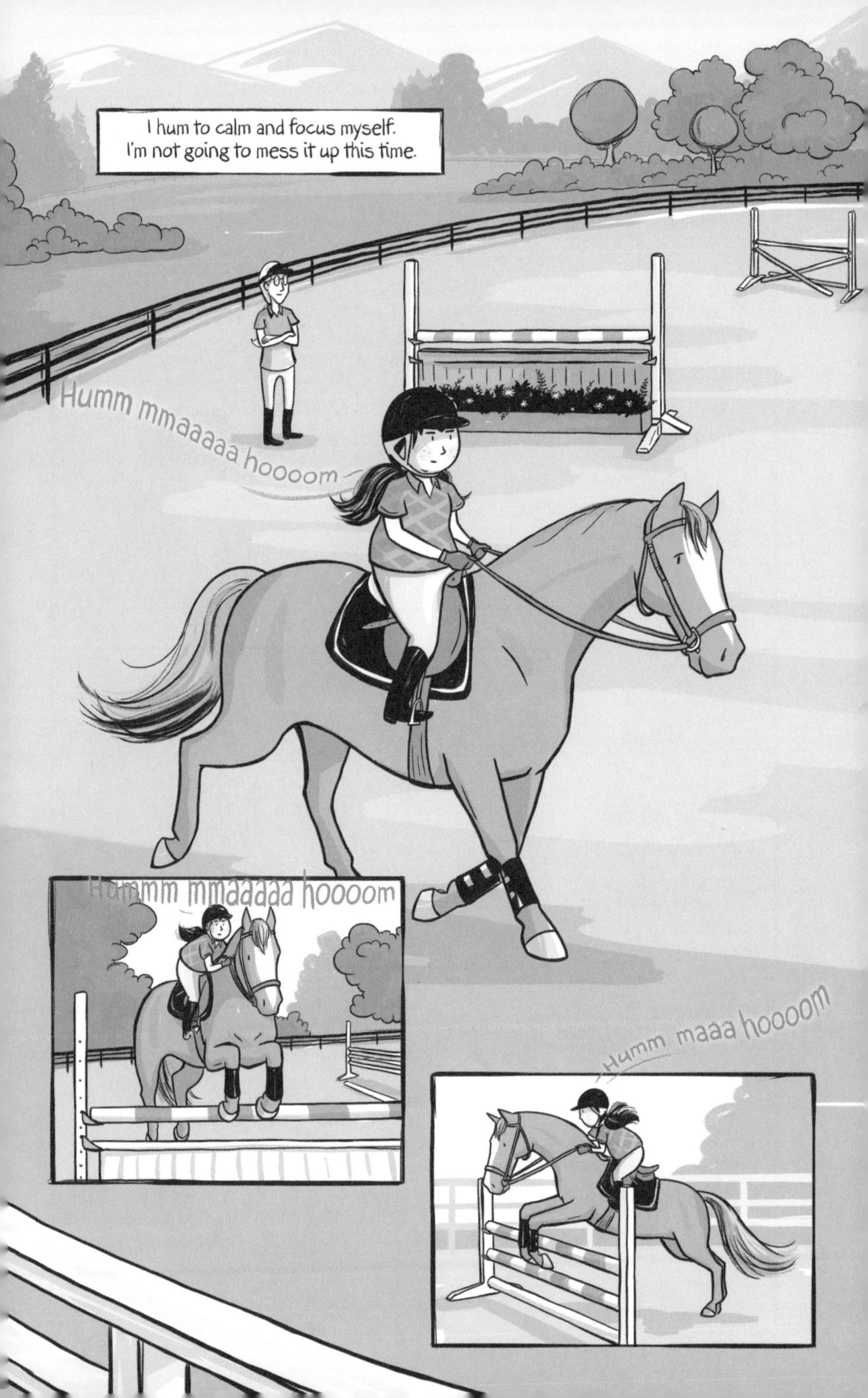
I hum to calm and focus myself.
I'm not going to mess it up this time.
Humm mmaaaaaa hoooom
Hummm mmaaaaa hoooom
Humm maaa hoooom

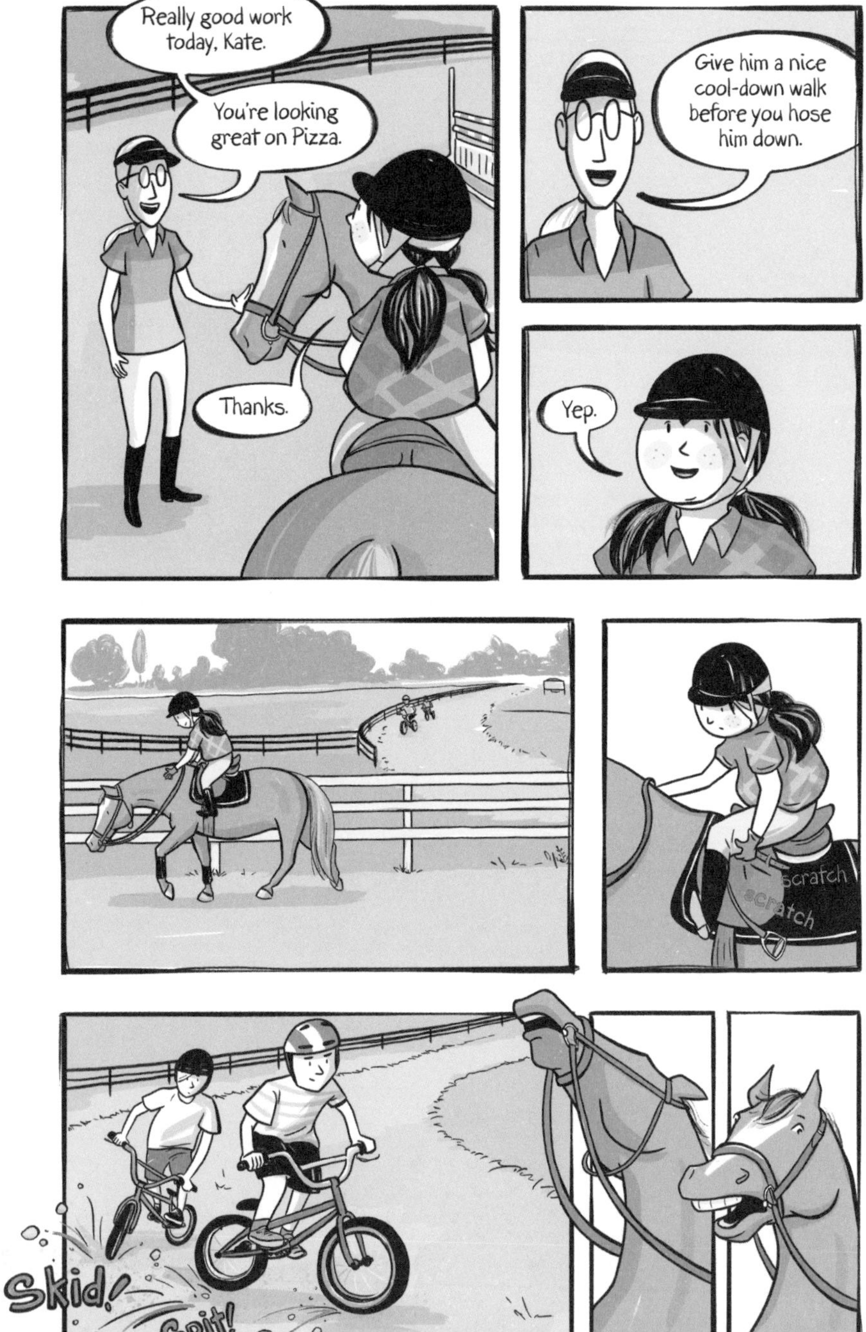
Really good work today, Kate.
You're looking great on Pizza.
Thanks.
Give him a nice cool-down walk before you hose him down.
Yep.
scratch
scratch
Skid!
Spit!

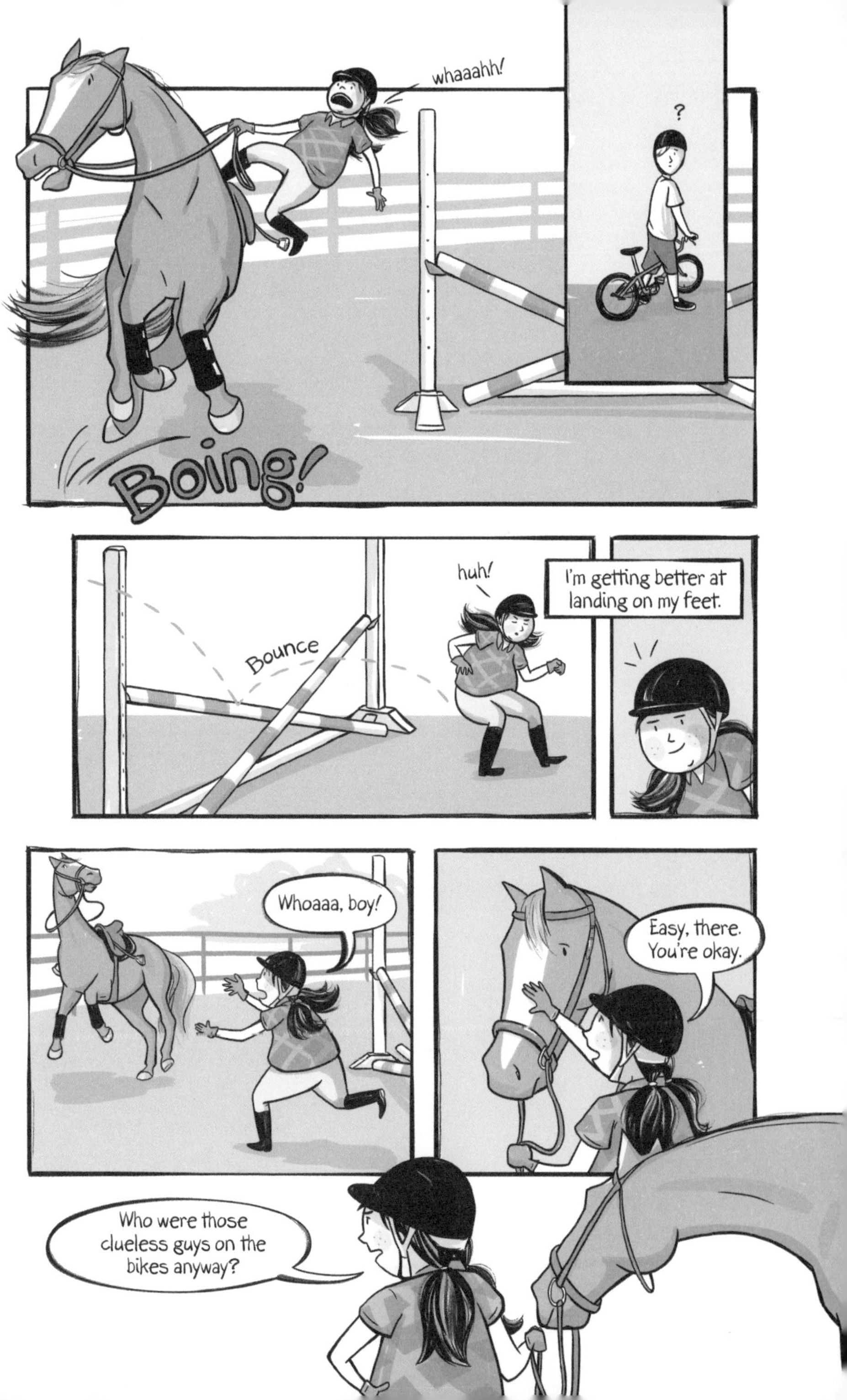
whaaahh!
?
Boing!
huh!
Bounce
I'm getting better at landing on my feet.
Whoaaa, boy!
Easy, there. You're okay.
Who were those clueless guys on the bikes anyway?

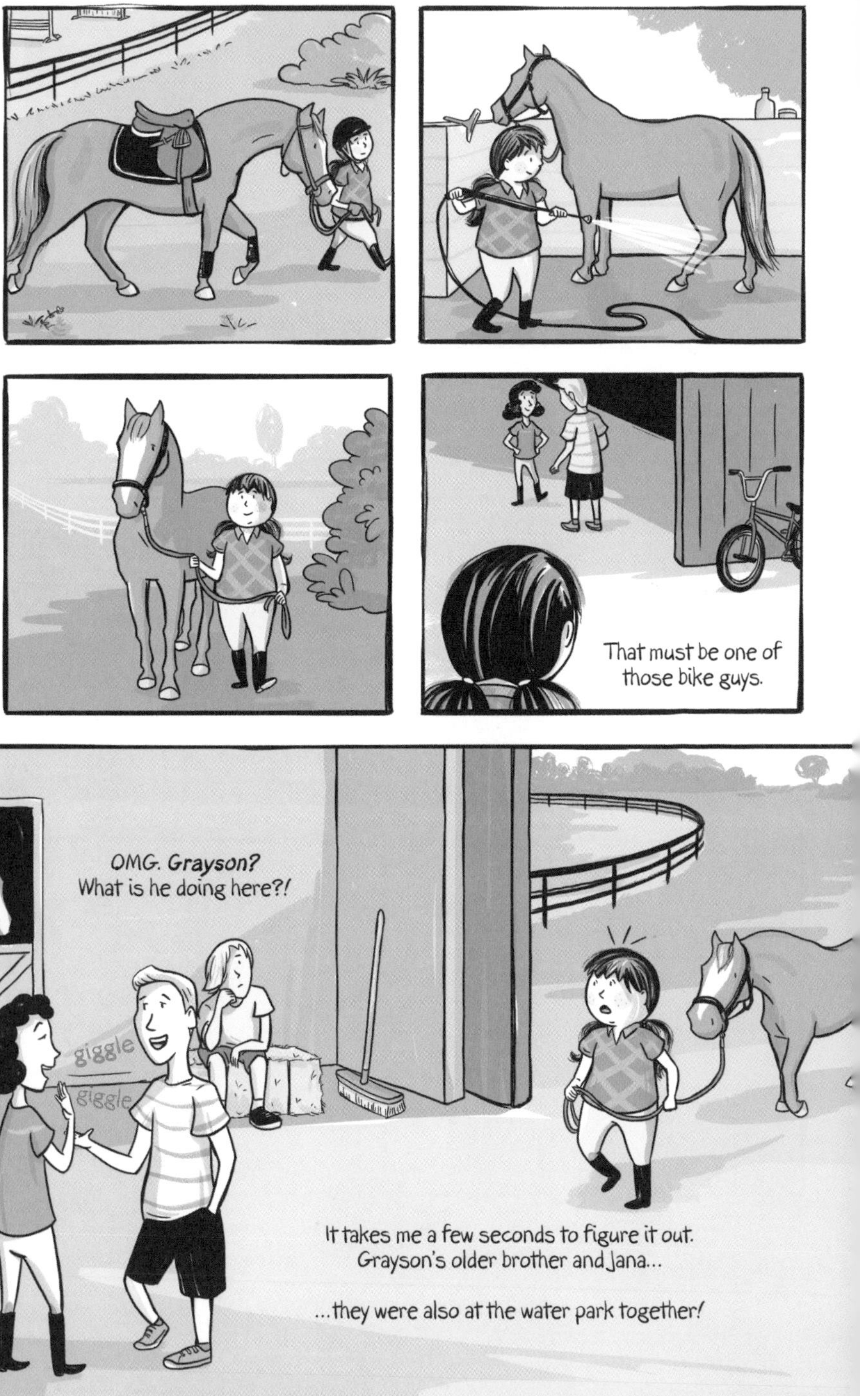
That must be one of those bike guys.
OMG. Grayson? What is he doing here?!
giggle
giggle
It takes me a few seconds to figure it out. Grayson's older brother and Jana...
...they were also at the water park together!

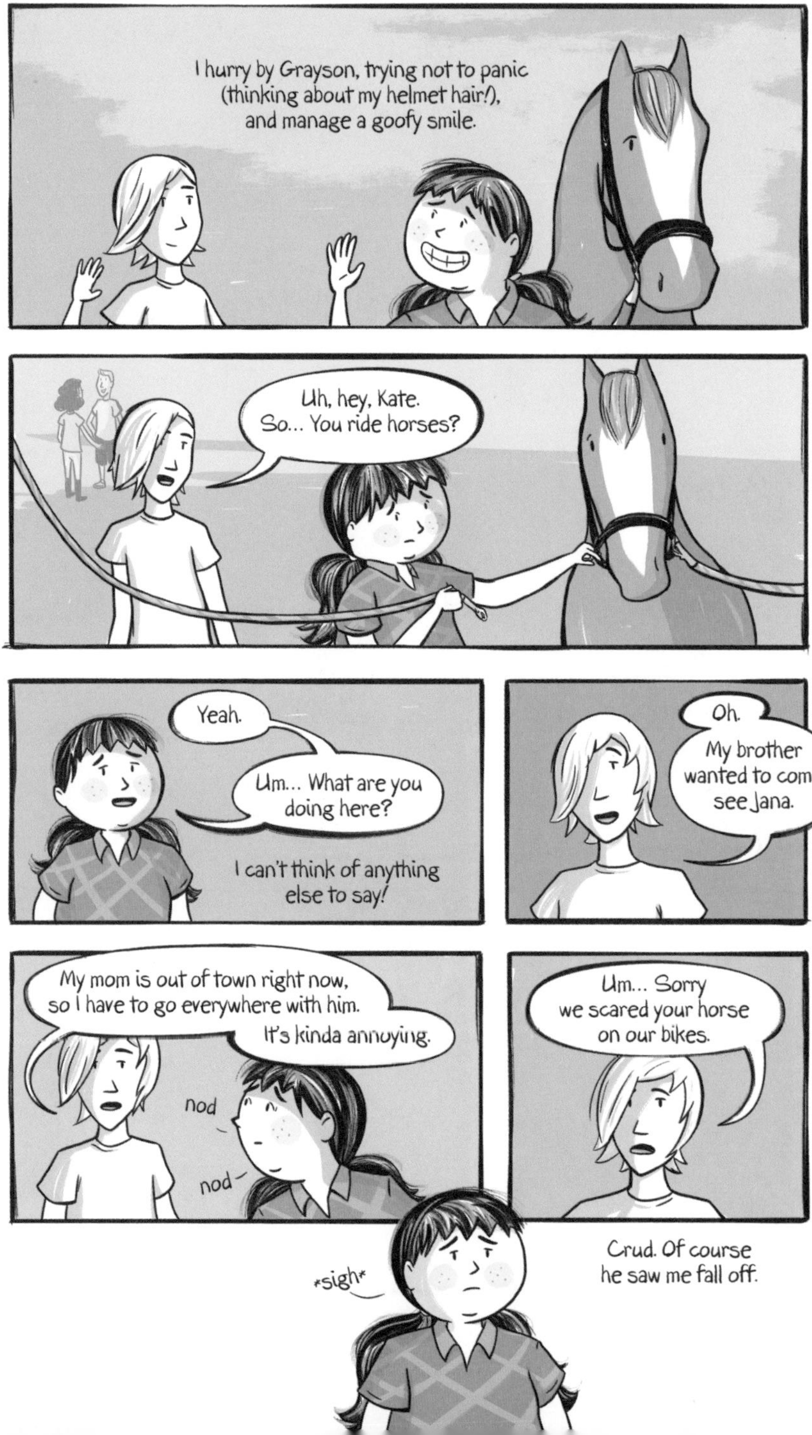

I hurry by Grayson, trying not to panic (thinking about my helmet hair!), and manage a goofy smile.
Uh, hey, Kate. So... You ride horses?
Yeah.
Um... What are you doing here?
I can't think of anything else to say!
Oh.
My brother wanted to come see Jana.
My mom is out of town right now, so I have to go everywhere with him.
It's kinda annoying.
nod
nod
Um... Sorry we scared your horse on our bikes.
sigh
Crud. Of course he saw me fall off.

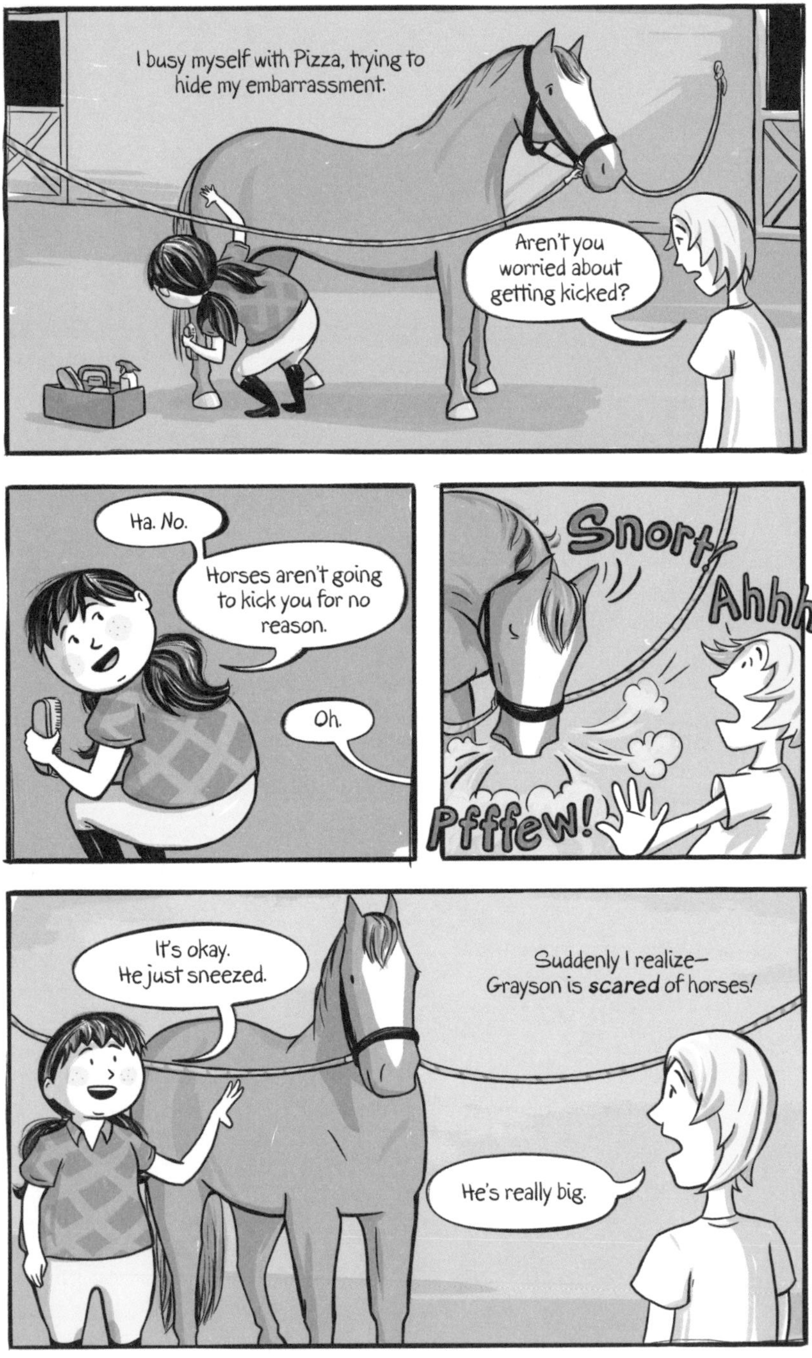
I busy myself with Pizza, trying to hide my embarrassment.
Aren't you worried about getting kicked?
Ha. No.
Horses aren't going to kick you for no reason.
Oh.
Snort!
Ahhh!
Pfffew!
It's okay. He just sneezed.
Suddenly I realize—Grayson is *scared* of horses!
He's really big.

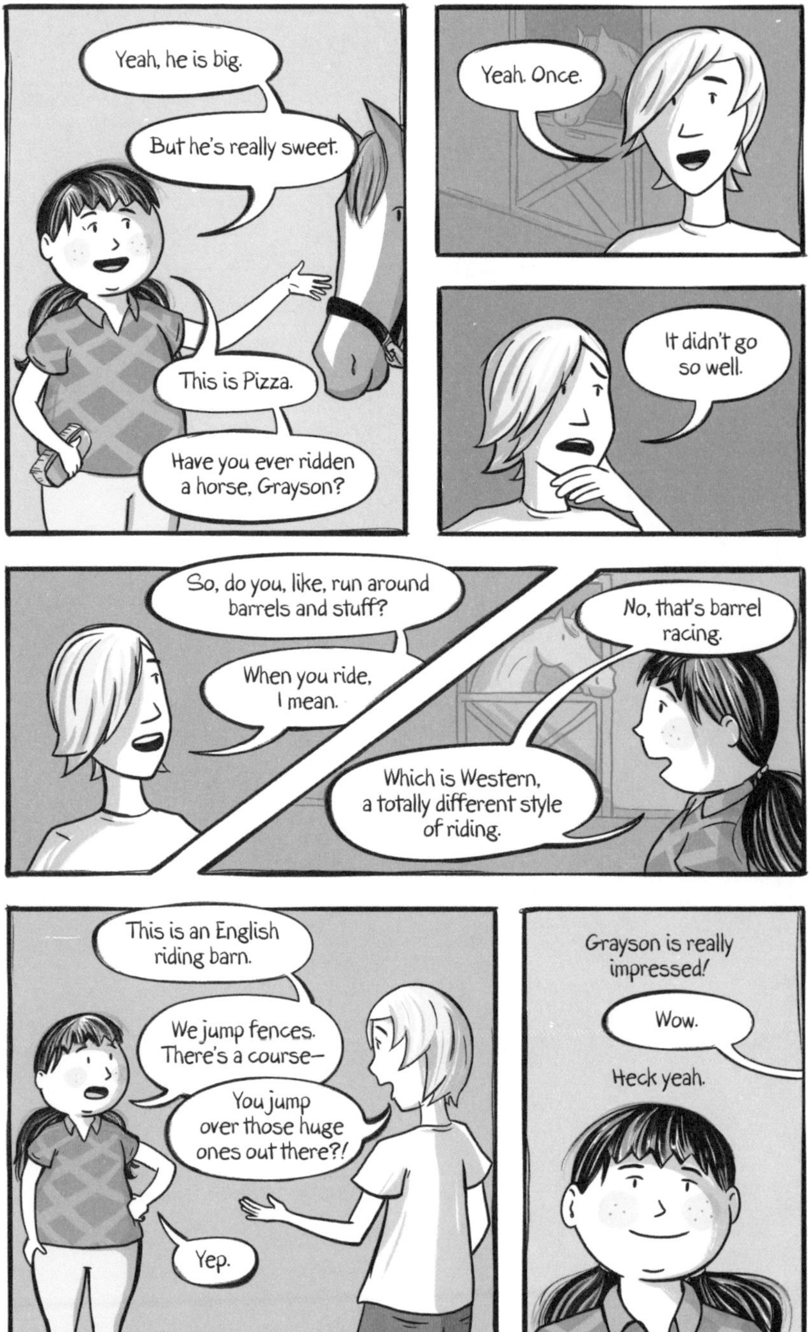
Yeah, he is big.
But he's really sweet.
This is Pizza.
Have you ever ridden a horse, Grayson?
Yeah. Once.
It didn't go so well.
So, do you, like, run around barrels and stuff?
When you ride, I mean.
No, that's barrel racing.
Which is Western, a totally different style of riding.
This is an English riding barn.
We jump fences. There's a course–
You jump over those huge ones out there?!
Yep.
Grayson is really impressed!
Wow.
Heck yeah.

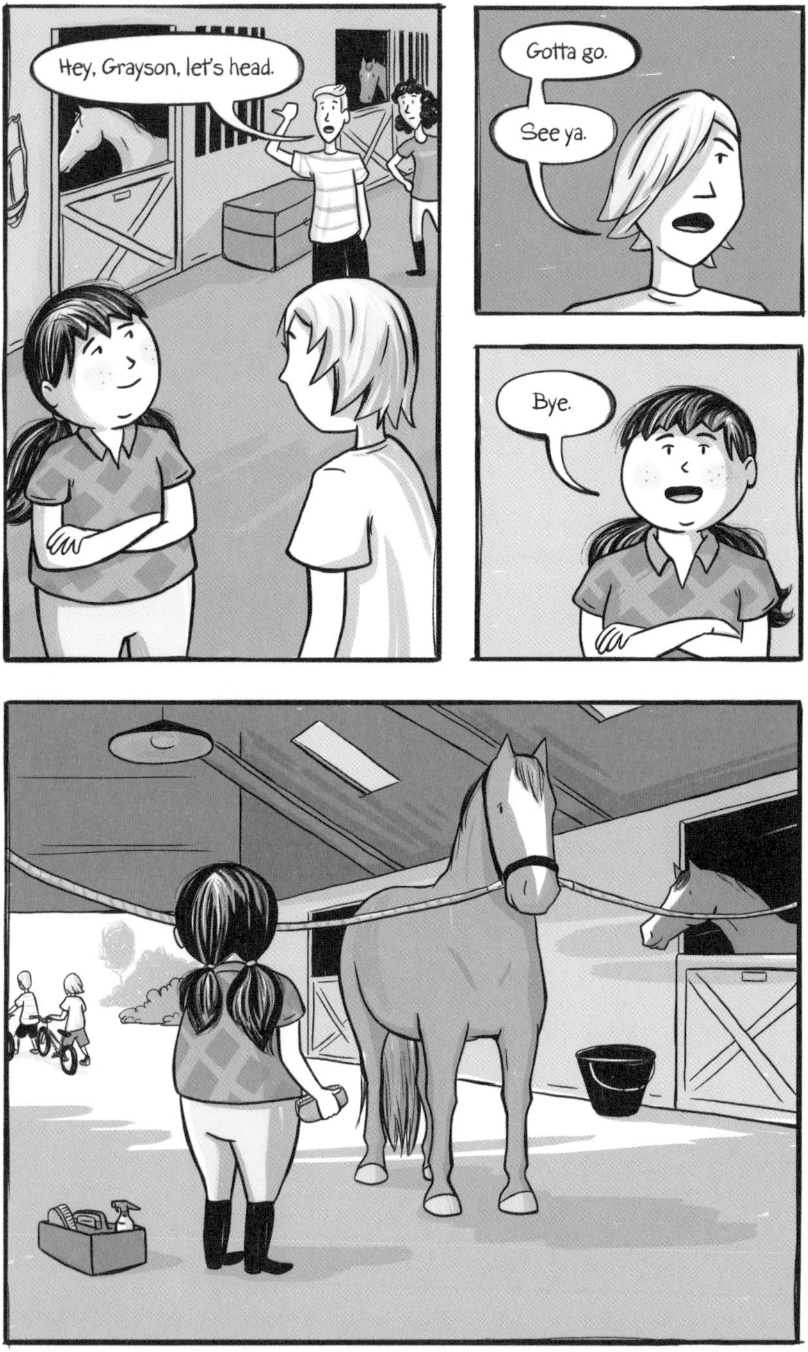
Hey, Grayson, let's head.
Gotta go.
See ya.
Bye.

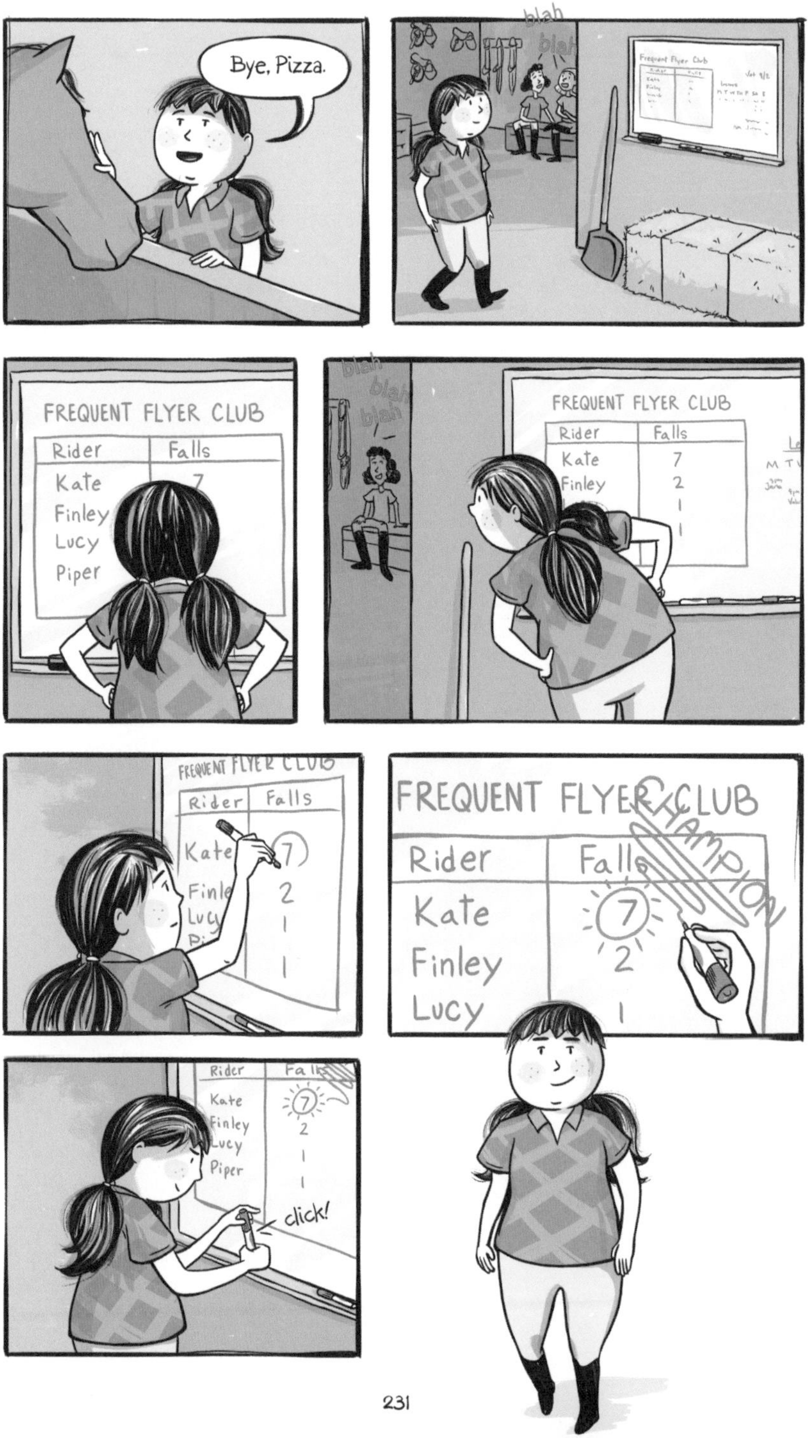

Bye, Pizza.
blah
blah
FREQUENT FLYER CLUB
Rider
Falls
Kate
7
Finley
Lucy
Piper
blah
blah
blah
FREQUENT FLYER CLUB
Rider
Falls
Kate
7
Finley
2
1
1
FREQUENT FLYER CLUB
Rider
Falls
Kate
7
2
1
1
FREQUENT FLYER CLUB
CHAMPION
Rider
Falls
Kate
7
Finley
2
Lucy
1
Rider
Falls
Kate
7
Finley
2
Lucy
1
Piper
1
click!

Chapter 10
Fly Through

Oxer

Two vertical fences placed near each other to make one single wide jump. Also called a spread.

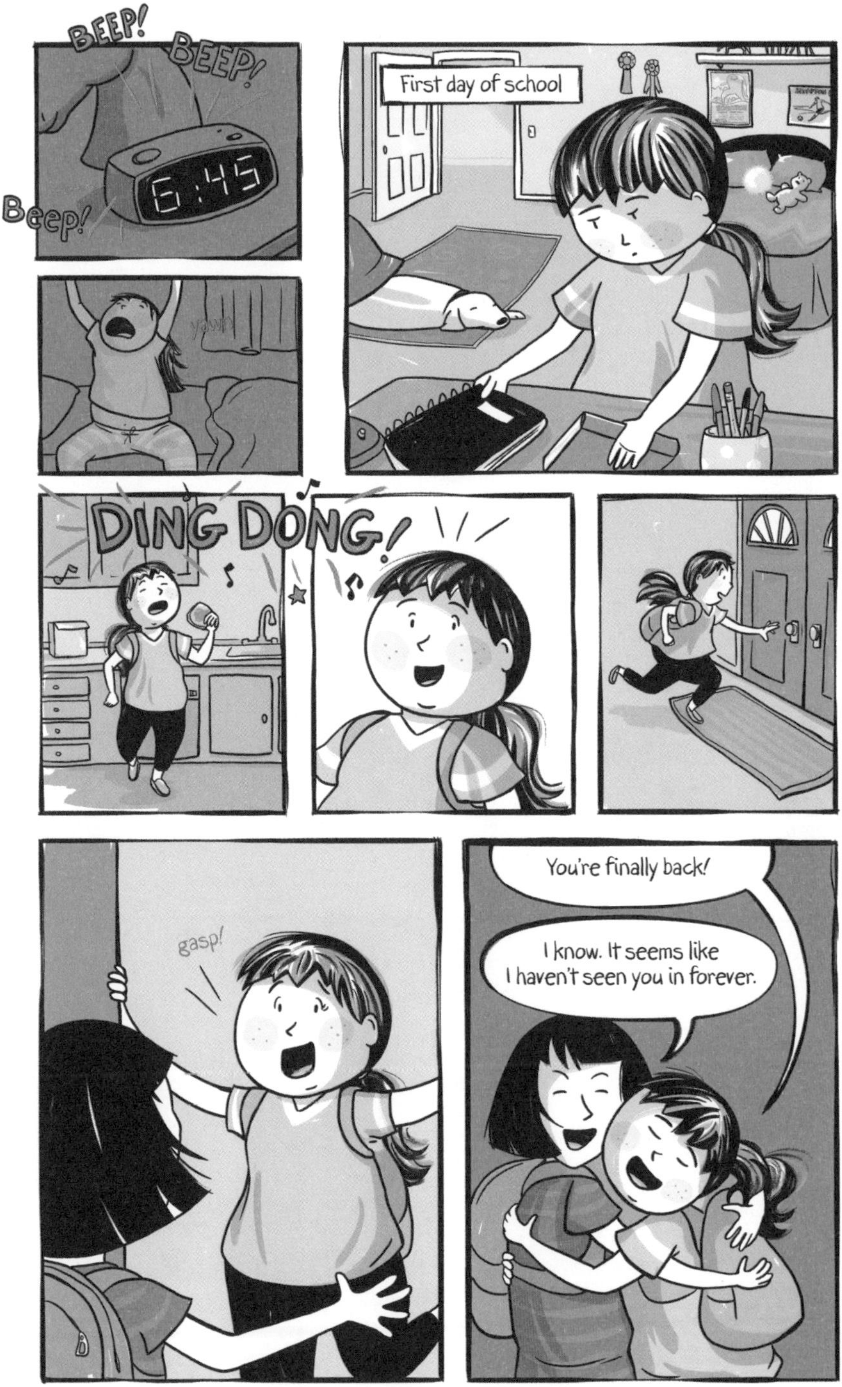
BEEP!
BEEP!
Beep!
6:45
First day of school
yawn
DING DONG!
gasp!
You're finally back!
I know. It seems like I haven't seen you in forever.

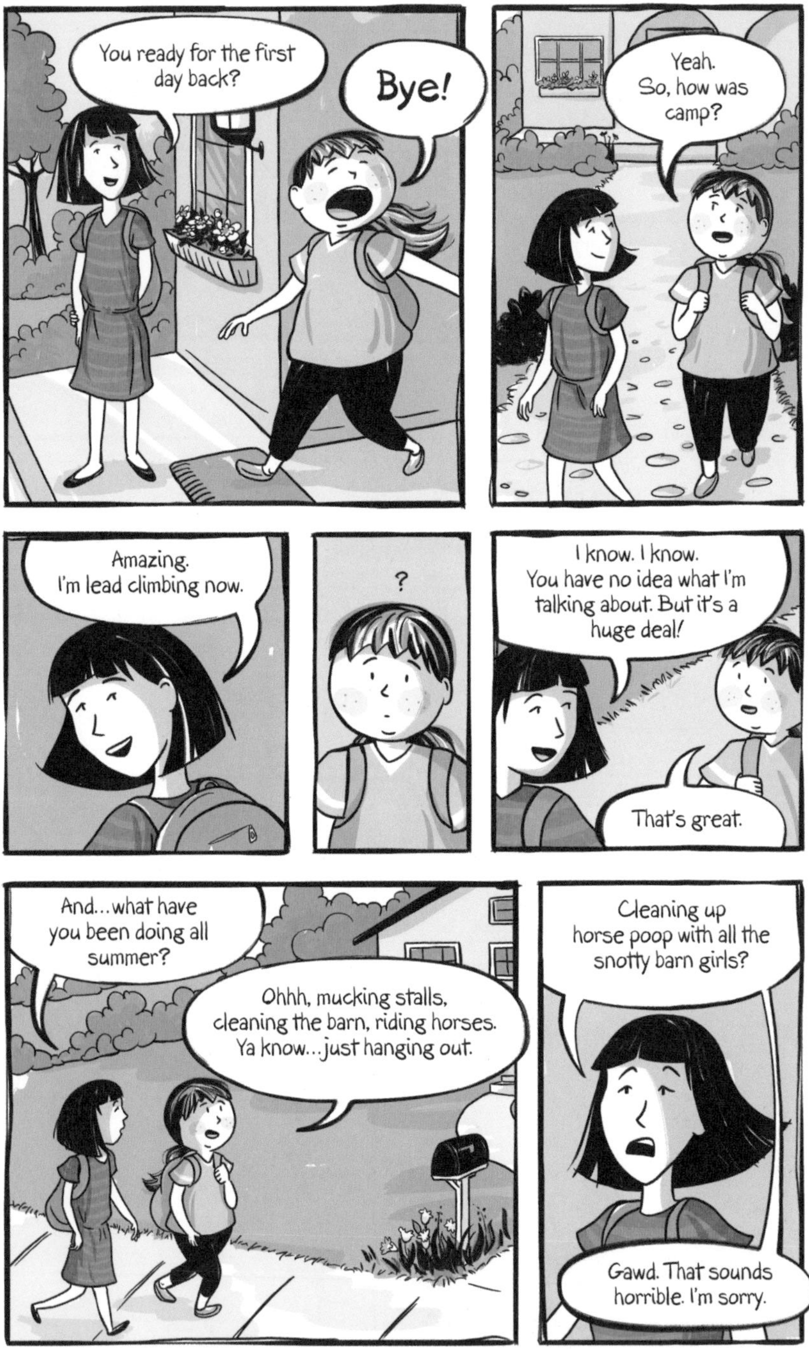
You ready for the first day back?
Bye!
Yeah. So, how was camp?
Amazing. I'm lead climbing now.
?
I know. I know. You have no idea what I'm talking about. But it's a huge deal!
That's great.
And...what have you been doing all summer?
Ohhh, mucking stalls, cleaning the barn, riding horses. Ya know...just hanging out.
Cleaning up horse poop with all the snotty barn girls?
Gawd. That sounds horrible. I'm sorry.

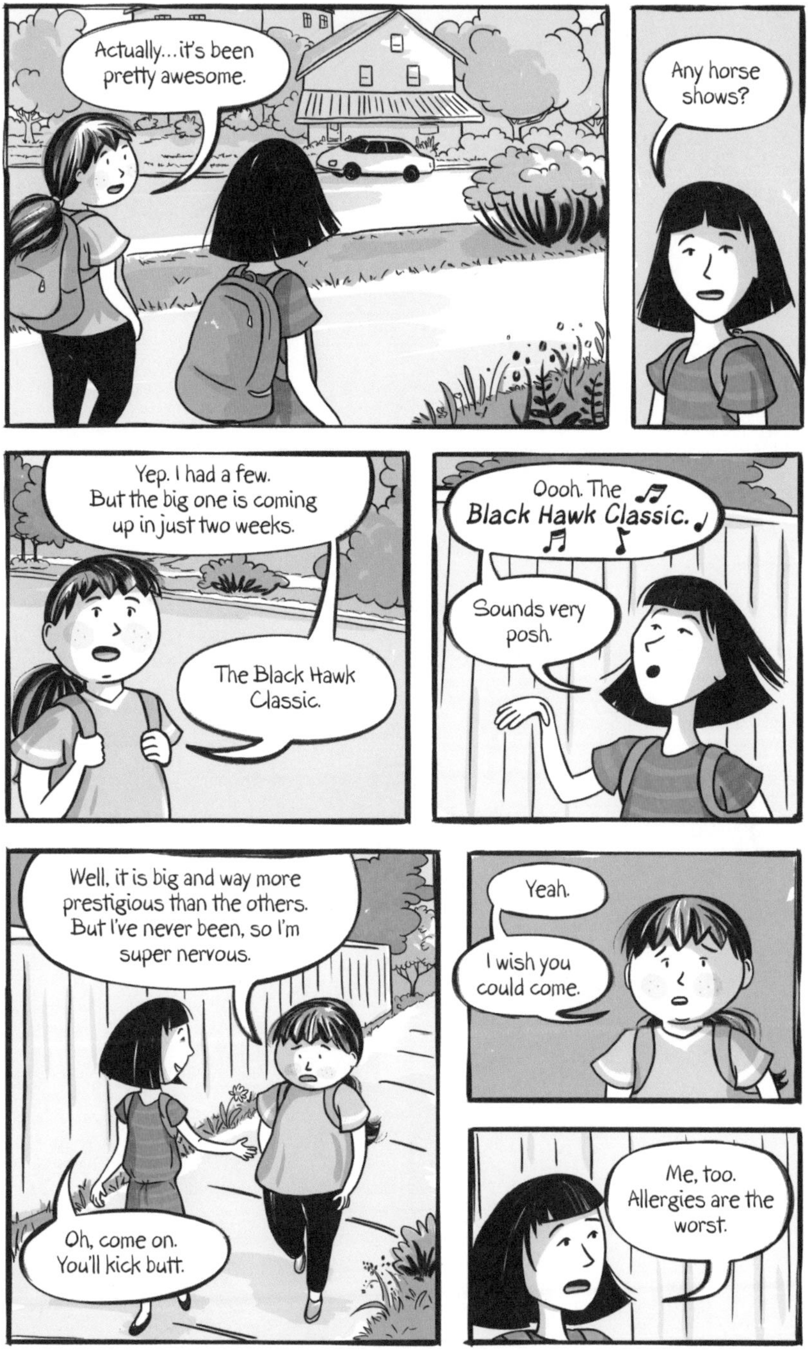
Actually... it's been pretty awesome.
Any horse shows?
Yep. I had a few. But the big one is coming up in just two weeks.
The Black Hawk Classic.
Oooh. The Black Hawk Classic.
Sounds very posh.
Well, it is big and way more prestigious than the others. But I've never been, so I'm super nervous.
Oh, come on. You'll kick butt.
Yeah.
I wish you could come.
Me, too. Allergies are the worst.

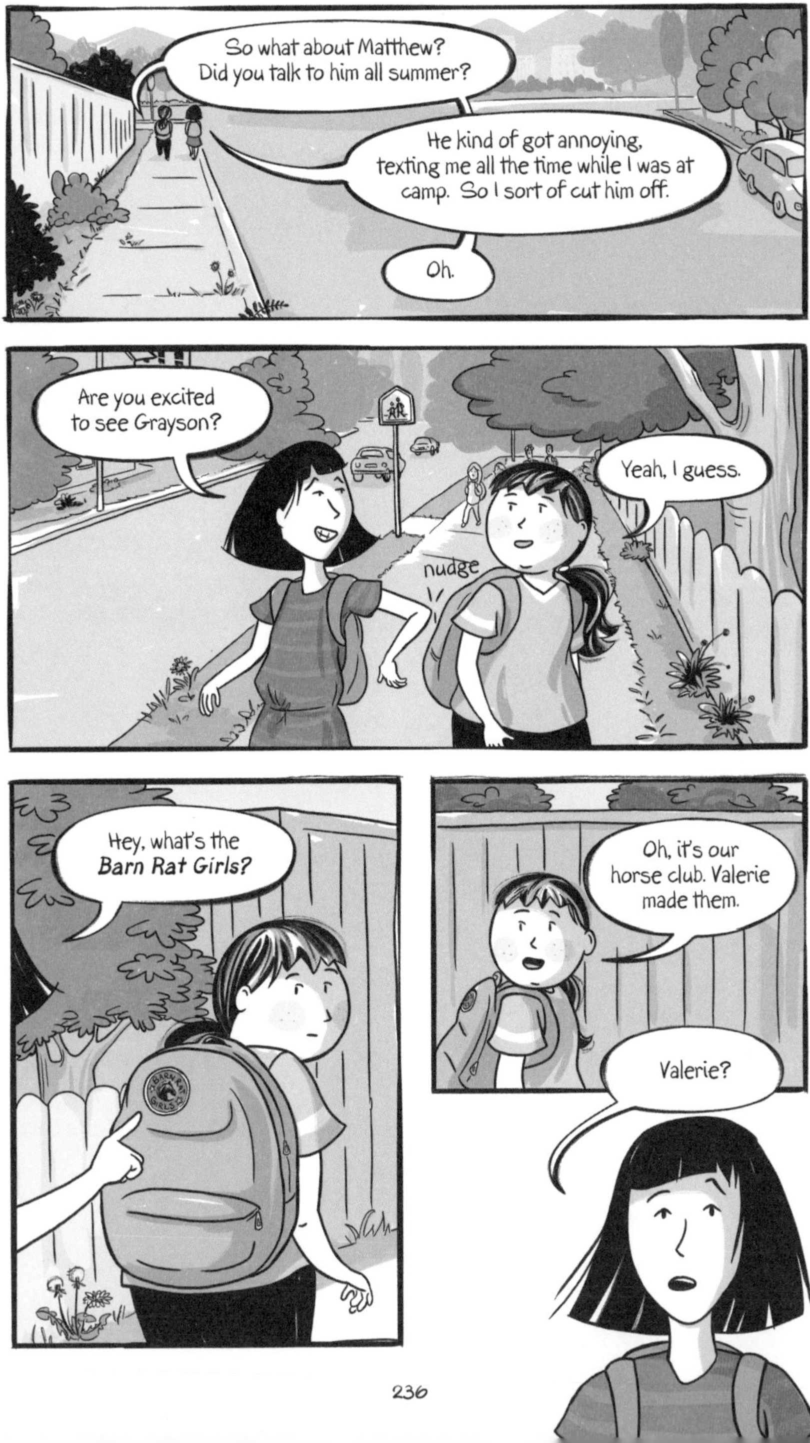
So what about Matthew? Did you talk to him all summer?
He kind of got annoying, texting me all the time while I was at camp. So I sort of cut him off.
Oh.
Are you excited to see Grayson?
Yeah, I guess.
nudge
Hey, what's the *Barn Rat Girls?*
BARN RAT GIRLS
Oh, it's our horse club. Valerie made them.
Valerie?

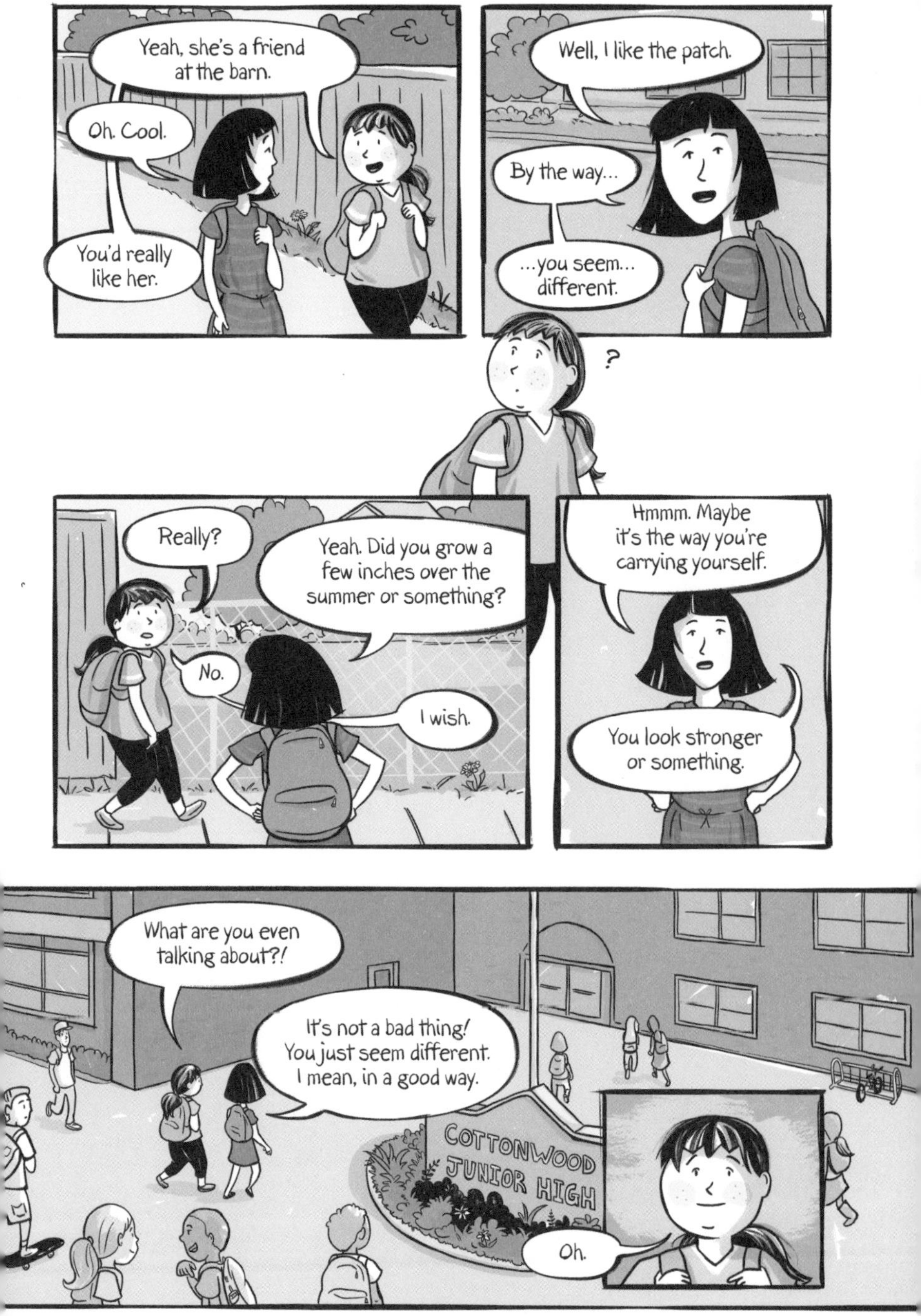
Yeah, she's a friend at the barn.
Oh. Cool.
You'd really like her.
Well, I like the patch.
By the way...
...you seem... different.
?
Really?
Yeah. Did you grow a few inches over the summer or something?
No.
I wish.
Hmmm. Maybe it's the way you're carrying yourself.
You look stronger or something.
What are you even talking about?!
It's not a bad thing! You just seem different. I mean, in a good way.
COTTONWOOD JUNIOR HIGH
Oh.

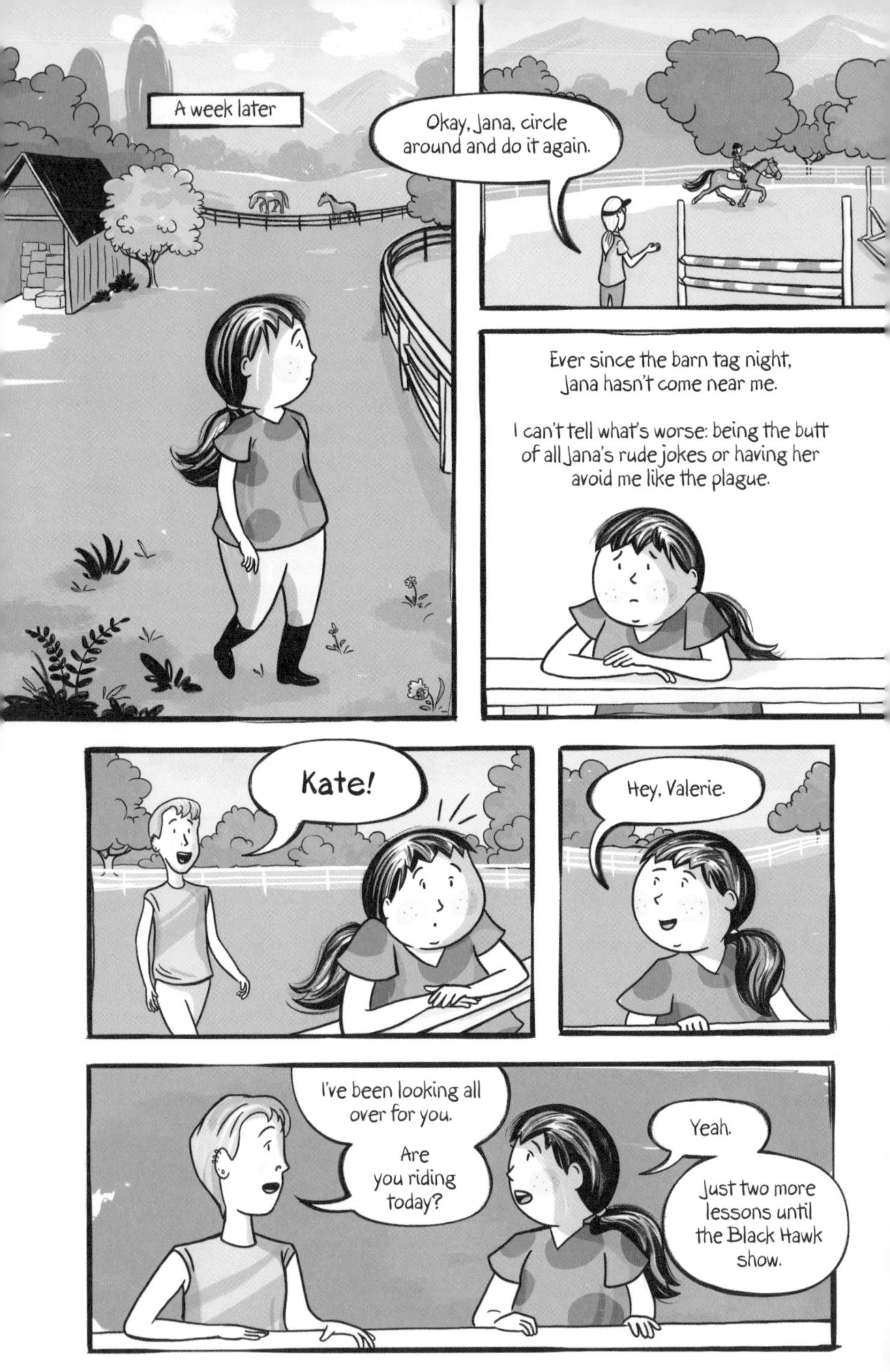
A week later
Okay, Jana, circle around and do it again.
Ever since the barn tag night, Jana hasn't come near me.
I can't tell what's worse: being the butt of all Jana's rude jokes or having her avoid me like the plague.
Kate!
Hey, Valerie.
I've been looking all over for you.
Are you riding today?
Yeah.
Just two more lessons until the Black Hawk show.

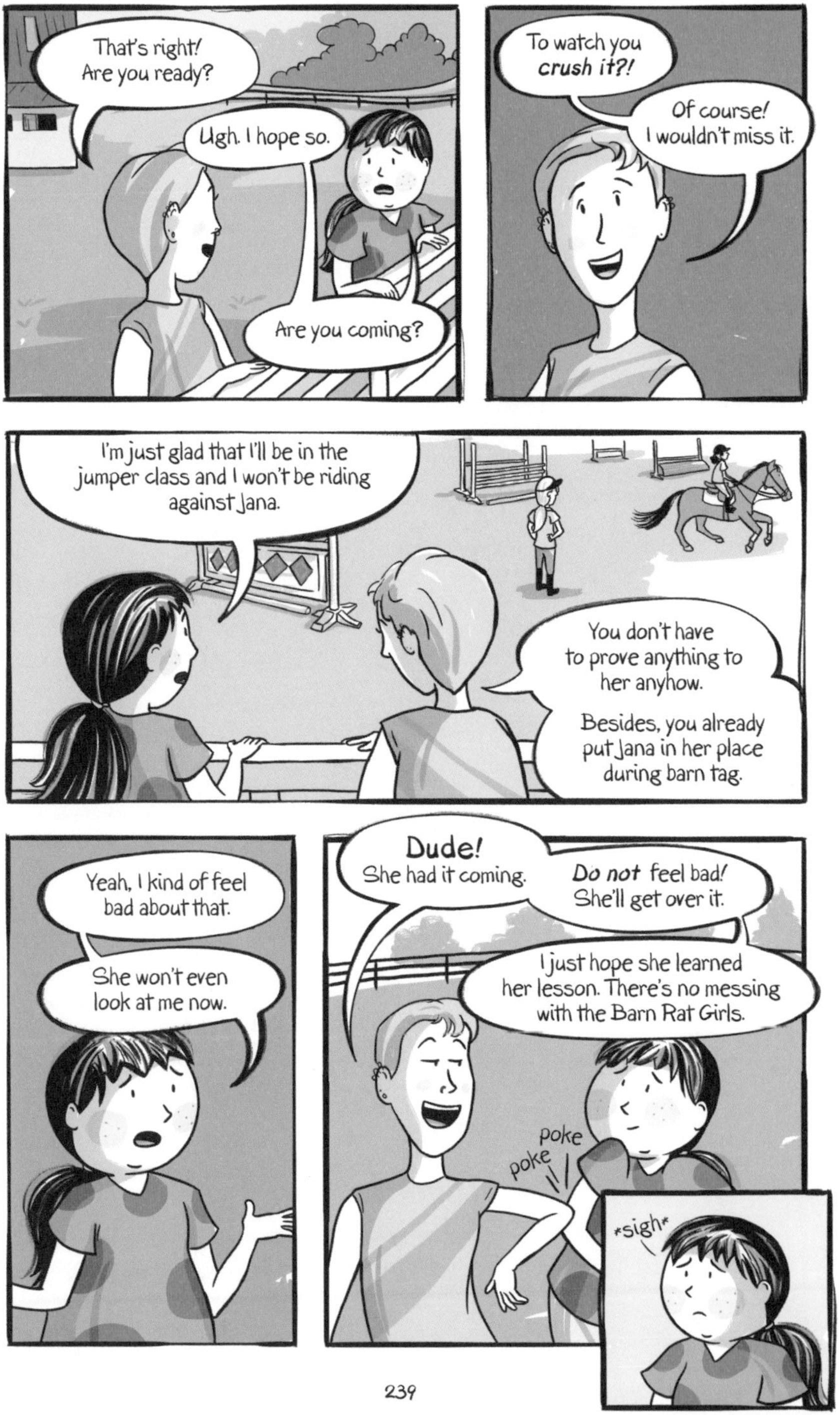
That's right! Are you ready?
Ugh. I hope so.
Are you coming?
To watch you **crush it?!**
Of course! I wouldn't miss it.
I'm just glad that I'll be in the jumper class and I won't be riding against Jana.
You don't have to prove anything to her anyhow.
Besides, you already put Jana in her place during barn tag.
Yeah, I kind of feel bad about that.
She won't even look at me now.
Dude! She had it coming.
Do not feel bad! She'll get over it.
I just hope she learned her lesson. There's no messing with the Barn Rat Girls.
poke poke
sigh

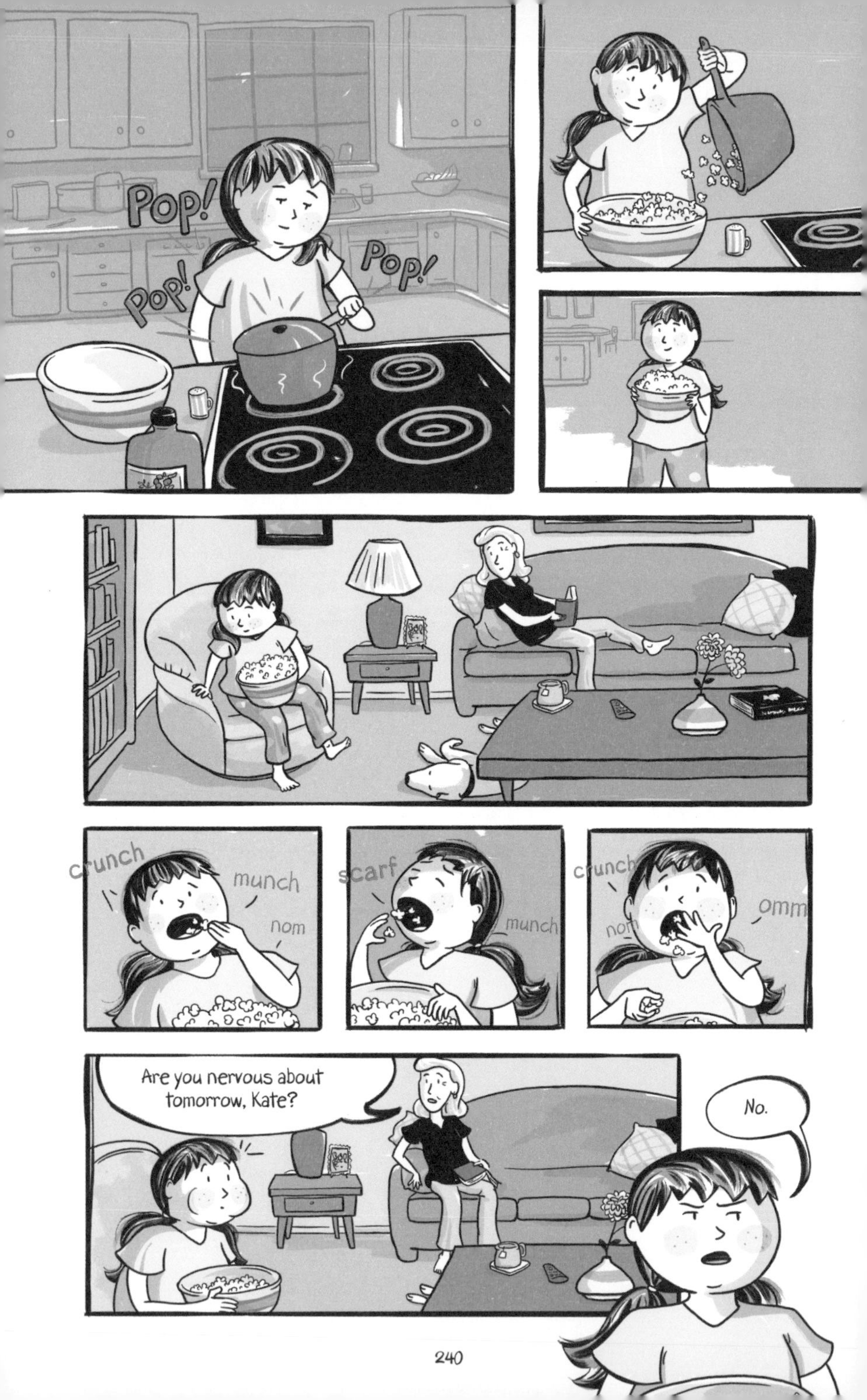

Pop!
Pop!
Pop!
crunch
munch
nom
scarf
munch
crunch
nom
omm
Are you nervous about tomorrow, Kate?
No.

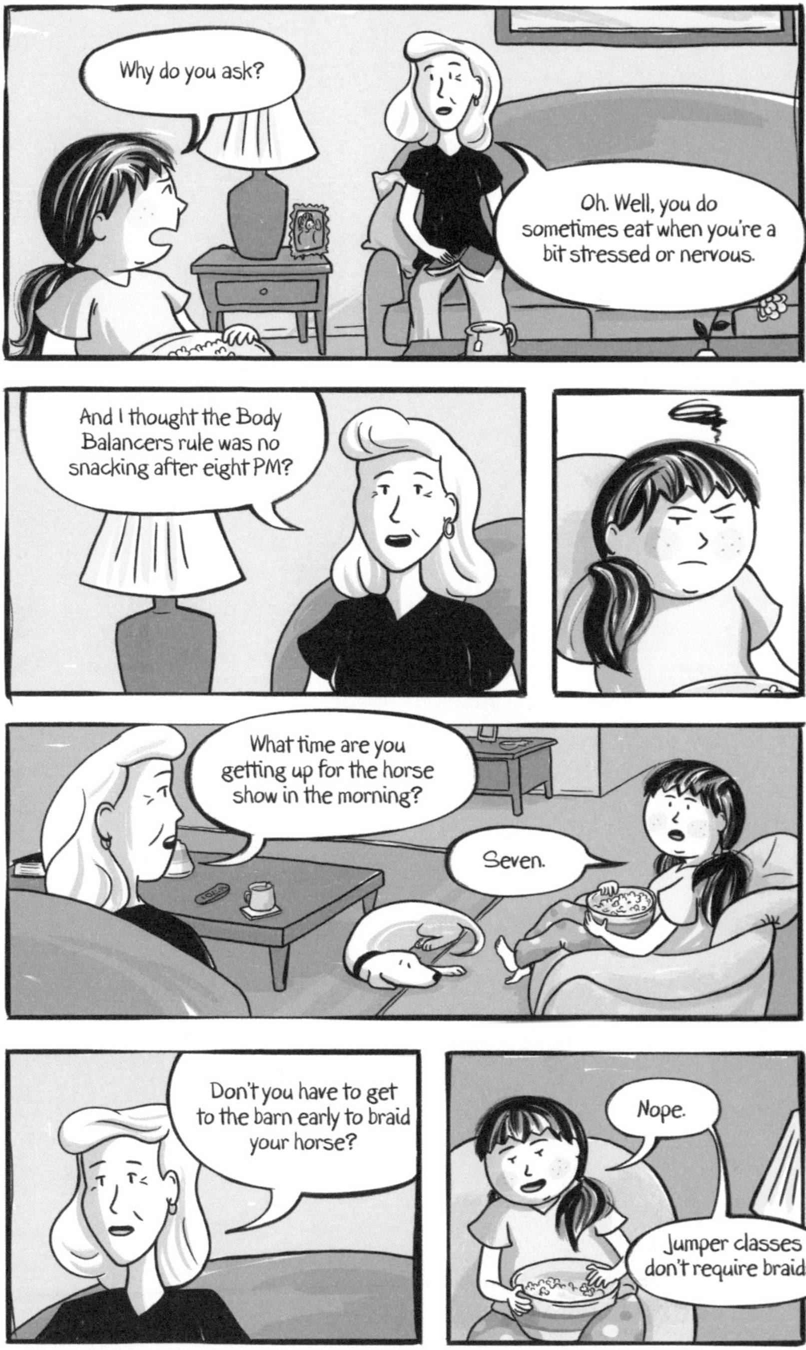
Why do you ask?
Oh. Well, you do sometimes eat when you're a bit stressed or nervous.
And I thought the Body Balancers rule was no snacking after eight PM?
What time are you getting up for the horse show in the morning?
Seven.
Don't you have to get to the barn early to braid your horse?
Nope.
Jumper classes don't require braids.

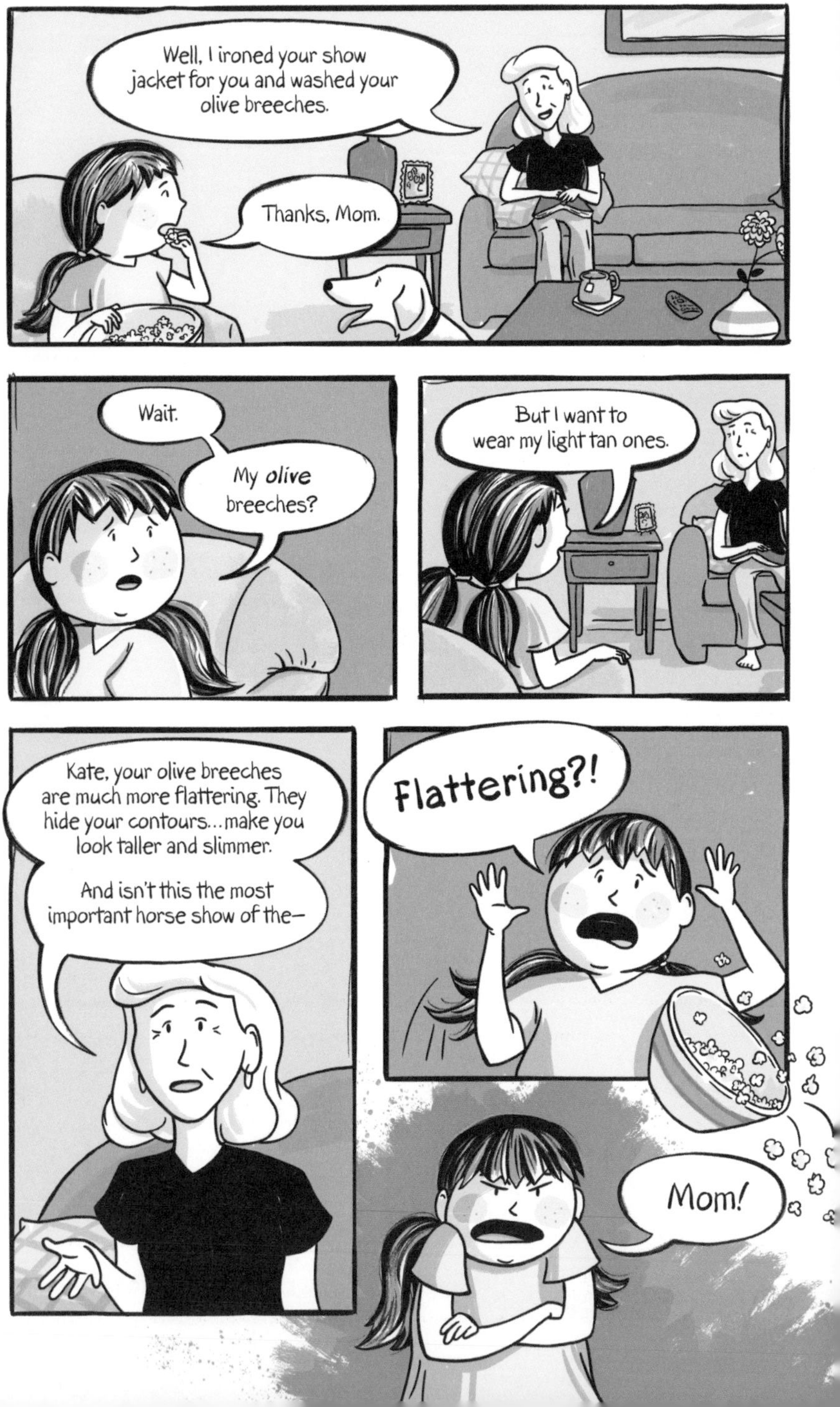
Well, I ironed your show jacket for you and washed your olive breeches.
Thanks, Mom.
Wait.
My *olive* breeches?
But I want to wear my light tan ones.
Kate, your olive breeches are much more flattering. They hide your contours...make you look taller and slimmer.
And isn't this the most important horse show of the–
Flattering?!
Mom!

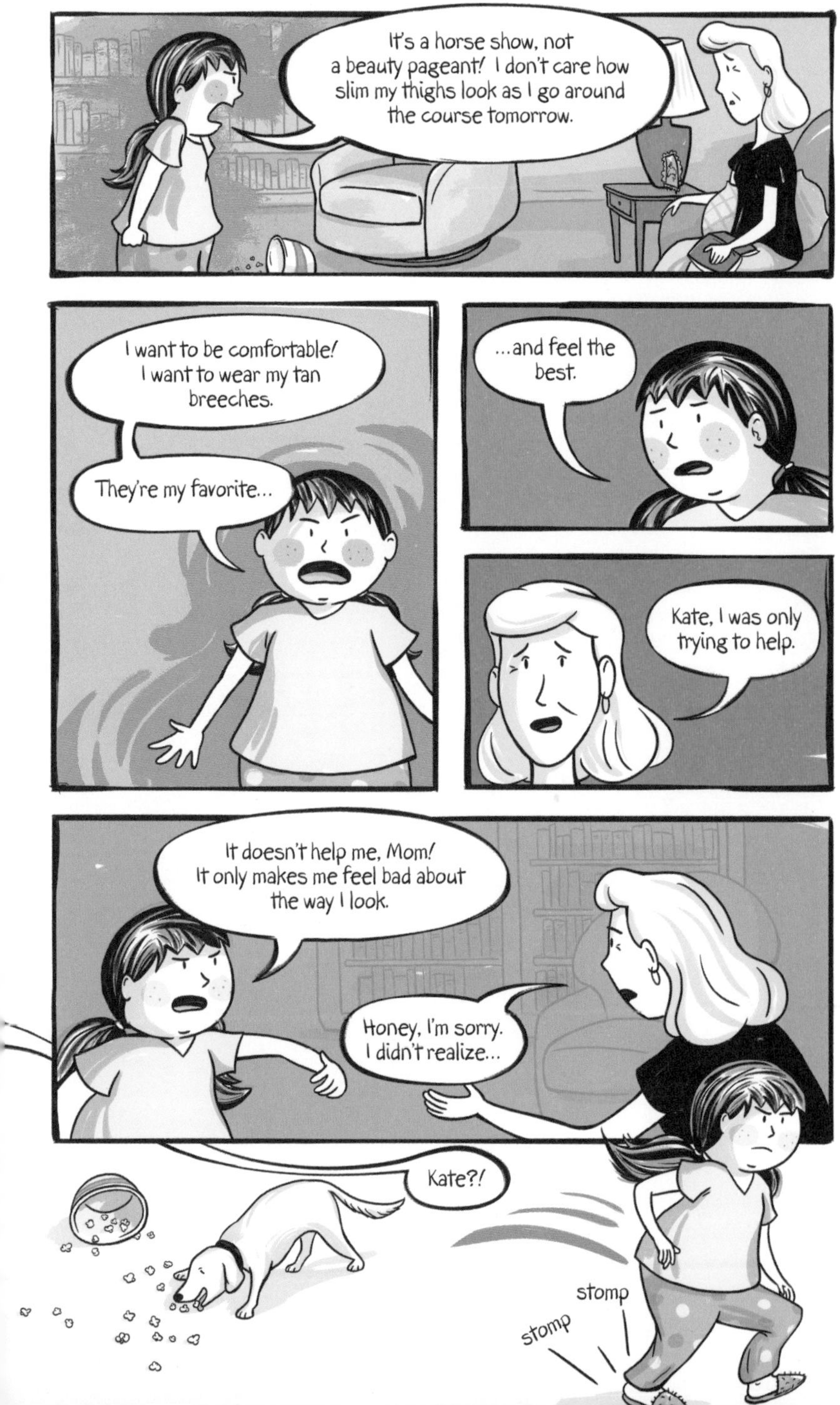
It's a horse show, not a beauty pageant! I don't care how slim my thighs look as I go around the course tomorrow.
I want to be comfortable! I want to wear my tan breeches.
They're my favorite...
...and feel the best.
Kate, I was only trying to help.
It doesn't help me, Mom! It only makes me feel bad about the way I look.
Honey, I'm sorry. I didn't realize...
Kate?!
stomp
stomp

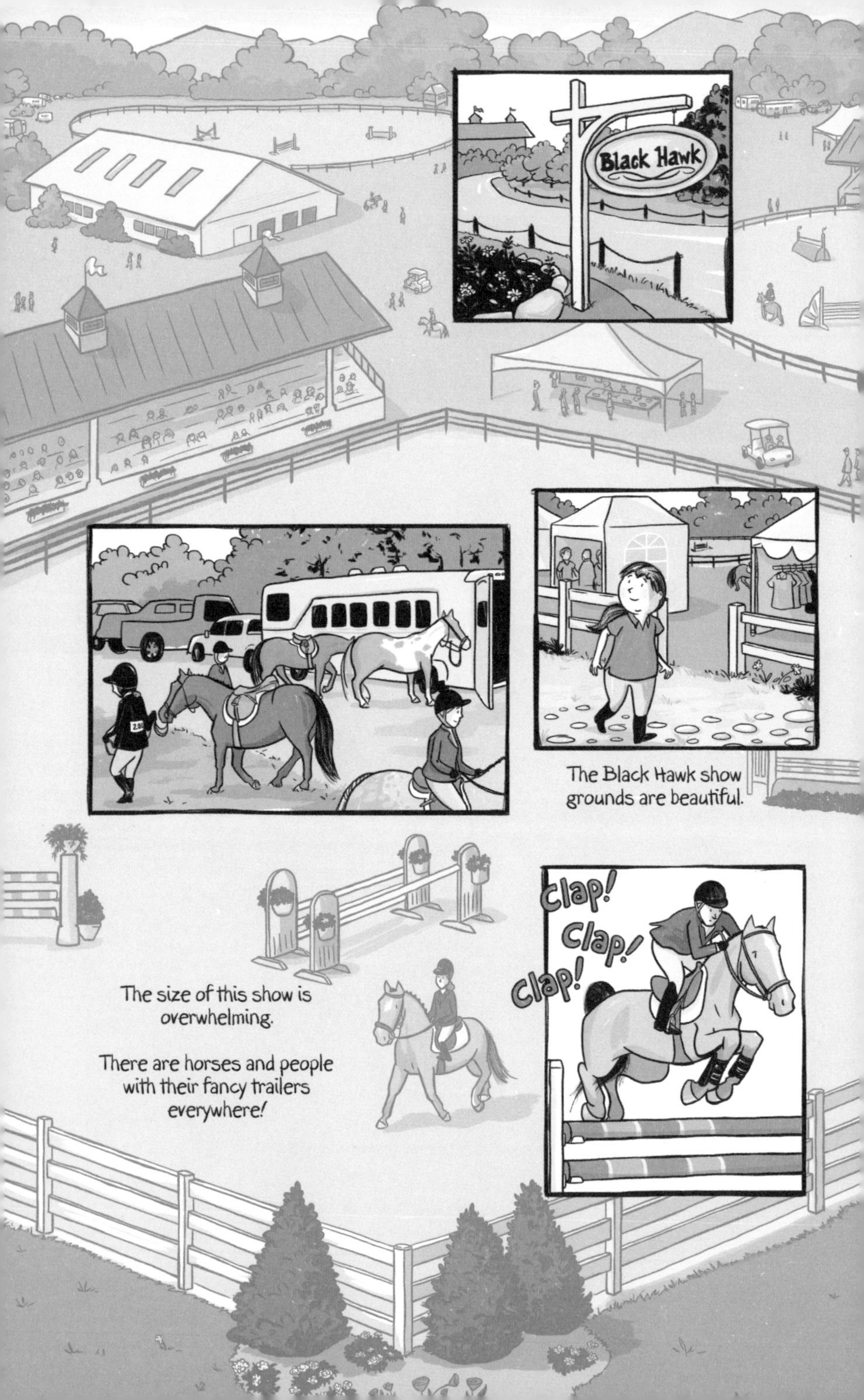
Black Hawk
The Black Hawk show grounds are beautiful.
The size of this show is overwhelming.
There are horses and people with their fancy trailers everywhere!
Clap!
Clap!
Clap!

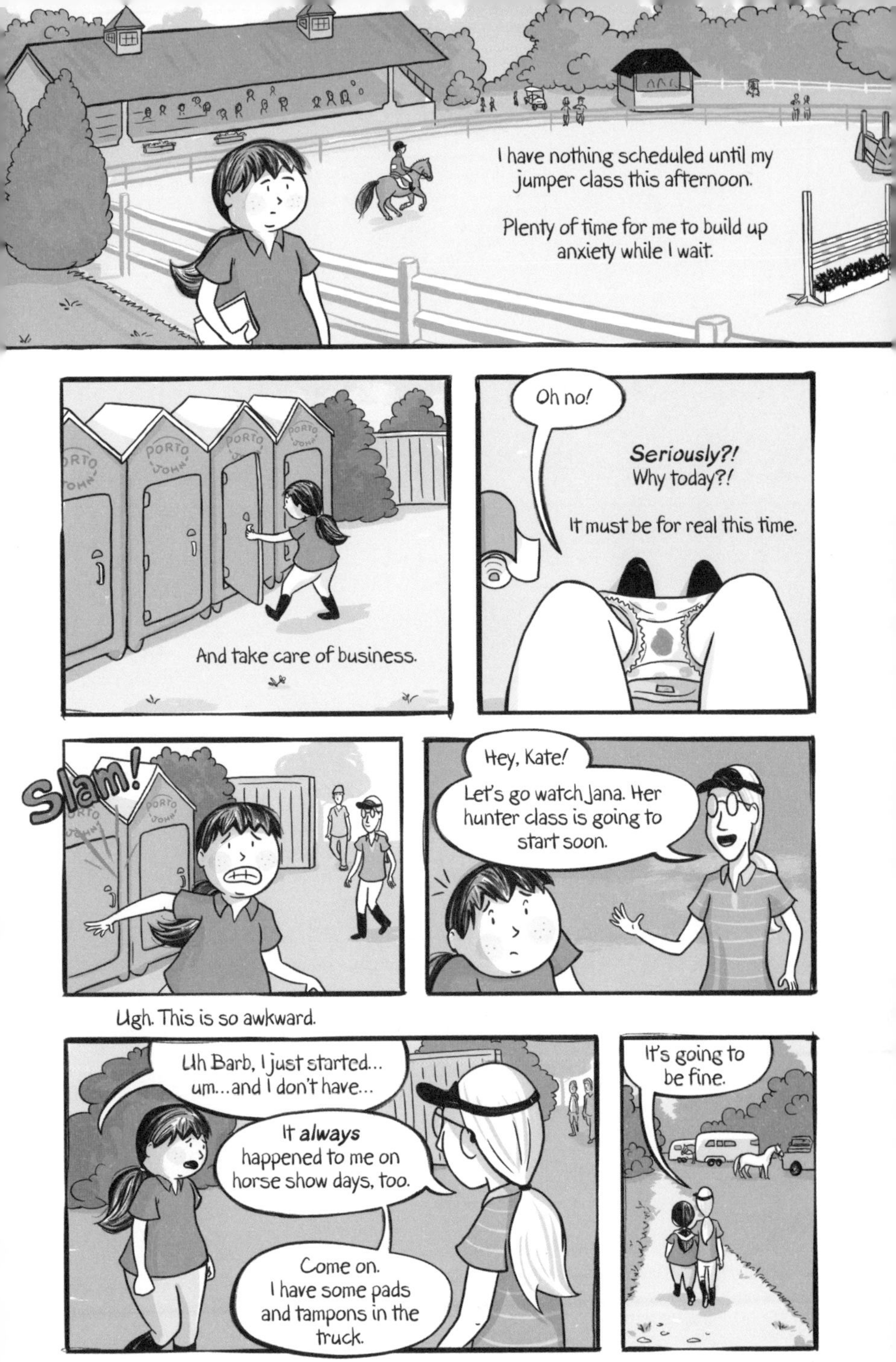
I have nothing scheduled until my jumper class this afternoon.
Plenty of time for me to build up anxiety while I wait.
PORTO JOHN
And take care of business.
Oh no!
Seriously?!
Why today?!
It must be for real this time.
Slam!
Hey, Kate!
Let's go watch Jana. Her hunter class is going to start soon.
Ugh. This is so awkward.
Uh Barb, I just started... um... and I don't have...
It always happened to me on horse show days, too.
Come on.
I have some pads and tampons in the truck.
It's going to be fine.

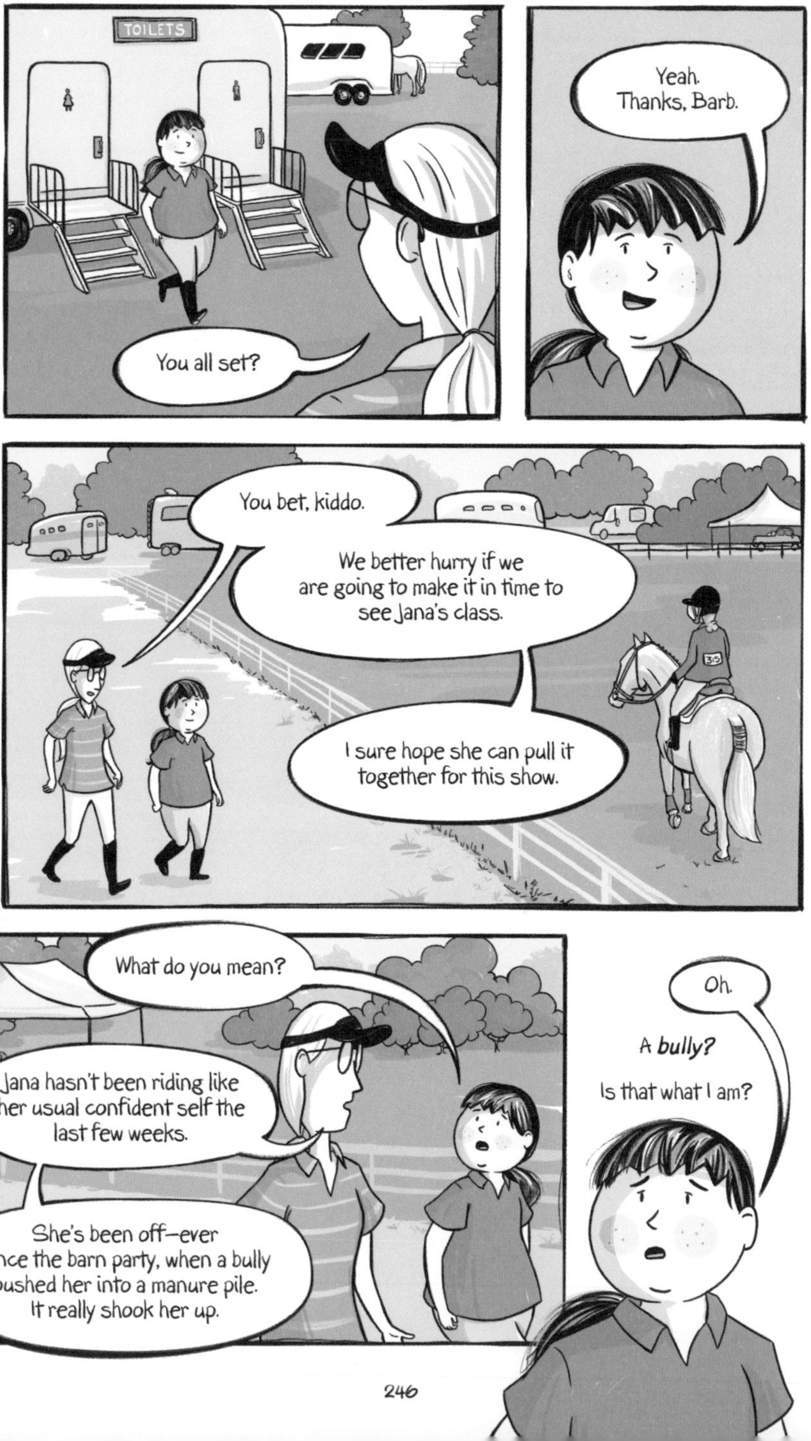
TOILETS
You all set?
Yeah. Thanks, Barb.
You bet, kiddo.
We better hurry if we are going to make it in time to see Jana's class.
I sure hope she can pull it together for this show.
315
What do you mean?
Jana hasn't been riding like her usual confident self the last few weeks.
She's been off—ever since the barn party, when a bully pushed her into a manure pile. It really shook her up.
Oh.
A *bully?*
Is that what I am?

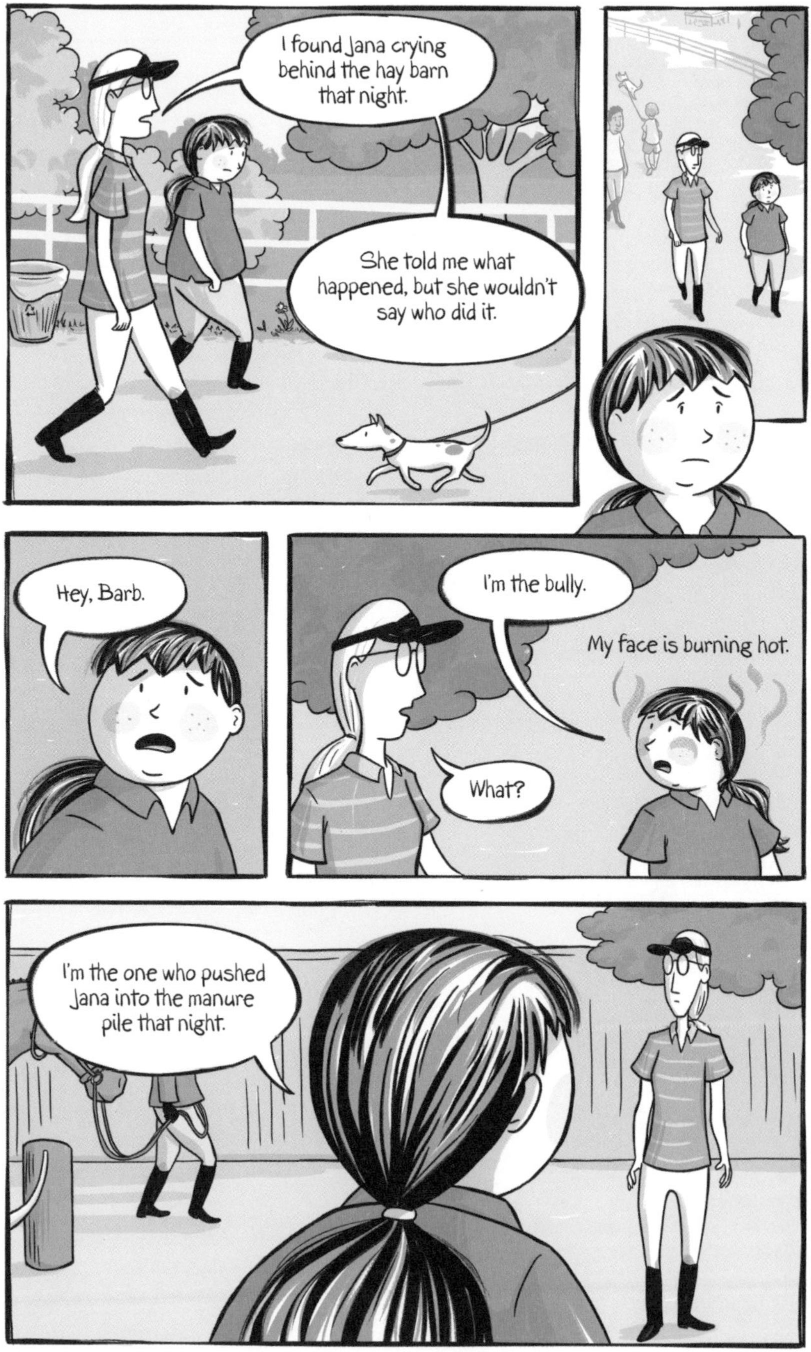
I found Jana crying behind the hay barn that night.
She told me what happened, but she wouldn't say who did it.
Hey, Barb.
I'm the bully.
My face is burning hot.
What?
I'm the one who pushed Jana into the manure pile that night.

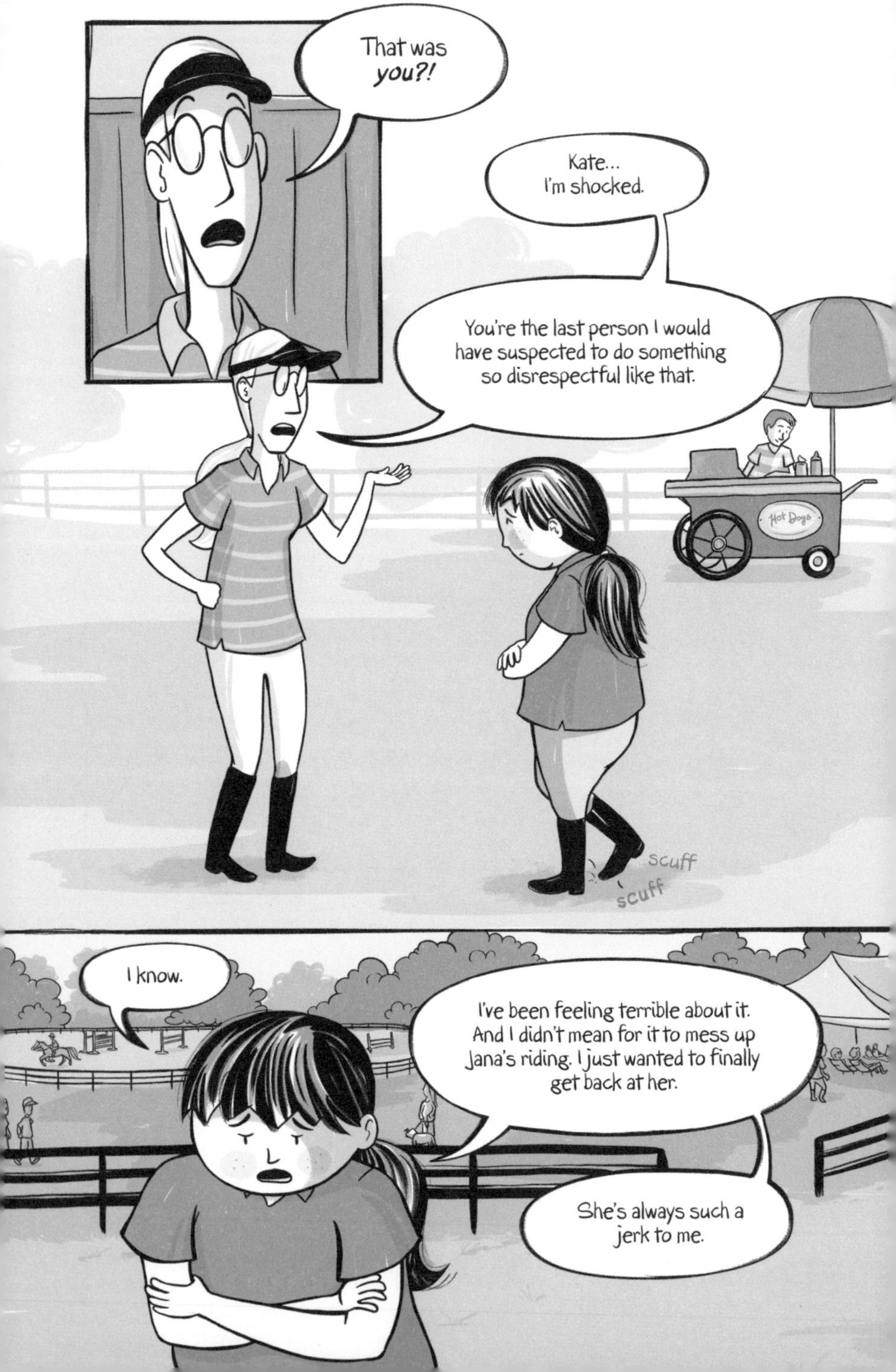
That was *you?!*
Kate... I'm shocked.
You're the last person I would have suspected to do something so disrespectful like that.
Hot Dogs
scuff
scuff
I know.
I've been feeling terrible about it. And I didn't mean for it to mess up Jana's riding. I just wanted to finally get back at her.
She's always such a jerk to me.

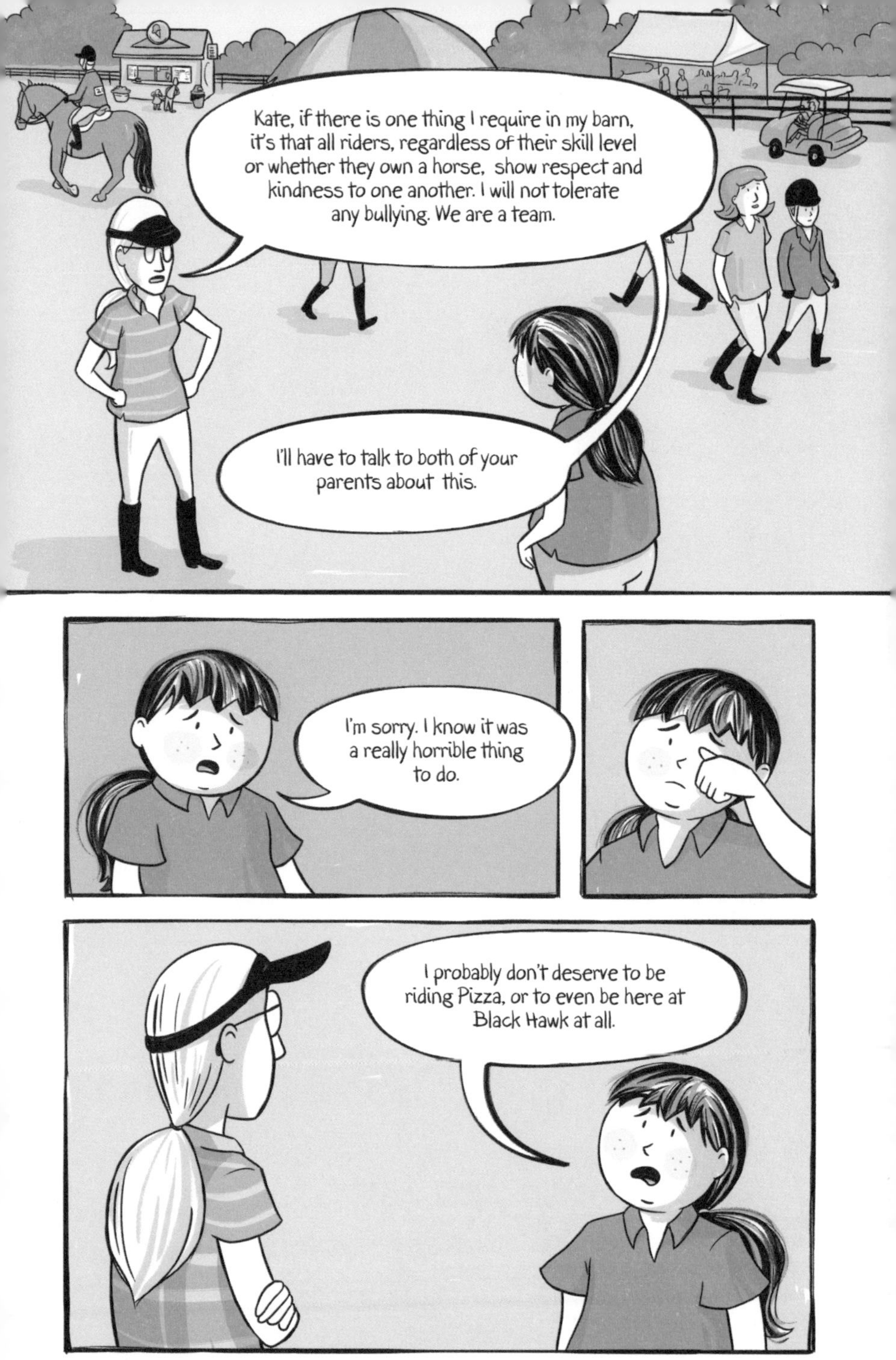
Kate, if there is one thing I require in my barn, it's that all riders, regardless of their skill level or whether they own a horse, show respect and kindness to one another. I will not tolerate any bullying. We are a team.
I'll have to talk to both of your parents about this.
I'm sorry. I know it was a really horrible thing to do.
I probably don't deserve to be riding Pizza, or to even be here at Black Hawk at all.

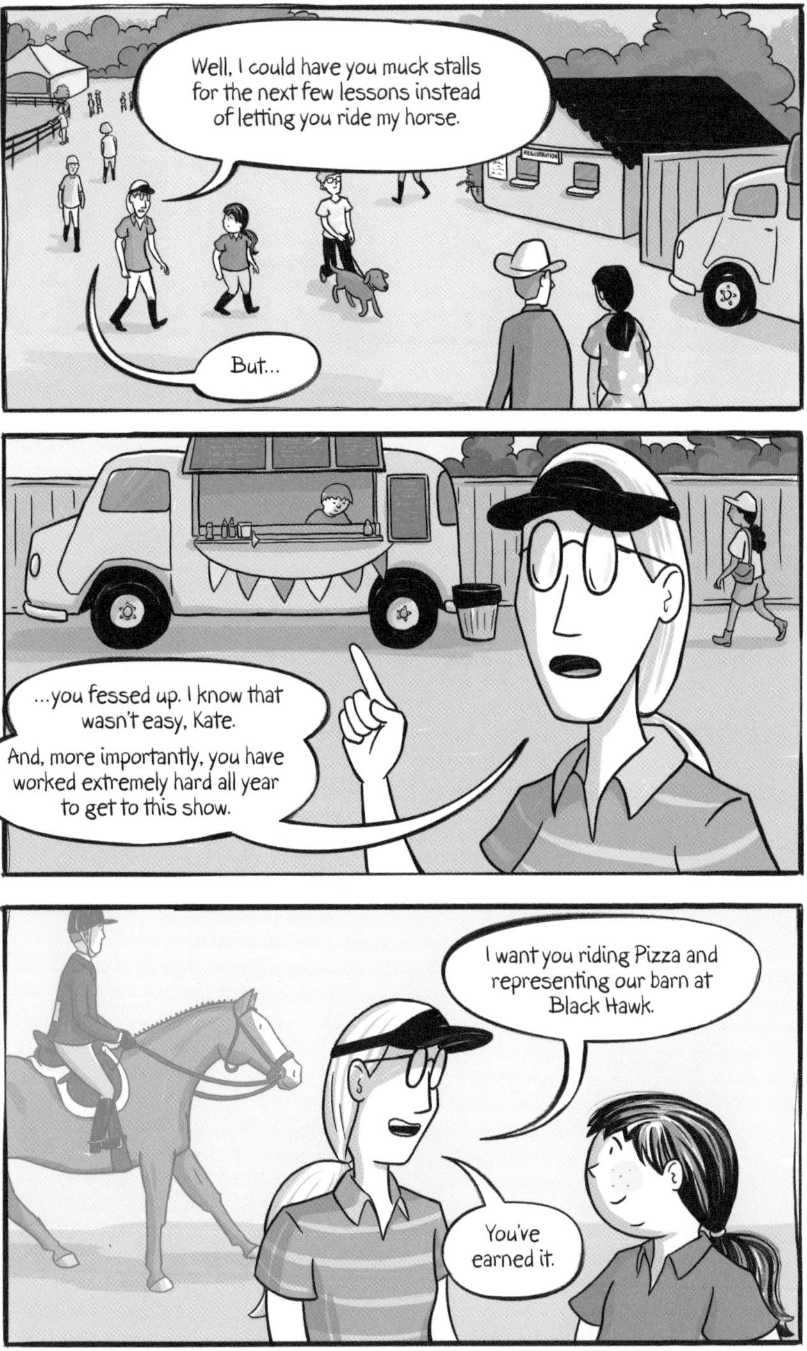
Well, I could have you muck stalls for the next few lessons instead of letting you ride my horse.
But...
REGISTRATION
...you fessed up. I know that wasn't easy, Kate.
And, more importantly, you have worked extremely hard all year to get to this show.
I want you riding Pizza and representing our barn at Black Hawk.
You've earned it.

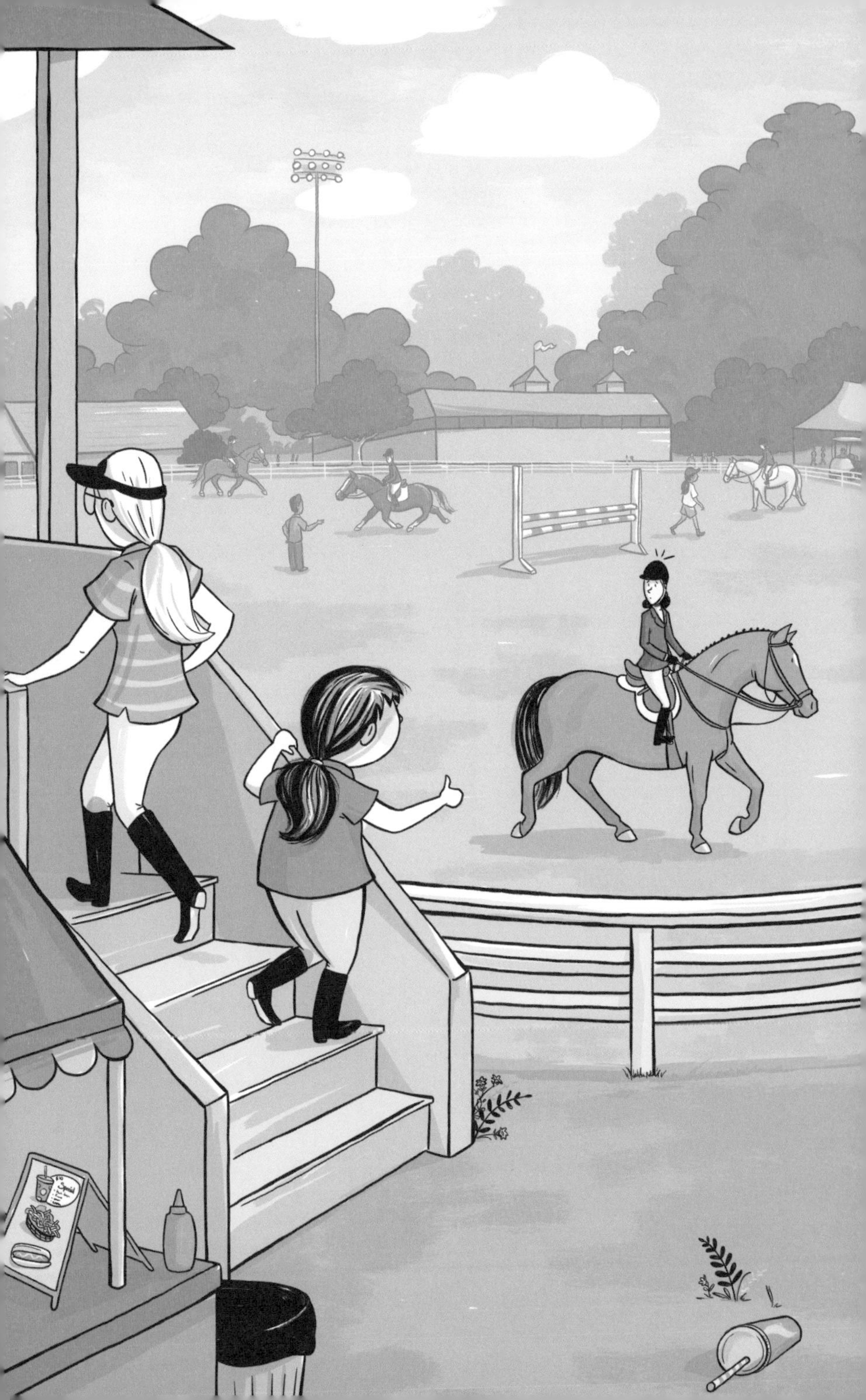

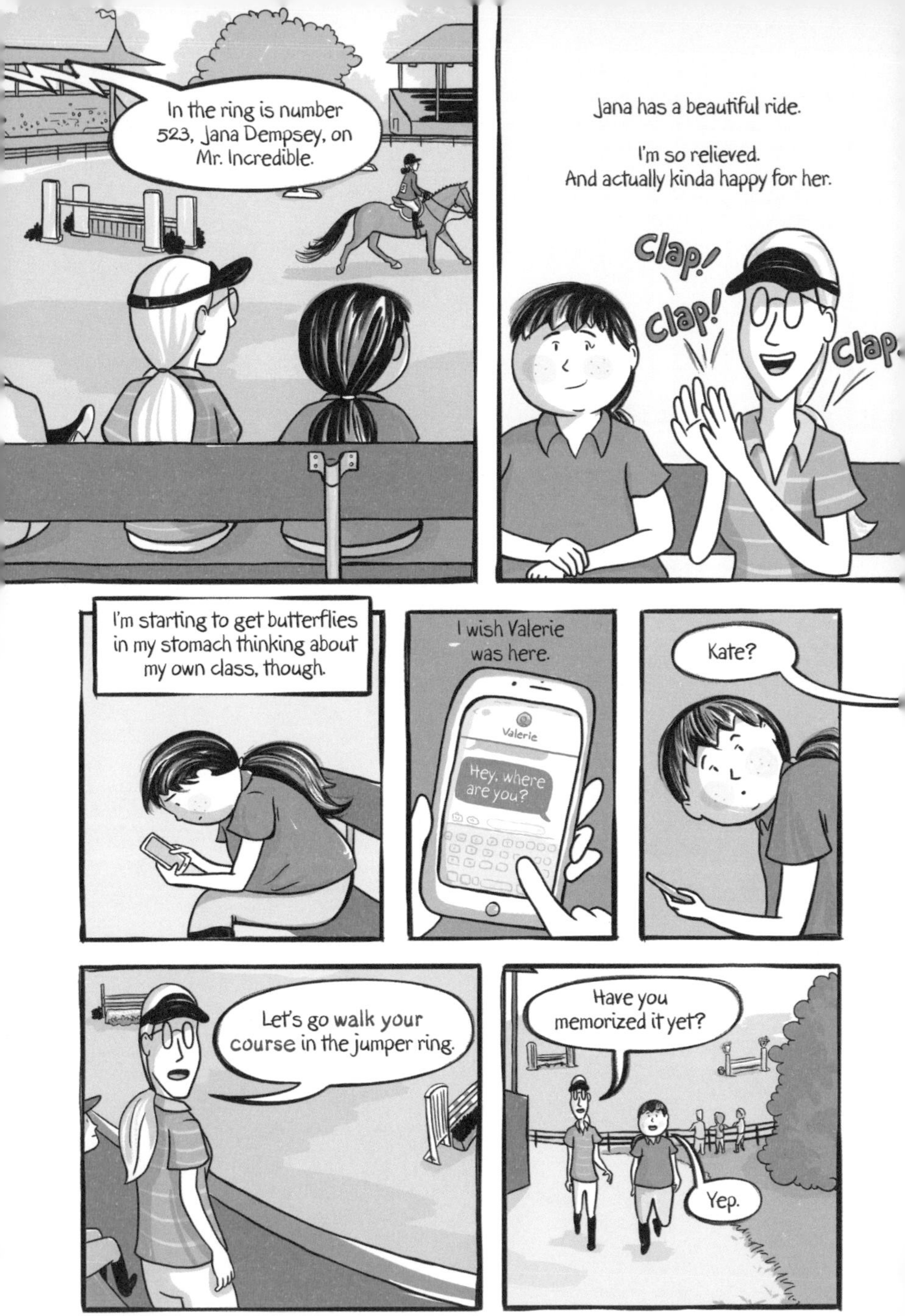
In the ring is number 523, Jana Dempsey, on Mr. Incredible.
Jana has a beautiful ride.
I'm so relieved.
And actually kinda happy for her.
Clap!
Clap!
Clap.
I'm starting to get butterflies in my stomach thinking about my own class, though.
I wish Valerie was here.
Valerie
Hey, where are you?
Kate?
Let's go walk your course in the jumper ring.
Have you memorized it yet?
Yep.

Walking a course: Following the course on foot in order to plan how you will ride during the competition (usually by counting the strides between jumps).

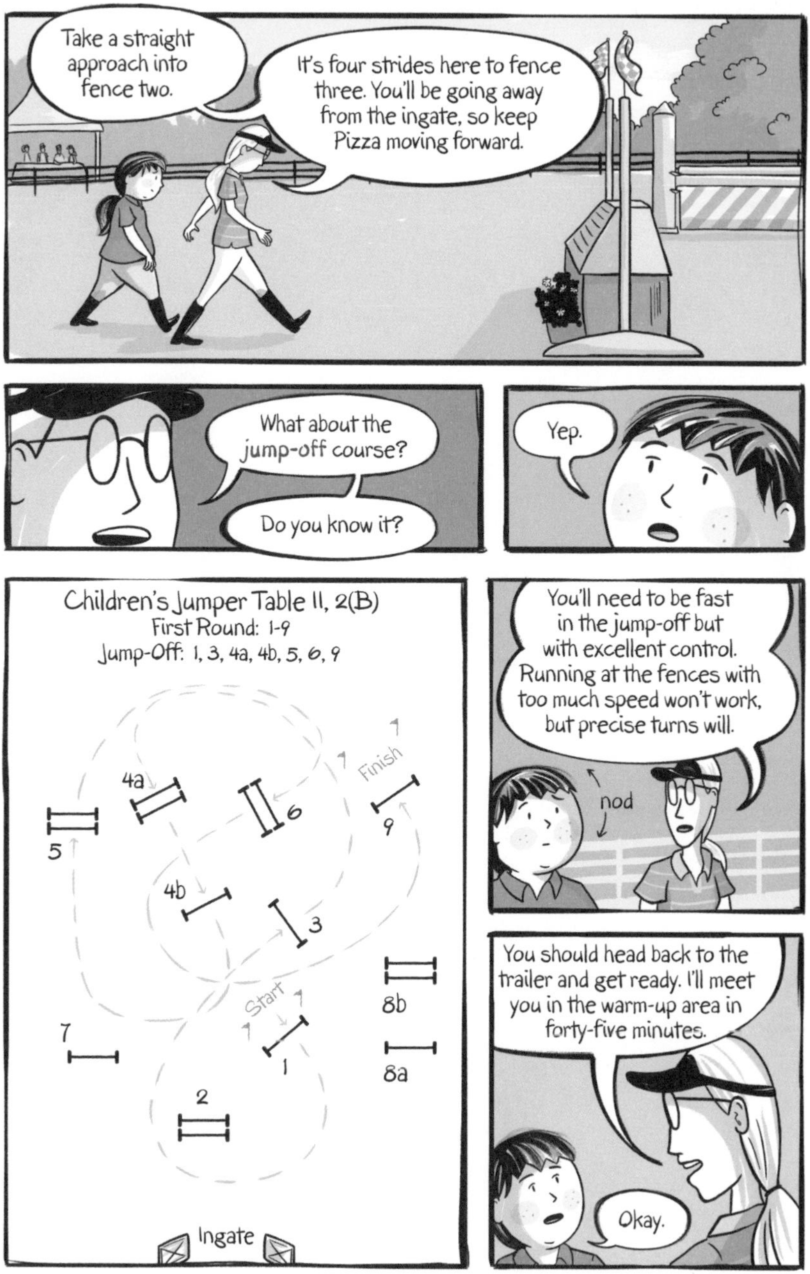
Take a straight approach into fence two.
It's four strides here to fence three. You'll be going away from the ingate, so keep Pizza moving forward.
What about the jump-off course?
Do you know it?
Yep.
Children's Jumper Table II, 2(B)
First Round: 1-9
Jump-Off: 1, 3, 4a, 4b, 5, 6, 9
4a
6
Finish
9
5
4b
3
8b
Start
7
1
8a
2
Ingate
You'll need to be fast in the jump-off but with excellent control. Running at the fences with too much speed won't work, but precise turns will.
nod
You should head back to the trailer and get ready. I'll meet you in the warm-up area in forty-five minutes.
Okay.

Jump-off: The second round of a jumper class, in which all riders without faults (no rails knocked down or time penalties), advance to ride another shortened version of the course to determine final placement. The rider with the fastest time wins the class.

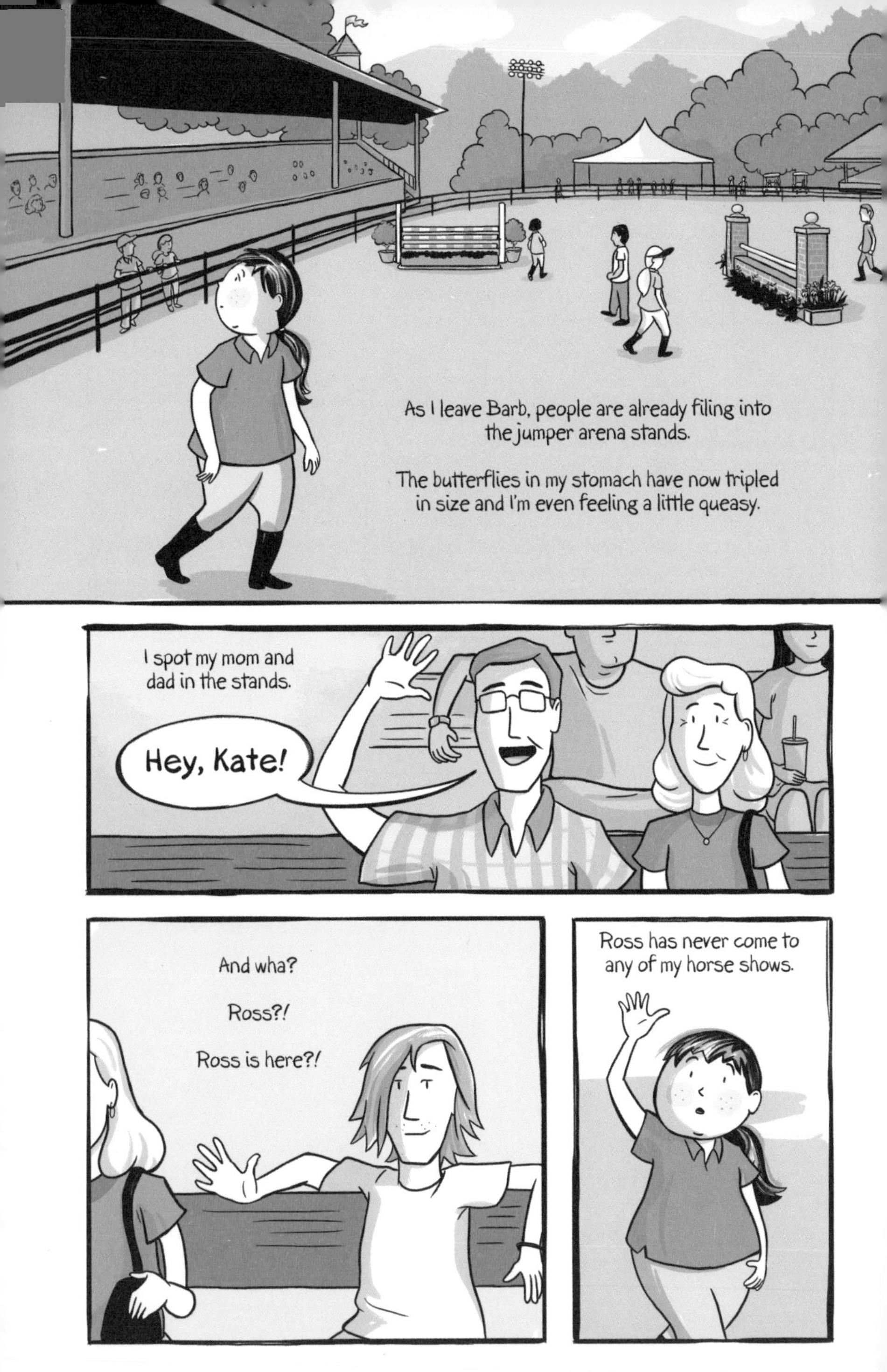
As I leave Barb, people are already filing into the jumper arena stands.
The butterflies in my stomach have now tripled in size and I'm even feeling a little queasy.
I spot my mom and dad in the stands.
Hey, Kate!
And wha?
Ross?!
Ross is here?!
Ross has never come to any of my horse shows.

Thirty minutes later, I've got Pizza ready. I have myself ready. I do a time check and see a text from Valerie.

Valerie
are you?

strep throat. 😞

Hey girl, I am soooo sorry I can't make it. I'm home sick with strep throat. 😞

Good luck! I know you and Pizza are going to crush it! 👊 👊 👊

I want to hear all about it. Call me later!!! 💙

The butterflies are gone from my stomach, but it feels like they left a heavy stone behind.

Humming might help?

Hmmm maaa hoo

After my warm-up, I watch some of the other riders go in my class.

I'm last. The wait is agonizing.

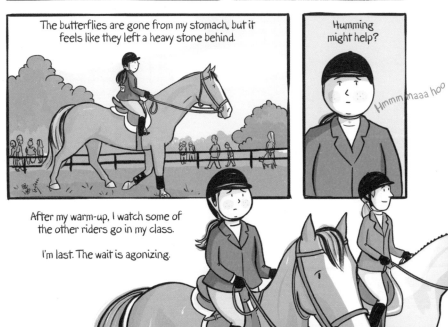

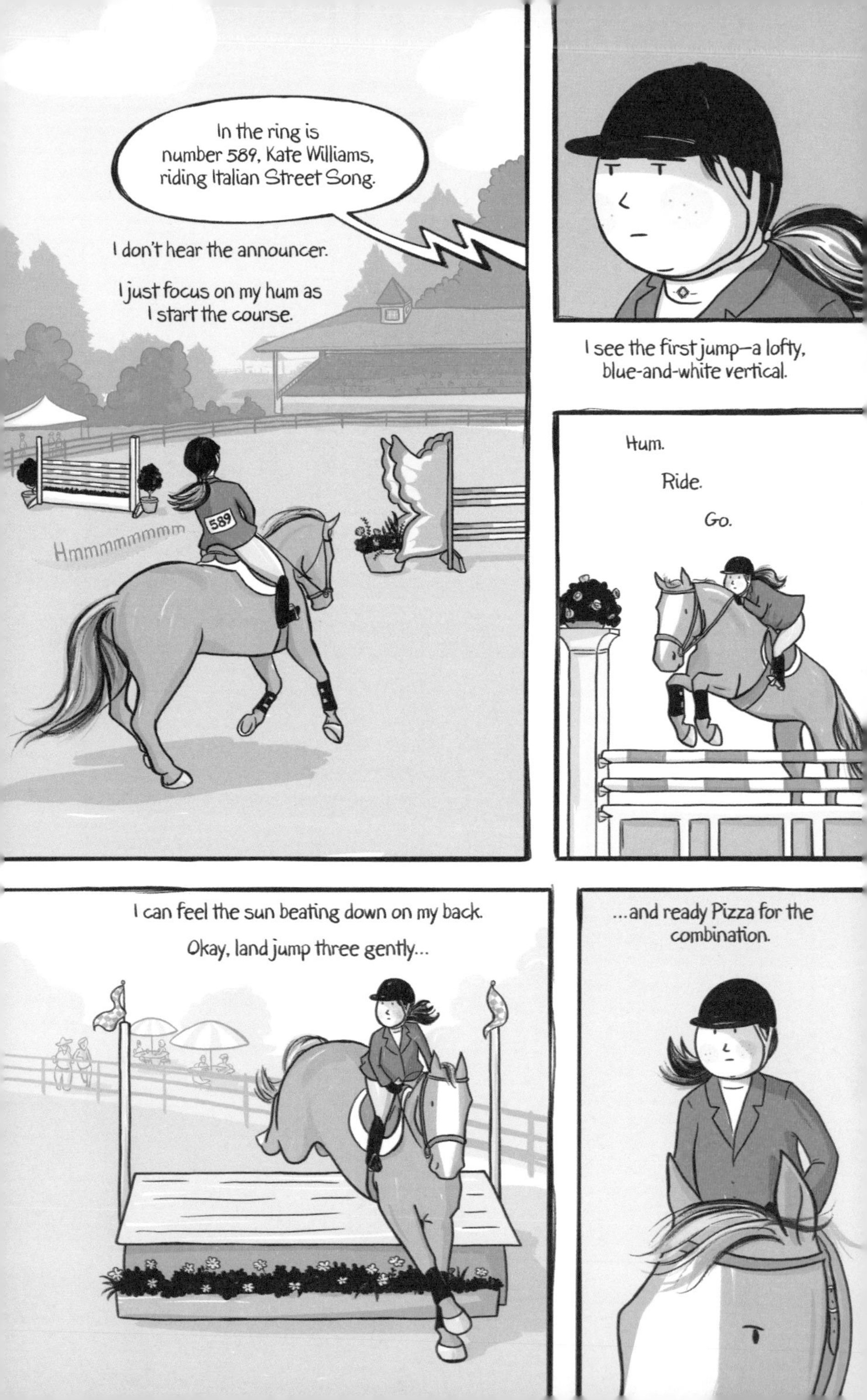
In the ring is number 589, Kate Williams, riding Italian Street Song.
I don't hear the announcer.
I just focus on my hum as I start the course.
589
Hmmmmmmmm
I see the first jump—a lofty, blue-and-white vertical.
Hum.
Ride.
Go.
I can feel the sun beating down on my back.
Okay, land jump three gently...
...and ready Pizza for the combination.

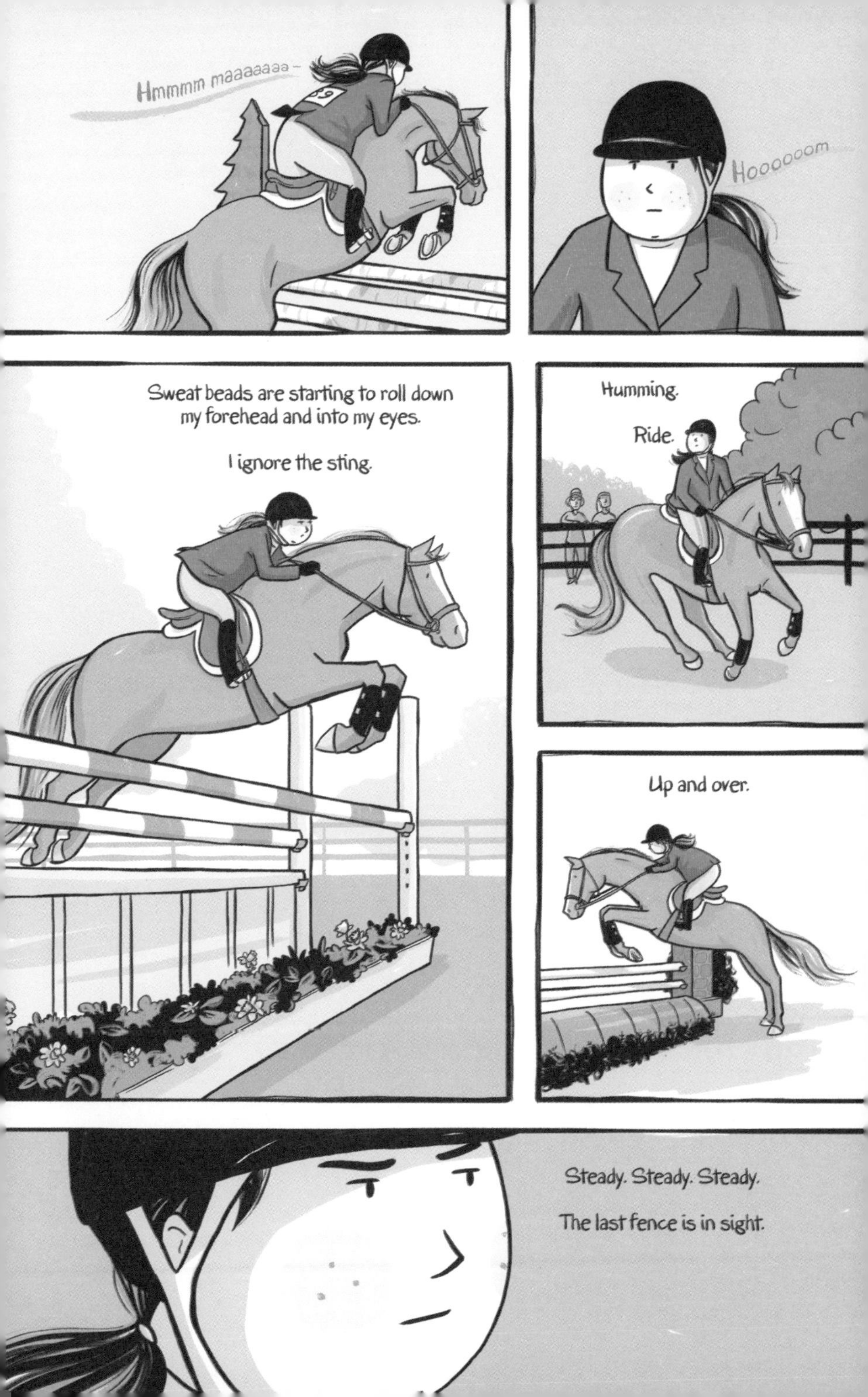
Hmmmm maaaaaaa~
Hoooooom
Sweat beads are starting to roll down my forehead and into my eyes.
I ignore the sting.
Humming.
Ride.
Up and over.
Steady. Steady. Steady.
The last fence is in sight.

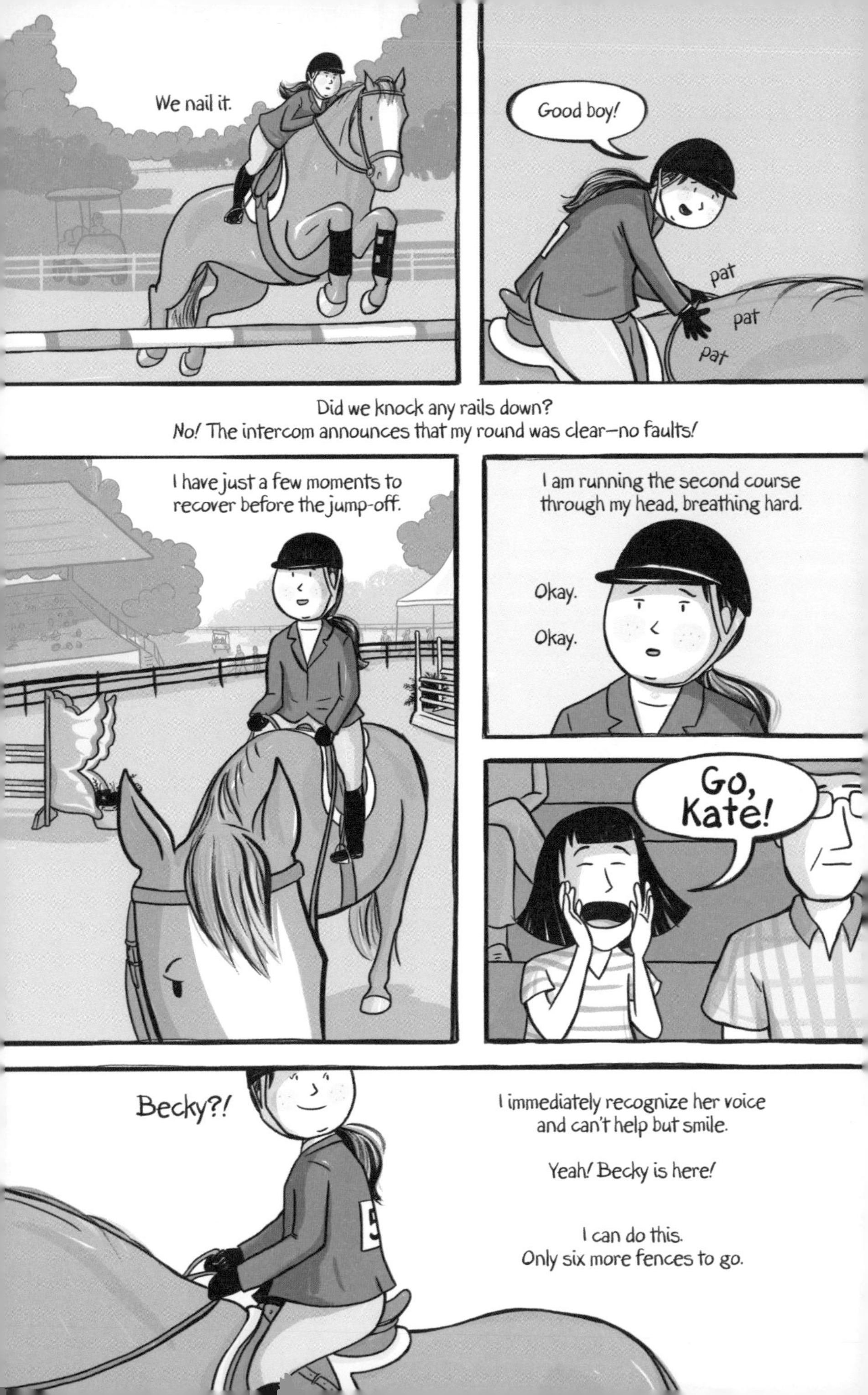
We nail it.
Good boy!
pat
pat
pat
Did we knock any rails down?
No! The intercom announces that my round was clear—no faults!
I have just a few moments to recover before the jump-off.
I am running the second course through my head, breathing hard.
Okay.
Okay.
Go, Kate!
Becky?!
I immediately recognize her voice and can't help but smile.
Yeah! Becky is here!
I can do this.
Only six more fences to go.

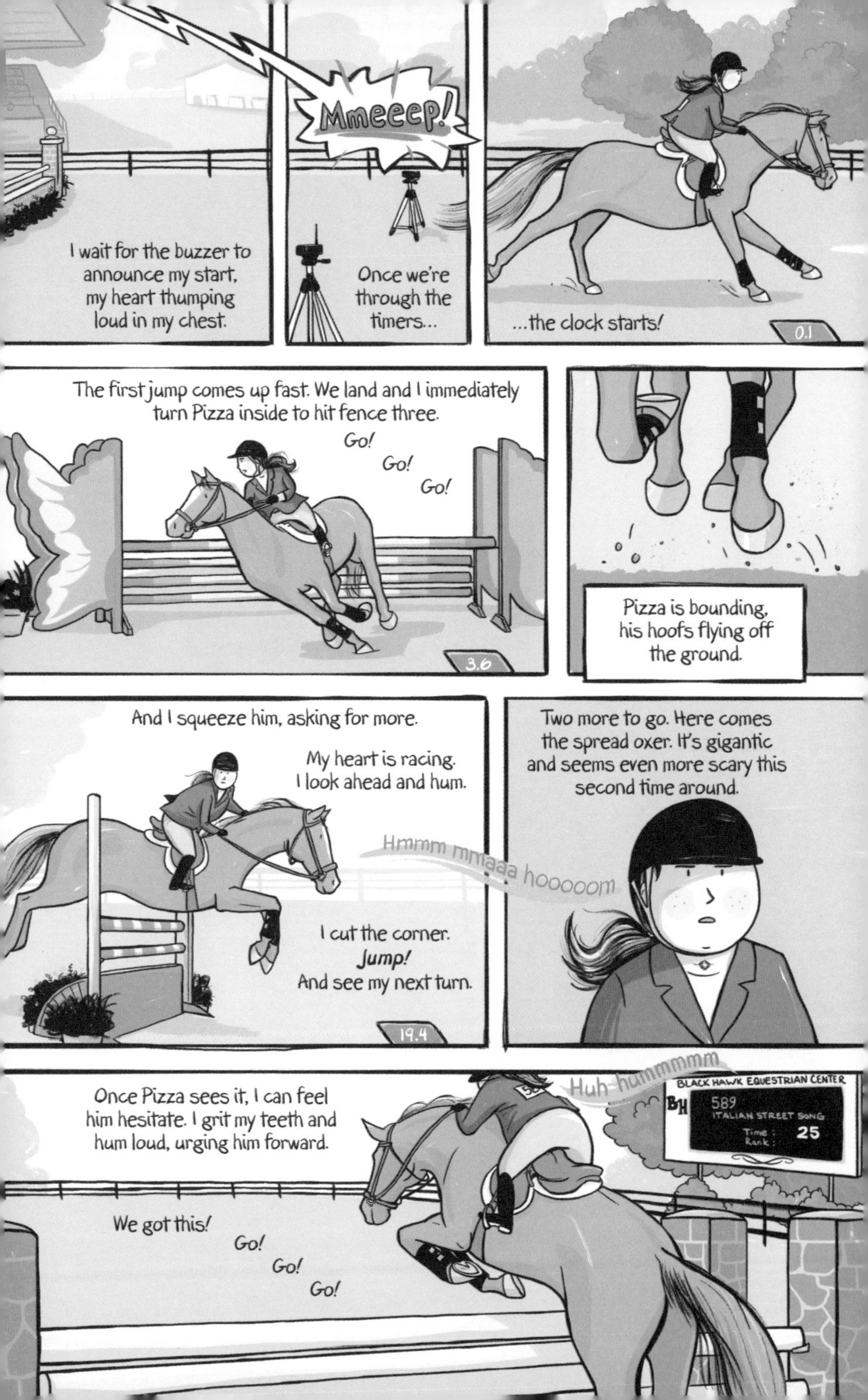
I wait for the buzzer to announce my start, my heart thumping loud in my chest.
Mmeeep!
Once we're through the timers...
...the clock starts!
0.1
The first jump comes up fast. We land and I immediately turn Pizza inside to hit fence three.
Go!
Go!
Go!
3.6
Pizza is bounding, his hoofs flying off the ground.
And I squeeze him, asking for more.
My heart is racing. I look ahead and hum.
Hmmm mmaaa hooooom
I cut the corner.
Jump!
And see my next turn.
19.4
Two more to go. Here comes the spread oxer. It's gigantic and seems even more scary this second time around.
Once Pizza sees it, I can feel him hesitate. I grit my teeth and hum loud, urging him forward.
Huh-hummmmm
BLACK HAWK EQUESTRIAN CENTER
BH
589
ITALIAN STREET SONG
Time:
Rank:
25
We got this!
Go!
Go!
Go!

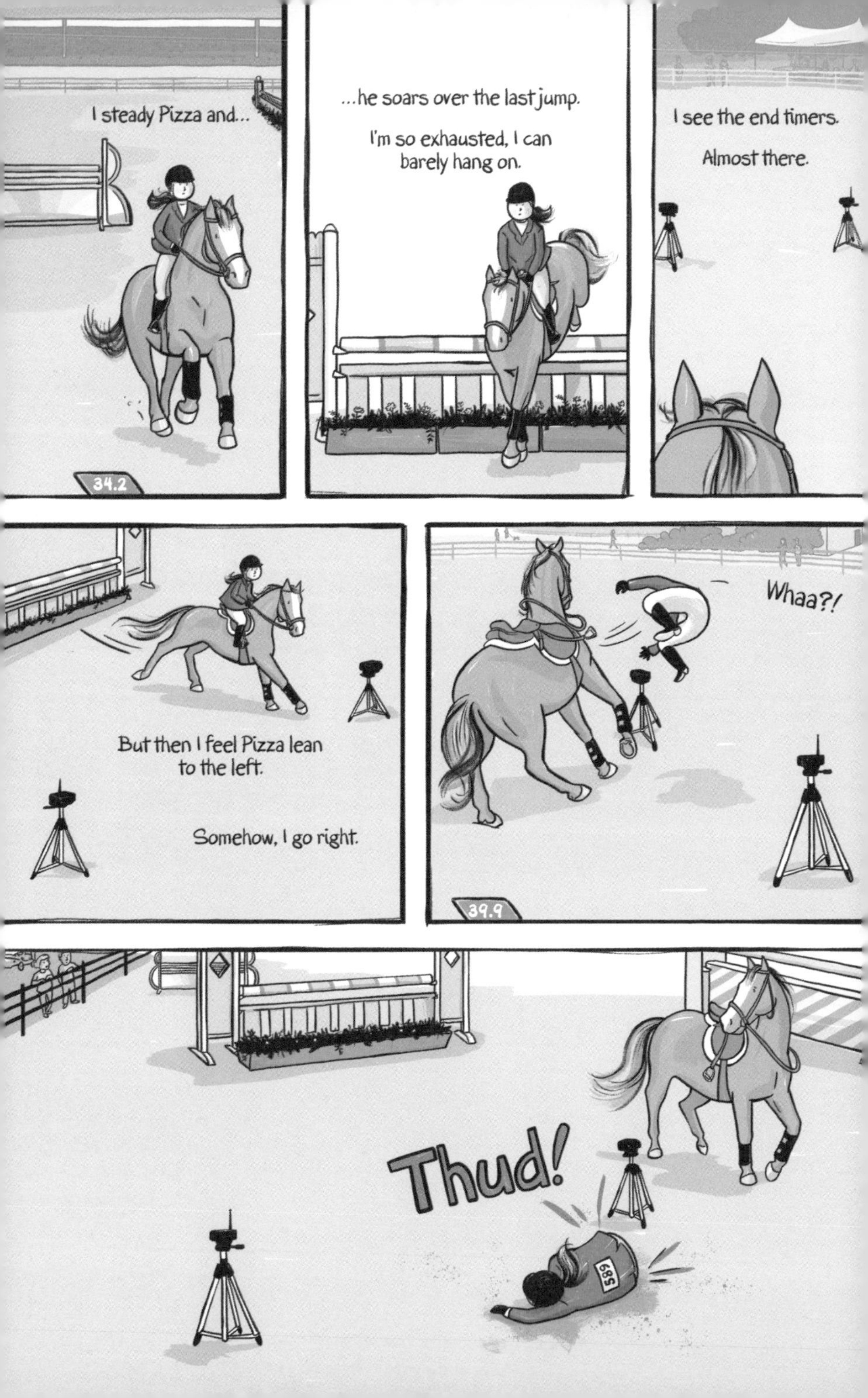
I steady Pizza and...
34.2
...he soars over the last jump.
I'm so exhausted, I can barely hang on.
I see the end timers.
Almost there.
But then I feel Pizza lean to the left.
Somehow, I go right.
Whaa?!
39.9
Thud!

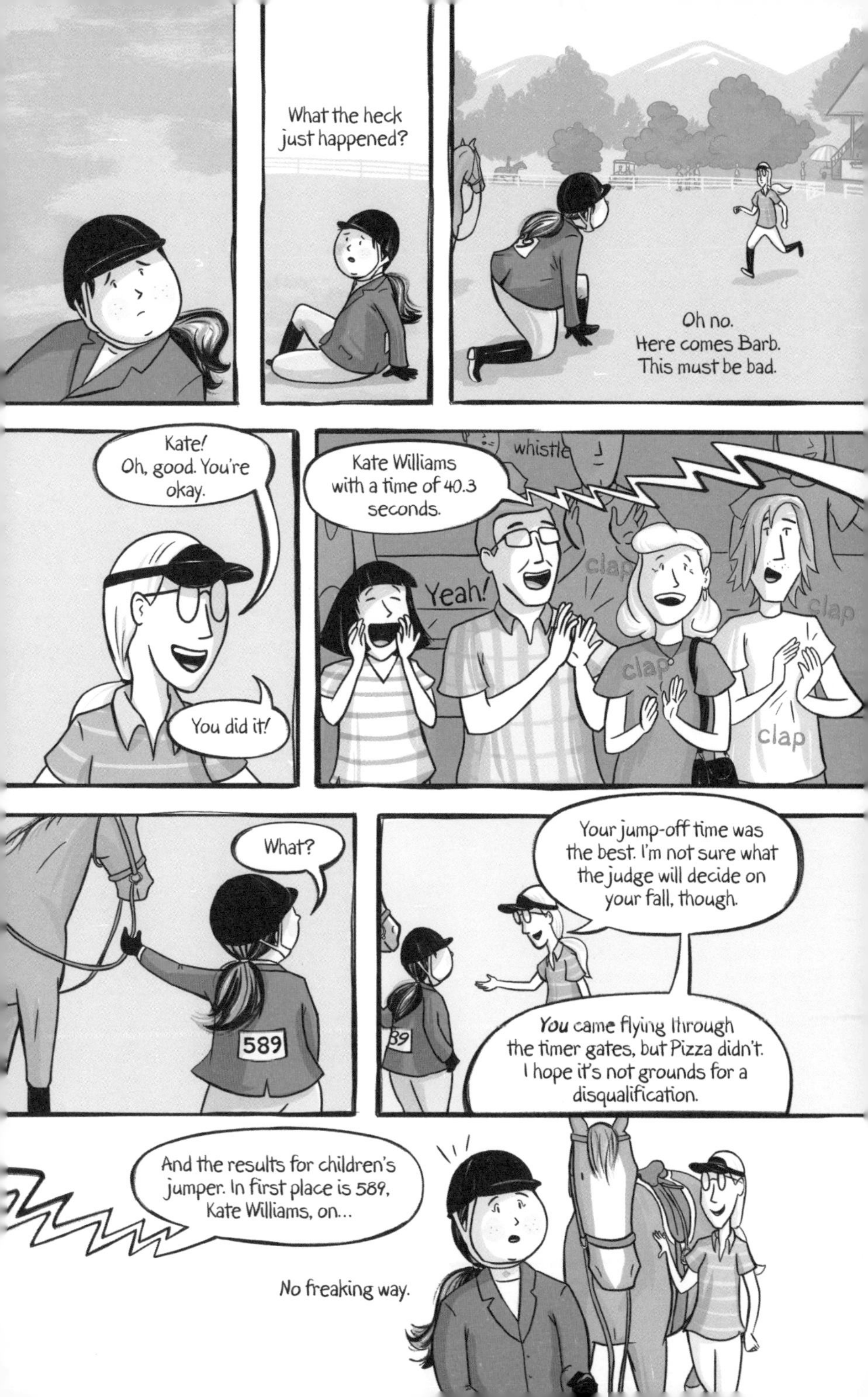
What the heck just happened?
Oh no. Here comes Barb. This must be bad.
Kate! Oh, good. You're okay.
You did it!
Kate Williams with a time of 40.3 seconds.
whistle
Yeah!
clap
clap
clap
clap
What?
Your jump-off time was the best. I'm not sure what the judge will decide on your fall, though.
You came flying through the timer gates, but Pizza didn't. I hope it's not grounds for a disqualification.
589
And the results for children's jumper. In first place is 589, Kate Williams, on…
No freaking way.

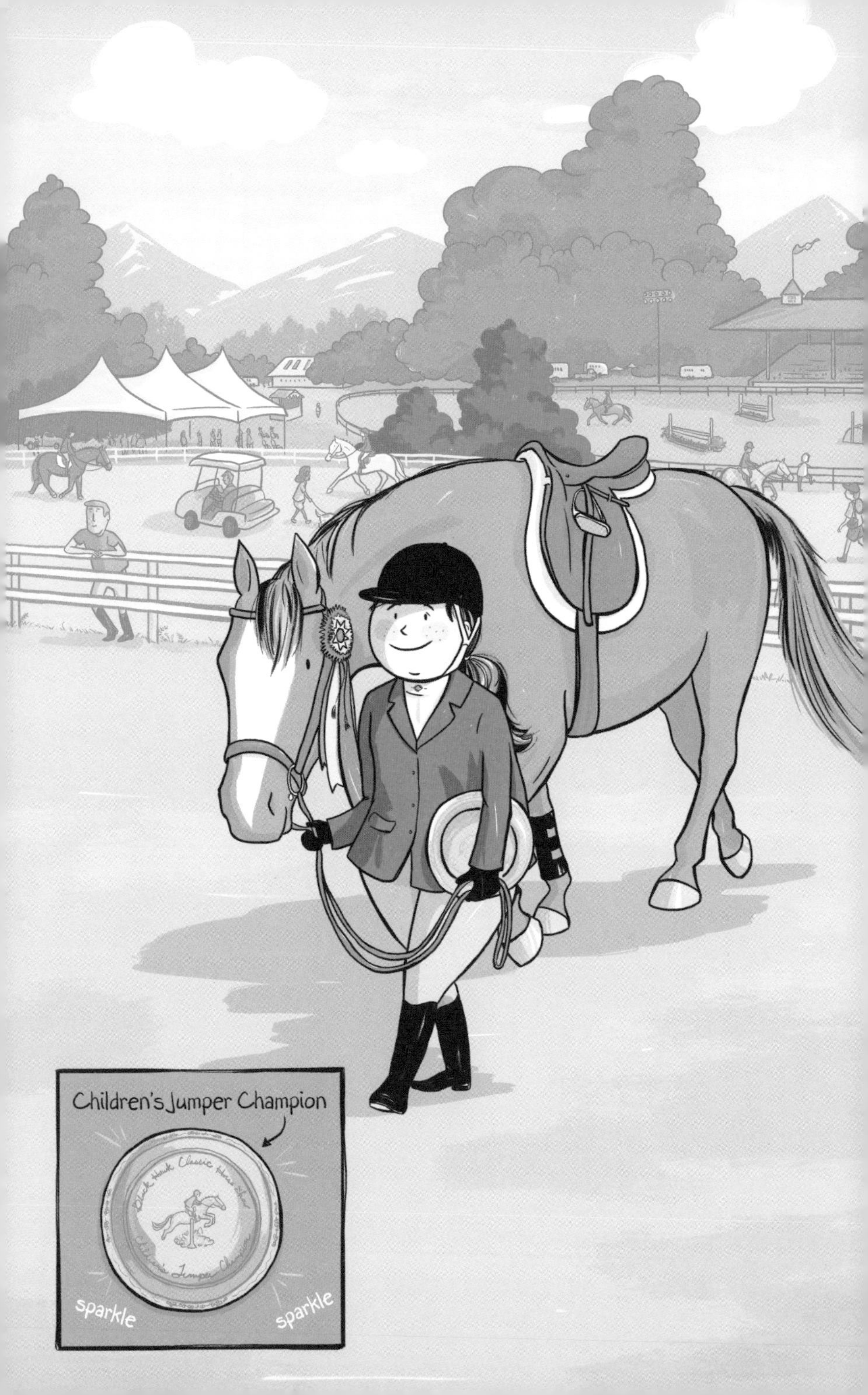
Children's Jumper Champion
Black Hawk Classic Horse Show
Children's Jumper Champion
sparkle
sparkle

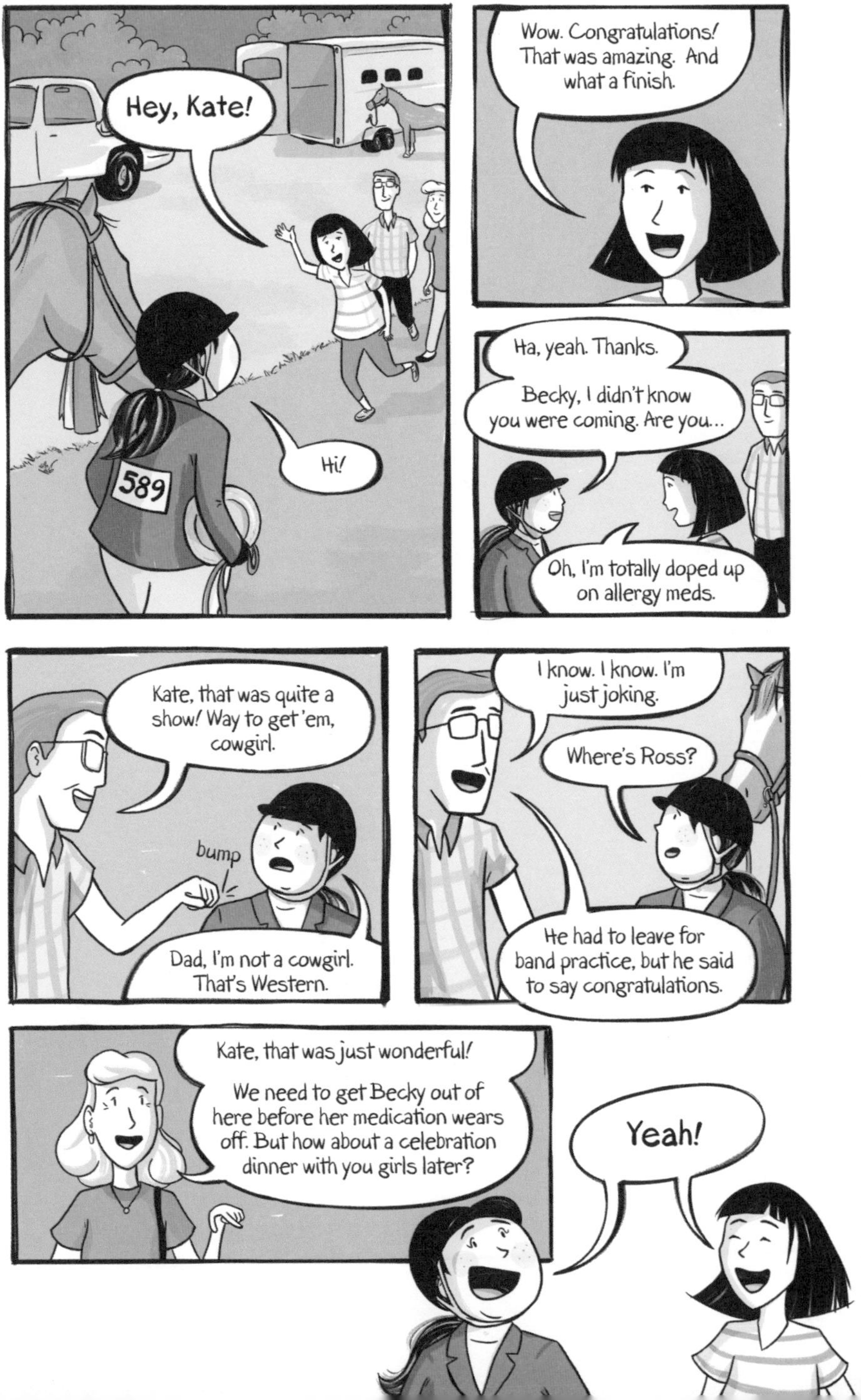
Hey, Kate!
Hi!
Wow. Congratulations! That was amazing. And what a finish.
Ha, yeah. Thanks.
Becky, I didn't know you were coming. Are you...
Oh, I'm totally doped up on allergy meds.
Kate, that was quite a show! Way to get 'em, cowgirl.
bump
Dad, I'm not a cowgirl. That's Western.
I know. I know. I'm just joking.
Where's Ross?
He had to leave for band practice, but he said to say congratulations.
Kate, that was just wonderful!
We need to get Becky out of here before her medication wears off. But how about a celebration dinner with you girls later?
Yeah!
589

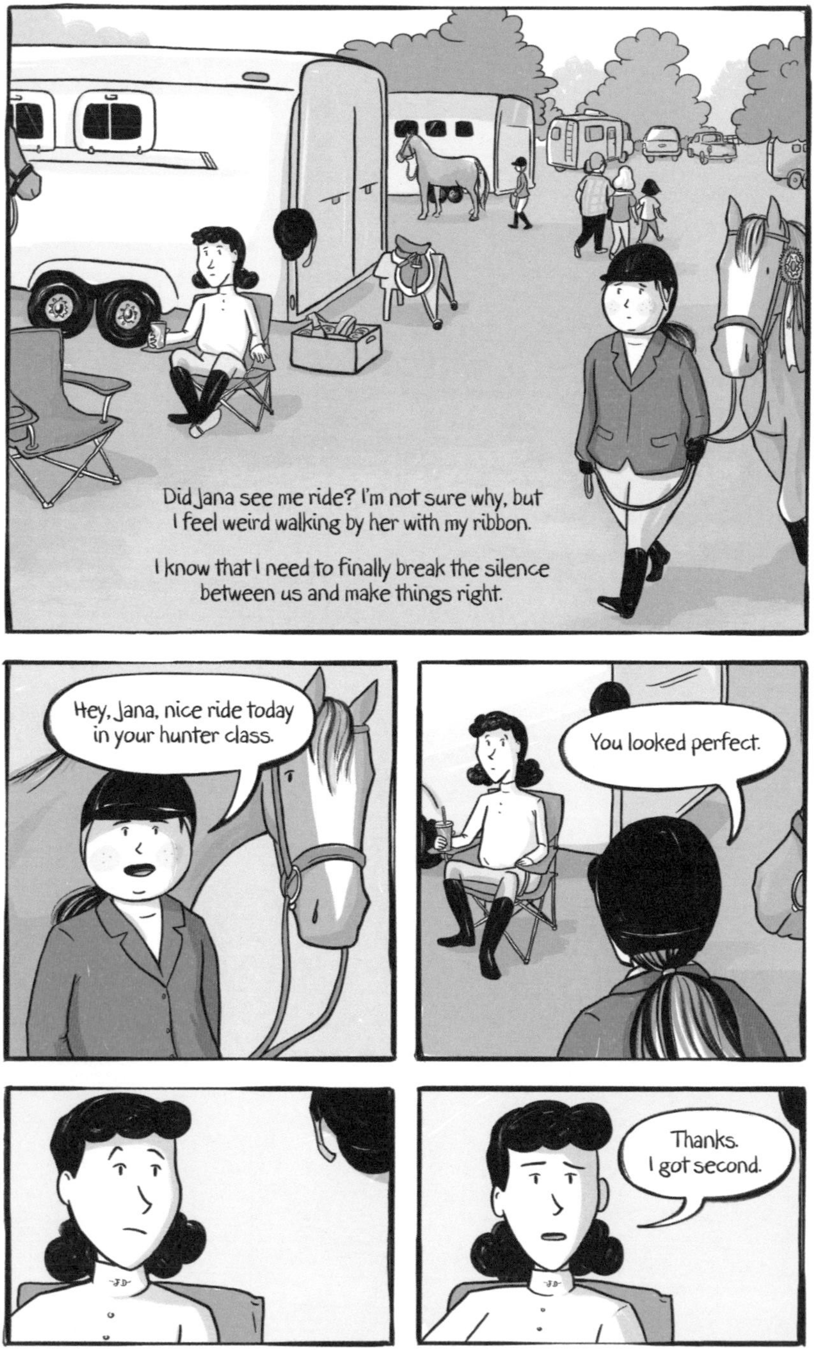
Did Jana see me ride? I'm not sure why, but I feel weird walking by her with my ribbon.
I know that I need to finally break the silence between us and make things right.
Hey, Jana, nice ride today in your hunter class.
You looked perfect.
Thanks. I got second.

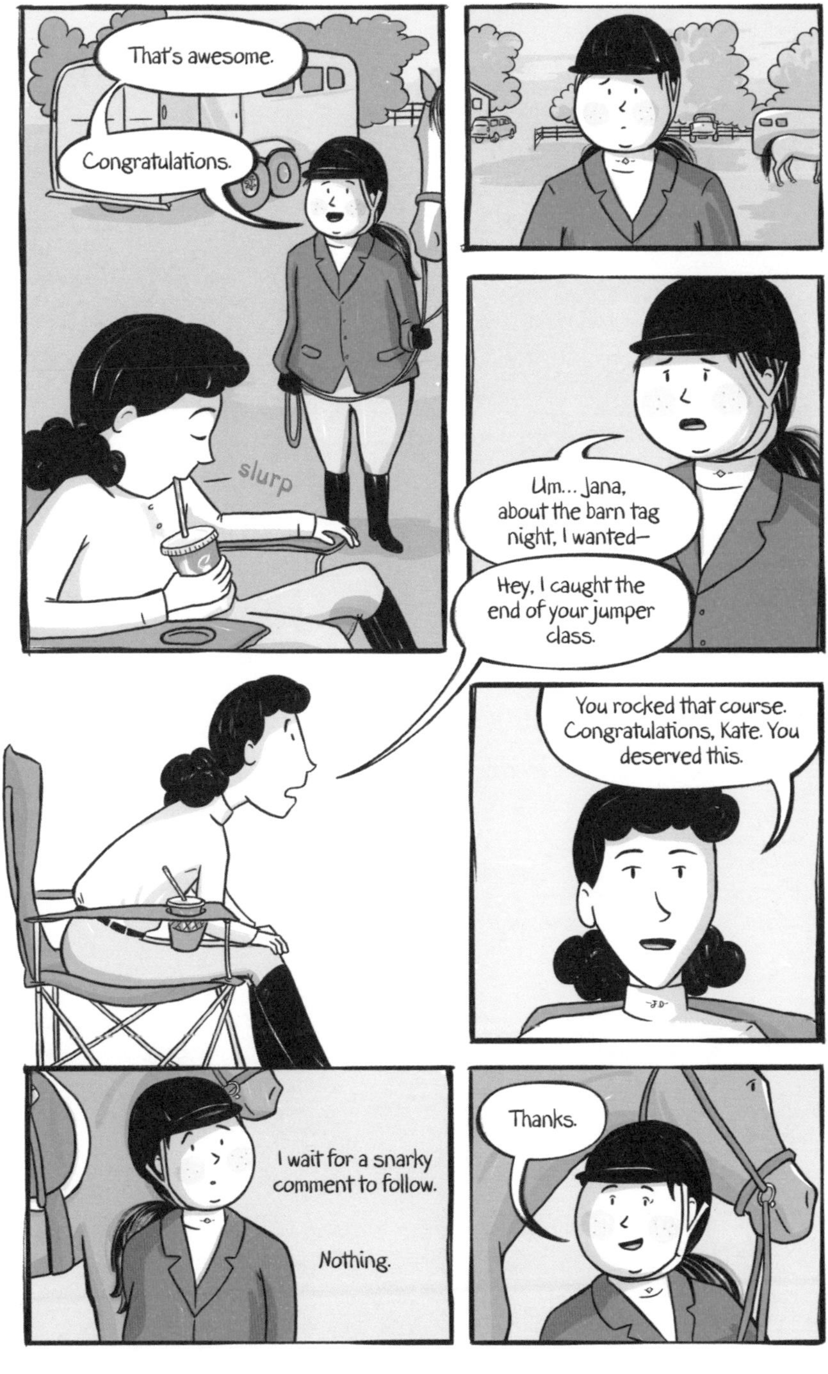
That's awesome.
Congratulations.
slurp
Um... Jana, about the barn tag night, I wanted—
Hey, I caught the end of your jumper class.
You rocked that course. Congratulations, Kate. You deserved this.
I wait for a snarky comment to follow.
Nothing.
Thanks.

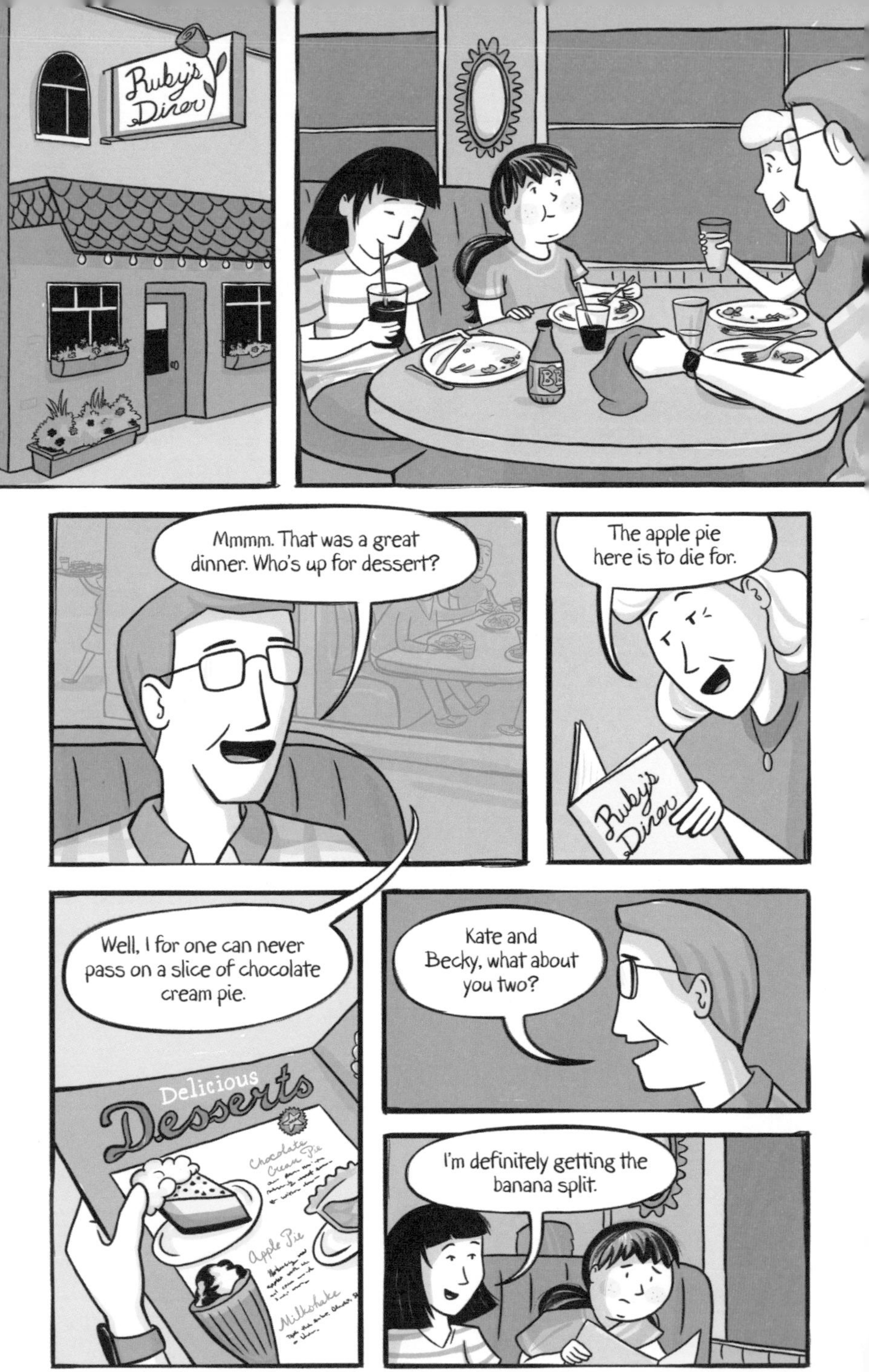
Ruby's Diner
Mmmm. That was a great dinner. Who's up for dessert?
The apple pie here is to die for.
Ruby's Diner
Well, I for one can never pass on a slice of chocolate cream pie.
Delicious Desserts
Chocolate Cream Pie
Apple Pie
Milkshake
Kate and Becky, what about you two?
I'm definitely getting the banana split.

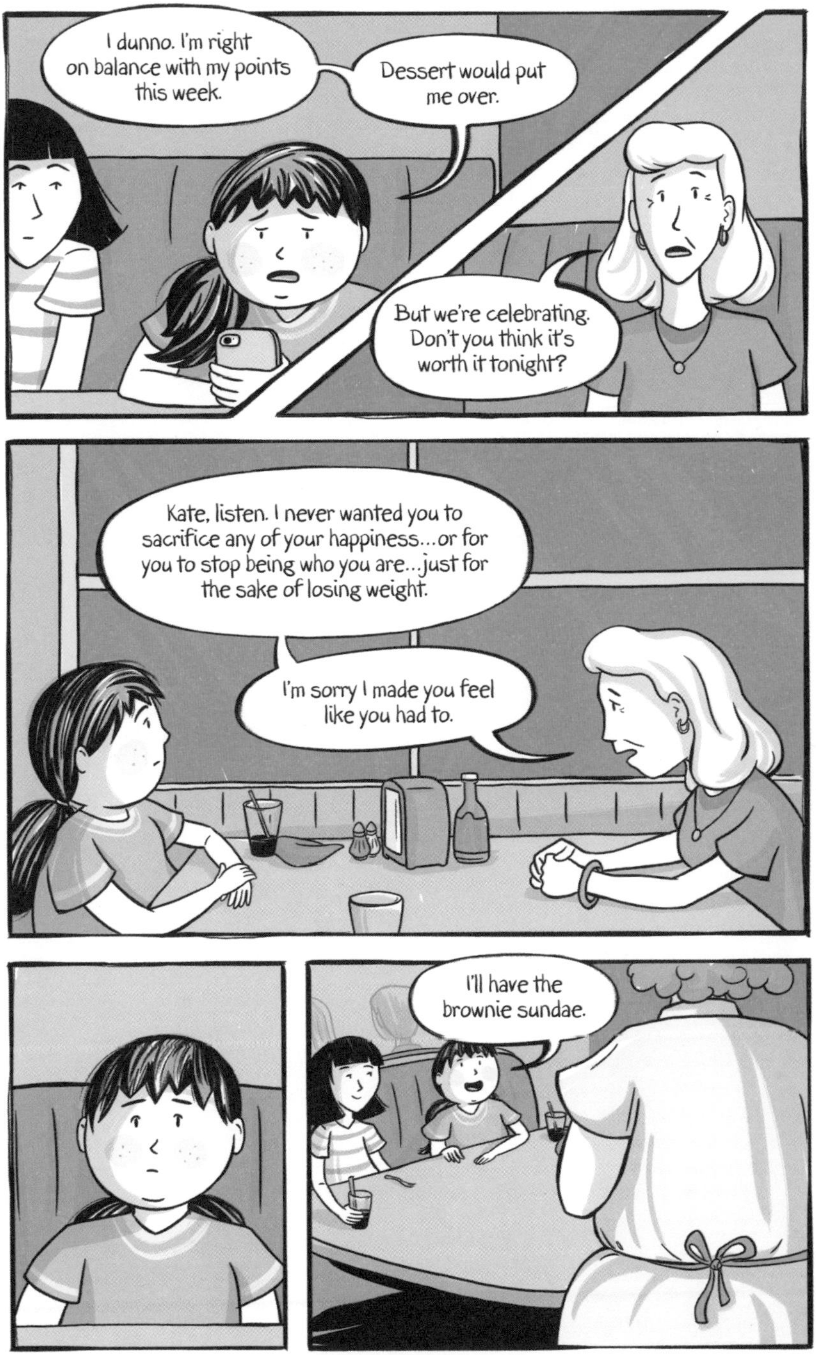
I dunno. I'm right on balance with my points this week.
Dessert would put me over.
But we're celebrating. Don't you think it's worth it tonight?
Kate, listen. I never wanted you to sacrifice any of your happiness...or for you to stop being who you are...just for the sake of losing weight.
I'm sorry I made you feel like you had to.
I'll have the brownie sundae.

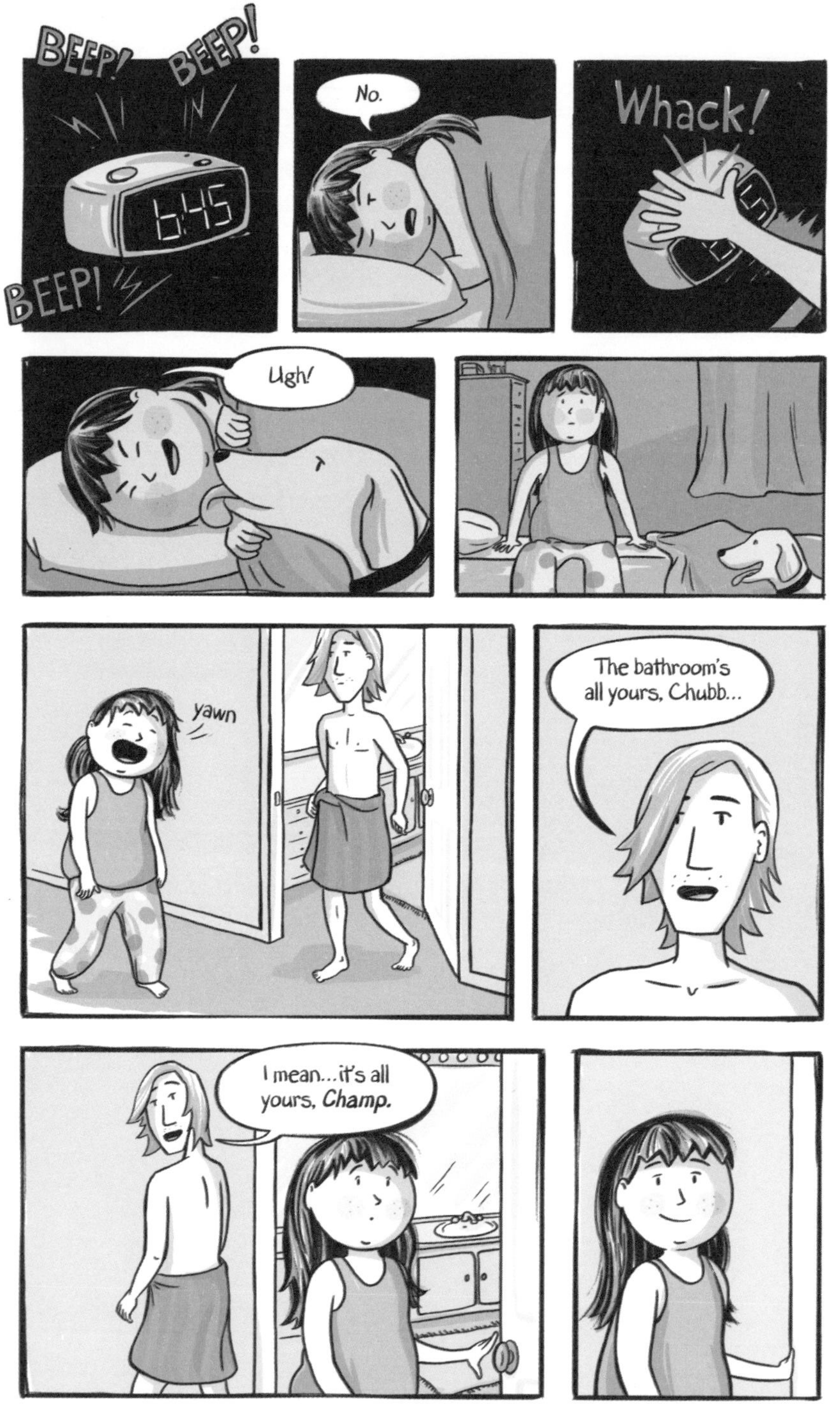
BEEP! BEEP!
BEEP!
No.
Whack!
Ugh!
yawn
The bathroom's all yours, Chubb...
I mean...it's all yours, *Champ.*

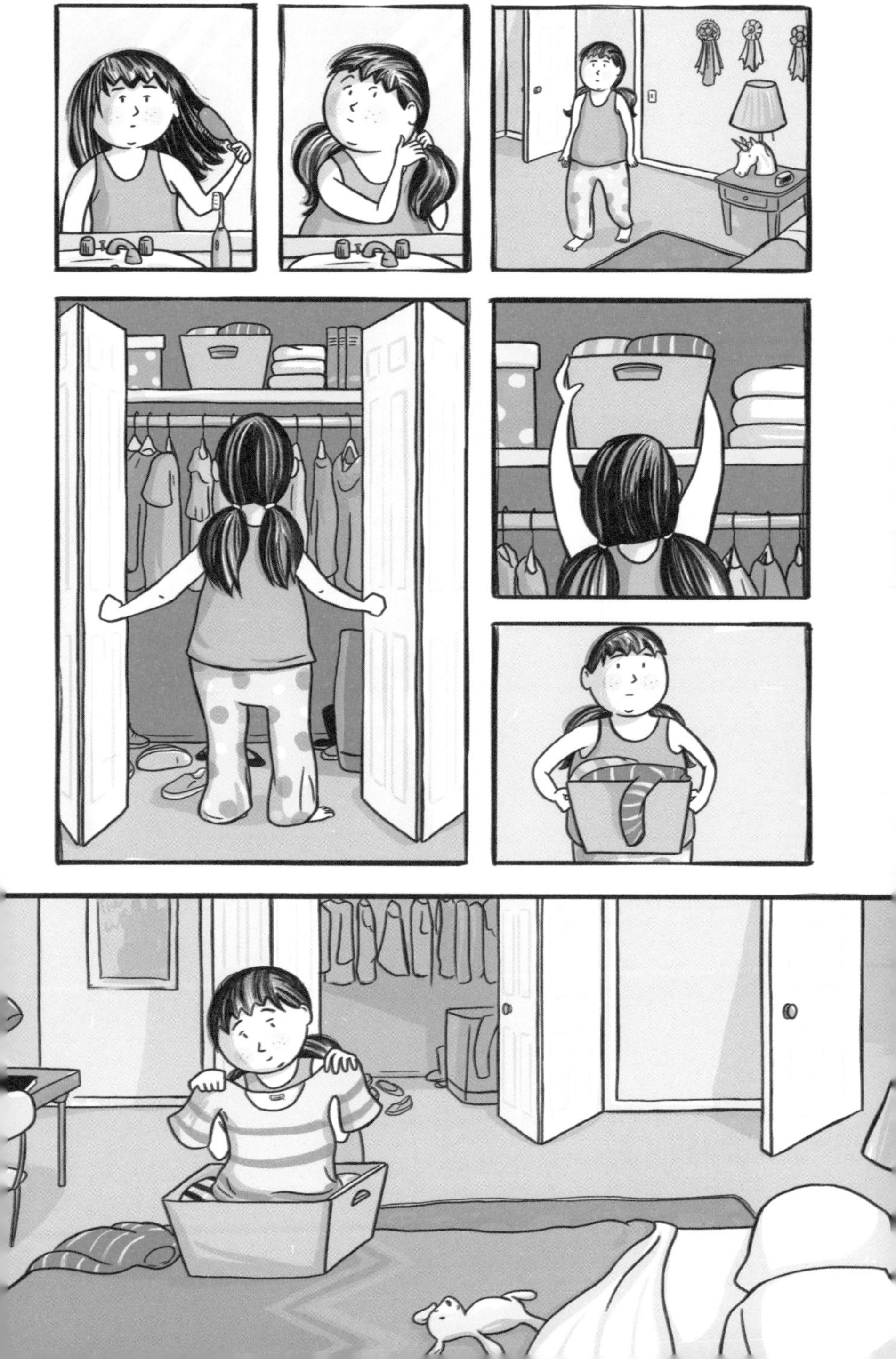

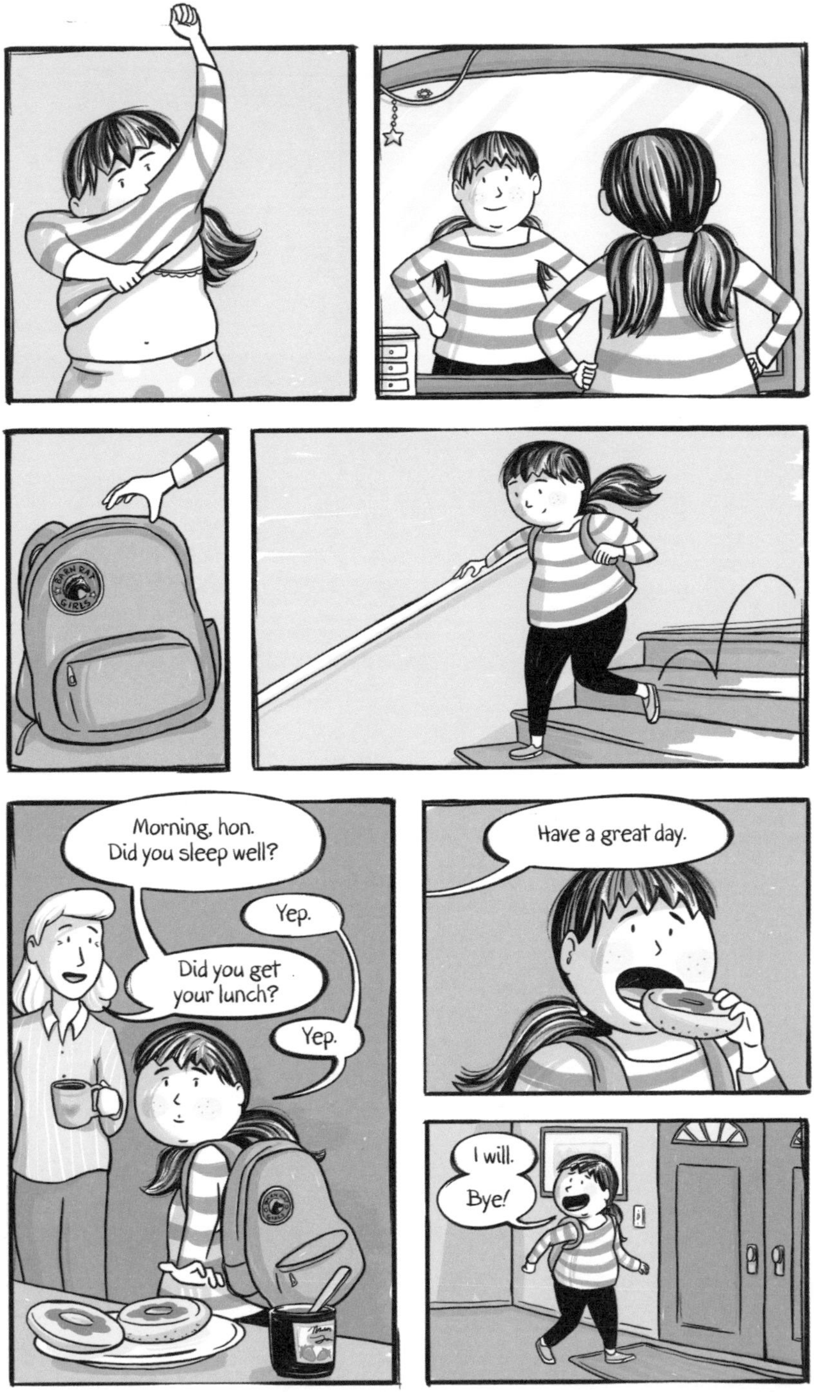
BARN RAT GIRLS
Morning, hon.
Did you sleep well?
Yep.
Did you get your lunch?
Yep.
Have a great day.
I will.
Bye!

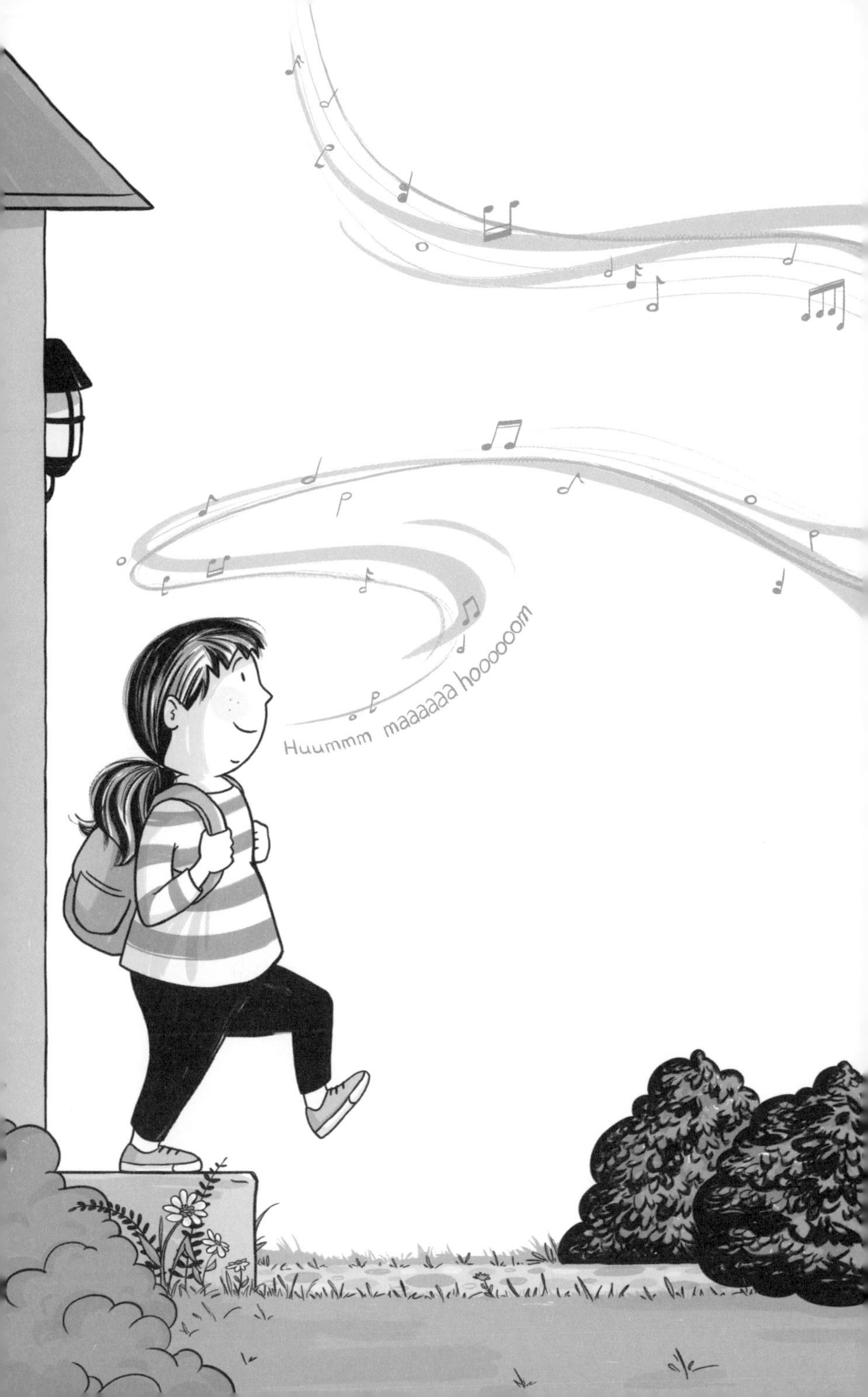
Huummm maaaaaa hoooooom

Author's Note

Although this book is not a memoir, it is inspired by many of my childhood experiences that actually did happen.

It all started at Trefoil Ranch, where I rode horses at camp the summer before starting fourth grade. From then on, I was a bona fide horse nut. I hung horse posters and calendars all over my bedroom walls. I drew endless pictures of them and started collecting models. I devoured horse books and subscribed to riding magazines. Every year I asked Santa for a horse for Christmas. I begged and pleaded for lessons and eventually began riding regularly at various barns. At the age of fourteen, after years of chores, lessons, and showing, I was extremely lucky and finally got my very own horse.

My years spent with horses are some of my most cherished memories. Anyone who shares the passion for these magnificent creatures understands how strong the bond between horse and rider can become. But along with the love and devotion come the hardships, like falling off. There are ten times that Kate falls off her horse in this book. All of those falls are based on true stories. Five of them are my own, and the others I collected from friends. Falling off is hard, and can be terrifying, but getting back on is by far the most difficult part.

The relationships that develop between riders at barns can be hardships, too. The Jana in this book didn't actually exist—not at my barn anyway, where I was fortunate enough to experience a genuine camaraderie and form some lifelong friendships. That's not to say I never encountered any bullying, it just wasn't in the riding arena. I was a chubby kid throughout my childhood—the subject of fat jokes and name-calling that happened at school, dance class, the swimming pool, and all around my neighborhood. I still see myself as "the fat kid," and probably always will. It's an identity that even today as an adult I have found difficult to shed. I know I'm not alone in feeling body insecurities or being called names. My hope in writing Horse Trouble is that it might let some kids know that they're not alone, either.

There is no doubt in my mind that riding horses gave me the strength both physically and mentally to persevere through many of my crummiest situations in childhood. I could always escape through horses, but the grit and tenacity I gained from riding them, being thrown off, and climbing back on again...and again, forced me to become confident and trust myself. Horses not only made me strong, but they helped me decide who I should be, giving me a strong sense of self. Maybe this story can help other kids to do the same. At least, I hope that it will be an inspiration to follow your passion through the best and worst moments, whether it be playing sports, performing on stage, creating cool stuff...or even just loving a big, four-legged animal.

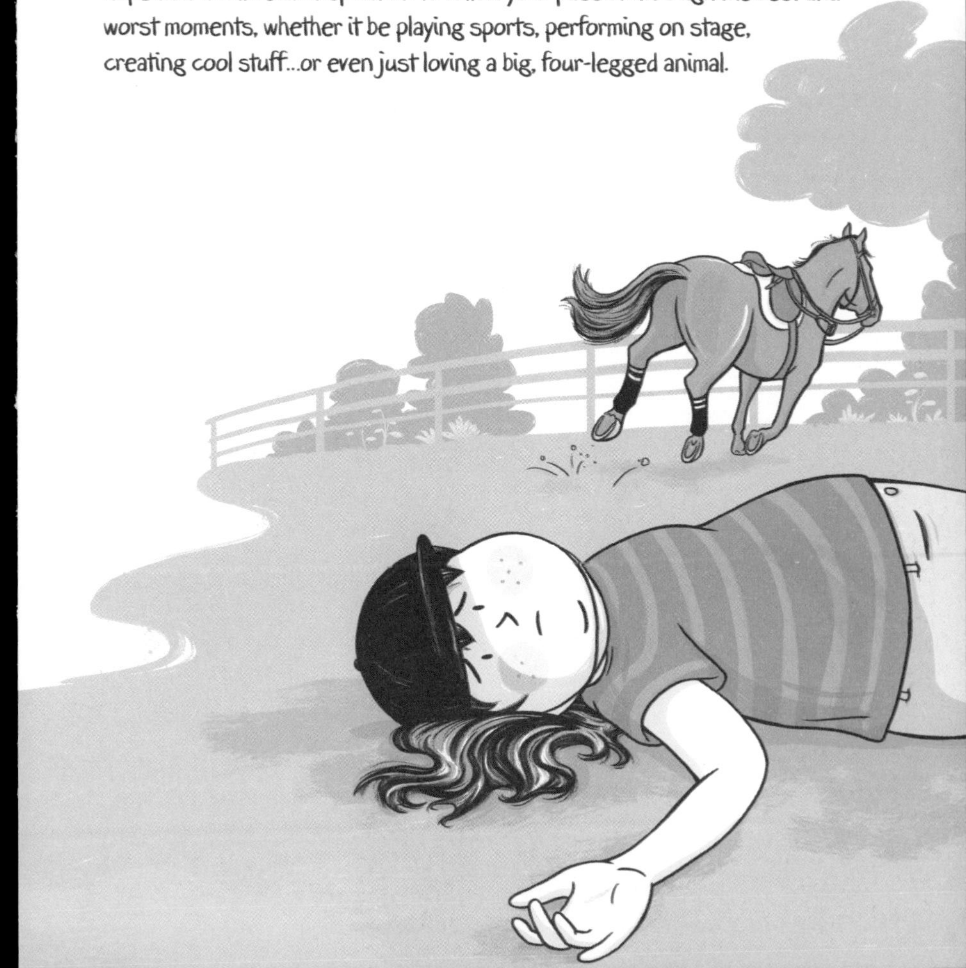

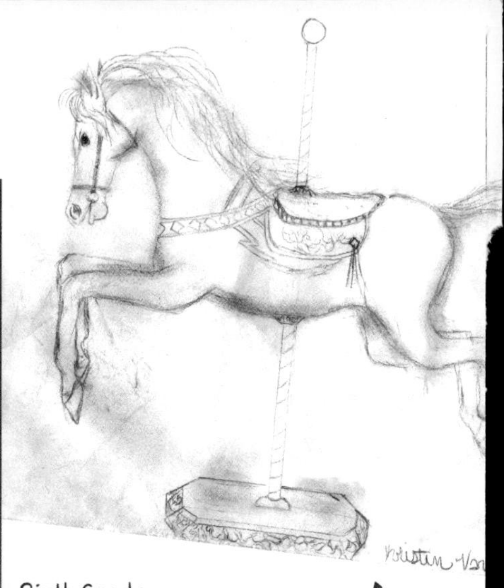

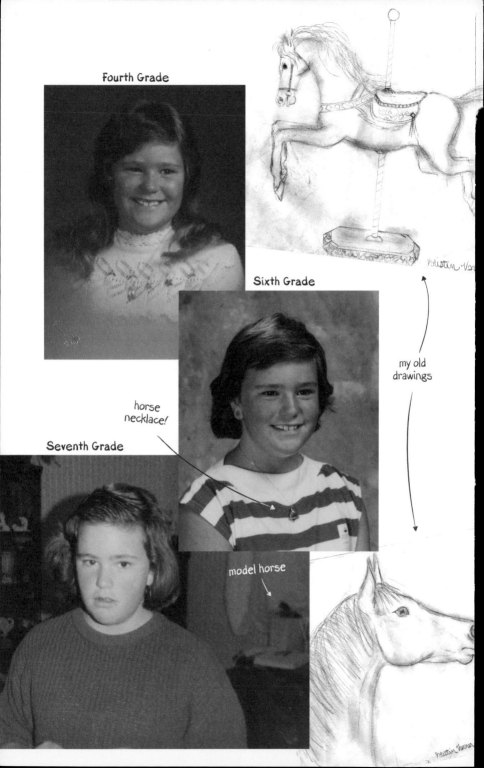

Fourth Grade

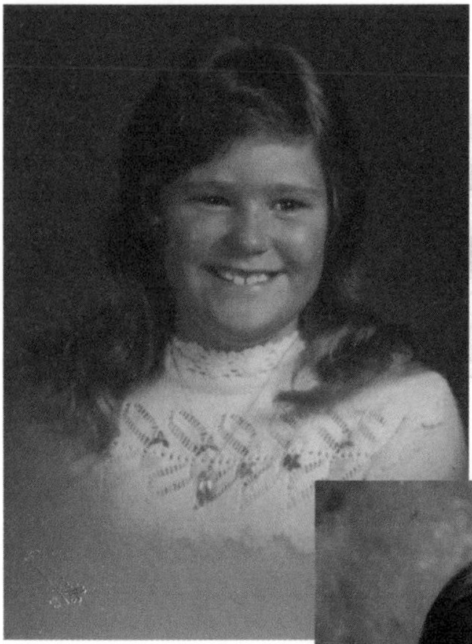

Sixth Grade

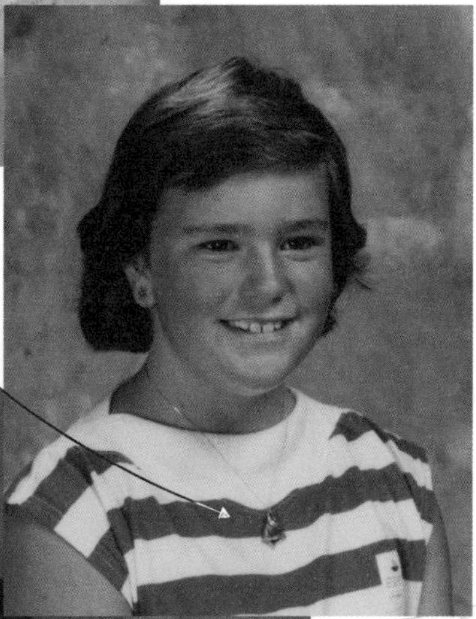

my old drawings

horse necklace!

Seventh Grade

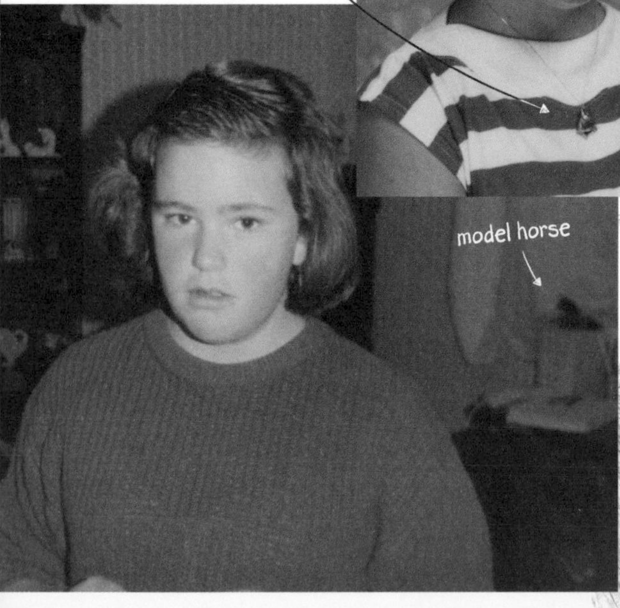
model horse

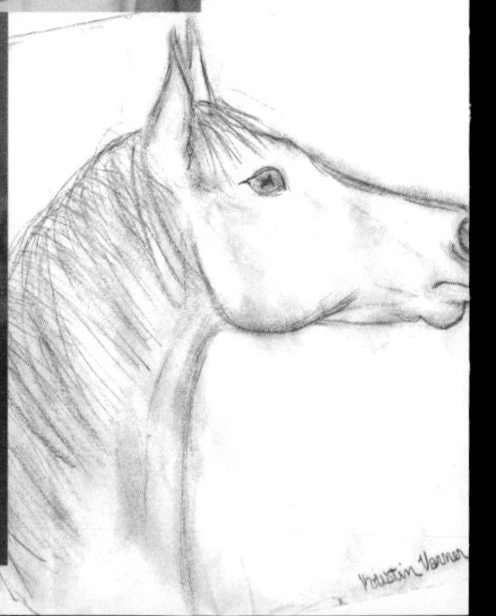

Riding my horse, Doc

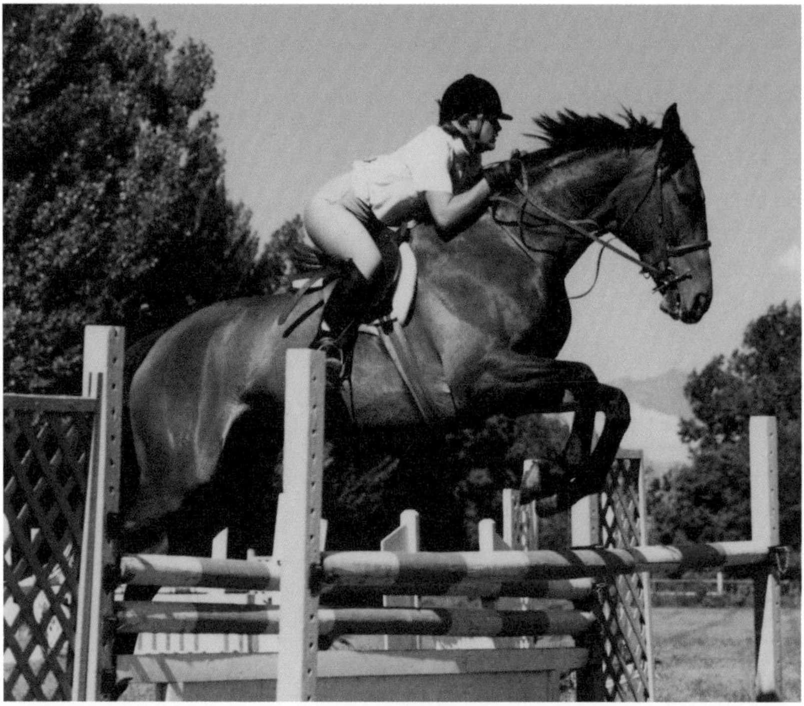

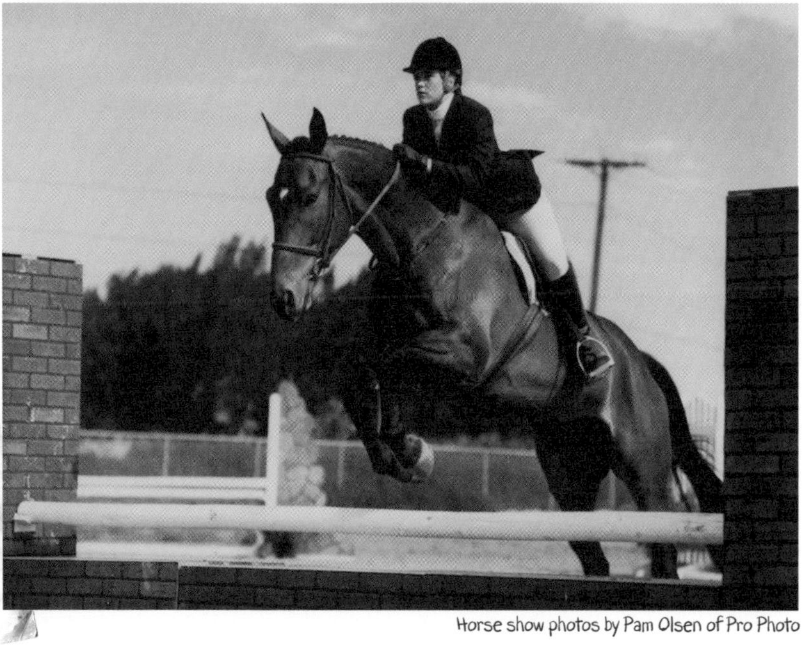

Horse show photos by Pam Olsen of Pro Photo

Early character sketches

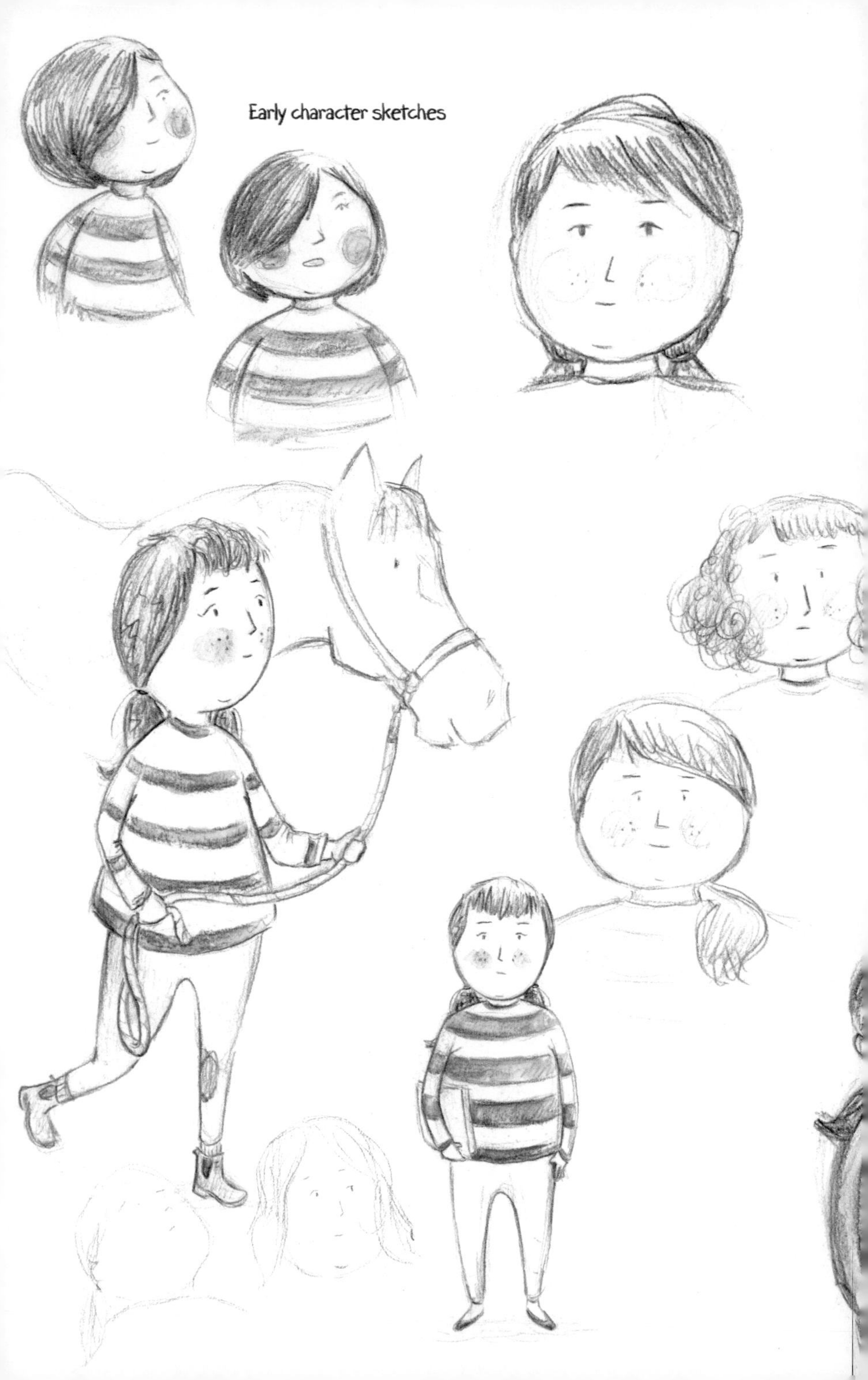

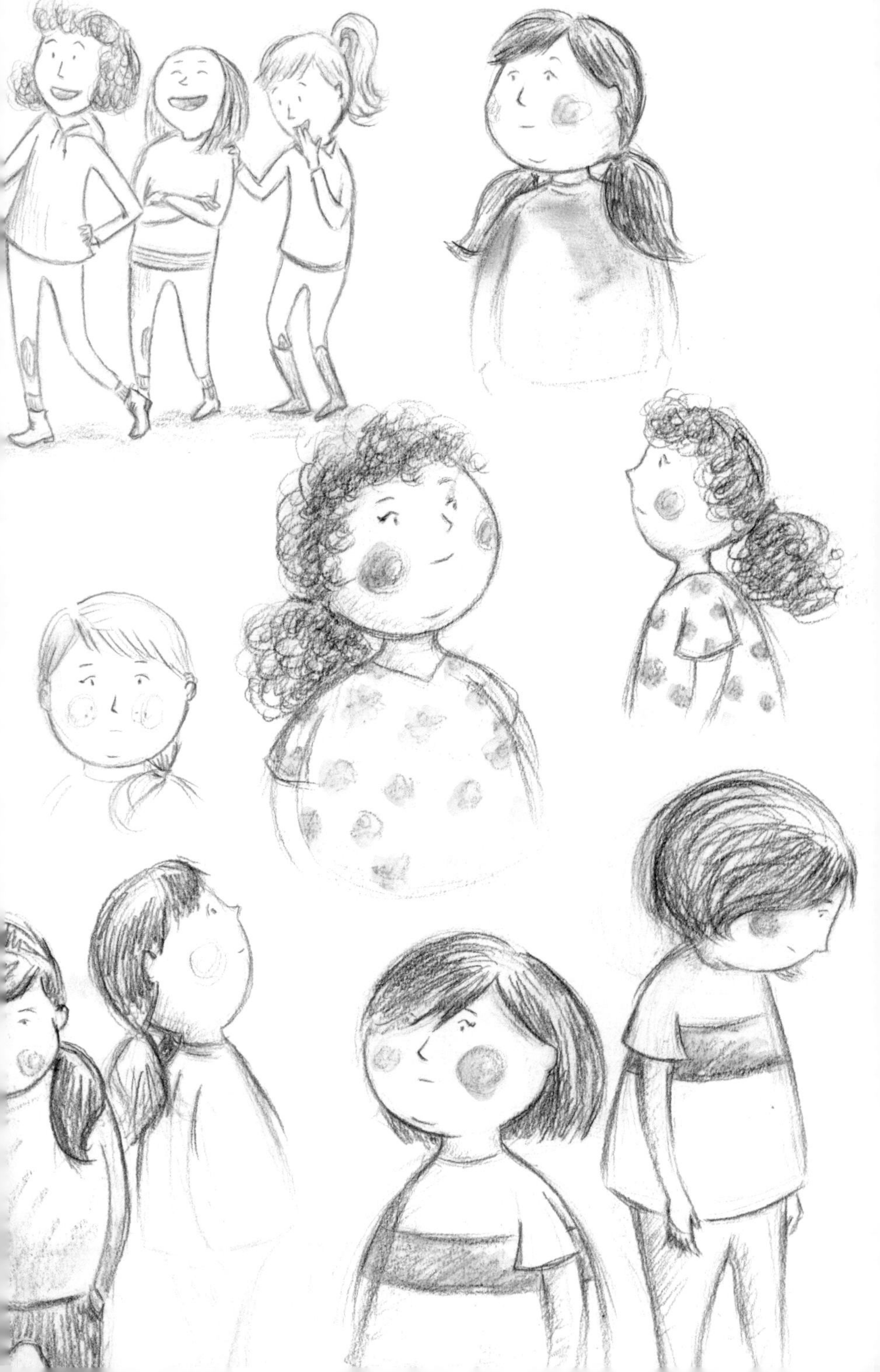

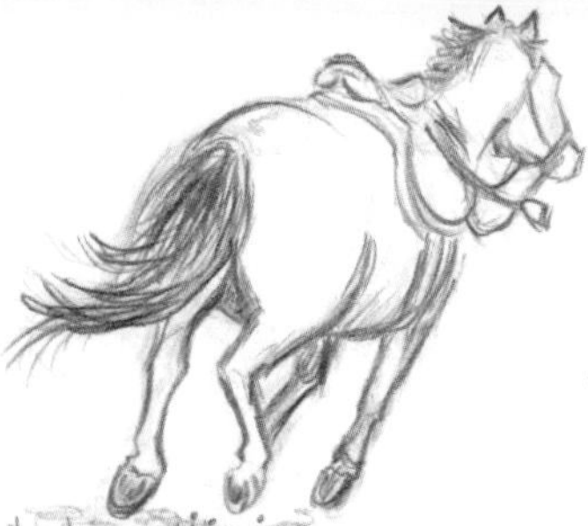

Cover Sketches

A lot of sketches were done for the cover of this book! These are just a few of them.

The original title was *Ten Times I Fell Off My Horse* (*Horse Trouble* is a little shorter).

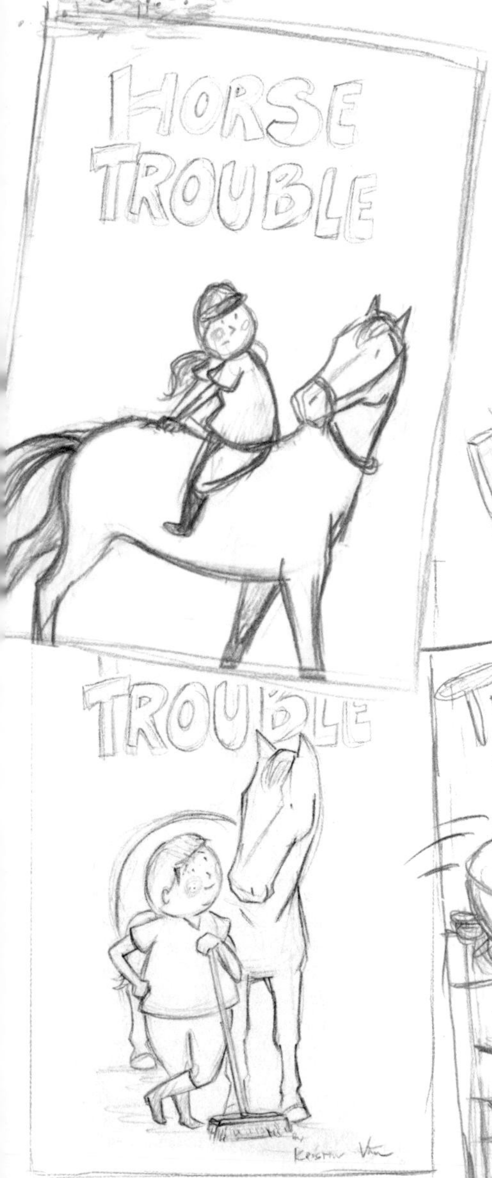
HORSE TROUBLE
TROUBLE

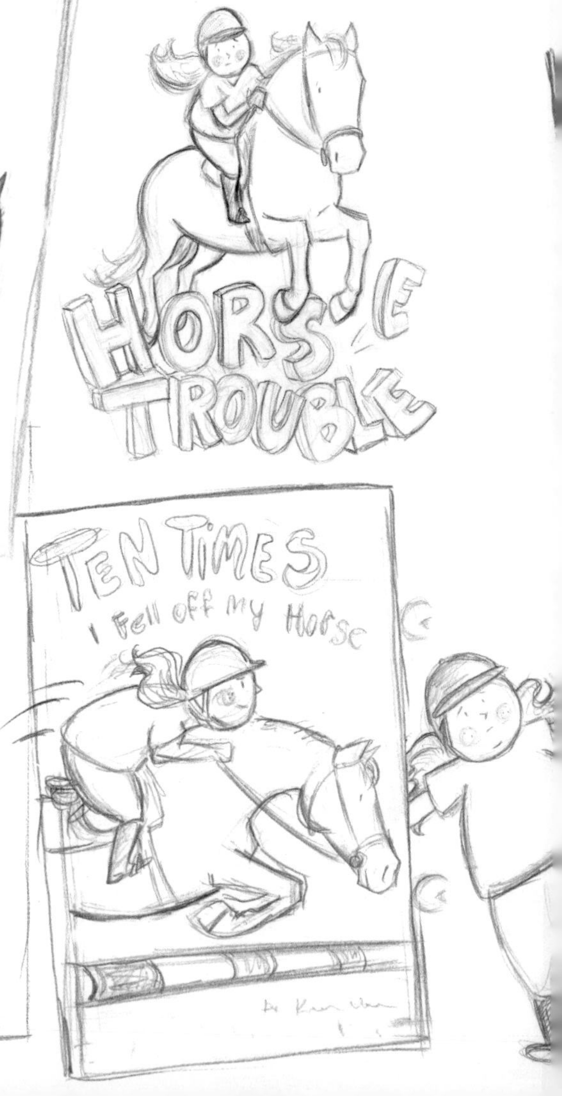
HORSE TROUBLE
TEN TIMES
I Fell off My Horse

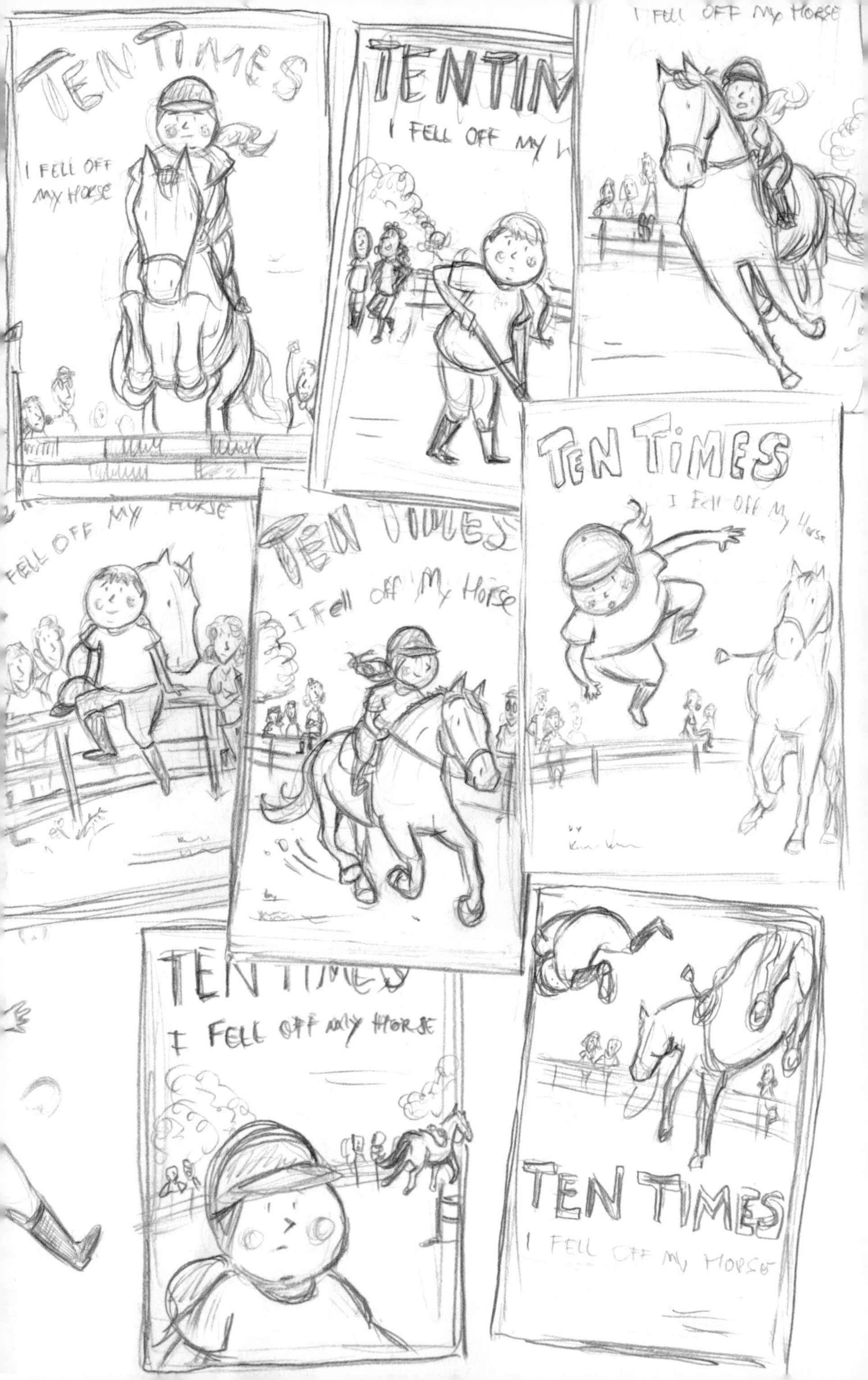
TEN TIMES
I FELL OFF MY HORSE
TENTIM
I FELL OFF MY H
I FELL OFF MY HORSE
FELL OFF MY HORSE
TEN TIMES
I FELL OFF MY HORSE
TEN TIMES
I FELL OFF MY HORSE
by
TEN TIMES
I FELL OFF MY HORSE
TEN TIMES
I FELL OFF MY HORSE

My Process

① The first stage of the book is the script. I print out each chapter to determine the page turns and story layout. I will often scribble out dialogue or make changes to the text as I go.

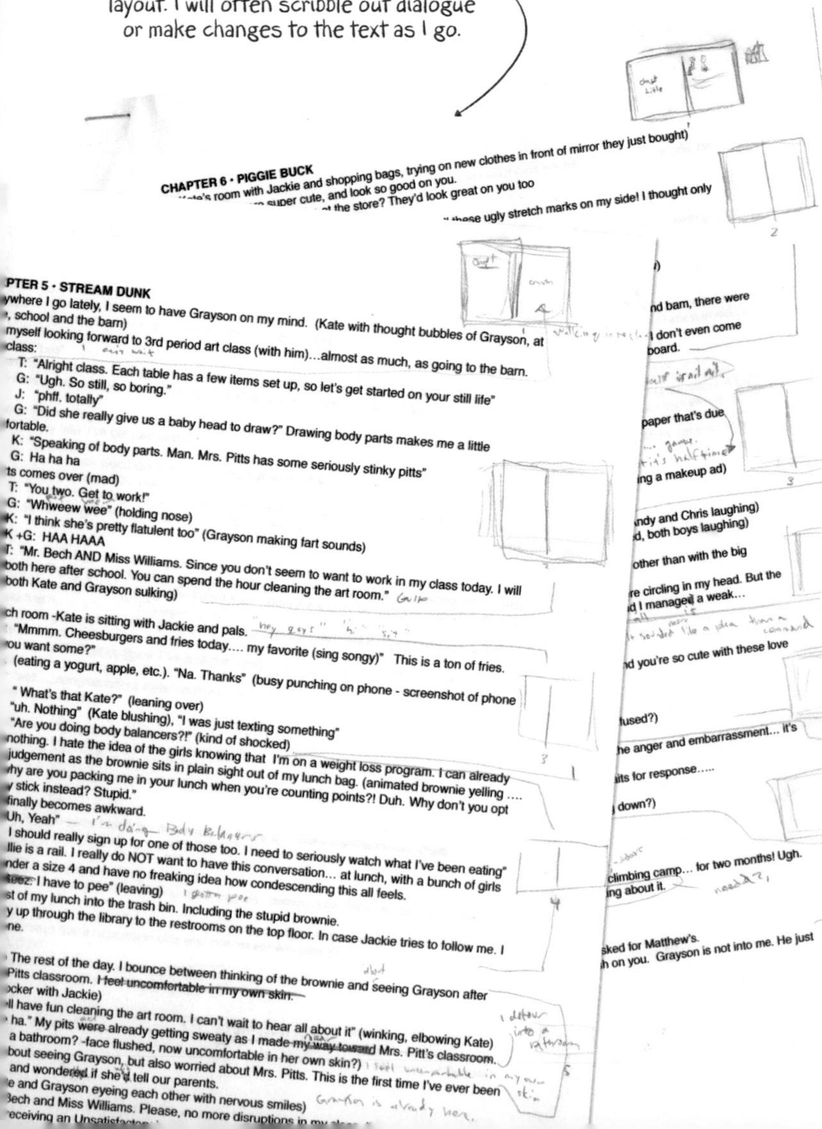

CHAPTER 6 · PIGGIE BUCK

...te's room with Jackie and shopping bags, trying on new clothes in front of mirror they just bought)
...— super cute, and look so good on you.
...— the store? They'd look great on you too
...those ugly stretch marks on my side! I thought only

...PTER 5 · STREAM DUNK

...ywhere I go lately, I seem to have Grayson on my mind. (Kate with thought bubbles of Grayson, at ..., school and the barn)
...myself looking forward to 3rd period art class (with him)...almost as much, as going to the barn.
...class:

T: "Alright class. Each table has a few items set up, so let's get started on your still life"
G: "Ugh. So still, so boring."
J: "phff. totally"
G: "Did she really give us a baby head to draw?" Drawing body parts makes me a little ...fortable.
K: "Speaking of body parts. Man. Mrs. Pitts has some seriously stinky pitts"
G: Ha ha ha
...ts comes over (mad)
T: "You two. Get to work!"
G: "Whweew wee" (holding nose)
K: "I think she's pretty flatulent too" (Grayson making fart sounds)
K+G: HAA HAAA
T: "Mr. Bech AND Miss Williams. Since you don't seem to want to work in my class today. I will ...both here after school. You can spend the hour cleaning the art room."
...both Kate and Grayson sulking)

...ch room -Kate is sitting with Jackie and pals.
..."Mmmm. Cheeseburgers and fries today.... my favorite (sing songy)" This is a ton of fries.
...ou want some?"
...(eating a yogurt, apple, etc.). "Na. Thanks" (busy punching on phone - screenshot of phone

" What's that Kate?" (leaning over)
"uh. Nothing" (Kate blushing), "I was just texting something"
"Are you doing body balancers?!" (kind of shocked)
...nothing. I hate the idea of the girls knowing that I'm on a weight loss program. I can already ...judgement as the brownie sits in plain sight out of my lunch bag. (animated brownie yelling ....why are you packing me in your lunch when you're counting points?! Duh. Why don't you opt ...y stick instead? Stupid."
...finally becomes awkward.
...Uh, Yeah"
...I should really sign up for one of those too. I need to seriously watch what I've been eating"
...llie is a rail. I really do NOT want to have this conversation... at lunch, with a bunch of girls ...size: I have to pee" (leaving)
...st of my lunch into the trash bin. Including the stupid brownie.
...y up through the library to the restrooms on the top floor. In case Jackie tries to follow me. I ...me.

· The rest of the day. I bounce between thinking of the brownie and seeing Grayson after ...Pitts classroom. I feel uncomfortable in my own skin.
...ocker with Jackie)
...ll have fun cleaning the art room. I can't wait to hear all about it" (winking, elbowing Kate)
... ha." My pits were already getting sweaty as I made my way toward Mrs. Pitt's classroom.
...a bathroom? -face flushed, now uncomfortable in her own skin?)
...bout seeing Grayson, but also worried about Mrs. Pitts. This is the first time I've ever been
...and wondered if she'd tell our parents.
...e and Grayson eyeing each other with nervous smiles)
...Bech and Miss Williams. Please, no more disruptions in my class
...eceiving an Unsatisfactor...

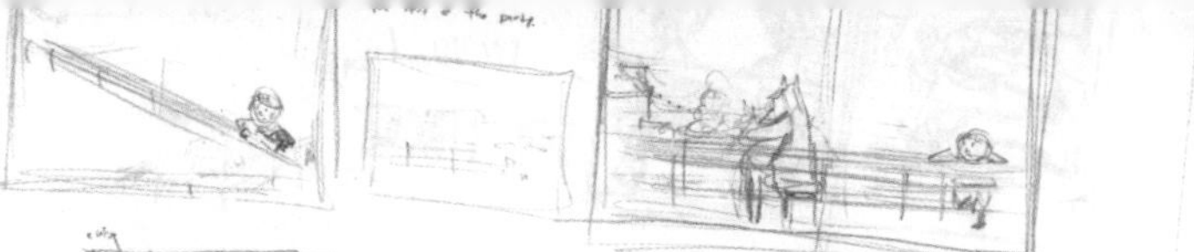

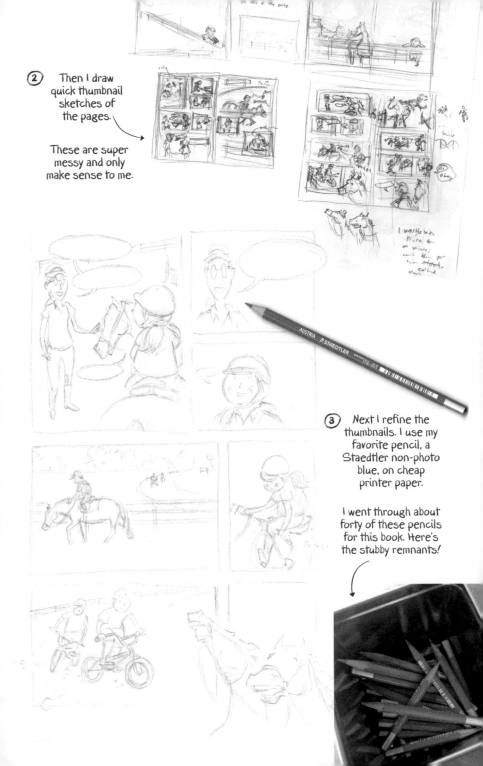

(2) Then I draw quick thumbnail sketches of the pages.

These are super messy and only make sense to me.

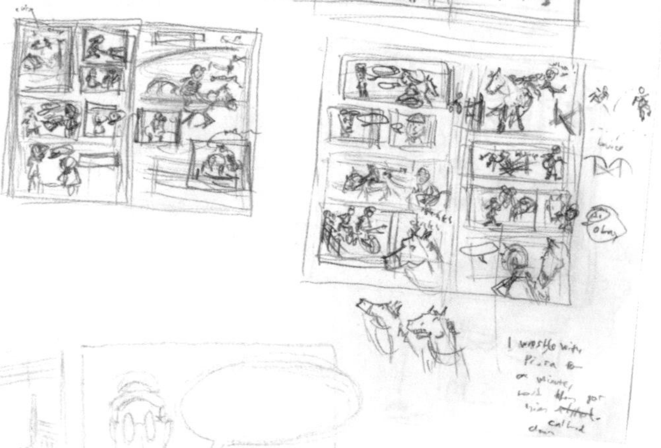

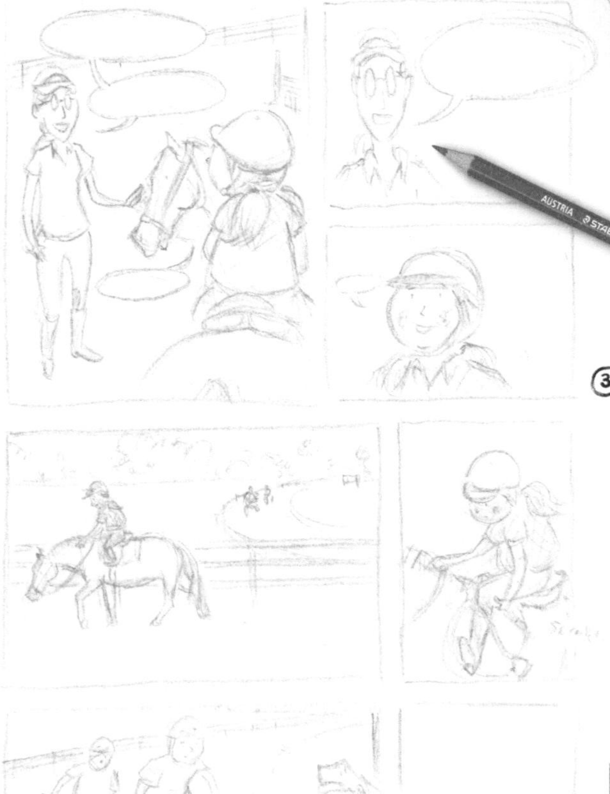

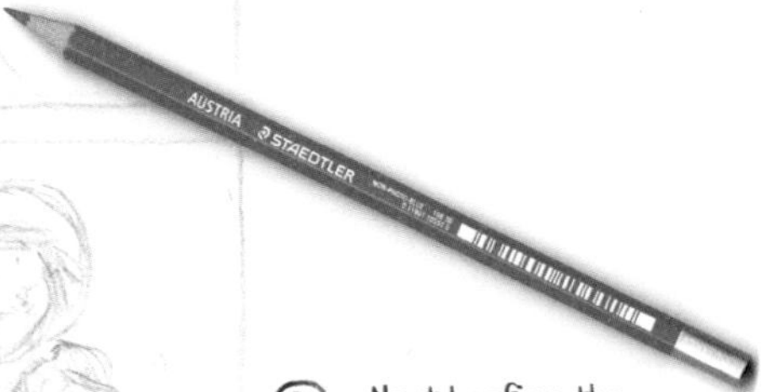

(3) Next I refine the thumbnails. I use my favorite pencil, a Staedtler non-photo blue, on cheap printer paper.

I went through about forty of these pencils for this book. Here's the stubby remnants!

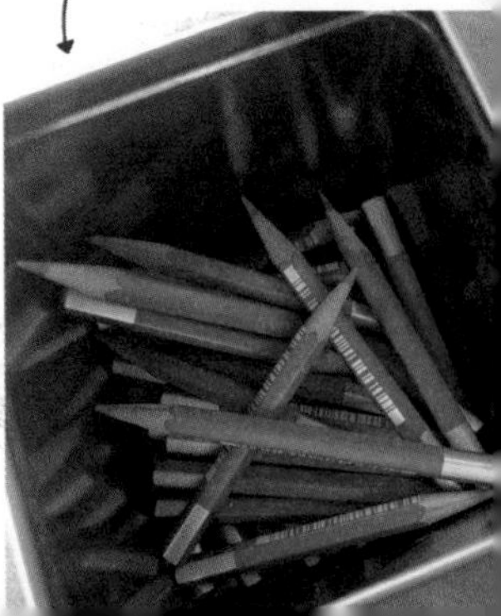

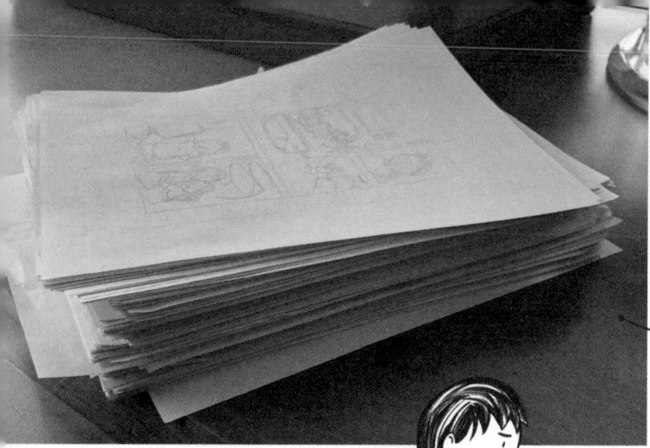

(4) All the sketches are scanned into my computer There are about three hundred pages in this stack.

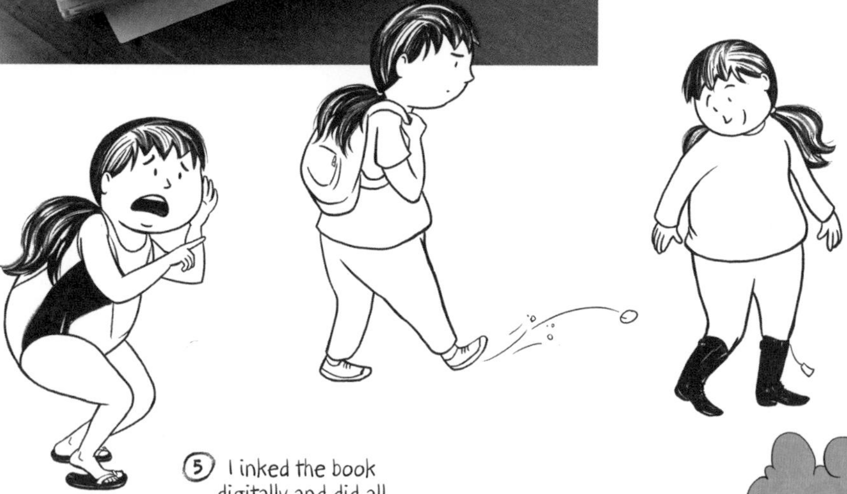

(5) I inked the book digitally and did all the coloring in Photoshop.

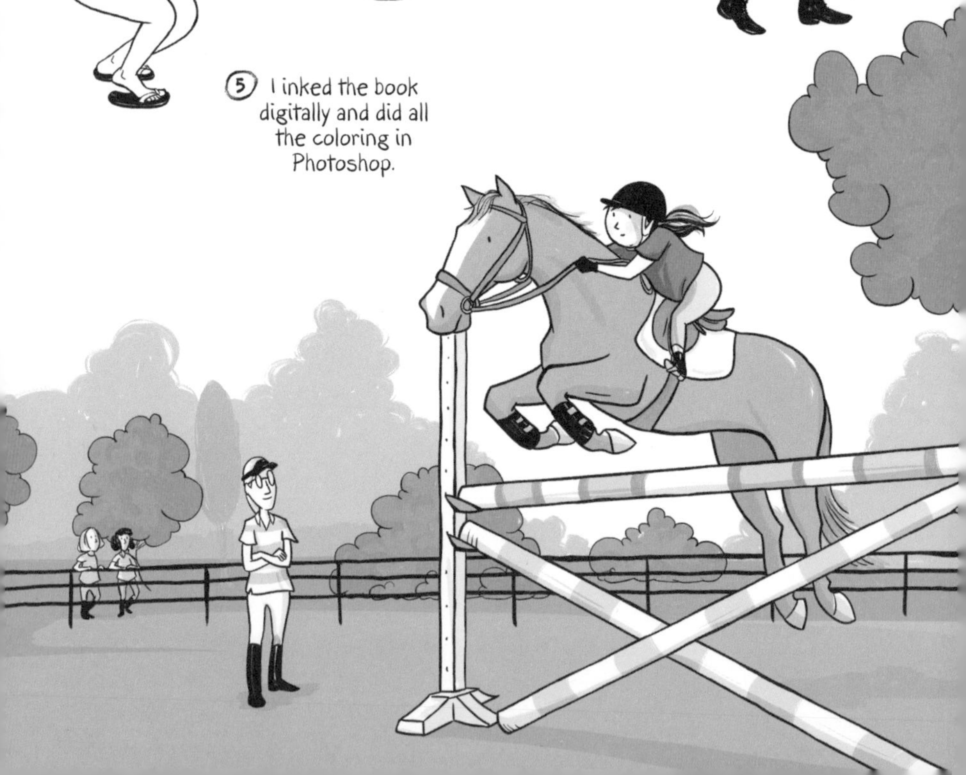